Renato!

Also by Eugene Mirabelli

The Way In

The Burning Air

No Resting Place

The World at Noon

The Passion of Terri Heart

The Language Nobody Speaks

Renato!

A Novel

Eugene Mirabelli

With an introduction by
DOUGLAS GLOVER

McPherson & Company
2020

FIRST EDITION

This is solely and completely a work of fiction.

Printed in the United States of America.
Published by McPherson & Company,
Post Office Box 1126, Kingston, NY 12402
www.mcphersonco.com

1 3 5 7 9 10 8 6 4 2 2020 2021 2022

Library of Congress Cataloging-in-Publication Data

Names: Mirabelli, Eugene, author. | Glover, Douglas, 1948- writer of introduction. | Mirabelli, Eugene. Goddess in love with a horse. | Mirabelli, Eugene. Renato, the painter. | Mirabelli, Eugene. Renato after Alba.
Title: Renato! : a novel / Eugene Mirabelli ; with an introduction by Douglas Glover.
Identifiers: LCCN 2020028693 | ISBN 9781620540428 (paperback)
Subjects: LCSH: Painters—Massachusetts—Boston—Fiction. | Sicilian Americans—Massachusetts—Boston—Fiction. | Older men—Fiction. | Widowers—Fiction. | Emigration and immigration—Fiction.
Classification: LCC PS3563.I68 R43 2020 | DDC 813/.54--dc23

LC record available at https://lccn.loc.gov/2020028693

The author thanks Antonio D'Alfonso, founder of Guernica Editions, for publishing *The World at Noon*, the novel in which progenitors of the Cavallù family first appeared. In addition, *The American Poetry Review*, *The Michigan Quarterly Review*, *Arba Sicula* and *Fantasy & Science Fiction* helped to establish the Cavallù genealogy, as did the editors of the *Sweet Lemons* anthology. The author also thanks Andrei Codrescu, founder and editor of *Exquisite Corpse*, which first published sections of *Renato, the Painter*. Thanks also go to *Fantasy & Science Fiction* magazine for publishing an episode that was later anthologized in *The Year's Best Science Fiction and Fantasy*, and further thanks to the *New England Review*, the *Journal of Southern New Hampshire University*, and the *Drexel Online Journal* for opening their pages to parts of this work as well.

for Margaret
& the children
& the children's children

Renato!

[INTRODUCTION]

The World As It Comes

by DOUGLAS GLOVER

RENATO*!* opens in Sicily in 1860 on the wedding night of Angelo Cavallù and his seventeen-year-old bride Ava. She is on her knees saying her prayers in the candle light when she catches sight of Angelo without his pants for the first time and realizes that from the waist down he's a horse. Angelo assures her (and the reader), "God created horses just to show us what He could do in the way of power and beauty... Horses have strength and grace and intelligence, horses have courage and endurance, horses have fidelity. Besides, I'm not wholly, not —" Then he admires her sturdy legs and adds, "We will be superb at making love."

This loopy, exuberant, joyfully erotic scene seems an outlandish place to start a novel that deals substantially with an aging twenty-first century Boston painter who may or may not be descended from Angelo Cavallù, but it has the effect of exploding the frame of the novel from conventional to marvelous on the first page. As the narrator serenely informs us, "Sicily was a beautiful land where strange and terrible things happened every day of the week." Angelo and Ava spawn an irrepressible dynasty. Cavallùs join Garibaldi's revolutionary army, marry goddesses who are also prostitutes, and colonize Boston's North End. A Cavallù by marriage designs an early airplane, another tries to invent a time machine. And the hero of the book, Renato Stillamare, Cavallù by adoption (it seems), turns up in a basket on the front step during family dinner.

You fall for *Renato!*, well, because you want this family. Maybe just by reading this book some of those Italian genes will rub off on you. Maybe you'll wake up in a Cavallù kitchen in Sicily or Boston, a putanesca sauce on the stove, and a beautiful woman or darkly handsome boy with hooves instead of feet will gallop in and make your life magical. At the very least you want to live a while with a writer who writes with such panache, such swagger, and surprise. He dances down the page with a mischievous tilt of the head, flirting with the reader, but always in control (there are so many generations to count, so many children, courtships, lovers, mysteries, and adventures). That controlled chaos is a kind of grace.

Eugene Mirabelli is of an era. He was born in 1931. I used to think of him as an Italian-American Philip Roth or Saul Bellow. He has that tang. He published three stylish early novels — *The Burning Air*, *The Way In*, and *No Resting Place* — between 1959 and 1972, but then entered a prolonged gestation before rebirthing himself as an entirely different novelist. His annus mirabilis, his watershed moment, was 1994, the year he published *The World at Noon*. It was as if, in delving always more deeply into who he is, Mirabelli has reinvented the peculiarly Italian, extravagantly melodramatic and often comic vision — the opera — in the novel form. By fusing the tale of American mid-life domestic chaos with the extravagant genealogy of the Cavallù clan, he creates a wonderful interplay of narrative planes, present and past, myth and reality, youth and age. He is a master of montage, sudden narrative breaks, interwoven plots and themes. And he couples this complexity with a sense of tranquil acceptance; not a superficial shrug but a genuinely comic (loving) accommodation to life and death. The Cavallù family, Sicily, and Boston's North End are Mirabelli's Yoknapatawpha County, the country of his imagination.

Renato!, the book in hand, assembles three subsequent novels — *The Goddess in Love with a Horse*, *Renato, the Painter*, and *Renato After Alba* — unified around the title character, Renato (means reborn in Italian) Stillamare, painter, lover, and repository of the family history, the baby in a basket, the last Cavallù (except he's not). The montage structure and the fact that Renato is the narrator throughout makes it easy to link them as a single book, the old story lines and characters recur, new ones are added. The teeming generations proliferate, lovers age and die but not before stumbling into all sorts of diversions and entanglements along the way. Mirabelli has a spontaneous gift for story telling. The overall structure — the sudden shifts of story line and rapid changes of time and place—has the feel of life itself.

Four main narrative lines surge in and out of frame: the annals of the Cavallù generations (multiple stories), the marriage of Renato and Alba, the mystery of Renato's parentage, and Renato's quest for a gallery show on Boston's Newbury Street, not to mention little essayistic asides on everything from Sicilian history to physics, side stories of artist friends, former lovers, and children, and the long list of meals cooked and eaten. Parallels and echoes abound. In "Renato, the Painter," now the middle part of the novel, Renato reluctantly offers a room in his studio to the daughter of an old friend. They are cranky roommates but end up having sex once, after which she falls in love with his paper maker. To balance things, his wife Alba has a fling with a chef. But this little affair is deftly repeated in a different tone in the third part when Renato, desolate after Alba's death, befriends a young barista who has just lost her husband to cancer. Sex is not part of this equation; the story is sweet and sad and wonderfully human.

Each part climaxes with a mass gathering, a chaotic reunion of family, friends, and loves, a moment of generosity and good will that is both an echo of the vibrant fecundity of the Cavallù ancestors and a ritual act of renewal through kinship and friendship (one is reminded of the weddings that close Shakespeare's comedies). And at the end of "After Alba," Fate (the author) decrees that Renato Stillamare will finally have his Newbury

Street show. Sadly, Alba is no longer there to share his triumph, which is less of a triumph for that fact. Afterward Renato visits with his barista friend who's just gotten married. He thinks of Dante and Donne and remembers his uncles Zitti and Nicolo arguing over the nature of reality, particle accelerators, and the behavior of electrons. "Still," he muses, "the closer we get to the bottom and beginning, the clearer it becomes that what we take as solid in this world is mutable and evanescent. It comes and goes. Human love is the only thing that lasts, as steady as Mount Monadnock and beautiful as daylight."

This truly is a wise and comforting book, funny and sad, wonderfully intelligent but wearing its intelligence lightly, whimsical yet thoughtful. For all its dizzy proliferation of story, *Renato!* is grounded in a sober sense of the real: the passage of time, the aging of the flesh, the way couples change toward one another, and the inevitability of death. Love is the lodestar from first to last. But when Renato speaks of love, the word is protean, not singular, not just passion and sex, although that's certainly part of it, but marriage, children, friends, and work. "The gods," he thinks, "have given us love instead of immortality"—a line that could serve as an epigraph. It's rare to find a book, especially in our time, that so emphatically says yes to life, to the world as it comes.

DOUGLAS GLOVER is the author of four novels, including *Elle* and *The Life and Time of Captain N.*, and six collections of short fiction. His most recent book is *The Erotics of Restraint: Essays on Literary Form.*

Renato!

BOOK ONE

The Goddess in Love with a Horse

1

THE FIRST TIME AVA SAW ANGELO NAKED WAS ON their wedding night (11 May 1860) when he strode into their bedroom, accidentally revealing to her startled eyes that from the waist down he had the hindquarters of a stallion. Now Angelo was no brute. He was a miller and this was in his house in Carco, Sicily. He had knocked gently and he had thought he heard her whisper Come in, but when he opened the door the room was ablaze with candles and Ava was still on her knees in prayer at the bedside. She lifted her head and saw — Angelo was wearing only the fancy shirt he had married in — saw those supreme flanks, hocks, fetlocks and horny soled feet. The blood drained from her face. For a moment she wavered and flickered, then she murmured the last words of her Hail Mary, blessed herself and stood up. "Amen," Angelo said, taking her cool hand in his. "I have something to tell you."

"Your legs —" she began.

"Remember," Angelo broke in. "God created horses, too. In fact, horses are among the most noble of God's creatures. Horses aren't soaked in blood. They don't have fangs or claws. They don't kill and they don't eat other horses. Horses are peaceful, more peaceful than men, not cowardly like sheep or stupid like oxen, but serene and powerful. God created horses just to show us what He could do in the way of power and beauty, and when He finished, He admired His handiwork. He admires horses. Horses have strength and grace and intelligence, horses have courage and endurance, horses have fidelity. Besides, I'm not wholly, not —"

"Your bottom half—" she began again.

"There've been other unions, but they were horrible mismatches and produced mongrel beasts. Harpies, manticores, bull-headed minotaurs. Only Chiron, the centaur, was a scholar and teacher. Besides, as I said—"

"Your thing—" she began once more.

"Don't let the great size frighten you." His voice was gentle, almost complacent.

"A horse?" she asked, astounded.

"A stallion," he said. He was quite frank about it. Sicily was a beautiful land where strange and terrible things happened every day of the week.

"I will not bed down with a horse!" Ava snatched her hand from his and ran around to the far side of the bed and stood there, watching him.

"It's been a long day and we're both tired," Angelo said, keeping quite still so as not to frighten her.

"So?"

"And when we're tired we should go to sleep."

"I'm never going to sleep. Certainly not with you," she said, her voice trembling.

"You look so fierce," Angelo remarked, simply to make her feel better. He had begun to stroll very slowly down the room on his side of the bed. "You look—"

"Not tonight, not tomorrow night, not ever!"

"Wild" he continued. "Like an animal. I like that, of course. An animal." He paused at the foot of the bed and smiled at her. "You are a magnificent woman."

Ava had almost started to say something but now she hesitated, her lips still parted, distracted by what he had just said.

"A splendid woman," he continued. "It's hard to believe that when I first saw you your legs were so thin I thought they would snap in two. You were always running after your aunt and everywhere she went you would follow her, trotting after her like a foal."

"Because I was ten years old," she protested.

"And now you are a woman of seventeen with beautiful teeth and strong round arms. And, I imagine, sturdy legs. We will be superb at making love."

Ava clapped her hands over her ears.

Angelo laughed. He praised her hair — told her it shimmered like a river at midnight — then spoke quietly about her luminous eyes, her gleaming shoulders something, her something breasts, and so on downward, dropping his voice softer and softer, so that Ava who had opened her fingers just a bit to hear him had to open them more and still more until, straining to catch his last words, she forgot herself and said, "What? What flower? — Stop! Don't come any closer!"

"Calm yourself," Angelo said. He seated himself on the low chest which stood against the wall by the foot of the bed. "How long do you plan to stand over there?" he asked.

"As long as I want to."

"Of course. But why not sit on the bed? Filomena scented the sheets with lavender, just for us."

Ava seated herself guardedly on the edge of the bed, watching him all the time.

"This is a pretty room, isn't it?" he said, looking around. "I whitewashed it myself a week ago." In fact, it was a pretty room. In addition to the bed there was a low dresser, a rush-bottomed chair, and in the space between two shuttered windows there was a washstand with an oval mirror hung above it. Angelo said, "The candles look nice, too. I didn't expect you to light them all at once, but they do look nice. Like a church at High Mass. Maybe that's why I'm so sleepy. Church always makes me sleepy," he confessed. "Or maybe it's my age. I'm no child and at my age —"

"What are you doing?" Ava cried, jumping up.

"I'm unbuttoning my shirt. I'm going to bed."

"Bed? What bed? Stop!"

But Angelo was already on his feet, rampant, and now he

threw off his shirt, letting it billow onto the chair, and there he stood naked while a dozen shadows of him reared and plunged on the whitewashed wall at his back. Ava had started to cover her eyes but it was too late. Now she simply looked at him and the candle flames grew calm again and the shadows grew still. His flesh was a rich chestnut color and his hair was black — black on his head, black in his beard, black everywhere. His shoulders gleamed, at the base of his throat there was a little hollow filled with golden shadow and on his chest the pattern of hair spread like the wings of a crow. His navel was deep and dark, his legs — ah, those splendid stallion legs — his flanks so smoothly muscled that as he walked the flesh shimmered, and the short downy hairs on his rump, the curling hairs on his thighs, the tassel-like hairs on his fetlocks, all sparkled like coal, and in the center, of course, as if the darkness of night had taken beastly shape — But Angelo was blowing out the candles one by one and it was becoming harder to see. He stopped when there was only the solitary chamber stick burning on the chest of drawers. Then he leapt into bed, stacked two pillows behind his back and sat with the sheets pulled to his chest. He looked at Ava. "I'm going to sleep," he said.

"I'm not sleepy."

"Would you like to rest on the top of the covers?"

She came and sat on the edge of the bed, her back to him.

"Give me your hand," he said.

"What are you going to do?" she asked, half turning.

"I'm going to sit here like we used to sit on the bench in your aunt's garden. What did we ever do there? Now give me your hand."

"All right," she said. She lay back on the covers against him and got comfortable. "But don't try to reason with me," she added.

"Of course not." He put his arms about her and took her hands. "Now that we're married, there's a secret I can tell you."

"I already know your secret," she said.

"Now listen. This is what you don't know. When a man of my kind, a man of my nature — when a man who is part stallion makes love to a woman, she inherits three gifts."

"Everything I ever inherited is in that ugly chest."

"These gifts come because he makes love to her. They come with his lovemaking, with his —" Angelo hesitated, hunting for the proper word.

"What three gifts?"

"Her childbirths will be easy, her milk will be sweet, and she will be beautiful forever."

"Angelo, you liar." She laughed.

"These talents will be yours by nature," he continued, undeflected. "And they'll be passed on to our daughters and their daughters, too, if we make love often enough."

"And the boys? What would they inherit?"

"My sons will be like me, of course." His breath was soft behind her ear. He went on talking in a voice gentle and resonant and even dreamy, speaking of his father and mother and the village where they lay, which was deep in the heart of Sicily, and in the hour or so that followed he told about those spirits hidden in the hills and fields around the village, told about the patron saints and beasts and, while his voice grew even sleepier, he talked about his relatives, not all of whom were horse, for one was a famous tree and another was a rock and there was an aunt —"

"Yes?" Ava said, turning to him. "Go on. I'm listening."

But Angelo was asleep. She turned all the way around and crept cautiously over the covers to study his face: his beard, his lips, the hard wrinkles at the corner of his eyes. A handsome man, she thought. His breathing was deep and slow, for he was fast asleep, but the guttering candle made the shadows on his face waver as if he were stirring and about to wake up. So Ava lay on the covers and listened to his soft, slow breathing and watched the candle flicker out and strove to keep awake.

Angelo awoke early and found Ava sleeping like a statue at

his side atop the bed covers. He gazed at her in the milky light, at her flushed cheeks and parted lips — how young she was! — cautiously lifted his hand to caress her, but changed his mind and slipped softly out of bed. In the dim hall he pulled on his work pants and boots, then groped his way down the dark stairs to wash in the courtyard. He hoped that a brisk walk on the hills would relieve the painful energy compressed in his legs, his thighs. He pulled on his shirt and flung open the gate and abruptly a horse and rider materialized out of the gray air. "He has landed," the rider told him.

"Ah!" Angelo said.

"Yesterday at Marsala."

Angelo wheeled and ran back into the courtyard, pounded once on the stable door, once on the kitchen door, then clattered up the stairway to his bedroom. "Garibaldi has landed at Marsala and I'm going to join him!" he cried, throwing off his shirt. Ava reached for the latch on the window shutters, staring at him. Angelo sat on the bed to pull off his boots and pants, then flung on his wedding shirt and strode out to the hall. He returned clothed in the fancy shirt and his best pair of velveteen pants. "I have waited all my life for this," he said, pulling on his boots. He crossed the room to Ava who stood by the open window, still staring at him. "You're crazy," she said soberly. Angelo took both her hands in his and kissed her lips. "Remember that I love you," he told her.

"Garibaldi is an animal, a beast," she said, her voice rising.

He laughed. "Then he has come to the right place."

"We will die," she wailed.

"We have always died. But today you should be singing."

Ava wrenched her hands from his and began to beat her fists on his chest, shouting "Go, go, go, go, go —" She had broken into sobs.

"I have never been so happy," he said, putting his arms around this sturdy young woman who wept for him.

Angelo kissed the crown of her head and rushed down the

stairway to the dining room. There he tossed back the lid of a black oak chest, peeled away the linens and flannels and came up with an antique bird gun, then he strode into the yard, pulling a heavy pistol from under the big flower pot by the door, and was shouting *Filomena* as he crossed to the stable where the boy had saddled the gelding. He mounted, took the bundle of food which Filomena handed up to him — leftovers from the wedding wrapped in oilcloth — and went out through the gate at a canter, leaving the boy at the stable door, Filomena in the middle of the yard, his uncles and half-brothers asleep indoors, and his virgin bride face down on her bed, beating her pillow.

Garibaldi had landed on the western shore of Sicily and everyone knew what he had come to do. He was a simple man with a simple desire. He would drive the King's troops first from that great island and then from the Kingdom of Naples and the forlorn southern peninsula, so that these lands could join with those in the north and become one Italy, a single nation as it had been ages ago. The King had 24,864 well-equipped troops waiting in Sicily. Garibaldi had come ashore with only 1,000 volunteers, some in red shirts and others in street clothes, and for guns they had junk — antique smooth-bore muskets, 100 Enfield rifles and 5 ancient cannons without gun carriages. At dawn the next morning he walked his patched-together army inland through seas of green corn and beans to Rampagallo, and the following day he trudged with them past silvery groves of olive trees up to the sun-baked highlands of Salemi. They spent the night in Salemi, some in houses and others in monasteries and still others under tents in the orchards outside. The next day their numbers increased a bit as volunteer squadre came up from the countryside, armed with flintlocks or pruning hooks, and somewhere among them was Angelo, Angelo Cavallù, *our* Angelo. He was dusty, for his horse had collapsed of exhaustion and Angelo had trotted over the hills and into town on his own two feet. That afternoon he saw Garibaldi dismount, stroll across a corner of the piazza and pass through a doorway: a pleasant-looking man with a rich honey-color beard, clothed in a loose red shirt — a man who moved with the effortless grace of an animal. Garibaldi was content at that moment, for he had just ridden in from a survey of the ground along the road to Palermo and now he was going to study a big map of Sicily which one of his officers had found. Until then he had not had a good map. That night, when he folded the map and went to bed, rain had begun to fall, but when he awoke at three the next morning the rain had ceased and it was beautiful. He pulled on his pants, drank a cup of coffee, called in his officers, told them what he planned to do and sent them to rouse his little army. He had been walking up and down the room and now he burst into song. Here was a fifty-three-year-old man about to attack an army of vastly superior numbers in a battle in which defeat meant death and he sang like a lover going to meet his mistress, because he was about to have his heart's desire.

That morning Angelo marched with the squadre down the road and through a valley where everyone bought oranges and lemons, then they left the road and trudged up a stony hillside. From the top of their bald hill they looked across a shallow alley to a steeper, terraced hill on top of which brightly uniformed troops were gathered in squares — there and there and there and there and over there. They were too many. Angelo's disheartened squadre, which had never been in a battle before, drifted quietly off to the side to watch how it was done. Over there, General Sforza ordered his trumpets to sound and ranks of identical soldiers began to step down the hill, to wade across the stream at the bottom and mount toward the volunteers, firing as they came. Over here, a bugler blew that fancy musical reveille which Garibaldi loved so much and a handful of his skirmishers began to fire at the oncoming troops. Of their own accord, the rest of Garibaldi's men, who had been sitting on the stony rubbish high on the hill, stood up — men in red shirts, men in street jackets, some even in top hats — and now they were running down at the troops in a burst of musketry. Angelo galloped after them. The Garibaldini drove the army back across the stream and part way up the terraced hillside. Then everything slowed. The afternoon grew slack and there was only the irregular clatter of gunfire, or once in a while the top of the enemy hill blossomed into white puffs of smoke and cannonballs shrieked past, and the sun roamed aimlessly overhead. It grew hot, terribly hot. Every so often Garibaldi's redshirts were driven down, or they climbed further up, but their numbers always diminished and now there were not so many — in fact, there were only a few hundred crouched on the steep hillside, pressed together here and there beneath the ragged terraces. Angelo sat with his shoulder against his own bit of loose stone wall, sucking the juice from his last orange, and he peered higher up the hill to where Garibaldi huddled with his bare sword and a crowd of his outlandish army. The terrace wall they clung to was nearest the summit and royalist troops were firing volley after volley down on them, even throwing rocks. He is a lion, thought Angelo, but I am only part of a horse and maybe not the best part at that. What do we do now? A rock hit Garibaldi on the back and he stood up, his sword flashing. His men stood up beside him. Now Garibaldi was climbing the terrace, his men were climbing the terrace. They were rising up everywhere on the hillside, rising and climbing through the ragged noise, crawling higher and higher, clawing up over the last heap of stones into a hazy white smoke filled with crackling gunfire and screams. Then there was the long hilltop slanting off and royalist troops running away, streaming down and away to the far valley, fleeing.

❦

Angelo marched here and there and elsewhere with Garibaldi for two weeks while the old fox outwitted the King's generals and drove the royal army from Sicily, then Angelo walked home. He wore a stained slouch hat and such tattered velveteen that when he turned in at the gate only his dog, Micu, recognized who it was, circling him and barking excitedly and leaping while Filomena and the boy stared. His bride cried, "Angelo!" from an upstairs window, "Angelo!" from the doorway, "Angelo!" as she threw her arms around his neck. He kissed her forehead and each cheek and said, "Tell Filomena to start heating water because I am going to take a long, long bath."

In the house they poured pots of steaming water into the copper tub which Angelo had dragged to the side of the bed. Ava laid out the towels, brush and soap on the table between the windows and turned to go, but Angelo took her wrist in one hand and gently closed the door with his other. Without a word he shed his shirt, pulled off his boots and stepped out of his pants. Ava stood at the window, staring out, and heard his gasp as he lowered himself into the scalding water.

"I cannot wash my own back," he said in a reasonable voice.

Ava turned hesitantly, a light flush on her cheeks, and took the soap and brush from the table and knelt behind his back. She lifted a cupped handful of water and let it trickle onto his shoulder, then another handful and another and one more. She dipped the soap into the water and slid it tenderly all the way across his back from the tip of one shoulder to the tip of the other. "Ah, that's good," Angelo murmured. Ava pressed her wet palm to his warm back and rubbed in a circle, making suds. "The first time I saw Garibaldi I was so close I could have reached out and touched him," he told her. "He's an old man, older than I am, but he moves very lightly, like an animal. — Would you like me to tell you what I've been doing for two weeks?" Ava dipped the soap into the water and swept it up and down his marvelous, silken back, enjoying herself. "Yes. Tell me," she said absently.

Later, when he had finished with his stories and his bath, Angelo stepped from the tub, letting the water sluice from him in streams as if he were a mountain, then he toweled himself dry and fell asleep in his bed for a day and a night. He dreamed. Maybe the dreams came from his aching muscles or the marrow of his bones or maybe they came from his blood, which was, after all, the mingled blood of men and beasts, of Siculi and Greeks, Romans, Carthaginians, Byzantines, Arabs, Jews, Normans, Spaniards — in other words, pure Sicilian blood. Occasionally his magnificent legs twitched and he gave a deep resonant groan, because he was dreaming not only his own story but the cruel three-thousand-year history of all Sicily. He was having a nightmare. At last he awoke and in the pale blue dawn he found Ava sleeping at his side, on top of the covers, an arm flung over her head and her hair spread loose upon the pillow.

He kissed her lips. Before she could rub the sleep from her eyes, Angelo said, "Come with me. I'll show you the world in the morning." He began to open the shutters. Ava stood there in her white chemise and watched him as the room filled up with light. She wanted to look at those equine hindquarters, those powerful flanks and long shins, wanted to see the dark whorls of hair on his chest, the satin nap on his underbelly, his black pouch and stallion thing. His flesh was the color of bronze and smooth beneath her fingertips as a chestnut fresh from its hull. Suddenly he knelt and scooped up the hem of her chemise, standing and lifting it so rapidly that she barely had time to raise her arms before the garment was unfurling in air, falling into a shadowy corner of the room. He put a warm hand on her haunch and when she lowered her eyes he kissed the nape of her neck. Now he whispered a few words in her ear and she tossed her head back, laughing. Who knows what happened next? Her births were always easy, her milk was always sweet, and she remained beautiful into old age. Their daughters inherited these traits. Their sons had legs like their father.

2

No one has been able to write a complete history of Sicily. Every historian who tries, fails — they sink into bewilderment or go mad with rage or collapse in grief, weeping. The agony that is Sicilian history is too terrible to think about. Ages ago Greeks with swords and chains invaded the island paradise and wrote about the locals who had cleared the forests and were farming. That's the last glimpse we get of Sicilians living free. In the next two thousand and six hundred years one greedy army after another came ashore to kill, imprison and brutalize them. After taking over, the new land-owners inscribed laws, contracts, leases and taxes on the flesh of the poor to enrich themselves and to immiserate the landless, so that each impoverished family had to turn against all others to survive. Some of the dispossessed went back to the caves of their ancestors, and others lived in the fields with nothing but the tattered clothes they wore to show they were people, not beasts. By 1860 a handful of idle nobles and their henchmen owned almost the whole island, receiving their legitimacy from the Bourbon King who sat in Naples, across the water in Italy. That was the year Angelo married Ava in May, the same month that Giuseppe Garibaldi landed on Sicily's western shore with a thousand volunteers. Garibaldi swept eastward to the great city of Palermo and from there to the eastern edge of the island, the city of Messina. On the shore at Messina you can look across the water to the city of Reggio Calabria situated on the southernmost tip of Italy. The city lies just above the watery horizon and behind it the brown, sun-dried land rises toward the harsh mountains beyond. In the old city of Reggio, off the main avenue, on one of the narrow side streets, there used to be a house — to speak plainly, a whore house, a bordello — called the Conca d'Oro (the Golden Shell), a well kept house with accommodating women, a friendly place.

3

THE FIRST TIME FRANCO WATCHED STELLA UNDRESS (20 August 1860) in her room at the bordello Conca d'Oro, her freshness and beauty struck him so hard that he fell to his knees, opened his arms and asked her to marry him. "I've never seen anyone so beautiful and I love you," he said. Stella looked at him, her face as serene as polished marble, and began slowly to unpin her hair. The room was filled with dusky golden light which filtered through the shuttered windows. "Marry me," he whispered. "Marry me," She held the pin in her teeth and calmly watched him while her hands searched in the coiled mass of her hair and when she had found the last one she laid all the pins in a sea shell on the bed table. She had worked a few years and was no longer surprised at the way men behaved in her room. "What do I say?" she asked distantly.

"Say yes."

"Yes," she recited, her loosened hair turning languidly about her breast and arm, unrolling over her wrist, across her thigh.

"Diva," the young man murmured. "Goddess."

"Yes. I am a goddess." She was matter-of-fact about it. Of course, the people of southern Italy never made much of the difference between mortals and gods, and you never knew when a man might become a god, or a goddess become a woman, or vice versa.

Franco knelt slowly forward and kissed her feet, embraced her legs as if gathering an armful of long-stemmed flowers, and plunged his face into her dark—

"But first you must wash," Stella told him, firmly turning his hot cheek aside so that he might see the big white pitcher and bowl on a very low little table. "Over there," she said. Franco staggered to his feet, his head filled with the odor of lemon flowers and brine. He poured the water into the bowl, set the pitcher down with a hollow clink on the marble, and began to scrub his face. "Not your face! Not in *that!*" Stella cried.

Franco straightened up and turned, water streaming from his bare shoulders and chest onto his trousers.

"What?"

"Not your *face*, caro. Wash—" Stella sighed and took up the towel that lay folded on the table and began to dry his chin. "You're new here?" she asked.

Franco was distracted by her nakedness so near to him, by the way her long hair fell upon her breasts, turned about her arm and uncoiled heavily to her knees. "Yes!" he said, getting his wits together. He told her he came from a village in the Calabrian mountains, but that he had traveled around and picked up an education and, as a matter of fact, in a short time he was going off to teach mathematics. He said he believed in mathematics and he thought he would like teaching it. Just now he was down here in Reggio — "the home of Pythagoras," he noted — merely to stroll around and enjoy the cafés and views of the sea. This Reggio was a city of vistas and he had discovered he was crazy about looking at the sea. Then he unbuckled and, because he was shy, turned his back to her before he stepped out of his pants.

"Maybe you'll see the Fata Morgana," Stella said, coming around to watch him. "The castles float in the air far above the water. It's famous."

"An optical illusion, a mirage," Franco said, hurriedly soaping himself.

"Of course it's an illusion. Morgana conjures the castles out of thin air. That's why it's called Fata Morgana, because she's the one who creates it."

"I'm a rationalist," he informed her. "I'm a freethinker and a mathematician and I don't believe in — What are you looking at?" he asked, covering his drenched privates with his hand.

"Don't worry. It won't fly away. Here's a towel." She walked idly to the shuttered window and peered between the slats at the balcony and at the sunny strip of street below. "I don't know anything about rationalists or freethinkers, but the Royalists don't like them. Have you seen all the soldiers?"

"They don't frighten me."

"They say Garibaldi has come over from Sicily."

"They've been saying that for weeks."

"How long have you been here in Reggio?" she asked, peeping again through the shutters to the sunny balcony.

"Three days," he said. "How long have you been at the Conca d'Oro?"

For a while she did not answer. "Forever, I think."

"That's not true."

Stella turned to him as if she were weary, the golden light spreading up like a fan behind her. "All my life, this life, I've been here."

Franco studied her face to see what she meant, but in that topaz shadow he could never make it out. She seemed made of honey-colored marble and so remote he felt half afraid of her. "You are the most beautiful woman I've ever seen," he whispered.

Stella smiled. "Yes. I'm a goddess. And you are a very young man — a rationalist, a freethinker and a mathematician." And taking Franco's hand she led him to her bed, drew up her long legs and sank back upon the white pillows as if bedded in clouds.

Franco was young and enthusiastic and they made love for a long, long time, but even with a goddess it comes to an end — unless you are a god, which Franco was not. Stella arose and went to the big mirror that stood by the bed and Franco, leaning up on his elbow, watched her draw on her blue silk robe.

"If you were my wife —" he began.

"I wouldn't respect you. How could I respect anyone foolish enough to marry a whore?" She was brushing her hair in long slow strokes.

"I believe in the future, not the past. I don't care what you've done."

"Because you don't know what I've done. If you want to

marry me you must come back tonight and watch me at work."

"Are you serious?" he asked.

"You can hide on the balcony and watch through the shutters." She took a pin from the fluted sea shell on her bed table and began to coil her hair upon her head.

"And then —"

"Afterward, you must tell me everything you saw," she said.

"Why?"

"So I'll know that you really watched. And then —"

"Then I'll ask you to marry me," said Franco, swinging himself from the bed.

"Then you won't ask," said Stella.

Franco returned early that night. The room looked just the same as it had that afternoon, but now there was an oil lamp burning on the low table beside the wash basin and Stella had her hair up in a large braided knot.

"Did you think I'd come back?" he asked cheerfully.

"Yes," she said.

Stella set a bottle of brandy and two glasses on the low table. She was wearing a white dress which left her golden shoulders and arms bare to the hazy lamplight. She poured out the brandy and they each took up a glass.

"My name is Franco Morelli and I live in our house in the town of Morano in Cosenza," he announced.

Stella looked at him in surprise. "My name is Stella Maria DiMare and I live in the bordello Conca d'Oro in Reggio, Calabria." She smiled.

They touched glasses and drank.

"You're a handsome young man. Did your mother ever tell you that?" she asked.

"I don't know. My mother died when I was a child."

"Oh. I'm sorry. My own mother died when I was born," she added.

"My father is a carpenter and cabinet maker."

"And my father was a fisherman," she said. Stella smiled, remembering him. "He used to tell me that he found me at sea. Other children were found under cabbages, but he used to say that he pulled in his nets one morning and there I was, swimming with all the fishes. I loved that story. He used to carry me on his shoulders. He died in 1848. I think it was during the bombardment. He sailed out and never came back."

Stella sat on the foot of her bed, Franco sat in a stiff chair, and they talked and talked, getting to know each other. Actually, Stella did most of the talking, for no one had ever asked her about herself and now she discovered that she liked to converse on that subject with this young man. In fact, she talked so much that she forgot where she was and remembered only at the last minute. "Oh! the time! I've got to tell mother superior you ran down the back stairs," she cried.

Franco jumped up and met himself in the tall mirror that stood by the bed — a flushed young man in a whore's bedroom. How odd that a flat mirror reflects so little of the truth, he thought.

"Hurry!" Stella said, unlatching the shuttered doors to the balcony. "This way. And be careful of the bird cages out there. Whatever you do, don't make any noise. After my last customer leaves I'll open the doors and let you in. Watch out for my doves!"

Stella shut the doors and adjusted the louvers so that Franco, out on the dark balcony, could peer in and see all that went on in the lighted room. Franco crouched among the bamboo bird cages and wondered how he could watch and not watch at the same time, for on the one hand he felt it was dishonorable to spy on the woman he loved and on the other hand he had given her his promise to spy in order to win her. He was turning this round and round in his mind when he heard the bedroom door open. He peeked between the slats and began to watch.

Well, what can I tell you? Stella's first customer was a cranky Neapolitan businessman whose limp thing wouldn't get hard no matter how she handled it, until he gave her an order to do thus and so with this and this. Next came the elegant son of a local landowner, a youth with a long nose who confused top with bottom, front with back, and one thing with another. And after him there came two Royalist officers, big men who tossed off their uniforms and shoved each other around like playful athletes before they set to work on Stella. It grew to be a very long night.

When her last customer had gone, Stella unlatched the doors to the balcony and whispered to Franco, *Come in*. He arose slowly and unsteadily from the lattice of shadows amid the bamboo bird cages. She poured two brimming glasses of brandy, drank one straight down and handed the other to him. But Franco stood wordless in the balcony doorway, his face white as a sheet of paper, his eyes dead as stones.

"Ah," Stella said gently. "I can see you've had a hard night."

Franco stared straight ahead, as if he were deaf, dumb and blind.

"I like you," she said. She looked at him, then sighed and drank down his brandy. "Actually, I love you and I'm sorry I didn't tell you before," she added.

He walked uncertainly into the room.

"Listen," she told him. "Garibaldi has landed and there's going to be a big battle tonight. You've got to get home."

"That's what I want, a good fight." He seemed to awaken.

"Did you hear me? Garibaldi has landed. When the troops find out they'll be shooting at anything that moves. You've got to get home."

"I'd like to kill a few troops myself," he said. "A few Neapolitans. Some landowners. A couple of officers." He laughed and his eyes brightened.

"Carissimo," she said, putting her hand to his cheek. "Garibaldi is immortal but you are not. Stay out of it. Go someplace safe."

But Franco had already crossed the room and now he threw open the chamber door and vaulted down the stairway, strode through a maroon parlor of gilded chairs, torn playing cards and overturned wineglasses, and burst into the street. He ran, turned away from the bordello and ran down whatever avenue opened for him, ran through a city of crumbling masonry and stucco and shuttered windows with no sound anywhere except his own clattering footfall. He ran where the streets themselves led, rushing now down a cobbled alley to a yet narrower passage that hurled him headlong into the Cathedral Square which abruptly swirled into a crackling chaos of gunfire, screams and plunging horses.

Garibaldi had landed. Everyone in Reggio had known he was coming, the only question was when. Italy is separated from Sicily by the Straits of Messina, and the northern end of the Straits is so narrow that anyone on the Italian side could climb a hill and look over the water to Garibaldi's camp and watch his men hammering together supply rafts, or inspect his makeshift flotilla of steamboats, fishing boats, rowboats and barges pulled up on the sand. The desolate King in Naples knew he was coming. He had ordered his warships to patrol the Straits, and he had packed 16,000 handsomely dressed troops into that part of Italy. The old general at the castle in Reggio certainly knew he was coming. He calculated that Garibaldi would cross the Straits and rush up from the shore to the streets of the city. That's why he positioned his colonel and the men of the 14th Line out front, had ordered them to bivouac in the large Square before the Cathedral. He figured that Garibaldi was an ordinary mortal.

On the morning of August 19 Garibaldi did appear, but not on the shore opposite his camp and not at the narrow northern end of the Straits at all, but on an empty stretch of beach thirty miles to the south. The Royal Navy never saw him. He simply appeared, materializing quietly out of the limpid dawn air with his men on a patch of sand that sloped gently up to a wilderness of cactuses and aloes. Eventually Royalist warships came up over the horizon and drew near and since not even Garibaldi could hide a steamboat on an open beach he and his crazy quilt army were discovered. The warships blew apart the grounded steamboat, but by then the entire army on the beach had vanished. Garibaldi had a simple plan. First he would march north to rendezvous with partisans already in the countryside, then he would transform all his men into substanceless shadows. The next night some would slip past the soldiers who guarded the city gates and once inside would glide noiselessly toward the Cathedral Square. He and the others would condense out of the black night air on the hills behind Reggio. When the redshirts and the Royalists were in blind battle in front of the Cathedral, Garibaldi and the rest of his army would sweep down upon the city and it would be theirs. The plan worked like a miracle. And Franco just happened to rush into the Square the moment the fight began.

The morning after the battle was quiet in the bordello Conca d'Oro. Stella sat in the half-shuttered light of her room with her forgotten sewing in her lap and gazed blankly at the dirty wall. She tried not to think of Franco, because whenever she did her heart felt hollow and heavy at the same time. She sighed and wondered what the next thousand years would bring and she was trying not to think at all when there was a BOOM and one of the shutters burst into splinters above her head. It took her a moment to realize that somebody had fired a shotgun at her balcony doors. "Stella DiMare!" he cried. She jumped up and put her cheek to the margin of the shutter, peering into the narrow street below. "Stella DiMare!" Of course it was Franco standing there, a pistol in his belt and a shotgun in his hand, shouting up at her. She pressed her back against the wall. "Yes!" she cried.

"My name is Franco Morelli from the town of Morano in

Cosenza!" There was another BOOM as the top of the other door to the balcony exploded, filling the air with wood chips.

"I remember you," Stella shouted, her eyes shut against the soft patter of bird shot and plaster falling from the ceiling.

"Thank you," he cried. "I've come back to tell you what I saw in your room last night."

She opened her eyes. "And what did you see?"

"A jackass, a dog, and two pigs!" he shouted.

"Very clever! You're the cleverest young man I know."

"And you," he called up to her. "I saw you, diva."

Stella opened the shredded balcony shutters and stood there a moment, looking down on him. His necktie was gone, his shirt was open, his jaw was dark with a day's stubble — a handsome young man. She said nothing. Her face was as calm as the sea when night is over and morning about to begin and her eyes shimmered with sadness.

"Oh, yes. Everyone looked at you but I'm the only one who saw you. I know you for what you are. Diva. Goddess. I keep trying but I haven't shot anybody yet," he cried. "Will you marry me!"

Stella looked into Franco's face and smiled, then she turned and unlatched the door to one of the bamboo cages and withdrew one dove and another. She tossed them into the air where they blossomed in a flurry of white wings, then beat their way in a soaring helical sweep skyward, circle upon circle, one following the other like melody in a round. She smiled because she loved Franco. Now she flung open the other cages and as the doves shot up around her like rockets she leaned over the rail to say, "Yes, I will marry you." But by then the street was empty and Franco gone.

Franco had run off before Stella had answered, because he was afraid she might say no. In all other ways he was brave. The next day he hiked out of the city and up the hills northward, climbing to join the Garibaldini camped on the slopes high above the Straits. Franco chose a patch of ground sloven with broken mud banks, cactuses, tangled vineyards and orchards, chose it because the view was splendid. Below him on the lower terraces of the mountain were the Royalist troops, and way down below the Royalists flowed the blue waters of the Straits, and on the other side stood the lilac headlands of Sicily with smoky Mongibello (Mt. Etna) to the south and the great Tyrrhenian Sea like azure enamel to the north horizon. Franco sat back against a crooked olive tree, his shotgun across his knees, but the call to advance and fire never came. Instead, the men of both armies — the redshirts in the balcony, the Royalists in the lower tiers — watched an artillery duel between the distant cannoneers on the Sicilian point and the warships of the Royal Navy. The following day Garibaldi gave the order to advance without firing. The men stood up, stretched and began to descend, step by step, upon the Royalist troops. Franco couldn't believe what was happening. Now and again cotton puffs of smoke appeared below and cannon-balls shrieked up at them, thudding into the mountainside, and every so often he heard the crack of enemy rifle fire, but everyone continued to step carefully downward with their weapons silent. At one point word was passed along that they were to halt, so they halted. Franco sat on the ground and stared glumly at the town below, knowing that if the fight continued in this fashion he would never get to shoot anybody. Then he saw Garibaldi close at hand on the brown hillside where he stood talking with three of his officers. He had a full golden beard, wore a loose red shirt stained with sweat and he carried a long sword, was using it just now to make a sweeping orchestral gesture toward the gray mountains further north. Two of the men broke off and headed up the hill while Garibaldi and the remaining officer began to walk down toward the enemy. His voice was strange, more like music than speech, and Franco remembered it for the rest of his life. Word came again to advance without firing, so they did, and in a little while the King's soldiers threw down their rifles and surrendered. In a few days Garibaldi was to gallop north to Naples, disarming and sending home ten thousand Royalist troops on the way, and when he rode through the mountain provinces of Calabria, Basilicata and Campania, men would come forward to touch his hand, women would hold babies aloft to receive his blessing, and he was greeted as a god.

Now Franco trudged down the last hillock, crossed a dirt road and walked onto the empty shore. He broke open his shotgun, unloaded his pistol and laid them on the dry pebbles. Nearer the water he saw something like a discarded banner lying on the sand and when he looked more closely he saw that it was a forgotten pile of laundry, a woman's white dress and blue robe folded loosely and anchored there by the handful of sea shells heaped upon it. He tried not to think of Stella, but everything reminded him of her. He sighed. He pulled off his shoes, threw off his shirt and waded into the water. He washed his face, his scorched neck, his arms. The scent of brine and lemon blossoms, the swaying of the sea anemones, the convoluted drifting braids of tawny seaweed— everything reminded him of Stella. He gazed at the waves that came forever forward to meet him, waves that still rise and curl and, curling, fall like scalloped shells upon that beach, and as he watched a wave broke into foam and it was Stella who stood before him, wringing the seawater from her hair while she waded ashore. "Franco," she called to him. "You are a rationalist, a freethinker and a mathematician and I am the goddess who says yes." They had many children, each one as beautiful as her mother.

4

WE KNOW THESE THINGS BECAUSE A GRANDSON OF Angelo Cavallù married a granddaughter of Stella DiMare on the dock in Boston in 1904, and the stories were passed down from one generation to another. Angelo, half man and half stallion, loved to tell the story of his wedding night, and his son Fimi told it to his own son Pacifico and Pacifico, who married on the dock in Boston in 1904, used to tell it at his big Sunday dinners where his children heard it and they, in turn, told it to their children. As for the story of Stella DiMare, a woman so beautiful her looks could stun, Stella refused to be ashamed and told all her children — seven daughters — the true story of how she had met their father in the bordello Conca d'Oro. Her daughter Diva told it with sympathy and amusement to her own daughter Marianna but Marianna, who married Pacifico on the dock in Boston in 1904, could never be coaxed to tell it at their big Sunday dinners, or only rarely and only if the children had left the table, for she had told them a different version. It was a very nice version, but not true.

These stories were first written down by Nick Pellegrino. His mother Marissa was one of Pacifico Cavallù's daughters, but Nick didn't hear them from her. His mother didn't know what to make of a great-grandfather who was part horse or a great-grandmother who worked in a house of prostitution, and she was too embarrassed to tell such tales to her son. As it happened, Nick heard them from his aunt Regina (Gina) who was one of his mother's sisters. When Gina was a girl she was told that Stella DiMare was a singer with the voice of an angel, that the Conca d'Oro was an opera house and what Franco witnessed that night was a production of Verdi's *La Traviata*, the opera about a Parisian courtesan.

As I said, a very nice version. But the facts about the Conca d'Oro got passed along from older sister to younger and the true story always came out. As I said, Nick wrote down these tales and we should all be grateful for that, but he got certain things wrong — like names, dates, generations, and that fable about getting married on the dock. Of course, when he heard these tales from his aunt he was twenty-two, she was thirty-two, and they were both lying naked on her sunny bed after making love, so he may have been too unfocused to remember much. Gina was the youngest of all his aunts. Gina's mother, Marianna Cavallù, had nine children — first came four girls, then four boys, and only then came Gina. She was as beautiful as her sisters and as wild as her brothers, so ungovernable that she ran away from her mother, or was sent off by her father, to live with one of her older married sisters, the thought being that her older sister would be better able to control her. That sister was Nick's mother, and Nick always said he had a crush on Gina since he was five years old. By the time Nick was twenty-two, Gina was a restless widow, her husband having been lost at sea in World War II. After the war Gina owned a café in the fishing town of Gloucester, on Cape Ann, in Massachusetts. That's where this happened in the summer of 1952.

So there's Nick in white trousers and a sky-blue open shirt, a handsome kid with scratchy stubble on his jaws. And there's Gina with bare arms and a tight white jersey with a dab of shadow beneath each nipple. He grabs her breast, gives her a kiss on the mouth, and she slaps his face hard — *whack! whack*! — this way and that. *"Four years at college and you've learned absolutely nothing!"* she cries, her eyes brimming with tears. He came back later with his arms full of flowers and over the next few days one thing led to another, as it will. Gina liked to talk after making love, liked to loaf on the bed and gossip about anything at all. She would lean back against the heaped pillows, the wisps of hair in her armpits damp and curled, a valley of sweat glistening between her breasts. And in the faint warm aroma of fresh dough that rose from her flesh after strenuous love making, she would light a cigarette and take the clam shell ashtray from the bed table and place it on her stomach, right over her deep sweat-filled belly button. "You have beautiful legs," she told Nick one day. "You inherited those legs from your great, great grandfather. Did you know that? Stop fidgeting and let me tell you something." That's how he first heard those stories.

Their love making was their special secret and they never guessed that everyone in the family soon sensed that something was going on. Gina's brothers figured that Gina and Nick were banging each other and it might be illegal or revolting or only very foolish, but there it was and somebody should break them up before anyone else found out. Gina's sisters felt she was overly fond of Nick, maybe way too fond, but that was only because he was he was young and so full of life, and because after Gina had learned how her husband had been swept from the deck of his Coast Guard ship she had gone crazy and her heart had frozen. Now her heart had thawed and that was all to the good, but somebody should break them up before it went too far. Nick's mother seemed to be the only one who believed that Nick, whom she still thought of as a rather sensitive boy, merely had a crush on Gina. Nick's father asked Gina's brother Mercurio, the brother closest to Nick in age, to drive down to Gloucester. "Don't bawl out Gina," he told Mercurio. "But when you have Nick alone, talk to him — don't ask what's going on, don't ever talk about that. Just remind him he's finished school, he's grown up, and now he has to get serious. When the subject gets around to women, tell him you don't like men who take advantage of women, younger or older. That will start him thinking. He won't listen to me, because I'm his father and he thinks I don't know anything about —" Here he broke off and searched for the right words. "Women and romance. But he'll listen to you," he said.

So Mercurio drove down to Gloucester in his red sports car, spent a night with Nick driving from one roadhouse to another, and the romance between Gina and Nick came to end. And Gina's sisters were right: Gina's heart had thawed. She no longer thought of her husband being swept into the black Atlantic, no longer heard him shouting in the icy water while the ship vanished behind a mountainous wave, no longer watched while he thrashed and bobbed and froze to death. Many years later — the soft summer of 1985 — at the double wedding where Gina married Marshfield Thomas and Gina's granddaughter Aurora married Jens, Nick learned from Mercurio that the whole fam-

ily had known something was going on between Nick and Gina back in 1952, and Nick's father had sent Mercurio to Gloucester to bring it to an end.

5

NOW LET ME GO BACK AND PICK UP THE LOOSE END of that earlier story, the one about Angelo Cavallù and Ava, and continue from there. Angelo and Ava Cavallù named their first child Giuseppe Calatafimi Cavallù — named him Giuseppe (Joseph), not after Italy's patron saint, Joseph, minimus husband of Mary, mother of Jesus, but for the great Giuseppe Garibaldi, and named him Calatafimi for the place where Garibaldi and Angelo and the other Red Shirts had fought their way up a hillside to blow away the Royalist army. This Giuseppe Calatafimi was called plain Fimi. He was born with thighs and legs like a horse, but not so emphatically as his father, and now at eighteen he was already a hand taller than the older man. Young Fimi wasn't a scholar, it's true, but he did know two short prayers by heart, had his multiplication tables up to nine times nine, could do long division, and though he barely knew how to read he could sign his name with a handsome flourish. Furthermore, he was like a young god with animals, could calm a spooked horse by sheer talk, call goats and pigs and bulls to his side, or whistle a bird so it ate from his hand, and about a year ago he had discovered he could do much the same with young women — farm girls, house maids, serving girls in taverns.

One night in the spring of 1879 Fimi couldn't fall asleep. He felt thirsty, or perhaps hungry, he couldn't tell which, or maybe he was getting light-headed with the scent of lemon blossoms from the neighbor's orchards, or possibly it was his legs which were growing tense with compressed energy. He got

up and pulled on his pants, careful not to wake his brother. He crept down the hall past his sisters' bedroom, groped down the back stairway to the kitchen and across the cool stone floor to the dirt courtyard, then ran across the courtyard, leapt the back gate, and galloped out to the field. Pieces of the moon flickered on the stream which separated the Cavallù land from the neighbor's orchards. He sat low on the gravel bank and the cool touch of the water on his feet and ankles soothed him. The stars looked hazy and he wondered if the scent of lemon blossoms had thickened the air. He was getting drowsy when a patch of night from the shadowy orchard came splashing across the stream to slip past him. Or it would have slipped past if he hadn't stood up. "Hey!" he whispered. "Who are *you?*" he said.

The person stopped as still as a stone. "No one," she said at last.

"You must be someone," Fimi said, walking over to get a better look. "I've seen you before. You work for the Baldos," he said.

"So?"

"What are you doing over here?"

"Nothing."

"Where are you going in the middle of the night?"

"Palermo."

"Ah! You're the girl the DiSecco woman bought. How do you like being a lady's maid?"

"Work is work. It's the school part I can't stand."

Fimi laughed. "You'll get a good husband out of it. That's the deal, isn't it?"

"I don't plan to get married to some old *contadino* with cow shit on his boots. I'd rather die in Palermo than live out here."

"You have a long walk ahead of you. Why don't you —"

"If you come a step closer I'll crack your nuts!"

Fimi laughed. "Tough city girl. Take it easy. Sit down and we'll talk. Only talk. It's a good night for talk."

But she had already turned and was walking into the dark field.

"By the way," he said. "If you're looking for the road to Palermo, it's down the slope, not over where you're headed."

"You're lying," she said, hesitating.

"Don't get lost. —Look at the moon. It's only a slice. Wait a few days, there'll be more moon and you'll be able to see where you're going. And you never know who's sleeping in those fields."

She glanced at the moon, then came back and sat on a stone somewhat above him, out of his reach. "I still think you're lying," she muttered. As a matter of fact, he was. She hadn't lived in the country long enough to know which way the moon grew and tomorrow night it would be even thinner. Fimi asked her name. Cinderella, she said tartly. And I'm prince Cavallù, he countered. He reached for her foot and she swung it out of reach. "Come on. What are you afraid of?" he asked her.

"They say you're animals."

"Who says?"

"Everybody. Signora DiSecco and her brother."

"No one would call DiSecco or her brother Baldo animals. We think of them as vegetables."

"And I know about the vendetta between Signor Baldo and your father," she said.

Fimi laughed. "There's no vendetta — maybe one of our sheep strayed onto Baldo's land and came home to us naked, so a few days later a barrel of Baldo's lemons suddenly turned rotten, then one of our goats got shot, then a few of their trees got chopped down. That's all. No vendetta," he assured her. "My father and Signor Baldo get along like brothers."

Fimi had edged up beside her; she watched him closely from the corner of her eyes, but she didn't move.

"What do you do for the signora?" he asked, simply to keep her talking.

"I prepare her bath every morning, light her bedroom lamps every night, and do everything else in between. Whatever she wants."

Fimi murmured sympathetically, brushed her cheek with his hand and she snapped at him, biting his little finger almost in two.

"Aiiii! —You work a long hard day," he said when he could, sucking the blood from his finger. "She beat you much?" He took a rag from his pocket and wrapped it around the finger.

"No. If she gets angry she locks me in my room with a book and won't let me out until I've copied a whole page, word for word. But she's all right, mostly all right. Sometimes she'll give me one of her old dresses to keep and she even leaves the beads on it. Like this one," she said, smoothing the fabric over her knees. "She gave me this. It's very nice, isn't it?"

"It's very black. I can hardly see where you leave off and the night air begins."

"She wears black, only black, for her dead husband."

Fimi's fingertips brushed her shoulder just an instant. "Ah, that's you," he said. "In the dark I couldn't tell. You were going to say something about the terrible work."

"The work isn't terrible," she told him.

"Then why are you running away?"

"It's like being in school!" she said irritably. "She tells me, Don't use that word, it's vulgar, and don't stand like that, don't show so much skin, don't use that word again, say this word, wash your hair like this so it shines. —Then I have to sit on a stool while she stands behind me and brushes my hair. She says, You can call me Signora Sofia when there's just us two. —She loves to brush my hair."

"Of course she does," Fimi said.

"All day the house is quiet as a tomb and at night everybody sleeps. What else is there to do out here? And they're too old to do anything anyway. Signor Baldo is old, his man is old, the cook is ancient, both maids are antiques, the overseer is decrepit, the watchdog is blind. I never see a living person —" Abruptly she stopped talking because Fimi had stroked her hair gently, just once. Now there was only the sound of the water rippling around the rocks in the stream. Fimi stroked again and she resumed talking. "They've divided the house, so Signora DiSecco has half and her brother has half. Signora has a room with nothing in it but books and that's where she reads and the only noise is scritch-scritch-scritch when she writes. Signor Baldo has a room, too, but not so big as hers, where he keeps his ledgers and his guns — he's very proud of his guns — and that's where he writes down the number of every little thing he owns, how much of this, how many of that, how much it costs and how much it sells for."

"They're very strange people, both of them," Fimi agreed, laying back in the long grass. "The stars look bigger tonight. And they look wet. Look. Lie back," he said, putting a warm hand on her arm. As soon as the girl lay beside him he rolled onto his elbow to face her, waiting while she talked ever more rapidly about DiSecco and Baldo, how they sat at opposite ends of the long dinner table and argued about everything and when you heard them stop it meant that Signor Baldo had shaken open his newspaper and his sister had turned to her book. Fimi brushed her forehead with his lips, kissed her cheek, her mouth. During the next half hour one caress led to another until Fimi's Cinderella abruptly shook him aside. "Jesus," she panted. "Jesus Christ! I've got to go. If Signora DiSecco finds I'm gone she'll lock me in my room and won't let me out till I've copied a whole damn book." She threw herself on Fimi, saying, "You'd better be here tomorrow night," and bit his earlobe, then leaped up and *splash-splash* vanished into the dark.

❦

Now, to be fair, I have to say something about Signora Sonia DiSecco. At eighteen Sonia had married Major DiSecco, a handsome reckless spendthrift who was killed four years later, ambushed with his entire troop by the brigands he had been pursuing. Sonia, stunned with grief, returned to the Baldo villa to live with her unmarried brother. Her grief receded but something in her remained awry, broken or missing. As a school girl Sonia had admired the British for aiding the Italians against the Bourbon Royalists during the Risorgimento, but now her admiration grew to a passion that embraced all things British — Parliament, Shakespeare, beef, tea, the adversarial judicial system, Isaac Newton's calculus, the poetry of Percy Bysshe Shelley, and on and on. She had never heard English spoken, but had taught herself how to read it and had recently begun a translation into Sicilian of Mary Wollstonecraft's *A Vindication of the Rights of Women*. She believed ardently that education ennobled people and was exhilarated when compulsory two-year primary school was legislated in 1877 — now everyone would have to complete second grade! And since we're talking about Sonia, I must add that she had not *bought* her maid in Palermo. The girl's parents had many more children than they could care for, so Sonia alleviated their poverty with a little cash and took the girl in as a helper and ward, all with the understanding that Sonia would educate her and find her a suitable husband. True, usually it was a poor girl from the country who was brought in to the city this way, but Signora DiSecco was never conventional.

Fimi waited by the stream the next night, but she didn't come, nor the following night when the moon was pared down even more. He decided to go to Signor Baldo's to find her, to see her even if only from a distance — and he wanted to make his exploration look innocent. So in the middle of the morning, while everyone was busy doing one thing or another, Fimi led his favorite horse — a spirited mare, glossy as a chestnut — led her without a bridle or saddle, walked her across the field by the hank of her mane in his fist, splashed across the stream and into the lemon orchard and broke out the other side. There he let go of her mane, whacked her rump and ran behind her, shouting and whistling as if trying to catch her, driving her toward the back of Villa Baldo whose new roof tiles loomed over the greenery just ahead. The mare burst through the screen of aloe bushes pursued by Fimi who chased her past the row of bee hives, past the doorway where the dog lay sleeping and the stucco wall and the grape arbor under the second-floor windows, then around the well and through a clutter of clucking hens, back to the bee hives and around again. Signor Baldo had popped up at a window at this end and — Ah, ha! — the girl was at a window at the other end, her arm cradling some books. Fimi stopped running, pulled off his shirt and as the mare came around the well he began flapping his shirt at her, whistling, shouting *Ai! Ai! Ai!* while memorizing the second-floor window where his Cinderella stood. When he had completed the survey, Fimi grabbed the mare's mane, brought her to a halt and came in a running leap to mount her. He was out of breath, his naked chest heaving and glistening with sweat, but he laughed he was so happy. Only after he had whipped his horse with his shirt and was cantering away did he see Signora DiSecco standing in the dappled shade of the grape arbor, pen in hand, watching him.

The moon was only a sliver that night and the sky thick with stars when Fimi crept into the Villa Baldo grape arbor, clambered up a post, pulled himself through a mat of vines and crawled along a thick vine-tangled beam toward the casement window which looked like a black mirror. He tapped on the glass, waited a few moments. He put his nose to the glass and peered in, saw nothing at first and then — ah! He drew back and the casement swung out with a hushed scraping sound. He swung his legs over the sill and dropped into the room. Fimi heard the rustle of falling fabric, the click of beads, and turned to see the dark shimmer of starlight on her hair and a gleam of flesh. "Where —" he began to say, but already her hands were on his shirt and with half a word, or maybe not a word but a panting breath, she ripped his shirt open, the buttons snapping off pop-pop-pop, then her arm was around his neck and her full weight pulled him down to his knees, down upon her, down upon the floor.

Everyone wants details, but the story has been handed around so many times the details have rubbed off. All I can tell you is that after their hushed and half-stifled frenzy she kissed his wounded ear and panted *mio stadduni* or *picu stadduni* — my stallion or little stallion. And that's all. As for Fimi, the love-making that night was the wildest in his life, until the next night which was even wilder, and so it went night after night after night. He wanted it to go on forever, but it came to an end two weeks after it had started. It ended the day that Signora DiSecco, who rode horses the way men do, went galloping by on the road to Palermo, and half an hour later her brother rattled past in a buggy, headed to Palermo too. By evening everyone had learned that the girl Signora DiSecco had bought in the city had run away. Whether she had returned to the poor neighborhood she had come from, or whether she had gone someplace else, or had been waylaid by the men with nothing who slept in the fields, Fimi never knew, but he knew it was over.

Now a few words about Signor Baldo. He wanted a wife. At the death of his father he had taken over the estate — a crumbling farmhouse, surrounded by disorderly orchards and a withered vineyard — and made it profitable. Now he was prosperous, almost forty years old and he wanted a wife. He hadn't been able to marry, he complained, because his young sister occupied half the villa and her rants upset every decent family between Trapani and Palermo. Baldo was courting a woman named Isabella (quiet, ample shape, good-size vineyard) but when Isabella's pious family were finally seated at his table his sister Sonia had lectured them on the virtues of universal literacy. Isabella's father had laughed angrily at Sonia, informing her that if her personal maid ever learned how to read there would be no privacy for Sonia or anyone else. Sonia had then become inflamed and ridiculed the pope for forbidding Catholics to vote or to run for office. It was Sonia's passionate rudeness, not her radical opinions that bothered Baldo. In fact, he liked to confess that in his youth he had read Mazzini and had admired Francesco Crispi, the young Sicilian revolutionary who had wanted to make Italy a republic. But Mazzini was an idealist and when Crispi grew older and wiser he helped to make Italy *not* a republic but a monarchy. Twenty years had passed: now the king and his politicians were far away up North and had forgotten about Sicily, as usual. Baldo's favorite story was how when Garibaldi and his Red Shirts came ashore to liberate Sicily the first thing they did was ask for a map. *"Sicily wasn't on their maps!* You see, the Northern Italians have always felt, deep in their hearts, that Italy stops at the beach in Reggio Calabria. On the other side of the water is the Island of Sicily which to them is not quite Africa but not really Italy, either. So nothing changes here. The important thing is not politics," said Baldo. "The important thing is to work, to have children, and to hold your land from generation to generation."

One day — it must have been two or three months after the girl ran off — Baldo and his sister Sonia DiSecco arrived at Angelo Cavallù's place. Angelo stood in the wide front doorway, his hands on his hips, not knowing what to expect. He was older than when you saw him last; now he had vigorous gray hair and the physical aplomb of a sturdy Arabian horse. Baldo was dressed neither formally nor informally, but was wearing a long face and carried what looked like a polished cigar box in his hand. His sister Sofia was dressed in black, as usual, but in addition she wore a black net veil. Angelo and Baldo noded stiffly to each other; Baldo drew his sister forward, Angelo bowed to her and led them to the sitting room. *"What?"* Angelo asked him. *"Private,"* Baldo answered. Angelo turned and led them farther to his private back room — one big window, a desk, four chairs, a shelf of jumbled ledgers, papers, wine glasses, and in the corner a large oak gear from the mill, a splintered oak axel, an egg shaped stone with a groove so you could bind it to a stick to make a hammer, two bamboo fishing poles, and other such things. He brought a rush-bottom chair and placed it beside Signora DiSecco who remained standing, her back as straight as when she rode horseback. Baldo opened the box — "A gift," he said — and placed on the desk a revolver with a dark grip and a very long barrel, setting it down ever so gently, as if it might break. Angelo took it up and looked at it without expression. "Remarkable," he said politely. "How long is the barrel?"

"Nineteen centimeters, at least," said Baldo. "It's American. A Colt Single Action Army revolver. Very powerful, very reliable. Six shots. I have another just like it."

Angelo took three wine glasses from the row on the top shelf, went to the wood cabinet that had a black iron key in its keyhole, pulled open the door and removed a bottle of wine. He set the three glasses on his desk beside the Colt Single Action Army revolver and filled them. He nodded to Signor Baldo to speak.

"Your son Fimi is the father of the baby now growing inside my sister Sofia," Baldo told him.

For a moment nothing happened. Angelo frowned and sank ever deeper in thought, motionless. Then, as if merely to break the lengthening silence, he handed a glass of wine to Sofia and to Baldo. Sofia lifted her veil to drink, revealing her red-rimmed eyes. Angelo drained his glass, threw open the door to the back courtyard and cried *"Fimi!"* then slammed the door shut, rattling every pane of glass in the house. About a minute later Fimi strolled into the room, closed the door behind him and looked around with his hands on his hips, clearly puzzled. Sofia cried, *"Mio stadduni!"* — my stallion! Fimi looked at her, the color vanished from his face and he crashed to the floor in a faint. Sofia dropped to her knees, cradled Fimi's head in her lap and wept. Baldo drank a bit of wine, appeared to savor the taste, then drained his glass. Angelo stood with his arms folded, looking down at the couple on the floor.

Fimi opened his eyes and scrambled to his feet and Sofia stood up, tossed her veil aside and wiped her eyes. Angelo put his hand on his son's shoulder and they went out to the hard dirt courtyard. From inside the room Baldo and Sonia watched Angelo and Fimi talking and gesturing wildly while the sun beat down like a hammer on an anvil. Finally they ceased talking and Angelo returned to the silent room where Baldo and Sonia stood exactly as before — she with black glistening eyes, he with his empty wine glass at his chest. "Donna DiSecco," said Angelo, holding the door open. "Fimi will now show you our cork tree. One hundred years old, at least." Sonia lifted her chin and walked out to Fimi who waited in the checkered shade of the distant cork oak, calm and brave, like a man about to be hanged.

Angelo refilled Baldo's glass and his own, then placed two chairs facing each other in front of the desk. They sat down. Angelo took up the Colt revolver, ran a finger along the bluish barrel, squinted into the cylinder — it was unloaded — turned the weapon this way and that in his hand, then abruptly set it down as if he had just then remembered what they were doing here. Up to now they had been speaking a mixture of Florentine Italian and Sicilian, but now they spoke only Sicilian. "You want your sister to marry an eighteen-year-old?" he asked.

"An eighteen-year-old who is the father of her baby, yes," Baldo said, clapping a hand on each knee.

"Be reasonable. There must be a different way. She's eleven years older than he is. Your sister is twenty-nine and —"

"She's just barely turned twenty-eight and your son is almost nineteen. That's scarcely nine years difference," he said, leaning forward.

"How would Fimi support a wife? And where would they live? In a mud hut like mezzadri?" The *mezzadri* were sharecroppers who were allowed to use the land, but only for a few years at a time so they wouldn't improve it, and they had to give most of what they produced to the land owner — an ingenious system.

Baldo leaned back and spread his arms. "You're a successful miller. He's your son. You're his father. His problems are your problems, not mine."

Angelo studied the floor at his feet for a minute, then handed Baldo his glass, took up his own, and they drank. "That jackass Major DiSecco went through your sister's dowry in six months. What could she bring to a marriage now?"

"A complete library," Baldo said. "Much of it in English."

Angelo smiled, showing all his large square teeth.

"Many of the books have fine bindings," Baldo continued. "Including a couple illustrated with geometric diagrams, the pages written in a pagan language, maybe Moorish, from the old days. I hate to think of giving up all those books. The room will be bare and hollow without them. But she loves her library." He sighed with regret for the loss of those books, then drained his glass and set it gently on the desk.

"She also loves that straw-colored wine you press from the little vineyard — a hectare, I think — on the road to Alcamo. I'm sure she'd enjoy sharing that patch of grapes with her young husband."

"That's four hectares and it's the only vineyard I have! I can't give that up." Baldo shook his head. "That little patch of grapes would seal the marriage," Angelo said with finality. He drained his glass and set it on the desk so hard it rang. "Your sister will no longer command half your villa! You'll be able to entertain decent families and their chaste, fertile daughters, one of whom has a vineyard of twenty-five hectares waiting for her."

Angelo sat back in his chair, folded his arms and watched Baldo. Baldo, who sat with his hands capped over his knees, looked somberly at the floor a while, then looked up speculatively past Angelo at the ceiling even longer, then looked at Angelo.

Sonia Baldo DiSecco, widow of that jackass Major DiSecco, and young Giuseppe Calatafimi Cavallù, called Fimi, were married July 30, 1879. Their child was born sometime in March, or maybe earlier as some say, in 1880, a remarkably large sturdy infant, and was named Pacifico (Peaceful) to embody the peace and reconciliation of the two neighboring families. It was an interesting marriage.

6

Signor Baldo intended an insult when he said that the Cavallù family were animals, or that the males, anyway, were animals, or were at least half horse — or whatever it was he said. Baldo was one of those conservatives who strove to keep up the old social distinctions between men and beasts, but many Sicilians didn't see things that way. The people who managed large estates rarely made a difference between the work animals and the workmen on their land — they cursed them, beat and fed them the same, housed them the same — and, frankly, the poor saw no distinction between bosses and beasts. Society was fluid that way. As for Signora Sonia Baldo DiSecco Cavallù, she loved her young stallion, her *stadduni*, and in the frenzy of love making would drum her heels against Fimi's hard hindquarters, spurring him on.

Ordinary Sicilians lived close to their animals. In country towns many of the dwellings were made of stones covered with painted stucco and these houses, typically huddled together on steep hillsides, would have two floors, so the cows and goats were brought in below and the Christians lived above; that way it was warmer in winter, too. Poorer families had only one floor and they bedded down alongside maybe just one skinny cow or sick pig and maybe things happened that no one talked about.

Calogero Zitellone (Zitti), who married Angelo Cavallù's

great granddaughter in Massachusetts, believed that the story about the half-stallion ancestor depicted the same kind of metamorphosis that Ovid wrote about. "These things happened when the world was new and was just beginning to take shape," he said. "They're true stories, but so distant in time that you have to interpret them to reveal the truth." Nicolo Pellegrino, father of Nick who wrote down those first two tales, raised his eyebrows. "You think somebody mated with a horse?"

"I was talking about metamorphoses, changes brought about by the interference of the gods — or, as you would say, genetics."

"Human's don't mate with animals," Pellegrino said.

Zitti gave a short, derisive laugh. "Never?" he said.

After the slightest hesitation, Pellegrino said, "Not successfully. If a human mates with a horse you don't get anything or you get a monstrosity."

"Sometimes you get a monstrosity and sometimes you don't," Zitti said. "These ancient stories are true, but nowadays people don't believe what they don't see. There's hardly a horse in Boston anymore, and no cows. There'll come a day when people will have gotten so far from horses and cows they won't believe they ever existed. They won't know a horse turd from a cow flap, and that's true ignorance."

Zitti (philosopher, philologist, inventor of an onomatopoetic language) and Nicolo Pellegrino (aeronautical engineer, balloonist) were academics who relished disagreement, and that conversation took place in 1935 in Lexington, Massachusetts, in Pacifico Cavallù's green back yard as the two men walked down the bocce court, retrieved the balls and got set for another throw.

Signor Baldo was right when he said nothing much changed in Sicily, not even after the glorious Risorgimento. Garibaldi was disregarded and the idealistic Mazzini, elected to parliament, wasn't allowed to take his seat. In 1866 groups of armed men began to march toward Palermo again. The revolutionary gangs were made up of clerics, mafiosi, some local princes, angry young men looking for a fight, stray followers of Mazzini and some nostalgic Bourbon crackpots hoping to restore the old Royalists. Angelo Cavallù stayed home and repaired his mill. In Palermo the revolutionaries managed to burn police records and land leases, which was all to the good, then the Italian navy sailed in, lobbed a few shells into the city, and 40,000 Italian troops took over. European maps printed after 1870 show the Italian peninsula and Sicily all one color, because the old kingdoms and dukedoms, and even the part around Rome previously ruled by the pope, all had been put together like a grand geographic jigsaw puzzle. But neither the Italians nor the Sicilians believed in a monochromatic map and no one threw away the old flags.

7

STELLA DIMARE (WOMAN OR GODDESS — EITHER WAY, her looks could knock you over) and Franco (mathematician and free thinker) were married in 1860 in Reggio Calabria. We don't know how many children they had, only that each one was as beautiful as her mother, and that the first was named Diva and the second, Morgana. Diva, born in 1861, married a fisherman named Remo Moretti in 1881 and the couple settled in a seaside town west of Palermo. The following year Diva's unmarried sister, Morgana, visited her and the next month, early in May, Morgana went to Palermo. This is what happened there.

Morgana was in the kitchen, in back, that night (May 11, 1882) when the police broke into the front room where the men were meeting. Morgana, hearing shouts, the thud of fists and the tumble and crack of furniture, jumped on a chair, stepped onto the kitchen table, reached up and pushed open the skylight and pulled herself onto the roof. She pressed the skylight shut and crouched there, her heart pounding so hard she could barely breath. As she peered into the kitchen one of the police thugs entered and swept the coffee pot and the neatly arranged cups from the table to smash on the floor. Then he went to a shelf, took one dish at a time and hurled it at the floor or the wall, while with his other hand he held off old Signora Felice who continued to flail and grab at his throwing arm, shouting curses all the while. Morgana backed away, then stood up to look around, and little by little her trembling ceased. She could see beyond the uneven terrain of roofs to the black waters of the harbor and, way off, the dark bulk of Monte Pellegrino. She crept across the flat roof, climbed over a low wall that separated this building from its neighbor, and then continued across the next roof.

Orlando Vela, a young school teacher who also wrote newspaper articles and poetry, was in Palermo too. That same night (May 11 , 1882) he was on a balcony in an unbuttoned shirt, pulling on his socks, jamming his feet into his shoes, and even before he was finished he heard voices from the bedroom — a grumpy baritone, a mollifying soprano. He climbed over the balcony rail and twisted around so he was perched there, clinging to the rail while facing the double doors which were now bounded with narrow yellow line of lamplight. He glanced down and saw a twenty foot drop to the paving stones, then looked up to find the margin of the roof only a few feet above his head. Orlando edged sideways closer to the building, steadied himself with a hand on an iron lamp bracket, climbed onto the balcony rail and hauled himself up on to the roof. The moon was half full, the sky lightly sprinkled with stars, and Orlando felt such exhilaration that he almost laughed. He felt like singing as strolled across the roof and lowered himself gently onto another that was a criss-cross of clothes lines and damp laundry.

Morgana and Orlando were making their way across this same roof, ducking around pale sheets and shadowy garments, when they bumped into each other.

"Good God!" Orlando said.

"Back off or I'll kill you!" Morgana said in a harsh whisper.

"Hey, take it easy, take it easy!" he whispered. "What have you got there? A pen? You're going to kill me with a steel nib pen?"

"Try me, I'll blind you."

Orlando laughed, Morgana lunged at him and he caught her, had his arms around her like a hoop.

"What's *wrong* with you?" he whispered, his mouth at her ear. His sense of decorum made him release her, but he still kept her wrist in his fist and was holding her at arms length, hoping she'd drop the pen, but she continued to twist and kick in furious silence until he let go. "Are you crazy? What did I ever do to you?"

"Nothing and don't try." She was panting and held the pen underhand, like a knife pointed at him, while she massaged her wrist with her other hand.

"Who are you?" he asked.

"You don't need to know. Just get out of my way."

"You sound Calabrian. You don't come from around here."

Morgana said nothing.

"Excuse me, signorina." Orlando bowed ever so slightly "Please allow me introduce myself. I'm Orlando Vela, the poet. I also write articles encouraging the spread of telegraphy, the building of paved highways and the completion of the railroad. And I teach school," he added as an afterthought.

"Railroads? It took five years to lay five miles of track. Then ten more years to lay the next ten miles! You still can't get from Messina to Palermo in a straight line." Morgana had relaxed somewhat and now she dropped the pen into the folded sheaf of papers that filled her pocket. "Because until you change the social system and control the power of the land owners and the so-called notables, you can't make progress in anything," she concluded.

"Are you some kind of female railroad engineer?"

"Are you some kind of police spy?"

"Do I look like a police spy?" he asked.

"You look like a boy who got dressed in a hurry. Your shirt's buttoned wrong, your collar has popped out. I won't disgrace myself speculating on what you've been up to. I'm sure it's not poetry or journalism or teaching, not at this hour."

"And who are you running away from? A boorish husband? It's usually a boorish husband. But in your case, I suppose not. You have no husband. Police spies? Yes, that's possible."

"Clever signor Vela."

"You're the secretary for a revolutionary group," he said, re-buttoning his shirt.

"There's no revolutionary group. Only a dozen people who gathered to listen to a talk by a French socialist. I took notes for the committee — the group, I mean."

"You must have been the only woman there." Orlando tucked his shirt into his trousers and smoothed out the wrinkles.

"In every revolutionary movement, in every progressive period, you'll find women there," Morgana said. "The police broke up the meeting. I don't know what happened to the others."

"I'm glad you got out."

"I'd gone to the kitchen to get coffee for the men. While the fighting was going on in the front room I got away," she said.

Orlando smiled. "In every revolutionary movement, in every progressive period, women will be sent to make coffee for the men."

"You should put that cleverness to better use, signor Vela."

"Signorina, I'm at your service." He put his hand over his heart and extended his arm in an operatic gesture.

"Fine. How do we get off this roof? I can't go back the way I came."

"Neither can I."

They walked quietly to the end of the aisle of laundry, then patrolled the edge of the roof, searching for a way down, and discovered a terrace about eight feet below. "If you permit me," said Orlando, "I can hold your hands and lower you until there's only a short distance more to go, then you could drop down and not get hurt."

"I can lower myself down," Morgana told him.

"Excellent. By the way, when you drop onto that terrace everybody in the house is going to wake up."

"I'll get off before anyone comes. It's a short drop from the terrace to the street," she said.

"Where will you go?"

"That's not your concern," she said.

"I suggest we can stay here until dawn, then we can leave. Because, you know, it's not a good idea to be on the street in Palermo when it's still dark, not even for a brave socialist revolutionary."

"I should have stuck you with my pen," Morgana said. So they stayed on the roof and continued to talk in whispers, though to be exact, Orlando did most of the talking and mostly about a long poem which he was writing about Daedalus and Icarus, father and son, who made wings of sea gull feathers and flew to Sicily. He was writing it not in Italian, he said proudly, but in Sicilian. Eventually the sky lightened and they were able to see each other more clearly, this slender but sturdy young woman with the remarkably clear eyes, and this young man with his playful smile and rather boyish pink cheeks, now darkened with overnight stubble, like sandpaper. As they got ready to descend, Orland said, "Please allow me to accompany you and no one will bother you."

After a moment Morgana said, "Thank you, Signor Vela."

"If you tell me your name, I can pretend you're a cousin from Calabria. But I have to know your name, Signorina."

"Morgana."

"A beautiful name, a name with poetry in it. Later I'll tell you the story of Morgana the sorceress who created the —"

Morgana cut in, saying, "I know the story."

"Fine. This morning you can be Morgana Vela, my cousin, my father's brother's daughter."

"We'll need another story when we get to my sister's house. We can discuss that later. I'm sure I can come up with some good ideas."

8

MORGANA'S OLDER SISTER, YOU RECALL, WAS NAMED Diva and she was married to Remo Moretti and they lived in a harbor town west of Palermo. Diva and Remo had children, among them a daughter named Marianna. Now one day in the summer of 1901 this young Marianna Moretti brought her family's bread to the *furnu*. The *furnu* was a bake house on the edge of town, a place with a large brick and stone oven where you brought your uncooked loaves to have them baked. Whenever Diva made a batch of bread dough, she would knead it and roll it and fold it into good round loaves, then put the loaves in a basket, cover them with cloth, and give them to her daughter Marianna to carry to the *furnu*. This day the baker, Grasso, was being visited by his friend Pacifico Cavallù. They had been in the army together, had been stationed in Naples, and together had visited cities even further north, and had got acquainted with different places, different people and different ways of doing things.

Now the sun was hot, so hot it was cooking the figs on the trees, and inside the *furnu* was even hotter, so here they are outside, their chairs tilted back against the broad trunk of a chestnut tree, having a lazy debate about women. "As you go south, the women get darker and more sensual," Grasso said. "My brother-in-law was with the army in Africa and he tells me that Ethiopian women actually crave sex. I noticed up north, where they sun isn't so strong, the women have lighter skin and lighter hair, like in Venice and Milan, and they get temperamentally colder, less sensual. Sicilian women are by nature sensual, but they lie about it and pretend they have no interest in sex. You have to release it in them. You can't do that with a woman from northern Europe. They're essentially frigid."

"Are you serious? All the women in Sweden are pale and blond, but they can't all be frigid," Pacifico said. "Otherwise there'd be no Scandinavians,"

"I'm speaking in general. In general, northern women are not as sensual as Mediterranean women."

"Northern women are more elegant."

Grasso thought about that a while. "In a way, yes. But I prefer sensuality. — What kind of women do you think you'd find in North America?"

"Women from Palermo, women from Naples, women from Rome, from Torino," Pacifico said.

"You can find them all there."

Grasso laughed. "I don't need to go to America to find those women." Then they debated how much money you might need before you could afford to marry a decent Sicilian woman, and that led to talk about the great Sicilian problem which is poverty and rebellion, poverty because no job pays enough and rebellion because landowners pay no taxes on land while poor people have to pay a tax on flour or they starve.

"Nobody ever starved in America," Pacifico announced.

"Here we go again. You really believe that?"

"It's true."

"Are they giving away bread in America?" Grasso asked. "Because the day when nobody starves is the day they give away bread. If you have rich people and poor people, sooner or later somebody poor is going to starve."

Pacifico laughed. "You should write a book on economics."

"You're the one who wants to get rich. I'm interested only in earning an honest living."

"Earning an honest living isn't so easy," Pacifico said. "Not in Sicily. In fact, it may be impossible."

They talked about the land owners who proclaimed that there

was no poverty and the way to get rid of the Sicilian problem was to abolish compulsory education. Grasso went inside to check on some loaves and came out a few minutes later, mopping his face with a cloth. A young woman with a parasol showed up in the distance — that was Marianna, of course — walking toward them in a steady but unhurried pace, a little girl by her side.

"You're serious about leaving?" Grasso said.

"Everybody's leaving," Pacifico said. "Except the government and the mafia," he added. He gazed in meditative silence across the dirt road to the distant terracotta hills. "Because it's the same thing. They call it mafia at the bottom and government at the top. But it's all the same."

"Death and taxes," Grasso said.

"What about death and taxes?"

"God created death to punish Adam and Eve for disobeying him when they ate the fruit from the tree in the garden. Right?"

"That's the way the story goes," said Pacifico.

"I think God invented taxes at the same time."

Marianna's back was as straight as the back of a woman carrying a jug of water on her head, but she walked with the basket of unbaked loaves on her arm and in her other hand an upraised blue parasol with a fancy lace fringe. Her sister was carrying a book and kicking a stone ahead of her as she walked. Marianna was eighteen and wearing what had been a loose sea-green summer shift, but since it had been cut and sewn three years ago it was no longer loose.

"They don't have so many taxes in America," Pacifico said.

"They're socialists?"

"Capitalists."

Grasso and Pacifico stood up and Grasso greeted the young woman. When the baker and Marianna, plus her little sister, went into the bake house, Pacifico decided to stay in the cool shade of the chestnut tree, then abruptly followed them and got entangled in the swaying curtain of beads in the doorway. The baker took Marianna's loaves and put them in a big flat pan along side other unbaked loaves which were waiting their turn to go into the oven. The only way you could tell your bread from anyone else's was by the way you had marked your loaves — by cutting an initial or some other zigzag into the dough crust — so Marianna glanced at the other loaves and scratched a quick M on each of hers. "You have beautiful penmanship, young lady," said Pacifico. Marianna looked at him a moment, then laughed and said, "I know how to write, sir, if that's what you mean."

"What happens if you take home someone else's loaf?" he asked, just to prolong the conversation.

"I wouldn't do that."

"You might do it by mistake and not even know you were doing it," he told her.

"Then I'd bring it back," she said, turning to leave, her hand on her little sister's head.

"But what if you ate it before you discovered it belonged to somebody else?" He spoke hurriedly because she was already at the door. "That would be stealing and stealing's a sin," he said in a rush.

"There'd be no sin if I gave my own in exchange for it," Marianna said over her shoulder.

They went out and Pacifico, trailing behind her, was caught again in the beaded strands swaying in the doorway.

He got outside and, at a loss for something to engage the young woman, he turned to her young sister. "What's the name of your book?" he asked her.

"That's mine, sir," Marianna told him. "She doesn't read things like that yet." She took the book from her sister and put it in the basket under the cloth.

"Ah. Well. Now you've put the book to bed," Pacifico said. "I'll never know what it is."

Marianna laughed. Pacifico was twenty-one, wearing a white collarless shirt, and he had fledgling beard on his chin and jaws — a stranger, an interesting man, handsome. He looked about to speak and even started to open his mouth, but said nothing, so to help him out she said, "If you're interested, it's called *The Lady of the Camellias* and it's by Alexandre Dumas, the son. He's a well known French author, famous for his novels," she said with school-girl pedantry, "But this is a translation. Because I don't know how to read French. It's the book Giuseppe Verdi made into *La Traviata*."

"A wonderful opera!" Pacifico exclaimed, relieved to be able to engage her this way. "It overflows with emotion. I saw it in Naples."

"I haven't seen it," she said, drawing back a strand of hair that had fallen across her cheek. "That's why I decided to read the book."

"And how do you like the book?"

"It's an interesting story of society, but sentimental. My teacher advised against reading it because of the immorality."

"Oh. Well. I. Well. What are your favorite operas?"

"I've seen only *Cinderella*. That's by Rossini. —I'm afraid I interrupted your discussion of socialism with your companion," she added.

When Grasso came out he found Pacifico and Marianna standing under the chestnut tree, talking, while the little sister idly opened and collapsed the parasol, then opened it again, a frown of concentration on her face. Grasso walked over, took one of the two empty chairs and dragged it to another part of the shade under the tree. Fifteen minutes later Marianna began her walk home, the empty basket loose on her arm and the upright parasol in her other hand. Pacifico watched her and without turning to look for Grasso, he asked, "Who is she?"

"Marianna Moretti. I take it you didn't spend all your time discussing economics or North America."

"She's amazing."

"Her father's a fisherman but rather well off. If there are fish in the sea they swim into his nets first. If there are any straggler fish, they might get netted by the other boats, or might not. No one knows why he's so lucky with fish. They sent Marianna to school, which was the right thing to do, but after she was finished they got her a tutor, which, you know, may have been too much. Now she walks around with a French parasol. That's how she is. She's pretty, if you like her type, but restless."

"No, no, no, not restless, *ambitious*," said Pacifico.

He asked Grasso for a bit of paper, so they went inside and the baker tore a strip from a blank page in his account book. Pacifico wrote in his neatest, most careful script — *You have stolen my heart, P. Cavallù.* Then he pulled a wad of dough from somebody's unbaked loaf, folded it around the paper and placed it on the pan beside Marianna's loaves. "When she comes back for the bread, make sure you put that in her hand, like that, with the end of the paper sticking out," he told Grasso.

Grasso looked at the lump of dough with the bit of paper sticking out like a tiny flag. "What's in the note?"

"Nothing."

"I'm not going to give that young woman something to read unless I know what it is. I'm not a fool and neither is her father." He unfolded the dough, read the line, refolded the dough around the paper. He sighed. "It's got your name on it. If her father gets ahold of it, only God knows what will happen."

"If she reads it before she gets home, he'll never see it. Make sure she reads it, that's all. —Now I have to go," Pacifico said, sweeping aside the curtain of beads in the doorway.

"She's going to be back later today to pick up her bread. Why don't you wait?"

"I have work to do and I want to be here tomorrow when she comes back."

"The Morettis aren't so rich they can bake bread every day. She won't be coming here tomorrow," Grasso said.

"She's smart. She'll be here tomorrow."

Marianna understood Pacifico's note and was back the next day. A year later Marianna and Pacifico were properly engaged and when Pacifico sailed from Palermo to the United States they began a correspondence that lasted until she, too, sailed from Palermo, and in 1904 Marianna Moretti and Pacifico Cavallù were married on the dock in Boston, Massachusetts.

9

Angelo Cavallù, born with the flanks and hind legs of a stallion, died of old age in 1900, died sitting in a plain wood chair under his favorite cork-oak in the courtyard of his home in Carco, Province of Palermo, Sicily. No one knew precisely how old he was and no one was able to recall when his family had arrived in Carco, only that they came from central Sicily. Despite the arthritis which afflicted him in old age, he and Ava made the difficult trip to Sicily's central region, the lands around Enna.

Enna is the place where Demeter, the warm breasted goddess of corn and grain, had her daughter Persephone stolen from her. Hades stalked slender Persephone, coming up behind her as quiet as a shadow, clamping a cold hand over her mouth and dragging her underground, after which her griefcrazed mother ceased to bless the harvest, so crops withered and nothing grew until Hades agreed to release Persephone, though only for half the year, for which six months Demeter allowed fields to bear again.

Angelo was interested in Demeter not for her grief — he'd seen enough of her grief in Maria, Sorrowful Mother of Jesus — but because she had mated with Poseidon and given birth to Arion, the horse. Nowadays Poseidon is known as the god of the sea, but back then, when the world was new, Poseidon was the god of horses. Demeter had been fascinated by his rippling power and gentleness, had caressed the dark hair that trailed over the nape of his neck like a storm cloud, and in their passion they mounted each other this way and that way for a whole year — bringing forth the horse, Arion, and a daughter whose name cannot be said. Angelo had long ago guessed that the blood of Poseidon flowed in his veins and had gone to Enna with the hope of finding others like himself and, maybe, his true ancestry. He was unsuccessful.

Stella DiMare, widow of Franco Morelli but still a woman so beautiful her looks could stun, was carried away by the tidal wave that swept the port of Reggio Calabria in 1908. At 5:20 in the morning of December 28th, the Monday after Christmas weekend, a colossal earthquake began to rumble beneath the waters that separate Sicily from the toe of Italy, and beneath the cities of Messina and Reggio, collapsing walls, toppling towers and flattening houses until both cities were rubble. Ages ago people there said earthquakes were Poseidon's work, and called him Poseidon, Earth-Shaker. In 1908 maybe 100,000 or 200,000 people died, no one knows how many. The quake shook the center of Reggio to pieces, crushing to death about 35,000 out of 40,000 people. Immediately afterward a huge wave swept into the port of Reggio to demolish the harbor front and, as it rolled out, Stella was seen carried upon its back — seated as if she were riding side-saddle, somebody said — and turning toward the devastated city she raised her arms in a slow, broad embrace or gesture of good-bye. She was among those never seen again. Today the streets of Reggio make a neat grid and the inner city has been wholly recomposed with fine examples of Art Nouveau, neo-classical, neo-Gothic, Fascist, and contemporary architecture.

10

ALDO AND MOLLY MET BY ACCIDENT ON MONDAY, January 10, 1910, in Boston. At the sound of her shouting he had come rushing up the stairway — past the gentleman stumbling down with his hand cupped under his bloody nose

— pushed open the door and saw Molly who cried, "Another one?" Aldo ducked when she threw, so her scissors stabbed the door frame where they vibrated with a thrumming sound. "I'm come to rescue. Not to fear me," Aldo told her. "What makes you think I'm afraid!" she said, tucking in her blouse. They heard the thunder coming from the foot of the stairway. "Your friends are coming," Aldo said reassuringly. Molly slammed shut the door and turned the key in the lock, saying, "It's the bitch and her halfwit son coming to crack our heads."

"I think we shall go," Aldo told her, looking around. There was a dressmaker's dummy in the corner, a table heaped with ledgers and papers, and by the wall a fancy brass bed over which hung a picture of the Virgin Mary with her arms out, ready for an embrace.

"And who are *you?*" Molly asked him.

Aldo jammed a chair under the doorknob. "We shall go out the window," he said. He shoved the window up and cold air poured into the room. "It's not far," he added, looking down to the alley. He turned to Molly and said, "Give me your hands and I can —"

"I can do this myself!" she told him. She straddled the window sill, twisted herself to face outward and teetered there a moment. Aldo muttered something, snatched her wrists and, lowering her as far as he could, dropped her onto the shallow crust of snow. Then he dropped down beside her, or beside where she had been, for she was already gone. Aldo caught up with her as they came out to the street. They trotted along the crowded sidewalk, Molly always half a step ahead. "Young lady —" he began to say.

She stopped and whirled on him. *"What do you want?"*

"You have no coat. You will freeze," he told her. "I'm not going back there, if that's what you mean!"

"I will get it for you," he said. Aldo had already started to take off his coat, to give it to her, but she waved it off.

"Grand. You and Saint Michael go back and fetch me my

coat. —Don't say I didn't warn you," she called after him.

Aldo ran back down the street and returned a few minutes later with her coat which felt so like a thin rag in his hand that he was embarrassed at the weight of his Chesterfield with its lustrous black velvet collar. Molly said thank you, slipped into her coat and turned away.

"I hope you will come with me to lunch," he said.

She shrugged, turned back to him and said, "Sure. Why not?"

The first time they had a good look at each other was when they were seated at a table at Sweeney's. Molly's face was milk white, but her high cheeks were such a fiery blaze that he wanted to reach out and feel their heat. Aldo's face was dark and ugly — or maybe just dark, Molly couldn't decide. "You're an Eye-talian," she announced.

"Yes. In this country I'm an Italian."

"And what would you be in Italy?"

Aldo had a dazzling smile. "In Italy I would be a Sicilian."

"What's a *sicilian*?"

He laughed. "That's a long story."

When he laughed his face lighted up from inside — that's the way it looked to Molly.

"My name is Aldo Vela and I'm an aeroplano designer," he said. It was clear she didn't understand what he was talking about. "You know, aeroplano. Avion. A flying machine. I design it. Them. I design flying machines." His hands went soaring this way and that, over the table.

"You went to Mrs Faolain's to design flying machines. Oh, sure," she said.

"For cloth. Fabric for the wings. I'm looking here and there to find where they buy it. —And you are a seamstress. Miss—" Here he paused, waiting for her to give her name.

"Molly," she said at last.

"Ah!" He laughed, apparently delighted. "A beautiful name. Molly."

"And I'm an accountant, not a seamstress. Mrs Faolain keeps

two sets of books. Or tries to, arithmetic being a great puzzle to her, but she thinks she's being cheated by somebody someplace, so she hired me to sort things out. That customer mistook me for one of her slut seamstresses. That's how he got his fat bloody nose. I'm telling you I'm tired of it."

"Oh," Aldo said, aware that he didn't have a good grasp of what she was telling him.

"I expect Faolain's got another set of books for the poor girls and the flashy gentlemen they take upstairs to the fitting rooms."

"Ah," he said slowly, as it became clear to him.

"But you're an accountant," he added, brightening.

"Yes, and you're a designer of flying machines," she replied, tossing her hands around to parody his gestures.

During lunch Aldo asked how she had decided to become an accountant. "It's what I can do," she said. "I have a head for numbers and I know how to read a ledger. I knew my numbers before I knew the alphabet." She asked him what a *sicilian* was. He told her *Sicilia* is an island and the unlucky people who live there are called Sicilians. "Italy is shaped like a big leg in a boot," he said. "And at the toe end of the boot is the island. The boot is kicking the island — that's Sicily —forever," he said, kicking his leg out. So he had got away, first to Torino, at the top of the Italian boot, where he had raced automobiles, then to France, where they made the best aeroplanes. Molly, too, had traveled, first from Mayo to Dublin, then to Canada. "A great Irish cemetery," she called Canada. "The city of Montreal is nothing but gray stones with priests and nuns tucked in between them. That's why I came down here. — Tell me about flying machines," she said, to change the subject. He laughed. "What would you like to know?" he asked her. They talked and talked and when they finally stood up Aldo swept Molly's chair aside and helped her into her coat, taking the opportunity to study her shimmering copper-colored hair such as he had never seen before, not even in Venice. Out on the sidewalk he said he'd like to see her again. She gave him the address of her rooming house. "You can come by on a Sunday afternoon and Mrs Murphy will give you permission to wait in the front hall at the foot of the stairs. They'll think you're Eye-talian, because they don't know about Sicily. Tell them you've come to go walking with Molly O'Neill and don't say anything else."

❦

Aldo was twenty-five years old. The famous day he met Molly he was wearing his French three-piece suit and he had money in his pocket, but things weren't going well. The expensive coat wasn't his. He owned a cheap coat, one change of clothes, two pairs of Zeiss racing goggles, one pair of leather driving gloves, a silver pocket-watch and a suitcase holding the detailed plans for an aeroplane. He ate with his relatives, the family of Pacifico and Marianna Cavallù, in their second-floor flat on Prince Street in the Italian section of Boston. At night he slept on a canvass cot in the back room of Pacifico's general store. During the day he helped at the store or studied his English language manual or borrowed Pacifico's lavish Chesterfield coat and visited Pacifico's business friends and their acquaintances, trying to get them to invest in his aeroplane enterprise. Frankly, he was getting discouraged and restless. The men he saw were eager to meet somebody who had flown through the air and lived to talk about it, and some were even curious about his proposal to build flying machines, but when they learned that Aldo didn't have an aeroplane — No? Not even one? Only those complicated mechanical drawings? — they lost interest and sank back in their chairs. Occasionally, for solace, he would visit a friend who owned a motor garage, and there among the consoling familiar smell of gasoline and the basso *bumbumbumbumbumbum bumbumbum* arias of pistons they would talk about engines.

As for Molly, she was about twenty-three and when she met Aldo she was in a tan shirtwaist with plain business cuffs and she had another, just like it, hanging in the corner of her room.

All her other belongings were in her suitcase which the landlady, Mrs Murphy, kept locked in an unheated room by the kitchen. When Molly wanted a change of clothes, Mrs Murphy would unlock the room and watch as Molly took one garment from the suitcase and replaced it with another — that was Mrs Murphy's House Rule 1 — so if Molly or any other woman left without paying her rent, she left without her suitcase. Molly made enough from her job as bookkeeper at Faolain's Fine Fabrics to pay for her room and one meal a day and still have pocket money left over. Of course, after having given that fancy Dan a bloody nose, and after having kneed another gentleman in the groin two days earlier and having slapped one across the face a week ago, she didn't have that job anymore.

On Sunday afternoon Aldo and Molly rode the trolley and subway to the Boston Public Gardens which, of course, were frozen solid. They walked the shoveled paths and stood on the little bridge over the swan-boat pond, looked at the gray ice, the empty trees and the fading sky. "What's it like in Paris in winter?" she asked.

"It's gray. More gray even than Boston."

"What about Torino?" she asked a moment later.

"In winter? Not much better. But fine in the mountains, if you like mountains."

"I thought Italy was sunny and warm."

"In the summer, yes. Especially where I come from."

"Sicily," she announced.

"Brava, Molly! Yes, Sicily," he said, using the English word. "In the summer, in August, it's so hot, if you pick up a drinking glass that has been too long in the sun it will scorch your hand. And the sirocco, when it blows from Africa, the wind carries sand from the desert and the sky turns yellow with sand."

She laughed. "Oh, sure! Sand blows over from Africa."

"It's true, it's true! The sand gets everywhere, like powder.

You can comb it from your hair. You can feel it in your teeth when you bite." He snapped his jaws shut and made a show of grinding his teeth. "It's true."

"All the way from Africa to Sicily. And Ireland, you know, is made of emeralds."

"It's not that far!" he protested. "In Italy they say we are Africans."

Molly looked at him, taking in his dark face.

"Lucky Aldo. You can pass for Eye-talian in this country."

Aldo, distracted by her gaze — she had clear green eyes — lost his tongue for a moment. "Tell me about Dublin," he said.

"Dublin is a sewer, but much improved from what it used to be," she said. "Or so I was told."

They walked through the frozen Gardens — there were only a few people, coat collars up, hurrying this way or that — and crossed the street to Boston Common where a ragged man, poking at a fire in an iron barrel, was selling roasted chestnuts from a soot-blackened tray. Aldo bought a small bagful of chestnuts. "Here," he said, giving a hot chestnut to Molly. "Put this in your glove, inside. And this. To keep your hands warm." Fifty years later she could still tell you about those warm chestnuts.

"What happened to your good coat?" she asked. "The one with the velvet collar."

"It belongs to my cousin Pacifico."

She put her arm through his and they walked to the subway. "How was the flying machine business this past week?" she asked.

Aldo shrugged and wagged his hand. "So-so. I hate asking for investors. It's too much like begging."

"I hate looking for work."

"The Aviation Meet began the same day we meet, you and I. Did meet. A big aviation show. That was a famous day. Did I tell you?"

"What aviation show?"

"In Los Angeles. You know Los Angeles?"

"I know Dublin and Montreal and Boston."

"The meeting goes on for ten days. Everybody flies. Louis Paulhan is there winning prizes. I met him in France."

"Aldo, tell me this about your machine — if you haven't built it, how do you know it will fly?"

He laughed and squeezed her arm hard in his, relishing the solid feel of her flesh and bone through the cloth. "I know, because I designed it."

❦

The Los Angeles Aviation Meet was a spectacular event displaying all sorts of fantastic aircraft. Glenn Curtiss, already famous for his speed, won prizes for the fastest flight with a passenger aboard and for the swiftest start. His flying student, Charlie Willard, won at precision take off and landing. Aldo's acquaintance, Louis Paulhan, set new altitude and endurance records and came away with the most prize money, over fourteen thousand dollars. Aldo respected Curtiss because he designed and flew his own aircraft, biplanes that were pushed by a powerful water-cooled 4- or 8-cylinder engine, but Aldo didn't care for the look of Curtiss's planes, boxy constructions of struts and wires with a clutter of air control surfaces, nor did he like the huge Farham that Paulhan sometimes flew, another powerful pusher with a roaring 7-cylinder radial engine. He loved the lighter Bleriot monoplane with its 3-cylinder engine up front and its elegant outstretched wings — true, you might get a whiff of exhaust, but that was better than having the engine slam into you from behind when you made a crash landing. He had designed his own plane along those lines. He had hoped that the news of the Los Angeles Air Meet would encourage businessmen and entrepreneurs to invest in aeroplanes, but they didn't, at least not in Boston. Los Angeles was far, far away and the flying machines in the newspapers were as remote and implausible as the sunny Los Angeles weather. In February Aldo went to the Aero Show at Mechanics Hall (demolished around

1960) and was able to examine a biplane made by a yacht builder from nearby Marblehead. It was a sturdy craft and looked like it might be air worthy, but it had never flown and was oddly designed with half a dozen vertical fins along the upper wing. The builder, Mr William Starling Burgess was there, too, a rich Yankee with a ruddy face, and Aldo didn't go near him.

❦

Aldo and Molly were fast going broke. One Sunday afternoon, in a corner of the Museum of Fine Arts where they had gone to get warm, Molly unpinned her intricately braided hair, combing from it every bit of jewelry ever given to her (not much, really: three gold rings, a pair of gold ear rings, a copper fibula, two enameled brooches, and a silver chain with silver Celtic cross) which she had hidden in there so she could smuggle all past her landlady, for Molly was behind in her rent and was preparing to decamp from Mrs Murphy's rooming house. Molly wouldn't accept the money Aldo offered to give her or loan her or whatever, so he went around to Faolain's Fine Fabrics to get Molly's back wages for her. Mrs Faolain gave a short harsh laugh and told him to get lost, told him if he or his whore ever came through that door again she'd have the police on them. Aldo vaulted the counter, yanked open the till, counted out Molly's back wages and vaulted the counter again, but by then Mrs Faolain's carbuncled son and two other louts were running at him. Aldo grabbed the smallest one by the wrist and whirled him around, twisting the kid's arm up his back. *"Get out of my way by God I break his arm off!"* Aldo barked, jerking the arm up so far the kid danced on tiptoe, trembling and pale. The other two wavered and Aldo hurled the kid head-first at them and shot out the door.

Molly kept hunting for a job as an accountant, but the small shops would never let anyone outside the family look at the books, if they kept any books, and the big companies weren't hiring — not women accountants, anyway. "What they want is a man in a green eyeshade with garters on his sleeves," Molly said. In late February she went to the garment district and began cutting cloth and breathing lint fifty-six hours a week in the same small sweatshop she had worked in when she first came to Boston. Aldo offered her money again, telling her that at the end of the workday at least she could return to a decent room. "No!" she said sharply. *"I don't want your money! Who do you think I am?"* They had stepped inside the Boston Public Library to get warm and her voice rang against the stone pillars and marble mosaic. Aldo flushed, as if he had been slapped. "Una donna tenuta!" he said. "You think I want to make you a kept woman! Is that what you think?"

"I didn't mean it that way. Come back here, Aldo!" she cried, catching his shoulder and kissing his neck as he turned away.

That spring Aldo not only worked in Pacifico's store, but he got another job as well. He got this other job when he was at his friend Tito's motor garage looking at a new Firestone-Columbus automobile — an unusual automobile with a fifty-inch track, six inches narrower than most, and the steering wheel on the left, unlike other vehicles. Aldo had taken off his jacket, folded back his cuffs, and was examining the engine, a four-cylinder high-speed job, when in walked the owner, a tall angular Yankee named Blanchard. Blanchard thought Aldo was one of the mechanics and after talking with him about the car Blanchard asked if Aldo could turn it into a racing vehicle. Tito came over and said, "Yes, we can make it into a racing car, no problem." Tito and Aldo worked on it nights, removed the fenders and headlamps, braced the frame and put in a bucket seat. Tito asked Blanchard where he was going to race. "Not me," Blanchard said. "Maybe I own a race horse, but that doesn't mean I'm a jockey. Someone else will have to drive this buggy."

"I can drive it for you," said Aldo. "I used to race cars in Torino."

The race was on Cape Ann, a private road race from Gloucester up the shore road to Rockport and down the inland road back to Gloucester. Aldo drove recklessly well and finished less than a second behind the winner, out of the money. But Blanchard was pleased, gave him a two-hundred-and-fifty-dollar bonus above his pay for the race and asked would he drive for him on Long Island. Aldo was now richer than he'd ever been since leaving France. He said Thank you and No. He knew the best drivers in the world would be competing in Mr Vanderbilt's race and Blanchard would pay him well simply to be there, but he hadn't been interested in speed since he began to fly. The exhilaration of automobile racing was in the speed — it was all about going fast in the dirt, while flying was about sky and air and he was starved for that. "And now I have a thing to show you," Aldo said. The next day Aldo showed him the detail drawings for his aircraft. "I'm impressed," Blanchard told him. "But I'm committed elsewhere. —By the way, who drew these plans?"

"I did, of course," said Aldo.

Blanchard spoke to one of his friends and a week later Aldo was offered a job in the drafting department of a bridge fabricating company. Drafting is tedious pains-taking work — make one blot or smear and you've ruined the whole damned sheet — and it's not at all like flying, but he took the job.

❦

So Molly and Aldo came to know each other, told each other where they had come from, what they had done — some of what they had done, anyway. Aldo's mother was a beautiful woman and *her* mother, a goddess so beautiful her looks could stun a man. That woman, his grandmother, never aged and was an embarrassment to her daughters until the tidal wave of 1908 rose up in the port of Reggio and carried her away, somebody said, as if she were riding a horse. Aldo's father was a teacher, journalist and poet who, among other achievements, wrote a poem about Daedalus and Icarus, but in Sicilian, which limited its readership and, unfortunately, he never quite finished it.

He was beaten one night by Premier Francesco Crispi's thugs who threw him into a filthy prison cell where he died the next morning. Crispi, you should know, intended to restore energy and virility to Italy by stamping out socialists and everyone else who disagreed with him. One day when Aldo was a boy his mother pointed out the villa of the man who had ordered the beating. After that she sold everything they owned and moved from Sicily as far as she could, settling in the distant city of Torino where Aldo later attended the Scuola di Applicazione per gli Ingegneri (Technical School for Engineers), became infatuated with automobile engines, did some racing and won a few, then crossed over to France because that's where they were making flying machines and he had fallen in love with flying. Shortly after that his mother married Giancarlo Mattei, a rather young industrialist.

"She'll not be lonely in her old age and that's good," Molly said.

"I can assure you my mother has not been lonely for the last ten years," Aldo told her.

"Ah, you don't care for Mr Mattei?"

"I behaved badly when I first met him and it became a habit. He's all right. He paid for a Bleriot flying machine he knew I wanted, but I refused it. Maybe I was wrong. It's stored in crates at a factory in France."

As for Molly, her father was a part-time typesetter and part-time horse trader with one patched boot in the city and the other in horse shit. Her mother, a country school teacher with a love of poetry and a fine singing voice, was herself an O'Neill from county Tyrone. "We have in our veins the blood of Irish kings, we O'Neills, including the one who captured Saint Patrick, and if that O'Neill had more than a boulder between his ears he would have killed the old man and saved Ireland a lot of grief." Before Molly was born her mother had given birth to five boys — two died as infants, one talked sedition at a meeting of the Irish Republican Brotherhood and was killed in a brawl outside a pub the same night, another became a merchant seaman and poet, and the last inherited the farm. When Molly was fifteen her mother died of TB and a couple of years later Molly went to Dublin to escape her father's rage and to live with her cousin Peggy who, two years later, gave her own papers to Molly so she could sail to Canada.

11

IN MAY OF 1910 ALDO AND MOLLY WERE MARRIED IN a civil ceremony. The marriage certificate — an 8 by 11.5 inch sheet of paper, folded, and now falling apart at the creases — with elaborate print and elegant handwriting, says Aldo Vela and Moira O'Neill were *united in* MARRIAGE *according to the Laws of the State of Massachusetts*, and the back of the document bears the bright red seal of the Justice of the Peace. They couldn't live in the Italian North End, partly because all of Aldo's friends and relatives spoke Italian and Molly didn't understand more than five words, and partly because the rooms and hallways were filled with strange cooking smells that made her gag. Aldo took her to an Italian restaurant where she tasted little bites and, as she didn't get sick, the next Sunday they ate at the Cavallù's crowded table where everyone talked at once, Pacifico kept slapping her shoulder and roaring with laughter, Molly drank too much wine and Marianna held her while she threw up in the kitchen sink and the children came running to watch.

The newlyweds rented a third-floor, cold-water flat (bedroom, kitchen, sitting room — tenants' toilet bowl, out and down the hall) over by the Fort Point Channel in a hodgepodge neighborhood of Yankees, Irish, Italians, Syrians, Greeks and, at the end of the street, Chinese. Boys played stick-ball in the street, girls played hopscotch on the sidewalk, and the old folks sat on the stoop, keeping an eye on everyone. In the evening,

Aldo would take off his jacket, necktie and collar, tuck a dish towel in his belt for an apron, and cook dinner — that way he could let Molly rest, wean her from those Irish scraps she ate and feed her decent Sicilian food. Two weeks later Molly found a job as a clerk-secretary in the accounting office of a brick company, which paid more and was less tiring than the sweatshop, but Aldo continued to cook anyway.

A formal photograph (taken at the *Broadway Studio, 913 Washington St. Boston*) from around this time shows Molly and Aldo in almost identical suit jackets, white shirts and upright starched collars, the only difference being that Molly wears a ribbon bow tie, stiff and flat, whereas Aldo has a four-in-hand. And here they are in June — not in a photo but in reality — on a hot Sunday afternoon, lolling on their open bed sheet, Aldo with a towel across his privates and Molly in a chemise. "I'm happy," Aldo announced. "Very happy. —I can almost believe in God," he added.

"Does Saint Thomas list this as one of the proofs of God?" Molly asked, her voice languid.

"I don't think so." He laughed. "Saint Thomas's book is so long, I think he spent all day and all night writing it and had no time for this. Besides, he was celibate."

"Fancy that," Molly murmured. "Celibate."

"Maybe there is a God." He thought about it a while, sighed. "You never know. Maybe there are many."

"If there is a God he's lazy or cruel, I don't know which. God had a long time to fix things, but in the end it was the garment workers union did it. Did something, anyway."

"You are cynical, Molly." Aldo got up, wrapping the towel around his waist at the same time. "It's very strange I'm so restless. I'm more happy for the first time in my life and I'm ready to do. I'm very ready. Maybe that's happiness." At the bureau he opened a small cardboard box and took a cigar.

"The Italians are the only ones who smoke those little things," Molly said.

"And Sicilians," Aldo added, opening the match box. He lit

the cigar and came back to sit on the edge of the bed.

"They look like twisted twigs dipped in tar," she said, kneeling up behind him.

Aldo smiled and breathed out a soft plume of smoke. "They're not elegant. Neither am I."

"Oh, yes you are, Aldo, yes you are," she said, pressing against his back, wrapping her arms around his neck. "My elegant Sicilian boyo."

Later Molly was at the dresser combing her hair while Aldo went on talking about Glen Curtiss who, last Sunday, had flown from Albany, in upstate New York, southward to New York City and Governors Island. "He followed the river down to the city. That's a hundred and fifty miles, you know." Aldo said.

"Yes," said Molly, "I know. You told me. Two or three times."

"Which is about two hundred and fifty kilometers," he continued.

"And he won ten thousand dollars," she recited.

"And the glory."

"The money would be nice even without the glory," she said.

"Paulhan won ten thousand pounds, the British money, in that London to Manchester flight," he told her.

"And we like Paulhan better than Curtiss, right?"

"Right. —By the way, I think Pacifico wants to invest in my flying machine."

"Is that what you two were talking about?"

"He asked how much I was making at my job and asked if I could afford to build my flying machine. He said he wanted to discuss something financial with me next Sunday."

Pacifico Cavallù was five years older than Aldo. Aldo sometimes called him his cousin but, strictly speaking, they weren't cousins. Pacifico's wife, Marianna, was the daughter of Diva, who was the sister of Morgana, who was the mother of Aldo. So Aldo and Marianna were cousins.

Pacifico had arrived alone in Boston's North End eight years earlier with the names and addresses of a couple of other men who had come over from Carco, plus a letter of credit from a bank in Palermo for a sum of money which he calculated would pay his expenses for six months. He rehearsed the English his mother had taught him, looked for work and was signed up by a New Englander named Bowman who was rounding up laborers for a train ride to Maine where they would hack a road into the woods, the cost of the train ticket being deducted from their first week's wages. Three months later Pacifico was back in Boston with calluses on his hands, this time speaking more English and working alongside Bowman to gather another dozen Italians for road building. Pacifico and Bowman came back to Boston a month after that with enough money to buy train tickets for two dozen workers, Pacifico acting again as his go-between and this time convincing Italians fresh off the boat to line up for a ride to their new jobs in the Maine woods. A month later the pair were back in the North End of Boston once more, but after they had corralled two dozen Italians and after Pacifico had got his pay, he and Bowman shook hands and said goodbye, Bowman herding the new workers to the railroad station while Pacifico walked down Prince Street to a general store he had looked into on his previous trips. The store was owned and managed by an Italian who didn't speak English as well as Pacifico, so Pacifico took over the task of dealing with the American suppliers, talking to them, writing business letters and getting acquainted with how stores worked in New England. Nine months after getting the job he made his first payment toward buying the store and wrote a letter that night to Marianna, telling her he was now well established in Boston and they could marry as soon as she came over. Marianna booked passage as soon as she could and came down the gangway onto the dock in wintry Boston early in 1904, accompanied by her mother, Diva, who returned to Sicily only after having seen for certain that Pacifico did not have another wife in this country and that her daughter was properly married. By 1910 Marianna had borne four children and Pacifico owned not only the general store but the building it was housed in and he was beginning to think about money the way a composer might think about music, not dismissive of the mathematics of it but focused avidly on composing a great structure by the power of his imagination.

Now Pacifico and Aldo sat at the corner of Pacifico's dining table, which had been cleared of everything except their after-dinner espresso cups plus a platter bearing a rope of figs and a handful of walnuts. "I'm starting a travel business and an import business," Pacifico said quietly in Italian. "Want to join me?"

"Join you? Me?" Aldo was stunned.

"I'd provide the capital, of course."

"Pacifico, I'm an aeroplane designer, a flyer."

Pacifico looked at him skeptically. "You've found investors?"

"No."

"Then the flying machine can come later. You have a wife and soon you'll have children." He was decisive.

"That's why I have to do this now, not later," Aldo told him, slapping the table top for emphasis.

Pacifico was amazed. "Then your answer is *no*?"

Aldo hesitated, searching for a way to say no without hurting Pacifico's feelings. "I've already ordered an engine from France," Aldo said.

"Ah," said Pacifico. He gazed meditatively at the cigar in his hand, then gently tapped the ash into the saucer of his espresso cup. He doubted that Aldo had even thought of ordering an engine.

"A Gnôme rotary. It's the best kind," Aldo added.

It grew quiet in the dining room. Kids' voices floated up from the street below the open window; Molly and Marianna were speaking English in the kitchen.

"I'm sure you'll do well," Pacifico said at last. He relaxed, adjusted himself comfortably in his chair. "And your wife is Irish — that could be an advantage. I had no idea when I came here that the city was run by the Irish."

Aldo smiled. "Molly has no connections here. She's an Irish woman who married a Sicilian and not even in church. She has friends, of course, but no connections."

"Ha! The Irish. The men are *mascanzuni* and their women are holy virgin mothers. —You have financing plans for your flying machine?"

"I'll improvise."

Pacifico laughed and slapped Aldo on the shoulder. "Bravo! Like Garibaldi."

"Exactly."

That evening Aldo told Molly, "Now I know what I'm ready to do and why I'm so restless and even more happy." Early the next morning he sent a cablegram to the Société Des Moteurs Gnôme in France ordering a 7-cylinder rotary Gnôme Omega engine, after which he detoured to Tito's motor garage to tell him about the engine — "Can I set it up in here?" Aldo asked. "Sure, if I get to play with it too," Tito said. Thence to his job at the New England Iron Bridge Company where, in the long room in which he worked there was a disused drafting table heaped with busted drafting equipment, so Aldo bought the table and everything on it for two dollars, and at the end of the workday had it carted to his apartment where he crowded it into their little sitting room. After dinner he drew the first full-size template for a wing rib while Molly looked over his shoulder.

The engine arrived in July. The mechanic, Tito (for the record: his full name was Benedetto Evangelista Campi), was a short but well proportioned man, rather like a jockey. He'd never touched a rotary engine, had never even seen one, but from Aldo's description of how it worked he guessed the inventor must have been a comedian. Every engine he had worked on had a row of cylinders in which pistons shot up and down, and the pistons were linked to a drive shaft, so their motion rotated the shaft which turned a power wheel. But in the rotary engine the cylinders were arrayed in a vertical circle, like numerals on a clock face, and each piston was connected to the drive shaft that passed through the center of the circle. But the drive shaft didn't rotate. When the engine started and the pistons began to fire up and down, the shaft stayed absolutely still while the engine itself — the cylinders and pistons, the linkages to the drive shaft, the stream of lubricating oil — the whole insane engine rotated around what should have been the drive shaft. Tito and Aldo worked on the engine five nights in a row and then five more — tore it down and reassembled it — and late in the afternoon on Saturday they had it ready to test. It started with a bang-bang-bang, then fell silent, jerking and bobbing on the test stand. That happened four times. On the fifth try it started with the usual *bang-bang-bang* and then burst into a wonderfully rapid thundering drum roll — such music! Aldo tossed his oil rag in the air and shouted *Bravissimo!* while Tito stared at the blurred whirl and began to laugh.

Months ago Aldo had found a cabinet maker who said he and his son would be willing to work evenings, and Tito knew of an empty motor garage — actually a disused horse stable the owner had hoped to rent out as a garage — in which they could assemble the wood and wire frame of the aircraft. Aldo had decided on American spruce, a strong and reasonably light wood. He'd never chosen which fabric to cover the frame with because, you recall, when he'd last been looking at cloth he'd heard a woman shout from upstairs, had dashed to the rescue and vaulted out the window behind her, his Molly. Since then he'd gotten in touch with a cousin, a tailor from Palermo whose father, also a tailor, had opened a shop in Cambridge many years ago. It turned out the father had died and the son, Enzo Capellino, was supporting his widowed mother and his two sisters — both sisters were getting married next year and both needed dowries — so, yes, the tailor would work nights, stretching fabric over the frame.

Now Aldo would roll out of bed early, shave, drink a cup of cold coffee and hurry to the stable to work for two hours, then hop a trolley to his job at the bridge company, and in the evening, after a brief dinner, he'd return to the stable where he'd meet the cabinet maker and his son, and usually Tito would show up, simply to help. As for Molly, after a day at the brick works she'd come home and prepare dinner — Irish corned beef or cold potato soup, Italian everything else. One evening she went to a free lecture at the union hall with Kate from the garment factory, and a couple of times she went to a slide-show at the library with her friend Maureen from Mrs Murphy's rooming house, but usually she sat outside on the front steps and read. The flats were hot as ovens, so everybody came out to get air, bringing a kitchen chair or just sitting on the front stoop until long after the gaslights came on in the dark.

At bedtime, while Aldo was hunched over his drafting table again, Molly would wash up, slip into her chemise, tie her hair in paper curlers. But tonight instead of going to bed she opened the cardboard Parodi box on the bureau and took out a cigar. It tasted oddly sweet on her tongue. She struck a match, lighted the cigar, inhaled, choked, coughed, then padded barefoot behind Aldo and blew a stream of smoke over his shoulder. "Mr Engineer, what do you do if your flying machine crashes?" she asked him.

"Hey! Oh, Molly, Molly, Molly. *You're smoking a cigar.*"

"I can see there's no fooling you." Her eyes had begun to water from the smoke and she held the cigar up away from her face. "Please take this vile thing."

"Hey, you're going to set your hair on fire," he said, taking the cigar.

"What if it crashes?"

"What do you mean? My machine? The one I'm making?" He was astonished. "It won't crash."

"But what if it crashes and you get hurt?"

"I've crashed before. Everyone who flies has a few crashes. Nobody gets hurt. —You're beautiful, even with those papers in your hair."

"Don't distract me, Aldo. You never told me you crashed."

He laughed. "It's nothing to brag about. I was just learning to fly. I'm like *you*, I'm not afraid."

"But it's only some thin, thin cloth holding you up in the air."

"That night dress is only some thin, thin cloth, but it works. Also, you're beautiful. Is it true the lace is made by Irish nuns?" Aldo had begun unbuttoning his shirt.

Molly glanced down at her lacy bodice. "I hope not."

"Here. Hold the cigar. I'm going to wash. —Santos-Dumont built a fine aeroplane out of bamboo poles and thin cloth. He was the first to fly." He stepped into the kitchen and turned on the tap water.

"It was the Wright brothers were the first to fly, you know."

"That's what they say now," he said from the kitchen. "But Santos-Dumont is a better man, more simpatico. And a generous heart."

Molly sat on the edge of the bed and blew a plume of smoke toward the ceiling. "You can't say he was the first to fly just because he's a nicer man."

When Aldo had finished scrubbing himself at the sink he came to the bedroom, naked save for the towel around his waist. "The Wright brothers have no passion. —Come here, signorina." Aldo took the cigar from Molly and stubbed it out in the ashtray on the bureau. "Do you know what's on my mind?" he asked her.

"Yes." She laughed and looked into his eyes. "Should I be afraid?"

❦

The next evening Molly accompanied Aldo to the old horse stable to see the flying machine which at that point looked like nothing much. Aldo told her the part resting on saw horses was the body; it looked like a delicately constructed ladder lying on its side, maybe ten times longer than it was wide. "On an aeroplane like this one, the French call it the *fuselage*," he explained. The two identical wing sections, which would be joined to the fuselage to form the solitary wing, lay on long makeshift tables. "Beautiful, isn't it?" he said. "See how the wing swells up from the leading edge, that lovely curve up and then this gentle sweet descending slant to the trailing edge — that's where the beauty is."

Molly smiled at Aldo's pleasure in his own handiwork. "How did you know how much to curve it?"

"I looked around. I looked at Santos-Dumont's wing sections. I looked at birds, large birds that glide. Then I try for a beautiful line."

"I've been reading a library book about these flying machines and —," Molly began to say.

"Books, books! Books are full of theory —," Aldo said.

"This one is full of numbers and —"

"Numbers are even worse than theories!"

"But the Wright brothers —"

Aldo laughed. "Are there anybodies duller than the Wright brothers? I think not. Everybody in this country is wild about the Wright brothers and their ugly flying machine. In France we called those machines *canards*. In English that means goose. The Wright brothers have a machine that sticks way out in front the way a goose's head sticks out. And no wheels. Maybe it's more like a flying sled."

Molly smiled. "Aldo's aeroplane will be beautiful."

"Exactly!" He laughed.

"But before they flew, the Wright brothers performed many experiments and —"

"Ah, yes. Experiments. I'd rather fly. Those are my experiments. — Now let me introduce Enzo to you. He's the tailor I told you about. We're going to start cutting and fitting the fabric tonight. Enzo," he called. "Vieni qui."

Enzo, an energetic compact man with a downswept mustache, greeted Molly with a smile, saying, "Mi piace molto—.'

"In inglese," Aldo told him.

"How do you do, Signora Missus Vela!" Enzo said, bowing ever so slightly as he shook her hand.

Aldo's flying machine was ready to fly in late July or very early in August. No one remembers precisely when it was, only that it was a sunny breezeless Saturday and that Molly was wearing a green dress and had let her hair down because Aldo had once said he liked to see her bright hair against the green of that dress. The flying field was a freshly cut meadow in Lexington, a somnolent village about fifteen miles north-west of Boston. (Paul Revere had ridden through in the early hours of April 19th, 1775, to awaken everybody, banging on doors and crying out that the British were coming, but the town had long since fallen back asleep.) It took Aldo, Tito and Enzo about forty minutes to uncrate and assemble the machine, then a half hour for Aldo to check and re-check every bolt and wire. Finally, Aldo climbed into the cockpit and they started the Gnôme — a tricky, dangerous business.

Aldo taxied down the field, jouncing on the brown stubble while Tito jogged along side. At the far end of the meadow Tito turned the aircraft around and Aldo taxied swiftly up the field, coasting to a stop beside Molly and Enzo who together turned the machine around again. Aldo roared swiftly down the field, lifted gently into the air for a few seconds — rolling crazily this way and that — then settled down onto the field again. After a few level runs, never rising higher than twenty feet, Aldo said he was ready. Tito ran back up the field to join Molly and Enzo. Aldo smiled, gave them a casual salute and raised his voice over the steady drumbeat of the engine and shouted *I'm going now!* Molly smiled and waved broadly, waved hugely, and as soon as Aldo had turned away and the aeroplane began to move she thrust a hand inside her bodice and clutched the silver Celtic cross that hung there.

The aeroplane roared rapidly down the field and lifted gently into the air, skimmed over the scrubby bushes at the far end, rose higher and higher and began a very gentle turn to the right, disappearing beyond the nearby elm tree tops. The sound of the engine dropped to a muted patter and eventually the aeroplane reappeared against the distant sky beyond the barn at this end of the field, vanished behind more trees and after what felt like a long time it emerged above the far end of the meadow, having completed a wide languorous circle. Now the aeroplane turned toward the field, dipping a wing on the inside of the turn, but even as the aeroplane approached it began sliding gracefully sideways and down, as if following a path pointed at by the lowered wing tip. Molly and Tito were already running down the meadow when the flying machine landed to the sound of snapping wood and the crunch of the undercarriage. Aldo clambered out beside the smashed wing, pulling off his goggles and saying, "I'm all right, I'm all right."

"Your face has got —" Molly cried, out of breath, reaching for him.

"It's oil," he said, wiping his cheeks with his sleeve.

"Oil from the engine. Tito, we need to add a windscreen or something."

"Gesú!" Tito said, panting. "Che malu furtuna." What bad luck, he said, while Enzo, who was at the wrecked wing, called out that it wasn't so bad, not so bad. "Non c'é male."

"Oh! There's *blood,*" Molly cried, "You're bleeding! Look."

"What? Where?" Aldo said. Then he laughed.

"No, no, no. That's from your hand. Molly, Molly. You cut it. See?"

And, in fact, she had clutched the little Celtic cross so hard that it had sliced into her palm. "Love has made a coward of me," was all she said.

On a Sunday in August, warm and windless, Aldo took Molly up in his aeroplane. They had a private joke, those two, about the song "Come, Josephine, in My Flying Machine," which Molly had told him was the dirtiest song she had ever heard, though everyone was singing it. "Explain," Aldo had said, sitting up naked on the edge of the bed to light a cigar. So Molly knelt up — also naked, but holding the sheet to her breasts — and sang a few phrases which, in fact, could be taken two ways. Aldo blew a gust of smoke toward the ceiling and laughed. "Oh-ho! I'll remember that when I take you *up, up, a little bit higher,*" he sang, handing her the cigar. But this Sunday, as she was seated and buckled in the aeroplane, he was not joking, not worried, but businesslike. Then they rolled and bounced along the field with the roar of the engine, went faster and faster and sailed over the bushes and trees into airy space. After a while she saw she had entered a wondrous three-dimensionality, an expanding volume of light and air, and where she had lived before was gone beneath her, looking smaller and ever so flat.

Aldo's aeroplane was about twenty-three feet (seven meters) from nose to tail with a wingspan of twenty-eight feet (8.5 meters). His detailed drawings vanished long ago and these dimensions come from Molly's household account book, an ordinary school notebook with lined pages where she recorded each penny spent on codfish or trolley rides or anything else. She stopped tracking household expenses on Sunday, July 31, 1910 — they were flat broke, anyway —simply drew a double line under the monthly total and right below that, on August 8, she began to jot notes and numbers about the aeroplane. Molly believed in her heart that if she could pick out the right numbers and arrange them the right way a pattern would make itself visible, at least visible to her, and she would uncover the aeroplane's strength's and weaknesses, the same as in her accounting work. In Montreal she had become adept at gathering her employer's numbers by the bucketful (invoices, bank statements, accounts receivable) until they poured down the page, page after page, and where other people saw only the confused surface of a muddy river, she saw what those numbers meant, saw the dangerous snags and shallows underneath, and the safe way forward, though no one asked for what she knew.

Now she jotted down every number she could get about the aeroplane. Some parts were easy to assess — the weight of the Gnôme rotary engine, 165 pounds (75 Kg) — but other parts were difficult to give a number to, such as that beautiful curved surface of the wing. She had measured the curve from front to back with her sewing tape, but it was the lovely curvature itself she wanted to calculate, not its simple dumb length.

"That's what keeps the aeroplane up in the air, isn't it?" she asked Aldo. "Because the air pushes up against the hollowed-out underside of the wing and keeps you, keeps the airplane, from falling — wouldn't you say?"

Molly in her nightdress, the one with the lace not made by Irish nuns, was at the kitchen table, writing in her notebook, and Aldo was seated behind her, bathing in an old metal washtub on the floor.

"I might say that, or I might not," he told her, soaping his chest, his belly, his privates.

"Or I might stab you, Aldo, with my pen!" She started to turn toward him, but faltered.

"When the aeroplane is on the field, the wheels keep the nose up, so the wing is tilted up in front and down in back, like a kite. So when I start rushing down the field the aeroplane sails into the air like a kite." He stood up, took the kettle from the stove and poured the last of the hot water into the tub, sat down cautiously. "But when I'm flying along straight, the wind passing over the wing is as important as the wind under it."

She turned, prepared to look boldly at him. "Why?"

"Everyone has his own theory. That's why there are so many different flying machines. And many of them actually fly —" and here his hand, palm down, rolled from side to side — "more or less."

Her eyes had averted themselves all on their own, so she returned to her notebook. "What's Aldo's theory?"

"Aldo can't do theory and fly at the same time. Theories are for theoreticians and bicycle mechanics. The wing, *my* wing, mine is a great bird's wing!"

"You'll be wanting your gravestone to say it was birds inspired you?"

"And Louis Bleriot, also a great inspiration." Aldo heaved himself to his feet, letting the water sluice down, slosh and splash. "Towel, per piacere, please," he said.

Without turning, Molly handed him the towel — somewhat damp from her earlier use, it's true — and closed her notebook. "Another Frenchman you admire because he crashed so many times and lived to crash again."

AND HERE'S ALDO! "Do you know what we call this part when we are children, just little boys, in Italy?"

"Oh!" Molly clapped her hands over her eyes. "Now how would I know that?"

"It's called *ucellino*, meaning little bird." He began to laugh. "Oh? Are you blushing, Molly? Molly, Molly — my Molly!"

"Holy Mother of God, who have I married?" she said, keeping her eyes shut but throwing her arms around him, pressing her cheek to his hot wet chest.

12

ALDO HAD DECIDED TO ENTER THE HARVARD-BOSTON Aero Meet which was going on from September the 3rd to the 13th. He told Mr Argyle at the Iron Bridge Company, and Mr Argyle said that after the Aero Meet was over Aldo could apply to the drafting department and, if they were short handed, he could have his old job back, then he stood up behind his desk and briskly shook Aldo's hand. Aldo owed money all over Boston. He didn't know exactly how much he owed because at the end of every week he handed over his invoices and most of his cash to Molly, letting her pay this one or that one, or not pay, whatever she decided. They were now eating at Pacifico's table twice a week, taking home the leftovers wrapped in wax paper and skipping lunch most days. Frankly, Aldo didn't care what he had in his belly or his pocket so long as he was building his aeroplane, and as for Molly, she said, "I'm fine, I'm fine. I'm not eating tripe every night or hunting for coal by the railroad tracks, so what have I got to complain about?"

Aldo wasn't interested in competing for a prize at the Aero Meet; he wanted to demonstrate his aeroplane, sell it and find buyers for other aeroplanes he hoped to build. Best of all, at the Aero Meet he would re-join the brotherhood of flyers and possibly — who could tell? — talk again with people like his friend Louis Paulham. Of course, you know, Louis had exited the United States back in March, one running jump ahead of attorneys hired by the Wright brothers, but maybe someone from the Voisin factory would turn up, or Louis Bleriot himself. Every flyer in the world was invited but no one knew for certain who would actually be there, not even the organizers.

After all, anybody with money and a theory of flight could build a flying machine. Some constructed machines that flew like box kites or gliders, others assembled wings, maybe two or three, and stacked one above the other, but the trick was to control the flight so it didn't end in a crash. Some liked to control pitch by putting elevators in the tail, others had them on outriggers, left and right. Some popular designs had elevators cantilevered way out front of the main wing, so the aircraft looked like a flying duck, the *canard* design — and by the way, *canard* means duck, not goose, our Aldo was wrong about that. As for controlling turns, many designers followed the Wright brothers and used thin cables to warp the wings, twisting each wing somewhat up or down to increase or decrease the slice it took to the air, causing the aeroplane to turn left or right — let's be honest, causing the contraption to roll, slew and slide left or right.

Louis Bleriot, the same Bleriot who Aldo admired, designed his first flying machine around 1901. It had wings that flapped explosively but it never got off the ground. His second, a biplane on floats pulled by a motor boat, caught a wing in the water and smashed. His third had wings shaped like big bottomless tubs mounted in tandem like beads on a string — it never took off. But in his fourth, a *canard* design with varnished paper wings, he did fly six yards. After he crashed that one, Bleriot constructed an aircraft with two sets of wings, one behind the other, in which he flew many yards, climbed to sixty feet, stalled, crashed. He limped back to his drawing board and designed more machines. In 1907 he built his seventh aeroplane — called the Bleriot VII, of course — with the engine up front, wheels under the engine, a single pair of wings and a tail with a rudder and elevators. It flew. Indeed, all his subsequent planes flew, even the one with rice paper wings, though it's a fact he went crash, crash, crash, and crash. Early in the morning on July 25, 1909, Louis Bleriot climbed into his Bleriot XI in Calais, France, flew across the English Channel and landed in Dover, England — crash landed. He had become the first person to fly the English Channel, thereby winning £1,000 from the London *Daily Mail* and rescuing himself from bankruptcy.

Aldo Vela's 1910 aeroplane had its 50 horsepower Gnôme rotary engine up front, the wings about shoulder height to the pilot, then the long fuselage with a rudder and elevators at the end. The only part of the fuselage that was covered with fabric was the section around the cockpits; the rest was bare to reduce drag, so it's true the aeroplane body looked like four delicate ladders laced together, edge to edge, by a fragile crisscross of piano wire. But the great wingspan, longer even than the fuselage, with its slightly uplifted wing tips, gave it a soaring bird-like appearance — a great, grand bird.

In August Aldo crashed three more times, during which he broke the left wing tip, collapsed the wheels, crushed the right wing tip, and busted the tail skid so often he finally replaced it with a wheel. The rotary engine was lubricated by oil shot from the crankcase to the cylinders and then sprayed out to the air where it was blown back into the pilot, so he designed a loose fitting semi-circular shield, or cowl, that fit over the top of whirling engine and deflected the oil — smelly castor oil, because castor oil didn't contaminate gasoline. Aldo made a hard landing at sunset on the first day of September, so the aeroplane was not ready by opening day of the Harvard-Boston Aero Meet.

But on Tuesday, the fourth day of the Aero Meet, Aldo and Tito did get there and assembled the aeroplane at Aviation Field. Along one margin of the field a crooked row of large boxy canvas tents housed the flying machines. Aldo had no tent, but he'd hung tarpaulin, roof-like, from four poles to shelter the engine and the cockpit of his aeroplane. Harvard Aviation Field was a temporary airdrome, a square mile of ragged turf on a flat patch of empty land that stretched into the southern waters of Boston Harbor. When they had finished assembling the aeroplane, Tito squinted across the field to study the grandstand, then he took in the thin line of trees by the road and the flat expanse of grayish sea at the far end of the field. "Very uninteresting land," he said. "Nothing grows here, you know?"

"Who cares so long as it's flat?" Aldo said, wiping his hands on an oil rag. "I'm happy."

"And all these people who come to watch the meet. How is it they don't have to go to their jobs?"

"Stay here and admire the women's hats. I'll be back," Aldo said.

Aldo walked from tent to tent, partly to examine the other flying machines by mostly on the lookout for pilots, designers or mechanics from France or Italy. Forty minutes later he was back beside his Vela aeroplane.

"Well?" Tito said.

"Everybody is English. I found some French aeroplanes, but nobody to talk with."

Molly came with her friend Kate, both of them calling out and waving from a distance as soon as they spied Aldo's place in the line of tents, and Enzo the tailor came in a handsomely cut suit and bowler hat, along with his two placid sisters in long coats. Pacifico and Marianna arrived somewhat later, and Pacifico had a hand-held Kodak camera that unfolded with a little bellows, so it could take fine photographs. Aldo made two demonstration flights that afternoon — soft landing each time — and for the remainder of the day he talked with Molly, his friends and relatives and whoever came by to ask questions about the aeroplane.

Molly returned to work at the brick company the next day, but was so distracted by clairvoyant thoughts of Aldo falling from the sky that she asked to be excused so she could go to the aero meet. She wasn't given leave, so she took off her paper cuffs, quit her job and made her way to the flying field. She knew her mere presence couldn't protect him, but she felt he was safer with her there, so every time Aldo took off she stationed herself at the edge of the field and traced his long slow flights, the steep leaning turns and flowing passages, herself as watchful as a sentry until he landed.

One morning when Aldo was tightening wires along the fuselage he heard two young men questioning Tito, or trying to. One of the men wore a stiff straw boater and the other was hatless. What they heard from Tito was — "It's air cool. Rotary. It spin around in the air. It's much lighter, because it use-a no water."

The one in the straw boater turned to his friend and said, "It use-a no water! —You're wasting your time, Tommy. He's just a wop Italian. I'm going to the next tent."

But Tommy stayed, turned to Tito and spoke in carefully articulated French, saying, "Excusez! Où est le propriétaire de cet avion?"

Tito merely looked at him.

Aldo spoke up in French, saying, "I'm the owner. What's your question?"

"Thank you," the young man continued in French. "I like your aeroplane. I was wondering about the engine."

"The Gnôme? It's fifty horsepower and it's air cooled, which means that we get a lot more power with a lot less weight."

Aldo was wearing a leather jacket over a thin sweater and his Zeiss goggles hung below his throat — gear from his automobile racing days.

"You're the flyer?" the young man asked, delighted.

"Yes."

"Is this a Voisin machine?"

"No, no. It's a Vela. I designed it."

"In France?"

Aldo smiled broadly and said, honestly, "Yes."

The young man — thin nose, spot of color on each cheek, flax hair — asked if it was difficult to learn to fly. Aldo told him it was no more difficult than learning to drive an automobile. The man, hands in his jacket pockets, peered into the cockpit a few moments, then walked slowly around the aeroplane, looking at it attentively. He asked Aldo a few more questions, smiled, said, "Merci beaucoup," and walked away. Aldo turned to Tito and said in Italian, "If that one comes back again, bring him to me. He's interested."

The Harvard-Boston Aero Meet went broke, but it was a success for most of the flyers and all the spectators, including circumferential president William Howard Taft, even though he was too heavy to be lifted an inch off the ground by any of the flying machines. The Englishman Claude Grahame-White won a lot of prizes, took mayor John Fitzgerald for a flight over Boston harbor, and made a little extra cash by charging passengers for a fifteen-minute ride. Another Englishman named Roe made a flight in a machine that had three wings in a stack, but it crashed. Wilbur Wright came with his team, partly to fly and partly to keep his chill eyes on Glen Curtiss, whom he was suing. Aldo talked with other pilots, among them Charlie Willard, who was said to have graduated from Harvard, but who was for sure a former race car driver. And he had a good time with Didier Masson who had been a mechanic for Aldo's friend Paulham and who was now flying every chance he got. On the last day of the meet the pilots organized an egg dropping contest, the only contest Aldo enjoyed. He relished making turns and shallow dives that mocked the maneuvers he had watched a few days earlier when there had been a target battleship, reduced in size but true in shape, and flying machines had successfully attacked it with plaster bombs, thrilling government observers. "Bravo!" Aldo had said. "What happens when the target shoots back?"

"If there had been a prize for the most beautiful aeroplane," Molly told him. "We would have won it."

"Yes, we could have won it," he said, pleased that Molly had said we.

Thomas Pickering, the man who questioned Aldo about his flying machine, had returned two days later with a different friend. Pickering hailed Aldo in French, asking permission to show his friend "cet avion magnifique," and of course Aldo agreed, replying in French. During Pickering's previous visit Aldo realized that Pickering would be more interested in doing business if he believed Aldo wasn't Italian but French. Pickering and his friend, a man named Adams, examined the aircraft, were obviously fascinated and asked one question after another. Aldo's French was more fluent than Pickering's and as they wound up the conversation Pickering asked what part of France he was from. "Nice, near Italy," Aldo announced. "In fact, I raced automobiles in Torino, in Italy, before I designed aeroplanes. My mechanic is an Italian, a very good man."

The next month Aldo began to give flying lessons to Pickering at the farmer's field in Lexington, sailing over the scarlet sumac and yellow birches into the spotless air, into wide sweeping curves and lazy figure eights, doing the maneuvers again and again, at last returning down a long shallow slope to land on the straw colored field. After two days Aldo felt comfortable enough with his student to switch to English. "Your English is very good," Pickering exclaimed. "And — do you know? — you have an Irish accent!" Pickering turned up one afternoon with two friends, Norman Prince and Chad Washburn, both of them interested in aeroplanes and both astonished that Pickering was taking flying lessons. The first Vela aeroplane was purchased for $4,150 in November, 1910, by Thomas Pickering of Duxbury, Massachusetts. Chad Washburn purchased the next one, and after that the orders came flying in one after the other, came in flocks, to the Vela Aeroplane Company.

Sunday morning and they're boldly, bravely naked, those two. "We're going to be rich," Aldo announced, stretching back on the bed, folding his hands behind his head.

"For sure," said Molly, brushing her hair at the mirror. "We'll not be able to shut the dresser drawers, they'll be so stuffed with money."

Aldo laughed, swung his legs off the bed and stood up. "Maybe not that rich."

"Rich enough to eat ice cream every day?" she asked.

Aldo had drawn aside the window shade and was peering at the clear blue sky. "Yes, that rich."

"Let's put on our Sunday best and get our ice cream," she said, pulling a slip from the dresser. "Before the money's gone."

They got into their Sunday best, took the trolley and subway to the Café Mondello. Molly looked around at the gold flocked wallpaper, the bright spacious mirrors, the gas chandeliers with electric bulbs. "I feel rich already," she said. "Like one of those grand horizontals in Paris." Aldo, unfolding his newspaper, murmured that this was a respectable Italian café and not a French bordello, and only the puritanical Irish would confuse the two. He scanned the headlines of *La Notizia*, folded the paper and put it aside. "My father would have liked this newspaper. Very socialist." Molly, who had been watching the family (mother, father, little boy) at the next table, smiled and turned to Aldo. "You loved your father," she said.

"Of course. Everyone who knew him loved him. Especially my mother. My father was a wonderful man."

"I loved my mother. I can say that." She spoke slowly, as if meditating. "But I cannot say I loved my father. Sometimes I felt sorry for him and a lot of the time I feared him. I just tried to stay out of his way. He had terrible rages, the old man. But your father was a gentle person."

"He liked people," Aldo said. "Above all, he loved my mother and me. He was a poet, you know. He was a journalist, of course, and a teacher, but at heart he was a poet."

"It must have been hard for you, a young boy, to lose — I mean — when he died —"

But Aldo cut her off, saying, "They beat my father to death! They broke his bones. They broke his head. If my father had a thought when he was dying it was to take care of us, of me and my mother. I couldn't protect him, but at least when I grew up I could avenge him."

Molly opened her mouth to speak, then stopped. "A poet," was all she said.

The waiter greeted them in Italian, briskly swabbed the small marble table top, took their order and dashed off.

"My father wrote a long poem about Daedalus and Icarus in Sicilian," Aldo told her. "He never finished it because he kept changing it. —You know the story of Daedalus and Icarus?"

"Not I."

"You were taught it in school, but you've forgotten it." He looked surprised. "It's about flying and —"

"Do you know Saint Patrick who drove the snakes out of Ireland? Do you know Saint Brendan who sailed to America in a stone boat?"

"No," he admitted.

"All right then," she said, satisfied. "Now you can tell me."

"It happened like this. It happened that Daedalus and his son Icarus escaped from an island prison by making wings from the feathers of sea birds. The old man was clever. He was famous for that. They glued the feathers together with bees' wax to make wings. Daedalus warned his son not to fly near the sun because it would melt the wax and his wings would come apart. But his son was enchanted by flying, drunk on flying — I can understand that, I feel the same way myself — and he flew too close to the sun. The heat of the sun melted the wax, the feathers tore off, he fell out of the sky and into the sea and drowned. That's not the end."

"I don't like the way this story is going, Aldo."

"Neither did my father. In the old story Daedalus couldn't rescue his son, so he flew on and discovered Sicily. —It's a Greek story, and the Greeks think they discovered Sicily, even though we were already there. — My father didn't believe a father would watch his son struggling in the sea and not rescue him. He revised and rewrote that part over and over again."

"It sounds like an Irish poem, I'm sorry to say. Such grief."

"In my father's last version, Daedalus swoops low over the waves so Icarus can grab his father's ankles and he holds on as his father pulls him from the sea. His father uses all the strength in his old arms to beat his wings, lifting him just above the waves and over the sea to the shore of Sicily. Sometimes his tired wings touch the water, he was so —, but he —" Aldo's eyes had begun to glisten and his voice wavered. He dried his eyes and laughed. "So. Anyway. In my father's version, Daedalus tells his son to change his name and he, Daedalus, will tell everyone that his son is dead, drowned in the sea. That way, the cruel and stupid king who imprisoned them will not bother to send thugs to hunt Icarus down, and Daedalus is so old and in such grief that the king won't bother with him either. They were political prisoners, you might say, and Daedalus made up the story of his son's drowning in order to save him. Now you know the story of Daedalus and Icarus, the true version."

The waiter swept in with their spumoni — heaps of pastel hues, like frozen flowers in crystal dishes.

"Now *this* is spumoni. You will never find finer ice cream than this," Aldo told Molly.

They decided to move to a new flat, a bigger place. "Because, Aldo, this apartment has gotten so tight I have to leave my shadow outside when I come in."

"I was going to suggest a move," he said.

So in May of 1911 Aldo and Molly left the Fort Pont Channel place and moved to a larger thirdfloor flat in the West End, a neighborhood of Irish and Italians. "Ah, this is big enough to swing a cat in!" Molly said. Aldo was selling his aeroplanes, giving flying lessons, putting money away and feeling prosperous. Their landlord lived on the first floor, a veteran of the War Between the States (28th Massachusetts, part of the Irish Brigade) who had fought at Gettysburg and been wounded in the slaughter at the Wheat Field. He despised Republicans, especially Theodore Roosevelt. "That braggart loves playing at war. He loved playing war with Spain. Oh, yes. Him and his cavalry. He thinks it's a sport. He hasn't seen men die by the tens of thousands. I've seen it. I was there." Aldo doubted that men had died by the tens of thousands at Gettysburg, but he was polite. "That was a large war, the war between the states," he ventured.

"Jaesus, Mary and Joseph, it wasn't no sport!"

"We will have no more wars," Aldo said decisively, handing him the envelope with the rent money.

"Thank you. —And they weren't all dead, either. They were dying and it took all day. Oh, yes. But who wants to remember? Even I forget. And that's the truth. —I need to go pee."

There was a ghost, a young Irish woman in a mossgreen head shawl, who sometimes appeared early in the morning seated on a step at the second floor. You could see her by looking up from the foot of the stairs or looking down slantwise from the third floor, but as you walked up or down the stairs your view was cut off at the turning of the staircase and when you reached the second floor she had vanished. Almost always she had vanished, but sometimes you had to step around her.

"How can you believe such things?" Pacifico asked, refilling her glass.

"Such things?" Molly said. "Would you be asking can I believe in a man whose hind end is the back half of a horse? Or a goddess who makes her bed in a whore house? Would you be asking me that?"

Pacifico gave a roar of laughter and slapped the table top in approval. "If you ever got to talk with this ghost, what would you say?" he asked, leaning slightly forward.

"I'd say, *In God's name what do you want.* That's the way you speak to haunts. You always begin with *In God's name.*" She tossed back her head, drank the last of her wine, banged her glass back on the table. "That's what I was taught."

"The Irish converse with the dead," Aldo told Marianna. "They have grand funeral parties, too. We went to an Irish wake — an uncle of Molly's friend Kate had died — and it was like nothing in Italy or Sicily. They drink whiskey like it was mother's milk. Have you noticed all the funeral parlors in Boston are owned by the Irish? They open funeral houses the way we open restaurants. If you want to know anything about the dead, ask the Irish."

When Aldo paid the next month's rent he asked about the ghost. "Oh," his landlord said, brushing aside the question with a wave of his hand. "She's no banshee if that's what you're worried about."

That evening Aldo asked Molly what a banshee was.

"You've been listening to the Irish Brigade, have you? A banshee is a woman spirit who foretells a death in the family."

"Did the nuns teach you that or did you learn it with your accounting?"

"I know it because I'm an O'Neill. The banshee works only for the O'Neills, and the O'Briens, O'Connors, O'Gradys and Kavanaghs." She laughed.

"I thought everyone knew that."

"What happens if a Miss O'Neill has married a Mr Vela from Sicily? Does the banshee still work for the former Miss O'Neill?"

"We don't know yet."

13

The Vela Aeroplane Company moved closer to the West End where the owner himself worked full time and Tito half-time, along with a handful of employees, building aircraft. Over the next few years Aldo improved his aeroplane (landing gear, engine) but it remained essentially the same craft. It was beautiful to look at, easy to handle and graceful in flight. It took to the air readily and flew slowly. Yes, slowly — Aldo had designed it that way. Other aeroplanes flew faster and faster and faster. Speed wasn't important to Aldo, quite the contrary. Speed meant flying in a straight line from here to there, pausing to look at nothing, but he wanted to lazily meander, to circle the foursided clock on the train station tower, climb higher into the sky, or drift low over the tall grasses that leaned with the flow at the river's edge. "This is a fair-weather aeroplane," Aldo used to say. "It's made to carry a couple to a picnic in the country, not to carry important mail or bombs. It's an aeroplane for holidays or romances and adventure." One of his improvements was a wicker basket, attached to the fuselage, to hold lunch and a bottle of wine.

In 1913 he designed his "Dragonfly" aeroplane, a ship somewhat similar to Louis Bleriot's second 1907 machine. It had two sets of wings, one pair behind the other, and a long tail. The design was prompted not by a wish to imitate Bleriot, but by Aldo's desire to reproduce the seemingly weightless beauty of nature's dragonfly. The aeroplane's wings were clothed with glittering translucent silk, and it flew well enough, but it remained a curiosity and sold only three copies. On the other hand, the basic Vela aeroplane sold very well. The wood frame was sheathed with plain linen which gave it a light dun or golden hue, but fancier models with cushioned seats had wings as gorgeous as orioles, tanagers or jays. For half a dozen years it was the most familiar aeroplane in all New England, New York and Pennsylvania.

Molly learned all she could about aerodynamics and gathered every number she could — all to keep Aldo from falling from the sky. She read books from the library and articles in *Aero*, but having gathered all the numbers there seemed no way to balance accounts, no established theory of flight, only a multitude of facts. Everyone knew that the curvature of the wings, the convexity of the upper surface — what the French called *cambrure* — was essential, but no one knew how much of a curve to make. She had read someplace that a propeller was simply a rotating wing, an idea that surprised and pleased her so much that she laughed out loud. A skimpy handful of people built wind tunnels to test their theories; everyone else built aeroplanes and flew them to see what would happen. Pilots crashed all the time, many got killed and no one worried. But Molly worried and in her nightmare an aeroplane lighted up the sky, plunging to earth like a meteor trailing fire.

"All life is risky, uncertain," Aldo said.

"But numbers are certain," she told him.

Flying delighted her just as Aldo had said it would. She felt there was a whimsy to it that no one had ever remarked upon. As for Aldo, she could tell he felt much more than delight —

flying exhilarated him, the expansiveness of the view enlarged his soul and charged his intelligence. When others flew they were carried aloft in a flying machine, but when Aldo flew, he was the one flying and the machine was mere ballast — his feet on the rudder bar and his hands on the lever were sensate parts of the aeroplane, just as the wires stretching to the fuselage and wings were spliced to the coils of his brain. He was a man with wings. Given the chance, he would turn somersaults in the sky and hobnob with angels and gods. Before she met Aldo she had never feared because she had nothing to lose, but now she saw how she could lose everything.

❦

Pacifico's wife Marianna had elegantly shaped breasts tipped with large rose nipples that were ever overflowing with sweet milk, and it seemed there was always a child suckling. Now she was breast feeding Dante, her fifth — or possibly Sandro, her sixth — handsome boys with thick black hair and eyes that glistened like fresh ink. Marianna was a smart, good looking, fertile woman. Maybe that's why one morning Molly told Aldo, abruptly, "My monthlies are as regular as the tides."

Aldo hesitated, his coffee cup half way to his mouth. "Your monthlies?"

"The bloody curse that God —"

"Ah! I understand," he said, nodding yes, slowly lowering his cup into its saucer. "I understand."

"Do you understand you will never have any children?"

"What do you mean?" he says, startled.

"I mean I got an abortion in Dublin when I was seventeen."

"Oh? *Oh!* God. Well. I don't —"

"If you thought you were marrying a virgin," she says tartly, "I'm sorry to disappoint you."

"What?" he says, looking at her, puzzled. "What!" he cries, reaching across the table to grab the throat of her shirtwaist, yanking her to her feet. *"Don't talk that way to me! Don't talk that way to me ever again! Understand?"* And he flings her back into her chair so hard it slides back a foot.

"Holy Mother of God!" she cries, whirling up and turning on him. "I have a past, you know!"

"Exactly! A past. That is *past*."

"I'm me — past, present and future!"

"Be calm," he tells her. "Sit down. Be calm."

"And who are you to teach me that?" she says, and snatching up the first thing she can get her hand on she hurls a wet dishrag at him.

Aldo caught the rag, quietly mopped the spilled coffee, rinsed the dishrag in the sink, squeezed it and hung it over the hook. "Tell me more," he said.

She sat down and gave half a laugh. "At the time I felt so relieved and free and happy and I thought — *so there is a God after all and he loves me.* I was happy, so happy. Now I think I'm cursed."

"No, no, no curse on you," he muttered.

"I murdered an innocent. I'm barren and it's my —"

But Aldo reached slowly across the table and put his hand to her mouth, stopping her.

"This is not the Dark Ages," he told her. "There's no more curses. I married you because of you, not because to have children. Yes," he added a moment later, as if discovering that he agreed with himself. "That's true."

"I murdered —"

"Molly, Molly. Listen to me." He put his hands flat on his chest. "I'll tell you what murder is. Murder is when you beat a man to death because you don't like his opinions. My mother and I, we moved from Sicily to Italy, to the north, far away to the north, to Torino. You know that. And before we left Palermo, my mother pointed out to me the house where lived the man who made my father to be beaten senseless and thrown into a filthy cell to die. I told you that, too. What I didn't tell you was that when I was a student at the engineering school in Torino I took a trip to Roma and from there to Napoli and from there I sailed to Palermo. I carried five wine bottles — very good looking wine bottles — filled with gasoline. In Palermo I walked down the avenue where my mother had pointed to the villa. It had looked like a prison castle when I was a kid, but it was only a bourgeois villa with a tile roof and some ugly wrought-iron growing over the ground floor windows. I strolled in the park along that avenue and asked who lives in that villa over there, and they told me, and it was the same man. That night I did what I had come to do, and the next morning I sailed from Palermo to Napoli and so back to Torino.

"A month later my mother calls me into her room where she is standing beside her writing desk with a letter in her hand. She had received the letter from one of her socialist friends in Palermo describing how a certain villa had burned to the ground and everything in it was ashes. The man lived, but with many shattered bones because he ran in the smoke and fell down the stairs. Somebody had even shot the horse dead when it was pulling the carriage through the gate.

"My mother asked me if I had been to Palermo. I said yes. She didn't say anything for a long moment, then she says, *You know the army and the police are everywhere. You could have been taken for a revolutionary. If anything happened to you I would die. Do you understand? Now promise me you will never go to Sicily again.* I promised. Then she kissed me on my cheeks, here and here, and she embraced me for a long time.

"That man with all the broken bones, he never got well. He died in pain." Aldo poured more coffee into his cup and lifted it, saying, "And — you see? — my hand doesn't tremble." He took a drink and set the cup neatly in its saucer.

"I should like to meet your mother some day," Molly said.

❦

Aldo and his mother exchanged letters every month or so — short but gossipy letters about her daily routine, local politics, a wedding party or a funeral, the ailments of friends, the birth of children, certain opera singers, and so on. In August of 1914 he received a different kind of letter from Morgana. She was writing, she said, a day after learning that Jean Juarès, the great French socialist, had been gunned down in Paris by a crazed assassin. She admired Juarès, not simply because he was a socialist — the world had many kinds of socialists — but because he was wise, compassionate, peace loving, brave, resourceful and persevering. Sometimes it was difficult to realize that such people lived among us. Juarès had seen how monarchs and ministers were maneuvering, preparing their countries for war, and he had warned against such foolishness. He knew that hush-hush meetings and secret compacts guaranteed not peace but vengeance. He knew that if war came, ordinary people who wanted only to marry, to have a job and a family, would be sent to battle others like themselves. The murder of Juarès was a signal that a great war was about to begin. Her own mother used to say the gods employed death of a gallant man that way, as a sign their entertainment was about to start, like dimming the houselights before the opera curtain rises. She reminded Aldo that she was a pacifist, and she hoped, pleaded and begged he would not join in the fighting. The world was going to soak in blood. She told him to take care of his wife — *Stay by her side because the war will make her conceive and she will need you all the more.* — but if he ever did cross the Atlantic his mother would be waiting in Torino to embrace him and cover his cheeks with kisses.

As a matter of fact, on June 28, Austrian Archduke Francis Ferdinand and his wife had been assassinated in Sarajevo by a Serbian nationalist and, using that as a let's-pretend pretext, Austria-Hungary declared war on Serbia, after which Russia — allied with Serbia — began to mobilize against Austria-Hungary. These old wars are hard to keep straight and easy to forget, so here's the way it happened. On August 1, as Morgana was writing her letter to Aldo, Germany declared war on Russia, and two days later Germany also declared war on France. On August 4 Britain declared war on Germany. On August 6 Austria-Hungary declared war on Russia and on the same day Serbia declared war on Germany. On August 11 France declared war on Austria-Hungary and was joined the next day by Britain. Other nations, too numerous to remember, got in on the war. The following year, on April 26, 1915 , Italy joined Britain and France against the Central Powers, and two years later on April 6, 1917, the United States declared war on Germany. By mid June, Aldo had arrived in France and was on his way to Tours, southwest of Paris, to train American pilots at the flight school.

Aldo had closed the Vela Aeroplane factory and Molly had begun working for the city of Boston, a job she got through Kate McCarthy who had connections to the ward boss under the mayor, James Michael Curley. Aldo left Boston near the end of May and Molly, despite her monthlies having been as regular as the tides, had no menstrual flow, though it should have come right then, nor did it come in June, not a drop of blood. She was writing one or two or even three letters a week to Aldo, but she never mentioned what had happened, or had not happened, because what it seemed to mean seemed impossible. Then one morning as she was descending the stairway on her way to work a wave of nausea lifted her stomach, made her dizzy, and she had to hold the rail all the way from the second floor landing to the front door.

Three nights later she wrote *Dearest Aldo, who I love more than ever you will be as amazed as I am for I am pregnant and we are going to have a baby. I went to Dr. White. And I talked with an old midwife from county Tyrone, my mother's own county, and the old woman asked me the same questions as Dr. White and a few more personal as well. — Marianna calls it a joyful miracle and Maureen says it's like the barren woman in the Bible who gives birth when she's a hundred years old, or some such age. Maureen has a good heart but the Bible never did me any good & frankly now that I'm carrying a baby I'd sooner cross the street than be on the same side as a priest.*

Marianna and Pacifico have invited me to live with them, but I'm fine here in Boston, especially as it is so convenient to walk to work. Not that Marianna would notice one more baby among the eight or nine she has or will have when my time comes. I miss you more than ever I know you have to be over there. I know the Italians and Irish will never agree about this war, except that it is terrible. I miss you so much. Aldo Aldo. I write Aldo Aldo because I remember how you say Molly Molly when you want to tell me something. Now I have told you my news. Love, Molly.

As soon as Aldo read Molly's letter he dashed off a note to her, writing that her news made him happier than he could express, especially in English. *I feel as if I am filled up and overflowing. I am so happy as the day we married, which will always be the happiest day of my life. The war cannot go on forever and now that the United States is sending troops the war will soon be finished. I'll be home before our baby is born.*

He wrote again that evening, urging her to visit the doctor often and maybe visit Marianna's doctor and to move in with Marianna and Pacifico outside the city before the baby came. He wrote that he was getting acquainted with routine at the base. The French were generous and were delighted that the Americans were arriving in France. The newspapers had reported about the American infantry battalion marching in Paris on the 4th of July and how one of the officers had said "Nous voilà, Lafayette!" and the crowds of French had gone crazy with joy.

The young American pilots here for training are idealistic and enthusiastic but — the remainder of the sentence was blacked out by the French censor. *The aeroplanes we use for training are* — this part was blacked out — *with clipped wings. They clip the wings so the aeroplane can't take off. The student pilots run the machine up and down the field and learn the controls, but the poor plane is like a baby bird that flaps and flaps but can never fly.*

My head is full of thoughts of you and the baby. Do you think the baby will be a flier? I'm sure of it. Boy or girl, it makes no difference, nowadays women are fliers too. It will be wonderful.

Molly had never disagreed with Aldo; that is, she'd never disagreed profoundly. True, she'd had arguments with him and at times raged against him, cursed him, thrown things at him — a thin book, say, or a medium size dish, absolutely no knives — and in a burst of anger had once locked the bedroom door against him, which led to his kicking it open with the heel of his shoe, hurling the door around so hard the knob punched a hole in the wall, but nothing you'd call a *profound* disagreement. Yet ever since that letter in which he said her baby would fly an aeroplane Molly had felt a deep and fearful disagreement with Aldo, and it was growing much like the infant in her womb. She would not have her child fall from the sky like one of those angels God threw over the edge. Her child would never fall flaming from the sky because she'd never let her child fly up there.

In mid-December one morning as she started down the stairway she was startled to see the ghost on the second floor landing. While Molly descended her view was cut off by the turn of the stairway, but when she reached the landing the specter was still there, sitting hunched on the step in a mossgreen head shawl. Molly pulled the skirts of her coat aside to keep it from brushing against the specter, held her breath while she stepped carefully around it and, struggling to keep her balance, clutched the rail and made her way down to the door and out to the freezing rain. She didn't tell anyone what she had seen and she didn't write to Aldo about it. The next morning when she left the apartment she spied the apparition again sitting on the step at the second floor landing and nearly pitched headlong down the stairway. She grabbed the rail, descended to the second-floor, drew in her coat so as to not brush against the thing, whatever it was, and made a falling run down the stairs and out to the frozen street. "No, damnit!" she said. Then she turned around, yanked open the front door and lumbered up the stairs (she was 30 weeks pregnant, remember) to the second floor landing which was utterly vacant. She stamped down the stairs, muttering Damn at every step until she was out the door. Then she went off to work.

Molly wrote to Aldo that night, telling him about the apparition, but phrasing it in a playful way so he would not think she was wholly daft — yet informing him about it all the same — then taking it back at the end by saying the spirit was so solid looking it must have been real, no ghost, just some poor biddy taking refuge from the freezing cold weather. Knowing that Aldo would worry about her health and sanity and would think she was seeing weird things because she was living alone, she added that she'd already arranged to stay with the Cavallùs out in Malden. That Saturday she visited Pacifico in his corner office over the new store and — presto! — Molly agreed that she would take the train the day before Christmas and would stay with them until well after the birth of her baby. "Brava, Molly!" Pacifico said. "Marianna will be delighted to have company. Two babies will be twice more fun than one. I'll call doctor Balboni! —And I'll send a note to Aldo to tell him the good news."

"Oh, no. Let me," said Molly.

On February 25, 1918, around four in the morning, Molly was awakened, or half-awakened, by crying. The sound seemed composed not of one voice, but of many women's voices blended together, wailing and keening — something like wind shrieking at the edge of a door or like a woman in anguish. Molly lay listening to the sound and thought it strange that Marianna was not coming down the hall to comfort whichever child it was. She pushed aside the bedclothes and walked down the dim hall toward the crying which was softer now, more like a moan, and glancing down the stairway saw the woman in the moss-green head shawl seated on the second step down, for it was she who was voicing grief. Molly bent down and whispered at her ear, "Go fuck off," then straightened and stepped into the bathroom. She picked up the first thing to hand, which was a tin cup half filled with water, turned and emptied it over the banshee — if that's what it was or had been, for it was gone now. Molly returned the cup to the sink and had started to walk back down the hall when the first contraction came, making her reach to the wall for support, squeezing her till she gasped.

Marianna had heard no wailing. But she did hear Molly cry out, so she shook Pacifico awake, then she stepped out to the hall and nearly bumped into Molly who, as Marianna always said, had been awakened by contractions and whose waters had now broken.

It was late in the afternoon when Brendan Neil Orlando Vela was delivered, covered with blood but safe, into this world. As for Molly, she lay in an exhausted stupor, awake without thought, feeling her body adrift on a gentle tide of air, or maybe it was only life ebbing away from her, she didn't know which. They brought the infant and laid it between her arm and her breast, and later they took it away. She slept, too tired even to dream. Late the next day she wrote a note to Aldo, simply the date and *My dearest Aldo, we have a son, a family. Love from your Molly.*

By the time the letter had crossed the Atlantic and traveled to his base at Tours, Aldo was in Issoudun. He had been directed to deliver a Nieuport aeroplane to Issoudun where a group of pilots from the United States was being trained. The French had been flying Nieuports but were now flying the faster, more robust Spads, and were giving the old Nieuports to the Americans who had no planes of their own. Early in the morning of February 26 Aldo took off from Tours and flew toward Issoudun, climbing steadily while the land beneath him spread farther and farther like a blue expanding map. Somewhere near Issoudun a feather of flame blew from the engine, curled up and blew away, then another and another, much like feathers torn from the engine cowl. Instinctively he shoved the stick and sent the plane into a long plunge toward the earth. The allies had no parachutes and there was no way a pilot could escape from a fiery plane except by jumping to his death. A radiant burst of flame reached toward him from the engine, flowed over the arm he lifted to protect his face, curled along side his cheek and neck, lingering to set his flesh afire — then it was gone, as if he had driven out of reach. There came a huge CRACK sound as a slice of fabric tore from his wing, he pulled up, leveled the Nieuport, saw the broad field of the Issoudun aerodrome ahead and everything was strangely quiet and soft, as if he were falling asleep. That's about all he was able to recall. The Nieuport made a smooth landing and even before it had rolled to a stop three men had rushed onto the field and pulled him from the cockpit.

Aldo's mother, Morgana, made her way from Torino to Issoudun, took a room in a hotel. By the time she arrived he was out of danger, was free to walk the hospital grounds, and was thoroughly familiar with the extent of his disfigurement. Fire had eaten the flesh along his left forearm and hand, damaging the nerves to his fingers; he was receiving painful physical therapy for his hand. His left eye was blind. His left cheek, ear and neck had also burned, and much of the flesh of his ear had had to be surgically removed. As the seared flesh healed it took on a blotchy, mottled appearance and it tightened, tugging his lips on that side into a grimace. He talked about the war, about Molly and his son, about one thing or another, but not about the mess of his face, not until the day his mother was about to leave for Italy. They were at the train station, standing side by side on the platform, sheltered from the falling rain. "I want to meet your Molly someday," Morgana said. "You should bring her to Italy as soon as this war is over. I'm sure I'll like her. And I want to see my grandson."

Aldo burst out, *"My face will frighten my son, my own face — it will give him nightmares!"*

For a long moment Morgana remained as she was, gazing at the railroad tracks that gleamed in the rain. "Would you take your father back from the dead if his face was burned like yours?" she asked, not turning to him.

"Yes," he said. "Of course."

"Your son —"

"I know, I know," he said, not waiting for her to finish.

"This terrible war isn't going to last forever, and when it's over you can bring your family to Italy. — Now are you going to let me kiss you or not?"

So here they are one summer morning a year later, Aldo and Molly, loafing side-by-side on a rumpled sheet in the bedroom in their West End apartment, both of them naked as the day they were born. Or they were a moment ago. Now Molly has slipped into a wrapper and left the room, and Aldo has a towel around his waist and is at the bureau, putting on his eye patch. He lighted a cigar, one of those black twig-like Parodi cigars, and he was assessing himself in the bureau mirror when Molly came in carrying a tin tray with two cups of espresso. "I'm still in pretty good shape," Aldo announced.

"You figured that out, did you?"

"And there are many things to enjoy," he continued.

"Now what would you be thinking of?"

"This cigar. That espresso." He set down the cigar, lifted the little cup and took a drink. "Would you like me to sing *Molly Malone* for you?" He spoke in a thick brogue. "It's about a poor Irish lass, don't you know, a working girl."

"I married you to get away from all that. And you'll wake the baby."

Aldo smiled, though I have to admit the left side of his face remained in a grimace. "In Dublin's fair city," he sang. "Where the girls are so pretty —"

"I'll go get the baby," she said, stepping out to the hall. Aldo drained the little coffee cup and stretched out on the bed sheet. Molly returned a moment later with Brendan Neil Orlando Vela whom she laid on the bed between Aldo and herself. The baby squirmed around, got up on hands and knees and began climbing over Aldo's stomach, up his chest, into his face. They put him down again between them. “He’s going to be an adventurer,” Molly said, brooding. “He’s going to live a life full of danger.”

“That’s all right. I protected him.”

“When?”

“In France, when my plane caught fire. That was me, not him. So he’s all right, safe and sound. I protected him forever.”

“Forever?”

“Yes,” he said. “Because I took the disaster.”

“You can’t say he won’t have aeroplane disasters just because you did.”

“I fooled the gods,” Aldo said. “It was me who fell from the sky, not my son. The gods always want to kill sons, anyone’s sons. I fooled the gods.”

“That’s not a logical argument, Aldo.”

“You think the gods are logical? Oh, Molly, Molly. The gods aren’t logical. They’re capricious, full of passion, ambition and rage.”

“So are we. Does that make us godlike?”

“At our best,” said Aldo. “Yes.”

14

ALDO WAS RIGHT, HE HAD FOOLED THE GODS. IN World War II his son Brendan, a fighter pilot, was shot down off the eastern coast of Sicily and survived without a scratch. Brendan flew with the 1st Fighter Group, the same unit to which Aldo had been flying that Nieuport in 1918. In 1943 the 1st Fighter Group flew P-38 Lightnings, a plane with an unusual design that delighted old Aldo. The P-38 had twin fuselages in parallel, with the pilot between them in a nacelle on the wing. It was a nimble fighter with four machine guns and a cannon, and it could climb skyward faster than any other aircraft, friend or foe. Brendan's squadron had completed a bombing run (15 July 1943) and was strafing targets of opportunity on the coastal road between Augusto and Catania. He came under ground fire, pulled up and was attacked by two ME-109s. He was climbing for the sun when his left engine exploded, shredding part of the wing and shattering his canopy. He unbuckled his seat belt, pulled the hatch release and was blown out of plane which began a long plunge earthward. Brendan fell from the sky while the glittering blue sea and the dun-colored land rolled this way and that beneath him. He pulled the rip cord, his chute opened and he landed on a quiet stretch of beach — so far as anyone can figure, it was the same quiet beach where Daedalus and Icarus had landed a few thousand years before.

Brendan was on his knees in the sand, hurriedly burying his chute and Mae West when a patrol of Italian soldiers turned up. He raised his hands and, speaking in Italian, said, "We're friends! Don't shoot!" The soldiers, scruffy and unshaven, held their rifles on him, looked him over. The sergeant asked where he was from, meaning what unit; Brendan, speaking in Italian, said he was from Boston. One of the soldiers asked Brendan if he knew a barber in Boston, his uncle, named Antonio Stella. Brendan explained that Boston was a big city and he couldn't know every barber but, he added, after the war he'd definitely look him up. The soldiers began arguing among themselves as to where they should take Brendan and then somebody remembered that they hadn't searched him for weapons, so the sergeant searched him and found he had only a pair of sunglasses, a pack of cigarettes and a Zippo lighter. The sergeant gave everything back to him. Brendan offered cigarettes all around; they lowered their rifles but declined the offer. "Where are the Germans?" Brendan asked. The sergeant sighed and looked tired. "Where are the British? Where are the Americans? And when will they get here? That's the real question." In the end Brendan was handed off to an Italian truck convoy going to Catania and from there was passed on to Messina where he was kept under guard in a small hotel with a group of other Allied officers. When the British and American troops entered the city, the guards surrendered to the prisoners, and Brendan rejoined the Twelfth Air Force.

Aldo had fooled the gods so well that even his godson was protected. Mercurio, Pacifico's son and Aldo's godson, was a gunner on a B-24 in the 98th Bomb Group, Ninth Air Force. While returning from a raid on the rail yards in Rome (19 June 1943) the B-24 caught fire as they were approaching Palermo and everyone bailed out. The others were never seen again, but Mercurio landed on the Via Imperatore Federico, ran up the street and vaulted over the wall into his father's garden. Three days later the US Seventh Army took Palermo and Mercurio linked up with his bomb group.

The Vela aeroplanes were already old fashioned when Aldo halted production in December of 1916. They were meticulously handmade and were certainly the most beautiful flying machines of their time, but by the end of the Great War Aldo's concept of a low leisurely flight over a slowly unrolling landscape — that was gone forever. In the 1920s he designed luxury aircraft for wealthy patrons who in an earlier era would have been content with yachts, and in 1933 he bought a Beech Model 17 "Staggerwing" plane and began a passenger-and-freight service, flying here and there across New England. His company survived the Great Depression and World War II and he had a fleet of four or five aircraft when he sold out in 1953. Molly worked in progressive politics, sometimes in the local Democratic party, other times in more radical movements.

I never noticed it at the time, but looking back I see they were a handsome couple. Molly had thick white hair, clipped somewhat short and brushed back. Aldo had had facial surgery in the 1920s which permitted him a more symmetrical smile, but when aroused to anger or laughter there was still a tug at the left corner of his mouth and an animal flash of teeth. We kids — this must have been in the late 30s — used to beg him to take out his glass eye, so as to frighten us and, when he did, we'd shout and run away — shocked, horrified, delighted. In his later years he preferred to go without his glass eye and to wear a black eyepatch.

Now let me show you three of those black-and-white photographs taken by Pacifico at the Harvard-Boston Aero Meet back there in 1910. This one shows a group lined up in front of Aldo's aeroplane — here, from left to right, are Enzo (bowler hat) with his two serene sisters, then Tito in blazing white shirtsleeves, Aldo and Molly and Molly's lively friend Kate and, at the farthest right, Pacifico's regal wife Marianna. This other one shows the Vela aeroplane viewed from the front left side, the convex upper surface of the wing quite noticeable. (The kid looking at the tail section is just a passerby, but — who knows? — if he's twelve he could be Nicolo Pellegrino who became an aeronautical engineer and married Pacifico's daughter Marissa in 1929.) This last photo is an unposed snapshot — Aldo wears a leather jacket with a scarf or long oil rag over his shoulder, and he's pushed his goggles up onto his forehead. He's turned toward Molly who has a hand on his arm and is saying something to him. The empty cockpit is visible to the right and you can make out the back of the pilot's chair made of woven cane. Molly died in 1961 at age seventy-four, Aldo in 1968 at eighty-two. You can fool the gods, but only for so long.

Everyone died. Louis Bleriot, whom Aldo admired for designing and enthusiastically test flying one machine after another until he finally got one to really go, died in 1936 at age sixty-four. Aldo's French friend, Louis Paulhan, who won prizes at the Los Angeles Air Meet in 1910, and who won the *Daily Mail*'s £10,000 London-to-Manchester competition the same year, died in 1963 at age eighty. Claude Grahame-White, the good loser in the London-to-Manchester flight, won prizes at the Harvard-Boston Aero Meet and died in 1959 at age eighty. Charles Foster Willard, the Harvard graduate who raced cars and flew aeroplanes, that same Charlie Willard whom Aldo met at the Harvard-Boston Aero Meet, died in 1977 at age ninety-four.

The West End landlord who fought at Gettysburg died around 1920 and was said to have been eighty years old. He was the one who had seen men die by the tens of thousands during three summer days in 1863.

15

ENZO AUGUSTO CAPELLINO — ENZO THE TAILOR, THE same Enzo who helped Aldo Vela stretch fabric over his aeroplane frames, that Enzo — invented something even more astonishing than a flying machine. It was used only once, and that was in Cambridge, Massachusetts, in May of 1928. All this happened because of Lydia Webster Chase — shy, tall, beautiful Lydia.

Lydia Chase was the daughter of Prescott Chase, a retired professor of botany at Harvard University. Enzo and Lydia knew of each other only because her father had his shirts and suits made in Capellino's shop. One day in 1908, while being fitted for a summer-weight linen suit jacket, Professor Chase happened to make small talk about gardening. Now, young Enzo Capellino was an avid gardener and he invited the professor to walk through the sunny patch he cultivated behind his shop. Old Professor Chase was delighted by this tangled paradise of Sicilian fruit trees, grapevines and vegetables, and in return he invited Mr Capellino to visit his garden, a half-acre of flower beds, cool moss and ferns and fish pools, gravel walks and willow trees which lay behind his large square house on Kirkland Street.

In the years that followed, the elderly professor and the young tailor visited each other's gardens once every June, exchanging seeds and cuttings. A certain decorum clothed these visits, partly because Professor Chase had been taught to treat social inferiors with polite formality and partly because Mr Capellino had been taught to show deference to his elders, and the professor was clearly a generation older.

In May of 1927 the professor's daughter, Lydia Chase, visited the tailor's shop for the first time, bringing with her the measurements for her father's summer shirts. Enzo looked up from his cutting table that day and saw a tall, slender woman dressed in white, a beautiful woman with a distracted look about her. She moved with an elegant awkwardness, as if — as if — as if, he thought, she were a large-winged crane or snowy egret, a creature who would be superbly graceful the moment she took flight, for air would be her natural element, not earth. Enzo himself was so distracted by her that it was not until after she left that he looked at the measurements she had given him. He saw that they were much shrunken from a year ago.

Miss Chase returned to Mr Capellino's shop a few weeks later to pick up the shirts. Enzo understood from the terribly diminished measurements that the professor, her father, was very sick. He wanted to solace Miss Chase, who was clearly even more distracted than before, but found that all he could say was, "I hope Professor Chase is well." To which Lydia replied, "Thank you." She flushed slightly, hesitated as if to say something more, then turned and left the shop, bumping ever so slightly into the door on her way out.

Prescott Chase, Harvard Professor Emeritus of botany, veteran of the Civil War, died in December of 1927 at the age of eighty-four and was buried next to his wife and son in Mount Auburn Cemetery. Prescott's old friends had already died or were ailing and housebound, and Christ Church, though small, looked quite empty. Lydia's women friends attended the service, as did five of the professor's former students and the President of the Charles Downing Horticulture Society. After the service, as Lydia followed the coffin past the empty pews, she noticed a solitary man standing halfway to the back of the church. He was of medium height, or somewhat shorter, and he was gazing at her with enormously sad, sympathetic eyes. It was not until she was home and had closed the door behind her that Lydia remembered him as the tailor, Mr Capellino, upon which she suddenly burst into tears.

Lydia's friends visited her regularly that December, but by the last week of January, 1928, the only visitor she had was a librarian from Harvard who had asked to examine her father's books and papers to see if there was anything valuable she could give to the university. She was lonely.

The figure of Mr Capellino refused to abandon Lydia's memory, so in February she visited his shop. He was even shorter and darker than she had recalled, and the shop more cluttered. But when he stepped forward to greet her he smiled, his face lighting up so much at the sight of her that she forgot what she had planned to say and fumbled with pleasantries about the weather. As for the weather, sleet and freezing rain had kept everyone else at home, so the shop was empty. Lydia recovered herself and said she hoped Mr Capellino could help her choose a necktie as a gift. Enzo explained that he had no neckties.

"No neckties?" she echoed, glancing about with a worried look.

"Please make yourself comfortable, Miss Chase," he said. "I'll make tea."

Lydia sat in a chair beside the cutting table and removed her gloves. Enzo brought out a ceramic tea service whose brightly painted teapot was in the shape of a hen.

"My mother died many years ago and my father needed somebody, needed me, to take care of the house, take care of him and the house," Lydia blurted out, as if she had been asked.

"I understand," Enzo replied gently, pouring tea. "I was eighteen when my father died. I had to take over the shop to help my mother and to make dowries for my two younger sisters. My sisters married seventeen years ago, and my mother died three years ago, and here I am today."

Lydia nervously twisted her gloves in her lap and wondered what to say next. "You garden on summer evenings," she ventured.

"And I read on winter nights," Enzo said.

After a moment she asked, "Have you ever wished to escape time, Mr Capellino, so as to change your life?"

"Often," he said, looking up at her.

"Would you change things in the past or the future?"

"You cannot change the past, only the future," he said.

"Somebody should build a time machine to go to the future," Lydia said, smiling for the first time.

Enzo was enchanted by her smile. "I will do that," he told her.

❦

One afternoon Enzo looked up from his jumbled cutting table and there was Lydia, standing tall in the middle of the shop. Snowflakes melting on her black cloche hat and on her long black coat gave her the appearance of — the appearance of — Yes! Enzo thought, the appearance of the night sky clothed with stars. She asked Mr Capellino for help in choosing a pair of gentleman's leather gloves. He explained that he didn't carry gloves. "No gloves?" Lydia said, looking about vaguely.

"No one will be coming here in this blizzard," Enzo said, quickly bringing out a painted coffee pot shaped like a rooster. "Please make yourself comfortable."

He was pouring coffee from the brightly colored pot when Lydia asked him, "Have you thought about the time machine?"

"I've thought about it for years."

"How would it work?" she asked.

"Einstein has written about the fabric of spacetime," he began.

"Einstein? The fabric of space-time?"

Enzo set down the pot. "Those are his words, yes. And I wondered about this fabric. He said it was curved, and I know something about fitting pieces of flat fabric over a curved surface. And as I thought about it, evening after evening, I came to see that the past is like a tightly woven bolt of cloth, endlessly wide and endlessly long and endlessly deep."

"And the future?"

"The future is being woven in this passing instant, right now. When we say *now* we refer to the edge where the threads are being brought together. A time machine will permit us to get just ahead, just a wee bit ahead, just a thread's breadth ahead of now. And once there, we can weave life any whichway we want, to please ourselves." He had never felt so confident and he broke into a smile.

Lydia had discovered she deeply enjoyed talking this kind of nonsense with Mr Capellino. "And what would it take to leap the distance of one thread ahead of now?" she asked with a smile.

"A lightning bolt," he said, laughing for the delight he saw in her face.

Lydia stayed talking with Enzo rather longer than the last visit and enjoyed herself more than she had in a long time.

The next time Lydia and Enzo met, a gust of wind blew Lydia's umbrella inside out just as she came in the door. She was gasping for breath and her face was drenched with rain. Enzo produced a dazzling white handkerchief and dabbed gently at her cheeks, but after three dabs the couple became embarrassed at how close they were to each other. Abruptly Enzo busied himself in fixing her umbrella while Lydia composed herself. She asked did he have any books, and Enzo laughed and answered no, no books, only men's clothing.

"The man who came from Harvard is cataloging my father's library and putting *all* the books in order," she said, looking around as if seeing the shop for the first time. "He's very good at making things neat and orderly. Perhaps you could use —"

But Enzo interrupted to tell her, "They are like diamonds in your hair, those raindrops." That was the first time he had ever said anything like that, and he was as surprised as Lydia by his boldness. He went off and returned with a tray and two glasses. "A little sweet wine from before Prohibition," he explained.

Lydia sipped from her glass, coughed and put her hand to her chest as the wine went down. "How would one get a lightning bolt?" she asked.

"I'll make one."

"Is that possible?"

"Yes, certainly. Before my parents immigrated to this country they lived in Palermo and saw Augusto Righi demonstrate his lightning machine at the University. My father was very impressed by Righi. He saw the demonstration twice and told me about it many times. My middle name, Augusto, is after Augusto Righi."

"The machine made lightning bolts?" Lydia asked, beginning to smile.

"Little lightning bolts, yes. Or, as you might say, very large sparks." Enzo, too, began to smile.

"How would one make a time machine?"

"It's the same as with making a suit. First I make the pattern, then I make the finished suit — or in this case, the machine."

"But how does it work? I mean, how does lightning make the time machine possible?"

"The lightning bolt makes a tiny rip in the fabric of space-time, in the precise present, in the now. And if you are right there when it happens, as close as you can get, you will suddenly find yourself on the frayed edge of the fabric of space-time. It stands to reason."

Lydia felt unreasonably happy. "When the time is right, I would like very much to see your machine."

"I'll invite you."

Lydia stayed and talked with Enzo until he closed the shop and then she walked home, reflecting on all the turns their conversation had taken.

Augusto Righi (1850-1921) is probably best known for his study of electromagnetic oscillations. His principle teaching post was at the University of Bologna, but he also taught at the University of Palermo in the years 1880-1885. The machine which Enzo Capellino's father saw Righi demonstrate was most likely the one designed by Righi to accumulate weak electric charges. Essentially, the apparatus consisted of a rubber belt looped between two metal pulleys set one above the other, and at the upper end of the loop the belt traveled through a small opening into a hollow copper sphere, leaving its electric charge there. In theory, there is no limit to the voltage which can be accumulated on the sphere. Probably the earliest precursor of Righi's apparatus was a device built by Walckiers de St. Amand in France in 1784. His machine was simply a silken belt stretched between two rollers, so that when you turned the rollers the silk moved, rubbing against small cushions positioned at the rollers, thereby accumulating an electric charge.

Enzo had long known that if he brushed his hand across certain materials, such as fur or wool or silk, an electric charge accumulated, so that if he then reached for a piece of metal a spark would jump from his finger to the metal, giving him a tiny shock. In his tailor shop he had noticed that he was able to get a particularly large spark by drawing wool cloth across the brass yardstick which formed the end of his cutting table, so he planned a machine with a broad continuous belt of thick wool looped tightly between two brass rollers and, of course, at one end there would be a large hollow copper sphere, pierced with a hole so that one of the rollers could be fixed inside.

The sky was blue and the air warm when Lydia next visited the tailor's shop. The clothing dummy in the window — the top half of a cheerful man who had worn a Harris tweed jacket all winter — now wore a white jacket with bright azure stripes; furthermore, he had a straw boater on his head and his stiff hands were holding a cardboard sign (*On Vacation! Will return in future.*) The door was unlocked, so Lydia walked through the shop and out to the garden where Enzo, in his shirt sleeves, was bent over a gleaming brass roller at least a yard long. His back was toward her, so she called out, "Mr Capellino, hello." He straightened up and turned around, smiling. "You make my name sound so beautiful," he said. "Please call me Enzo."

"And you may call me Lydia, if you wish," she replied.

"Lydia, I'll get us something cool to drink." He dashed up a rickety flight of outdoor stairs and entered the floor above the shop. Lydia looked around at the curved sheets of metal which lay here and there, and at the tangled garden which was just beginning to come into blossom. Enzo returned with a painted tray bearing a bottle and two glasses half filled with ice.

"You are actually building an actual time machine," Lydia said, clearly surprised.

"Actually, yes." He poured something as dark as coffee from the bottle into one of the glasses and handed it to her.

"Now, I hope you will accept this," Lydia said, handing him a large flat parcel. While Enzo unfolded the wrapping paper, she told him, "The librarian from Harvard says that the bookcase behind my father's desk has a number of valuable books about botany and horticulture. Dwight — he's the librarian — knows about these things, about how valuable the books are. Right down to the penny. He said somebody might steal one of the volumes and he wants me to donate them to Harvard for permanent safekeeping. He's not interested in this one and he let me take it from the house. It's my father's garden diary, all about the flowers in back of our house. Twenty years of notes and drawings."

Enzo gently opened the worn volume. "This is wonderful, truly wonderful," he murmured. "It's a treasure, a treasure," he said, tenderly turning the pages. "I appreciate your thinking of me," — he was pressing the notebook to his chest as he said this — "but this valuable journal should remain in your family, in your hands," he said, giving it back to her. "Your father was a great botanist. He loved his plants almost as much as he loved you."

Lydia's eyes glistened and there was an awkward silence. Enzo raised his glass. "To you," he said cheerfully and he drank.

Lydia raised her glass. "To you," she echoed. The beverage was like liquid fire and not sweet. "*Well!*" she said, gasping from the drink. "Well, well, well. Please tell me about your machine."

Enzo described how he was building a hollow metal tube which would be about four feet in diameter and stand about twenty feet tall. Inside, at the bottom of the tube, was a brass roller driven by an electric motor. A broad belt of wool ran from the bottom roller, up the tube and over another brass roller, then down the tube to the bottom roller again. And at the top of the tube there would be a great hollow metal sphere to gather the electric charges which would fly from the cloth, he explained. "That's the hard part," he added.

"The electric charges?"

"No. The hard part is getting the sphere to rest just right at the top of the tube. It's already fallen down twice. I think I've misplaced some pieces."

"It's best to keep everything in its place, because then there's a place for everything. That's what Dwight says."

"Oh, yes. Dwight," murmured Enzo. "Would you like a little more wine?"

"Is it legal to drink this?"

"Oh, yes. My father made this many, many years ago. Before Prohibition. He loved to make wine. Shall I refill your glass?"

Lydia, began to laugh — a remarkably rich musical laugh. "Ah, Enzo, please, do," she said, holding out her glass. She was,

Enzo realized, just the slightest bit drunk. The days were getting longer and they enjoyed each other's company until twilight when Lydia said goodbye.

Under the hot sun Enzo had stripped to the waist and was working on the starter switch of the time machine when Lydia walked into the garden. "Hello, Enzo," she said. "I received your invitation and here I am." The 1920s fashion for women was all flatness and no curves, which struck Enzo as comically wrong, yet as she came walking in her sleeveless dress, one hand swinging the long strand of large green beads she wore around her neck, she was the most desirable woman in the world. As for Lydia, she wondered why she was there, saying hello to this short bronze man whose shoulders glistened with sweat and whose thick chest hair — well, Enzo had already snatched up his shirt and was buttoning it while she took in the great time machine. It stood erect in the center of the small garden, a thick twenty-foot column topped by a sphere which had been beautifully proportioned to the shaft but, as Enzo explained to Lydia, it had fallen a few times and was now somewhat reshaped. Indeed, it resembled a blunt arrowhead pointing skyward. "What do you think?" Enzo asked her.

Lydia shaded her eyes with her hand and gazed up at his apparatus. "It reminds me of something. I can't think what. It's rather like — Oh! — It does look rather like a, or like the —" Lydia hesitated, searching for the proper term. "Yes, like a stamen, the stamen of a great flower."

Enzo stood beside her, also looking up at it. "Ah, I had not thought of that," Enzo said slowly. "But, yes, I suppose it does."

"And it will make lightning?" she asked him.

"Yes, at the top. I'm sure of that."

"And the lightning will tear the fabric of space time, make a little rip in it?"

"Yes, I'm sure of that, too."

"And you'll be able to leap forward into next year or the year after that?"

"Ah," Enzo sat down on a small garden bench.

"I'm not so sure of that. I've been working without sleep for the past five days. But I hope so." Indeed, he did look tired.

"I hope so, too," Lydia said.

"I'll get us a cool drink," Enzo said. He went up the wobbly flight of outdoor stairs and into his rooms above the shop and came back down with a basket of ice which cradled two large bottles of wine and two glasses. The day was warm and there was an uncertain breeze that blew strongly one moment and vanished the next, leaving only a dry stillness. Lydia sat on a cast-iron garden chair and Enzo sat on the small wood bench and they drifted in a long winding conversation as they drank the cool wine.

Lydia asked him about the metalwork at the top of the outdoor stairway. "It looks like a big bird cage," she said.

"Ah, that's a protective cage," Enzo said. "After starting the machine, I'll go up those stairs and get inside it. At that height I'll be level with the top of the lightning machine and close to it, but the lattice of metal will protect me from being hit."

Lydia looked worried. "Are you sure you'll be safe? Won't you be electrocuted?"

Enzo smiled. "I'll be safe. My only worry is that the rip in the fabric of space-time won't be big enough for me to slip through."

Lydia looked at the metal column with its banged up arrowhead crown. "How strange," she said reflectively. "Here you are on an ordinary Monday afternoon. You're about to leap forward in time, and no one knows."

"You're here and that's the world to me. Now it's time I tested it." Enzo strode to the machine and pressed the starter button. The motor began turning the brass roller so the great wool belt began to move, rising up inside the tall metal cylinder, passing over the roller inside the metal sphere and down again. Little by little the speed of the rollers increased, the belt blurred and the air was filled with a humming rattle. Enzo drank off the last of his wine, tossed the glass over his shoulder — he discovered that he could make these bold gestures with complete confidence so long as Lydia was nearby — and mounted the trembling stairway to the lattice cage. He stepped into the cage and looked down to the garden to discover that Lydia's chair was empty. She was running up the stairs. She called to him, but the humming of the machine had grown louder.

"The librarian is going to ask me to marry him," she said. "I don't know what to do. I haven't been able to sleep for days."

"I can't hear you," cried Enzo from inside the cage, plainly shocked at what he had heard.

"He wrote me a letter last week, saying he was going to ask me this evening."

"The librarian!"

"Yes, Dwight has a schedule and this evening he's going to ask me to marry him. What do you think —"

"I think he's an unpronounceable clump of consonants," Enzo shouted over the growing thunder of the machine.

"Dwight says the future is known to people who make schedules."

"Will you marry a man who has a place for everything and everything in its place? A time for everything and everything in its time?"

"I'm forty-one years old and no one has ever proposed marriage to me," she said, lifting her voice against the crackle of sparks.

"I'm forty-three and have never dared propose marriage to anyone. I've achieved nothing!"

A bluish glow hovered over the row of phonograph needles which were fixed a hairsbreadth from the flying surface of the belt and long thread-like sparks began to flare from the bent edges of the sphere atop the machine.

"You have made this wonderful machine," she cried.

"But it may work no better than I have!"

Enzo threw open the lattice door and started out to meet her just as Lydia started in, the two clutching each other as the first lightning bolt unfurled and snapped overhead like a colossal whip. The hair on Enzo's chest burst into flame, scorching Lydia's breasts. The world overflowed with light as every nail and rivet, every garden tool, the cast iron garden chair and even the garden itself surged toward them, all the while flaring apart, coming undone. "Yes!" Lydia thought — or maybe she actually cried aloud — "Yes! We're at the front edge of *now* and these are the raveled threads of space-time." And everything melted like a meteor into the rising dark.

When Enzo opened his eyes he was flat on his back in the garden. He realized that his arms were around Lydia, her arms over his shoulders and her eyes closed in sleep. The collapsed remnants of the lattice cage lay upon them like a shredded blanket. Lydia opened her eyes and sat up. She looked at the blue sky, glanced down at her singed dress and the string of melted beads, then looked at Enzo. "We're alive and it's a beautiful day," she said. "Yes," said Enzo, looking at his pocket watch whose fused hands said three o'clock. "And I wonder *which* day it is." They went through the shop and out the front door to the street to ask the first passerby what day it was and what time of day. It was three in the afternoon on Tuesday, May 22, 1928, precisely twenty-four hours forward from where they had been. "You've worked wonders, Enzo. We've jumped a day ahead and we're free to make whatever we want of our time."

"I propose marriage," he said, smiling up at her.

"I accept," she said, returning his smile.

Then they set off to get dinner, because they both felt wonderfully hungry, quite famished in fact, as if they had been asleep and had not eaten for a whole day.

In June of 1928 a man buying a seersucker jacket asked Enzo what the equipment in the back yard was for. When Enzo told him that it was a machine for generating lightning bolts, the man became extraordinarily interested and asked so many questions that Enzo, in a burst of confidence, began to tell him about the fabric of space-time, upon which the man gave a short laugh and said the tailor didn't know what he was talking about.

In 1929, a year after Enzo and Lydia had made their jump forward in time, Robert Van de Graaff built a small electrostatic generator at Princeton University, capable of producing around eighty thousand volts. At the inaugural dinner of the American Institute of Physics, he demonstrated an improved version of the same apparatus. It resembled in all essentials the very much larger and more powerful machine which had stood behind Capellino's shop three years earlier. In 1931 Van de Graaff joined the Massachusetts Institute of Technology and began assembling a double generator composed of two twenty-three foot high columns each containing two belts and supporting an aluminum sphere six feet in diameter. This machine, capable of generating 50 million electron volts, was housed in its own building at MIT and, after some changes, was used as an atom smasher. In the 1950s MIT donated it to the Boston Museum of Science and in 1980 the Museum installed it in the Thomson Theatre of Electricity where it currently produces spectacular demonstrations of man-made lightning.

Enzo and Lydia were married on Saturday, June 23, 1928, and their daughter, Abigail Santuzza Capellino, was born in autumn of the following year. They lived in the large square house on Kirkland Street, and Enzo continued to work as a tailor for some months, then sold his shop in order to devote himself to the extensive Chase gardens which were succumbing to overgrowth and weeds. Old Professor Chase's collection of works by Charles Downing led Enzo and Lydia to an interest in pomology, and they became quite expert in that field, publishing a number of papers on apple species of New England and New York.

Although they wrote for scholarly horticultural journals and for garden club magazines, neither Enzo nor Lydia ever published anything about their time transit. They remained silent about the event partly because they enjoyed their privacy, and partly because they came to know how dangerous the experiment had been. They were lucky to have awakened with nothing worse than hunger pangs, as if they had merely been asleep for a day, but they feared some other experimenter might not survive. Despite the protective metal latticework, technically known as a Faraday cage, the couple were fortunate not to have been electrocuted — much as Ben Franklin, flying his kite into an electrical storm, had been fortunate. Lydia and Enzo enjoyed taking their grandchildren to the Museum of Science in Boston to witness the lightning bolts thrown off by the electrostatic machine there, and a lightning flash during a summer storm always remained a happy sight for the couple. Enzo Augusto Capellino (1885-1970) and Lydia Prescott Capellino (1887-1971) escaped time for a day.

16

PACIFICO CAVALLÙ, SON OF YOUNG FIMI CAVALLÙ AND the mature, learned and passionate Sonia DiSecco, grandson of Angelo Cavallù (man from the waist up, stallion from the waist down) and seventeen-year-old Ava, that same Pacifico arrived in Boston in the early spring of 1902. Three weeks later he was in the frozen Maine woods, part of a crew hacking out a road for dray horses. The crew was made up of Sicilians, Calabrians and Neapolitans. The foreman was a Maine man named

Nadeau, a drunk who knew a dozen words in Italian, enough to get the job started, but on the third morning he didn't appear. The workers were standing with their hands in their pockets by the ice-covered tool shed when a boss turned up and asked who among them spoke English. Pacifico said he spoke English. "Read that sign over there," the boss said. And Pacifico said, "Pelletier engineering and construct company. Abasolutely no drink on the —" And the boss cut him off, saying, "Fine. You're the new foreman."

After he had been on the job three months Pacifico's muscles were hard as rocks and the boss — his name was Bowman, you recall — called him aside, told him to come along to Boston to round up more Italian workers. "We're running out of Irish and this time of year the Frenchies quit to go work on their farms. We'll take the train tomorrow morning. Shave good and put on your white shirt." Three days later, on the train back from Boston, Bowman took out a roll of bills and peeled off an extra day's wages which he gave to Pacifico. Pacifico said, "Next time we go, you tell me ahead of time and I can have Italians lined up and waiting when we get there. Save you time."

Bowman smiled just a bit. "Maybe I like staying in the city for a couple of nights on company money," he said.

"Maybe you can stay in the city on company money and not to worry, because I will have a crew at the train station when you ready to go back," Pacifico told him.

"You can do that?"

Pacifico laughed. "Leave it to me," he said.

Pacifico went to the city with Bowman three times, acting as go-between each time. On their third and last trip Bowman paid him on the crowded sidewalk in Boston, as agreed. "I don't judge a man by his name," Bowman told him, handing him his wages.

"Neither do I," said Pacifico with a quick smile. "Any time you need workers, let me know. I'll have them waiting when you get here."

"Well," said Bowman. "I'll do that."

They shook hands, then Bowman shepherded the workers to the railroad station and Pacifico walked around the corner to Prince Street, to a general store where he'd lined up a job on his previous trip to Boston. The store — you remember this — was badly managed by a fretful Neapolitan who didn't speak English as well as Pacifico, so Pacifico's job was to cope with the American suppliers, talk to them, write business letters to them, and translate documents from the Shawmut Bank credit department. He also worked behind the counter and hauled barrels up from the cellar. Nine months later he made his first payment toward buying the business and that same night he wrote a letter to Marianna Moretti, telling her he was established now and they could marry as soon as she arrived. Marianna came down the gangway onto the snowy dock in Boston early in 1904.

According to Nick Pellegrino, the couple were married right there on the dock. Maybe it happened that way — their breath making cloudlets in the freezing air, the Justice of the Peace holding out a pen in one hand and in the other a marriage certificate, two customs officers as witnesses, blowing on their hands and stamping their feet to keep warm. But we all know Nick was told that story by his aunt Gina as they lay naked and sweaty on her sun-filled bed, so maybe Nick wasn't listening attentively and got it wrong. Furthermore, the family's spoken history has always said that Marianna's mother came down the gangway one step behind her daughter, and that the couple married in a church. So Nick wasn't listening. Or maybe Gina *did* tell him that tale, but only because it's a common immigrant story and people like to hear it.

Or maybe it's true. Maybe Diva Moretti didn't come down the gangway one step behind her daughter, didn't spend the next three weeks chatting with this old lady and that little girl throughout the North End to satisfy herself that Pacifico didn't already have a wife tucked away someplace. Maybe Diva didn't care if her daughter's marriage was attested to only by a scrap of paper signed by a faceless notary, and didn't care if there was no ceremony in Saint Leonard's church where the priest spoke Latin to God and Florentine to the parishioners. After all, Diva was the daughter of Stella DiMare, a goddess so beautiful her looks could stun, and half-divine Diva cared little about Jesus and even less about the Pope and his priests. But family history says they married in a church and that their signatures are on the registry at Saint Leonard's, or if not at Saint Leonard's then Saint Stephen's, or if not Saint Stephen's then certainly Sacred Heart, or in one of those other churches that long ago closed its doors and are gone from the North End.

Pacifico and his bride lived in the front half of a flat that was up a narrow flight of stairs (the bottom steps smelled of piss) off a littered alley from jam-packed Hanover Street. He enjoyed showing Marianna around the city. "All around here is called the North End," he told her. "Because it's the north end of Boston. If you go down any of these little streets you come to the ocean and fishing boats, just like Palermo — but with ice and snow." They threaded their way along the crowded sidewalk. "And everybody lives beside everybody else, the Irish there, the Jews along Salem Street, the Italians here." He laughed and put his arm around her waist. "That's the way it is in this country, everybody rubs shoulders with everybody else." As the weather warmed they walked farther into the city and he pointed out the Customs House tower, took a ride on the underground train, went into the gold domed State House, admired the sacred Cod Fish ("In the beginning they were fishermen, like your father's family," he explained.) then Boston Common and — now that it was spring — the Public Gardens with its tranquil pond and slow gliding swan boats. As they turned homeward they passed through noisy North Square. "This is where I was hired for my first job. And this is where I gather the workers for Mr Bowman to go to Maine."

"Why are they taking the top off that building?" Marianna asked.

"That used to be the Banca Italiana, but now it's going back to being Paul Revere's house. He was a famous man in this town, a patriot and silversmith."

"Like Cellini?" she said.

"Not so fancy as Cellini. Very simple. But very elegant. I'll buy you one of his bowls someday," he added.

Ten months after they married Marianna gave birth to their first child, Lucia Sicilia Cavallù. The following year Pacifico made his final payment to purchase the store — the business — he worked in, and three months later moved his growing family (another child, Marissa, had arrived) from their cramped two-room flat to the top apartment over the newly named P. Cavallù General Store. The store was the first floor of a three-story building of red brick. Pacifico painted the store's walls and ceiling a blazing white, added more lights, re-arranged the dry goods and brought in newspapers, sheet music and books. Business improved. The owner of the little building, Mr Samuel Levine, appeared every couple of months, a stout vigorous old man, exploring a roundabout route between the barrels, crates, crocks and boxes. "You're doing very well, Mr Cavallù. Whenever I come here you're busier than before. So many customers you have. You're prospering?"

Pacifico laughed. "You'll be raising my rent."

"*Not* Sam Levine. I want you to stay right here," he said, patting the counter and smiling. "So you can make lots of money and keep paying the rent on time. Unlike some people I know. —How are your little girls?"

One day, between customers, Pacifico asked him, "Have you ever thought of selling this building?"

"Have you ever thought of buying?"

"Me?" Pacifico looked surprised, operatically surprised. "No, no, no. I don't have the money to buy a building like this. —But if I did buy, I'd never have to pay rent for the store. I'd never have to pay rent for my apartment. And the tenants on the second floor would be paying their rent to me." He smiled.

"So you've thought of buying," Mr Levine said. He pressed the button on the tall gas-pipe cigar lighter and a short flame flared at the top. He leaned forward, lighted his cigar, let go the button and leaned back. "So I'll think of selling," he added. He exhaled a happy cloud of smoke, smiled and went out the door as two others came in.

A week later old Mr Levine walked in, paid for a cigar, slid a folded sheet of note paper across the counter, then angled his way between two customers and out the door. Pacifico looked at the dollar amount his landlord had written squarely in the middle of the little sheet, then he re-folded the paper, jammed it into his back pocket and went about his business, wondering all the while if he could raise such a sum of money. At the end of the day he sat down at the counter, took up a pencil and made a series of calculations on a flattened paper bag. The next morning he went around to the Shawmut Bank on Water Street, then to the Banca Italiana and then to an Italian money lender, and when he got back to the store he fished the note from his back pocket, drew a neat line through the Mr Levine's price and wrote a much lower number beneath it. Six days later, when Mr Levine was lighting his cigar at the gas jet, Pacifico slid the folded note back across the counter to him. Mr Levine tucked the note into his jacket's breast pocket, patted the pocket, and edged out through the throng at the door. A week later Mr Levine slid the note back across the counter to Pacifico. He'd drawn a line through Pacifico's bid and written a higher price below it. Nobody knows how many times the note passed back and forth between the two, but on the final occasion, just at closing time, Mr Levine slid the note to Pacifico, saying, "I've come to the bottom of the paper. There's no more room. That's as low as I can go." He lifted his arms a bit and let them drop dejectedly to his sides, dramatically helpless.

As soon as they were alone, Pacifico unfolded the note — unfolded it carefully for by now the edges were frayed and one of the creases had torn — studied the dollar amount written at the base of that column of crossed-out sums. After a long minute Pacifico said, "Good!" and Mr Levine cried, "*Very* good!" and they shook hands vigorously. Pacifico gave a great laugh, snatched the stool from in back of the counter and gave it to him. Old Sam Levine seated himself with a grateful sigh and Pacifico Cavallù sat on an upturned crate, two plain drinking glasses and a dark bottle of wine between them. They drank. Sam winced, held up his glass and studied it, as if the color of the wine might explain the raw taste.

"Home made," Pacifico explained, clapping Sam lightly on the shoulder. "Sicilian!"

The older man hesitated, then tossed back his head, drained his glass and unbuttoned his vest. "Fine. Fine wine. — When I arrived here the North End was all Irish. Whiskey drinkers," he explained. "That was thirty, thirty-five years ago I arrived. Maybe longer. The years go by faster these days. The Irish were here but they were moving out. They needed to sell," — here he turned his left palm up — "we needed to buy," — he turned his right palm up. "We made deals." He clasped his hands. "The Irish had come up in the world and wanted to move out to the country, out to South Boston."

"I notice a lot stayed behind," Pacifico said, refilling the glasses.

"True." He signed. "A lot stayed behind and will never get out and even more moved in. The times are changing. I never thought the North End could be more crowded than what it was back then. But it's more crowded today."

"And now it's you moving up and moving out," Pacifico said.

Sam smiled and raised his glass. "First the Irish, then us, and next you."

That was early in 1908. By 1911 Marianna had given birth to Candida, which made four kids, and she had another rising in the oven — or maybe she already had five — and Pacifico had added more bookshelves to the store, more clothesline with dangling sheet music, more cans of expensive tobacco and rows of fancy pipes, cigarette compacts, more tinted stationery paper and gold-nibbed fountain pens, mother of pearl picture frames, more fancy combs, hair brushes, pocket knives, large Italian playing cards, and he was now selling guitars, mandolins, harmonicas, player piano rolls, Victrola records, hand guns, ammunition, Venetian glassware and mirrors. He worked twelve and more hours a day, scanned the newspapers, took a book (biography, history, epic poetry) upstairs when he quit, washed up, ate dinner and played with the kids. Marianna, a baby at her breast, kept the accounts and prepared the meals. They still lived in the apartment (three windows up front, three windows in back) but nowadays Marianna sent the wash out and no longer had to haul on the pulley rope, heavy with damp or frozen clothes, and her fingers, which used to bleed that way, had healed. And by the time Dante was born, which made five — or maybe it was Sandro, which made six — they were able to hire Signora Bruno, who had been a scholar in Italy, to teach Lucia how to read Italian.

"God rested on Sunday," Pacifico told Marianna. "You can lie here or go to church. I alone, solitary and by myself, will do the cooking for the family," he announced.

Marianna sighed contentedly and settled back, her loose black hair uncoiled this way and that upon the pillow. "You cook beautifully, *caro*, but you don't clean up afterward," she said.

"Because I have to talk business with the men. Otherwise I'd never learn anything."

"Ah, yes. And what have you learned?"

"That I want to have a bank, the Cavallù Bank."

Marianna laughed, then stretched and sat up and saw his sober face. "Or are you serious?"

"Listen, I thank God I have a good back and two strong arms, but if I was still swinging a pickax we'd be living in a hole in the Maine woods. Now we have this store — we buy at one price and sell at a little higher price — and we have this building where we rent out one flat. We're doing well but our money is in mandolins and cigars and combs and in these brick walls. When I get my bank, my money will be in money."

"I can remember one day when you patted the front of this building. Remember? You said you liked to be able to reach out and touch your wealth. You said you liked it solid. Like *me*, you said and you tried to pat my culino. Remember?"

"You're right. I did." Pacifico reflected on it a moment, then laughed. "First I'll buy buildings, they'll bring in money, then I'll make my bank." He rolled out of bed onto his feet, the floor creaking under his weight. "Now, while you lie there recovering from our love-making, I'll make you a café au lait." He pulled on his trousers, leaned into the crib to kiss Dante and already had one arm into his shirt as he walked out the bedroom door.

At those Sunday dinners they had Marianna's cousin Aldo and his Irish wife, and one of Pacifico's young journalist friends, and often doctor Balboni and his wife, or Bartolo, the lawyer, and his wife. When dinner was over and the women had gathered in the kitchen, the men would huddle at the head of the table to talk politics and finance. By the end of the year Pacifico had purchased the building at the corner of Prince and Hanover, a structure big enough to hold not only the expanding P. Cavallù store, but also an importing business, a travel office, a photographic studio and two or three other business he hadn't thought up yet.

By 1914 the Cavallù family had moved into a compact two-story wood frame house in Malden, a crowded town a few miles outside of Boston. It was an ordinary house with one step up to a broad front porch and another step up to the glass-paned door, on either side of which was a large window with a bright hand-painted shade (on the left, the Bay of Naples with Mount Vesuvius steaming in the background and on the right, the city of Messina with Mount Etna flaming in the background), and behind the glass door stood the grand rock of Monte Pellegrino, keeping guard over the placid blue harbor of Palermo. At

Pacifico's direction, a squadron of carpenters and plasterers refashioned the front sitting room with crown molding, elaborate cornices and a fresh ceiling, and on that ceiling an artist — the same who had decorated the window shades — painted four acrobatic angels sailing skyward in a circle of vanishing perspective, their billowing garments of purple and gold trailing to the four corners of the room. It was in this house, at the top of the stairway to the second floor, that Molly had whispered *Fuck off!* to the banshee and poured water over her, and in this house that she recuperated after giving birth to Brendan. Of course, by then Marianna had given birth to Sandro, Silvia and, I think, Mercurio, making eight, and she wasn't through yet.

Pacifico's importing business had started years ago when he asked a cousin who was coming from Sicily to bring along as much popular sheet music as he could pack into the bottom of his suitcase. Now he had people in Palermo who bought whatever he wanted and every other month fifteen crates were unloaded onto the pier in Boston, trucked to Cavallù Importing Company and dispatched from there to the shelves of Italian shops in Worcester, Providence and Hartford. The new travel office, run by the cousin who had brought the sheet music, was busy from the day it opened. The window displayed a three-foot-long ship model, a passenger vessel of the White Star Line, with finely detailed lifeboats, loading machinery, ventilation ducts and lounge chairs, one deck upon the other up to the great black funnel. Pacifico's daughter Bianca stood at that window one summer evening, marveling at the ship, and she remembered into old, old age how it looked when night filled Hanover Street and tiny lights inside the ship came on and the portholes, row upon row, shone over the dark sea.

Of course, no immigrant fresh off the boat was rich enough to make a voyage back to the old *paese*, but anyone could afford to send a picture showing how well they had done, so the photography studio always had customers. It was up a flight of stairs and down the hall, a room divided between a salon, with two large windows, and a laboratory or darkroom in which to develop and print the photographs. The salon had a bellows camera mounted on a tripod and two different canvas backdrops to choose from, plus a handful of props such as white paper roses or leather bound books, the most important prop being three dark vests (small, medium, large) and a glittering watch chain which signaled prosperity when draped across a vest.

❦

At first the Cavallù bank was no more than the black iron safe at the back of the P. Cavallù General Store on Prince Street, a safe big as a bedroom bureau and so heavy only Pacifico could move it. When you hauled open the iron door you found the store's tin cash box, a shelf of banged-up ledgers and a shoe box with a stack of envelopes containing bills, plus silver and gold coins, each envelope bearing the name of the depositor. The North End Italians were intimidated by the shimmering marble and glittering brass of Boston banks, and even if the frozen Yankee behind the barred window was polite — and how could you tell? — you never found out who was actually running the bank or where your money went when you slid it under the bars to the teller and, furthermore, they wanted a minimum deposit that was something like a month's wages. On the other hand, these depositors knew Pacifico Cavallù and were welcome at his store and they could see where he kept their money. You could go to him, show him your passbook and ask to see your cash. He'd bring you a little buff colored envelope with your name on it and your money inside.

"Can I count it?"

"Certainly. Go ahead and count it."

You could add up the bills and coins and see that it matched the sum in your passbook.

"How do I know this is my money, the money I put in the envelope?"

"You just counted it," said Pacifico.

"But how do I know it's the *same* money I gave you."

"Does it look the same?"

"Yes."

"Exactly. It's the same," said Pacifico.

"When do I get the interest on my money?"

"After every three months. July is the next time."

None of the depositors had much money, but there were a lot of them and the little sums all added up, so by 1917 the words *Banca Cavallù* appeared in gold leaf on a new plate glass window on Hanover Street. The bank's board of directors included a grocer, a lawyer, a doctor, a newspaper editor, a café owner and a confectioner — each one a friend chosen for his business acumen and his willingness to trade his hard coin for paper bank stock at a hundred dollars a share. The bank made small loans to Boston Italians, sometimes without collateral, but Pacifico or one of the board members knew exactly the character and circumstances of every man the bank loaned to, and every loan paid off. By 1919 the bank had doubled its assets and the older Cavallù girls were enrolled in Notre Dame Academy, the school attended by Mayor Curley's daughters and the daughters of LaMarca who owned the Prince Spaghetti Company.

Then, in 1920, the devil himself turned up in Boston calling himself Charles Ponzi, a sharp dresser with a straw boater hat, a pinched waist jacket and glittering necktie pin. He tapped his walking stick on the pavement and announced the creation of the Securities Exchange Company which would make poor people rich. "Give me a hundred dollars today," he said. "And in ninety days I'll give you a hundred and fifty." Pacifico chose a jacket with threadbare cuffs and rode the subway downtown to the Securities Exchange Company's office on School Street. He said he was a clerk who wanted to invest, asked to see Mr Ponzi and asked him how the company could guarantee those remarkable profits. Mr Ponzi, smiling and relaxed, was happy to explain. "I used to be just like you," he said. "A hard-working man who was never able to get rich. Then one day I noticed that international postal coupons, which can be bought in this country for, maybe, a penny, can be sold in, say, Bulgaria for six cents. So I trade in international postal coupons, lots of them."

"Ingenious!" Pacifico said, breaking into Italian.

"And quite legal," Ponzi said, now in Italian too.

"And you share this secret method."

"Because I want others to enjoy being as rich as I am."

After a few more pleasantries, they shook hands and Mr Ponzi escorted him to the door. Pacifico returned to his bank, hung up his old jacket and put on his proper one, then he went home. "I visited Ponzi in his office today," he told Marianna. "The man is a fraud."

"You didn't have to go to his office to find that out," she said, taking the newspaper from him, a baby on her hip.

"I wanted to see what he looked like. He's thin, has no weight. I could pick him up with one hand and rattle him till his money fell all over the floor. He's going to ruin us."

"Calm yourself. Here. Hold Regina," she said placidly, handing him the baby. "By the way, have you thought about us moving to a bigger house?"

Word got around that Mr Ponzi was, as a matter of fact, paying his investors a fifty percent profit after only ninety days, just as he promised. Newspapers reported the astonishing success of the Securities Exchange Company and in no time investors began crowding into Mr Ponzi's office, their fists full of money. And many of those investors were withdrawing their savings from Banca Cavallù.

"You want to withdraw *all* your money?" Pacifico asked.

"Yes."

"Do you mind if I inquire why?"

"I'm going to make an investment."

"In Mr Ponzi's company?" Pacifico asked.

"I'd be a fool not to. So I need my money, all of it."

"Does anybody know this Ponzi? Does anybody know

what place he comes from? Does anybody know his family?"

"All my money."

Pacifico sighed. "All right. Look. I'm giving you your money. Here. See? —This is silver. And this is gold, right? Now when you give this to Ponzi he's going to give you a promissory note printed on cheap paper and when you bring it back to his office in ninety days he'll be gone and your dollars will be gone, too."

"No. He's paying back in forty-five days now."

"Here. Go!"

Millions of dollars poured through the Securities Exchange Company as Mr Ponzi paid off his May investors with the money he was receiving from his June investors, and he paid off his June investors with the even greater sums he was taking in from his July investors. Dollars continued to drain from Banca Cavallù. Pacifico told his bank teller to step aside and he himself took over disbursing cash to his depositors, chatting amiably with each one and counting the bills and coins as slowly as he could. Banca Cavallù had $1,507.30 in ready money when federal and state authorities closed in on Mr Ponzi, the Securities Exchange Company collapsed, and dollars began to flow again to Banca Cavallù.

"Listen," Pacifico said to Marianna. "You remember Cavagnaro who had a little bank in New York? He sold it to Giannini. And who is Giannini? Giannini is like me but he lives in California, which is a very long state, and he owns very many banks up and down that long state of California." Pacifico was standing at the bathroom sink, naked to the waist, whipping his shaving brush round and round in the shaving mug. "We can do the same thing here. First in Boston, then Rhode Island and Connecticut. What do you think?"

"What about the buildings on Unity Street?" Marianna asked. She was in a pale yellow nightdress, standing at the door with Regina at her breast. "What about the buildings on Charter Street?"

"The buildings? What about them?"

"You haven't collected real rent from some of those tenants in months."

"We're doing fine. Attilio collects from each flat each month." Pacifico stopped abruptly, his shaving brush half way to his cheek. "Hasn't he been doing his job?"

"Attilio's an honest young man. He's also a gentleman and maybe too nice for the job. This month three different tenants put him off. He came away with an inlaid chess board, a silver candy dish and a parrot in a big brass cage."

Pacifico relaxed, laughed. "He's soft hearted. That's no sin. But I'll talk to him." He ducked past Marianna, his face covered with lather, and began cranking the gramophone.

"Fine. What am I supposed to do with all the junk he's collected?" Marianna said. "Attilio puts the rent money in your bank and brings everything else here. Where do you think the broken clock came from? We can't cram another thing into this house.

We don't have enough room for the kids."

Pacifico returned to the sink, giving the baby a kiss and Marianna's buttocks a slap as he passed. "I'll buy us a bigger house," he announced. He swished his razor in the washbowl water and began to shave, pausing now and again to sing along with Caruso whose golden voice, sounding small and distant, floated up from the graceful horn on the gramophone.

So we come to the house where this chronicle ends and my biography begins. It was a big square three-story structure with a porte cochère on the left and a columned porch that traversed the front and wrapped around the right. (The villa in Italy also had three storeys, but was built of stone, stucco and tile.) This was in Lexington where Paul Revere had roused the farmers, maybe a mile from the meadow where Aldo flew his newly built aeroplane back in 1910.

On the right of the Cavallù house in Lexington there were

other broad lawns and large houses. On the left stood Saint Brigid's Catholic Church and beyond that, the parish house. And now comes the story I was told so many times I've got it word for word. It's 1930, it's early March, it's evening. It snows. Then came the moment I've heard about over and over again. It comes like this. It comes *knock, knock, knock* by the heavy brass knocker on the big front door. That sentence and what follows has to be said exactly as written. Pacifico Cavallù pushes back his chair and slowly gets up from the long table, his white linen napkin still tucked in his vest as he strolls across the big square hall and pulls open the front door. Outside it's all black sky and freshly fallen snow and, down at his feet, a large oval laundry basket with a mound of blankets and—"Good God!" he says. Now there's a clatter of dropped silverware and the scrape of chairs and everyone comes running to the door to get a look. Bixio begins to bark and Nora, the housemaid, has to climb a chair to see over the heads of the grown-ups. For a moment everyone crowds the doorway but nobody moves—Pacifico is still peering into the dark where a few silent snowflakes tumble through the doorlight—then Marianna steps past him, warily lifts the basket and carries it on her hip to the dining room.

There were fifteen people in the Cavallù house that night. First of all there were the parents—that's Pacifico and Marianna Cavallù—Pacifico at this end of the table, a sturdy man with beautiful eyes and a short iron-colored beard, and big Marianna at the other end, a woman such as you might find carved on the prow of a ship, with her broad face and her hair in a black braided crown. Their children ran in age from ten to twenty-five and were known for being handsome, quick-witted and rash. They were seated on both sides of the long table—Lucia and Marissa and Bianca and Candida and Dante and Sandro and Silvio and Mercurio and Regina, along with Marissa's husband Nicolo, an aeronautical engineer, and Bianca's husband Fidèle, a stone cutter. And, of course, there was Carmela the cook and Nora the housemaid. That's two in the kitchen, thirteen at the table and me on the front piazza.

Mother Marianna shifted the wicker basket from her hip to her place at the table and everyone continued to speak at once, saying, "Look at those big eyes it could have died out there in the cold why our doorstep such big eyes for such a small little baby what kind of mother would leave her baby but why our doorstep could have died under these thin blankets came to the wrong house and so strong the way it holds my finger take a look take those off and that one too and my God swaddling clothes unwrap the poor thing and let's take a look. *Sfasciarlo! Sfasciarlo!*"—Unwrap it! Unwrap it! Then the women sang "Ah-ha!" And the men chorused "Oh-ho!" and Regina, the youngest, said, "Look at his little *ucellino*,"— birdie—while Mercurio, a year older, frowned and blushed.

"He's going to be strong," Pacifico said. "You can tell by the legs."

"A Calabrian," Marianna said. "They wrap them that way in Calabria."

"Mamà, they wrap them that way in Sicily, too," Lucia informed her.

"No. Not like that. That baby is Calabrese," her mother insisted. "He's been washed and rubbed with olive oil and then swaddled."

"It's terrible and I'm not ever doing that to mine," Marissa said.

"Anyway, he wasn't born in Sicily or Calabria. He was born right here in Massachusetts," Lucia said.

The naked infant was nested back on the blankets in the wicker basket, which was handed up over the espresso cups, crushed walnut shells and dried figs to Pacifico. The table quieted while he unhooked the watch chain from his vest, drew out the gold timepiece and lowered it delicately alongside the baby's head, close by his ear. For a moment no one drew breath, then the infant turned toward the tick-tick-tick. Pacifico, his face still heavy with concentration, abruptly hauled the watch up and lowered it down the other side. Again the infant turned his head and twisted about to find the ticking. Pacifico, hoisted the watch once more and held it directly above the baby's face, rolling the chain between his fingers just enough to start the gold and crystal flashing. The infant stared up, fascinated. Pacifico slid the watch back into one of his vest pockets and looped the heavy gold chain across and then glanced up. "É bello," he concluded. "He's fine."

Marissa's husband Nicolo, a logical man, asked, "Did anyone look for a note?" Now everyone looked. They unfurled the blankets and gently shook them out, they went back through the big front hall and the vestibule to see if a little leaf of paper had dropped to the floor when they had trooped in, and they even went out onto the porch. There was no note. Regina had taken one of the blankets which wasn't a blanket at all, but only a cheap kerchief. "Look at this. Can I keep it?" she asked. It was a square of thin blue cotton printed with a fanciful map of Sicily, one of a thousand such kerchiefs. "How does it look?" she asked, pulling it around her shoulders and turning her head to see the effect. "What do you think? Can I keep it?"

"No. It doesn't belong to us," Pacifico told her. "And neither does the baby."

Marianna had taken the kerchief from her daughter and now she began to fold it. "Some poor confused woman didn't know which side of the church the parish house was on. If it wasn't so late we could take it over right now. Father McCarthy can find a home for it."

"Not Mr McCarthy," Pacifico told her. He refused to call any priest Father.

"All right. Father Basilio, then."

One by one they fell silent as they watched Marianna tuck the kerchief around the baby in the basket. Carmela came and set a pan of warmed milk beside Marianna, looked without curiosity at the infant and then hobbled back to the kitchen. Nobody spoke. Bianca's husband Fidèle lowered his little finger into the baby's warm hand, which closed tight around it.

"We can't give him back," Bianca said, breaking the silence. "We can't just give him *away!*"

"He belongs with his mother," big Marianna said firmly. "And his mother doesn't live here."

"But maybe the father is here," Candida said. "After all, it could be Dante or Sandro or—" She shrieked and ducked aside as Dante lunged across the table to throw his wine in her face, Sandro already on his feet, his chair crashing backward. She swept the wine from her cheek with the back of her hand. "All I mean is—"

"Candida!" her mother cried.

"She talks too much!" Silvio said.

"You!" Dante said.

"Me? What about me?" Candida retorted.

"You know what about you," Sandro said.

"*Basta.* Enough," Pacifico said, holding up his hand, palm outward.

The baby went on crying loudly in the sudden silence. Bianca swathed him in his blue map-kerchief and lifted him from the basket, cradling him in her arms, while her husband Fidèle brought up the pan of warm milk. He sat down beside his wife and sank a twisted corner of his napkin into the milk, saying, "He's hungry. Let's give him something to drink."

I was adopted by Bianca and Fidèle who named me Renato, which means reborn, and here I am all these years later, a man who doesn't know who or where he came from, writing a genealogical history of his family.

I've been told that every adopted child wants to find out, sooner or later, who his birth parents are but, frankly, I've never had that desire. What I know is that your true parents are the ones who bring you up, teach you your alphabet and your numbers, praise you and kiss you, or whack you when you misbehave, then they set you on your way and weep to see you go. Furthermore, like many kids adopted as infants, I grew to somewhat resemble my parents and people who didn't know better would say, "He has his father's looks," or "He gets those big eyes from his mother." I'm happy to say my mother was Bianca and my father was Fidèle, called Fred.

My father and his sister were orphaned when their parents died in the Spanish influenza epidemic of 1918. My father was nineteen and his sister Vivianna fourteen. My father took his father's place in the family, carving stone and cutting tile, while his kid sister kept house and did the cooking. At seventeen Vivianna married the man who had got her pregnant, but her baby died a few days later and her husband took off. She worked here and there as a secretary, but after a few months she'd quit and take off, mailing her friends a stream of picture postcards by which they could chart her zigzag course down and up the coast or out to the Mississippi and back again. She even worked briefly for Pacifico in the summer of 1929 while my father and mother were on their wedding trip in Europe. Before my parents returned to Boston Vivianna went off and never came back. Her last postcard, mailed in 1930 from the minor honky-tonk town of Las Vegas, had a picture of the Hotel National, a bare two-floor shoebox with a striped awning over each window. *Here I am but not for long. Leaving for San Francisco on Monday & will write from there. Love to all, Viv.*

All my father ever said about Vivianna was that she was clever and restless. And, my mother added, she was attractive. Some years ago I found five snapshots of her forgotten in a stack of business documents in a large old envelope labeled *P. Cavallù & Co.* Two of the snapshots were taken indoors and they're dark; in one, Vivianna, her hair fashionably bobbed, sits in a swivel chair beside a broad black desk, and in the other she's by a window where the light leaves almost half her face in shadow. To be honest, they're lousy photos. The remaining three snapshots were taken out of doors on a breezy summer day. Her pale blouse opens wide at the throat and her hair blows across her cheek in a short dark crescent. The sun is bright and there's no blurring, even though she's turned her head and is laughing. In this other snapshot she represses a smile, trying to hold still for the photographer, and in this last one — caught unaware, her skirt flapping in the wind — she's stepping down from a boulder to a beach, most likely the same beach that shows in the background of the other outdoor shots.

After I started writing this little genealogy I began to look through the photos, letters, souvenirs and junk that got passed down the generations. I didn't come across anything new, nor was I able to fit everything together like a jigsaw puzzle. There were too many pieces missing. But I did notice that the man who ran the photography studio in the Cavallù building vanished the same time that Vivianna did. The photographer was Pacifico's half brother, Tancredi, the son of Pacifico's father, Fimi Cavallù, and a girl who worked in the kitchen — una picciotta di cucina — *not* Pacifico's mother, the passionate and learned Sonia DiSecco. Nonetheless, Sonia insisted that Tancredi, whom she had named, be brought up in the family and treated like any other Cavallù.

Tancredi was born in 1905, arrived in Boston in the summer of 1926 and left early in September of 1929. The story goes that he had always wanted to be a painter and that he had been driven crazy by having to photograph fat men in vests and a thousand little girls in First Communion dresses. The story also says that he didn't return to Sicily but went to Paris, and that might well be true. The only artifacts to survive from the studio are an ornate black oak chair and a French magazine, *La Révolution Surréaliste*, dated October, 1927, with *Tancredi* scribbled inside the front cover. The cover was grimy, but the pages were clean and there was a startling photograph jammed deep inside — a naked young woman whirling away with something in her hand, maybe a blouse or a shift. Her arm and hand are blurred, her flying hair is trimmed just like Vivianna's and that slender back could well be Vivianna's too.

The background is no help, a disheveled bed and an empty doorway.

Maybe Marianna was right and I was abandoned on the wrong doorstep by a confused woman who mistook this house beside the church for the one on the other side. Maybe it happened that way, a silhouette setting the basket ever so gently by the door, bending over it a long moment, then rising to knock, knock, knock and run away, glancing over her shoulder to see the door open and fill with light. If that's true, I thank my guardian angel who steered her to the Cavallù door. On the other hand, maybe Marianna was wrong and maybe the woman didn't mistake the grand Cavallù establishment with light pouring from every window for the tidy narrow gray parish house on the other side of the church, and maybe she knew very well at whose doorstep she was laying this infant. Maybe I resemble my mother and father because I'm the child of my father's wild kid sister and my mother's uncle. Or a man even more unlikely. Who cares?

I've never seen a photo of Tancredi, and all the family ever said of him was that he briefly managed the photography studio, fled to take up painting in Paris, and that he was a *briccuni*, which is Sicilian for rogue or rascal or worse. As for Vivianna, for a short while she was a hectic young woman in family stories and now she's just an image in five Kodak snapshots and a blurred 7 x 9 photo used as a bookmark in a French magazine.

❦

Pacifico and Marianna had nine children — Lucia, Marissa, Bianca, Candida, Dante, Sandro, Silvio, Mercurio, and Regina — and two homes, the big house in Lexington and the villa in Palermo. As it happened, the Second World War broke out while Marianna was in Massachusetts and Pacifico was in Sicily on business, and they weren't reunited until the war ended and Marianna sailed to Palermo. Pacifico died in 1948 after a good meal (melanzana con mozzarella), seated at his dining table with the plans of a cargo ship spread open in front of him. The villa had deteriorated, had leaky plumbing and loose wiring, and he'd rented out half of it, but he wasn't broke. On the contrary, he'd put together a group of like-minded friends and had acquired a surplus vessel from the United States Navy intending to start a shipping company. At this distance it's impossible to look over his shoulder to see if the ship was an LST, as some say, or a smaller craft. He died that summer day, his white beard pressed against his chest as if he were deep in thought, just before Marianna returned from the kitchen with his cup of espresso. As for Marianna, she lived long enough to welcome some of her grandchildren into the long garden behind the villa. She died early one morning in 1955, having seen her grandmother, the goddess, standing tiptoe on a big scallop shell that floated on the waters off the beach at Mondello, standing and beckoning as if she weighed nothing at all.

BOOK TWO

Renato, the Painter

Q. Who made you?
A. God made me.

—Catechism of Christian Doctrine

PART ONE
In which I am Introduced to my Parents, the World, & the Woman I will Marry

1

I WAS MADE IN THE USUAL WAY, THOUGH WHETHER I came here head-first or tail-first I don't know, since my mother didn't stay around long enough to tell me, and my father, if he knew me at all, never came by to admit it, but my life having turned out the way it has, I suspect I came out tail-first and that my head still dreamed in the dark while my legs went thrashing about in the light of this world. One way or the other I got out whole and got my bellybutton neatly knotted, and what happened over the next few days or weeks I can't even guess at.

And here I am, more than seven decades later, a vulgar old man with white hair on his privates and no time to wonder where I came from or where I'm going, because I'm too busy trying to make a name for myself. The parish house was on one side of St. Brigid's Church, the Cavallù house on the other, and my guardian angel, she—for surely angels are sexed—steered me to the right place. I was adopted then and there by Bianca and her husband Fidèle Stillamare. When I turned thirteen my parents gave me a diary in the hope that I would learn to spell if I wrote a paragraph at the end of each day, but after a few entries I quit writing and used it for a sketch pad, and have never succeeded in keeping a journal of any kind. Yet here I sit, writing any which way—*scribble, scribble, scribble.*

When I was growing up we had two autobiographies in our bookcase, a square brown one by Benjamin Franklin and a fancy red-and-gold one in Italian by Benvenuto Cellini, since each man had done great things in his way, though wise and prudent

Franklin, a friendly guy, had no fire in his veins and Cellini, a good swordsman and sculptor, beat his women and bragged about it. My father admired Franklin for his hard work and scientific curiosity, but my mother liked Cellini for entertainment, forgiving him his sins because he was an artist and artists were heroes to her.

So I had thought to write a book of my life and views after I had accomplished some great works and grown famous, which was an innocent thought with no vanity in it, for I was only a kid. We natural-born princes of the world, we work for the glory of the work itself and for nothing else, still I had thought I would be famous by now or at least better known. And I don't have forever like I used to. My friends have begun to die off and my best and closest and dearest Mike Bruno is gone, gone, gone. Anyway, I have sat down to write this chronicle and not about myself alone, for I've never lived alone for long and hope I never do, and now will get on with this.

2

I DON'T KNOW WHO BIANCA AND FIDÈLE HAD ENVIsioned when they dreamed of their first-born child, but they got me instead. They unwrapped me, my mother used to tell me, like a precious gift that had been laid at their doorstep, and they gave me my birthday that same wintry night in March, and so it has been ever since. My father liked to say he was just a stonecutter, but he was many other things as well—a mason and tiler and glazier, a sign maker, a carver of letters in stone or wood, designer of alphabets, graphic artist and sculptor. We lived on the edge of town in a farm house on a long five-acre lot that went down to the dry bed of the old Middlesex Canal. Seventy years ago you could drive the back roads of these little towns outside Boston and when you came to houses with a vegetable patch out back, two or three fruit trees and a grape arbor made of iron pipe, you knew you were among the Italians and, in fact, you might be passing my home. *Stillamare's Cut Stone & Tile Company* was in the barn out back and employed two or three workmen, depending on the jobs my father had gotten. In winter he ate lunch with his men in the shop at a bench where my mother had set a pot of steaming coffee, and in summer at a table with a pitcher of iced tea on it under the big maple tree by our kitchen door.

In my earliest memory I'm playing in the dirt at the edge of our vegetable garden—even now I can smell the damp gold dust on the underside of the tomato leaves and get the warm taste of the bright red tomato which a beautiful woman, one of my mother's sisters, has bitten open and sprinkled with salt and offered to me. In those days we spoke Italian in the kitchen and English when we walked downtown. Italian sounded old-fashioned and worn out, like our pots and soup spoons, whereas English was modern and sounded cleaner, but whenever I said anything like that my mother would slap me across the top of my head, saying, "*Senti! In paradiso si parla la lingua di Dante.* In heaven the angels speak Italian. Not English, Italian! *Non dimenticare mai.*"

By the time my brother Bartolomeo was born I was four years old and already prince of our five acres, and a few years later I became king of the fields and woods. I knew the route of hidden creeks and the whereabouts of old stone walls that had crept into the woods years ago and been forgotten. On a rainy day I could run all the way from the Common to our house and not get wet, because I knew where to cross the streets and backyards in a zigzag that went beneath an endless canopy of jutting eaves and elms and lilac bushes. I knew a friendly gray boulder shaped like a throne and knew a huge beech tree that had been half-uprooted in the Big Wind of 1938 and now grew at a slant, so you could walk up the trunk through a colonnade of branches, and I loved certain maples in whose slowly swaying branches I would be happy to rest even now. I knew how to call to crows, and when I called, they came. I knew where to find wild apples, blueberries, pears, Concord grapes, tadpoles, woodchucks, rotted stumps, quartz crystals, mica and clay, and I knew where snakes went to shed their skins.

My grandmother Cavallù, my Nana, had nine children and when all of them had married I had sixteen uncles and aunts, and when they had children I had lots of cousins. My cousin Nick and I were about the same age, and my cousin Veronica about three years younger, and we spent a lot of time together when we were kids. We saw each other on the holidays, of course, but also every Sunday afternoon when our families would congregate to talk or play bocce and then sit down to coffee and, if we were lucky, some pastries and gelati. Furthermore, the three of us were shifted from house to house whenever our parents, still young and hot, wanted to have a weekend alone, and each spring another uncle or aunt got married and soon we were joined by more cousins, so there was troop of us children. Nick and I were the ringleaders of this pack, and if Nick wasn't around it was me and Veronica.

In August our families drove to the Cape where we used to swim or go digging for clams or pick beach plums, and if we stayed out of the way we could watch my father and uncle Nicolo and uncle Zitti pitch horse shoes—the iron shoe would rise from my dad's hand as lightly as a bird, and from uncle Nicolo it would whirl on its way, but from uncle Zitti it would tilt and veer and tumble and you never knew where it might land, because he was a philosopher and thought so much. Or we could watch our younger uncles build huge kites of bamboo and colored paper which they would launch from the sand dunes while their women, in swimsuits on the beach far below, waved encouragingly and smoked cigarettes, or lay back to sunbathe with a magazine spread open upon their face. (And now my nose, all on its own, suddenly remembers the exciting sharp odor of the gun smoke when the men were shooting clay pigeons, the tangy smell of Veronica's rubber bathing cap, and the gentle scent of the kitchen olive oil we used for suntan lotion.) Back home in February we would skate across the frozen marsh and through the woods, or if it rained we would play indoors, sprawled on the floor, drawing pictures on those glossy white oblongs of cardboard that uncle Zitti let us ransack from his freshly ironed shirts. I thought that everyone grew up this way, and it was only later I learned that the kids I went to school with didn't have a bunch of cousins to play with on weekends, but had to make do with whoever happened to be living in the neighborhood, a terrible thin social life.

My father saved my report cards and when I looked at them just now (pale yellow cards with his strong handsome signature on the back six times each year) I was astonished at how badly I had done. *He is inclined to waste time, and gets mischievous with his neighbors*, wrote grandmotherly Miss Blodgett. The reports show that I didn't obey promptly, didn't use time and materials wisely, didn't cooperate and was only average when it came to working at a given task. I was slow with number facts and even slower with letters. I didn't hate letters, quite the contrary. My father, being a sign painter and carver of inscriptions, loved the shapes of letters and numerals and he inspired that same love in me. On any day of the week our backyard had parts of the alphabet strewn around, leaning against the maple tree or stacked in a heap by the barn door, so I learned the names of letters, learned how to draw them and got to know their different personalities, but I didn't learn how to read and never asked to. When the time came, my mother took me to Hancock School and introduced me to Miss Gosling. There were six grades (Miss Gosling, Miss Blodgett, Miss Ouellette, Miss Keane, Miss Tennyson, and Miss Shea) and reading was dinned into me for six years and eventually it took, though I never did learn how to spell.

The world was filled with things and each one had a face and a way of gesturing for attention—certain intricately carved chairs, house-fronts, waters that winked or waved, trees that beckoned, muttered, sighed—and each one waited to be read, greeted or listened to. It turned out you didn't pay attention to these things or to pictures of them, but only to printed words. And after I learned to read words, those other things withdrew with injured dignity and even the boulders clammed up, refused to speak.

I loved to draw. I loved getting down on the floor on my stomach with a pencil and a sheet of my father's design paper or my uncle's shirt cardboard. I could draw better than anyone else, but it didn't count because they didn't teach it in school. Instead, we brought autumn leaves to class and traced them, then colored in the outline with wax crayons. In winter we cut snowflakes from folded tissue, or drew snow trees with white chalk on gray paper, and in spring we traced the bottom of our ink wells to make the sun and flowers. Our third grade class made a mural about Hiawatha's camp, but I wasn't allowed to work on it, even though I was the best at drawing, because I was slow at numbers and reading. Of course, everybody knew that tracing and coloring were for children and we soon put that behind us and had Art Appreciation instead.

In Art Appreciation the teacher would show us a picture of a famous painting, like *The Angelus* by the famous French painter Jean Francois Millet, and she'd read to us about it. Then each of us was given a miniature picture of it with stick-um on the back which you licked, then you stuck it onto a sheet of construction paper. *The Angelus* was about a man and a woman working in a plowed field when they heard the church bell ringing, so they bowed their heads, and if you looked closely you could see the church belfry on the horizon. That was Art Appreciation. We Appreciated a lot of pictures like *The Age of Innocence* or *The Blue Boy* or the one about a dog that rescued people who fell off the dock into the sea, but they weren't very interesting and when we were through I decided I couldn't be a painter after all, because it was so dull.

We did a lot of singing and that was a joy. The teacher would blow a note on her pitch-pipe and we would hum it till her note and our humming blended together perfectly, then we'd sing. Also, we got a lot of poems by heart, which I still think is the best way, so I can still recite *The Ride of Paul Revere* and *To A Waterfowl*. And in penmanship we learned to lick a new steel nib just once before dipping it into the ink well, and we practiced the Palmer Method with an eraser balanced on the back of our writing hand.

Each time the teacher gave me my report card it surprised and frightened me how low the marks were, because I knew that my mother would read it and hand it back, saying, "You'll have to give this to your father yourself." And after my father read it he would shout, "Do you want to be a ditch digger? That's where you'll end up, digging ditches! Is *that* what you want?" That's where dumb Italians ended up. No, I didn't want that. Being a ditch digger would mean working beside people like that pig Norman Oldacre who liked to make loud farts and told bathroom jokes and who took me aside in the school yard one morning and beat me up so hard my eyes watered.

But I didn't feel stupid and I knew that the stupidest kid in my class wasn't me but fat Collins. The teacher told him he was the cow's tail because he always came in last, but Collins just sat there being fat and smiled and blinked his sleepy-lidded eyes and said nothing. He wasn't my friend but I thought it was cruel to call him the cow's tail and make fun of him just because he couldn't memorize. I felt I could learn anything and that I was as smart as everybody else and even nicer than some other kids—certainly nicer than Eddy O'Toole who said *fuck* even though he was an altar boy at St. Brigid's, or Betty Bender who talked back to the teacher, or Carol Shepherd who stuttered, and as good as Jack Sawyer or Sue Meadows or that too-sweet girl with the permanent raspberry stain on her cheek whose name I've forgotten. I used to watch the shadow of the window sash creep ever so slowly across my desk and my mind would wander.

It's hard to believe, but years ago the town pried all the slate from the classroom walls, sold our desks and turned the school into expensive condominiums with big windows. When we were there the janitor used to sprinkle green sawdust in front of his broom when he swept the black oiled floors, and the stair treads had scoops worn in from our shoes. The Boys' Room had a wall made of brownish copper with water drizzling down it. You peed against the wall and the water washed it down to a gutter where it drained away past a white cake of disinfectant that smelled so strong it made you hold your breath. The sign over the paper towel box said *Why take two when one will do?* There was a tall skinny kid, three years older than everyone else, whose father used to beat him in the street and he had to keep his head shaved because he got lice. This kid caught me by the woods one day, twisted my arm behind my back until I took off my clothes and went swinging on the vines with him, then he unfolded his jackknife and said he'd get me if I told, but happily he was killed in boot camp three years later. Just before Christmas all the classes came out to the hall and each grade sang its own Christmas carol. The first grade had little voices so they sang *Wind in the Olive Trees*, the second grade was stronger so it sang *O, Little Town of Bethlehem*, and so on up to the sixth grade which sang *O, Come, All Ye Faithful!* When finally we were in sixth grade we were the last to sing and we stood very quietly in the hall and listened to the carol floating up from the little kids downstairs, singing in their sweet voices, and the songs went from room to room, getting stronger and richer and closer, and I felt this is what they meant when they told us about the angel chorus in heaven, this was what it sounds like.

Before I leave Hancock School I should introduce Miss Keane, my striking fourth grade teacher. All the gentle ancients at the school wore droopy sacks in mottled purples and moldy browns, illuminated by a lace collar or a pale cameo brooch, but handsome Miss Keane liked to wear silky white blouses that looked good to touch and a narrow black skirt that hissed excitedly against her stockings when she marched —tap! tap! tap!—down the aisle to see what we were doing. If we all had performed well, she would smile and take off her Mexican silver earrings and tell us about her trip to Mexico. But when we misbehaved she would angrily erase the blackboard, her bracelets jingling frantically, then snatch up her pointer and smack it to her white palm in rhythm with our chant, not ending till we reached *nine elevens are ninety-nine.*

From Miss Keane I learned the multiplication table and how to spell some words, not many, and about volcanoes and cave men. And I learned that in Europe they thought it shameful to work with your hands (as my father did) and they looked down on a person who wore mended clothes (as I did), but here in the United States all citizens were created equal and it didn't matter what your last name was, because you could go to a public school and learn things and grow up to be whatever you wanted to be. Later, when I was in old Miss Tennyson's fifth grade, Miss Keane would step into my darkened bedroom and tie me naked to the bed, my arms like Christ crucified, then she'd pull my stiffened thing—like this, and this, and this! *this!*—until it fluttered in a strange soundless thunderbolt of pleasure, and sometimes Sue Meadows and Betty Bender slipped in behind her to see what was going on, their eyes shining with curiosity.

3

I SEE THAT I'VE LEFT OUT THE WAR THAT WAS GOING on in the background and that had been going on for as long as I could remember. In the candy store the bubble-gum came in flat squares with nice cards underneath, colored picture cards that showed Japanese soldiers shooting the Chinese families they had roped together for the War in China. As I understood it, Mussolini had asked my mother and my aunts to give him their jewelry for the War in Ethiopia, but they had laughed at him—because they were so beautiful, I supposed, and didn't want to give up their bracelets and rings—though later my mother explained that it was because we despised the Fascists and admired Haile Selassie. In the newspaper there was a photograph of young men lounging in the street with their arms around each other's necks and little Italian flags in their hands: *These young men say they would be willing to fight for Italy in its war with Ethiopia.* All my aunts and uncles were shouting at once and my grandfather slapped uncle Silvio because Silvio was in the photo, but later everyone sat down to spumoni and coffee and went back to talking in English. Uncle Silvio had made a mistake, and we shouldn't talk about it in English. My grandfather and aunt Lucia sailed to Palermo to see about the villa, then the War broke out in Europe, too, and they couldn't get back, but Nonno wrote to us how ashamed he was when Italy invaded France, "a stab in the back" everybody called it. Every Sunday during coffee uncle Nicolo would ask, "Do you think we'll get dragged into this one?" and uncle Zitti would say, "We're already in it, Nicolo. We're already in it."

I was eleven years old when the Japanese bombed Pearl Harbor one Sunday afternoon and that meant we were actually in the War. The next spring my father enlarged the vegetable garden. A lot of people began vegetable gardens, which were called Victory Gardens the way the new bicycles were called Victory Bikes and later the letters from my uncles (shrunk to the size of a post card and covered with tiny writing) were called V-mail. My mother put up blackout shades and made soap, because it was scarce. We had ration booklets, we had buckets of sand at the ready in case the house was hit by an incendiary bomb, and we had the car headlamps painted black on top, like sleepy eyelids, so that our coastal ships wouldn't be silhouetted against sky-glow. Nick and Veronica and I had fathers too old to be drafted, so each summer we still went to Cape Cod and stayed there while our parents came and went by turns, but our young uncles couldn't come and the Coast Guard patrolled the beaches and forbid trap shooting or flying kites, because you couldn't carry guns near the beach and the kite string might actually be the wire aerial for a secret radio which could be used to contact German submarines. At night Nick and I would lie in our cots on the screened porch and watch the searchlights and listen to the *bam-bam-bam* of the anti-aircraft guns striking sparks from the black sky during practice.

There was a rusty target ship run aground about a mile offshore and while we played on the beach we could watch the B-25s make solitary bombing runs at it and see puffs of white smoke. If we were lucky the last bomber would make its final turn shoreward and come at us low. Then Nick and I would scramble to the top of the sand dunes and watch as the plane roared gloriously along the beach, its wings on a level with the top of the dunes, the pilot with his hand raised in a slow salute to the women who had dropped their magazines and were waving as he thundered past. We knew that German submarines were stalking off the coast, because once in a while we could feel a subtle shuddering boom—it could be day or night—and once in a while the tide crept in black with diesel oil, bearing bits of charred rubbish, but we weren't supposed to talk about it. Aunt Regina's husband, uncle John, was lost in the North Atlantic where the sea freezes you to death before it fills your lungs with water, but his body never washed up on our beach. Little by little it became clear what the War was and how I was going into it, and like other boys I began to pick up this and that about combat, not about killing so much as about how to dig a foxhole and how to lie flat when the artillery rounds came in, how not to be afraid of fear, how to identify planes, how accurate the German 88s were, how to Breathe, Aim, Sight, Shoot, how never to leave your rifle, no matter how heavy it got, because the M-1 rifle was the infantryman's friend. Uncle Silvio sent us *Yank, the Army Magazine* and there I read about army life and studied the full page pin-up photos of cheerful girls in bathing suits and high-heel shoes. On my bedroom wall I had a big map of Europe which I stuck pins into to follow the progress of the War. Uncle Mercurio's B-24 was hit over the Mediterranean and he bailed out, parachuting down past Monte Pellegrino and into the Via Imperatore Federico, so he was able to run down the street and vault over the wall into his father's garden and rush upstairs to hide until General Patton and the Seventh Army marched into Palermo. We saw pictures of the rubble in southern Italy; my father cleared his throat but didn't say anything, my mother wept and threw the magazine across the room. The Italians surrendered and later the Partisans caught up with Mussolini, shot him and trampled him and hung him upside down at a gas station, killed Clara Petacci and hung her upside down too, right there, you could see her underpants. The Germans retreated slowly, leaving Rome and then Florence, but they counterattacked in France, coming through the snow. The Germans were barbarians, but the Japanese were worse, barely human. We knew what the Japs had done in China and the Philippines and none of us kids wanted to fight in the Pacific. Uncle Silvio liked to go in with the first wave right under the naval bombardment and dig in before the Japs had time to come out of their bunkers. On Iwo Jima we had to crawl on our bellies over the sand and pumice, one inch at a time, and flush them out with flame throwers and kill each one separately, because they wouldn't surrender. But no one wanted to hit the beach in Japan, Silvio said. We felt such powerful joy when the atom bomb obliterated Hiroshima, the pleasure lingering for days as the smoke hovered over the city and later the black rain fell, felt it again when the next bomb erased Nagasaki, and felt relief when they surrendered. I was sixteen when we gathered on the Common and the ministers of the town gave thanks to God for our victory.

4

MY FATHER AND MOTHER REFUSED TO BELIEVE I was as stupid as my report cards said I was, and they still hoped I would go to college, so over the next six years I not only had to practice reading and writing, I also had to bang my head on algebra, chemistry, physics, more algebra, plane geometry, solid geometry, trigonometry, French and Latin. The geometries delighted me, but I did badly at everything else and terribly at Latin. I stumbled over *amo-amas-amat*, trudged into Gaul in the last rank of my class, straggling further and further behind Caesar, then drowned as everyone else sailed off with pious Aeneas to found Rome.

My grandfather believed *his* children were born with the talent to write a sonnet, drive a car, draw, dance or fight, the same as they were born with the capacity to speak and sing (that's my grandfather, standing hairy-chested at the washbowl, scissors uplifted to trim his beard, singing an aria while Caruso accompanies him through the graceful horn of the Victrola in the bedroom) and since his children did do those things—some things better, some things badly—they assumed that *their* children could do them, too. Now, as often happens with adopted children, I had come to look rather like the people who were bringing me up, most strikingly like my mother, and my ability as a draftsman seemed to be an inheritance from my father, which pleased us both, and when I turned fourteen he said, yes, I could take drawing lessons, for I had been pestering him about it for months.

I began with Mr Horgan, a very stout man with crankily brown hair and a large oatmeal face, brightened here and there with fresh razor nicks. He had come to live in his parents' empty house; they had died long ago and the house, a huge structure with two chimneys at each end, was falling apart—the gutters hanging from the eaves, the white paint peeling from the clapboards. Each Saturday morning I would grab a fist-ful of pencils, hug my biggest drawing pad under my arm and ride my bicycle one-handed to the edge of town to ring Mr Horgan's bell. One of his young housemaids— housemaids is what he called them—would come to the door in bare feet, wearing nothing but one of Horgan's big shirts, look at me and shout over her shoulder, *Hey, Frank, the kid's here!* Mr Horgan, his paint-smeared shirt tucked crookedly into his corduroy pants and those pants tucked unevenly into his boots, would begin muttering resentfully as he limped out the door, and he'd continue to drop sighs as we walked together down the rutted driveway to his barn and mounted the jittery stairs (Horgan in front) to the loft where he had his studio. He would hum and groan and mutter irritably as he groped under the eaves, gather-ing up things (a cracked pottery jug, a chipped bowl, a tarnished silver cigarette case with a broken hinge, a ratty shawl) which he would set on the round, elevated piano stool which he used for a stand. When he had arranged each object precisely as he wanted, his resentment—I assumed it was resentment at hav-ing me there —would evaporate and he'd fall silent. Then he would sit on a tall stool with his drawing board in his lap and I would sit beside him on a somewhat lower stool with my pad, and we would draw the assembled pieces. During those periods of friendly silence, defined by the soft scratching of our pencils, I used to tremble with bliss and anxiety as I struggled to get my drawing right. When we finished, he would give me a complete critique of my sketch, his thick fingers dabbing here and there at my pad (I'd erase his smudges when I got home), then he'd show me what he had done and we'd discuss his work awhile. When the lesson was over he would continue to talk, but more amiably now, asking a question or two about my school work as we went down the quaking stairs (Horgan in back) and out the gravel driveway to my bicycle.

Mr Horgan taught me three things. First, always look at-tentively at your subject. "And don't just look at it, *watch* it. You might see it do something nobody has seen before. Listen to it, and if you get a chance, touch it, smell it, bite it and taste it!" Second, block it in. "Get it down on paper all at once, no matter how. Get your hands and arms and legs around it! Be *passionate*. The rest is details." Third, show that the shadows and the shady sides aren't really black. "If you can see it, there's some *light* on it, and if there's *light*, there's *color*. Remember this, Renato, *God made colors, not lines, colors!*" And I would have showed the passionate colors, except that Mr Horgan made me use my graphite pencils until, after six months, he threw his heavy freckled arm around my shoulders and said, well, by God he could look at my black-and-white drawing and see the colors I wanted to represent, so why didn't I bring some paints with me next time.

One day Mr Horgan auctioned off all the antique furniture in his house and the next day he auctioned off the house itself and drove to Montreal with pretty Miss Dewey, the librarian, leaving his housemaids with no place to stay. My father rarely said a word against anyone and was especially reluctant to knock another craftsman, but after Horgan had gone he announced that I could learn a lot more from a commercial artist, so the following September I began to take lessons from Mr Quill, a small brisk man with wispy hair, bright eyes and perfectly circular glasses.

Mr and Mrs Quill lived in an old-fashioned house (tall turret, scalloped shingles) where they worked together illustrating children's books. Mrs Quill would open the front door— "Good morning, Renato. Did you have a nice walk?" —and after I had wiped my shoes on the doormat or knocked the snow from my boots, whichever it was she wanted, she would lead me up the bright oak stairs and down the hall to their studio, a neat white room with two drawing tables face-to-face, each with its own slanted drawing board and jar of pencils. There Mrs Q would vanish and Mr Q would take over, talking cheerfully about what we were going to do that day. Beside his drawing table he had placed a small desk for me and laid a few things on it, maybe a row of paper knives or a set of French curves. He began the first lesson by giving me instructions on how to sharpen a pencil properly. The Quill Method was to pare away the wood until there was a long spindle of bare lead which he then briskly filed to a point on a pad of sandpaper.

Mr Quill really enjoyed teaching me things, like how to use a T-square and triangle or how to draw a pen along a ruler without smearing ink all over the place, all of which was useful but gave me a headache. He knew all the rules of perspective—"Invented by you Italians, Renato!"—and in the subsequent weeks I drew dramatically foreshortened cylinders, cubes, pyramids and cones. Perspective enchanted me. Under his guidance I sketched a shoe carton, drew the plan view at the top of the paper, the elevation views at the side, then projected lines from those views so they crisscrossed in the middle of the sheet and magically gave rise to a perfectly proportioned three-dimensional box. Whenever Mr Quill would say, "Now you try it," I'd sweat about snapping off a pencil point or busting his screw press, but I was filled with satisfaction at knowing how to do so many things. By the end of the year I had incised linoleum blocks and printed them without smudging, had made monotypes, lithographs, serigraphs and dry point etchings—many of them of Hodge Podge, the Quill's sleepy orange cat.

I didn't take any drawing lessons senior year, because I was too busy with basketball practice and track and working on the school paper and acting in the senior play and fooling around with my friends and having a good time. I still have my high school yearbook, a tall thin volume bound in glazed blue cloth stamped with gold letters (our school colors: blue and gold) and the numerals 1948, but I'm not about to open it. I know the certificates awarding me my sports letters are tucked inside, along with the big photo of Debby Field and me at the Senior Prom (a gardenia corsage strapped to her wrist), plus the graduation program which lists four student speakers under the heading "The Outlook of Youth in the Atomic Age." And

I've seen the gray photos, each face looking so young and at the same time much older than high-school faces nowadays, with our old-fashioned hair styles and our 1948 looks. I opened the book a few years ago and discovered that looking at those banal photos and reading the names of classmates I thought I had forgotten compressed my chest as if a gravestone were standing on it, made my eyes water, and left me confused that these ordinary people whom I did not love could make me feel such loss.

5

I'M SURE THERE'S NOTHING IN HEAVEN MORE FILLED with innocent wonder and delight than an angel with his first erection, but it might not look that way to us fallen mortals, for as the Catechism says, *Our nature was corrupted by the sin of our first parents, which darkened our understanding, weakened our will, and left in us a strong inclination to evil.* Those first parents were Adam and Eve, and my nature had come cascading down from them to me and only God knew what had happened along the way. My mother suspected I had been conceived out of wedlock in a blazing passion which had burnt my natural parents to a cinder and left me an orphan on her father's doorstep, so she worried and kept on the lookout for signs of the same pyromania in me.

Now one lazy summer morning my mother came to rouse me from bed, pulling the sheets into a heap to be washed, and discovered me with my *ucellino* as stiff and springy as a willow twig. For a moment she was shocked, actually turned to stone by the sight of it. Then she broke into a rage, bawled me out for wasting my strength and ruining my health, began weeping and swatting at my head while I dodged around the room, snatched on my shirt, my pants, hopped down stairs, pulled on my socks and sat outside on the back steps to tie my shoes. A few years earlier she used to interrupt my play to kiss my neck, would ruffle my hair or bite my ear, and she still loved to gather me from the tub and hug me in a towel, letting whole navies run aground at the drain while she rubbed my head till my hair was dry. But my mother prided herself on being a thoroughly modern woman and not some immigrant *cafone* who swaddled her baby and hung garlic around its neck to ward off the flu. She followed the latest theories on how to raise a boy and learned it's his spermy fluid makes him virile, so a boy who wastes it wastes himself, leaves himself with weakened muscles and a drained personality—meaning there's scientific and hygienic reason to stop his fun.

My father didn't have as refined an education as my mother, who had gone to Notre Dame Academy and Regina Caeli, but he had learned his lessons in Boston's public schools and public streets, which may explain why he worried less about my growing up. My mother, still striving to bring me up right, spied her old volume of *Getting Ready to be a Mother* under my school books and snatched it up, whirling around to whack me with it and then stumbling over the boots and ice skates in the back hall, her undone hair snaking out every which way while I scrambled into my mackinaw and ran out the door. That fascinating book (photos of woman milking her breast, pages 122-124) didn't reappear in its proper place in the upstairs bookcase, but while searching for it I discovered a sturdy brick-like volume that had not been there before, Gray's *Anatomy*. The *Anatomy* pages were stunning. I was enchanted by the intricately detailed engravings by Dr. H. Van Dyke Carter: the bones, musculature, blood vessels and nerve paths —handsome bodies portrayed as if they had been flayed alive, and in some views the artist had even drawn little hooks to peel back and hold open the flesh, making me recoil with pain. Still it was very interesting, all of it. And I was hypnotized by a meticulous view of the labia wide open, the secret clitoris, and the mons veneris with each small wildly curled hair separately depicted. My father, guided by his love of craftsmanship and his pragmatism about my growing up, had chosen the book and put it there for me.

My fourth grade teacher no longer visited my darkened bedroom and neither did my classmate Sue Meadows, but Betty Bender, who talked back to the teacher, she came night after night. In class it seemed I was holding one end of a thin rope and she was holding the other end and the rope was stretched so tight that we could feel every tug and vibration. At night she would step barefoot into my bedroom and undress hurriedly on the braided rug in front of my bureau, because her own bedroom had been demolished by something —a flood, a hurricane, the whole town wrecked, trees every which way, power lines down—and our unwitting parents insisted that we share a bed, so I'd reluctantly lift the blanket and she'd slip into bed in her white cotton underpants and undershirt, her freckled shoulder brushing my arm. *You'd better not take them off*, I'd mutter, sore at being disturbed. *I can if I want to*, she'd hiss, pushing down her underpants. Then everything would rush together, thrilling up to a big pulsing jolt of pleasure. And I wasn't able to keep the stuff from spurting onto my hand like I had a year ago.

Nick and I were crazy about our aunt Regina who was as reckless as her brothers, more beautiful than her sisters and the youngest of them all, being only ten years older than we were. When Gina was fifteen she ran off, or was sent off, to live for a while with her married older sister, Nick's mother, so Nick always bragged he had been in love with her since he was five. Now that Gina was a war widow, she lived with her daughter Arianne over her café in Gloucester. One empty Sunday afternoon when everyone else was at the beach, Nick and I lighted up a couple of cigarette butts from the clam shell ashtray on Gina's bed table and, seizing the moment, began to explore her bedroom. We peered into the closet at the dresses. "Yum, yum!" Nick said, reaching into a bodice. I laughed. We wandered over to the bureau, lifted the stoppers from the perfume bottles to get a whiff, unscrewed the jar lids to dab at the cremes, peeked into the jewelry boxes, and then gently tugged open the top drawer, pausing whenever it squeaked. It held a clutter of ring boxes, gloves, menstrual pads, a hair brush, some loose snapshots, a pearl necklace, kerchiefs, and so on. The second drawer was a tumbled bed of silken cloth, white and pink and gold, that slowly resolved itself into bras, underpants, stockings and garter belts. We gazed in silence, then I choked on the cigarette smoke and began coughing and had to stub the cigarette in the ashtray. Nick had pulled a dusky stocking up his forearm and was wiggling his fingers inside it. I studiously untangled one of the bras, a satin thing with a filigree of lace, then shoved up my jersey and flattened a silky cup onto my nipple. "Look," I said, "We're kissing." Nick had unbuckled and stepped out of his pants and now he began to sort through the drawer. I threw myself on her bed, rolling my head in the faint scent of perfume that rose from her pillow. When I looked up, Nick was wearing one of Gina's underpants over his tense privates. "Oh, God, oh, God, oh—" he gasped, stripping the pants off. "I'm getting a hard-on!" Voices floated up from the back door, Nick grabbed his pants, we shot out of there.

Later that afternoon, while the grown-ups were lingering over coffee in the front room, Gina stepped into the kitchen and pinched my cheek so hard it made my eyes water, holding me that way and whispering in my ear "You kids do that again and I'll break your neck! *Capito?*" Then she slapped Nick on the head and walked out. "What did you *do?*" Veronica asked us. We didn't tell her. "Let's go out," Nick said. We went downstairs and sat outside on the back step and watched Arianne and Bart and Tulio and the other little kids playing in the alleyway. Veronica came and sat beside me on the step for a while, toying with the charms on her bracelet, but she got bored because we wouldn't tell her what we had done, so she picked up a stone and went off to draw a hopscotch pattern for the other children.

"Veronica's all right," I remarked.

"Veronica's a *child*," Nick said scornfully. "She's too young."

I thought about that a while. "She has breasts."

We watched Veronica on her hands and knees, scratching the hopscotch lines on the pavement. She was wearing a pale yellow sundress that made her arms and legs look very brown. I liked Veronica.

"I like Gina better," Nick said. And, as a matter of fact, five years later Nick and Gina were banging each other on her bed, which is another story but not this one.

6

VERONICA'S MOTHER WAS MY MOTHER'S SISTER, Candida, a handsome athletic woman who had won prizes for archery and swordplay, being skilled at épée in her youth, and her father was Calogero Zitellone, called Zitti, a professor of philosophy, amateur philologist, author of the epic poem *Luna* and creator of an onomatopoetic language. Our families used to meet on Sundays, sometimes at Veronica's home and sometimes at mine, but most often at Nick's because Nick lived in the big house which our grandparents had filled before the war and everyone was used to going there. Uncle Nicolo sat at one end of the table, uncle Zitti at the other, and all the other aunts and uncles and cousins sat along the sides while the little kids, who had been fed earlier, crawled around our legs.

The three old men—my father, uncle Nicolo and uncle Zitti—had married into the family and were more serious than the younger uncles. Zitti and Nicolo disagreed about everything. Zitti was a tall slender man with bright lively eyes, a compressed smile and gray hair which he combed back in thick, vigorous waves. "Your theory of reality is all wrong," he announced one Sunday afternoon. By then half the chairs at the table were empty and everything had been cleared away save for a silver coffee pot, a broken rope of figs and a nutcracker.

"I don't have a theory of reality," Nicolo replied. He was an aeronautical engineer, balloon enthusiast, author at twenty-eight of a book on electronic orbits, unfortunately based on a concept of the atom which was swept away a year later, a short man with a flawlessly bald head, absolutely round and bare, like the dome at MIT where he taught. He had taken off his spectacles and was polishing the lenses with the white square of his handkerchief. "I'm simply telling you what is."

My father, who could crack walnuts in the crook of his arm, was making toy sailboats for little Arianne, making them from walnut shells with toothpick masts and paper sails. He had been holding a lighted candle upside down so the wax would drip into the empty walnut hull and now he stood a toothpick upright in the cooling wax and waited, listening to them.

Nicolo put on his glasses, rimless squares like the cursors from a slide rule. "On the atomic level reality is mostly empty space. There's very little stuff down there and when you penetrate closely it vanishes into mathematics."

"Of course it vanishes, because what you're talking about is the *surface* of reality." Zitti made a fluttering gesture with his fingers. "The fog of appearance, the mist that hovers over the true reality so that we can grasp it with our senses. I think my theory deserves more attention. —What do you think?" he asked, turning to my father.

"Try carving stone all day," my father told him. "By God, you'll learn all you need to know about reality."

Mercurio came walking through the dining room with grandfather's old bird gun, the one with the fancy engraving on the stock. "Who wants to go shooting? Are you going to sit around the table all day and discuss verbs? Or is it socialism this time? Come on, let's go shooting. There's pheasants out there."

Dante followed with a long-barreled six-shooter, the gift from Signor Baldo to Angelo Cavallù in 1879. "It's a beautiful day for shooting," Dante said. So Mercurio and Dante went down to the fields to shoot while my father stayed behind with Nicolo and Zitti to play bocce on the gravel court.

I found Nick and Veronica and together we climbed the narrow back stairway to explore the rooms at the top. Nick's family occupied rooms on the first two floors, but they kept the rest of the big old house vacant. We used to slip in by the wine cellar, where the air smelled of damp earth, and go up the back stairs past the warm kitchen and the quiet bedrooms to the topmost landing where a small window looked way off to the old graveyard, the brown fields and the black woods. Up there the rooms were chill and empty, except in one corner we found a schoolroom map of Europe and fifteen copies of a history book, and in the closet of another we found a pair of riding boots spattered with dried mud, a couple of bamboo fishing rods, a stuffed hawk, and a leather flying helmet with goggles, which we examined closely, because we knew the story of how our grandfather had become enraged at Mercurio's reckless stunts and had torn the helmet in half with his bare hands, and these rooms lead to others tucked beneath the eaves, and it was under those slanted roofs that we came across the baby carriage with the little port-hole windows, the big leather suitcases and, best of all, the huge steamer trunks covered with stickers from the Cunard line and White line. The trunks had been upended, so that when we tugged them open the lid swung out like a door to reveal a cramped dressing room with flowered wallpaper, a mirror, a stack of drawers, elastic pockets and a shallow closet with an interior of watered silk. It was while ransacking these little boudoirs with Veronica—Nick busy with his skeleton keys at the next trunk—when she would laugh or try to elbow me aside, the sweet scent of her bath soap mingling with the odors of tobacco and perfume that rose from the drawers, her breath on my cheek as we tried to decipher the rapid Italian scrawl in some forgotten letter—it was then that I became more and more tensely aware of her.

At our house one Sunday afternoon Veronica and I sat on

the floor in my bedroom and while the voices of our parents came floating up from the living room we worked together on a giant jigsaw puzzle. Tulio, Bart, Arianne and the other little kids kept dashing in and out, but eventually they went outside to play in the snow. We worked the puzzle in silence a while. "Remember what we talked about last time?" I asked her, pressing a piece into the ragged edge nearest my knee.

Veronica glanced up from the puzzle and looked at me a moment, a slight flush on her cheeks. "Yes."

"Well?"

"Turn around and don't peek," she said sharply.

I turned around, listening attentively to the rustle of her dress and the jingle of her bracelets—sounds which have aroused me wild ever since. "All right," she said quietly. "You can turn around now."

She smoothed the hem of her skirt down over her knee and watched me, her discarded white underpants lying rumpled at her edge of the puzzle, then she swept them into her fist. I stood up, my legs trembling, and sat down beside her. She turned to look at me again, smiled briefly and waited.

What can I tell you? That afternoon she was wearing a white sweater and a dark green plaid skirt, white ankle socks and black shoes with a strap. Uncle Zitti wouldn't let her wear perfume, so she used lavender-scented bath soap, fresh and sweet, which I had come to like.

After we had said our good-byes at the front door, I rushed to my desk with my head in flames, grabbed my colored pencils and—my prick stiffening in anticipation—began to draw that gentle cleft and mound fledged with hair. Her flesh tones were impossible to render and I had to compromise on pinkish ivory, and she hadn't much more hair than on the back of a man's hand, but it was fascinating and I got it all —some hairs in small, precise semi-circular lines and others merely suggested by thicker shading. I don't know what happened to that sketch. I suppose I burned it to get rid of the evidence and now there's a hundred of my canvasses I'd set fire to if I could have that scrap back again.

In the cottage by the beach I pulled on my swim shorts and looked up to see Veronica disappearing from my bedroom doorway. I grabbed a towel and followed her into the kitchen, saying, "You were *spying* on me."

"No I wasn't!"

"I *saw* you, Veronica."

"You left the door open and I just happened to be walking by," she said, ignoring me.

"You just happened to be peeking in, you mean."

She put her beach towel on the counter and began to pour olive oil from the big gold Filippo Berio can into a saucer. She was in her swim suit and around her neck she wore a leather string with a bit of coral. Everyone else had started down the road to the beach and the cottage felt unusually hollow and quiet. She dipped her fingers into the saucer of oil and began to rub it onto her shoulders.

"Do you want some?" she asked quietly, trying to be friends.

"Nope."

"Do my back," she said, turning away. She pulled down the straps of her swimsuit, revealing the pale negative of the suit on her russet shoulders.

"Don't you ever say *please*?"

"Please," she echoed.

I caught the warm scent of her skin and dipped my fingers in the olive oil and spread it on the back of her shoulders. She turned and yanked her swimsuit straps down, pulling it all to her waist. Her breasts were startlingly white. I looked. She started to draw the suit back up.

"Wait!" I cried.

She dropped her hands to her sides and waited. I drew my fingers slowly across this breast and then that one. "Jesus, I didn't mean to mess you up with the olive oil. I'm sorry," I said.

"That's all right. I don't mind."

Her nipples had begun to stiffen.

"What does it feel like when that happens?"

She shrugged. "Watch," she said. She plucked gently at the nipple. "See. It gets hard."

I put my hand over her breast. "Something else gets hard, too," I muttered.

"What? What else gets hard?" she asked, beginning to giggle. "Show me."

"You, too."

"Oh, no! *You* first," she insisted.

"How far do you want to go?"

"No farther than last time."

"That's what you always say, Veronica. Come on."

"I'm not stupid, Renato."

I can still call up the secret pallor of Veronica's breast and the tender blurred pink hue of the corolla around the nipple —a color I sweated to reproduce again and again the following autumn, working the chalk broadside to the paper and then rubbing it around and around with my fingers, blurring it, grinding my hand into the weave of the paper in a futile effort to bring back the firm give of her breast beneath my palm.

One freezing Sunday Veronica led me down to the ice rink where we sat on a bench and watched the skaters going round and round while she told me about a kid she was dying over, a boy two years ahead of her who had skated with her one afternoon and when it got dark and the street lights came on he had walked her home. They had stood on the sidewalk in front of her house and looked at the black sky full of stars. He had said he was going to phone her, but eleven days had gone and still he hadn't called. She had seen him in the school lunch room twice since then, but he wouldn't look at her. Veronica sat beside me with her head down and watched her own boots scuffing back and forth at the snow, but I couldn't think of what to say and felt stupid. We walked back to her house talking about other things, about Nick's going to college and me off to art school.

Just before we went inside I told her the boy was crazy not to call her and wasn't worth spit and there were a lot of guys who wanted to date her. "You're good-looking, you know," I added.

"Oh, sure. Tell me another."

"No. I mean it."

"You're just saying that because I'm your cousin."

"No. I mean it. I think you're good-looking."

"Since when?"

I shrugged. "Since always. I always thought so."

Veronica looked at me—she was wearing her Sunday coat, the red one with the black velvet collar, her cheeks red from the cold and her eyes glistening black. She smiled and said, "I'll make us some hot cocoa."

7

THE FIRST TIME I WENT ALL THE WAY I WAS SEVENteen, fresh out of high school and working on the fish pier at Newburyport. I was in the hot sun stacking crates of chopped ice and flounder when a girl in a swimsuit came walking along with her arms full of flowers. I said Hi and she said Hi, then she looked around and asked me did I know the *Saint Rafael*. The *Saint Rafael* was a fishing boat, a dragger. I pointed to where it was tied up and watched her walk down and go on board. She had long legs, a streak of mud on one of them. A while later she came walking back, her arms empty, and she put a hand up to shade her eyes and looked at me, frankly curious. "Renato Stillamare," I said. She gave me a quick, open smile—she had sea-green eyes and the bridge of her nose was sunburned—but she kept on her way, a kid with long legs.

After dinner I went down to the breakwater to hook up with some friends and saw her strolling with a couple of girls her age, all in striped jerseys and white shorts, and I said, "Hi." They giggled and nudged each other. The next evening she was down there alone so I asked her how old she was. "I'm going to be fifteen," she said.

I laughed and said, "Is that the same as fourteen?" She blew the hair out of her eyes and looked off at the horizon and started to walk away. "Please stay. I like you. I really like you," I told her. Her family grew flowers to sell, but she was good at languages and planned to become a diplomat and travel all over the world. I told her how I was going to the Museum School in the fall. She thought it was amazing that I wanted to be a painter and asked a lot of questions about the school and about Boston. That night we were sitting in the field up back of her family's greenhouse and when she lay back I kissed her, put my hand on her breast. I could feel her heart hammering so hard she could barely get her breath, but she wanted to show she was a grown-up and no kid, so she didn't move or say a word, just watched my eyes. She had never made love and I let her think I had. I pressed in by inches while she winced and turned her head aside—I could see she was gritting her teeth, but when I hesitated she gasped, "*Do it!*" and I did it. Afterward we held hands and walked down the long field to her house while she raked her fingers through her hair, combing out the burrs and pieces of straw. She told me her secret Algonquin name which she had named herself, but I could barely hear because I was thinking over and over what we had done. When I got home I didn't wash my hand but lay in bed with my fingers on my lips, breathing her fish odor, then I pulled a towel under the sheet and beat off.

The next night while we were walking along the breakwater with our ice cream cones she said, "I'm still bleeding." I broke into a sweat. "Maybe it will stop tomorrow," I told her. I didn't know what to do. That night in bed I tried to pray to the Virgin for help and then to Jesus and God the Father and then to the Virgin again, but all I could think of was her and then I had to beat off into the towel. She stopped bleeding and we banged each other night after night after night. One of her eyes was ever so slightly larger than the other, making her face asymmetrical and beautiful in a way I couldn't understand. It got so when I'd see her walking to meet me I'd feel a terrible weightlessness in my guts, as if I had stepped off the pier and were falling, and I'd get sick with desire. I was afraid I was going crazy and I wanted to phone my father, but I knew he'd tell me If that's the way you feel, stop seeing her. But I didn't want to stop seeing her, couldn't stop myself from seeing her, and by the end of August it was a relief to get pulled away, to go home and head off to art school.

8

AND LOOK AT ME NOW, A BALD OLD MAN WITH HAIR sprouting from his ears and a face like a truck had run over it. I have a nearsighted left eye and a farsighted right, broad hands, short fingers, a hairy torso (inside there's a polypropylene patch for hernia repair), good feet and good legs and this thing, this third thing with, alas, a prostate the size of Middlesex County. If only my friend Mike were alive, we'd have some great talks, for he was a man who understood these matters. And I should add that my eyes are full of shadows — not metaphors, but real shadows from a clotted vitreous humor.

Now let me introduce this dark-haired critic with the sweeping eyebrows and high cheekbones and that lovely narrow waist; this brainy, sensual and high-handed woman, my wife — whom everyone feels sorry for, because she married me. She claims she weighs the same as the day we married and maybe that's true, but she uses henna on her hair and a crayon on her eyebrows. "God dims our eyes as we grow older," she informs me. "It's his way of doing us a favor." Her outline has been redrawn so she now looks less like Botticelli's young *Flora* and more like Giorgione's *Profane Love*, saturated with what she knows.

What are we that we should be so mindful of these things? Half egg and half tadpole, that's us—at our best we're like those Atlantic salmon we saw at dawn, leaping against the falls on the Connecticut River. We marveled at their power to hurl themselves skyward against that falling tonnage, but it was sad to come upon those same old fish above the falls, in the limpid pools and shallows where they lay emptied, dying. I've felt that way after the children have returned and run off again to their distant worlds, when the house has grown calm once more and I'm alone in the clear silence with nothing to do, moving these old fins now and then to steady myself.

9

I ENROLLED IN THE SCHOOL OF THE MUSEUM OF FINE Arts in Boston. My uncle Nicolo, knowing my love of drawing, yet believing in mathematics, gave me a book called *Descriptive Geometry*, a sorcerer's manual of graceful solids —hyperbolic paraboloids, helicoides, volutes—and stereoscopic projections which, when made properly, would pop up from the page and hang in mid air. When I finished that book he quickly gave me another on the geometry of René Descartes, showing how to pack the long trajectory of a falling star into the nutshell of a quadratic equation. "Descartes? *René Descartes?*" uncle Zitti cried. "Descartes is another French blockhead!" For Zitti despised everything French and believed that the few *Francesi* he did admire, such as Montaigne or Napoleon, were really Italian. But uncle Nicolo was already pressing me to read *An Introduction to the Calculus*, a cabalistic book whose pages were covered with beautiful symbols—sigmas and deltas, arrows, lazy infinity signs and tall, graceful summations. "That's no way to prepare for life," uncle Zitti muttered, frowning at the group of wooden balls that lay on the bocce court like a diagram of planetary motion.

"The realities of the world are reflected in words, in literature," said Zitti. He held a bocce ball at arms length and squinted along the top of it toward the little ball, the *pallino*, which lay off to one side about half way down the powdery gray gravel court. He yanked his arm back, ran two steps forward and shot underhand with a leap, hurling the ball so vigorously that it caromed off a side board and whizzed past the pallino. He cursed softly, the same as when he played horseshoes down the Cape.

"You need geometry, you'd do better," Nicolo told him, mopping a squared handkerchief across the sweaty tanned dome of his bald head.

"Listen," Zitti confided to me. "I'll give you a reading list. A good list. Short but good. It will be based on my method, very practical."

My uncle's first list began with Emily Dickinson, followed immediately by John Locke and Henri Stendhal ("Stendhal was essentially Italian and had a miserable childhood because he was born in France," he informed me) and it concluded with Ovid's *Metamorphoses*. I've kept all twenty of his neat handwritten lists and I owe my liberal education to him.

One warm autumn day uncle Zitti and I were in the field back of the big old house to watch uncle Mercurio and Coral, his wife, take turns with the bird gun. I told Zitti I thought the books he had me read weren't practical at all. "Oh, yes. Very practical. Later in life. You'll see." We watched as Mercurio scaled an old dinner plate high into the air—Coral fired BOOM and the plate went SMASH, exploding to bits. Uncle Nicolo waved vigorously to Coral to put the gun down, calling out to her, "They don't allow shooting in town anymore! Too many houses! Too many people!" Mercurio scaled another dish up over the field and Coral blew it to pieces. "You'll see," Zitti told me. "The unexamined life isn't worth living," he added, quoting one of his favorite philosophers.

But I was living the unexamined life and enjoying it hugely.

I found outdoor jobs every summer and indoor work in winter, so I bolted from home and rented a room in Back Bay, within walking distance of my friends and the Museum School, for we were making art and talking about it deep into the night over coffee and lousy French cigarettes at the Commonwealth Cafeteria where the avenue was like a boulevard and the buildings had mansard roofs and that was our Paris.

Furthermore, I had met a young woman named Sophia, a student across the river in Cambridge, and had begun to go out with her. I hadn't had much success with women, which isn't surprising since I wasn't able to separate my hunger for flesh from my craving to paint and was always confusing what I wanted to do. In fact, I had already spent a couple of drizzly afternoons trudging back and forth across the long bridge over the Charles, trying to nerve myself for a vault over the rail, in despair over some woman or my prospects for fame, I never knew which. I was mad for paint and it didn't matter to me whether it was oil or acrylic, so long as I could get the color I wanted, and I could draw with a crayon, a brush or my own stiffened prick, as I learned when I was so foolish as to dip it in ink and swab it on the wall, and that May one of my paintings won a prize and I got into a group show at the Upstairs Gallery in Boston just before the little place went broke.

10

ONE DAY I WROTE A LIST OF THE WOMEN I HAD made love to, wrote it not from stupid vanity but in despair and madness, for I was crazed with influenza, my head banging like a loose door when I lifted it from the pillow—lying there sweaty and unshaven and rank, I made the list to show myself that although I was nobody and might die in that stinking loft at least I had been loved by these women. I'm sure you would have done something finer and more spiritual for solace, but I was me at twenty-five and my brains were cooking in my skull: when my friend Max brought me a bag of food I snatched the drinking glass from my bedside table and threw it at him, and when he said, *Hey! Stop that!* I grabbed the aspirin bottle and hurled it at his head, which it grazed before exploding against the wall. When the list of women turned up a few years later at the bottom of a paintbox I tossed it out, but then added a few more names and tucked it away again, because I didn't want to be the kind of man who fucks and forgets, and long after I was married I came across it rewritten and folded as a bookmark in an old sketchbook, so I kept it. Yesterday I searched all over the place and couldn't find it, shook out every mildewed sketchbook and portfolio, and this morning I tried to recompose the list and was embarrassed to find that I had lost the names of some of those women or remembered only a nickname, and when I thought I had gathered everyone, two others turned up to remind me that there might be more I had forgotten. I hadn't thought of those young women for forty years and recalling them made me slump in my chair and grow melancholy, and I don't know why, because all I remembered was how trusting we were with each other and that's nothing to be sad about.

True, I did meet one or two cold bitches who would turn a man's heart inside out just to see what it contained, and I knew it instantly afterward, while still on my knees, pulling out and panting, "*What am I doing here?*" I confess I've been mostly fortunate, for God gave me this thing—this young prick, this old whatever, call it what you want—that knows when to hang back out of shyness, and shy privates have rescued me where my brains have often failed. But the women I remember best were good-natured and far more patient than I, which reminds me that I want to apologize to them, finally, for my moodiness, my endless ranting about galleries, for implying that a bad time in bed was never my fault, for my sullen silences, for my throwing paints and brushes, smashing furniture, slamming doors, for destroying someone else's books or stealing their cigarettes or underwear, for my waking a body at three in the morning just to talk, and a hundred other stupidities.

Now let me go back to when I was a student, grinding and polishing my talent till it was bright as the blade of an ax. In Boston one winter day I ran into the girl from Newburyport, the one I had known in the summer, now buttoned up in a long black coat with a black beret pulled down to her ears. We stood on the arctic pavement, stamping our feet and beating our arms to keep warm, and I learned she was in her first year at Boston University and planned to major in comparative literature, a subject in which she could use her French, and she liked living in Boston. I felt so many different ways at once and I can't recall what I said. Afterward, as I was trotting away, I thought it would be nice to phone her and go out for a cup of coffee and a longer talk and I don't recall why it never happened.

Of course, by then I was going around with Sophia and that would have been reason enough. I wish I could give you Sophia as she was then, her looks and also her talk, for she had a way of talking that dazzled me like acrobatics. She enjoyed words, including dirty ones, the way another woman might enjoy oranges or cherries, and when we made love it was mostly what she said that brought me to a frenzy. She claimed to like the way I said whatever I was feeling—"I love you because you're so rash," she told me—but there were feelings I didn't have words for and whenever I tried to tell her about those things she would say, "If you don't have the word for it, you don't really have it." More than once I secretly had to look up a word she had used. One night after she had gone home I cut up my dictionary, took a scissors and cut out word after word until the pages were in shreds, then in a flush of embarrassment I stuffed them back into the book. The next time she said, "If you can't say it, you can't have it," we were naked, kneeling face to face on my bed. I wrestled her onto her stomach, a position she never liked, and while she thrashed and began cursing me I grabbed the dictionary from the bed table and shook it open over her so words swirled down in a blizzard, making a word-drift in the saddle of her beautiful back.

I saw the girl from Newburyport two years later at a big party. By then Sophia and I had broken up or, to be precise, Sophia had dumped me after some lapses on my part, after scolding me every other month, calling me a truant and a delinquent because I had gotten involved with other women, mostly during those times when Sophia said we should lead more independent lives. The party was in the West End, the old brick West End that used to be, for the neighborhood no longer exists, the people thrown out and their homes demolished to make way for the rich; anyway, the West End, the rooms small and so crowded it took me half an hour to edge into the kitchen and that's where I bumped into the Newburyport girl again, and we said *Oh!* and *Hi!* and I felt the same confusion as before. I put a few chunks of ice in my drink and asked if I could get her something. "Fill it with gin," she said cheerfully, holding out her glass. "Gin and what?" I asked. "Just gin," she said simply. We went out the kitchen door and sat sweating on the back steps under a hot copper sunset. She said she was still at Boston University, but was now majoring in art history with a minor in French and hoped to go to Paris next summer. She was waitressing this summer. I said I had finally finished at the Museum School, was working as a carpenter and waiting to get drafted. I wanted to talk about Sophia but decided against it, so we sat there not talking, just looking at the fading sky and the wilted flowers. She lit a cigarette.

"Ka-gi-gi," I said. "Just now I remembered your Indian name, the Algonquin name you named yourself. Ka-gi-gi, the raven."

She looked at me. There was a fine glaze of sweat beneath her eyes, like when we made love that first summer, and for a moment I thought I could smell her skin, which started a little panic in me. She let the smoke drift from her mouth and she said, "I was fourteen. I hated my real name."

"You have a beautiful name."

"Yes? Well, I didn't think so at the time."

"Did you come with somebody tonight?" I had come alone and thought maybe she, too, was single this evening and would leave with me.

"He's inside."

"You shouldn't drink that way," I told her, more sharply than I intended.

"What way?"

"You shouldn't drink so much gin so fast."

Abruptly she went and poured her glass into the flower bed and came back to sit closer beside me on the steps, where we exchanged phone numbers, and for a time that evening I kept her in sight, attempting to figure out who she was with, and I even trailed her out to the garden and listened to her throwing up in the dark, after which I began talking to a hefty young woman in a black sun dress, a badly drawn version of Sophia, and I ended up at her place. I was drafted that fall, did my Basic Training at Fort Dix and was soon discharged because of allergies which disappeared when I became a civilian again.

I spent the next six months in New York, painting and meeting people (Max, Karen, Sue, and Wilson, but especially Max—good guy, good painter), then returned to Boston and met Odine, a tall woman with swan-white skin. By then I was achieving great things in abstract expressionism and psychotherapy, I thought, and Odine didn't lecture me about other women, didn't call me names the way Sophia had, but was nonjudgmental and told me I was *sick* and, she explained, I was *sick* because I had started life as a foundling and it was my insecurity about who I was that compelled me to seek out women, for under the guise of hunting for a fresh bedmate I was really searching for my mother. And her diagnosis was probably right, I thought, because I had all the symptoms, but my having this ailment didn't bother Odine and I was grateful for that.

Odine had begun an M.A. in contemporary philosophy, a

densely mathematical matter, so one night she came over to tell me about Carl Friedrich Gauss (1777–1855) and his thoughts on the intrinsic geometry of surfaces, a subject I found much more interesting than the usual discussion of our relationship. Gauss could calculate the curvature of a surface by drawing a triangle on it and measuring the interior angles and he had actually used the technique in his great land survey of Germany. To test this I tore off Odine's silk jersey, grabbed a black crayon and drew the triangle ABC with its apex (A) at the top of Odine's long spine and its base (BC) running from her left hip bone to her tenth right rib, but before I could make a good survey she had rolled over and pulled me in, and by the time that business was over the phone was ringing. It was Ka-gi-gi, the raven, the girl from Newburyport, saying I'm at the airport. Can I come over? I just got in from Paris and all I want to do is sleep. —Or do you have someone there? (I waved to Odine who had finished brushing her hair and was going out the door.) "No, that's fine," I said.

Her face was thinner than I had remembered and the faintly asymmetrical sea-green eyes were darker. I told her I'd sleep on the floor and she could take the bed. She smiled and said, "Don't be crazy. And I wouldn't impose on you, but you're the only person I know who still lives around here."

"How's Paris?" I asked.

"Paris is great unless you discover you're pregnant right away. That's why I came back. And now, actually, I'm afraid to go home. I mean, I don't want to be a problem to my poor parents. I don't know what I'm going to do. And I suppose I'll wind up waitressing again. —My head is throbbing from those damn engines," she added, just before she drifted to sleep on a couple of folded blankets, her head pillowed on her bunched-up raincoat.

The next morning when I woke up she was at the window, gazing down at the street. I made the coffee, poured her a cup, and did all the talking, for she was amazingly quiet and didn't say a word, just smoked her cigarette and didn't touch her coffee. "I began having these cramps in Paris and now I'm bleeding," she said at last, a quaver coming into her voice. Her eyes began to glisten and fill, brimming. I ran down to the street for a cab, went with her to the emergency room where a doctor said it was a miscarriage, and I stayed with her until a nurse took her away. I visited her in the hospital the next day but she was sleeping, a hospital ID bracelet around her wrist, so I just stood there and watched her, and grew sad remembering how seven years earlier I had been wild about her, and now I felt only this hollow in my chest and even when I took a deep breath the hollow didn't fill. I came back the next day and we talked, but not much, and the following afternoon she went home to Newburyport. That September I sent her an invitation to a show I was in, care of her parents' address in Newburyport, but she didn't answer or turn up at the gallery and I supposed she had gone back to Paris.

I was laboring on abstractions during those years, didn't do any figurative work and have no paintings of Odine from that time, which is too bad because she had an interesting body, formal and precise and clearly articulated, her breasts high and rather flat, sweetly tipped, and her skin so white and inviting that I sometimes took a grease pencil to it and drew the bones and musculature that lay beneath the surface. I always liked Odine and I hope she's okay and doing well in this world, and if she reads this I want to say Thank you for being so patient and letting me learn anatomy with you. Later that fall she went to Stanford to continue her studies and I to New York to hook up with some friends, Max among them.

The first deKoonings I had seen were at the Museum School in 1953 and I had thought, Oh, wow, I can do that. Now in the city we tried to meet those painters and though we visited a lot of galleries we never connected with important people, and a couple of times I even went to the Cedar, which was supposed to be a great place for that crowd to drink and pick up a quick fuck, but I could never drink much or pick up a woman in a bar. I had hoped to get my work looked at by other painters and maybe by a gallery or a buyer, but after a few months I ran out of money and took a part-time job illustrating manuals and catalogs for a hardware company which, I told myself, was a good way to learn graphical precision and discipline, but it was soul-destroying work and I longed to be outdoors pulling lobster pots or stacking crates of fish, and though I had friends I felt lonely much of the time and used to press myself into the corner of my room to feel the walls embrace me while I wept.

I got sick and sicker: my head throbbed, my guts felt like they had been pulled inside out, I couldn't stand up at the washbowl or walk but had to crawl back to bed. Two days later my friend Max came by, took one look and came back with a bag of food, which is when I threw the drinking glass at him and tried to brain him with the aspirin bottle. Another afternoon he came around with a bottle of ginger ale and a box of crackers and he had with him a woman named Bena who returned alone the next day—simply to cook me a meal, she said. Bena was a large but firmly built woman— "Statuesque, Renato. The word you're looking for is statuesque," she said, seating herself slowly on the margin of my bed—with dark hair and dark eyes. Maybe she would have looked overweight if she had gained a pound here or there, but she never added even an ounce and remained properly large-bodied, larger than any woman I had known. When I had taken the straps of her slip from her shoulders, had rumpled the bodice down to her waist and had begun to push it further down, she stretched and smiled and murmured, "No. It can't get past my hips. It comes off the other way. Over my head—" and indeed it did. Even after I left the flu behind, got off my bed and began to get around, Bena insisted on coming over to cook a meal again and again. She didn't care for my drawings of some young women I had been going with a few months earlier—"Scrawny. Malnourished," she called them—but she liked my abstractions, talked about them intelligently, and also said she believed that my desire to paint was an unconscious stratagem, a way for me to remain a child forever and avoid adult responsibilities and, unwittingly, to destroy myself. "You like to draw pictures. You want to play with colors and shapes forever." She didn't think any the less of me for this, quite the contrary. "I admire you. Artists are eternally young," she told me one evening while I watched her unpin her hair and remove her blouse. "People have known this for a long time. Artists are children. They are children in their delight at the world and in their spontaneous creativity," she said, reaching behind her back to unhook her bra. "And what's important is to keep them from self-destructive tantrums." Her breasts had the largest and darkest aureoles I had ever seen.

Bena used to come by my place after her shift at Beth Israel where she worked as a dietician, and I'm sure her potato pancakes, her matzoh balls and all that chicken soup helped me get stronger. I was sorry she had that lunatic theory about artists being happy children, spontaneously drawing pictures and coloring inside the lines, because other than that she made sense, mostly. I hadn't gotten my full weight back, but I felt good and my mind was clear, very clear. I knew I wasn't destroying myself, knew also that the New York art business was rotting my soul and making me sick and I knew it would be good for me to leave. So, early one morning, before Bena arrived, I packed everything I wanted into my suitcase, broke up all my paintings and crammed them into the huge metal drum I used for a trash barrel, then I poured kerosene into the drum and set it on fire. It made a surprising lot of black smoke, so I shoved the drum over to the window and pushed open all the window vents. The flames crept up into the smoke and the ceiling began to blacken. I poked into the barrel with a broomstick, hooked one of the flaming canvasses and pitched it out the open window, then pitched out another and another and so on, letting them sail this way and that down to Greene Street. It was exhilarating.

"Hey, Renato!" somebody said, and she wasn't in Newburyport or Paris but here in my doorway.

"I thought you were going to Paris!" I said.

"I'm leaving tomorrow. What are you doing?"

"I'm getting rid of some rotten sick bad paintings."

She gave me a quick smile. "I was on the sidewalk hunting for your address when these pieces of fire began to fall out of the sky. I thought it might be you."

"Want to go out for breakfast?" I asked her.

She said yes, so I picked up my suitcase and my paintbox and we walked down to the street where she waved off some athletic guy in a chrome yellow sports car. I asked who he was and she said "Just a friend who gave me a ride down here. Let's eat I'm starved." We ate breakfast in a deli and I asked what had she been doing for the past nine months and she said she'd been waitressing around Newburyport and now she was going back to Paris to study art history. Her father had been ailing but he was better now. I was sorry to hear about her father whom I remembered only as a tall man who loved to grow flowers. I told her I was sick of New York and was leaving it for good, and that I planned to go home for a few weeks, then go to Cape Ann where my aunt Gina had a café and I'd work outdoors and not paint for a while. I started to tell her all sorts of things I had been brooding about, but I broke off for fear of boring her. "I have your parents' address," she said. "And here's where I'll be staying when I get to Paris." She wrote it on a paper napkin and slid it across the table to me.

"I don't know how to write letters very well," I told her, stuffing the napkin into my breast pocket.

"Send me drawings," she said.

11

I SAVED HER LETTERS AND HAVE THEM STILL, DOZENS OF tissue paper pages covered with type which varies in hue from clotted black to foggy gray, lots of words xxxxxed out and others scribbled in the margin with long inky tails pointing to where they belong. In her first letter she wrote about the Parisian neighborhood where she was living, about her rooms and her roommate and the view outside the window and she signed with the name she had hated as a kid, Alba. *Alba is the ancient Celtic name for Scotland which is where my parents came from*, she added. I replied with a plain, unshaded line drawing of my bedroom and the window that looked into the old maple tree, and I wrote around the margin *Alba means dawn in Italian and I've always liked your name and my last name isn't Stellamare it's Stillamare*. Her next letter was about her classes at the institute and about her roommate, Dolores, known as D, and she concluded by saying that she had always thought my name was Stellamare because that would mean star-of-the-sea, which was a beautiful image and, frankly, Stillamare looked like a misspelling to her. I made a line drawing of my father's shop front, Stillamare's Cut Stone & Tile Company, and on the back I wrote that *stilla* was the Latin word for drop, like a raindrop, and Stillamare means drop-of-the-sea, and as a kid I had been called Trin, which was short for Trinacria, which is the ancient name for Sicily. I left out the part about my being found swaddled and wrapped, one of the wrappers being a cheap kerchief which had a map of Sicily printed on it. Alba's letters continued to arrive at two- and three-week intervals, and I learned more about her studies for the "doctorat," which wasn't a doctorate but a master's degree, about her roommate D, and about a scruffy bookstore near Notre Dame with an espresso machine at the back. The bookstore was a meeting place for all sorts of down-and-out artists and poets, including a scornful writer from England who sounded bogus to me. The writer was forty years old, a savage intellectual who held all social conventions in contempt, and although I wasn't surprised when Alba moved in with him I was sore at her and then mad at myself for feeling that way and grateful that I didn't have to write anything but could send an old block print of my coffee mug and overflowing ashtray.

I talked my brother Bart into coming with me for a weekend visit to Montreal, just so I could listen to people speaking French and pretend I was in Paris. The city was made of gray stone with fancy iron-work stairways going up ten or twelve feet to the front door, because of the deep winter snows, we figured, and there were small green parks and streets with cafés with tables set out on the sidewalk, and we had a great time. Two weeks later I rode a train back to Montreal, rented a room, and looked up a old man named Boisvert, a paper-maker I had known at the Museum School, and through him I met some other people who worked with handmade paper and among them a young woman named Denise. Denise invited me to a party where everyone talked politics, mostly about how to throw out the British and establish a country where everyone was French, and afterward she took me for a walk around the old quarter and then back to her room. She gave me her lighted cigarette to hold, then crossed her arms and grasped the hem of her jersey and started to pull it up. I said *Wait!* and told her I was only visiting Montreal, only for a couple of weeks. She had paused and now she smiled, saying "C'est bon cela," and pulled the jersey off. Denise had reddish gold hair and a wonderfully compact athletic body which she enjoyed, the same as she enjoyed making paper or arguing politics. I stayed in Montreal a few weeks and learned something more about paper-making, but when the cafés folded their umbrellas and pulled in their chairs I decided to head homeward. Denise came with me as far as the sidewalk outside the train station where we hugged and said goodbye, then she turned away and I went inside and that was the last I saw of her for many years. Every decade or so I find anew my old sketches of Denise, including a surprisingly vivid one I did with a ballpoint pen on a sheet of stiff cream-colored paper: Denise standing with her back to me, dressed but barefoot, combing her hair. I hope she's alive and well: she never minded if our love-making was imperfect, or if I was stupid about Quebec politics, or if I talked too much about Alba.

I spent the winter on Cape Ann, living at my aunt Gina's. This was after her affair with my cousin Nick and before she met the man she eventually married. Nick never guessed that we knew about him and Gina, but Gina had figured it out, Gina knew, and once when we were dancing at a jukebox she asked me, "What do they say about me?" I played dumb, but she said, "You know what I'm talking about." So I told her, "They say Nick had a crush on you and they wish you'd go get married to somebody." The music had stopped and Gina lit a cigarette, took a flake of tobacco from her tongue, saying, "They want me to marry a professor or a banker or someone and can you see me doing that?" and we both laughed. That winter I painted her café walls and fixed the wobbly chairs and tables, and I made some big ink drawings with a brush, including a few of Gina and my cousin Arianne, and one large painting of the harbor from the café terrace. When I wasn't working I walked up and down the steep streets of Gloucester (which wasn't the pretty place it is now with those new brick walks and brass historical markers, but was a busy crowd of trawlers, draggers, screaming gulls, chopped ice, fish —the whole town smelled of fish) and every so often I'd ride the train to Boston to hook up with my friend Bill Boyle or Dave Katz or Peter Constantine or all three together.

By the time spring arrived we had made plans to head north up the coast, working odd jobs and painting along the way, but Boyle got falling down drunk and broke his wrist, and Katz panicked at the prospect of living outside a city, so in the end it was just Costas and me. It wasn't so easy to find odd jobs and it turned out that whenever we did work three or four days we earned barely enough money to cover our expenses for the next two, so we quit working and paid our way up to Boothbay Harbor, the place where Robert Henri and his crew had made some good paintings in the Twenties and Thirties. We never did reach Monhegan Island, but Costas produced some good paintings, whereas I merely doodled in my sketchbook or sat on a huge rock and stared out to sea, like a stupid gull hoping to hatch something from the rock I was sitting on. We went broke in mid-July and decided to hitchhike down Route 1 toward Boston, which we did, catching one ride from Boothbay Harbor to Portland, and another from Portland to the Massachusetts line, and there we rented a sweltering room over a restaurant kitchen for the night. Costas went to sleep while I sat in a chair by the open window and smoked and brooded, for it had become clear to me that I had no life to go back to, that there was nothing left for me to do at my aunt Gina's café, and nothing for me at all in my old room at home, no woman I wanted and nothing I wanted to paint. I thought how I had painted so many canvases and had fucked so many woman and how it all added up to nothing. The next morning we went out to Route 1 together and I hung around talking with Costas until he caught a ride to Boston, then I walked back to the restaurant and talked the owner into hiring me to patch up the murals on the dining room walls.

The restaurant, Lorette's Farm, was an old rambling structure of joined buildings that stretched back from the road with each succeeding roof down lower than the one before, like an extended telescope. The dining room occupied the first floor front, and Mrs Lorette plus her daughter lived on the second floor, after which came the kitchen with my attic room, followed by the pantry, the dressing room for waitresses, and storage sheds and so on. The dining-room murals, which depicted workers along the Merrimack River, had been painted directly onto the finished plaster twenty years ago and had been washed down with soap and water every season thereafter, so the paint was now half scrubbed away and, to speak politely, they had never been beautiful, but they did reflect the civic esthetics of the 1930s, the same as those WPA murals in post offices around the country, and I was sorry years later when the place burned to the ground.

I worked on the murals only at night, after the dining room

had closed, and then only for a few hours at a stretch, so that the paint odors wouldn't drive off customers, and during the day I sat by the window in my stifling room and read one of the books I found up there, Beauparlant's *History of Quebec*, or I lay naked on the cot and dozed, or tried to, for on bright days the room became an oven and I couldn't sleep until after the sun had gone down. My boss, Mrs Avril Lorette, was a strong woman with a handsome face seemingly drawn with black lithograph crayon and then redrawn and overdrawn, so that all the lines were bolder, the eyebrows and lashes thicker and the shading darker, even producing a duskiness above her upper lip. Her energetic daughter Nancy was seventeen, an earlier version of her mother, a lighter print, as the art critics say, with white highlights produced by the confectioners sugar she used on those pastries which she made each morning— "Before the busybody spies are up," she told me, laughing—a time when we could do what we wanted, so we did, morning upon morning, for we both had good healthy appetites. At ten each night Mrs Lorette would rap briskly on my door to wake me just when my room was getting cool enough to sleep in, and if I didn't promptly pull on my pants and go to the door she would come in and shake my shoulder, her hands scented with the blissfully cool odors of carrot greens, celery, fennel and apple. If I didn't open my eyes she would lightly scratch the nape of my neck, and if I still refused to open my eyes she'd pat my bare behind, singing "Up, up! Get yourself *up*," and she'd give it a sharp little whack. So one thing led to another in a chain of logical entailment, just as the old philosophers promised they would, and I wound up doing with Mrs Lorette what she expected me to do, the same as I did with Nancy.

By the end of August I was about finished with the mural and fatigued by what you might call my duties to the Lorettes, and I thought it would be best for me if I just slipped away without elaborate good-byes, so one morning I crammed my shirts, socks and underwear into my paintbox and quietly folded my easel. I ducked from my room through a small door which opened into the low attic over the pantry and I crept cautiously toward the bright square window at the end of the crawl-space over the attached shed. I was creeping along a rafter, dragging my easel and paintbox when unwittingly I set my knee on a rotted timber and plunged through the ceiling into the room below. I staggered around in a rain of crumbling plaster, splintered lath and two-hundred-year-old dust, and bumped into Alba. "*Renato!*" she cried.

"I thought you were in *Paris!*" I said.

"I got back a month ago and began working here last week. What are you doing?" she asked, brushing plaster bits from my shoulders.

"Murals. But right now I'm running away," I said, grappling with my easel and paintbox.

The Lorettes' voices came from an upstairs room, shouting at each other.

"You're running away from Mrs Lorette?"

"Her, too."

"From Nancy Lorette? From both?"

"Not my fault. It's complicated," I said.

"You mean you—" Alba had begun to laugh. "With both of them? I'll bet it's complicated."

"Got to get going," I said, briskly.

She gave me a quick smile. "You can take Jack's car."

"Who's Jack?"

"He is," Alba said, nodding toward a thick-necked athlete in a red-striped jersey who came stumbling through the doorway with a large, heavy sack on his shoulder. "Give him the keys, Jack."

We heard Mrs Lorette louder now, shouting in my room over the kitchen and kicking my bed to pieces. Jack slid the sack from his giant shoulder with a grunt, and tossed me the car keys. "The Chevy pickup," he said, wiping his neck with a handkerchief. "Don't let it idle too slow, it'll stall."

"Leave it across the river at the Union Garage," Alba told me, squeezing my arm. "Now go. Quick!"

Back in Boston I found a fair size place, a room with a view of the Charles River in slices between the other buildings. Some hours the river was gray and other hours it was yellowish or green and some times it was so blue you wanted to dunk your brush in it and slap it all over everything. I had been invited to participate in a group show in Cambridge and when I brought them my stuff I saw that the show was going to be good and that my work looked especially strong. I invited Alba to the opening and she came. I had never seen her dressed in style before and had never even thought of her that way, but here she was walking toward me in a suit— trim jacket, the blazing white of her throat and the stiff rise of her breasts, tight skirt—her hair in a thick glossy French twist, silver button earrings, flashy bracelets and high heels. It was a satisfying crowd and I met the other painters as well as the owner of a gallery in Boston and some brainy people from Cambridge. I introduced Alba to my father and mother and Bart, then afterward we five went to a Greek restaurant to celebrate and when dinner broke up they drove off, after everybody had hugged everybody, leaving Alba and me on the sidewalk.

I felt terrific. We walked along the river and talked of what we had been doing for the past nine years, walked until Alba's high-heel shoes hurt and she paused, took off her shoes, and we walked some more, then stood with our elbows on the guard rail above the silent, flickering black water and were still talking when the street lamps snuffed out, for by then the sky was milky blue and the scumble on the far side of the river became the uneven brick heap of Boston with the hill and the small gold dome of the State House, the thin tower of the Custom House (for it was still the old city of 1890), and the big chunk of the Hancock, light spilling between the low buildings and through the fog onto the motionless water. We just stood there looking at the silence and light, I don't know how long. "Do you ever think about that summer?" Alba asked.

"It was crazy. We were out of our minds," I said, still looking across the water.

"I was a kid. I thought it was supposed to be that way."

We were standing side by side at the guard rail and when our arms brushed I turned and found she was watching me, waiting. Her face was bare again the way it had been years ago and I could see all there was to see, one eye almost invisibly larger than the other, the dark sea-green irises flecked with uneven rays of lighter green and blue, the high contour of her cheek, the nakedness of her lips, and I got light-headed and kissed her mouth and had to grab the rail to keep from plunging. "I just want to paint, that's all I want to do now," I said.

"Anyway, I'm going to Paris—" she began.

"What!"

"—in two weeks. A formality, but I really want that doctorat."

I felt very strange, almost dizzy. We began to walk across the Mass Avenue bridge in the early morning light, the sky growing ever more spacious as we approached the middle of that long, flat span, all shadows evaporating from the air and the river brightening. My eyes weren't right and I couldn't figure out what was happening, except that the far end of the bridge seemed to be going farther and farther off, so when a cab came along I flagged it down and we rode the rest of the way to my place. As I opened the door to let her in I saw how stark the room was, but Alba said, "Oh, I *like* this."

She was looking at the low wall I had hammered together, just plywood and two-by-fours with my bed and books on this side, the other side all workspace. "The building's condemned, so the rent's low, is why I live here," I explained.

"What a terrific view," she said, walking to the windows that looked between the tenements and across the river to Cambridge. There was a dark streak on one of her legs where her stocking had a run in it from walking without shoes, the same as the mud on her leg the first day I saw her. I followed the stocking up to where it must be attached to her garter belt, searching for any shadow on her skirt which would show where a strap or clip pressed into her flesh. She had begun to walk slowly about, looking at the paintings that leaned against this chair, the table, that other chair, the stepladder, the paintings that stood this way and that way all around the room. She said, "I love being here. All the colors. And these are so much bigger than the ones at the exhibit. I—" and she broke off as I had put my hands inside the lapels of her jacket to wrench it open, so the silver button leapt off and hit the floor, ringing like a bell, and I yanked the jacket down her arms and pulled it off, and by then we were whispering so swiftly not even our guardian angels could have heard. I tore off my shirt, unbuckled my pants and lifted out just as she stepped from the fallen circle of her skirt. She started to unfasten a garter clip, saying, "Let me take this damned—" but I grabbed her away.

"Do you believe in God?" she asked afterward. We were naked on our hands and knees, looking under the bed for her missing button. I told her I hadn't made up my mind about that. She said, "I mean, is life just things bumping into other things and everything happening accidentally? Because if it is, then how did we meet and keep on meeting? If it's all just atoms banging into other atoms it doesn't make sense. But I feel it must make sense." All I knew was that I wanted to have her for the rest of my life. "There must be a meaning— ah!" she cried, holding up the button. She got to her feet and shook her head vigorously to untangle her hair, then began to pull a comb through it, which was a pleasure to watch, remembering how she used to rake her fingers through that mop to catch out the straw after we had laid in the field up back of her house. "I was only fifteen," she said, as if I had spoken.

"Fourteen, Ka-gi-gi, you were still fourteen."

"I should get dressed. And I should phone Susan and tell her where I am. Where do you keep your phone?"

"I missed a few payments and they shut it off."

I pulled on my pants, set a pot of coffee on the hot-plate, then broke open an English muffin and dropped it into the toaster for breakfast. Alba had put on her skirt and jacket and was gathering up her loose stockings and the garter belt and bra. "Home," she said, looking around, smiling. "Have I already said I like this place?" she asked. "I clean every week. It's clean junk," I assured her. We had another cup of coffee and a cigarette, then lay on the bed facing each other so I was able to look at her, look at her hair or her mouth or her eyes, which is one of the things I used to do with her years ago and which I had liked best, just lying with her and looking and talking or not talking, and I said, "Stay forever," and she began to speak as if she were running out of breath and at last she says, "Choose me," and I say, "I am, I do," and she shut her eyes and I kissed her shut eyes and her mouth and her trembling breasts, for her jacket had fallen open, and there was a *knock, knock* at the door and a *knock, knock, knock*. Alba sprang up, brushing her skirt smooth and clutching her jacket shut. "Pin, a safety pin, do you have a pin?" she whispered. I told her there were pins on the bureau, buckled my pants and trotted barefoot to the door. It was a man from last night at the gallery (straw-colored hair combed straight back, round face with circular eyeglasses), but I couldn't recall his name or anything else about him. "Gruenfeld," he said amiably. "We talked last night at the opening."

"Yes," I said.

"Good," he said. "Well, as you know, I—"

"God, yes! You have the gallery on Newbury Street. You said you liked the show. Now I remember."

"*Your* work. I liked *your* work. I tried to call first but the phone company claims it never heard of you and since you did say to come by any time and since I do like to make my visits on Mondays—" Then he turned and introduced me to the thin and rather bony woman who had been standing off at his side, and she shook my hand. "If we could just take a look around. Or perhaps there's a better time," he ventured.

"No, no, no! Come in, come in!"

I brought them in and there was Alba in her crisp suit and high heels, standing by the stepladder to sip her coffee, her unfastened hair shining in the sun. She carefully set the coffee cup on a step, smiled and came forward with her jacket neatly pinned shut so I could introduce her to Gruenfeld and the woman. I saw her bra and underpants trying to hide themselves under her rumpled breakfast napkin on one of the steps of the stepladder. "We'll just look around," Gruenfeld said cheerfully. Alba returned to her coffee and I sat on a stool and we watched Gruenfeld and the woman move slowly from canvas to canvas, his partner silent and Gruenfeld saying only *This is interesting* or *This is what I mean* or *Look at this* until twenty-five minutes had passed, after which he came over and took out a miniature notebook, wrote his gallery's address and phone number, tore out the page and gave it to me, saying I should make an appointment to have lunch with him and talk about my future, because he wanted to give me a show, then I walked them to the door where we shook hands and they left.

I turned around and said, "I'm a painter," for I had never known for sure, and Alba said, "I knew it all along."

She was hanging her jacket neatly over the back of a chair and her breasts shone in the sun, and now she unfastened her skirt and of course she had nothing on underneath. I threw off my clothes and pulled her down onto a warm blanket of sunshine so I could look even more, because her flesh had no shadows but only variations of light, light everywhere, shifting from milky white to cream to pale coffee to warm bread color, and that thick dark whorled mass of secret hair, uneven patches of color on her cheeks and her eyes glistening from the heat of her own flesh, her body so naked and incandescent that I must look again and again and again, filled with the power and exhilaration of seeing everything at once.

Alba went back to her place that afternoon and returned the next morning with a small suitcase and two boxes of books. I painted through fall and winter, though sometimes we fooled around, as when we smeared ourselves with paint and rolled us in big sheets of Japanese paper to print our own version of gyotaku, or when I cast a papier mâché bowl from Alba's rear, or painted the world's hemispheres on her breasts, or dunked my brainless prick in ink and drew on her back, but mostly I painted and painted better then ever, better than anyone else, had a successful show at Gruenfeld's gallery on Newbury Street and, when our building had to be demolished, we got married and went to France and there Alba picked up her doctorat (a fancy page of paper that they signed and tore from a book, like a check) and thence to Italy and Sicily and back to France, returning to the States in time to set up my first exhibit in New York. Oh, Alba, *this* Alba, *my* Alba.

PART TWO

The Summer of my Seventieth Year, in which there are Unpredictable Complications, One Exhibit, & Many Pregnancies

12

THAT WAS THEN, THIS IS NOW. SHE LIVES ON HER side of the river, I live on mine. Our kids have grown up and left home, the old cat has died and joined the dog, we've sold off the house and now we're living happily ever after, Alba and me, for I'm here in Boston with my own bed, three easels and five hundred paintings, while Alba is in Cambridge with everything else. We didn't plan it this way; we never had the leisure to plan anything in our lives. It just happened that when my friend Mike Bruno died I quit teaching and began to spend more time painting in my studio and it grew easy for me to sleep there because that way I'd be where I wanted to be when I woke up. Our children disapproved, said we were getting silly in our old age and complained that they didn't know where to send their letters home. They wanted us to stay put in the worn-out old house where they had grown up, us to keep watch over their forgotten school prizes and sports trophies while they explored the globe for adventures.

Skye, our daughter, who attended three different graduate schools and then dropped out to marry a nomadic anthropologist, likes to think of herself as a settled homebody who grows vegetables, bakes bread and raises children and, indeed, she has four children, but in the last decade they've trooped through seven different countries, haven't stayed at the same address two years in a row, and won't so long as her husband can find a grant or fellowship to keep them in rags someplace else. Brizio, our son, who has weighed dark matter at the Harvard astrophysics lab and untangled string theory at Stanford, this prince among intellectuals has disguised himself as a carpenter working for a solar house company and is living with a daft young woman who grows herbs for a living. And Astrid, the comet in our planetary family, Astrid, who liked to call herself Galaxy, started out as a singer in a rock band, then married a guitarist but had the marriage annulled seven days later so as to take up fashion modeling, made a lot of money at modeling but quit to keep house for a widowed photographer, a sexy sexagenarian from whom she learned all sorts of things, even photography, and from whom she parted amicably to become a photographer herself, at which she was quite good, and later she became a movie publicist, moved in with a very young cinematographer and became a video director in advertising, then broke up with the boy cinematographer and now has her own business as a publicist-producer-director of low budget-documentaries. Those are the sedate children I've scandalized by moving into my studio.

When Mike Bruno pitched over and died he left a great empty room in my heart, actually a dozen messy rooms. That round, jovial man had been my best friend for thirty and more years. He had a sunny temperament dappled with melancholy, had huge appetites, a lavish mind, a dozen deep interests and a hundred flaws. He knew more about the history of art than anyone anywhere and could recall in detail every painting he had ever seen. He loved cookery and women and talk—God, how he loved to talk!—but above all he loved to look at paintings. I walked into the Newbury Street gallery where my first exhibit was still fresh on the walls and saw that restless soul looking at one of my paintings, shifting from foot to foot, opening and closing his fists, shaking his head, then he turned to me and began to talk about the work, remarking on this detail and that brush work and this passage and that color, sweeping his hand this way and that across the canvas as he lectured. He saw it all, he liked it. I told him I had painted it. "Good! Good! I'm Michael Bruno. Let's get lunch," he said, shaking my hand.

The last time I saw Mike he was propped up in his coffin,

looking neither dead nor asleep but as if he were keeping his eyes firmly shut to reproach us for making so much noise. "No, he liked noise. He loved the sound of people having a good time," Finn insisted. "Then I wish we were having a good time," I told him. But I won't go on about Miles Michael Bruno or bring him up again.

13

THIS IS NOW AND I HAVEN'T HAD A ONE-MAN SHOW in a Newbury Street gallery in twenty-five years. The Strand Gallery opened on Newbury a year ago—blond oak floor, radiant lights, crap on the walls—and I thought I'd give it a try. I gave them twenty slides to look at, twenty slides from which you could have picked twenty superior to the dead stuff on their walls. The gallery never got back to me, so I was back to the gallery to collect my work. And here's youthful Mr Bell, smiling and pushing a lock of fine, light brown hair from his brow. "Ah, Mr Stillamare, good to see you again!" he said buoyantly. Bell was in his late thirties, a bright-eyed man with a freshly scrubbed look about him. "We've been slow and I apologize for that, but we really like your work. I wish we could take on more painters. Come into the office, come in, come in. Let me move those. Sit here. Let me move that, too. There. Now, how have you been?"

I had no idea what Bell was up to with this chummy chit-chat, but I sat down and told him I'd been fine.

"Good. We like those slides. Very interesting work, very interesting."

Bell sat half on and half off the right front corner of his desk and swung his leg a bit to show we let no formalities come between us pals and also to show who was patron and who petitioner, and all the while he chatted amiably about the season and the weather and he wondered if you could sit at the cafés on Marlborough Street this early without freezing. His office was small, crammed with flat files, cabinet files and shelves of what looked like archive boxes, but everything was as nicely packed, latched and tucked away as in a yacht. The door beside his desk was open enough for me to get a narrow glimpse of a bigger office. I was about to ask him to give me back my slides when he stood up, saying, "I'm going to—adjust these blinds—dim these lights—turn on the projector. I want to review a few of these and have you tell me about them. Just tell me whatever you want to. All right? I'll ask questions from time to time. All right?"

He frowned briefly over a handwritten list on his desk, then began to project the paintings onto a patch of white wall across from us. We went through three huge Cape Cod landscapes, abstract in their flattened simplicity, two free renditions of a gold Filippo Berio olive oil can with a foreground of sliced tomatoes, two big scenes of couples sprawled on an open bed, another of a solitary seated male with his limp cock over his thigh, and five large canvases of women in the bath or shower. Bell had opened the window blinds and was instructing me on how hard times were for galleries when the door beside his desk swung open and here was Sonia Strand herself. "Sonia, this is Mr Stillamare."

"We like your work, Mr Stillamare," she announced, her voice a scratchy baritone.

I said thanks and we shook hands, her touch firm and startlingly warm. She looked to be in her very late forties, a tall woman with a wide bush of ruddy gold hair, blue crystal eyes and a dark red mouth.

"And I'm sure Peter has already told you we're carrying as many painters as we can—more than we can, I think—and our calendar is crowded as is." She went on that way for a while, then asked Peter would he please take her calls while she talked with Mr Stillamare. Then she shut the door and we stood in the middle of her office while she ran her hands up her temples and through those glittering bronze corkscrews of hair and looked around the room bewildered, as if she had forgotten what she was doing there. In fact, she did look out of place, this tall well-built woman not in a suit but in a heavy columnar dress with thick vertical stripes from top to bottom, as if she were a caryatid from some Greek temple. Her desk, actually a long glass table, was a cluttered patchwork of overlapping letters and notes and photographs, anchored here and there by glittering enameled boxes and a gold pocket watch, large and fancifully engraved. A sloppy buttress of unframed canvases leaned awkwardly against one wall, a chrome and black leather sofa sat against another, and a low table with a stainless steel coffee maker stood by the window. Her cloak, tossed over the arm of the sofa, looked to be lined with peacock feathers. "Say! Would you like a cup of coffee?" she asked, struck with the idea.

"Sure. Why not?" I said.

"Exactly!" She smiled. "Please call me Sonia and I'll call you Renato. Right?"

"Right!" It was her gallery and her party, after all.

So we stood at the window and drank from crummy paper cups while she told me that I had not been in many shows recently, but the ones I had been in were excellent, very well known and widely respected and, furthermore, it was apparent that my work had been evolving all that time. She toyed with a long silver chain and pendant that hung from her neck, saying, "I wish I could be more hopeful. The public is so strange these days. They flock to the openings, they look around and I know they like what they see or they wouldn't keep coming back. But they leave without buying."

She informed me for a while about the public, then settled herself on the shining folds of her cloak in the corner of the sofa and turned an open hand toward a nearby chair, a piece of Baroque bric-a-brac, suggesting that I should sit too, which I did. I guessed that she didn't have a cold but that her voice had a natural rasp to it.

"And yet there are buyers who would be interested in your work," she was saying. "I know them. It's all a matter of marketing. Painters don't like to hear that when they're young. But you understand."

She hesitated, for it was on the tip of her tongue to ask me how old I was exactly. I smiled and waited, wondering if she had a plan for this conversation or if we were going to talk in circles until she got bored and sent me out.

"You knew Cyrilly," she said.

I said Yes, I did.

"A wonderful woman."

I said Yes, she was.

"I met her when I was just a college student, but she was so kind. She really helped me. She seemed to know everybody in New York, every dealer and buyer."

I said Yes, she did.

"How did you happen to get associated with her?"

"I met her here in Boston. She was working with a man named Gruenfeld. A year or two later she opened her place in New York."

"Those were good years for the art business," she said.

We talked about Cyrilly, Sonia Strand telling me how tough Cyrilly could be when making a deal— "And yet she had that lovely light voice, so musical, not like mine," said Sonia—and how loyal Cyrilly had been to her painters. I said, "Yes, she was remarkably loyal—" and I was about to expand on the theme of loyalty to painters but was cut off. "I know," Sonia said, sighing. "That was a different era. The art world has changed a lot since then." I don't recall how much longer we talked or what we talked about, for I was getting impatient and didn't care if it showed. Sonia touched my arm and went to her desk, saying, "Just a minute. Don't get up." She left behind a light floral scent, at odds with everything else about her, and stood at her desk to look down for a long moment at one of the loose papers there, her hand absently holding the oblong silver pendant that hung almost to her waist. "You know," she said, without looking up. "I can't tell much from a photograph, I need to look at the painting itself. I like to look on Tuesdays." She turned to me. "What's a good day to visit you?"

"Next Tuesday."

"Next Tuesday it will be," she said crisply.

I told her how to get to my place and we shook hands, Sonia Strand giving me that firm warm grip while I looked directly into the blue crystal eyes, then I picked up my slides and headed back down Newbury, slanting over toward the Daily Grind.

14

THE DAILY GRIND IS HALF LEFT AND HALF RIGHT, which is to say that the counter is in the middle of the floor and you can turn left past one-hundred-pound sacks of green coffee beans and crates filled with tea, or you can go to the right, past a playpen set there first for the owners' kids and now for the toddlers of the hired help, and that side has a dozen little square tables, each painted a different color, clustered by the window. When I entered, Garland glanced up from the counter and said, "Hi, Ren," then she frowned and went back to her accounting problem, cross with the numbers for not coming out right. Garland is always about to fly apart and on a hectic day her eyes enlarge and her cheeks become a luminous pink while her fine hair flares out as if electrified and she's crazily beautiful, but not now.

I went to the men's room and had a long, merciful piss, all the while brooding on my sullen prostate and what might lie ahead for it and for me, wondering had anyone thought to write a poem on such a thing, as years ago I had written one about my upstanding young prick, then I shook off the last drops, washed up and went to a table by the window. Garland said, "You got mail," and left a couple of letters on the table as she went past. One envelope was from Scanlon and the other was just a folded sheet of lined notepaper sealed with a strip of tape, nicely fashioned by, it turned out, a former student who used to make frames for me. *Hi, Ren! We are just passing thru on our way home and can't stop, but we had hoped to find you here. Come visit us! Love, Daphne.* She had included a photo of herself, the angular gamin on the left, and Laura, a softly rounded rosy-cheeked lawyer, standing side-by-side in Daphne's pottery studio, each with an arm around the other's shoulders—in her Christmas card she had said they hoped to get married—and on the back of the photo she had written, *This is our family.* I liked Daphne. I opened Scanlon's envelope with the table knife and stuck the snapshot inside so as not to lose it.

One of the waiter kids came over, put down a cup of coffee, took my order and went off, the back of his gold shirt saying, *Property of Jay Gatsby.* I unfolded Scanlon's letter and settled down to enjoy it, knowing it was going to reveal his newest theory of painting, because Scanlon concocts a new theory every time he starts painting in a new direction, which he does every eighteen months in his endless search for what he calls the market. Ten years ago he had been on the way to becoming famous, but then the market shifted, his dealer got busted for hoarding cocaine, the gallery folded and Scanlon found it harder and harder to get a show. Scanlon says we all theorize and most of us don't know it, but Scanlon knows it and writes his theories in his letters and his notebooks, so if his paintings ever get famous his notebooks and letters will get famous, too. I couldn't theorize and paint at the same time, even when I was his age. The only good painter I ever knew who talked intelligently about his own paintings was Ben Shahn, about whom you hear nothing anymore, but he was a thoughtful man with an expressive black line, though his colors were more faded than I like, and he could really talk.

I was halfway through my sandwich when somebody came

up and asked was I going to have a painting group this summer; I said no and went back to looking at the wild sketches Scanlon had included with his letter. Scanlon's sketches are always better than his finished paintings. Then I drank a second cup of coffee and watched the waitress (elongated torso with the slightly protuberant abdomen of a child) reaching and bending and ducking as she cleaned the empty tables; no abrupt squats or jagged pokes, but all fluent and harmonious, a pleasure to observe. Her swimsuit top revealed a tendril of tattoo on her shoulder, so I asked what it was and she said "A snake eating its own tail. It's a symbol of immortality, I think." She turned her back, pulled down the strap and looked over her shoulder at me, expectant. "Beautiful design. Great colors," I said, and she smiled with satisfaction and pulled up the strap, though in fact all tattoo colors are lousy.

I had half a cup more and sat there watching a kid in the playpen, but all the while thinking about a solo show in the Strand Gallery and about Sonia Strand coming next Tuesday to see more of my work and I thought I'd better tell Alba about this and ask her advice on how to manage it, because Alba is good at managing things, having practiced for years on me, then I went to the other side of the shop to see Gordon. "Don't ask me what I'm doing. I don't know what I'm doing," he said placidly.

Gordon Levy is forty-something years old, tall and thin, with a 1930s Art Deco face composed of a few smooth planes. I asked him what was wrong with the roaster, and he said nothing was wrong but he had decided to take it apart to clean it and he would never do that again. The only part of the machine still in place was the fancy front end, a solid piece of cast nickel scrollwork, which I suggested he put in the window as an art object. I held one of the curved metal plates around the barrel while Gordon screwed it back in place and we got to talking about the art market and the coffee market and tattoos. He said he'd met a woman who began with a single flower tattooed on her butt and every year she added another kind of flower. "When I got to know her she had an entire garden back there," he said. A young woman came up to us — a sharp face with a head of waxy black hair that stuck out in all directions—the same one who had come up to me a while ago when I was at lunch. "Listen, don't go to pieces," she said, a nasty edge to her voice. "But when I asked over at the college they said I could find you here. That's why I came over here."

"The answer is still no," I told her, amiably enough. "I don't teach anymore."

She stared at me, a line of mascara along her eyelashes, a silver rivet through the flange of her nose, some rings through her eyebrow. "That's not the point. You were my father's teacher. That's the only reason I even talked to you," she said, lifting her chin and compressing her lips now as if she were about to spit at me.

I started to ask who her father was but she had already turned and was striding to the door, leaving behind the afterimage of her oily black leather jacket and chrome studs. The door crashed shut behind her and there was a moment of silence, then Gordon glanced up from the coffee roaster where he was still trying to adjust a metal hoop. "I didn't know you went for that type," he said.

"Can I use your phone?"

I phoned Alba, told her how things had gone at the Strand Gallery and said I would really like to talk to her about it, said I needed her advice about what to show Sonia Strand and how to present it (all of which was only the truth), and asked her about tomorrow. Alba said That's great news, but I'm going to the cooking class tomorrow and I won't be free until two o'clock. I asked her where should we meet at two. Well, she said, I can get over to the Daily Grind by two-thirty. That's where you're phoning from, isn't it? I said, "Yes, two-thirty tomorrow. Thanks, Alba."

15

WHEN I GOT BACK TO THE STUDIO I FOUND A POSTcard had arrived from my daughter Astrid, calling herself Galaxy again (*Am coming to Boston—will get in touch, have lunch together—love Galaxy*) which postcard I wedged into the door panel so every time I went out I'd see it and not forget, then I began to sort through my paintings to decide which ones to show Sonia Strand, but the idea of my work in her gallery intoxicated me so much that I couldn't sort anything from anything, so I quit and walked from the studio to the back room, back and forth I don't know how many times, then decided to tack the photo of Daphne and Laura onto the cork board but there wasn't any space, since I didn't want to take down any of the other snapshots or notes, so I tucked it into the frame and I taped Scanlon's sketches to the wall where I sometimes put my own stuff. Then I took out a big canvas and began slowly to prime it, a soothing routine, and I was still at it when a key grated in the lock and the door rattled open and here was Zoe, saying, "Hi, it's me." I said Hi, Zoe, and turned back to the canvas to keep the placid rhythm of painting the undercoat. I love Zoe and like everyone else I love she can get on my nerves by interrupting my work. She set a bag of groceries on the seat of a kitchen chair and came over to put her hand on the back of my neck, saying, "Feel that? I didn't wear gloves. It was so bright and sunny I didn't realize how cold it was. I'm freezing.—What do you think?" I told her summer wasn't here yet, and I went on painting.

"No, what do you think of this?" She stood beside me and ran her hands up through her hair, watching me.

"You got a haircut."

"Like it?"

It had been shaggy before and it was still shaggy, but shorter now, cropped in a way to make it look like a close fitting feather cap, but maybe I'm not describing it well because I didn't especially like it. "Very sleek. Aerodynamic," I said and went back to painting.

"I'll get vain if you keep flattering me this way. I discovered my hair is getting thin, Ren. I never conceived that would happen. It's not falling out, you know, it's just getting thinner, each hair is actually thinner than it used to be. I'm getting old."

I told her she was young and beautiful. Zoe was in her mid forties, actually rather late forties, late late forties, and had a firm body that she exercised relentlessly to keep trim. She also had pale gray-blue eyes that Alba had once called wolf's eyes, which I thought was an unkind remark but which Zoe took as a compliment. On the inside of her right wrist there was a birthmark, a raspberry stain like a splash of paint, which I had first seen when she was eighteen, and I'd told her it meant she was destined to be a painter and, in fact, she was now a graphic artist with her own studio, which is not the same thing as being a painter, but closer to it than when she was re-designing secondhand clothes or sewing what she called soft sculpture. Now I have to tell you something and it's no secret—Zoe is my daughter Astrid's mother.

"Astrid won't like it, probably won't," Zoe continued. "She's so critical of me."

"Astrid loves you."

"I know she loves me. I also know she's unreasonably critical of me," she said, walking away. "And she won't listen to anything I say."

"She sent a postcard inviting me to lunch. She didn't say when. It's on the door."

"She never says when till the last minute. She phoned me. She's inviting all of us to lunch—you, me, Alba," she said, glancing at the postcard.

We three hadn't had a meal together in months. I began turning the idea this way and that, trying to decide whether I liked it or not.

"Astrid likes us all together, you know," Zoe continued. "She always wants that. She's certainly not pleased with you for moving to this studio."

I ignored that last remark and continued to paint. I could hear Zoe taking things from the grocery bag, putting this and that on the shelf, and I heard the soft thud of the refrigerator door and the heavy clink of wine bottles. Zoe remarked that Astrid was calling herself Galaxy these days, as if she were still singing with the band or modeling again. A minute later she added that maybe it was good for Astrid's business, because it was different and distinctive. I went on painting. Then Zoe said she was worried because Astrid was so thin and needed to gain weight and was living too fast and maybe was taking pills to keep up the acceleration. I reminded her that Astrid was a vegetarian and took scrupulous care of her body and was fussy about what she put into it and wasn't the kind of kid who took pills. Zoe said she wished Astrid had more room in her life for the non-material, the spiritual. Now Zoe was patrolling the edge of the studio, pausing at the big corkboard to study the photo of Daphne and Laura, then glancing across the other photos and notes, stepping carefully around the ink stone and paper on the floor, then moving past my grandchildren's crayon work to examine Scanlon's sketches. I told her she had been in motion ever since she came in and she should get herself a glass of wine.

"The only reason I'm here," Zoe said lightly. "The only reason I'm here is, well, I thought I'd stop in, see how you were getting along. That's all."

I said I was getting along fine and I told her about Sonia Strand wanting to see more of my work.

"Hey, Ren, that's great! Tell me more."

I gave up trying to paint. "Pour a couple of glasses of wine," I said. I figured if she wouldn't let me paint, and if she had come over to see how I was, we might as well drink and talk and let one thing lead to another, my bed being right here beside us.

Zoe filled two glasses and handed one to me, saying, "By the way, I have to be at a meeting in Cambridge by four."

"Then we should drink fast and act impulsively—if you're in the mood."

"Oh, I'm in the mood all right. But I have to get there early and meet with Derek ahead of time to plan things."

"Shit!" I said. I had hoped to avoid this, but I have to tell you that Zoe and the enterprising Derek Mallow had been playing footsie under the conference table for months; that's a fact. "Thanks, Zoe. Thanks for the *visit*. Goodbye!"

"Why are you mad at me?" she says in an injured tone, so I tell her, "You come up here with food and wine and now you tell me you can't stay! You come over to tell me you can't come over? I have better things to do, Zoe. I want to *work*," and by now her cheeks are pink and she cries, "This thing came up at the last minute. You're not being *fair*!" and I tell her loudly, "So I'm not being fair. I was working," and then she whips back, "It would help if you had a phone—"

"*Fuck the phone!* I'd never get any work done."

Zoe walked to the middle window and stood there looking out, her arms tightly folded and her shoulders hunched forward and, of course, she looked especially vulnerable since the haircut made the shape of her skull so clear and exposed the nape of her neck. I finished cleaning my brush and I hauled the canvas back to the wall. "Why is everything so damn difficult with you?" I asked, setting her wine glass on the window sill.

"I came over because I was lonely for you," she said, turning to me. We kissed, but when I put my arm around her it was like embracing one of my kitchen chairs. "Anyway, what makes you think it's me who's the difficult one?" she asked, and took a drink of wine.

We stood at the window and talked of one thing and another. Zoe said it had been so sunny today it was hard to believe it was still so cold, and we talked about Sonia Strand and Peter Bell, then Zoe poured herself another glassful and said Astrid was working too hard, chasing after glitz and glitter, and wouldn't listen to her mother anymore; I told her that Astrid was young and energized by her work, which was what I believed, and Zoe relaxed somewhat and refilled my glass.

"Which do you like more, food or sex?" she asked.

"The angels in heaven envy us for both," I told her. "We should have both."

"Be serious, Renato! It's a test of age, because young people choose sex and old people choose food." I laughed, and Zoe put her hand over my mouth and said, "How about tomorrow? I could come tomorrow afternoon and we could have both." Maybe it was the wine, but her face had the same warm light as when she was a teenage kid.

But I thought about my getting together with Alba tomorrow afternoon to talk about which paintings, and I didn't know when that would finish, so I put down my glass and told her, "I have to see Alba tomorrow."

"I thought you were seeing her on weekends. I thought you saw her last Sunday," Zoe said petulantly. I said right, but I had to see her again. Zoe looked at me. "I liked it better when you two were living together. At least I knew what was going on," she said flatly. We talked about food and not sex, and when she had finished her wine she give me a brisk kiss on the mouth and left.

16

After Zoe left I turned to my ink-brush work— great sheets of delicious, handmade paper on which I was trying to draw using a Japanese calligraphy brush— and I had been going at it for I don't know how long when there was a knock at the door. It was the same woman in the greasy black leather jacket who had pestered me at the café, her black bristle hair sticking up in clumps, thin silver rings through her sooty eyebrow. "Hi," she said. I said Hi and we looked at each other. "Can I come in?" I said No and started to shut the door. "Hey, wait!" she cried angrily, shoving her boot against the doorjamb. She withdrew her boot. "All right, *please!* Please just wait a minute. Let me *explain.*" I held the door, waiting with my hand on the doorknob, and she said, "I got in from San Francisco yesterday and I don't know anybody around here except you." I told her she didn't know me either. "I'm broke. I maxed out my credit card to get to Boston," she said. I asked her had she tried Travelers Aid, told her they could take care of her better than I could. "I was hoping you could help me out," she said.

"You mean money," I said.

"No. I just need a place for tonight and then—" I had taken my hand from the doorknob and started to wave her off, no more than a gesture, but she flinched and threw up an arm to shield her head.

"Hey, calm down," I told her. "Who are you, anyway?"

Her cheeks had reddened slightly, but she gave no other sign that she had thought I was going to punch her. "My name's Avalon. We don't know each other but you knew my father. You and my father were friends."

"So you say."

"I have proof. Look," she said. She slipped a hand into her pants pocket and pulled out a beat-up wallet, flipped through her little album of cards and photos until she found what she wanted, then held it out to me. "Here's a picture of him when you knew him," she said. It was a black-and-white photograph of a young man with dark, rather long hair, cramming a suitcase under the front hood of a VW bug. The photo had been taken just as he turned to the camera and started to say something. The face was familiar, but maybe because the big hair looked so much like the late sixties that it reminded me of people I had known back then. "And here's one of him and you. —I know it's real, because that's the front of a stage I went and looked at today," she added. It was another black-and-white snapshot: me and that other guy clowning around, leaning back to back against each other, while behind us was the Charles River and a quarter circle of the open-air Hatch Shell where the Boston Pops plays concerts in the summer. "See. That's him and that's you, right? That's you and my father."

The photo or the smell of her leather jacket or something else about her began to stir some uneasy memory. "What's your name?" I asked.

"Avalon. Avalon Flood." In addition to the rings through her eyebrow and the rivet in the delicate bell of her nose, she wore a row of little silver rings through the rim of one ear and what looked like a miniature bolt through the lobe of the other one. "Flood," she repeated.

It had begun to come back to me. "I remember your father," I told her.

"He's dead. Can I come in?" Her gaze darted over my shoulder, this way and that. She left the door open behind her and came in a couple of steps and paused, looking around. "I guess you spend a lot of time painting," she said.

"I'm a painter."

"I know you're a painter! Sometimes I say stupid things." She shifted from foot to foot, shot a glance into the shadows of the other room, but stayed where she was. "Married?"

"Yes."

"Where's your wife?"

I told her my wife lived across the river in Cambridge, but Avalon seemed not to listen, her gaze flicking from this to that, around the room. She had a lean, sharp face with quick eyes, a good throat, and the rim of her jersey undergarment was clean. "Do you have a bathroom?" she asked. I said yes and she stepped back out the door and returned with a big lumpy backpack which she dropped to the floor, and at her other side stood this kid, a boy about seven or eight, maybe nine years old—who knows?—holding a big toy airplane. "This is Kim," she informed me. Kim had a round Asian face and steady, velvet-black eyes which regarded me with passive curiosity

"Hello, Kim.—Where did he come from?" I asked her.

"He's mine. I'm his mother."

"Great. Got any more out there?"

"No. Where's the bathroom?"

Later, while I was preparing the pasta, I asked Avalon about her father, Brendan Flood. "He was a computer programmer," she said. "He used to draw pictures for me when I was a kid, and he told me about the art school and about you, but he wasn't a painter." I remarked that when I knew her father he had been programming computers, yes, and doing a lot of other things as well and, I added, she might want to know that he was also a little cracked, not falling apart crazy, but cracked, and I had liked him for that, too. She said she could believe he was a little cracked, all right, because that would explain how come he married Sandra ("An airhead.") who, when Avalon was ten, drove away in their convertible and never returned, and it might explain why he later married Linda ("A bitch.") Anyway, when Avalon was fourteen her father died of melanoma cancer ("Too much sunshine. In the end he got burned to a crisp and that was the end of my dad.") so Avalon was sent to live with Linda's mother in Sacramento ("Because Linda didn't want me. She wanted to play around and she didn't want me there to watch.") but Linda's mother ("The bitch's mother.") didn't want her either and a year later Avalon was sent to live with Linda's unmarried younger sister ("An asshole.") in San Francisco. After a year there, Avalon moved in with a classmate ("Not too bright but not a slut, either.") and completed her high school courses in Sunnyvale. "I also took courses at San Francisco State," she said. She went on a while, but I wasn't much listening to her, thinking instead about Brendan Flood, whose whole life had come and gone.

After we had finished eating but were still at the table, she said, "I have two photo albums. That's all I have from when he was alive. Linda took everything else and sold what she didn't want. No one wanted the photographs, so that's what I inherited."

"Where'd you get Kim?"

She said nothing but looked at Kim who was at her side, warming up his airplane, wheeling it slowly into position with a soft, powerful hum. "He's very well behaved, isn't he?" she said, caressing his back as he taxied slowly down the table. "He's half Japanese, that's why," she explained.

"Is that why? Where's his father?

"In Japan, I suppose."

"You don't know?"

"As soon as Kim was born I took one look and knew who his father was, but by then he was gone. I suppose he went back to Japan. He was a student at Stanford, from Osaka."

"Kim is a Korean name," I told her. "The Japanese and the Koreans hate each other. Who named him Kim?"

"I named him after his father. Kimura. That was his last name. I couldn't recall his first name. It was something like —oh, I don't know—anyway, all I could remember was Kimura. So he's Kim. I think it's a good name for a boy, don't you? I'm teaching him about Japanese things so he will appreciate his Japanese background. Like, I'm teaching him how to use chopsticks. And he's learning Japanese. I got a teach-yourself book and taught him numbers in Japanese. —Kim. Kim, come over here." The pilot had been heading toward my fresh ink-on-paper work, but now he banked slowly and made a wide turn and began the long descent toward our table. His mother said, "I want you to count something. Please." She pulled him against her side. "See these things on the table? Just these. Can you count them?"

Kim kept a grip on his airplane. "There's five," he said quietly. "What's so great about that?"

"I want you to count each one in Japanese," his mother told him. "Like in one, two, three—only in Japanese."

He pointed at each of the dishes and wine glasses, this time saying, "Ichi. Ni. San. Shi. Go. Roku."

"There! You see?" Avalon had turned to me in triumph. "Isn't he a smart kid?"

I said yup, a wonderful kid, let me show you where you two can sleep. I took Avalon and her good-tempered bastard to the other room, which is where I stored my old paintings and everything else I couldn't cram into our expensive cement tomb in Cambridge, and I dragged a mattress edgewise from behind a wall of big canvasses. "This is great, isn't it, Kim? This will be fun. And now," she added, turning to me, "I want to give him a bath because we spent last night at a shelter and only God knows what low-class germs live there. Do you have a towel? Maybe two towels, actually." I got her two towels, and after she had given the kid a good soak and rubbed him dry she wrapped him in the other towel and seated herself on the floor of my studio, letting him fall asleep with his head in her lap. "Why did you come East?" I asked her. "Why Boston?"

"San Francisco isn't a good place to raise a child. It's all very advanced and enlightened and it's a freak show."

"So you just packed up and came to Boston."

"That's right," she said, caressing Kim's head, running her slow fingers complacently through his black bristle hair in rhythm with his breathing.

"And you looked me up because I knew your father."

"Actually, I looked you up because you knew my mother."

"Not me. I didn't know her. No."

"My father said you knew about her. He told you about her. He told—"

"Nope," I said, cutting her off.

"He told me so."

"What did he tell you?"

"My mother was an angel, right?"

17

I KNEW BRENDAN FLOOD AND I KNEW ABOUT AVALON'S mother, because when it was over Brendan told me about her. Whenever he spoke about her he said she was an angel, and I have no doubt she was—either that or she was crazy and Brendan was stoned. According to Avalon, her mother and Brendan met in August—which is absolutely true—an August so hot that asphalt melted in the streets and seven of the trees along the river burst into flame. The air was boiling in his apartment, so Brendan had propped open the skylight and was lying naked on his back on the bare floor, his hands clasped behind his head, trying to keep cool. He was staring up at the square of blue sky as if from the bottom of the sea when a body as naked as his own floated ten feet above the skylight, thrashing and clawing and choking—then it stopped thrashing and sank very gently head-first with the legs floating out behind, a swimmer whose lungs had filled with water, and came to rest with a white cheek flat against the skylight, the mouth wide open and the eyes like blue quartz. Brendan lay there trying to puzzle out what had happened, then he pulled up a chair and stood on it, reached out through the open skylight to grapple a leg and hauled the body down feet-first into his arms, himself crashing sideways onto the floor under the sudden weight. He got up and— What can I say? This was a bare-assed young woman, maybe eighteen, with a wingspread of over twelve feet.

A bitter stink of burnt feathers hung in the air and, in fact, Brendan noticed that the trailing vanes on both wings were singed away, revealing a sooty membrane underneath, and her right arm was seared. He rolled her onto her back. Her wide eyes were as sightless as two pieces of turquoise, as if she had drowned in air. He was wondering was she drunk or stoned or in a narcoleptic fit when she stumbled to her feet, knocking him aside. She glared at the skylight and began to howl —a freezing sound that started as a single icy note, solitary at first but soon joined by others all pitched the same and all in different timbres until it seemed a whole orchestra was shivering the room, cracking the windows, exploding bottles, glasses, light bulbs. Brendan had clamped his hands over his ears, had run as far as he could and continued to bang his head against the wall until the desolate cry ended. "Who are you?" he asked, gasping for breath.

She turned her stone eyes toward him and spoke, or tried to, but all that came out was a kind of mangled music.

"Stop!" he cried, ducking his head and clapping his hands to his ears again. "Stop!"

But she went on until there was nothing but shards of sound, then she shrugged and said something like *Oh, shit*, tripped over the mattress on the floor and plunged into a deep sleep. Brendan wiped the sweat from his eyes and watched to see if she would stir, then he righted the chair under the skylight, stood on it and pulled himself shakily onto the roof with the hope of spying some explanation. There was only the commonplace desert of tar and gravel. He dropped back into his room, chained the door and wedged the chair under the doorknob. He was trembling from exhaustion when he returned to look at her—one long white wing lay folded across her rump and the other spread open like a busted fan across the mattress and onto the floor. He crept slowly from one side of the mattress to the other and watched the light shimmer this way and that on the feathers as he moved, feeling ashamed of himself when he paused at the glimpse of gold hairs at her crotch. He had always understood that there was no difference of sex between angels, that angels were not male or female but pure spirits. He told me he didn't know what to think, much less what to do, and it got to be so quiet you could hear the faucet drip. So Brendan retrieved his little tin box of joints from the window ledge and sat on the floor with his back to the wall, struck a match and began to smoke, keeping his dazed eyes on her all the while.

She slept for two days and two nights, or maybe it was three days and nights, or maybe only that one day and night—Brendan lost track because he fell asleep himself. When he woke up she was sitting cross-legged on the mattress, looking at him with eyes as clear as a summer sky. "You need a shave," she told him, for her voice had cleared too.

"I've been busy," he said, startled.

She was looking around at the bare white walls and scuffed wood floor, at the banged-up guitar case and the old record player and the short row of records and books on the floor against the wall. "Yeah? Doing what?" she asked, skeptically.

"Thinking about things, meditating." He had gotten to his feet and had begun to search hurriedly for his underwear or his pants or any scrap of cloth to hide himself.

"You ought to eat more. You look like a fucking bird cage on stilts. What's your name?"

"Brendan Flood," he said. He hadn't found his underwear but quickly thrust a leg into his blue jeans anyway. "I've been on a fast. I've been meditating and fasting," he explained. "Who—"

"Meditating and fasting? Holy shit!" She laughed. "Who pays the rent here?" She sounded a lot like Avalon when she talked.

"Me. I work nights as a programmer. Listen—" he began.

"So what else have you been doing? Hash? Acid? Come on, Brendan. Don't look so surprised. I know you've been smoking grass. The air is full of it."

"Listen, who are you?"

"I'm an escapee, Brendan. Just like you. You can trust me. Jill," she added as an afterthought.

"That's your name?"

"They named me Morning Glory," she said sarcastically. "But you can call me Jill, yes."

"How did you get here?"

"Well, you've got a chair jammed against the door, Brendan. And I didn't scale the walls. I came in over the roof. Remember?"

He groaned and rubbed the heels of his hands against his closed eyes. "What day is today?" he asked, not opening his eyes.

"How would I know?"

He looked at those wings which stood like snowdrifts behind her shoulders. "Do those come off?" he asked.

"Are you being funny? This is me," she said, glancing down at her breasts, cupping and lifting them. "As fucking naked as I get."

Her flesh was the color of the dawn horizon, so beautiful it frightened him, but he gathered his courage and looked at her—her face, the hollow of her throat, her breasts and the honey-colored hair of her crotch. Yet at the first surge of desire he felt a chilly counter current, a fear that his lust was a monstrous sacrilege that would bring the wrath of God down on his head like a hammer. He escaped to the bathroom to piss and discovered a long gold hair stuck to the damp wall tile. He filled the washbowl with cold water and doused his privates, thinking to put out the fire and clean himself at the same time, but it was his brain that was ablaze and just when he was dunking his head it came to him that the creature in the next room might not be an angel at all, might be some delusion fabricated by Satan, whereupon his legs gave way and he pitched forward into the faucet and came up choking. He wondered if he were going crazy.

He went back to the room and found her seated cross-legged on the mattress reading one of his books, *The Poetical Works of William Blake*, which was where he kept his cigarette papers. She looked up and began reciting "And when the stars threw down their spears and water'd heaven with their tears—" but saw that Brendan was already aroused, up and rising. "Ah, you devil," she murmured, tossing aside the book to grasp his shaft. "Did he who made the lamb make thee?"

Brendan was doomed to remember their lovemaking for the rest of his life. It began simply enough when he threw himself to the mattress and pulled her onto her back, hoping to get a hand on her breast and a knee between her thighs, but before he could make his next move he felt her fingernails pierce his rump and felt his cock being seized as in an oiled fist and he slid in deeper and higher until he couldn't tell whether he was fainting or screaming with pleasure. He had staggered to his feet and was carrying her upright, her legs around him like a vise, stumbling now against the chair and then the table and now crashing against the wall and again the table, carrying her at last as if she were miraculously weightless or as if she were actually carrying him, as if he were on his back, hooped in her arms and legs, her wings beating slowly but just enough to keep them afloat above the mattress and table and chairs. And when he came it was a long, long rush in which his body gave itself completely away, such a long rush that he could feel the marrow being drawn sweetly through his spine from his distant fingers and toes, and at the end of it every one of his bones was hollow and his skull completely empty.

Later they lay side by side on the sweat-soaked mattress and Brendan, believing he had been turned inside out and the secret lining of his life exposed, told her all about his student days at Cal Tech where he learned Fortran and Cobol and other machine languages of lethal boredom, followed by his years on the road as a Zen guitarist with Zodiac, which had nearly driven him crazy, and how for these past three months he had fasted and prayed, waiting for God to give him a message or vision or signal of some sort. When he was finished he looked at Jill and she said, "I'm hungry. Are you hungry? I know I am. I'm starved." Of course, there was no food in the place. So Brendan pulled on his clothes and hunted up a pair of jeans and a T-shirt for Jill, but she refused to wear them because, she explained, she couldn't go out. "Going out gives me an anxiety attack," she said. "I get panicky and throw up or pee in my pants if I go out." So Brendan went out and came back with three hamburgers and some sliced pickles. He sat across from her at his wobbly table, bit into his hamburger, looked at her shining breasts and watched her eat. She tore through her food— "Are you going to finish that?" she asked him, glancing at his plate—and when she had downed the last half of his hamburger she wiped her mouth with the back of her hand and said she wanted to go up on the roof to take a look around. He asked her didn't she want to wear something, anything, to cover up, and so on. "For Christ sake, Brendan, this is 1967! The last dress I owned was made of colored paper." But she pulled on a pair of his shorts and Brendan set his chair under the skylight, gave her a boost and pulled himself up behind her.

Remember, this was Boston's Back Bay where the roofs are flat and the brownstones are built shoulder to shoulder with no space between them, so you can walk from roof to roof to roof for a quarter of a mile before coming to a cross street. Brendan watched her looking around and realized she might have come from just a few roofs away and nowhere more exotic. She had shaded her eyes with her hand and was gazing across the pipe vents, TV aerials, skylights and chimneys to the soft horizon. "What city is this?" she asked him.

"What do you mean, what city! This is Boston! Don't you even know what city you're in?"

She whirled on him, saying, "You're so smart and you don't even know what day it is! I never said I was smart. I never went to college. So fuck off!"

Brendan flushed. "It's the twelfth. Or the thirteenth. I stayed up all night to watch the meteor shower on the eleventh. So it must be Saturday. I think."

"What difference does it make what city it is, anyway?" she muttered, sullen.

So they dropped back into Brendan's place where he stepped out of his blue jeans and she peeled off her shorts and they knelt face to face on the mattress and began to make love again, and it would have been even better than before except that Brendan had begun to doubt that anything could be so good or that he could be so fortunate or that Jill (or Morning Glory or whatever her name was) could be what she appeared to be.

Three nights a week Brendan crossed the river to Cambridge where he worked as a computer programmer, but other than that, these two slept at night and made love by day, all day, every day. They ate of course. Jill still refused to go down to the street, saying she had a bad case of agoraphobia and dreaded open space, so Brendan went off for groceries and came back with take-out hamburgers and pizzas and Chinese, plus pasta to cook up right there. Brendan never gained a pound; in fact, he lost a few. "Are you trying to starve yourself to death?" Jill asked him.

"Food dirties the windows of perception," he told her.

"Because, do you know what they do to people who try to kill themselves but fuck up and don't do it right? They strap them down and do things to make them regret their mistakes. Believe me," she said.

When he asked her how come she knew about such things she said, "I'm an escapee. Remember?" which was what she usually said whenever he asked her about herself.

But mostly they made love. There were days when they clowned around, as when they lathered themselves in whipped cream and licked it from each other's flesh, and hours of heavy sensuality when he lingered and she opened to him with the languor of a flower and, to be sure, there were moments when he rushed her like the whippet that he was.

According to Avalon, Jill's feathers had begun to show color and in November she announced that she was pregnant. Now Brendan noticed that whenever they made love the points at the trailing edge of her wings glowed translucent pink and each successive time they joined the color reached deeper into the feathers, like dye soaking into fabric, until the wings themselves took on a pale rose cast, a shade which deepened each day and, in fact, the hue at the tip of each feather began to alter from red to maculate gold in the way of a spotted trout, and from that to a grassy emerald to an iridescent sapphire such as you see in peacock feathers, thence to a purple so luminous it tinted the room. Her eyes changed, too. Some days they were so clear that when he looked into them he saw sky, clouds, stars, albino doves. Other days they solidified into black mirrors and she would turn her blind face to the skylight and scream, then hurtle from one end of the room to the other, dashing herself ruthlessly against the walls until she dropped, the pulse beating furiously in her neck, her soundless mouth stretched open and her wide eyes like agates. When she'd come to, she'd shiver in his arms and though her teeth were chattering she'd grin and say something like, "I graduated from Boston Psychopathic with a degree in paranoia. What do you think? Am I a fallen angel or what?" He would pull her across his lap and hold her head to his shallow chest, rocking her until she drifted to a peaceful slumber, his brain spinning in confusion.

Brendan had never wanted a telephone in his place and now he couldn't afford one, so he called from a public booth at the nearby health-food store, searching for a gynecologist or obstetrician or plain medical doctor who would make a house visit, but of course there wasn't one to be found. He did come across a midwife's card on the bulletin board there, so he phoned her and, since she lived only a few blocks away, she said she'd come around to examine Jill the next day. But the next day when Jill found out who was at the door she barricaded herself in the bathroom and refused to come out till the midwife had gone. Jill informed Brendan that she didn't need a doctor or midwife. "What do they know? We can do this ourselves. You're smart. There are books on this," she said. He broke into a sweat, but bit his tongue so as to say nothing and went out and came back with five books on childbirth.

"No. Not these," she told him, exasperated. "There's this French doctor who helps women give birth under water. Get the one by him."

"You'll drown!" Brendan cried, remembering her face as

he had first seen it pressed against the skylight almost twelve months ago.

"Not the woman, asshole! The baby. The baby gets born under water in a tub. Get that one."

He didn't go looking for the book but it wouldn't have made any difference if he had, because several years were to go by before women gave birth in tubs of warm water at Dr. Odent's clinic in Pithivier, France. When Brendan awoke on August 11 Jill was flat on her back in labor beside him, her fingers deep in the mattress ticking, her hair stuck like gold leaf on her damp forehead and cheeks. He pulled on his jeans and jammed his feet into his sneakers and stumbled down the stairway, his loose laces whipping and snapping at each step, and ran to the health-food store where he phoned the midwife. Seven minutes later the midwife's car turned onto Brendan's street and began to nose hesitantly along the row of parked cars, looking for a place to stop, but Brendan pulled her from the wheel and hustled her up the stairway and into his flat. As the midwife later testified, Jill was seated naked on the wood chair under the skylight, the baby wrapped in a bloody dish towel on her lap. "Don't come any closer!" she cried, jumping up. She scrambled awkwardly onto the chair seat and stood wavering there as if under the endless impact of a waterfall, the swaddled infant now crying in her arms. "Brendan, take the baby. It's a girl, like me. —You stay back, lady!" she shouted at the midwife. Brendan received the baby from her. "We crazies are the only true rebels against God," she said, reaching toward the open rim of the skylight. Then this Jill, or Morning Glory or whatever her name was, pulled herself out to the roof and jumped off, finishing her long dive from the battlements of heaven.

18

LATE THE NEXT MORNING I HIKED OVER TO COPLEY College where I used to teach; I was hunting for anybody who knew anything about Sonia Strand and her gallery. By the way, if you're ever in the neighborhood take a look at the sculptured wall behind the reception desk. You can still make out road signs embedded in it, along with a guitar, peace symbols, a mailbox, wooden window frames, tambourines, multipaned glass doors, mirrors, transistor radios, cast human torsos (breasts, pudenda and bums), plus groups of big mismatched letters spelling out LOVE, up, down and sideways. I began to teach at Copley the same September the wall went up, a lively wall saturated with the happy playschool colors of the late 1960s and pierced with glass window panes through which you could spy naked children and women with long shinning hair and sunny breasts. The school was just getting started; we teachers were young, the students even younger, and we fooled around in ways which your more enlightened, progressive and prudish generation now forbids. As for the wall, the sex police purified our vision by covering that beautiful artifact—the best work in the building—with a coat of dead white paint and that's the way it's been ever since.

It felt strange to be back there, seeing all those students in the hall and no familiar faces. Then I bumped into Nils Petersen with a big poster under his arm. "Hey, man. It's been a long time. Good to see you!" he said, slapping my hand. "Are you going to be around later? I have to teach up in the lab in five minutes. Come along."

I like Nils. He's thin and wears his gray hair in a short pony tail, but on him it looks all right. On our way upstairs he raved about all the colors he was generating on his new computer. Years ago artists like Nils used to compose their work by hand, using pencils and rulers, and they separated colors by hand. The way you separated a color was by hiding all the others under a translucent ruby red sheet, because the camera was loaded with ortho film which couldn't see through red; of course, that meant you had to cut a separate ruby for each color—that's where the skill began. There used to be a special swivel knife made by the Ulano company and if you wanted to see a master at work you could watch Nils cutting a ruby with that knife. He had a meticulous dexterity that made me dizzy, and I still have a couple of things he designed, not the printed product but the master pages composed of layer upon layer of sweetly cut ruby sheets. Now the graphics room is called a media lab and Nils does everything on a computer.

We stopped outside the media lab where Nils tacked the poster on the bulletin board—*Pixels: An Exhibition of Computer Art.* I asked was he going to exhibit any computer art in the show. He said yes, so I said I'd go see it, and I meant it. Frankly, computer art is shit without the smell.

I asked him what he knew about the Strand Gallery.

"They have good cheese and expensive wine at their receptions," he said. "Why?"

I told him I was thinking of showing them some slides.

"Sonia Strand makes the decisions. She has a couple of people over there with her, but she's the one who does the deciding. That's what I hear. —Are you going to be around later?"

I said no, but I'd see him at the show for sure, or before then, so Nils went in to teach and I went off to the faculty lounge. The lounge hadn't changed—a leftover space with two scruffy bentwood seats and a busted armchair with tufts of cotton coming out the corners. The window sill held a coffee pot, a stack of styrofoam cups and a cigar box with coins scattered in it. I had turned to leave when a thirtyish woman in a bulky black bathrobe came in, Azarig Tarpinian behind her. He saw me and his face brightened, saying, "Well, well, well. Look who's here." The model seated herself in the armchair and opened her magazine. Azarig turned on the electric heater and asked her if she wanted a cup of coffee—she didn't—then he came over to the window, saying, "Hey, it's good to see you. We've made great progress since you've been gone. Now we're giving a course in the theory of painting. Not practice, *theory*." He laughed. Azarig is a large, comfortable looking man. We stood there talking while he made a cup of coffee. I said I had just bumped into Nils and he's deep into computer art.

"He's good at it, according to critics and people who claim to know," Azarig said.

"It's art without finger prints."

"You haven't changed," he said.

"My favorite old artist is the one who covered his hand with red pigment and pressed it against the wall in a cave in Chauvet. That was thirty thousand years ago. But I know how he felt just then. He felt like us. This is my hand. Look. This is me."

Azarig meditated over his cup of coffee, then glanced up and said, "You know about Hammerman?"

"He retired to the Cape. What should I know?"

"He had to go back to the hospital. They performed an orchiectomy. That's the fancy name for castration." Azarig turned away and looked out the window.

"It sounds barbaric," I said.

He shrugged. "They say it slows the spread of the cancer from the prostate. It's a treatment."

We stood side by side at the window, looking down at the street: the slow and uneven stream of cars, the pigeons descending, the people walking along in the bright sun, all as if nobody ever died. There was a rustle of paper as the model turned a page in the magazine she was reading. I asked Azarig how he himself was doing these days.

"I take something for blood pressure, something else for cholesterol," he said. "And you?"

"I'm all right. My prostate numbers aren't good," I admitted. "I'm supposed to get it checked again. The doctor hasn't found anything so far. You never know."

We agreed that God could have done a better job with the pump and the plumbing and, as a matter of fact, agreed that even Azarig or I could have done a better job, and then I asked what had he been working on, and his voice picked up as he told me about some figures he had done in wax and so on and so forth, and I asked him what he knew about the Strand Gallery.

He laughed. "Sonia Strand? She's interesting, like a big painted statue."

"I meant the gallery."

"Her husband was a dealer in gemstones down in New York. Her last husband, anyway. Precious and semi-precious stones, but not diamonds. After he died she moved up here and opened the gallery. You like her?"

"I don't know yet."

"The family came over right after the war. Her father was an art dealer. Viennese."

The model had put aside her magazine and was looking our way, trying to catch Azarig's eye, and when he saw her he glanced at his watch and put down his styrofoam cup. "It's show time," he said. Then he walked the model up the hall to life class and I headed downstairs where I bumped into Eloise Carol, author of "The Male Gaze as Rape," who believes that male artists assault their canvases, attempting to objectify and dominate whatever they paint, whereas women use their brushes to caress and nurture their subjects. We shook hands and I went out, happy to leave the old place, buy some paints, eat lunch and see Alba.

19

ALBA ENJOYS TELLING ME WHAT TO DO AND HOW to behave, so when I asked what she thought I should show to Strand she didn't hesitate. "Show everything from the past three years," she told me. "Keep everything else in the back room."

"You mean, *hide* the other stuff?" I said.

"That's *not* what I said! But if Strand liked those nudes, that means she likes big canvasses and lots of color, so put those up front. And when Strand comes to look, you should—" but I broke in to say "I've done a lot of work in the past three years and I can't put it all up front."

"Put the best up front, and when Strand—" she began, but I told her "All of it is good."

"I know all of it is good, Ren, but not all of it is best."

As I said, Alba likes to run things and if you don't watch out she'll run your life, but I figured she was probably right about the paintings. I looked at her, but she said nothing, merely waited, satisfied. I asked if she knew anything about Strand's confederate, Peter Bell, but she didn't, so we went back to re-arranging the pieces of gossip we had picked up about Sonia Strand. Alba asked me did I remember Leo Conti still had his gallery, and I said yes, I remembered him and had heard he wasn't doing so well. "And he remembers you," Alba said. "I think he'd like to see your work. In fact, I know he would. In fact, he told me so," she added, pleased and hopeful. I asked didn't she remember where his gallery was, and Alba said, "East Cambridge," and I said Not exactly the center of the art world, and she said, "East Cambridge has some interesting parts."

"A small old factory building is interesting?" I asked.

"If it has a gallery in it."

"Yeah, well," I said.

"I think it's worth looking into." I thought it was dismal, but I supposed Alba was trying to be helpful so I bit my tongue and didn't say anything. Besides, she looked fresh and attractive, which was a change, for she had put on a new sweater, soft and tight, and had swept her hair into a glossy French roll, all of this for me, or for the cooking class she had attended earlier today, which I doubted. Now she began to talk about Astrid, saying that she had phoned last night and we were all going to have lunch together. "She plans to come by your studio around noon, or maybe at one or two o'clock, but she couldn't say what day, exactly. Everything is up in the air," Alba added.

"Everything is always up in the air with Astrid. She's calling herself Galaxy again. I wish she'd settle down, get her feet on the ground."

"She sounded fine on the phone. She sounded happy and energetic," Alba said.

"She needs to focus her energies more. She zigs and zags and is all over the place, running after glitter. Maybe you could speak to her about that."

"Me? She has a mother. Why me?"

"Because she will listen to you, because you're not her mother."

"Renato, she's fine. She's a splendid young woman. She's doing well in New York. If you want, I'll remind her that when she was a year old she renounced Satan and all his allurements and empty promises. As her godmother I can do that."

One of the coffee kids, the Gauguin female with black eyes and cinnamon flesh, appeared at our table bearing a tray loaded with pastries; we didn't want any, so she drifted back to the counter. Alba was telling me about some country property she had looked at yesterday, a big farmhouse with out-buildings, which is what we had always talked about buying, only this one turned out to be on a corner between two roaring highways so she crossed it off the list and now the list had nothing on it. "But be honest, Renato. Are you still interested in our buying a place in the country?"

"Of course I'm interested. What do you mean?"

"You'd give up your studio here in Boston?" she asked.

"I'd have a studio in the country—in a barn, in an out-building."

"What about your famous privacy you're always talking about? And you do know what I mean," she added.

"I'd have all the privacy I'd need in the country."

"Damn it, Renato! I'm not going to shut my eyes if you go out to your studio with some fuckable, some, some—"

I cut in to hush her, saying, "Nothing has ever gone on in my studio that you didn't know about! More or less. And—."

"Oh, spare me!" she cries, looking around, exasperated at finding nothing to hurl at my head. "You want us to live in the country and you'll have your studio there, too?"

"Yes. *I* want it. *You* want it. —That's what you want, isn't it?"

"Well, I'm not so sure. I'm beginning to like the way we're living right now," she says complacently.

I came to a stop, not knowing what to think or which way to go. "Is that what this is really about?"

Alba turned away to look out the window, content to leave the conversation as it was, so that I could puzzle over it and worry about her meaning, that being one of her little stratagems, though I didn't fall for it. It was a bright day, chill and windy; we watched a man without a coat trot past, one hand holding a briefcase, the other hand clutching his lapels together at his throat. Here in the café, where it was pleasantly warm, the sun lay slantwise down Alba's arm and across our table and the air was fragrant with freshly roasted coffee beans. "Have you seen Zoe recently?" she asked.

"She stopped by the studio on her way to a meeting in Cambridge," I said, for I had learned how to tell the truth and get away with it. "She didn't stay long. She had to get there early, ahead of time, to prepare something."

"What's she up to these days?"

"We talked about Astrid, mostly. —Do you remember Brendan Flood?"

"Anything else?"

"Nothing much. —Listen, do you remember Brendan Flood?"

"Are you trying to distract me? Yes, I remember Flood. That was ages ago. Is he back in town?"

"No. He's dead but his daughter is here."

"Oh. That's a shock. Well. How's his little girl?"

"She's not so little anymore and she has a child of her own, a little boy." I told Alba about Avalon and Kim and suggested that Alba might like to help them out, or at least help me get them off my hands, but no. "Why should I always be the one who takes care of the strays you bring home?" she asked. I told her it was her nature to do so, that she had a generous heart and that, furthermore, I hadn't brought Avalon and her kid home but, I repeated, Avalon had knocked on my door and when I opened it she had thrust the kid inside. By then Garland had come from behind the counter, pulled a chair to our table and sat down with a sigh. Her face had a delicate pink flush with a glaze of fine perspiration and she plucked at her blouse to bring the cool air to her flesh. "Why do you put up with him?" she asked Alba. "I don't. Not anymore," Alba told her. Then they began to discuss pastry dough, how to make it fine and flaky, and I took off.

20

When I got back to the studio Avalon was standing bent over the table with a newspaper nailed flat under her palms while she studied the help-wanted ads, and without lifting her head she said Hi, and kept her frown on the small print, making a great display of concentration. Kim was lying on my bed, humming, his dirty bare feet propped against the wall and his eyes glazed with boredom. I had bought five little wood homunculi, each shaped like a bowling pin the size of my thumb, and these I dumped on the blanket beside his head. "Passengers," I told him. "They want to fly to anyplace you can think of." Avalon looked over her shoulder at me and at Kim, who had swung his feet down and was sitting up now. "I'm getting a job," she announced.

I said that was welcome news because—I reminded her—she couldn't stay here. I asked what jobs she had held in California, and she said Lots, and I said I had already guessed she had lots of jobs, probably lots and lots of jobs, and I asked her what was her last job. "I make silver jewelry, rings and chains and bracelets and things like that. I've got some in my backpack. I designed them. I'm a designer, you could say. —Don't look at me that way! I used to work as a designer in a shop on Fillmore. In San Francisco. I designed tattoos." Kim had trotted into the back room and was now piloting his airplane back to my bed where the bored passengers lay in a heap, waiting. "Kim, what do you say to Renato? What do you say when somebody gives you a gift?" his mother asked. Kim looked at me: "Do you want them back?" he ventured. I told him no, he could keep them. "Honey, what do you say?" his mother prompted. "Thank you," he announced, resuming his flight plan.

I took a roll of masking tape from the caddy and got down on my hands and knees to lay out a border on the floor, and Avalon said, "I used to work in a New Age shop selling crystals, herbal soaps, mind-body books, massage oil, things like that, and that's where I sold my jewelry. I've got some in my pack I can show you," she added. I asked what else she had done for work, and she said, "After I quit college I got on a crew putting down asphalt driveways in Orange County. That was my first full-time job. I developed a good body that way and afterwards I worked in a health and fitness club and they used me as a model in their advertisements, so I got into that, into modeling, and then into acting, in a couple of plays, intellectual ones, but that's a stupid life and it doesn't pay as much as waitressing, which is the other thing you do when you're an actor, you waitress even when you get a role. And I was a weather announcer on a TV station in the Valley. —What are you doing? What are you taping the floor for?"

I told her I was laying out a border and that I wanted her and her kid to stay on *that* side of it and not to cross over to my side, and when she looked blank at me I said, "I'm going to be moving a lot of canvases back and forth and I don't want you or Kim to touch anything. Understand? A gallery owner is coming up here next week to look at some paintings." Well, she said, you needn't be so grumpy about it. "Now you tell Kim," I said. She told Kim not to cross the taped line on the floor, not even where it zigzagged, not to cross it or Renato would go crazy. "Understand?" she asked him. Kim nodded yes and stared across the taped line, freshly curious about my work table, his black eyes like spots of wet ink.

I asked Avalon what kind of job she was going to go looking for, and she said she was looking for a job that paid well; I asked what was she good at. "I'm good with animals, for one thing. I worked for this old veterinarian and I was good at it, only she retired and I had to get another job. I learned a lot at the vet's and then I went to work as a lawyer's assistant, but all I learned on that job was I didn't want to be a lawyer. And I'm good at managing a shop. One place I managed was a photo shop in a mall, one of those places where you go and dress up in a costume and get your picture taken. I ran the shop right up to when I had Kim, then I didn't work for three months and when I went back there they wouldn't hire me again, because I insisted on part-time, so I could look after him." I asked did she ever think of learning something so she could get a decent job. "You mean like learn Russian, or the atomic table, or something? I already know a lot of things." I told her I was sure she knew a lot of things. "I don't know why you're so sarcastic. I do know things. I know five different kinds of massage. I know how to make rag paper. I know the Dewey Decimal system. So what?"

I turned away and began to clean the room, gathered up the big sheets of paper I'd been working on, stowed my ink dish and ink bar, and swept the floor. I fried rice and peppers for dinner that night, and afterwards Avalon cleared the table and washed the dishes and dried them and put them away, and that was all right by me.

Early the next morning I pulled canvases from the stack that leaned against the studio wall and I propped them up here and there, all around the room, so I could decide what to show Sonia Strand. Kim had come out and was sitting cross-legged on the floor, on his side of the taped line, watching me. A while later his mother came out in her jeans and undershirt and made him breakfast, then she sat at the table with a purposeful blank face, drinking a mug of black coffee and staring over his head and out the window. I said good morning. "I would have said good morning but I didn't want to bother you," she replied. I couldn't tell if she were being pious or sarcastic. I asked what did she plan to do for the rest of the day, because, I told her, I was going to be sorting through my work and I needed room to move around in and quiet to think in. "I'm going out to look for a job," she announced. I went back to my canvases and some time later I saw she was in a black sweater and had put on black eyeshadow and deathly pale lipstick. I ignored her and continued working, but soon enough I felt her from across the room in her black leather jacket with the chrome studs, just standing there, shifting from foot to foot, waiting, tense.

"Yes, damn it, yes," I told her over my shoulder. "I'll take care of him. Go!" She whispered a couple of words to Kim, kissed him and ducked out the door. I dragged some canvases from the back room to the studio and stood them against the others and kept shuffling them around until I noticed that Kim had flopped onto my bed and was lying on his back with his head over the edge, his face upside down, watching me. "Let's take a walk," I told him.

We left the plane and its passengers at the studio and hiked down to the river, which this morning was a dark metallic blue with a million tiny dents flashing and glinting on its surface, for a chill breeze was sweeping up from the harbor, and there on the grassy bank we discussed the changing shape of the clouds that scudded overhead ("They're made of fog," he informed me. "That's why they change shape."), and watched a solitary oarsman in a shell pulling up stream. I remarked that the figure in the shell seemed to be sitting on the water, like a waterbug, but Kim said he didn't know what a waterbug was, so I told him that if I moved to the country I'd invite him out and I'd show him some waterbugs. I said that I didn't really know him and asked him to tell me something about himself. "You know my mother and she can tell you," he said, walking off to pick up a stone. I said I'd much rather hear from him; so we discussed his favorite number, which was two, and trolley cars, which he also liked, and a TV show he used to watch called Doctor Who; so, between skipping stones on the river and talking on these and other topics, we passed a couple of hours, then went to a cafeteria on Mass Avenue for a bowl of soup and on to the studio.

Avalon returned late in the afternoon and was clearly discouraged, so I didn't ask if she had found work but suggested that her search might go better if she took some of that jewelry off her face, to which she retorted that I sounded old, and I told her yes I was old and I'd rather sound old than stupid. "Anyway," she said, "one shop I went to said they wanted to look at my designs, my rings and bracelets, so I'm going to show them next week." I asked her who was going to look after Kim if she ever found a job and had to go to work, and she said she would enroll him in school, and I said, "Which school? You're not going to be living *here* and you don't know where you'll be living, so how do you know which school?" I'll figure something out, she mutters to herself, and anyway the school year is practically over, and it's almost summer and—. "No it isn't," I tell her. "And that kid ought to be in school."

"Oh, for Christ sake leave me alone!" she cries and pulls Kim into the other room. Avalon didn't come out until an hour or more had passed; she had been wearing the black turtleneck jersey all day, but came out in a frayed black sweatshirt with the sleeves cut off. She saw I was frying some flounder, so she set the table for three and we sat down to dinner. She had gotten over her sulk and now talked easily, even drank a second glass of wine while telling me about Santa Cruz where she had hung out for a time. Her sharp face with those bits of glittering metal was about as beautiful as an ax blade, but her biceps were admirably firm and despite her head of black hair her forearms had a fine brownish-gold down.

Early the next morning as I was going out the door Avalon said, "You know that café where you were talking to the manager or the owner or somebody like that when I came in?"

"What about it?"

"You could tell them that you know me and that you know I'm honest and that I can waitress. I'll do it. And that way you'll get me and Kim out of here."

It sounded good to me, so on my way back from the river I went around to the Daily Grind and asked Gordon did he remember the woman in the black motorcycle jacket with chrome studs, the one who was pestering me a couple of days ago, had rings in her eyebrow and so on. "Sure," he said. "She was in here yesterday, asking for a job. Said you'd give her a good recommendation. I told her to come back next week." When I got back to the studio I told Avalon that I'd throw her and her kid out if she ever again used my name without asking me first. Her face went blank and she pulled Kim into the back room so fast he tripped and got dragged the last yard.

I sat myself on a stool in the middle of the floor and looked at the paintings set all around the room and I attempted to decide which ones to show to Strand, but since bawling out Avalon my brain had stuck tight as a piece of jammed machinery and I couldn't get it to think. I made a pot of coffee, which routine is always soothing, and poured myself a cup and just as I had seated myself again on the stool Avalon appeared in fresh black eye shadow and that ghastly pale lipstick, clutching a small rucksack in one hand and tugging Kim with the other as she slammed out the door. After they had gone, the studio began little by little to fill up with silence, and sunlight settled slowly on the edges and surfaces of things and sank into the paint so the colors resonated, and I was able to make choices.

Later that afternoon, when I dragged one of the canvases from the studio to its storage place in the back room, I stumbled over Avalon's backpack which lay on the floor by the mattress. The backpack was a huge lumpy green nylon thing, the size of a small trunk, with a padded harness, lots of straps and buckles and a multitude of pouches, zippers, loops, mesh pockets and, sure, an open space where the rucksack had been attached. She had been in Boston only a few days, but she was quick and I figured that by now she knew where to go to lay out the little square of black velvet on which she displayed her tawdry silver bracelets and cheap wire rings, and I could see her sitting on a stone step in Copley Square or maybe standing against a wall on Marlborough Street, that bright shifty look in her eyes and the scrap of black velvet with her glittering junk down on the pavement between her boots.

I was at the sink washing dishes when Avalon and Kim came in, the kid scooting past—"*Watch out I have to go the bathroom!*" Avalon was tired and her face being made up like a corpse didn't improve her looks. "Sell much?" I asked cheerfully. She shrugged. "Get arrested for not having a vendor's license?" I asked with the same cheer. "No, I did not get arrested," she said. She went to the back and when Kim came out of the bathroom I asked did he wash his hands, and he said he forgot and ducked back into the bathroom. Avalon had thrown herself face down on her mattress, still in her black leather jacket. "I made soup. It's in the pot on the stove," I told her. At first she didn't stir, then she slowly rolled over and wearily lifted her arm and said, "Pull," so I pulled her to her feet and she said, "Thanks," as she went to the kitchen. After they had the soup, Avalon gave Kim a bath, then read him a story from one of his tattered books and put him to bed. I was writing a letter to my daughter Skye. "Seeing as how you don't have a TV or anything, do you have any magazines?" Avalon asked me. I showed her the stack of *Art New England* and she looked through a few issues, then she sighed and said she guessed she was too tired to read, so she took a shower and went to bed.

I spent Sunday with Alba in her expensive concrete shoebox. The place is all window at one end and there we ate a nice brunch that included a crepe fancy, which she had learned to make in her French cooking class, and while we ate I talked in circles about which paintings I definitely wanted or maybe did not want to show Strand, and whether I was displaying too many or too few, and so on and so forth. As I said, Alba has good sense about these things and, furthermore, she likes to give instructions, so by the time we had a last cup of coffee she had told me which paintings she thought would go best. After brunch we pushed on through the *Globe* and the *Times*, dozed in the sun by the window, hiked to the Square and back again, then she made a light dinner and I washed the dishes. Now, the day having gone well, I asked did she want a brandy and, after turning my offer this way and that to inspect it, she decided she was going to take a long bath and I should bring the brandy to her in the bedroom when she called, so I waited and lit a few candles ("Please, Ren, the fewer, the better.") and we made love like old gods, which is to say slowly, luxuriously, majestically. ("You smile, Alba, but that's the way I'll remember it.")

When I got back to the studio around midnight every light in the place was ablaze. Avalon lay asleep on her side, her cheek on her palm, her body curled around a checkerboard drawn in chalk on the floorboards, and her son lay sleeping above her on my bed in his pajamas, his dangling foot almost touching her head. I picked up Kim and carried him to the back room and laid him on the mattress, then I went back for his mother. She wore no makeup and in sleep her profile had a neat, chiseled edge, her closed eyelashes like a single black brush stroke. I said, "Hey, Avalon," and waited, then said it again, but she didn't stir so I jabbed her butt with the toe of my shoe and she opened her eyes, then turned her head and looked up at me. "I put Kim on your bed," I told her. She scrambled to her feet, glanced around in a daze, then stumbled to the back room.

21

NEXT MORNING I SHUFFLED THE CANVASES, SO the ones Alba thought would do well were displayed better, and I took down Scanlon's drawings and put up some of my own, then I went out to phone Sam Geist, an old painter I knew. Geist used to get into town once in a while, but he was ninety-one or ninety-two now and didn't go out and, as I hadn't seen him for months and was feeling energetic and expansive, I phoned him. I got his wife, Rita, who said I hope you're coming over for a visit this time. He needs to talk to somebody.

I had expected that. I drove out to Geist's and Rita let me in, a thin woman in her eighties with a sharp face that had darkened but otherwise not changed much over the years, as if it had been hacked from wood. "This way," she said, admitting me to the overheated interior. "Sam," she cried. "Renato's here. He's brought pastry, the kind you like! —He dozes off," she confided to me. "Go in."

The room was as neat as a display in a furniture store window, except for the uneven jumble of framed photographs crowded onto a small table. Sam was wide awake, seated forward on the edge of his chair, watching me, his hands folded atop the gray aluminum cane that stood between his knees. His face had dwindled since I last saw him, but his eyes were glistening brightly, his white hair standing up in long tufts like soapsuds or a dandelion gone to seed and half blown away. "Come over here, Ren." His voice had a rustling whispery sound and his iron-cold hand startled me when I grasped it. "Rita, get the poor man a chair!" he croaked. They bickered over which chair I should sit in, then we all agreed to go down the hall to the kitchen. Rita stood in front of Sam and took his hands— "Are you holding? Hold on, Sam. Are you holding?"—pulled him waveringly upright and held him under his arms until he had braced himself with his cane. "All right," he said. "I'm all right! You're in the way, Rita!" We made a slow passage to the kitchen, a bare white room with an old-fashioned stamped tin ceiling, each plate and cup and bowl in its proper place on a shelf, a fresh white oil cloth on the table. Sam lowered himself unsteadily into the chair I held for him at the table, then Rita set out the pastries and began to prepare the coffee. "What's going on in your life?" Sam asked me. I began to tell him how I was trying to get Sonia Strand interested in my paintings, but he broke in to tell me about Newbury Street galleries ("Thieves!") and about some paintings he had seen in New York a few years ago ("Junk!") and about an article he had recently read in *Art News* ("Crap!") Rita brought the coffee to the table and sat down, asking how was Alba, so we talked about Alba and then Sam asked about each of my children in turn and by name. "He's showing off his memory," Rita said. "He's gotten vain about his memory."

"You remember Russo?" he asked me.

"Yes, I remember Russo." I had known Russo for decades and he had introduced me to Sam.

"I was thinking about him the other day. You know he wanted to get to be ninety. Because then he was going to have a big retrospective show. He thought if he got to be ninety he could convince some gallery to give him a retrospective. He died at eighty-nine." He hesitated, as if he had lost the thread of his story. "I don't know if that's comic or tragic," he said at last.

I asked him how old he was, himself.

"All that Communist crap," he said, his voice rasping. "If Russo hadn't spent all those years working for the Commies he could have had twice as much time to paint. You know, he didn't begin painting until he was fifty. He got out of jail is when he began to paint. When he was underground he used to spend a lot of time hiding in museums. Before that he thought he was a sculptor. I remember that huge concrete sculpture he made. He was twenty and thought he was Michelangelo. They put it on display in Grand Central Station. Then he joined the Communists. What a waste."

I said I had always liked Mike's work, most of it.

"He was a good painter," Sam said soberly, meditating on it. "He painted every day. Even to the end, he painted."

I remarked it was nice that the gallery at U Mass had one of his big canvases.

"But those political paintings, those aren't his best, those social statements. You remember whenever he talked about painting he got lyrical and talked about soul and spirit and the human heart. All that Marxist materialist shit would go out the window when he talked about painting."

I said yes. "I remember once—"

"I'd tell him, you're no goddamn *Communist*. You're a *Romantic!* His best paintings were those big peaceful ones, those huge soft colors." His hands had begun to tremble and his eyes glistened even more brightly.

I said I agreed.

"We talked a lot, you know," Sam told me. "We didn't agree but we talked. No one talks any more. There's no one to talk to." One of his eyes overflowed a drop, but he didn't notice it.

"Sam, take Renato to your studio so he can see what you've been doing." Rita stood up, removing her cup from the table.

"Everyone's dead," he barked. Later his voice resumed its usual strained whisper, a sound like rustling paper or dried leaves. "You remember that room where Russo used to paint? It was so small he nailed a mirror to the wall in back of him and when he was painting he'd take a hand mirror and look in it so he could see the mirror behind him and that way he could see what his work looked like at twenty feet." He began to laugh.

"He knows all that," Rita told him. "Show him your new works, honey." She began clearing the table.

"I got to pee," Sam told me. "Do you have that problem yet?"

Sam shuffled off to pee and when he returned we went outside and crossed slowly into his studio, a refinished garage in back of the house. It was the dead of winter in there. Bleak light from the overhead windows illuminated the cold stillness—the hardened dabs of paint on the table top, the row of old, crumpled paint tubes, the jar of dusty brushes, the paintings stacked deep against the walls. I held Sam's arm as he settled himself onto a piano stool in the middle of the room, then I switched on the electric heater. "Take a look at those," he told me, nodding toward a stack of painting. "Move them out. Go ahead. You won't break anything." I had seen them before, but I followed his instructions and pulled out the ones he wanted me to look at and I talked about those, telling him how much I liked the way he had shifted this perspective or had treated that patch of color, and so on and so forth, while he remained perched on the piano stool in silence, his hands at rest on the top of his aluminum cane, his eyes liquid bright, watching me.

Geist had painted the New England landscape for more than seventy years, smearing his paint onto the canvas in thick, energetic layers, simplifying the earth's ravines and hills and stony outcrops to elemental shapes, depicting the occasional farm house or barn as flimsy as a strawberry box and the new highway no more substantial than a ribbon laid across a rock. He was a good painter and for a while had been known as the Grant Wood of New England, a witless comparison that he detested. He liked the work of George Bellows and John Sloan, and painted in that tradition, but for the last several decades no critics had taken his painting seriously and his achievement had been forgotten. Just before we left the studio Sam led me to the work table and there he opened a portfolio of ink sketches I hadn't seen before—dried weed stalks, leafless trees and meticulous studies of bare, thin, twiggy tree branches which interlaced and overlapped and crisscrossed, seeming to reveal in their tangle a scrawled message or semaphore which remained never quite decipherable. I liked it all. "This is good, very good,"

I told him. Sam nodded in sober agreement, then he closed the portfolio and leaned heavily on my arm and we left.

22

THE VISIT WITH SAM DEPRESSED ME ALL THE WAY back to Boston, so instead of climbing upstairs to the studio I walked over to the cheap end of Newbury Street and into the stream of mostly young people, hoping it would do me some good. It didn't do me any good at all. I sat down among the empty chairs outside a café. It was sad to see Sam enfeebled and though I know it didn't pain me the way it pained him, still it gave me a lingering ache. He was fortunate to have a sturdy wife and two married daughters, plus a granddaughter who visited him once in a while. And for sure his five-inch obituary would appear in *The Boston Globe*, recounting his success in his youth, and listing which of his paintings were still in the so-called permanent collections of New England museums.

A waiter came out and asked what I'd like to order, but it was chill outside so I went in and got an espresso. Let me add that Sam Geist was in that generation of painters who came of age during the 'thirties and 'forties and saw their works turned into old-fashioned junk after the war. Geist always said it was émigré intellectuals who derided American painters as parochial and promoted instead "crap that could have been painted in a cellar in any country on the globe." He was thinking of Action painters and Abstract Expressionists and maybe he was right. No matter the history, Geist was forgotten because nobody big chose him to be remembered. Some painters can't afford a pot to piss in while others get rich selling their shit and it all depends on which one the patron chooses. Sam had been rather well known in New England and now he was watching his reputation getting erased bit by bit, which is rotten, but that's what happens if you outlive your patrons. Painters fight against invisibility and how long you live is how long the fight goes on. A year or two before Mike Russo died, he and his wife put together all their nickels and dimes to buy their first house and rebuild the attic into a studio, and in the pain of his final months the old revolutionary still dragged himself up the narrow stairway to paint because, he told me, "The object of art is to revolt against death."

As for me, I wasn't getting any younger sitting at this café, so I finally climbed up to my studio. I cut a wedge of cheese, took a handful of olives and walked up and down, reviewing the work I was going to show Sonia Strand, and after thinking about this for a while I went to the back room and dragged out a big bright painting (horizontal nude female across bottom foreground, shutters in middle open to black iron balcony, greenery and blue sky across upper background) which looked like a poster, *Travel To Southern France This Summer*, but might be the only thing she liked. I tucked the bogus thing in among the others, then I lay down for a nap.

I woke up hungry, ate the stale heel from a loaf of scali and decided to make pasta with tomato sauce for supper. I was tossing this and that into the sauce when little Kim comes through the door, announcing that he's going to school tomorrow, and a moment later Avalon comes in, smelling richly of coffee. She drops her black leather jacket on one of the hooks by the door and while one hand still clings to the hook she reaches down with the other and yanks off her boots, *thump*, *thump*. I asked how her day had gone. "I roasted coffee all day. I mean, I roasted coffee all day after dragging those goddamn sacks of coffee beans from the storeroom. You know how much those things weigh?" She was wearing a sodden T-shirt (DAILY GRIND), stained with sweat and coffee oil. "Look at this," she says, pulling from the jacket pocket a train of wadded white cloth which she shakes magically into a blouse. "I went in wearing this. I thought I was going to waitress. It's filthy!" I told her to take a shower. "Those sacks weigh two hundred pounds, some of them," she informs me, and she goes on to say that Garland—"What's wrong with that woman's nerves?"—told her to enroll Kim in school and to do it tomorrow morning or to not come back to work. Then Avalon pulls the sweatshirt over her head and walks to the back room, using the shirt to mop under her arms as she goes. I told Kim we were going to have pasta with putanesca sauce tonight. "I don't know if I like putanesca sauce," he said. I told him I certainly hoped he would like it and, furthermore, I said, I was going to show him three different kinds of pasta and he could choose which shape he liked best and we'd eat it for dinner. "Well. I guess you'd better let me see them," he said, very businesslike. Kim learned the difference between fusilli, conchigle, and rigatoni, pronouncing the Italian beautifully when he told his mother about pasta shapes at dinner, after which she brought out her paperback *Teach Yourself Japanese* and went over a lesson with him.

23

Sonia Strand had said that she would arrive at ten in the morning. My studio is the only door at the top of the stairs, but after Avalon and Kim had gone out I wrote my name on a big white rectangle of paperboard and tacked it to the outside of the door, then I left the door open a ways and took a shower, put on a fresh shirt, flung open the windows, made a pot of coffee, slammed the windows shut, and drank a mug of coffee while reading *Teach Yourself Japanese.* A little before ten I heard somebody coming briskly up the stairs and I went to the door just as Sonia Strand appeared—wide bush of ruddy gold hair, crystal blue eyes and that dark red mouth not out of breath—we exchanged hellos as she shook my hand and stepped inside. She was alone and I wondered whether that was a good or a bad sign, since most gallery owners appreciate a hireling or other sycophant with whom they can compare notes afterward. I took her cloak, the one with a lining that shimmered like peacock feathers, and asked would she like a mug of coffee, but she gave a large wave of her hand as to brush the offer away and said, "No. I'll get to work right now."

I retreated to the stove and poured another swallow of coffee into my mug while she turned her attention to the paintings, moving herself back and forth a bit in front of the canvas as if to get it in focus. She stood with her fist on her hip and her other hand ever so gently, almost invisibly, slapping a small black notebook against her leg. She was all business but not in a business suit, attired instead in another long columnar dress, this one sleeveless, with a checkered panel of stiff cloth across her bosom, each big square divided diagonally, half black and half white, reminiscent of a Weiner Werkstatte design or the score card for a bowling match.

"These paintings, it's always interesting to see them in their true size," Sonia said a bit later, sounding as if she had a chest cold. "You can tell a lot by looking at a slide, but not everything."

I assented.

"And I like your brushwork, too. That's another thing that never shows up properly in a slide." Now I remembered that the somewhat hoarse baritone was her natural voice.

In ten minutes she had examined most of the paintings whose photos I had brought to the gallery and presently she began to look at the others. I walked over to the canvases and asked did she want me to bring this or that one forward. She waved her hand and said, "You show me." I began shifting the canvases around, letting her look as long as she wanted, of course, before sliding a fresh one to the front. She said nothing but looked with complete steadiness at the work, one hand holding the little notebook, the other hand on her hip or toying with the flat, heart-shaped pendant of silver that hung from a thin chain almost to her waist.

"I wonder, can you take that one out and set it against the wall over there?" she asked.

It was the one that looked like a travel poster; I stood it against the wall.

"No, no," she said. "Turn it so it faces the wall. It's really not any—. I mean, it doesn't—."

I turned it, face to the wall.

"That's better, thank you."

She continued to look at the canvases for a few more minutes, and she asked what name or descriptive phrase I used for this, that, and the other one, which she then jotted in her notebook. She turned to me and smiled broadly. "These are wonderful," she said. "I really like them. I'm impressed by your work. Bold design. Rich colors. I'm impressed. Yes."

There was a space of silence.

"But what?" I asked her.

"No but. There's no but. I admire your work."

"Thank you."

"I noticed some drawings," she said, turning to look at the half-dozen I had taped to the far wall and forgotten.

"Yes."

She strolled over to look at the drawings, one in pencil and one in black crayon, the rest done with a black felt-tipped pen. "You like Klimt or Schiele?" she asked at last. She was looking at the nudes.

"Some of their work, yes."

She turned to me and smiled. "Ever been to Vienna?"

"Not yet."

She came and sat in a kitchen chair and looked around slowly at the studio, taking it in for the first time, and now her gaze lighted on me and lingered, as if I were someone new and interesting. She smiled. "I'd like to have you at the gallery, but I don't know if I can," she said. "Our calendar is filled, unfortunately. But I want to have you. I do want to have you. It's a matter of scheduling. I can't give you anything right now, but I'll look at our calendar and see what's possible. I'll tell you what our plans are and where we might do something. If you'll let me," she added.

"Of course I'll let you," I told her.

"Good! I'm glad you're so professional. Some painters seem not to know how a gallery works. I'm glad you do. You understand the constraints we have to live with."

Now Sonia smiled and tilted her head back, thrusting her hands into that broad mass of reddish gold hair as if it were so tightly packed it hurt her and needed to be loosened, her gesture so open and informal that I took it to mean she felt the difficult part of our meeting was over. She let her hands drop onto her thighs—*slap!*—bringing her flesh to my mind. Her gaze raked across my throat and chest, then returned to my eyes. She seemed to be waiting for me to speak, but I watched only to attend to her whims and didn't want to risk saying the wrong thing, and I wondered if I should ask did she want a mug of coffee now, and in the end all I did was smile at her. She said she supposed that we must have been to some of the same openings and she wondered why we hadn't bumped into each other before. I told her I didn't go to many openings. "Well," she said, "I'm going to send you an invitation to our next opening and I hope you can come."

"Of course I'll come." I went to the stove and refilled my mug with coffee and, as I had my back to her, I spread open my shirt below my throat to show some chest hair, for she seemed to be interested in that. "Can I bring you a cup of coffee?" I asked over my shoulder.

"No, thanks. I have to get back to the gallery now."

I sat in a chair at a polite distance opposite her. She asked did I photograph my work myself, or did I use a professional photographer; I told her I had shot most of them myself and my photographer friend, Michiko, had done the others.

"I could put you in with another painter," Sonia said a moment later. "That's one way of getting you onto the calendar.

But I'm afraid your work would overpower hers. You should have a show of your own."

"That would be great."

She had encircled her wrist with her other hand, and now she was idly stroking her arm, arousing the reddish blond hairs. "One of the shows we did last year was devoted entirely to drawings. I wish I had seen your work. Those nudes would have done very well. They're really not nudes," she added, reflecting on them. "They're actually naked men and women. Rather the way Klimt and Schiele drew them."

"That's one way of looking at them," I said, always agreeable.

"It's Klimt who made his models undress only part way—or is it Schiele I'm thinking of?" Her thumb continued slowly to massage the succulent white flesh on the inside of her elbow, stroking a blue vein.

"It doesn't matter. I know what you mean," I assured her.

"They weren't nudes in the classical sense," she said. "They were women who had taken most of their clothes off. They were naked and they knew it and the drawings showed they knew it."

I realized morosely that she wouldn't be interested in seventy-year-old me, but this is how she behaved with the up-and-coming young pricks so eager to get into her gallery, and it had become a habit with her.

"Your drawings are rather like that. Would you agree?" she asked.

I laughed. "Sure! Why not?"

She laughed too. "Exactly. Why not!"

We talked a bit longer and when she started to get to her feet I sprang up, pulled my chair out of the way.

"Thank you for letting me see your work," she said, gathering her cloak over her arm.

"Thank you for coming," I said.

"I'll get back to you in, say—" she broke off. "Well, it will be a few weeks before I can sort things out. But I'll be in touch. Soon."

While we walked down the stairway we talked about Vienna, Viennese cafés, and espresso machines. At the downstairs door we shook hands firmly, then she stepped out into the sun and I trotted back upstairs, happy. I began to haul canvases to the back room, but quit and ran over to the Daily Grind to phone Alba and tell her about Sonia Strand's visit. I told her how Strand had swept in and what she had been wearing and the way she had looked at the paintings and what she had said about getting a place on her calendar and what we had talked about and so forth. That's wonderful! Alba said, and I said, "I think so, I hope so," and Alba said That's terrific, Ren, that's wonderful. I told her which paintings I had put out and we talked back and forth about the Strand Gallery. Before we said goodbye, she told me Astrid had phoned this morning. She's coming to Boston the day after tomorrow, Alba said, and we'll come by the studio to pick you up at one-thirty. All of us, OK? she asked, and I said, "Great. See you then."

24

I DON'T KNOW HOW YOU CAN CONFUSE DRAWINGS BY Gustave Klimt with drawings by Egon Schiele. Schiele's line jerks and cuts like a knife being dragged through flesh —his own, I suspect—whereas Klimt has a fluid, caressing stroke. Schiele made a lot of interesting sketches of young girls, but wasn't careful and eventually got himself a couple of weeks in jail. All I know is, if you let them hang around your studio and do whatever they're forbidden to do at home, like reading a book or eating French fries or whatever, after a while they'll relax and sprawl this way and that and now you've got yourself a spicy little twelve-year-old model, plus a chance at prison time. Klimt was an ass man and said he knew some women whose fannies were more beautiful than their faces, which I believe, and he drew a joke caricature of himself, his head on a body which is all and only a woman's grand rear end. Not my passion, though I can still recall the glossy touch of a certain fresh rump and the kiss I gave her sweet blond asshole. Schiele was born twenty-eight years after Klimt, and twenty-eight years later they both died of influenza in Vienna. People talk about how tormented Schiele was, but to my mind there was more wrong with Klimt, since he never married but fucked all over the place and left fourteen bastard kids to take care of themselves, though maybe that was because he sprouted in claustrophobic hot-house Vienna and not out-of-doors Paris.

I would have relished talking with Mike Bruno about all this, about Sonia Strand and about Klimt and Schiele and Vienna in 1918 and everything else, but poor Michael was dead and there was no one above ground to talk with, certainly no one who would enjoy observations on the buttery privates of twelve-year-old girls or the smooth behinds of their mothers. Alba claims she understands this furnace in my head, and maybe she does, for she used to stoke it herself every other day and throw cold water on it between times. The company of men was what I wanted, so the day after Strand's visit I crossed over to Cambridge to have coffee with a couple of friends. The afternoon was rainy and gusty, and it was pleasant to sit by the café window with these guys (Kadish, McCormac, Winthrop) to watch it rain and to talk of this and that, but I never got around to telling them about Sonia Strand or my hopes to get a show in her gallery, much less how tired the brainless thing was getting. On the way back to Boston I felt so solitary—or maybe you could say I was just lonely for Mike Bruno—anyway, I felt better when Avalon and Kim came in the door.

25

NOW I HAVE TO SAY A FEW THINGS ABOUT ASTRID'S childhood, since she's about to arrive, which means I have to say something about Alba and me and Zoe, for our marriage hasn't been as neat and symmetrical as yours may be and our family is smaller, or larger, than it seems. We first met Zoe in 1968 when she was, let's say, seventeen. Back then my shows were getting good reviews and Alba, more beautiful than ever, was discovering how very much she enjoyed motherhood as long as she could also get out in the world, so out we went, making our way together like a pair of avid explorers. One night at a party Alba came up behind me, saying, "This is Zoe from Maine who's come to Boston to seek her fortune." Beside her was this mini-dress kid with flushed look of an excited child and ironed hair that hung past her shoulders like beaten gold. We shook hands and she said, "Your wife is wonderful, I've been pouring my heart out to her." We took her home with us, lighted the kindling in the fireplace, pulled the sofa cushions onto the floor, smoked a couple of joints and lay in front of the fire to stare at the flames and talk, or not talk but just sprawl together and, sure enough, one amiable caress led to another.

I won't go into details, not even the ones I remember. It turned out that Zoe had done threesomes before, but it was the first time for me and Alba, and it never could have happened—forget my happy dreams and gross appetites— never would have happened except that Alba had become giddy over Zoe and wanted to show off for her, wanted to demonstrate the beauty and power she had recently become sure of, wanted to impress Zoe in exactly that way. Alba will shrug and deny it, say that we were all stoned that night and that she was no more in charge than I was and that, after all, Zoe was the one who had done it before; but no matter what we did in the dark heat of the fire, each of us like a hesitant bather sinking cautiously into a scalding tub, no matter how we turned or paired or rolled in that floating world, I saw Alba putting on the show with Zoe as our conspiratorial voyeur. Afterward we tucked sleepy Zoe under a blanket on the sofa and crept upstairs to bed to be in our proper place for the children, come Sunday morning.

We kept in touch. We had Zoe out to the house for a Sunday brunch, bumped into her at an anti-war rally that spring, and she came with us to a faculty exhibit and a few parties during the summer. And, yes, the three of us played around together more than once, but that fall she met a young man and moved with him to distant Seattle and we assumed we wouldn't see her again. Yet a month later we received a letter from her, beginning *Dear Alba + Renato (or can I say Ren)*, which told about life beside Puget Sound, so Alba began to exchange letters with her and once in a while I sent her a note or, more often, a sketch with a line or two on the back, so Zoe and I exchanged letters, too, which is how it came about that she had two correspondences, one with Alba and one with me. She had been in Seattle about six months when she wrote us that she had discovered she was pregnant; she felt fine, she said, but she wasn't going to marry the young man, a tidy roommate and traveling companion whom she liked but didn't love and who was already on his way to British Columbia. She'd begun reading a book about religion and decided that she was a deist, because she believed God had created the world but abandoned it and that's why it was such a mess.

Zoe went to nest with her mother in the old house in Penobscot, Maine, the same house her father had fled the day Zoe was born, which exit her mother blamed on Zoe, and after Zoe's baby arrived Zoe moved to Boston and invited us to her place. Her apartment wasn't much more than a closet with a skylight and little Astrid was asleep, bedded in a yellow plastic laundry basket in the corner. Zoe poured three mugs of instant coffee and we sat on rickety chairs around the footlocker she used for a table. "Astrid's almost eleven months old, actually. Not three months," Zoe told us with a fleeting smile. I was puzzled, that's all. Zoe was kneeling by the basket and now she folded the blanket away from the baby's head, as if to show us that she was, in fact, almost eleven months old. I was about to say, "Time flies," but everything fell to a strange silence and slowness. Zoe drew the sleeping baby ever so gently from the yellow laundry basket and seated herself on a wood kitchen chair, cradling the baby in its blanket. She glanced at me and at Alba, then lowered her head to the baby and her face glowed, as if the baby were a lighted candle. Alba had not moved. "She was born in Seattle," Zoe told us, looking up. "I should—I would have said something, told you, but I. You both. I'm sorry. I didn't know what to do." Alba didn't move but asked Zoe what she was telling us, and Zoe confesses she was already three months pregnant and knew it when she left for Seattle, then Alba slowly asks Zoe does she need to tell us anything else, and Zoe says no, nothing else, and at last everything comes to a stop and I ask Zoe, "Am I the baby's father?" and Zoe looks at me and says yes. Alba's lips were pale, her face white. "What do we do now?" Alba asked.

None of us knew what to do. Alba and I drove home in silence and later that night as we were undressing for bed she turned to me and spoke for the first time. "I have only one question," she said. She was naked, with her arms across her breasts and her hands tucked into her armpits as if she were chill. "Did you ever get together with Zoe when I wasn't there?" she asked. Her face had turned to stone. I said, "No," which was the truth. She looked at me, then she dropped her hands and turned to get into bed and I said, "I'm Astrid's father and that means—" but she cut me off, saying, "I know what that means."

We told the kids. Fabrizio was two years old and didn't care one way or the other about this trivial infant, whereas Skye was six and happy to have a baby sister, accepting as another grown-up oddity that her sister had me for a father and Zoe for a mother—though she did privately question Alba about it and some days later questioned Zoe about it, too, before being satisfied that this genealogy was known and understood all around. We got our parents together: my mother clapped her hand to her forehead and burst into Italian, saying I already had a good wife and now I was ruining everything, then my father twice cleared his throat as if to speak but said nothing, while Alba's mother looked alternately angry and bewildered.

On days when I wasn't there, Alba had Zoe and the baby come to our house, for Alba can be wonderfully generous, devious and calculating, all at the same time, though she can't tell you which is which. I don't know what went on in her mind, nor do I know how Zoe felt about Alba, how much was friendship or gratitude and how much was strategy. As for Alba and me, we slept on opposite sides of the bed for a few weeks and when, later, we did make love it was stark as knives. Then one Sunday—I don't know how deeply she planned this or if she simply had a whim—Alba had Zoe and the baby Astrid come to Sunday breakfast with all of us, so my whole family was together for the first time. And that night, for reasons I don't understand, I was aroused mindlessly, as if by Alba in heat, and I caught her in the bedroom and didn't quite get to the bed but took her to the floor, which pleased her just fine.

Now, as everyone tells me, Alba is a beautiful and easy-going woman, but let's be clear about this, Alba likes to manage people and she was managing the three of us so well there were moments I suspected she was enjoying herself more than she let on. She informed me one night that they had agreed Astrid would be baptized in May, that Alba would be godmother and that I should ask Mike Bruno or somebody to be godfather. After the baptismal party little Astrid stayed mostly with us, with our kids, while her mother took courses at Mass Art every morning and waitressed the rest of the day, spending her nights in a sleeping bag at a friend's place in Boston or, on weekends, in our fold-out bed. Zoe took Astrid and decamped to Boulder for a while, returned to Boston, left for Los Angeles (we had Astrid each summer), came back to Boston, moved to

Taos (now we had Astrid during the school year) and settled in Boston, during which fifteen or twenty years she had two marriages, two divorces and one miscarriage. Amid all her coming and going I had grown fond of her, and I told her so. "And I, of you," she said.

Alba believes that if you're a romantic you love only one person because the one you love is so radiant and blinding you can't even see the rest of the world, but if you're not a romantic and not blind you can be in love with two or three at once. "It happens," she says with a shrug. Zoe doesn't think so. "No, no, it's the other way around," says Zoe. "It's the romantic who tries to love more than one at a time, but it's all make-believe. Because in this world, in my world anyway, we're selfish and vain and jealous. We want to be loved and we don't want to share."

26

WHEN I OPENED THE DOOR TO ASTRID'S SHARP knock-knock she gave me a tight hug, saying, "Hi, dad, let's go," and pulled me by the hand, the same as when she was seven, clattering breakneck down the stairs and out to the sidewalk where Zoe and Alba stood waiting beside a big yellow taxi. "Now we're all together," she declared. Astrid is a good-looking young woman and that's a fact: her hair was drawn back as tight and glossy as a chestnut fresh from the tree, her face angular and windswept, a streak of color on each cheek—our accelerated daughter. I gave her another hug, throwing my arm around her back and pressing her sharp shoulder blades to feel if she had enough flesh on her (she didn't), taking in the breezy scent she used. "Let me look at you," I said, backing off. Zoe said She's as beautiful as ever, and Alba said She's stylish too, and all the while I was thinking she's skinny as a stick. "Let's go," Astrid said, holding open the door to the big yellow cab.

As we rattled toward the restaurant Zoe prompted her to continue telling about the conference she had gone to this morning, so Astrid told us how well it had gone and who she was going to meet this afternoon, but before she could say very much we had arrived at the eatery, a glassy high-speed place with a continuous row of bars—salad bar, fruit bar, juice bar, bread bar, and so on—followed by a long dining bar, which meant you entered at this end, chose your food, ate it further along, and went out the other end. "Is this place designed like my digestive tract, or have I've got a terrible imagination?" Zoe asked. The women discussed Astrid's black velvet jacket and her white silk blouse, and it gave me an odd pinch in the heart to see how more aged Zoe and Alba looked now that Astrid was here. When I got the chance I asked my daughter about her current film project, and she told us about it and told us a lot more about trying to raise money to finance it, and went on about a young man, whom she had met last week, who owned *TrendSetters* or some other trash magazine and he knew people who had money to invest in movies. Later Astrid told us about a great party where she had met Abdi, the celebrated hair dresser— "And, mother, let me repeat that I do like the way you've cut your hair," she said—and Cindi Ross, the high-fashion model, and Ricardo Carlos, the same Carlos who had invented a new dance step last year. While Astrid was talking about the party, Zoe and Alba had glanced sideways at each other, then Zoe composed herself and said she knew the party must have been exciting but that, frankly, those people sounded, well, flashy and empty. Astrid replied that no, actually, Cindi was a hard worker; then she smiled and slid her hands slowly across the table to grasp her mother's hands. "Don't worry about me. I can take care of myself," she confided.

We left the dining bar and as I was going out the door beside Astrid I asked her, "How's life?" and she said, "You mean how's my private life, right?" and I said, "Right," and she said, "By the way, dad, speaking of private lives, how much longer do you plan to camp out at your studio?" I told her I wasn't camping out, I was living there so maybe I could do some real work before I died, and she said don't be so morbid; then Alba spoke up behind us, telling her that we were still looking for country property. "Yeah, well, I've heard that before," Astrid said, pausing so Alba and Zoe could join us. Alba and I insisted we were telling her the truth. "I hope so. And so does everyone else. Especially your children," Astrid said. In the taxi Alba asked had she heard anything from Brizio or Skye, and she said yes, she had gotten a long letter from Skye describing an expedition Skye and Eric had taken up some mountain in Indonesia, and yes, she and Brizio talked on the phone about once a month to catch up on things, and no, she didn't know if Brizio was planning to return to physics or to continue building solar houses, but she did know he enjoyed working outdoors.

When we got to Copley Square, we three got out of the cab so Astrid could drive downtown to her conference, then Astrid got out too, to say goodbye to us, we thought, but instead she stood by the open door, squinting in the sun, and she said, "Oh, by the way, you remember Harry?" She meant the randy old photographer she had lived with a few years ago, a widower decades her senior; we said yes, we remembered. "You remember I went to his funeral?" And we said, yes, we remembered that, too. "Yeah. Well. Anyway, you remember how I met his son at the funeral—actually, we had met before but we got reacquainted at the funeral—and how we had dinner together a month later?" No, we hadn't remembered that. "Yes, you do," she insisted. "His name is Wes and I'm sure I told you. Anyway, we had dinner, you know, and then we had dinner again a couple of days later, and so on."

She stood on the sidewalk with one hand atop the open door of the taxi, the other hand shading her eyes from the sun, and she smiled at us, waiting.

"And so on?" I said.

"And so we've kept seeing each other," she concluded, smiling. Alba said, "Oh, you mean—" and Zoe said, "You like him," and Astrid said, "Yup. I really like him and he really likes me." I asked did Wes know that Astrid had lived with his father, and she said, "Of course he does. I'm the one who convinced Harry to make up with him. When I moved in they hadn't spoken to each other for over a year." Zoe asked what his name was. "Wes, mother, Wes. It's short for Weston. And this—Wes and me—this is different." She smiled briefly, her sober gaze shifting from Zoe to me to Zoe. "I thought I should tell you." She tossed her head and raked a thin hand through her hair, then she laughed, her face becoming luminous. "That's wonderful," Zoe told her, and I said, "Yes. Great. That's great, Astrid."

"He's just right," Astrid told me. "You'll like him." Then she gave her mother an impulsive hug and kiss, gave me and Alba a kiss, squeezed my hand and ducked into the cab, waving goodbye, her phone already in her other hand as the cab shoved off. Zoe had taken a step into the street to watch the cab disappear into traffic and when she came back she asked if Astrid had ever told me about Wes or Weston or whatever his name was, and I said no, but I admitted that I had never been able to keep track of her friends, not even when she was in high school. Alba said she hadn't heard about Wes before today, but that Astrid certainly looked happy about him. Zoe and I discussed Weston for a while, then Zoe said, "Astrid always knows what she's doing when it comes to men, even when she's doing the wrong thing, and she wouldn't say this one was different from the others if he wasn't, so, well, anyway—" She broke off and looked to me for help. "He's different from the others and that's a good thing," I said. Alba suggested that we wait and see. We debated a little longer but in the end we all agreed to wait and see, because Astrid wasn't a kid anymore but a smart young woman and, besides, there wasn't anything else we could do.

27

God created Adam and Eve after working for five and a half days on everything else, because he wanted spectators to his achievement, needed at least a couple of people to say, "Oh, wow! That's *great!*" because above all else God is an artist, creator of heaven and earth and all things, as the Catechism says, and creators want others to enjoy and appreciate their works and would like themselves to be admired for their handiwork. It's a long and lonely trek to that place where you paint not for viewers who never come, but simply because you can, because you're good at it, and because there's pleasure in making the vision visible. It's a place you go to when there's no place else to go. God wouldn't have liked it there and neither do I.

Now, these days the prospect of my show at a good Newbury Street gallery energized me so much I would walk up and down, jittery in front of the canvass, trying to calm down enough to paint. There were mornings I felt in me the powerful legs—hindquarters I could say—of my great, great grandfather, the Cavallù who was man from the waist up and stallion from the waist down, but that's a story for another day and, besides, I'm his great, great grandson only by adoption. Every morning I'd trot a mile or two beside the Charles, then scramble up the stairs two at a time to my studio, eat breakfast and begin painting and keep painting until I was about to drop, at which time I'd stretch myself out on the floor to rest.

Once I fell asleep there and woke up with Avalon crouched over me, her ear to my chest and her fingers searching for my carotid artery while Kim stood in the doorway, his eyes big as saucers. "Christ! I thought you were dead!" she cried angrily. "Not yet," I told her. I got up and stumbled around and began to prepare dinner. Avalon watched me and when I fumbled a pan into the sink she said, "Hey, I'll cook," but I said, "No, thanks," and waved her off because, frankly, Avalon didn't know how to cook. Whenever she prepared dinner it turned into a bowl of noodles or a soggy mix of chopped vegetables and rice and, no, I didn't believe her when she said it was because Kim needed more practice with chopsticks. I was buying the food and she was paying for half of it; she made breakfast, I cooked dinner. But that evening we began to work the stove together and every evening after that I tried to teach her some Mediterranean dishes. "First of all, olive oil," I told her, holding up a bottle from Tuscany.

"Extra virgin," she says, reading the label. "You're either a virgin or not, so what kind of crap is an *extra* virgin?"

I asked her did she know what virgin olive oil was. "Pure," she says. "No," I informed her. "Pure is the grade below virgin. You get extra virgin by pressing unbruised olives. Virgin is more acid than extra virgin and—"

"Wait, wait! Let me guess. The less virgin you are, the more *acid* you are," she says, laughing at her own witticism.

"The important thing is taste," I told her, undeflected. "Extra virgin is like wine. It has a taste and a color from the soil where it grows. —Are you listening?" And so forth every evening.

Actually, Avalon listened more carefully than I guessed and caught on faster than I expected. "She's a worker," Gordon told me at the Daily Grind. "Doesn't talk much. Doesn't smile much, either. But she works," he said. I watched her drag a huge burlap sack of coffee beans across the floor toward the roaster. She was in her Army camouflage pants, baggy things mottled with green and khaki and black, and a white swimtop, her bare arms and shoulders glistening with sweat. "Everything stops when her kid comes in, so she can look at his school work and tell him what a great one he is. But she gets the job done," he told me. "Did you see her jewelry we've got by the cash register? She asked if she could sell it there and we said yes."

"Of course I've seen it. She wears a lot of it on her face."

"If you don't like her, why do you let her live at your place?"

"I didn't say I didn't like her. I just don't like her in my studio."

Which is why I visited Michiko Shimada. She sometimes rented out part of her place and, frankly, I was hoping to move Avalon and her kid out of my studio to anywhere else. I liked Michiko. She had come to this country from Osaka about ten years ago with her camera and not much more, had worked at odd jobs (waitress, artist's model, teacher of Japanese) and had established herself as a photographer. I don't think I'd heard her say five words in a row about abstractions such as politics or esthetic theory, but she brought a deep engagement to anything she looked at and was herself worth looking at, her body a stylized rendition of a body, the long mass of her hair a single brush stoke of black ink, the breasts and buttocks indicated by pale shadows, and that face a smooth bronze sheet on which were inscribed her lips, nose and eyes.

Now she opened the door to her studio and we exchanged *Konnichi wa*. She smiled broadly, a brilliant oblong smile, and said something that I didn't understand. I said *Foku de tabemasho*—let's eat with forks—meaning I'd used up all my Japanese. She made tea, we looked at her photos, talked about this and that, and I discovered Renato wasn't going to say anything about Avalon and Kim because, after all, he liked Machiko and didn't want to mess up her studio, her work and her life. As I was leaving, I invited her to dinner at my place and told her I had somebody she might like to meet. "Yes, thank you. And who is this somebody you want me to meet?" she asked. "Two somebody's," I told her. "A small boy and his mother." I don't know when I had begun to think that maybe she could hire Avalon as an assistant.

❦

One afternoon I was working when Zoe turned up to say Hi, and I said Hi, and went back to take a couple more swipes at the canvas, and she said Well, do you? and I said What? and she said I've already asked you twice—do you want to take a break now or do you want me to leave? and I said Yeah, and added maybe another brush stoke, and she said Yes to which? and I said Yeah, I need a break now. So Zoe turned to make coffee and I began to clean up and I was surveying the canvas when Zoe said, "What did you do with the coffee canister? And where did you put the grinder? Where is everything?" and that's when I knew I had better tell her about Avalon and Kim.

So I brought out the fancy Italian mugs Zoe had given me and set our chairs by the window, and there we drank coffee and took biscotti from a plate on the window sill while I waited for a good moment to tell her about Kim and his mother. Zoe said she was through for the day because nobody would call with a job late on a Friday afternoon and, anyway, she added, a nasty pain had developed again in her upper back, just at the edge of her wing bone, and she couldn't work anymore, even if she wanted to, and she didn't want to—only then did it break through my skull that Zoe had come here to yield herself to whatever comfort I might offer.

Now, one way to undo Zoe is to undo her knotted muscles. So I unrolled the frayed old futon while Zoe stepped out of her shoes, hung her jacket and blouse on a chair. She stretched herself face down on the futon, resting her cheek on her arm. "Do with me what you will," she said into the crook of her elbow. I unfastened her bra and began to massage her back, first smoothing the bra lines, then sliding my thumbs up into her trapezius and finally rolling the small muscle that edges her wing bones, that last causing her to groan with pleasure and to close her eyes. Later she turned her head to rest her cheek on the back of her hand, murmuring, "I've been meaning to ask, what's this taped line on the floor for?" That's when I told her about Kim and Avalon. Zoe didn't say a word. I massaged a bit longer, then slapped her clothed rump and dismounted. "The girl sounds like a tramp," Zoe said sharply. She sprang up and began to fasten her bra, keeping her back to me. I put my hand gently to the nape of her neck but she jumped away. "This is a bad time of the month for me, so fuck off," she said. She stepped into her shoes and strode to the back room, took a look around, returned. "I don't know how Alba stands you," she said, buttoning her blouse.

"Come on, Zoe."

"I'm tired and I'm annoyed. Hope you get along with the little boy," she added, snatching up her jacket. "Bye."

I got along well with the little boy. Kim was a good kid, if you had to have a kid living in your studio. I had given him a ream of cheap paper and a box of colored markers and after dinner, after he had finished his homework, he would stay seated at the kitchen table, drawing energetically and talking about what he was drawing, which was never trucks or dinosaurs, but diagrams, maps and floor plans. He drew the layout of his schoolroom for me, an elaborate plan which showed the location of the teacher's desk, his own desk, his friend Kevin's desk, the art supply closet, the big maps (these were shown in detail), the fish, the flower box, The Flag of the United States of America, and for his mother he drew an equally detailed plan view of the Daily Grind with the cash register, coffee roaster, coffee bags and café tables properly arrayed and labeled.

I had to go to Gloucester to rescue three paintings which had been languishing in the ratty back room of a gallery since last fall, so I drove up on a Saturday and brought Kim and his mother along to give them a change of scene. After I had stashed the paintings in the wagon, I drove up and down Gloucester hill, showed them Our Lady of Good Voyage with a fishing boat in the crook of her strong arm like it was baby Jesus (a wood statue I love) showed them where Gina used to have her café, then down to the harbor to walk out on the wharves, and over to the Fitz Hugh Lane house ("The only painter who could paint silence," I tried to tell Avalon) and to a shop so she could buy an absolutely necessary picture postcard of the harbor. After lunch we walked along a deserted stretch of Good Harbor beach, Kim racing up and down the hard sand while his mother searched for sea shells, then home to the studio just as a gusty rain blew in from the Northeast. The steep little town isn't the way it used to be when I was growing up, when the harbor was busy with fishing boats and seas were crowded with cod, but I could see Kim and Avalon liked it and had a great time.

As planned, Michiko Shimada came to dinner. I introduced Kim, who shook her hand in a grownup way, saying politely, "Hello, I'm pleased to meet you." And a moment later Avalon came from the back room, barefoot and in black velvet shorts belted with a chromium dog chain, a black elastic jersey top (very tight) and around her neck a black leather dog collar with pointed chrome studs. "Yay! Mom's all dressed up!" Kim exclaimed, delighted. I forgot to mention the pale lipstick and the thick black eyeliner. I introduced Michiko and Avalon to each other. Michiko smiled and said, "It's a pleasure to meet you," but Avalon had already turned away, saying, "Yeah, I'll get the wine." Kim went back to drawing his Metro map while we three stood at the window, wine glass in hand, and discussed the weather or, to be precise, Michiko and I discussed the weather while Avalon remained silent, as if absorbed in listening to us, her sharp gaze slicing back and forth from Michiko to me and back again. We sat down to dinner, the chrom neck studs and facial rings glittering in the candle light, and as soon as everyone's plate had been filled Avalon pointed her knife at Michiko, saying, "You're wondering what I'm doing here." She lowered the knife, her face seeming to push slightly forward toward Michiko. "I fit in fine here. No matter what anybody thinks, even if they think they're old friends with Renato."

I stiffened in my chair, hoping not to slap Avalon's face, and Michiko, her lips parted, hesitated to speak.

Kim announced, "I can name all the stops on the Red Line and the Green Line." He looked around the table, cheerful and expectant.

"That's *great!*" I told him, slapping the table top. "Let's hear them. Right now."

"Only the main line, not the branches," he said. Then he recited all the stops from Alewife to Braintree on the Red and from Lechmere to Riverside on the Green. Avalon watched her son avidly, her hand hovering an inch above the table, ready to caress his head the moment he finished.

"An intelligent young man," Michiko said.

"He knows Japanese," Avalon told her. "Please, Kim, count in Japanese."

At his mother's prompting Kim rattled off the numbers and the dozen or so words and phrases that made up his Japanese vocabulary. "Ah, good, very good," Michiko told him, smiling. "Yoku dekimashita ne! Yoku dekimashita," she said. Now Avalon smiled, told Michiko a little about Kim, swapped anecdotes with her about San Francisco, told her about her job with a photographer, drank down a third glass of wine, relaxed. The dinner went well and long after Kim had said, Can I be excused? and gone off to fall asleep over his maps, we sat there talking into the night. Our Avalon had become quite talkative, annoyingly so. She asked Michiko had she ever heard of sel gris or fleur de sel. No, Michiko hadn't. "Renato is teaching me about salt. He lectured me about olive oil and about vinegar, now it's salt. Sel is French for salt."

"Oh, *sel*, yes!" Michiko said. "I was taught some French in school."

"He's teaching me how to cook Mediterranean because, like, we're a family."

I looked at Avalon, hoping my stare would shut her up or at least slow her down.

"We're not fucking or anything like that," Avalon said.

"For Christ sake, Avalon!" I said.

"I have to think about my reputation. I don't want people to get the wrong idea."

"I know Renato for a long time. I won't get the wrong idea." Michiko smiled. "Not to worry, Avalon."

Afterward, after Michiko had left and we were at the sink, Avalon asked was Michiko as nice as she seemed. "Yes, I said. "She is. She's very nice."

"Are you fucking her?"

I stopped and looked at her. "What's *wrong* with you?"

"There's nothing wrong with me," says Avalon.

"Yes, there is. You dress like a whore and you're rude and you're insulting. And since you're so concerned with your reputation, which is laughable, you should move out."

Avalon's face went blank. She lifted her chin, then carefully hung the dish towel on the rack and went to bed without another word.

They didn't move out. Kim went to school, Avalon went to work. The prospect of my having a show on Newbury Street had energized me, so scores of new paintings blossomed in my head, and not only paintings but also drawings, tile designs, wood sculpture, a type-face and lines for a poem on my prostate. I'd get up early, trot by the river which would still be asleep and gray as glass, then back to the studio to paint, which I was doing better than anyone.

28

YOU CAN DRAW BY PISSING ON SNOW OR BY USING a computer, but pissing on snow is better because your art will express your humanity and mean something to anyone who sees it, so I would not have gone to the opening of *Pixels: An Exhibit of Computer Art* except that my friend Nils Petersen had some work in it and had asked me to come. Alba and I arrived to a thin crowd of mostly young people who knew one another and didn't want to talk with anyone old, so we passed invisibly among them to view the computer prints and to look at the screens' endlessly repeating images. After the tour we made small talk with Nils and his wife Hanna, during which I told Nils his work was the best in the show and I praised his multitudinous colors, which pleased him, I hope, then Alba and I visited the wine-and-cheese table which displayed not only wine and cheese but also platters of cold cut meats, gorgeous hillocks of sliced fruit, and a handsome young woman pouring white wine into a row of flimsy plastic glasses. More people arrived, including some from Copley College, and we had a pleasant chat with Azarig and his wife Anna, then later we bumped into Marc, a friend whose poetry I can't decipher, and his wife Simone, a performance artist, but forgivable because of her verve and knock-out good looks. Zoe arrived, greeted Alba with a great hug and me with a hasty hug followed by a quick turn away to dramatize her annoyance with me.

Later Alba and I talked with Sebastian Gabriel, accompanied as usual by his young daughter Cait, a gangly girl with braids and an eager smile, braces on her teeth. Sebastian is one of the finest papermakers in New England (he made the paper I used for my Genesis series) but thin, disorganized and failing at business since his wife walked out on him. I asked Cait if I could bring her a ginger ale and she said yes, then followed me to the soft-drinks. We conversed, agreeing that the animated computer designs were kind of dull but that it was interesting to meet all these artists. Katie sipped her ginger ale and told me, "My father makes beautiful papers, you know, but computers can't print on my father's paper. I don't know what we're going to do. He says we'll get by, but I worry about him. He's impractical, you know." I told her that great artists would junk computers and work by hand in order to use her father's beautiful paper, and I asked what she had been reading recently, for I knew she was an avid reader, and she told me about a five-volume story by Lloyd Alexander, the same epic my daughter

Skye had loved, so we talked about that brave tale or, rather, she talked while I listened and smiled and nodded, remembering Skye when she was that age.

I took another stroll around the gallery and discovered that most of the artists in the show used to design book jackets or advertisements, not that I deprecate the work of graphic artists; indeed, from my father I learned to admire particularly the work of Eric Gill, the British craftsman who designed the famous Gill sans serif typeface and who also cut clean and supple wood engravings, a religious man who took to wearing monks' robes, though I was disappointed to learn that he fucked not only his daughters but his dog, too. A while later Azarig and a witless cyberhead named Roth and I got into a discussion about the giclée reproduction method where prints are stored in digital form and then squirted onto paper by a computerized urinary machine. Azarig remarked that storing a print in digital form saved a lot of space and Roth began to rhapsodize about the technology of digital printers and about this great computer artist and that great video artist, and so on and so forth, and eventually he got around to asking had I made any use of these exciting new print processes. "Look," I told him. "Printing means scratching something up, smearing it with paint, then pressing it onto paper with your hands or your feet. It takes a certain skill. What you're talking about is machined crap." After which surly declaration I hunted around for Alba and finally spied her seated languidly and somewhat fatigued in a corner with Zoe who was talking and laughing, flashing her hands about as if she were juggling invisible balls in a private entertainment for the two of them, a typical Zoe maneuver when she's sore at me

I ended up at the wine table and while the young woman was pouring bogus Chablis into my plastic glass I asked her what she did in real life. "I'm an environmental scientist," she said, handing me the drink. "During the day I take the temperature of Boston Harbor but it doesn't pay much, so I do this one night a week. What about you? What are you in real life?" she asked. So we talked about personal identity and true life and after a while I began to think how our Brizio, living in disguise as a builder of solar houses, might like this comely scientist, for I certainly did, when a skinny young lout came up and said, "Mr Stillamare, I'm Frank Vanderzee. I admire your work and I was wondering if you were going to have a show where I could see more of it."

"You want to talk to me or to Winona here?" I asked him.

He had a good-natured smile. "You, actually."

"I've seen you someplace."

"Drinking coffee at the Daily Grind," he said.

"Yes, and you're a painter. —You need to eat more."

He smiled again. "If you could visit my place some time I'd like to show you what I've been doing."

He looked like a nice guy, but I had no wish, none at all, to see his work or anyone else's. I would have returned to my ontological chat with Winona but she had moved to the other end of the table, so I was stuck talking with this Vanderzee (chest hair boiling from the V of his shirt) and eventually I said I'd drop around to his place one of these days.

Later I was talking with Sebastian when Alba came up to tell me she wasn't feeling well—she was going home and did I want a ride back to my studio or did I want to stay here and find my own way home. I asked was it a headache or an upset stomach or what, and she said it felt like being seasick with a high fever and now all she wanted was to go to bed. I walked with her to her car—it had rained, the air was sweet and the sidewalk smelled of washed stone—told her I'd phone in the morning, then she drove off to Cambridge while I returned to the gallery, for though I dislike going to these gathering I also dislike leaving them, and there I had another hour of company before I made a midnight walk back to my studio, a pleasant walk on clean, drying streets, but also melancholy, because it reminded me of the homeward walks we used to take when we were young and the city was new.

The next morning I drove over to Alba's concrete dovecote, knocked on the door and waited, then let myself in. She looked dead in bed, propped up by two pillows with her eyes sunk shut and her arms just two peeled sticks on the blanket, her face as still and white as an old fashioned mortuary photograph. "Hey, Alba!" I croaked, shaking the bed, frightened. Her eyes opened, passive and uninterested. "I'll call the doctor," I told her. She shook her head no, whispered that she had thrown up during the night but felt better now, just tired, then she closed her eyes. Her forehead was hot and sweaty. I phoned the doctor and made an appointment for the following afternoon, which was the soonest I could get, then I drove back to the studio, left a note for Avalon, stuffed some clothes into an overnight bag and drove back to Alba's. The doctor listened to her chest, diagnosed pneumonia, cheerfully wrote out a prescription which he said was for a new, powerful medicine. Sometimes I watched Alba while she slept and knew my life would be over if she ever died. During the day I caught up on my reading, at night I rolled myself in a blanket on the bedroom floor and went to sleep; after seven days Alba's fever abated and I drove back to the studio, made a note that Alba should have a chest x-ray and I should have my annual physical, then dove into painting again.

29

OF COURSE, THE PAINTING DIDN'T ALWAYS GO WELL. There were times when I suspected I'd done my best work years ago and, as I hadn't been able to make a name for myself back then, I felt it was useless to go on now and, in fact, there were days when I didn't paint at all, or painted badly and made such a mess there was nothing to do but punch my stupid fist through the canvas and kick the stretcher to bits. A couple of decades ago I had done a series depicting a group of three people—some showed a woman and two men, others displayed two women and a man—where one figure was clothed and at least one other was unclothed, a psychological arrangement that critics said was derived from Giorgione by way of Manet, which was agreeable to me and profitable too, though in fact they were inspired by something else, and now in one of my lousy canvases I was trying to assemble a group of older figures, some of them unclothed, but the thing was no good.

Avalon and Kim were distracting me. There's the tent Kim made from an easel and a blanket, a teepee that stood in the studio for a week while he and his friend Anwar played at being Navahos, and here on the counter are a dozen of Avalon's bite-size buttons for me to swallow and choke on, and her blouse with a threaded needle through the cuff and, for all I know, three other invisible needles scattered where I slice my bread, and there's her underpants and bra hanging from the shower-head and, wedged between two of her cologne bottles, this sheaf of old papers, *my* sheaf of old papers, the reading list hand-written and annotated by my uncle Zitti. "What are you so grumpy about? It's only a book list, for Christ sake. I was only looking at it. I wasn't going to erase anything," she complained. *"Don't pry into my things!"* I told her, which was hopeless, since the back room where she and Kim slept was where I stored most everything. And here's Kim again, cross-legged in front of my father's open tool chest, a row of stone chisels on the floor arranged according to size; I explained the use of each one as I retrieved it, then I padlocked the chest. And here's Avalon, saying, "Why don't you talk to me? You're always writing letters. Every night, scribble, scribble, scribble." You might try it yourself, I say, shoving a sheet of stationery across the table at her. "Oh, sure. Who would I write to?" All right, so she had no one to write to. And when I needed to take a break, needed to go out to converse or go brood by myself, I couldn't enjoy the Daily Grind because Avalon would be there, trying to get the espresso machine to detonate, hauling sacks of beans or tending the roaster, her face glistening with sweat and her jersey—*my* jersey!—sagging dark and damp between her breasts and under her arms.

One night I got in late and there was Avalon, propped against my pillow on my bed, one of my old sketchbook-journals open on her lap, for at one time I had thought all artists kept notebooks and I had tried to keep one. I asked what the hell she was doing. "Kim's asleep and I didn't want to wake him with a light, so I'm reading out here," she explained, setting her wine glass on the floor.

"No, damnit!" I said, slamming the journal shut and yanking it from her. "Why are you reading this?"

"I was just looking at—" she began.

"Don't snoop!" I told her.

"I wasn't snooping, I just hap—"

"Does the word privacy mean anything to you?"

"You know, Ren, you'd be a lot nicer if you'd just loosen—"

"And you should ask before wearing my clothes!"

Avalon jumped up, grabbed her sweater at the neck and though I told her *Keep it, keep it, you can keep that one!* she was already pulling it over her head and threw it at me.

One night I was at the kitchen table writing a letter to my brother Bart when Avalon sat down across from me with a couple of books, but I went on scribbling and didn't look up. "Want to see my pictures?" she said briskly. I finished my sentence and gnawed on my pen awhile, trying to grapple the next clump of words, but Avalon stayed waiting so finally I gave up and looked at her. She had two small photo albums, the kind that hold one snapshot per page. "I know you're paranoid about being interrupted but it's getting late and I thought you'd like to look at my pictures." She was sitting up straight and businesslike with a hand flat on each album. Abruptly she dragged her chair around to my side—"Move over a bit," she said—slid my letter away and laid a shiny pink album in front of me. "I have lots of photos and you'll recognize my dad right away, of course," she told me, flipping open the cover. There were a few black-and-white photos of Avalon's father, Brendan Flood (puzzled smile, bushy hair), holding squinty toddler Avalon in his arms, then some color snapshots of Avalon standing alone on a brown lawn which looked like it had the mange, though the colors were so faded I couldn't see for sure, then pages of brighter color pics of Avalon and her father and the empty silhouette of another person who had been carefully scissored out, a neat decoupage which left not even a sliver of Sandra, the airhead, or Linda, the bitch.

Avalon said a few words about each photo— "That's me at the beach," or "That's us at the redwood forest," or "That's me again." —which explained nothing, and though I tried to focus on the dumb images I grew increasingly aware of Avalon sitting close against my side, her bare arm grazing mine each time she turned a page. We must have finished the pink album, for she closed it and placed in front of me the glazed lilac one. These photos were the same as the earlier ones except that little Avalon (blondish hair, by the way) was getting thinner, taller and more awkward, and she was making friends— "That's me and Jenny," or "That's Diego's band," or "That's Charlotte and me and Valerie," or "That's me in Diego's car." —page after page after page. Then she turned the last page, closed the glazed lilac cover and turned to me. I had never seen her so close before, the wire rings along the rim of her tender ear, the miniature rivet that pierced the delicate flair of her nose, the loops of wire through her eyebrow, and her eyes—the blue iris with smoky black specks which, for a moment, gave me the weird sense of being at the bottom of a deep well, staring up at the sky. She was looking at me in a needful, pleading way which I'd never seen her use before, as if now I were supposed to say something or do something, and I wondered if she expected me to kiss her for showing me the photo albums. I didn't move and she said, "How come you never introduce me to your wife or that Zoe person?"

"You're not going to be here that long," I told her. She stared blankly at me a moment, then swept up her albums and went to the back room. I finished the letter to my brother, then washed and went to bed, but didn't get to sleep right away and instead I thought about Avalon back there on the mattress, curled around Kim, and thought how strange she was and I wondered what misalignment of the stars had brought it about that she was here, what cosmic machinery had busted and left her and her bastard kid living in my studio. I knew Avalon was desirable in her way, though you wouldn't have seen it, and Alba came to mind and I thought how luxurious our love-making had become and later it was Zoe I was thinking about, which should have confused me, but by then I was drifting and so drifted to sleep.

One night I came home from Zoe's and saw that Avalon had stuck something big as a pasta bowl flat against the studio wall. "What's *that?*" I ask her. She says it's an air purifier. "What are you talking about? And who are you to nail anything to my wall?"

"It's an air purifier. It takes the poisons out of the air, because the—" she begins.

"What poisons? Are you out of your little mind?"

"The poisons are toxins that come from your paints. This place smells of paint and you've lived here too long to notice. Paint has toxins that—"

"I know about paint. I've been painting all my life. I'm a goddamned professor of paint."

"I read in—"

"Don't injure your mind with reading." I pull the *Artists' Air Sponge* from the wall and begin loosening the stump that stays behind.

"Kim is a growing boy. If he breathes toxins—"

"He won't breathe toxins."

"He sleeps in a room with a hundred big paintings stacked against the wall. I keep the windows open as much as I can in there, but it gets cold at—hey! What are you doing? That's mine!" she cries and snatches the *Artists' Air Sponge* from the big trash can.

Winthrop has no sense of smell and says it's the turpentine that did it to him, but I suspect it's the same ailments as have already turned his nerves into a tangle of sparks and dead wires, because my nose is still all right. There was a time when I did use lacquer paints and, in fact, I was crazy about them because I could float one delicious color on top of another, but the lacquers tainted the air and twice Alba found me knocked out on the floor and had to drag me by my armpits from the studio, so after the second time she said, "No more lacquers!" and that was the end of that.

On one of those days when things were going badly I threw my brush across the room and hunted up Winthrop to have lunch with. When I got back to the studio Avalon was in the middle of the floor, scooping up her scattered photo collection. "How come you're home at this hour?" I asked her. She had scrambled to her feet. "The coffee roaster. Gordon's fixing it. He said I could take the rest of the day off. It broke down again," she said, her cheeks glowing, her eyes darting this way and that. I saw the old blanket chest at the foot of my bed was open, so I knew the photos were my snapshots of Alba—half dressed, costumed or naked—and the loose envelopes on my bed were my letters. "Get out," I told her. Avalon held the photos out to me and they went flying when I grabbed her wrist. "I showed you *mine*!" she cried, jamming her heels against the floorboards. I had already turned away and was dragging her to the open door. "You can't do this, Ren!" I swung her hard and shoved, but she whirled— "You can't do this, you shit!"—and whacked my face hard, stinging. I began to pry her fingers from the doorjamb when abruptly she let go, trying to clutch at me while I beat back her furious hands, then she ducked down and grabbed my leg. "Get out of here and get out of my life," I croaked. I wrenched her thumb backward so her hand sprang open and I kicked her away and slammed the door, locked it. I was panting. I walked up and down the studio, trying to catch my breath, then got down on the floor and began to pick up the photographs. Avalon had begun to beat on the door, crying, *You can't do this, Ren. This isn't you!* but I went on gathering the photos. I sorted the envelopes by the postmarks and put everything back with the other stuff in the chest, though my head felt like it was going to explode. Avalon stopped pounding on the door and now in the silence she said, *If you don't open this door I'll kick it in.* I went to the kitchen sink and turned on both taps, my hands still trembling. *It's a flimsy door, Ren, and I'll kick it to pieces. You bastard! You fucking bastard! You*—I dunked my head in the sink and kept it there, the water shooting down on my skull, filling the bowl, overflowing, pouring down my legs. I came up for air and turned off the taps and the studio was silent.

I threw myself face down on my bunk and after a while my insides ceased trembling. I wondered if Avalon was still outside the door but then remembered she would have to go to the Daily Grind to meet Kim when he came from school, so I got up and looked at the clock over the stove and saw she must have gone by now. Her keys were on the counter at the end by the door where she always tossed them (tiny chain with a glassy tag: photo of Avalon on one side, her son on the other) but not her wallet, which meant it was still in her pocket, since she never carried a purse like other women.

I went to the back room to look around. A couple of weeks ago she had enlisted me to help drag the bookcase away from the wall, so it became a low wall itself and made a room within the room, an alcove for the mattress. The mattress was made up neatly on the floor, a bed without legs, and lying along side it was my old sleeping bag where Kim nestled down each night, though he often crawled into his mother's bed before dawn. Some of Kim's strange maps were tacked to the wall. Avalon had furtively removed half a dozen books in a row from my bookcase and laid them flat atop others to clear a space for her grooming tools (emery boards, lipsticks, clippers, crayons), and she'd done the same on other shelves, making spaces for Kim's toys and for her own treasures, hers being a chipped clam shell she had found during our walk on Good Harbor beach, an ugly photo postcard of Gloucester Harbor she had bought the same day, the cork from a bottle of Asti Spumanti we had drunk one night when I thought my painting was going especially well, plus other such prizes, including a brush I had thrown someplace and a mug that said *The Daily Grind* which she had probably stolen. I hauled Avalon's huge backpack to a standing position, grappled it up and lugged it through the studio and set it outside, leaning against the wall, then I took a wine carton and tossed in Kim's loose jerseys and pants and socks, also swept his toys and his mother's sundries into it, and set it out beside the backpack.

I locked the door and drove off in my wagon, not wanting to be near when Avalon came back to fetch her stuff. I don't know where I headed, but when I discovered I'd crossed the river and was in Cambridge I swung off the avenue and navigated the back streets to Zocco's place. Zocco wasn't in. I swung around and headed to Harvard Square, parked in an over-priced garage and walked to the Café Paradiso. No one I knew was there. I ordered a cappuccino and a cannolo and was satisfied to sit outside by myself, looking at the street and the crowds streaming past, and later I took out my pad and wrote a few pages to my son Fabrizio. When I returned to my studio the backpack and the box were gone; the pair of pants and the two jerseys I had bought for Kim lay scrambled on the floor by the wall, but at least she had taken all the toys. I figured if Avalon had her head screwed on right she had gone to the Daily Grind and asked Garland to take her in and Garland, being Garland, had said yes.

I felt good, relieved, free. For dinner I boiled rice and stuffed it into a pair of pepper halves, poured tomato sauce over the rice, ate up and washed it all down with Chianti from the bottle, belching as contentedly as I wanted, then I wrote a couple more pages to Fabrizio, after which I painted well and farted happily till midnight and went to bed. When I woke up it was still dark and I lay there wondering why I had awakened. I got up and went to the bathroom to piss, but for a long time there was only the clamping pain and no pee, then it dribbled for a while and left no relief but only a blurred ache. It came to mind about cancer in the prostate, the way it reaches into you down there and spreads, a horridly familiar thought which I tried to shake off, then I wiped the spattered rim of the john bowl with a fistful of paper, flushed it away and washed up. Instead of going to my bed I turned the other way and stood for a minute looking into the back room where the light from the hall illuminated a triangular piece of Avalon's mattress. I got back to my bed but I couldn't go back to sleep, even though my mind was calm and empty.

I thought about lying alone, as I was, in this black room with my blind canvases, and Alba across the river asleep in our big bed in that concrete mausoleum, thought about this being a stupid way to live, and about Zoe amid her down pillows on the thin hard mattress she said was good for her back, and I thought about my paintings and were they any good and could I make myself known before dying, and I thought about Skye and Astrid and Brizio, about their busy lives and their plans. I suppose I wasn't actually thinking deeply about these people but only picturing them for my own solace, knowing that they cared about me, for if they didn't care, then everything I had done would be gone and I would be nothing, just another old man with pee on his pants. It was a while before I got to sleep.

The philosopher Montaigne, perhaps Italian as uncle Zitti believed, says that your inner self is a place of contradictions and that to live well you have to learn to live with your inconsistencies, and he's right. Now, this next morning, I picked up Avalon's key chain with my studio keys on it, stuck them in my pocket and went around to the Daily Grind. Inside, the air was thick with the smell of roasting coffee beans. Garland was wiping the marble counter top and when she saw me she stopped and stood there watching me as I walked around the sacks of beans and on to the back of the store where Avalon was tending the coffee roaster. The gas jets shimmered like sapphires and there was a sound like gravelly surf as the beans slid endlessly inside the rotating drum. Avalon seated herself back against the stone window ledge, one boot on the floor and the other on a rung of the coffee roaster, her narrow eyes darting here and there beyond me. I thought to tell her that she never had a right to turn up at my door and I had no damn reason to take her in. I fished out her studio keys and started to give them to her when her hand slashed past, snatching them from my fingers and shoving them into her pocket. She settled back more comfortably on the window ledge, her gaze shifting around the room. "Thanks," she said, looking at me at last. "You're welcome," I said.

30

One day Avalon came home after work and said Zoe had left a phone message for me at the Daily Grind, which message was that Astrid is getting married and please phone me. "What does she want *me* to do?" I wondered out loud. "Sounds like she wants you to phone her," said Avalon. The next morning I went to the Daily Grind and phoned Zoe who said, We've got to talk about this, so you bring the wine, I'll make the dinner. I told Avalon I was going to have dinner at Zoe's. "She talks to me like I'm bizarre or something," muttered Avalon, scooping up a bucket of coffee beans. "Maybe because you gave her your life history when all she asked for was a cup of coffee," I suggested. "Only because she came in here to spy on me and I gave her what she wanted," Avalon said, pouring the beans into the coffee roaster.

Zoe's studio-office is front and back on the right, and the

rest of the old house is her home. That evening I knocked on her bright blue door (Blue Door Graphics) and she greeted me with, "Astrid barely knows the man and wants to marry him instantly. She said late spring or summer, remember, but yesterday she phoned to say she she's thinking of getting married right now." I followed her to the kitchen and began to adjust the corkscrew, her elaborate gadget of gears and levers, all the while speculating about Astrid. "Well, what do you think?" Zoe asked me.

"I don't know. Maybe she's pregnant. We should think about that."

"She'd tell us if she were pregnant," Zoe said, quite firm. "Wouldn't she?" she added, searching my eyes for the answer.

"I hope so. I think so. Sure." I went back to working on the cork.

"She's always told us when she was in trouble," Zoe continued.

"Yes, but getting pregnant isn't the same as getting into trouble, not when you're planning to marry the man."

"Maybe she only thinks she might be pregnant and is getting us ready, just in case."

"She might do that," I conceded. "Probably would. She's prudent that way, after the fact."

"Alba thinks Astrid has known this man longer than we know about."

"She's probably right about that. —Ah! Open at last."

"Fill our glasses. I'm starved." By the time we had finished dinner and washed up we had decided to recommend to Astrid, whom we must remember to call Galaxy, that she should live with Weston a while before marrying him and, furthermore, she should keep the key to her current apartment just in case living at Weston's didn't work. By fitting together the loose jigsaw facts we had of Galaxy's life since she left home, interlocking them with the meager handful of tidbits she had given us about Wes, we were able to compose that stretch when she was living with Wes's father, Harry, whom we had met a couple of times (bald head, bright eyes, springy step) and by prompting each other's memory we were able to figure when she could have met Harry's son and when, after Harry died (hang-glider, downdraft) she must have begun to see more and much more of Wes.

The dinner and the wine and our long, agreeable talking together had warmed my heart and I knew that Zoe felt the same warmth, because sharing our complaints and worries about Astrid always aroused her tender feelings and, in fact, any deeply intimate conversation opened her to amorous suggestions. So, being in the mood as I was, after I had dried the last dish I looked around the kitchen, thinking to prolong my stay and thereby let one word lead to another, though a single glance showed me there wasn't anything more I could do except say good-night and go back to the studio. "Oh, have another glass of wine. I'm going to have another glass," Zoe said, rescuing me.

I threw my jacket back on the hook and we took the bottle to the living room where Zoe slipped off her shoes and settled into a pillowed corner of the sofa, stretching her legs across my lap so I could massage her feet, which massage was always melting bliss to her. I held her heel in the palm of one hand and with the other I began to work on her toes, after which I sank my thumb into the long muscle of her arch, causing her to sigh with pleasure and to sink further into her corner, and so on till I wrapped my hand around her sharp ankle, holding it snug till the marrow of her bones went warm. Zoe stood up and reached under her skirt to tug her pantyhose off, rolling the misty material down her legs into a storm cloud which she swept away with a bare white foot, then she seated herself in her corner of the sofa again, the smoothing down of her skirt leaving a warm perfume to fade in the air like the after-image of her swan-white thighs. That's fancy language and I use it to show I was old but aroused and the wine had gone to my head. She slid her legs across my lap again so I could massage her calf muscles, and for a while she sipped her wine in silence while I worked on her hard, silken flesh. "I'm alone now, really alone," she told me.

"What are you talking about?"

She tilted her head back and drained the glass with one swallow. "Astrid marries Weston. What happens to me?"

"Astrid has been on her own for years and you're still her mother. Nothing's going to change that."

"But this is different. She's getting married and it's going to make a difference. I'm going to be right back where I was thirty years ago," she said, setting her empty glass on the floor.

"It's *not* the same as thirty years ago."

"No. Thirty years ago I had hope, I had a future."

"Christ! You're still *young*, Zoe. The one who's old here is *me*, not you. The day will come when you're my age and you'll wonder what you were talking about."

"You have a family."

"Yes, and you're part of it."

"You have no idea how hollow that sounds," she said, abruptly swinging her legs from my lap. She poured the last of the wine into her glass, drank it down and then seated herself on the floor with her back pressed against my knees. "Anyway, I don't want to be part of somebody else's family any more. I want to be the center of my own," she said, bowing her head, her hair so short, the shaved nape of her long neck so naked and vulnerable. I plowed my hand through her hair, trying to recall the thick shining weight of it when she was a young Renoir, then I began to massage her right shoulder which was always stiff and sore because of the way her beloved computer mouse monopolized her right hand.

"I want to get out and meet people, new people," she said.

"Has anyone stopped you?"

"No. But you undermine my confidence so I don't leave."

"You left and got married twice. And that's not counting the other times you left."

"I married two times, period. That not so much. Or so many or whichever's the right way to say it."

"And I don't know what you mean by undermine. I've supported you in everything you've ever done. When have I ever undermined you? What have I ever done to undermine you or stop you or hinder you or whatever it is you're talking about?"

I went to the kitchen, grabbed another bottle of wine, rammed in the corkscrew and wrenched out the cork, poured myself a glass. I was at the sink, staring through my reflection in the black window and thinking glumly how I should go back to my studio, when Zoe came in behind me, saying, "I used to have friends in San Francisco and Taos. I haven't been to San Francisco for five years and I can't even remember the last time I was in Taos." She reached past me to put her glass in the sink, taking care not to brush my arm with hers. "Are you coming upstairs or not?" she asked brusquely, not moving away.

I looked at her. Her hairstyle, that cruel scissoring which left only a close fitting cap of feathered hair over her skull, made her appear more fragile than she was, made her eyes seem larger, too. She looked at me and waited, her pale irises all depth and need one moment, but hard as opals the next.

"After I finish this glass," I said, sullen.

When I got upstairs Zoe was in her soft dark robe and as I entered she turned off the bedroom light, leaving on only the small lamp in the corner, its illumination as dusky as the perfume that now hung in the air, a rutting scent she knew I liked. I tore off my shoes and socks and had just tossed my shirt on the chair when she said, "I've been thinking."

"This isn't the time or place—" I began

"I want to say something," she insisted.

"Is that what we came up here for? For a damn lecture?"

She had seated herself on the edge of the bed with her hands in her lap. "You undermine me by saying you love me."

"Fine!"

"Because if you love me why should I go looking for somebody else to love me when maybe there's nobody out there who will."

"Fine. I won't say it anymore." I shucked off my pants.

"You say you love me and so—"

"You damn well know it," I said impatiently.

"So I've come to depend on it."

"You can depend on it." I tossed my underpants on the heap and was naked.

"Yes, up to a point."

"Have I ever let you down?"

"You know *exactly* and *precisely* what I mean!" She sprang up, flung her robe onto the chair—or tried to, for it billowed and fell short—and now we were both naked.

"You've known from day one—" I began, exasperated.

"Love everybody, love nobody! Who do you love, Ren? Or have you lost the list?"

"We've been here before, Zoe. This road leads nowhere."

"We've never been anywhere else!" she cried.

"You want me to forget about you? Is that it? What do you want? What exactly and precisely do you want?"

"*I want to be loved most!* I want to go somewhere where I'm loved most! Is that so vain? Is that so impossible?"

After her words, in that silence, I reached toward her but she slapped my hand away. "Am I supposed to go back to my studio now?" I asked.

"I didn't say that!"

"You want me to stay?"

"You want to leave? You expect me to drive over to your place at this hour?" She flung open the bed and stood there looking at me, her arms tense at her sides, waiting.

"Great. This is just great."

There are times I've wished *this* Renato were not *that* Renato. What can I tell you? We lay together in the frail light of the corner lamp, as wary as animals in an eclipse, and yet it gave me comfort to comfort her, to run my old hand gently through her hair, no matter her hair was short and thin, so she would know I knew who she truly was and knew she was desirable, and in a while she pressed her cheek to mine so we couldn't see each other but had to signal through our bodies and make conversation that way, one word leading to another. At breakfast she said, "You know this doesn't change a thing," and I said, "I hope you're right, I wouldn't want you to change," and she stopped with the toast half way to her mouth and she said flatly, "You're a bastard, Renato," and I said, "Yes, maybe. I was found on a doorstep."

31

I HADN'T HEARD A WORD FROM SONIA STRAND, SO I decided to go around to her gallery to show her I wasn't so old as to be forgetful or dead, and to ask when she was going to put me on her exhibition calendar. I pulled open the heavy glass door and here comes Sonia herself in gleaming trousers of crushed brown velvet and a blouse which looked to be sewn from a Renaissance flag, reaching out to shake my hand, saying, "Mr Stillamare! Renato, so good to see you." Her hand was soothingly warm and as she smiled her eyes wrinkled at the corners, her gaze lingering on me as if we were close friends who through some shared misfortune hadn't been able to see each other for months. "Come," she said. "I just finished a note to you and, since you're here, we'll save the postage—" She led me to her office, snatched up a stack of square white envelopes and plucked out the one with my name on it. "An invitation to our next reception. Please come. There are people I want you to meet and they'll be here. And I want them to meet you. You'll come?"

"Of course." I don't know anything more tedious than somebody else's gallery reception.

"And now—" We were standing in the middle of her office and Sonia put her hands on her hips and glanced around with a slight frown, as if searching for something. She wasn't quite so tall as I had remembered, but stood straight and tall enough to be imposing. The large glass table she used for a desk was blanketed with a quilt of overlapping letters, note cards, loose photo-slides and other such trash, all held in place by those fancy little enameled boxes she kept as paperweights. She opened the door to Peter Bell's cubiculum, said a few words to him, then pressed the door shut. "Say!" she said, turning to me. "Do you have time for an espresso?"

"Sure."

She smiled. "But not in a paper cup, right? The last time you were here I scandalized you with paper cups, I could see that, so I went out and purchased these little beauties, thin as egg shells. And in just a minute we'll have coffee." Sonia had gone to the espresso machine by the window and began to load it, her back to me.

"The reason I came by—" I began.

"I hope you came by to ask about your exhibit," she said, glancing over her shoulder.

"Exactly."

She finished with the machine and turned to me. "As you know, I've already written out a calendar for the year. And we're completely booked. You know that, too. But I don't want to wait until next year, I want to exhibit you this year— if that's all right with you," she added.

"That's all right with me."

"Wonderful! Now that means I'll have to write you in on top of somebody else. It will be a two-artist show. I'll try to choose somebody who won't be completely overpowered by your work. That won't be easy." She smiled. "But I can do it."

"And when would that be?" I insisted.

"This fall. Fall's best," she said crisply.

"Good," I said as crisply as she.

Sonia attended to the sleek little coffee machine while I took a couple of restless, irritable turns around her office, bumping into her Baroque side chair and nearly putting my boot through a painting that leaned against a tall file cabinet.

"Renato." There was a note of gentle rebuke in Sonia's voice;

she opened her arm toward the chrome and leather sofa. "Make yourself comfortable. Please."

I stayed standing. "I don't paint miniatures. You've seen my work."

"Yes, I've seen your work, and yes, you don't paint miniatures. What are you getting at?"

"How much wall space do I have if there's another painter here?"

"Don't worry about wall space," she said. "You do the painting, I'll provide the gallery. Now enjoy your espresso. Please."

Sonia handed me a cup of coffee, sipped her own and by way of conversation she asked had I seen the big show at the Fine Arts last fall (I had and I said so), and what had I thought of it (I had thought it was crowded and said so), and how about Zircon who was finally breaking onto the national scene at fifty-five (I'd piss on him if I could, but I kept mum about it), thus we stood in the middle of her office and made amiable gossip about nothing much and carried on our private calculations. What I knew for sure was that I had advanced toward an exhibition date, but had been maneuvered away from having the gallery to myself and now would have to share the space. So all the while we chatted I watched her eyes, those blue crystals, and listened to the pitch and timbre of her voice, which always sounded as if she had just awakened and I was the first person she spoke to, and I waited for her next move or for the chance to make a move of my own. "Actually," she said, "I'd love to put some of your drawings on exhibit, too."

"Why is that?" I asked, thinking how drawings sell for less than paintings and we'd both make less money.

She set her cup slowly and very gently on the desk. "Because your drawings are extraordinary. The ones I saw in your studio, those figures who look, oh, not like nudes at all, but like naked people, people who have taken off their clothes. In a sense, most nudes are still clothed. The conventional ways of portraying bare bodies are so—so high-minded, so sanctimonious, so non-sexual, that when we look at them we don't see nakedness at all."

"You're right about that."

"Thank you, Renato." She smiled slightly.

"But I don't want to use up wall space on drawings," I told her, my voice edgier than I intended.

"Think about it."

I laughed. "I'll certainly think about it."

"Be careful you don't crush that little cup in your fist."

"What?"

"Let me take your cup."

"Oh! Sorry."

Sonia set my egg-cup beside hers on her desk and continued across the room to open wide the door to the gallery and I followed her out. The stuff hanging on the walls—balanced designs, harmonious colors, meticulous brushwork, rigor mortis—gave me a headache and I wanted to leave, but I figured I'd better ask when were we going to talk about prices, percentages, and how many paintings. I began to say, "When are we going to—" but Sonia was sliding both hands into that wide bush of copper colored hair, shutting her eyes for a second. "You know," she said, opening her gaze onto mine. "We should discuss details—" I started to say I agreed, but Sonia hadn't finished talking. "In a week or so. As soon as I have time to sit down and write a letter. I'm *un*-believably busy right now, so there may be a delay, but don't take it amiss. Busy is good," she added, smiling.

Peter Bell walked up with a handful of mail and a letter knife with fancy enameled handle. "Good to see you, Mr Stillamare."

"Good to see you, Mr Bell."

"The weather is warmer. The cafés are setting out tables," he said, smiling.

"Must be spring," I said.

We shook hands and he trotted away to his kennel. Sonia had opened one of the letters and glanced inside, saying, "I'll need two-thirds of the selling price."

I didn't realize she was speaking to me until she glanced up from the letter. "Agreed?" she asked.

"You'll take two-thirds?" I said.

"Not always, but this time. Yes."

"This time, yes," I said.

Then we shook hands and I left.

❦

I phoned Alba and told her, "I've just finished talking with Sonia Strand about my exhibit and it's a disaster."

What are you talking about? Alba asked me. What happened?

"She doesn't want my work, she's taking sixty-six percent, she wants a handful of drawings, she's trying to get rid of me."

Is she giving you a show or not?

"No. Or yes, if I share the gallery with one of her farts."

What did she say, exactly?

"That I'm lower than whale shit."

Where are you calling from?

"Copley Square. Why?"

Why don't you go to the Daily Grind and —

"I don't goddamn want another goddamn cup of coffee!"

Or go see Winthrop or Zocco or Hay. Or I'll come around if you want.

"How about a long lunch?" I asked her.

I can't have a long lunch, I've got that cooking class. But tomorrow's good. Or do you need me to come in right now?

"No, I'm all right. Tomorrow where?"

Alba suggested Thoreau's Garden over in Cambridge and that was fine with me.

"Thanks, Alba. Sorry to bother you."

No bother. It's part of the marriage vows, she said.

❦

I hiked to the Daily Grind because I couldn't figure what else to do and along the way I thought about going around to see

Win or Zocco or D'Arcangelo, but I didn't know how much I wanted to tell them, because first I wanted to think some more about Strand and what she was proposing and what she meant and what I should do next, though I knew Zocco and the others would be sympathetic and so on and, on third thought, maybe I should talk about it to clear my head, or maybe write to Scanlon who was sure to offer advice, but in the end I decided not to tell anybody anything. I never had to think even twice about what I told Mike Bruno. When I got to the Daily Grind it was low tide (three tables, the rest empty) with Garland at the counter bent over a work schedule, scowling, scrubbing away with an eraser as if she were working on a botched crossword puzzle. I asked was Gordon around; she sighed into the page and said he'd taken the day off. Avalon was in back by the coffee roaster, folding empty burlap sacks and tossing them onto a pile that had mounted to her knees. She saw me watching her, wiped her forehead with the back of her filthy hand, saying, "What are you doing here at this hour? Why aren't you painting?" I told her I'd stopped by to see if I had any phone calls. "You look lost," she said. I asked Garland could I use the phone and without glancing up she handed it to me. I punched in Zoe's number and was informed by her machine that no one at Blue Door Graphics was available to take my call right now but please leave a message at the tone, so I hung up. I headed home to the studio, but I didn't feel like painting so as I trudged along I took detours and while I was browsing through a store window I decided to go in and buy Kim a compass, because he liked to draw maps and if he had a compass we could survey the neighborhood and draw some good ones. The place was stocked with boisterous outdoor gear —hiking boots, collapsible stoves, yellow pop-up tents, a rack of glittering canoes—and over to one side were a couple of neglected compasses at the end of a row of gadgets that could tell you your location based on signals from satellites nailed to the sky. I bought a compass, the real kind that works with a magnetized needle, and went to the studio.

That night, after we had finished cleaning the dishes and pans and after Kim had gone off with his compass, I sat at the table and wondered what to do. I tried telling myself that Sonia had not cancelled my show but only reduced it, which was true, but I didn't get any lift from that, none at all. After a while I remembered I had been meaning to write a letter to my brother about our mother and how to get her from his place to Massachusetts but I didn't feel like writing a letter to anybody about anything. Avalon said something and then went to take a shower and I sat there feeling tired. I was gazing mindlessly at the canvases stacked against the wall and at the big one braced against the easel, but all I saw was the broad area of canvas and stroke upon stroke of paint, and all I felt was how tired I was, as if my energy had been seeping away, ebbing away for months, and I had not noticed and now I couldn't move. I thought how I could die right then and the thought of dying meant nothing to me, meant only the end of this stupid struggle, a struggle so stupid I couldn't make out what it was for, or maybe I was too tired to see. I sat there a long spell, but if I had more thoughts I can't recollect them, because all I remember is me reading a book at the table when Avalon sat down opposite me. "You've been morose all day," she announced. Go away, I said. She went away, but after she had put Kim to bed she came back. "That's the same page you were reading half an hour ago, you're not making much progress," she said. When I looked up at her she handed me a glass of wine. "You need company," she said. I gave up and closed the book, whatever it was. "Why don't you ask me one of those cooking riddles?" she suggested. I don't know what you're talking about, I said. "Like the other night when you said, you know, a hungry man goes to the kitchen and all he can find is a piece of bread and a bottle of olive oil and something, I forget—but you know what I mean. Remember?" Oh, that, I said. "Well?" she said. I couldn't figure out what she was up to, but at last I said, "All right. A hungry man goes to the kitchen and all he can find is a stale loaf of bread, just the heel of the bread, stale, and a can of peeled tomatoes, and an onion. What does he do for dinner?"

"He puts the peeled tomatoes in a pot. Adds water." She hesitated. "Cuts up the onion and puts it in with the peeled tomatoes. That makes a kind of soup. He heats up the soup. And."

"And?"

"Drinks the soup and eats the stale bread?"

"No. He puts the stale bread *into* the simmering soup. It softens the bread, the bread soaks up the soup. It's delicious." I picked up the book.

"Ask me another."

"Why?"

She clamped her hands on mine to stop my opening the book. "Come on, Ren. A woman, a woman this time, goes into the kitchen and all she finds is—"

Her hands were not so big as mine, but blissfully warm, her fingers strong and smooth, and my flesh under hers looked like old leather gloves. I shied away from my hands, looked over to the kitchen counter and I tried to come up with a puzzle for her. "Some sugar, one fresh egg and a bottle of Marsala," I said at last.

"What's Marsala?"

"Sweet wine."

"She cooks the egg and drinks the Marsala!"

"You would."

"And you?"

"Drop the egg yolk in a pot, add a little sugar and beat it to a thick creamy yellow, add a spoonful of Marsala and whip it to a froth."

"Then what?"

"Then eat it."

"Raw? Eat the egg raw?"

"You can heat it if you want. You hold it in the air over the heat—just like this, see, so it doesn't cook—and add the wine and whip it up."

"Ren, it's still raw and it sounds gross."

"On the contrary, it's marvelous."

"Oh, sure. Show me. Let me see you eat a raw egg."

Avalon kept nagging until at last I got an egg and some sugar and began to whip up a zabaione, but I didn't have any Marsala so I threw in vanilla extract instead. I ate about half and then lifted the spoon to her mouth. She drew her head back. "I bet it tastes like when somebody comes in your mouth."

"You'll like it almost as much. That's sperm, this is egg. Taste it."

While I held the spoon, Avalon stuck her tongue cautiously into the zabaione, then took it into her mouth and swallowed. I finished that spoonful, then scooped another and held it out to her, and so the spoon went back and forth between us until the zabaione was gone, after which I refilled my glass with wine while Avalon asked in three different ways what had gone wrong today that made me so moody. I took a drink and passed the glass to her and told her nothing had gone wrong that couldn't be fixed by shoving a bomb up the ass of every gallery owner in Boston, and Avalon smiled, tossed her head back, drank down the rest of the glass and informed me that an artist's life is a hard life, as she well knew, being a silversmith herself, though she admits that her jewelry at the Daily Grind is actually selling, piece by piece, then she hands me the glass and asks what kind of writer is Alba, and I say she's a known essayist, an occasional restaurant reviewer, a sometime book reviewer, a now-and-then translator of French poets, a part-time curator of artists' books, a scribbler of pornography which she calls erotica and a former art critic who never lifted a finger to help her husband's career, and Avalon says that she herself never wanted to get married but now, seeing how Alba and I live, she thinks maybe she should get married because living apart that way she'd have somebody to write letters to, though she doubts she'd write as many letters as I do, even if she had a dozen kids. So the glass traveled back and forth between us until the bottle, over which we said goodnight, was empty and she went to her room; as for me, grateful she had taken me out of my black mood, I dropped into bed and lay there feeling tender-hearted toward her, but quickly fell to sleep and, except for rising once to pee, slept as forgetfully as an old log rotting in a field.

32

THE NEXT DAY I DROVE ACROSS THE RIVER TO Cambridge to have lunch with Alba at Thoreau's Garden though, frankly, I liked Thoreau's better when all it had was paper plates and a menu of bean sprouts and raw carrots, none of this fakery with rusted farm tools hanging on the wall. "That's because you're getting old and grumpy. Start eating, you'll feel better," Alba told me. While we were devouring a Greek salad I told her about my visit with Sonia Strand, made a vigorous re-enactment with every word and nuance mimicked from the original scene, so I was surprised when Alba calmly replied, "That doesn't sound so bad."

"Doesn't sound so bad? I'm going to end up with nothing! *No percentage, no wall space, no show!*"

"She didn't say no—let me finish, Ren—she didn't say no exhibit. She did put you on the calendar, which is what you went to see her about. You don't know what's going on at the gallery. I'm sure she has her own agenda and I'm sure we don't know it. She may have certain buyers in mind for drawings, your kind of drawings. She's asked for your work and she's not going to ask for work unless she thinks she can sell it, so she must think she can sell you. For all you know, she may be trying to get rid of that other painter, the one she's putting you in with."

Alba didn't say anything more, so I went back to my bowl and picked away at the greenery, thinking about what she had just said, all of which I supposed was more or less true but at the same time it didn't feel satisfying, and after a decent pause

Alba asked how was my salad and I said fine and asked how's hers, and hers was fine too. "We don't know her agenda," I said. "But we know it has to do with money. That's what the dealers are dealing in, money. There's painting and there's, there's—"

"Marketing and money," said Alba.

"I didn't think I'd end up this way. I would never have started if I had known I was going to end this way."

"It's not ended. You're not ended," she said calmly.

It meant the world to me when Alba said things like that, which is one of the reasons I married her, though I didn't know it at the time. "You don't think so?" I said.

"I don't think so. I'm sure you're going to go on painting."

"I'm tired. It's getting easier and easier not to paint. Days go by."

"I thought you were working. You were, weren't you? A while ago you were painting more than ever."

"I'm painting, but nothing's happening. I mean, I have this energy—it's good, it's good energy—but I can't connect, I can't connect it to— I've got some good ideas, some good pictures. I've laid them out, a few of them. They're good. I know what's good. But it's easy to put the brush down. It's easy to walk away from the canvas. It's never been that way before."

"It's been that way before," she said.

"Not like this."

"That's what you always say. —Listen," she said, reaching for her purse, a deep leather sack the size of a horse's feed bag. "Before I forget, we got a letter from Skye. They've really enjoyed Sydney—strange to think of it getting to be winter down there—but they're ready to come back to the States. Wait a sec. It's here someplace. Here. But read it later, Renato, not now. She says they should arrive here by late summer. That's the important part. The other parts are interesting too, of course. —Heard anything new from Astrid? I mean Galaxy, anything from Galaxy?"

"No. And I don't know if that's good or bad."

"Zoe seems more relaxed, as relaxed as she ever gets, anyway."

A Greek salad not only makes a good lunch but also provides a pleasurable distraction, because you can pursue this or that small sharp taste or swerve onto a wholly different one or, if you want, seek out a new texture or a fresh color, and then you're happily swabbing the inside of the bowl with a slice of coarse bread and feeling the vinegar on your tongue, but I was all the while thinking of the Strand gallery and the paintings on those walls and the paintings in the galleries up and down Newbury Street. "What I do," I was telling Alba, "I do better than anyone—I'll say it to you, I won't say it to anyone else—I do it better than anyone. I'm not saying I'm the only one who can paint, but I can paint. But what's the use of doing it when nobody is going to look? Nobody's looked at my work for the past thirty years. I've been developing and moving ahead and now I'm where I want to be, but I'm all alone here, because no dealers or buyers or lookers came along with me. Now if anybody happens to see my work it looks odd to them, because they haven't been watching it get this way for the past two or three decades. So why should I fucking paint?"

"I'm not saying you have to paint. But you certainly do it better than other painters. And there's people who do like your work," she added.

"Where?" I said, looking around.

"Have you thought about Conti's gallery right here in Cambridge?"

"Is that still standing? I thought they had knocked it down so they could sell the bricks."

"It's still there."

"I heard Leo Conti was flat broke."

"He's getting there. But Conti thinks of himself as a benefactor to the public, so he keeps the gallery open."

"He had a nice accounting business, too bad he sold it."

"He sold it so he could be a patron of the arts. If he goes

broke now, he goes broke satisfied that he was more than just an accountant."

"I don't want to show there."

"How about Mimi's Café?"

"Me?"

"For that series on paper. The Genesis series. They're finished aren't they?"

"They're finished but they're not going to hang in Mimi's Café."

We concluded with a cup of coffee and didn't say much, Alba taking an interest in the stamped tin ceiling while I studied the floor boards, or we looked past each other to watch the other patrons. "Why don't you come around to the studio and look at the paintings and tell me what you think?" I asked her.

Alba put down her coffee mug and looked at me in a friendly, good-natured way as if I'd just said the stupidest thing she'd ever heard. "No, Renato."

"I'm not going to bed with her."

"I admire your restraint."

"No one's there during the day except me. Anyway, you might like Avalon, despite what you've heard from Zoe."

She shrugged. "What's the point, Ren?"

"I could use your help. I need your help," I said. "I need you."

"Sure."

"My muse."

"I cannot believe you're this hard up," she said.

"You could stop by early in the afternoon, whip up an omelet for us. Make your cooking teacher proud. What's the chef's name?"

"Michelle," she said.

"Famous?"

"Famous in France," she said.

33

I DECIDED NOT TO PAINT FOR A FEW DAYS SO AS NOT TO spoil the stuff I was working on, because if I kept at it while I was feeling this low I'd just piss on everything and turn it to mud, so at the hour when I would have been walking up and down in front of a canvas, I stood at the kitchen counter and emptied the old glass Mason jar of all those slips of paper on which I'd written chores that needed to be done. I sorted the scraps (*fix CHAIR*, *See Urologist*, *buy 2 Tires*, *shower curtain*, *Make appt w/ urologist*, *socks et cetera*, *Umbrella*, *Urologist prostate exam*) and threw out the one in Avalon's jagged handwriting (*Get us a real toaster that doesn't burn my fingers every damn morning.*) I repaired the kitchen chair, then crammed the remaining notes into my pocket and got myself out the door. It was a balmy day, so I cranked down the car window and chugged along, trying to enjoy the weather despite my gloom. I bought the socks et cetera and shower curtain, then drove out to Tire World to get two new tires put on, then to a phone booth to make an appointment with my dentist, because I had a tooth which had recently grown sensitive to hot or cold, and I bought an umbrella. I got back to the studio by mid-afternoon and found in the mail a biggish envelope from Scanlon, which envelope I decided to open later as a treat. I ate lunch and then lay on the floor, a book under my head and my hands folded on my stomach, still glum but too tired to care. After the nap I got up and pissed and dribbled, which reminded me again to make an appointment with the urologist to get ye olde prostate poked, then I drove over to Cambridge to the Café Paradiso to read Scanlon's letter and to see if Winthrop or Cormac or Hay or anyone would show up.

Scanlon had stuffed his square manila envelope with a thick letter, a handful of photos, some drawings, a couple of slides, and a big glossy chromatic brochure of his show in Toronto that had just closed. He said he had rediscovered my studio address and had now written it into his Notebook—if you knew Scanlon you'd know it was an honor to be in his famous Notebook which, I figured, must be up around volume seventy-five. He wrote in detail about the show and mentioned a new strategy, which he'd tell me about later, for recapturing the position he had held in the art world a decade ago, and about how little he was getting for his paintings nowadays, and how the only honest way to make a movie about Gauguin's life would be to make a movie about five other painters who lived back then and leave Gauguin out of it, and how Elaine deKooning went around and fucked Rosenberg and Hess and Egan, and those guys were so happyfied they went out and told the world Elaine's husband was the greatest painter since Picasso, and Scanlon's question to me was this: would we have heard of Bill deKooning if Elaine had been a lousy lay? As I said, it was a thick letter, and at the end he wrote that he was coming through Boston on his way to Maine and he hoped I'd be free to have dinner or lunch or some other meal with him.

I sat by the window in the Paradiso, sipping the cappuccino and holding Scanlon's slides up to the light, one after the other. As usual, he had re-invented the way he painted and these canvases were completely different from the ones he'd last showed me and, frankly, though I usually like the way Scanlon paints, I'd like it even more if he evolved and deepened instead of zigzagging all over the place, chasing sales. Anyway, it would be good to see him again, to get acquainted with what was going on in New York, and I could tell him about my latest meeting with Sonia Strand and ask what he thought about the deal. I looked at the drawings and spent a long while with the fancy catalog that had accompanied his exhibit and, after I had finished a canollo, I ordered another cup of coffee. The waitress was plain and crabby, no pleasure to talk to, and the customers were a dull and depressing troop. I slid Scanlon's brochure back into the envelope and wondered how long I was going to go on trying to make a name for myself: I felt bone tired of the struggle. It was strange to have every art dealer in twenty-some years tell me that no one would want my work, and still to go on painting and to grow more certain my work was good, sure to last. I was amazed to be so convinced, seeing as half a lifetime ago I had exhibited in better galleries, gotten bigger notices and sold at higher prices. I knew my work was alive and lasting, the same as I knew my career was a miserable limping thing, and I sat there in the Paradiso and thought this is a little like dying, this long failure, this dwindling away to nothing, and like some dying man who can't believe he's dying, I still think my work is good and must survive. I heard a bark, realized I had laughed out loud at myself, and to cover that little eccentricity I coughed and cleared my throat, then got up and paid and left.

That week I cleaned house. In the studio I pulled and shoved everything into the middle of the room, then sponged down the walls and scrubbed the floor. I was pushing everything back against the walls when Avalon came in from work, Kim in tow. "How soon till you clean the storage room where you sentenced Kim and me to go sleep?" she asked. I told her I'd get my paintings out of there tomorrow and she could clean the room herself. "Hear that?" she said to Kim. "You got a lot of papers and stuff to pick up." The next day I lugged half a dozen boxes of gear and most of my paintings from the back room, careful not to disturb Avalon's precious trash, and when she got back from the Daily Grind she began cleaning. I was at the stove when I heard her singing—a low, warm voice—the first time ever. I strolled down to the back room to see if the voice was coming from Avalon herself or only from one of her electronic gadgets. It was Avalon who turned and stopped open-mouthed and the singing stopped with her, like a light going out. Kim was on his hands and knees on a map of Boston, playing with the compass I had given him. "Get a sponge. Join in the fun," Avalon told me. I announced I was going to make dinner and was wondering when she wanted to eat. "Anytime soon," she said, then she bent to dunk the sponge into the bucket and turned back to the window, but didn't sing anymore, which I regretted.

Next day while we were cleaning the kitchen Avalon said, "As long as you're so hysterical about improving everything around here, why don't you get a little tub for the bathroom?" I calmly pointed out that the bathroom had a shower and there wasn't enough space for a tub, but she said, "A person might prefer a tub, even a little wooden one, to soak in, with nice bath soaps, bubble-bath soaps." I told her I couldn't think of anyone who would want to slop around in a bubble bath. "You yourself might be just that person," she said. "You could soak in the tub and read your Melville and Ovid there, instead of reading them on the can." I asked her what the hell she knew about my reading habits. "Only whatever book I find on the sink when I go in there in the morning. And if Ovid is such a classy poet as you say he is, why do you read him in the crapper, isn't that a sacrilege or something?" I stopped scrubbing the grill and looked at her and was about to shout in her ear that Ovid was a *classic* poet, not *classy*, but she continued to say, "And I notice the book you use for a pillow on the floor has a book mark that hasn't moved for a month." It was a book on theoretical physics, just the right thickness. "I'm trying to learn what my son is doing," I said. "Or what he's not doing, since he abandoned physics and transformed himself into a carpenter."

"Why do we keep this weird-looking thing?" she asked. I told her It's a plate and well-bred people put their food on it when they're eating. "I know it's a fucking plate, but what's the design with the ugly face and three legs for?" But she wasn't interested and before I could tell her about Medusa, she had wandered over to the cork board and now was looking at the photos and postcards. She told me it was too bad the way I had jumbled everything – snapshots, letters, glossy Polaroids, old photographs. She studied a couple of the brownish-gray photos in cardboard frames. "Your ancestors don't look comfortable," she told me. I told her I didn't have ancestors. "I come from a long line of orphans and foundlings," I said. She asked what did I mean. I told her how I was adopted. "Who are these?" she asked. I told her it was my father and his kid sister, Vivianna. "She must have hated being dressed up like that," she said.

Then she was at the wall calendar, saying, "Why don't we get rid of these?" and she began fingering the papers I had pinned to the calendar. "They're always out of date," she added. Avalon had already unfastened the clothespin and now a flock of invitations circled around her, avoiding her wild grasp as they fluttered to the floor. "Listen while I explain again what the word privacy means," I told her.

She was right about the invitations being out of date, all but two of them, one from Finn and the other from Sonia Strand. Finn invited me to all his East Coast openings to demonstrate that he wasn't the sort of person who dumps unsuccessful friends when he becomes famous, and I accepted his invitations to show I wasn't mean-spirited about his good fortune or ashamed of myself. We had never been especially close, but I had liked Finn even though his work method drove me crazy. He would earnestly sketch and erase, sketch and erase for weeks until he had something presentable, then he'd draw a grid on it, transfer it to a canvas and work at it for several more weeks, then he'd call in friends and ask what they thought of it, then he'd scrape and repaint till any quirks were smoothed out, leaving it all as light and airy as a slice of white bread. The invitation from Sonia Strand was for the gallery's exhibit, *Transgressing the Boundaries of Desire: The Art of Judi Flowers.* According to the invitation, Judi Flowers broke through the decorum traditionally imposed on woman artists and portrayed the female body in a series of subversive sado-masochistic poses. When I drew women that way it had been called pornographic, but Judi Flowers' controversial work was a compelling critique of patriarchal something, I never learned what, because I threw out her invitation with Finn's and everything else.

❦

After three days of housecleaning I took another half day to go through my file cabinet, throwing out this and that until I had only one alphabetized drawerful (Automobile to Medicare to Social Security), then I slammed that drawer shut and drove over to Cambridge to get a cup of coffee and see if anyone was around. Tom Hay was sitting in the Paradiso with his chin on his chest, half reading a magazine propped against his cup, and when he saw me he brightened and sat up with a smile, a delicate looking man but true as a compass needle. He asked what I'd been doing and I told him I'd been straightening up my papers— "So I can drop dead now and everything will be in order, no problems for my wife and children. How have you been, Tom?" We talked about his children, his writing, his lower back, his publisher, his wife's blood circulation, my teeth, my prostate, my painting, my children. He asked had I seen Winthrop recently and I said no, not recently. "He's got some kind of neuropathic something," Tom said. "Oh, that. Yeah. But no tremor. Not yet anyway. He just moves a little cautiously, I notice. He's begun a new series of paintings. Good stuff," I said.

"Yeah, he's good. Frankly, I don't see any difference between his work and what's getting all the money and attention in New York. And you're good, too," he added. "How come you're not famous?"

"I don't know. You've written half a dozen books, why aren't you famous?"

"That's a total mystery to me, Ren. Maybe I'm not the right religion or ethnicity or class or sex—I mean gender, whatever they call it nowadays." Then he talked about critics and post-modernism and what he called the French Disease, by which he meant some weird French critical theory, and told me about a scholar in New York who wrote articles about non-existent books to show that advanced criticism was independent of actual authors or their texts. Later he got onto politics and was discoursing about those assholes in Congress when Karl Kadish came in and we pulled up another chair. Karl was wearing an old-fashioned vanilla straw hat and a puckered cotton jacket, white with blue pencil stripes, and tucked under his arm he carried a foreign journal printed on flimsy airmail paper. "I see by your jacket it's summer," Tom said.

"Someone has to keep track of these things," Karl said soberly, setting his hat gently on a nearby chair.

"When Karl takes off his necktie I'll know it's July," Tom told me. We asked about Karl's wife and children (his daughter married to a rabbi, his son to a Lutheran pastor) and what he, Karl, had been doing, which led to gossip about in-fighting at Harvard and thence to Indian tribes of New England and about the Red Sox and Updike's old essay on Ted Williams' last day at bat, about the old Celtics team with Larry Bird and Robert Parish and Kevin McHale and what a front line that had been. Tom was always contrary about sports, especially Boston teams, and he bad-mouthed Bird and Parish, so it wasn't as much fun as it could have been, but still it was good to talk. We were onto politics again and those assholes in Congress when Lou Zocco and Cormac McCormac came in together, shaggy Cormac's big torso and short legs giving him the appearance of a bear walking on its hind legs. Tom Hay waved them over but stayed only long enough to exchange hellos before he had to leave. Cormac was in a white shirt with the sleeves rolled up and big blotches of sweat under his arms, ebullient because yesterday he had gotten some pieces back from a new foundry and they looked good. He turned to me and said, "Hey, Renato, I bumped into your wife last week and she's looking great since you left her. More beautiful than ever."

"What are you talking about? I didn't leave her, I didn't leave anybody."

"Yes you did," he said jovially. "And now you're living in your studio with this young woman, wears black leather undies and brings you espresso in bed."

"Who told you that?" I asked him.

"I read it in the newspaper. Or maybe I heard it on the radio. I forget which."

"You split?" Zocco asked me, genuinely concerned.

"God, no. I'm spending a lot of time at the studio, is all. I'm living there, more or less."

"He goes home on weekends for a good meal," Cormac told him.

"Maybe it's not his fault," Karl suggested. "Maybe Alba threw him out and only lets him back in on weekends."

"Ah, women," Cormac said.

"Refresh my memory," I told him. "How many wives have you had?"

"Oh, them," Cormac said. "I'm a flawed man. I had hoped for something better in you."

"Where did you happen to see Alba?" I asked.

"At a fancy grocery store in the North End, sells gourmet vegetables, exotic meats, expensive edibles."

"And she told you we had split?"

"Of course not. She's too loyal for that. But she did look great—beautiful, glowing—so I deduced you had left."

"No, you ran into Zoe," I said flatly. "And she talked, told you some nonsense about me."

"That, too. Day before yesterday."

I asked Zocco where he'd been that I hadn't seen him for some weeks and he said he and his wife had been in France, so the conversation got onto the French and French cuisine, Kadish saying the French prepare a meal like lovers who expect you to admire their technique, whereas the Italians want you to enjoy it. "And the British hope you'll get it over with quickly and feel better afterward," Cormac added. Then we had another cup of coffee and talked about life on other planets orbiting other stars, and about women, the persistence of desire and did some old men have bull's balls or just an old habit, talked about Zocco's sailboat and Kadish's plans to retire and what Cormac should do about his beard, which, he claimed, was thicker on the right than on the left. Now if I was captured by love-starved Amazons and taken to their tropical island with only my paints and brushes, as often happened in my boyhood, I could be happy, but I'd miss most the company of men like these.

34

Cormac was only fooling around, playing for laughs. But I suppose if you had never seen Avalon and if you heard I was living with this woman, this athletic woman half my age, I suppose it would sound like I must be having a great time plowing her, this old bastard painter making a final surge heavenward before falling down, down, down to his jealous grave. Actually, I've never fucked all over the place. I've been loyal to Alba and to Zoe and haven't bedded other women, or so few as to be none when looked at in perspective, and aside from some accidental tumbles on the studio floor I've lived like a eunuch. As for these stories about Renato Stillamare—young Renato lolling about the studio with a couple of ripe, melon-breasted women, old Renato chasing around his easel after a firm little fanny, creased like a peach—these comic concoctions come from Michael Bruno who loved to tell stories. I'll say only this about Mike. One night he didn't answer our knock at his door (we'd come to celebrate Nixon's impeachment), so I went in, heard him lecturing on Dante, followed his voice up the stairs and found him sitting in bed with naked Pam on one side and naked Clarissa on the other, himself in the middle wearing only his eyeglasses, a huge volume of the *Inferno* open in his lap, and a platter of cold chicken at hand. The startled trio looked all agog at us, then Mike waves his glasses and says, "Join us!" But spoilsport Alba only laughs and says, "Next time, when there's more men."

The other one to tell lies about me is Alba herself. I don't mean when we've had a fight and she's still sore at me the next day and says serenely to our guests, "Oh, Renato would fuck a snake if he knew a way to hold it down. —Right, Ren?" I mean when Alba tells stories and doesn't finish, I mean the way she tosses out a remark or starts to say this or that and then breaks off, as if there's a thing she could say or stories she could tell about what a bastard I am, tales she won't tell because she's a loyal wife. Maybe she does this to dupe the world into believing I'm a beast and not an old man with a swollen prostate who gets aroused only to pee, a great priapic beast, and how with nothing more than her bitchy look and the crack of her whip she can control this wild hairy thing—not tame him, for he's not tamable, can't be housebroken—but managed, managed only by Alba. Or maybe she does it purely to help old me think better of myself, better a beast than a toothless, clawless, mangy, moth-eaten mongrel lapping water in his cage, which I am.

Frankly, Alba's good at cooking up spicy stories, knows how to serve them hot and how to tell me what I like to hear, goading me to join her in the telling. You can call them sexual fantasies or you can call them plain lies—no matter—she began these playful fictions years ago when our kids were safely in school and we could steal an hour to meet at the studio (the sun blazing in the window, our clothes in a heap in the corner) and she continues, when she feels like it, even now in the bedroom (a lighted candle on the bureau far away.) Not always, but sometimes as we embrace she whispers endearments, such honey-soft words that even my name sounds sweet in her mouth, calling me her god from the sea, her dark lover, her bull, yes, and her stallion, yes, yes, each whispered word more licentious than the one before, holding me in her warm cupped palm or raking me with her nails while telling me what this handsome, this hard, this silky sweet beast wants, needs, must have. She makes a drama about us and not only us but whoever else she guesses I fancy, arranges the props and directs us actors, and her breath is so warm on my ear when she whispers, "Would you like to do that? Would you do that to me?" for she knows what we would do if we dared, and her whispers are an incantation that transforms us so we are no longer acting but doing what we must because of who we have become. Alba says that in the final moments of our love-making, in those moments when the universe crushes together, she comes to know her fiction is truer than facts and that we are as she says we are whether it happens that way or not.

But it's a fact I had never touched Avalon and if Cormac had met her once he'd have figured I hadn't. Avalon's eyes were shifty and her expression too sharp, wary and predatory for anyone to think of her as an easy lay; furthermore, Cormac preferred his women to have what he calls rondeur, which is a foppish French word meaning roundness or, as they say in heaven where the angels speak Italian, rotondo, whereas Avalon was lean, angular. Then there's the off-putting silverware tacked to her face, plus her black-leather-and-chrome-spike collars, wristbands and belts, not to mention the clothing from some Army depot, dreary khaki which she had recently begun to enliven with blouses of velvet or lace or vinyl from a Déjà Vu boutique, one of those second-hand shops that are up one flight of piss-smelling stairs or down four damp steps from the street. Cormac wouldn't have gone for her; nobody would have gone for her.

As for me, I had thought of using Avalon as a model and I was thinking of it again. I was looking at the shaggy hair and the ax-blade face, the smooth notch in that nicely defined collar bone, the precise workmanship of her feet, her strong legs, the deep tense hollows of her arm pits, and that navel with a little silver ring at the lip, winking—taken all together, she made me want to paint, made me want to paint all sorts of things and not just herself alone. She didn't show off, didn't flaunt her body or display so much as a breast or butt, never mind anything else down there. On the other hand, she wasn't coy; a couple of times she burst into the bathroom to snatch her panties or bra from the rack when I was in the shower, and I once broke in on her own steaming Niagara, shouting at her, "Get out I need to pee!" and she shouts back, "You pee in the shower? You should learn to pee in the crapper! Try it!" and as I couldn't hold it in any longer I peed. But mostly she stayed out of my way.

Sometimes I wondered why I never thought to give her cheek a caress at the breakfast table or to pat her neat end when she went by, but I didn't. She was learning how to cook and how to keep house, and she had always been scrupulous about keeping herself and her kid clean. She loved her son and it had never entered her head to leave him on a snowy doorstep when he was two or three days old.

35

I WAS BORN WITH TEETH OF CHALK BUT MY YOUNG dentist, son of the gentle philosopher-dentist who used to work on my teeth, is a buoyant and energetic man who believes he can resolve any tooth problem. He peered at my aching molar and at x-rays, then cheerfully told me that the tooth needed root-canal work and a crown. I asked him how his father was and was his mother still sewing quilts, then I sank into the chair and let him stuff a rubber sheet down my mouth and grind away the silver amalgam anciently packed in the tooth. He bored deep into the nerve canals, took more x-rays, and crammed the hollowed chambers with gutta-percha, inserted a post, leveled off the tooth and took an impression of it, made a temporary cap, then told me to come back in two weeks to fit the permanent crown to the stump. Afterward, craving solace, I drove around to Alba's and she made tea for me to sip while the anesthetic wore off, and later she comforted me with dinner—fish, massaged with butter, sprinkled with oregano, fried in a pan, showered with lemon juice, garnished with watercress, washed down with white wine—after which I fell tranquilly asleep, made love when we awoke the next morning, then returned to my studio.

Alba's cooking had changed. It had always been satisfying, for she could give me whatever I wanted, but over the past few months her cookery had become fancier—or not fancier, but foreign and more sensuous—or maybe nothing had changed and I was just taking a greater interest in food because, as Zoe said, when you get older you get less interested in sex and more interested in food. Michiko laughed at all this and said, "Alba cooks wonderful dinners and now she's learned some new recipes from her cooking teacher, I think." Michiko, no clothes on, was kneeling at the low table where she had set the ink stone (suzuri) and ink bar (sumi), and now she loaded the brush (fude) and poised it vertically over the paper, her own image sliding left and right in the camera's view finder as I tried to fit everything inside the frame, from the coppery nape of her neck to the black point of the brush. I snapped the shutter, the camera clicked and whirred and fell silent. Michiko had swept a broad vertical line down the middle of the paper, ending her stroke with a deft push that left a neat feathered tail in its wake. "Remember," she murmured, not turning her head. "That's my camera and my film and I get to develop the pictures and throw away the ones I don't like." She paused, frowning slightly at her calligraphy.

"Just keep going," I told her. "This is good. Just keep going. It's good."

She suspended the freshly loaded brush above the paper again, studying her next move. "This isn't the way to do it," she whispered. "My teacher would be ashamed of me, to see this—this mess I am making." But she kept writing and I kept shooting. I went for the smooth concentration of her face, the shallow contours of her torso and the delicately spare design of her arm, wrist, fingers, those slender pale petal fingernails, and simultaneously the thick inky brushpoint and sweeping black strokes, the kanji on the paper being so like her precise body, that body being a kanji itself. When I had finished the roll of film, Michiko laid the brush aside and modestly drew her pants across her lap. I gathered up the scattered sheets of paper and turned away so she could get into her clothes. I studied her brushwork: "I recognize moon," I said, not turning around.

"Haiku by Basho," she told me. "I'm dressed for public now. —I still don't understand what you want to photograph for. Or what you're looking for."

I turned around. "Neither do I. But I'm sure there's a meaning in it someplace, a sign, something to read. Like that harpooner from New Bedford with tattoos all over his body."

Michiko smiled. "Are we going to lunch now? There's a noodle shop I want to try." So I took her to lunch at the noodle shop, then she went on her way and I went to my studio to not paint.

The harpooner was tattooed with hieroglyphics which explained the meaning of life, or so he said, but the man couldn't decipher them and neither could anyone else. Now Michiko's body was marvelously smooth and blank, but it incarnated the same sort of undecipherable text. "Man, I don't know what you're talking about," Scanlon told me, laughing. We were standing side by side in my studio, looking at canvases. "You mean you want people to *read* your paintings?" he asked.

"No, no, no!" I said.

"What then?"

"All I'm saying is that the body is different, truly different, from anything else you can paint. All I'm trying to do is paint it so it says—. What it says."

"Great," he said flatly. Scanlon is a short, large-shouldered man, with bright eyes, a small hooked nose and a thatch of mottled brown hair sweeping back from the top of his balding head, as if he were standing in a strong wind. He folded his arms across his chest and surveyed the final canvas that leaned against the deep stack by the wall. "Have I seen everything? You got anything else around here to show me? I like this big stuff.

You get a bargain when you buy a Stillamare. —Anything new in the back room?" he asked.

"The only new thing back there is Avalon's knapsack."

"Avalon's the woman you wrote me about, the one with the kid and no rent money. I remember. My memory is still pretty good. Did I remember to tell you I sold almost every painting in my Toronto show?"

"Twice already. But that's all right. It's good news. You can tell me again if you want."

"I'm not convinced yet, that's why I keep saying it. I still can't believe it. —I'm starved. Let's go out to lunch and you can tell me what you think of those photos I sent you."

We walked toward Copley Square, Scanlon discoursing on the international air of Toronto while I mutely wondered if I could have a sell-out show anywhere on the planet, then we came to an overpriced French bistro that Scanlon decided was right for us, and as soon as we had our napkins in our laps he said, "You haven't told me how things worked out for you at the new gallery, the one you wrote me about, the Strand, I think it was. What happened there?"

"I'm getting to that. I wanted to show you the paintings first," I said, uncomfortably aware that I was stalling.

"Good paintings. But my opinion doesn't count. What did the gallery have to say about them?"

"Your opinion counts a lot."

"Sure, sure. But what did the Strand woman say?" he asked again.

"She said a lot of different things. I'm still negotiating." I hesitated, wanting to talk about it and at the same time so embarrassed at my failure that I wanted to shut up. "Sonia Strand wants to give me only half the wall space, wants to cram me in with some other painter."

"Oh?"

"And she wants sixty-six percent of whatever I get," I confessed.

He frowned, bit his lip. "Tough tit to suck on."

"Exactly."

"Let's get some food in our bellies before we discuss this," he said, briskly looking around for a waiter. So we ate and talked some about the camping trip he and his wife were planning, and even more about Toronto and the photos he had sent me of his exhibit there. I preferred the work he was doing a few years ago, but didn't want to hurt his feelings by saying so and, anyway, he had devised a fine theory that showed how his recent paintings were at the front of a radical movement in contemporary art, and since his theory pleased him as much as his paintings, we conversed about the theory. Then we began talking about Sonia Strand. "Find out what she likes and give it to her," he says, quite off hand.

"She doesn't know what she likes. Galleries don't know what they like. All they know is what they think they can't sell," I say. "Because galleries don't go broke by turning down painters, they go broke by taking on painters they can't sell. So they learn right away what they can't sell. After that, they want to be astonished. Astonish me and if it's something I can sell, I'll take it."

"She's looked at your work, right? She's told you which ones she liked, right?" Then he leans forward a bit and drops his voice to confide to me. "Give her more of what she likes. —It works in bed, too" he adds briefly.

"Wonderful. When do I get to paint what I want, the way I want?"

"You've been doing that all your life," he says.

"No. I've been teaching in a second-rate art school all my life. I did what I had to do to make a living. I have two wives and three kids, remember? Now I'm old and I don't want to die pretending to be somebody else just to get into a gallery."

He puts down his coffee cup so hard it rings and he looks at me. "You think that's what I'm doing?" he asks abruptly.

"What?"

"You think I'm bogus because I'm finally able to sell again?"

"Of course not! Hell, I wasn't even—"

"Because nobody bought my other stuff. I know you liked those things, but I couldn't show anyplace except college galleries. Those paintings died a quiet death." He jerks his head aside, annoyed. "They were a waste of my time."

"How can you say that? They were good paintings, terrific paintings. You found a way to go. You've got to stay with it, go farther and farther, then it will develop and change naturally. Let the buyers catch up later. That's the only way to go."

"Yeah. Well. That's you, Ren. Not me. I'm interested in selling."

"You think I'm not?" I had to laugh.

"You know Magnussen's in Manhattan?"

I told him I didn't know spit about the art scene in the city anymore, and that was the truth.

"It's a good gallery. New but good. I sent him the big brochure from the Toronto show, the same as I sent you, and he asked to see my new paintings. I had a couple like the ones in the show, so I sent him slides of those."

I said Hey, that's great, told him it was terrific news, hoping I spoke with warmth and energy because, actually, I felt suddenly fatigued by his good news and ashamed of myself for feeling that way.

"Well, maybe he'll like my work or maybe he won't," he said with a philosophical sigh. "You never know."

I agreed you never know.

"I haven't had a good gallery for a decade," he said soberly.

I said yes, and oh, and well, and sank into thoughts of my own career.

Later, out of doors on the sidewalk, we agreed we should get together more often, and that a lunch in Boston or New York wasn't enough, and I congratulated him again on the Toronto show and the bid from the Manhattan gallery, then we said Take care and See you soon, turned and went our different ways. I walked down to the river and trudged upstream to the Fens and over to the Museum and then to my building, which isn't a terribly long trek as I'm in good shape for an old man, yet by the time I had climbed the stairway to the studio it felt like I should have died some while ago.

36

I GOT A BRIEF LETTER FROM LAUREL BRUNO, MIKE'S widow. It was just a hasty note, she said, because she had dreamed she was in the airport at Phoenix and Mike was there, too, and the dream was so vivid she wanted to tell me now and not wait until her next letter. She was so happy to see Mike, all the dreariness dropped away and she asked him What are you doing here? because even in the dream she knew he had died, so there must be some explanation. And Mike said I came to wish you bon voyage and to tell you not to worry, enjoy the trip. When she woke up she felt only a tinge of sadness, but when she was setting the table for breakfast she burst into tears and couldn't stop crying for a long time. She supposed the airport was in her dream because she was planning to fly to San Francisco to visit friends. Laurel wrote about her job and what she called the *ascetic* scenery of Arizona which, she added, she was still not used to. I read the note a few more times, then put it in the box where I keep things about Mike, just slid it in under the lid, so as not to look at the photos and letters inside.

The only time Mike returned to visit me was outside the Back Bay café where we used to meet sometimes. The air was amazingly bright and I said Let's get a table with an umbrella, and he said I can't stay long, but the sun's great, isn't it? I was heartsick because it was clear he didn't feel how much I missed him, but he was in good spirits, quite his round old self, and when I opened the menu it had a column of paintings the size of postage stamps. That was two years after he died and I haven't seen him since.

37

I BEGAN TO PAINT AGAIN AND IT HAPPENED THIS WAY. On Saturday morning Sonia Strand appeared at my door accompanied by two muscular louts who, I assumed, carried her sedan chair, but it turned out they had come along to manhandle one of my big paintings— "That one, the one with all the yellow," Sonia said—downstairs and out to Sonia's van, because she had a whimsical rich couple coming to her gallery, a couple who enjoyed previewing and sometimes actually buying canvases before they went on display. "And I think they might appreciate this one," Sonia told me over her shoulder as she—"Bye!"—drove off.

By the time I got back upstairs Avalon had escaped from the back room and was standing at the middle window, looking down into the street where the van had been parked. "Who was *that* bitch?" she asked without turning around. I told her the bitch was Sonia Strand who owned the Strand Gallery and maybe the bitch could sell the painting.

"That was one of my favorites," Avalon said crisply. "One of your best."

"One of my best? You've lived here all this time and haven't said ten words about my paintings and now you're a goddamned art critic?"

She turned and looked at me. "What are *you* so grumpy about?"

"You want a list?"

"Listen, I don't like Kim and me being shut in the back room every time there's a knock on the door." Her voice had turned annoyingly sharp.

"Quit complaining, Avalon, this was the only time and I already said I was sorry!"

"You. Did. Not."

"All right, goddamn it, I'm sorry!"

She stepped up to me and spoke in a harsh whisper. "You said you wanted to take Kim out to make maps, so do it." She bobbed her head once toward the back room to indicate where Kim was. "He's going over to Anwar's this afternoon and he's going to spend the night there. So if you're going to take him out, take him now."

I took Kim out. My plan was to search for a North West Passage to the Charles River, so we took our bearings outside the front door of the apartment building and headed toward the Fens, thence to the Museum and onward to the river. While we were tracking from the back of the Museum to the river he told me I had forgotten to shave. I told him I was giving my face a vacation this week. "There's no vacation for faces," he said. I told him, "Hey, are you counting steps or not? You're supposed to be counting." That kept him quiet until we reached the street corner. "How many steps?" I asked, flipping open my sketchbook. "The same as the last bunch, I guess," he said vaguely. "We're going to get lost if you don't do your part. Which way do we go now?" I asked him. He turned the compass on his palm, watching the needle veer and tremble. "Three-hundred and forty-five degrees," he said at last. When we reached the river bank we sat on a busted bench by the water and drew a map of our route based on his compass readings, and I asked did he think we'd be able to find our way back now. "I don't need a map to do *that*," he informed me. I told him that wasn't the point. "Your face is going to be white if you don't shave it," he said, cautiously touching my jaw. I stayed very still and squinted across the river, letting him rub my cheek as long as he wanted. "Wow, it feels weird and scratchy!" he said, taking his hand away.

"Listen, we were going to figure out how wide the river is without going across it. We were going to use a little geometry. Remember?"

"You were going to, but I'm bored now," he told me.

So our morning together didn't turn out quite as I had hoped, but at least we produced a map, and when we returned to the studio Avalon had prepared us lunch, which was grated raw carrots, diced tomatoes, chopped cucumbers, sliced green peppers and shredded lettuce, all of this wrapped cold in a flavorless tortilla. According to one of Avalon's holistic theories of food, vegetables should be kept near freezing, then scrubbed in cold water and eaten chill; that way they would invigorate the mind and raise us to a higher plane of consciousness. I unwrapped my tortilla, painted the inside with umber Dijon mustard, tossed in a handful of feta cheese and pickled olives and rolled it up again. Avalon was wearing my bathrobe, her hair turbaned in a towel. "I took a shower and I didn't want to get dressed till I finished lunch," she explained. "Because after I take Kim to Anwar's I'm going to Jenny's wedding. Remember?"

"Now I do," I said. Jenny was one of the waitresses at the Daily Grind.

"You've never seen me in a dress,"

"You showed it to me when you bought it. It's black."

"I showed it to you. That's not the same as seeing me in it."

"Mom looks funny in a dress," Kim volunteered.

"I'll bet she does."

"You two, a lot you know about dresses. It's a killer dress and I look great in it."

As it turned out, she didn't look bad. The dress was black, sleeveless, very short and very tight, held up with what they call spaghetti strings—two thin straps, thinner than my shoelaces—which left bare her shoulders, the hollow of her throat, the strong division of her breasts. Actually, she looked good, even in the black fishnet stockings. "What do you think?" she asked me, standing taller in new high-heels. "Am I a killer or not?"

"Mom, you're not a killer," Kim informed her.

Her hair had lengthened since I'd known her and no longer stood like a tar brush but—now black at the tip and pale at the root—it fell thickly every which way, tucked behind her ears and over the nape of her neck, making a tawny foil for the cruel silver rings and rivets in her ears, eyebrows and nose.

"You look fine, Avalon. Very Killer. Remember not to outshine the bride."

I drove them to Anwar's place where Kim jumped out and ran off without a good-bye wave, then I took Avalon to the Daily Grind where she joined two other waitresses, all three sharing a taxi to the wedding. I drove back to the studio, checked the mailbox and found a postcard from Sebastian Gabriel—you met him with his daughter at the *Pixels* exhibit—saying he had finished making the paper I had asked for and would I come to his place to take it away, please. I clothespinned Sebastian's postcard to the margin of the calendar to remind me to drive over to his place next week. After that I wrote a letter to my brother Bart about our mother's money, which we were managing, then wrote a note to mother, though it was impossible to know how much of my bland weekly gossip she actually retained, her nowadays being only a distraction, a confusing jumble of flimsy scenes through which she could see vivid dramas from thirty, fifty or seventy years past and, according to my brother, she was beginning to misremember or even forget those events, too.

I started out the door to mail the letters but remembered I wanted to take the dirty laundry out too, and as I was pulling the lumpy laundry bag from the back closet I saw my bathrobe was sprawled across Avalon's bed in a warm, cozy embrace of her pillow. I took the foolish thing away. On the floor at her bedside she had a thick paperback novel, beneath which lay *The Craftsman Entrepreneur: How to Sell Your Handiwork*, and under that was *Teach Yourself Japanese*. Avalon had taken over another shelf in the bookcase, stuffing my books sideways on top of each other to make room for a row of chrome-spiked, black leather chokers and bracelets (I tried on a few, none fit), a couple of covered cardboard boxes (jerseys, skimpy underpants) and a glassy jar of *Nuage D'amour* bath beads as a bookend for my copy of Montaigne's essays. She had a bottle of cologne which smelled rather like my after-shave, but she had no perfume. (Avalon had a way of lifting her head and flaring her nostrils to pursue an unfamiliar scent, and although she got used to wisps of Alba's perfume on me she never did accept Zoe's and would rub her eyes until they were red and blow her nose, claiming that she was allergic to something in the air.) She had used colored markers, the ones I gave Kim, to draw art nouveau flowers on a cardboard box where, I discovered, she kept each school paper her son had brought home, plus her journal (fake green leather, fake gold corners) which—please note!—I didn't open. I don't know how long I stood there, entranced by her things, the trinket details of her life that I couldn't look at when she was around, but at last I woke up and headed out to mail letters and take the dirty clothes to the laundromat.

I stopped at the laundromat, a lonely space with a desolate aisle of washers and dryers, plus a solitary woman folding towels, stayed only long enough to toss the clothes into a washer and then headed over to the Daily Grind. I sat in the sun by the window with coffee and a muffin while at a nearby table a little boy and his mother were discussing the possible outcome of a fight between Tyrannosaurus Rex and a plane equipped with rockets, the kid kneeling up on his chair and talking vigorously, one hand attacking the other; his mother listened attentively, then smiled, captured one of his hands, and began arguing a point. The kid sat back, one leg tucked under him, the foot sticking out beneath his bare thigh. I sank my chin on my chest, scribbled him onto my paper napkin, crumpled the napkin into my pocket and put the cap back on my pen. His father had come in and sat down beside him, one hand lightly on the nape of his son's neck, and now plowed gently up under the shaggy thick soft black hair. I looked out the window and was unreasonably happy.

I phoned Alba with the prospect of being with her for dinner and bedtime and Sunday brunch, but got only her recorded voice telling me she couldn't come to the phone just then but to please leave a —. I hung up, half remembering that she had told me she was going away this weekend, told me something about going with a woman friend to look at country property in Maine, or maybe she had said it was to a restaurant which had an especially fine cuisine or a clever chef or something like that. I phoned Zoe but got only her recorded voice and hung up. I went back to Edward Hopper's Laundromat, pulled the damp clothes from the washer and tossed them into the dryer, then went outside and sat on a bench to watch the people walking past until the clothes dried. When I got to the studio I looked into the bathroom with the thought of cleaning it, but it was quite clean (one tightly curled pubic hair, burnt gold, on the wall of the shower), so I wrestled the big unfinished canvases around till they faced me and I looked at them and they were good and I was back painting.

38

I PAINTED STEADILY AND WHEN THE OLD BONES AND sockets began to ache I walked up and down, then I made a pot of coffee, filled a mug and went back to painting. I don't know how long I painted. I went to refill my mug and found the coffee pot was empty, so I turned to the refrigerator to get something to eat. Avalon had a gallery of Kim's art posted on the refrigerator door, including his old sketch of me with brushes stuck every which way in each gigantic hand and a brush sideways between my teeth, and I had to laugh because here I was with a brush and an empty coffee mug in my left paw and three brushes in my right and I felt good. Maybe Scanlon is right when he says if you paint you have a theory of painting, whether or not you know it, and maybe he's right when he says you paint to exhibit, because nobody ever painted just to have something to hide, but I know for sure I paint because

I'm good at it. I opened the refrigerator door and ate a chunk of Romano, washed it down with three swallows of cold wine, grabbed a handful of olives, then went back to the canvas and when the light began to weaken I turned on the flood lamps and kept painting.

I don't know when Avalon came in, but I heard the water running in the bathroom and later I felt her standing behind and a little to my right, watching me try to work, then she came around to my left so close I could smell her ninety-nine-cent cologne, then back to the right, so I said, "Sit down and tell me about the wedding," simply to keep her out of the way. She was happy and went on prattling for I don't know how long, but after a while she said, "You're not listening," and I said Yes, I am, and she said, "What did I say?" and I turned around to look at her and tried to recall. She was still in the black micro dress and fishnet stockings, her arms folded, waiting. I told her Your make-up has come off. "Very observant, Ren. That's good in a painter. I washed it off an hour ago." I decided to give up and began to clean my brushes.

"Tell me about the painting," she says.

"What do you mean?"

"Tell me about the painting, the one you're working on."

"There's nothing to tell. It's a painting, not an event, despite what some moronic critics have said. You don't tell about it, you look at it."

"Try," she says. "Please. —Pretty please with goddamn sugar on it," she adds.

I went over to the canvas. "These figures, there's geometry and color and there's psychology. Now, the geometry, the depth as well as the flat surface, the way the bodies are arranged, makes the psychology, composes the psychology and— Never mind. See this? This is good, this whole passage in here, all through here. Good, very good. Nobody else can do this the way I do. Nobody." I paused to look at what I had done, where I had gone, and then began to look at what I had to do next and began to see how to go about it, which is one of the secret pleasures of the work. Then Avalon broke in on me. "That's it? That's all you're going to tell me?" she says.

"Are you hungry?"

"No, but you are," she says briskly. "I'll make something for you. I'll make zabaione."

"You?"

"You said you liked the way I made it a couple of nights ago. You melted my heart." She laughed.

"I'm not hungry. I changed my mind."

But she was already at the kitchen counter.

"I'm going to take a shower and go to bed. Goodnight," I told her. I pulled off my socks, tossed my shirt on the bed and went into the bathroom, had a great long, satisfying piss, stepped into the steamy blind shower and, as sometimes happens when the work is going well, saw the next passage and luxuriated in that streaming knowledge and even knew the brush strokes, toweled myself dry and started out to the studio with my pants slung over my arm—"Hey, there," Avalon says—stepped back to take our bathrobe, *my* bathrobe, from the hook. "I thought you'd gone to bed," I told her, wrapping up.

"I told you I was making zabaione," she says, going to the counter. "I put it in mugs, one for me and one for you. Taste it," she says, handing me a mug full of creamy whipped zabaione, a muted yellow cloud with a dark shadow to it. "Here's a spoon. Taste it."

It didn't taste bad. "What did you spike it with?"

"Rum," she says, lifting her mug to tap it against mine.

"Very original, Avalon."

"It's an art. Nobody else can beat egg yolks the way I do," she says, smiling at me.

I laughed and touched the side of her face, meaning only—I don't know what I meant, except to be friendly, but she was looking at me in such a way that I caressed her cheek and pushed up into her hair, hair so soft and thick it startled me and my hand jumped back. She looked at me for the space of a heartbeat, then stepped up close, watching me and waiting, so I stroked her hair again and yet again, cautiously so as not to frighten her off. "I like it here," she says quietly. "It's safe. I feel safe."

"Good. That's good." I stroked her hair.

"I'll move out, Kim and me, we'll move out as soon as school is over, you know."

"I know."

"I, Kim and me, appreciate every—"

"Let's sit down," I told her, going to a chair at the table.

Avalon sat down across from me, saying, "I'm saving a lot of money this way and I appreciate all the—"

"Finish your zabaione. And tell me about the wedding."

But instead she shoots me a glance over her mug and slouches down in her chair and placidly says, "I'm not talking to you."

"I'll listen this time."

So Avalon told me about the wedding, which was performed out of doors with everyone standing in a circle around Jenny and Mark which, Avalon said, was really good because, frankly, churches give her the creeps, not that she has anything against Jesus, though Jesus never stayed up the night with a sick child, certainly not his own sick child— "The wedding, Avalon, the wedding."—and about the reception with the long tables under the trees, and how everyone from the Daily Grind sat together and had a great time and there was dancing and on and on she went. I did try to listen, but in a while all I was doing was looking at her and seeing not the hard pins and rivets and rings but only her clean face and self, which I had never seen before, and all I wanted just then was to watch her and even after her voice had stopped I went on watching and "What?" she says abruptly, "What did I say wrong?"

"I like you, Avalon."

"Are you trying to get me into your bed?"

"I wouldn't even dream of it."

She looked sharply at me. "Why not?"

"I'm too old."

She thought about it. "That wouldn't stop you if you wanted to. You're not *that* old."

"I'm much older than you."

"Everybody thinks I'm leeching off you or they think you're fucking me, or both."

"What do we care what everybody thinks?"

She gave me a sudden smile and these little lights danced in her eyes. "*We* don't care," she announces, smiling, and I wanted to caress her face again, wanted to put my old gorilla hand through her hair. But instead I got up and went to the sink to wash out my mug and a moment later she comes up, puts her mug under the running water and begins to wash it. I guessed she'd go off to bed now and I tried to think what to say to keep her here; I wanted to stay up all night and I cleared my throat to speak, but nothing came out, and in the magnifying moment I saw the tense stretch of her dress, saw the smooth warm texture of her skin and the subliminal blue veins as if I were only an inch away. Avalon had dried her mug and now she set it upside down on the drain board, saying, "I was sort of surprised to find you here. How come you're not across the river with your wife?"

"Alba's away for the weekend. And I'm back to painting, so it's all for the best," I told her.

"Where'd she go?"

"I don't know."

"You're a pair, you two. What about the other one?"

"Can't you say Alba or Zoe? And Zoe's not *the other one*. She's Zoe. She's Astrid's mother and she's been a mother since she was seventeen or eighteen. She hasn't had an easy life and I thought you would have some feeling for that." I had tried to say something to keep her here beside me, but all I had done was bawl her out.

Avalon shrugged and half turned away. "If you weren't home when I came in I'd have put on some music. That's what I do when you're not around. The weekends you're away we get real loud. The big space in here makes it sound like, grand. You ought to try it, Ren. Get some rhythm in those old bones."

"I know what it sounds like in here. I used to do that." It came out defensive even in my own ears, but I didn't know what else to say. "You know the crate full of records back there? My player broke and they don't make players for those records any more, that's all. I used to have a great hi-fi. I played a lot of music."

Avalon laughed at me. "Hi-fi. Yeah, I bet you had a great hi-fi. Those old 78s are so godawful stiff they're like dishes, like platters. They're like old-fashioned crockery. They're antiques."

I kept her there, kept her there talking, though to be truthful it was me carrying on both sides of the idiotic conversation while Avalon was busy massaging her thigh or stretching this arm behind her head, then that arm, then pressing her hand hard into the small of her back and with the other hand squeezing the bare nape of her neck and the long muscle that slants to her shoulder. She was some package in that tense micro-dress, despite the chromium trash nailed to her face, and I wanted to caress her cheek again or close my fists on the warm satin flesh of her arms, sink my teeth in the succulent scruff of her neck. In a moment she was going away to bed and I started to touch her hair, but she watched me so I dropped my hand.

"That's all right," she says, matter-of-factly. "I like it when you do that."

"You're all right."

"But I don't know why you're so stingy with me," she says. "Everyone else gets a piece of you. I notice when you meet people in the street you open your arms so wide you smack me in the face. And at the Daily Grind you give everybody a touch or a pat on the shoulder. You put your arm around Michiko and kiss her. You give Garland a squeeze. The other day I saw you pick up one of the kids in the playpen and toss her in the air till she hiccupped, she was laughing so hard. But you won't even touch me with your little finger."

"That's not true, Avalon."

"Yes it is."

"It's because I don't want to start down that road."

"What the hell road are you talking about?"

"There's no fool like an old fool. I know it. I know it and I know me. I'll be damned if I—I'm going to bed."

"If you what, Ren?"

"I'm going to bed. It's past my natural bedtime."

"Let's stay up all night," she says.

"I'm going to bed."

So Avalon abruptly vanished to the back room and I turned off the rack of lights above the canvases and then the other lights, one by one, and crawled into bed. A short while later the dim light from down the hall went out and Avalon was in her bed, too. I lay here with no thought in my hollow head, only a desire to lie in the dark and be filled with the dark and be blotted out, but after a while my eyes adapted and the windows grew luminous, revealing the slanted stack of stretcher frames, the big easel, the kitchen chairs, and what looked like a string of glittering pearls forgotten on the floor beneath the table. I rolled over and faced the wall. I didn't want to think about the canvas I had been working on because then I wouldn't get to sleep, but if I didn't think about my work I'd think about Avalon and a minute later I'd be galloping down the hall to make a joke of myself, an old buffoon who still hadn't learned how to rein in the horse he was born on. I don't know how long I tossed back and forth between those tangled sheets, don't know if it was twenty minutes or an hour, not being able to rest my thoughts on any one thing except should I stay here or should I go there, thinking I'd be a fool to try it with Avalon and then thinking I'd be a bigger fool to stay here, then back again. At last I threw aside the bed covers, stumbled to my feet and pardoned Alba for her crazy flirtations, her lunch-and-coffee men friends, pardoned her passing fancies with this aging poet and that young athlete, pardoned the little sins she told me about and the bigger ones she didn't, pardoned her for doing whatever I was about to do. I turned to the hall and here was Avalon, saying quietly, "I heard you get up and I thought I'd meet you halfway." We stood there so close we almost touched and I felt, or maybe I only heard, her ragged breath, then she pulled her T-shirt up over her head, her elbow brushing my cheek and the warm smell of her skin filling my head, tossed the pale cloth into the dark and now she was as naked as I was. I held my gut tense, vain even in these shadows, but Avalon was already stepping past me to lift the bedclothes and get into my bed and I got in beside her.

How much do you want to know? We settled against each other awkwardly, our shocked flesh receiving volt upon volt until our bodies found alignment, front to front on our sides. "I'm clean, no problems," she says quietly. "Me too," I tell her. "You know I never fucked around—not in the last few years, anyway," she says. "Me neither," I tell her, kissing not the cruel rings in her eyebrow but the pierced flesh there, kissed her cheek, her ear, whatever she offered as she pressed her face this way and that against my mouth. Her hand glided from my shoulder to my hip to my flank with a caution so gentle it startled, just as the softness of her glittering shaggy hair had startled; she had a vigorous embrace and such tenderly inquisitive fingers as to doom a young man to her touch, and I was grateful to be old.

"I knew I would make it.—Oh, you sweet man, you lasted like nobody else," she says afterward, breathless and sweaty and happy, as if she had just won the Boston marathon. I told her Lasting is the only new thing an old man has, and rolled onto my back, exhausted, and let her rest half on me, the bed being so narrow, and after I got my wind back I got up naked and starving and looked into the white glare of the refrigerator. I took out a bottle of wine and the big end of a thick pizza we had made yesterday (a school of anchovies deep inside it, the whole topped with green peppers, gold onion rings and delicate pink leaves of prosciutto), then shut the door on the light. "I can do anything in the dark except eat," says Avalon, "so do you want the electricity or the oil lamp or those beeswax candles you're always telling me never to use?" I lit the oil lamp and Avalon put her plate ("The one with the ugly face on it," she says) on the near side of the table, where Kim usually sat, her knees bumping mine in a friendly way. The pizza was dense with flavors and the wine felt clean going down and the lamplight made Avalon's flesh as gold as a ripened pear, such as you would want to bite into, and "What are you scowling at me for?" she says. I'm not scowling, I tell her. "Yes you are," she insists, sinking her teeth into the pizza. It's the look I get when I'm hungry, I tell her. "If we run out of food you can eat me," she says and then she begins to laugh at her witticism, holding her hand over her mouth, swallowing, then laughing, coughing and laughing. "Be careful, you'll fall out of that chair," I tell her.

"Oh, God," she says, wiping her eyes, gasping. "I feel good." And she sinks back in her chair and sighs happily and looks at me and says, "Tell me again about my mother."

"I've told you about your mother twice a week. How many times do you want to hear the same story?"

"All right, tell me about my father when you and him hung out together." I was about to tell her You've heard all that, too, but seeing how happy she was I relented and said All right, then I refilled my glass and took a drink and wiped my mouth meditatively on the back of my hand, all the while trying to recollect poor Brendan Flood. I began by saying how the great thing about Flood was he did so many things, how he programmed computers, which in those days were huge monsters big enough to fill a room, how he wrote poetry, how he painted—no development there, but I didn't say that— and played the guitar and had his own band, how he liked to recite whole pages of Thoreau or William Blake or Allen Ginsberg because, like them, Flood was an angel-headed hipster burning to connect to the starry dynamo, and I told her about the urban commune he tried to organize and the peace march he led into a riot with the police, and how at a rally on the State House steps he ended his poem by tearing open his shirt to display LOVE in red lipstick on his chest, told her these and fifty other things, knowing I had forgotten hundreds more and regretting it. "What did he tell you about my mother and me?" she says.

"Have some more wine."

"But I like that story."

"No."

"Aren't you interested in your mother?" she asks me.

"You mean the one who left me on the doorstep or the real one?"

"Your birth mother," she says.

"No, not at all."

"Don't you want to find out why it happened that way?"

"I've never been curious about that. And there's nothing left to find out at this date. It's all gone."

"She must have had a reason for doing what she did and you should find out," she says. I told Avalon I wasn't interested, which was true, and that I was happy with the way things had turned out, which was also true, but Avalon went on anyway. "You should find out. Because maybe she wanted you to find out and to understand," she says.

I drained my glass. "If she wanted me to know something she should have left a note."

"I give up," Avalon says, letting her hands drop to her bare thighs with a loud slap. "And I have to go pee," she says, getting up.

Avalon went off to the john and in my head one thought led to another, so when she came back I asked her, "How many rings do you have down there?"

"Two," she says

"Don't they get in the way?"

"They didn't stop *you*, did they?"

I thought about it. "I felt them."

"You're supposed to."

Avalon drank her glass, tilting her head way back to get the last of it, and I don't know why it was such a pleasure to see her that way—her arm up, the tight pectoral and lifted breast and the underside of her jaw, her throat working beautifully. I supposed it would be impolite to ask why she had pierced those tender labial petals, but I asked anyway. "Why did you put them there?"

"Fun and games," she says, setting down her empty glass. "I was going through a phase, you'd say. Back then I used to have rings in my nipples, too, gold hoops, but I took them out when I got pregnant. You can breast feed a baby even if you have rings in your nipples, and I've seen it. But I didn't want to." She rattled on about piercing in San Francisco but maybe she saw I was heavy-lidded because she wound up with, "We're out of wine and I'm going to bed. What about you?"

When I came back from the john I blew out the lamp and got in beside Avalon, she lying hard against the wall, and told her If I roll over I'll crush you. "I'm not crushable, so you can relax," she says, her breath on my arm. I stretched out on my back and folded my hands behind my head, thinking to lie steady as a king carved on a tomb, fearful if I relaxed anywhere my old guts would rumble or I'd fart or I'd leak, as had begun to happen these past few years. I stared at the foggy ceiling or across the room at the tall gray window oblongs and in a while Avalon sank against my side and I wondered how she could make herself so weightless whereas my own bones felt so heavy, and then I noticed her breathing had slowed and deepened, for she was asleep and easy in her sleep, and I relaxed somewhat and thought how strange it was to be lying here with Avalon, as if the machinery of the heavens had slipped a gear, and I cautiously put my arm around her, and I felt better that way, and while trying to think of young men who would be fit to marry her I wandered off to sleep.

I woke up stiff. The air was pale in the studio and colors were just beginning to show when I lifted the blanket and slowly rumpled it down to look at more Avalon as she lay asleep on her stomach, her face to the wall. She had strongly defined scapulae and a long spine and—*lo and behold!*—two large symmetrical wings tattooed in white ink spread out and down to clasp the neat round of her buttocks. It wasn't a bad design in its own rapturous and vulgar way and I don't know how long I lay propped on my elbow, studying it, wondering what comic constellation of motives made her get tattooed in such elaborate feathery detail but in an ink so bland it was almost invisible. Then she awoke and my dawning prick bestirred itself, or maybe it was the other way around—no matter—for when Avalon slid her flesh warmly against mine and began to turn in welcome I closed my hand on the nape of her neck and took her from behind, kept her from seeing this old man's avid gargoyle face in the bright morning air.

39

MEDUSA'S ECSTATIC FACE (THOSE SHOCKED EYES, that gasping mouth) was on a plate that Avalon grabbed from the kitchen shelf only when she wasn't looking, because it was so ugly. I can't recall when my mother first showed me the cheap blue kerchief imprinted with the map of Sicily which had been wrapped around infant me on the doorstep, but from the beginning I was fascinated by the strange face in the center of the map above the word SICILIA —a face crowned with something curled or twisted, and from the head grew three muscular legs chasing each other around, so there were two legs spread near the bottom and one at the top. At first I took it for the head of Christ crowned with thorns. "No, that's Medusa," my mother told me.

I asked why Medusa was so angry. "Because her hair has turned to snakes, see, those are snakes," she said. "She was a beautiful woman and very proud of her long hair, very vain, but her hair was changed to snakes and now she's so mad that one look from her can turn you to stone." I believed it because my mother herself had flown at me with her black hair twisted every which way, her face white with rage and her eyes big, swatting at me as I dove under my bed or jumped out the door. "Perseus cut off her head and that's her head," she told me. She began to turn the edge of the kerchief and I cried, "*Wait! I want to look some more!*" but she was already folding it away, laying it deep in her cedar hope chest. "Benvenuto Cellini made a statue of Perseus with the head of Medusa, a bronze statue, which he cast all in one piece. He was a great artist, that Cellini."

My mother enjoyed telling me stories about Cellini, but I was more interested in Medusa. I came across the three-legged figure on a book cover at Veronica's house, on a cracked plate at Nick's, fashioned into a trinket on my aunt Gina's wrist, and drawn on every map of Sicily. Medusa was one of three Mediterranean sea spirits, the mortal one but also the most beautiful, so beautiful that the old sea-god Poseidon went mad for her, surged from the waves, and with sea water streaming from his beard and flanks — "He *ravaged* her on the floor in the temple of Athena," Veronica informed me — *ravished* her on the floor in the temple of Athena, whereupon Athena, that bitch so envious of Medusa's powerful beauty, turned Medusa's long black hair to snakes.

I asked why there were three legs that way, as if they were joined at the hip in back of Medusa's head. "Because there's three corners to Sicily," my father told me, hunched over the slate he was inscribing. "That's called the trinacria, that design. It stands for Sicily. Those three legs with the head of Medusa in the middle." I asked whose legs they were, which caused him to laugh and straighten up. "Those are nobody's legs. Go ask your uncle Zitti" he said, sweeping his leathery hand across the slate to brush away the grains. "That's the sort of thing he'd know."

Trinacria was an ancient name for Sicily. "Derived from the

Latin," Zitti told me. "Which is derived from the Greek, trinakrios, which means triangle—we used to call you Trinacria when you were little, but your mother put a stop to it—and the Greeks called the three-leg symbol a tryskelion, which means three legs." But no one could tell me whose legs they were. Years later when Alba and I were hitch-hiking through southern Italy we came to a museum displaying artifacts from nearby Pompeii, and among the rotted ax blades and block planes stood a small naked bronze man, grimacing as he staggered along with an ancient erection as big as either of his legs. "Now *that's* an accomplishment!" Alba said. The poor guy, corroded and grayish with age, had been supporting this burden for two thousand years, and when I saw him I knew those were his three legs running around Medusa's head. "But in every trinacria *I've* ever seen, each leg is just a leg," Alba insisted. I informed her she had to see these things as symbols. "If we're looking for symbols," she says, laughing, "Medusa's head isn't a woman's head with snakes at the top and a gaping mouth, it's her big hairy down-there."

Metamorphoses such as happened to Medusa happen often in Sicily, for it's a place where gods and goddesses, animals, women, men, spirits, and angels have taken each other by love or by force and made beautiful monstrosities since the beginning of time. Demeter, warm goddess of corn and grain, used to stroll the plains of Sicily and it was there in a field by the town of Enna—it's true, you can visit it—Hades stalked Demeter's slender daughter Persephone, clamped his cold hand over her mouth and dragged her underground, after which her grief-crazed mother refused to bless the harvest, so crops withered and nothing grew until Hades agreed to release Persephone, though only for half the year, for which six months Demeter allowed fields to bear again. The first to take Demeter was Poseidon, that same Poseidon who later ravished Medusa. But Poseidon in his youth didn't live in the sea; no, in his youth he was the shining god of horses. Demeter fell in love with Poseidon, fascinated by his rippling power and gentleness, and she walked beside him in the fields, caressed the dark hair that trailed over the nape of his neck like a storm cloud, and led him to her bed where they mounted each other this way and that for one whole year. From their union came the horse, Arion, and a daughter whose name can never be said, and the blood of Poseidon flowed in the veins of my great great grandfather Cavallù, who was born with the hindquarters of a horse. The only reason I'm confessing these things is so you'll know what's in Sicilian blood and how come I'm this three-legged man, corroded and grayish with age.

40

I GOT OUT OF BED AND SURVEYED LAST NIGHT'S WORK to see if it looked as good in the morning—it did—and I must have picked up a brush because I was painting when Avalon brought me a cup of coffee, saying, "God, don't you ever quit?" Not when the work is going well and it was going well till twenty minutes later when she said, "We have to go get Kim," so I dunked the brush and we drove off to get Kim. When we got there, Anwar's mother had invited Kim to stay through lunch, which was all right with Avalon, so we headed back to the studio and Avalon said, "I'm all dressed up, so why don't we get Sunday brunch at a nice place." In her eyes she was all dressed up, wearing her belly-button jersey top, the black one with silver threads in it, and her black velvet shorts with the chromium dog-chain belt. I stalled, told her I'd have to shave first. "You look fine, very distinguished, very mature. Let's go," she said. So we dined on over-priced waffles at Aujourd'hui, very mature me in shaggy white stubble and happy Avalon in black velvet shorts displaying a warm crescent moon of bare flesh beneath each rear hem.

Actually, nothing much changed in the way we lived—

each morning Avalon went off to the Daily Grind to roast coffee and sell espresso makers, while I trotted up and down the river, returned to the studio and painted; she still slept with Kim at her side, I had my bunk to myself. But early one misty afternoon here she was back in the studio, saying, "All right, I thought it over and bought some film, so let's get going." I loaded my camera, took about twenty shots of her in the silvery light while she pulled off her jersey, shucked her jeans, unhooked her bra and stepped out of her flimsy underpants, then took a hundred more right here or over there or just fooling around (she grabbed the camera, snapped a few of me) and ended with seven different shots of her standing in the middle of the bare floor with her hands clasped behind her head. I put aside the camera which, thinking of all the snapshots it had inside, purred happily as it rewound the last reel of film. I brought Avalon a handful of bra and underpants and with my other hand gave her lovable rump a pat—or tried to—actually, she cried "Ha!" and hopped sideways so I missed, then she waltzed around the easel and when I lunged after her she jumped past me, circled the table and dove behind the stack of big canvases that slanted against the wall, her tail gleaming for a moment as she scooted down the little tunnel at the bottom of the stack. We are made to the image and likeness of God, as the Catechism says and as I know when I'm painting well, and every now and then God just plays around, makes a fool of himself or herself or themselves.

"Now tell me about this painting," Avalon says one day, pulling up her jeans and buckling her belt.

"I thought we went over that."

"No, this other one. I have a problem with this."

"But I don't and I painted it."

"I don't want to be critical, but I—"

"Excellent decision!"

"How come some of them took off their clothes? I understand nudes, but this—"

"Do you like it?"

"I don't think it's a good idea to have kids that age in the same picture with adults when some of them are naked."

"Listen, do you like it or not?"

"I feel the way you do when something I make for dinner turns out weird and you eat it anyway," she says.

"Try the landscapes and still lifes."

I said earlier that nothing much had changed, but maybe I should have said the change was subtle and, now that I think of it, sometimes the change wasn't so subtle; like, one evening I was at the table writing a letter to Brizio when Avalon sat down and announces, "I forgot to tell you—I did you a favor—I made an appointment for you to see your doctor."

"You did *what?*"

"Because, Renato, every time I pick up the list of things we need to buy, like milk or cereal, there's always those little scraps of paper saying, *Make appointment to see doctor*, or *Make appointment to get poked*, or *Make appointment to get finger up ass*, so I copied down the phone number and phoned from work and they had a cancellation and I said you'd take it. I thought you'd be pleased. Next Tuesday at ten," she adds.

"Goddamnit, Avalon, mind your own business and leave me alone!"

"I wrote it on the calendar. You're welcome."

Kim had memorized his multiplication tables long ago, but he didn't have a single poem in his head, his teachers believing that poetry would take up too much space and that if he ever needed a poem he could look one up in a book, so we began to recite some lines each night after dinner. We had gotten to that place in Paul Revere's ride where there's *a hurry of hoofs in a village street, a shape in the moonlight, a bulk in the dark*, and Kim was having difficulty memorizing the next couple of lines which, frankly, aren't very memorable, but at last he got them and finished the lesson with *That was all! And yet, through the gloom and the light, the fate of a nation was riding that night!* Great stuff.

Kim dashed off and his mother said to me, "I read that poem you wrote about apple tarts." I asked her what she was talking about. "In the cook book, the one that's falling apart, I was looking through all those loose pieces of paper with recipes and one of them was a poem in your handwriting. It begins, like, *For apple tarts, my best advice is cut the apples up in slices*, and something like, *add cinnamon or other spices,* and I forget the rest, but I thought it was pretty good." I went to get the cook book. "Does the recipe work?" she asked.

"Of course it works, if you read the whole thing," I told her. Frankly, I was overly pleased with the little jingle, so I shuffled through the scraps of folded stationery and found it. "See—*lightly flour a rolling pin and roll your dough out flat and thin to fold those spicy apples in*—and so on and so forth." It seemed good at the time.

"Very clever, Ren."

I unfolded each square of stiff old paper (wine stains on the margin, herb leaves in the crease) and read the recipe, then turned it over and read the names scribbled on the back. Alba had written the recipe and our dinner friends had signed it, and we had kept the notes as souvenirs. Now I laid the open papers on the table and recalled as best I could each gathering, some in this studio, but the joyful spirits would not come when I called.

"What's wrong?" Avalon asked.

"Nothing. We had good times."

"You don't look it."

"They're gone," I told her.

"There'll be other times, other dinners."

"Too many of the people are gone."

"You have lots of friends left," she said, getting up from the table. "You're always having coffee with somebody at the Grind or else you're over in Cambridge with those guys or at somebody's studio and you're always writing letters to some friend." She had come back with the wine bottle and two water glasses and now she filled the glasses and handed me one. "Tell me about Alba."

I drank down half the glass. "I love Alba and would die without her."

"Oh, for sure," she says airily, dismissively. "But that's not what I asked."

"What's there to tell? Alba is big-hearted, good-natured, intelligent, and every year a little more bossy and prudish."

"She looks beautiful in the pictures," says Avalon.

"Those are old. She doesn't look that way anymore."

"Don't be a pig," she tells me.

"Alba's a beautiful, warm, thoughtful woman who keeps a dagger wrapped in her hair in case she needs something to shove in your heart."

"How come you're not living with her? I mean, why did you leave now, after all those years?"

"I haven't left, I'm just living here in my studio. Maybe I'm not living with her because I want to paint. Maybe I'm tired of being managed. Or maybe I don't like living with a person who writes gallery reviews for the *New England Newsletter*, celebrating assholes. My first mistake was teaching her how to look at a painting. Now she thinks she's a critic. I love Alba but she's a complex subject, too fucking complex to talk about, and I wasn't kidding when I said I'd be lost without her." I drank the rest and set the glass hard on the table with a bang and looked at Avalon who was still watching me. "Satisfied?" I asked her.

"No. But tell me about Zooey."

"Not Zooey. *Zoe*. Her name is *Zoe*. Is that so hard to say?" I drank another half a glass. "Zoe comes and Zoe goes. When she's single, she can't stand being single. When she's married, she can't stand marriage. She's broken out of two marriages and wants to try it a third time. She did try celibacy one year—bought some ugly dresses at the Salvation Army store, wore no makeup or jewelry, went off on a spiritual retreat run by monks and ended up in bed with the abbot. She's full of contradictions that make her interesting to men, except the ones she marries. I think the only person she trusts and loves completely is her daughter. Zoe needs a home, that's all. Or maybe not. She's a difficult woman, very difficult, too difficult to talk about."

"If you want to sit here drinking all by yourself just say so."

"No, no, no. When I'm drinking or eating I like company. —My idea of heaven is all my friends at a big table where every one's talking and enjoying a meal that goes on forever."

"Because you're Italian," she says.

"Sicilian. There's a difference. And the reason I like friends around my table is because I was born at dinner, at a long table with my grandfather at one end and my grandmother at the other and lots of people on both sides. Did I ever tell you I was born at a dinner table?"

"Yes, and I still think you ought to find out why it happened."

"I'm going to bed."

"Do I get a goodnight kiss or what?"

After that kiss and a bit more she went to her bed and I went to mine, where I stretched out in sweet tiredness, folded my hands behind my head, and listened to the rain patter on the window. I thought about my work and knew I was getting to where I had always wanted to go and, in fact, I was so close I could see the way there, could see it clear. I knew I wasn't going to get there because *there* keeps edging off the horizon, but that didn't bother me. I was grateful to have lived so long and to have learned this much. What I mean is, I had finally learned how to paint. I wanted to phone Alba tomorrow to tell her all about it. I wanted to show her the new work, the way I used to, so afterward we could eat and she could tell me what she thought about the canvases, which ones she liked and what she thought was strong or lame in each one, but even while I was thinking it I knew she wouldn't come, not to the studio, not so long as Avalon had a key to the place. And the more I thought about all this, the longer I envisioned it from Alba's slant, the more I wished I was a different me and not this same old man with one hand on a brush and his other in a bush. Despite all her foxy cleverness, Alba couldn't see through walls, couldn't see that I was going to my chaste bed like a monk each night, couldn't know I was living like a misfortunate castrato, more or less like a castrato, comparatively so. All she could figure, with Zoe's inventive help, was that I kept some skanky girl in the back room so I'd have a body to fuck whenever I began another canvas—though they both knew me better than that. Anyhow, all this was going to change. We knew, Avalon and I, that she was moving out with Kim after he finished the school term, though when I thought to calculate how soon that would be I discovered I didn't know the school's closing date. I wondered if the schools in Cambridge were better than in Boston and wondered if Alba would help find a place for them over there, but then remembered how high rents were in Cambridge and thought how Avalon needed to get a better job and thought about Kim, a good kid—had felt myself floating off to sleep, but beached to wakefulness again—and mused how strange that reading a recipe and a scrawl of long-ago names could wring my heart like it was a soaked dishrag. I thought of the big dinners we used to have in the studio, everyone bringing a platter of food or a bottle of wine, the bowl we made from a cast of Alba's peach fanny, when we were young and the future was radiant around us like an aura, and I thought it would be good to have a big dinner again and if Alba could find us a place in the country we could set the table outside in the shade of a big tree and began to think who we would invite and was adding names to the list when I floated off to sleep.

41

IN DR. CADOC'S OFFICE I PEED INTO A FUNNEL-SHAPED beer glass, then dropped my pants and, still standing, seized the top of the examination table in a hard embrace while the doctor, his hand in a tight translucent glove, pressed a lubricated finger to my anal ring and pushed strangely inward and continued to push ever and ever more deeply inward (my teeth clenched) to feel through the flesh of the rectal wall my faithful prostate gland hidden on the other side, then his finger turned in a slow relentless sweep (my mouth gasping open) and made one last push which forced—*expressed* was his medical term—a few drops of seminal fluid onto a glass slide which his other hand held beneath the drooping head of my abject penis; there was nothing unusual afloat in my urine or seminal fluid—"Everything looks clear. All you need is a blood test," he said, letting me out on parole.

42

ONE NIGHT AVALON SAYS, "I SHOWED YOU MY PHOTO albums and told you about me, and I'm not prying, Renato, because I know you get hysterical about your privacy, but why won't you tell me about you?" and I said, "What do you want to know? I'll tell you everything," and she said, "I know you're not curious about your birth mother—."

"Right."

"—Which I don't understand. So tell me about the one who adopted you."

I told her about my mother, Bianca, and how she had four sisters and four brothers and all of them were dead now except for two sisters, told how her father had come here from Sicily with nothing but an English dictionary in his pocket and how he worked hard and got himself a wife and a big house in Lexington and a villa in Palermo and nine children. "His name was Pacifico Cavallù and he's the one who found me on the doorstep. Everybody was sitting at the table in the dining room and there comes this knock at the big front door. Three knocks, like this," and here I hit the wall with my fist the way it had been done every time I heard the story. KNOCK KNOCK KNOCK. "There were thirteen people at the table that night. My grandfather got up with his napkin still tucked in his vest and went to the door and it was snowing and there I was. That was seventy years ago."

"And you still don't want to find out who your mother was who left you there, right?"

"I know enough. I know when the baby was born she went to leave it at the church, the parish house, but she made a mistake and left it at the wrong place. Because my grandfather's house was on this side of the church and the priests lived on that other side. She got pregnant by accident and left me at the wrong door by mistake, that's who she was."

"First of all, she didn't get pregnant by herself. And Second, maybe she didn't—"

"I'm grateful she didn't leave me in the snow and I'm grateful she got the wrong house."

"Let it go, Ren. Tell me about your father."

So I told her about my father, Fidèle, who was called Fred, and how he was an artist and master craftsman, a stone cutter, because his mother and father had died in the influenza epidemic of 1918, both mother and father on the same broiling August day, and how his father's last words to him were *Salvaguarde tua sorella*—Protect your sister—and how the day after the funeral my father wrote a letter to the Wentworth Institute to withdraw from the engineering classes he had been attending, after which he went downstairs to his father's shop and wrote to the dozen or so customers who had unfinished job orders, assuring them that he would complete his father's work. He cut and re-cut stones and set and re-set tile from seven in the morning till seven at night, six days a week, until he had learned how to do it right and had finished each order, and in the summer of 1927 he was the man who set the tile and raised the carved stone lintel over the door to Pacifico Cavallù's store on Prince Street. One of the Cavallù daughters brought him a glass of water and as he tossed back his head and was drinking it down she looked at the working of his throat and at his chest where the damp shirt clung, and when he handed her back the glass she said, "My name is Bianca, what's yours?"

"I like that Bianca," Avalon said. "But you told me once you came from a family of orphans and foundlings. So where are the orphans and foundlings?"

"My father's parents died when he was nineteen and his sister was fourteen. They were orphans. He had to take care of her and she was a wild one. Even at fourteen. That's why his father said to protect her."

"Who was the foundling?"

"My father's father."

"Where was he found?"

43

On the road from Palermo to Vuccarina there used to be a tavern run by a man and a woman, and they had a girl in the kitchen named Serafina. One hot afternoon (August 15, 1893) Serafina was plucking a chicken when a young man appeared out of nowhere and asked for a drink of water. "Water," he said hoarsely. She looked up to see him standing there—slender as a willow wand, with sunburned cheeks and pained, glittering eyes. "If you would be so kind," he added with a wan smile. Then he fell on his face in a faint. Serafina snatched the bucket of water from the sink, dropped to her knees and began to wash his face. "Oh, God," she murmured, loosening his collar with one hand and pressing the cool damp cloth to his forehead. "You're beautiful, beautiful, beautiful. Please wake up. Please." When he came to, the only thing the young man saw was Serafina, her wide sea-green eyes and her gold hair. He looked at her a moment, then shut his eyes and shook his head and opened them again.

"Don't move," she told him crisply. "I'll get you something to eat."

"No," he croaked. "Only water. I'm fasting."

"You're starving to death," she told him, dunking a cup in the bucket. "Drink this. There's food in the pantry that nobody else knows about. I'll go get it," she said, springing up.

The young man drank down the cup of water, then climbed waveringly to his feet and hauled the bucket to one of the long tables and seated himself there. The tavern door and both windows were open and he stared out at the dusty white yard, wondering where he was. The sun was beating down like a hammer and it seemed he could hear it going bam-*bam*, bam-*bam*, bam-*bam* in his head. Serafina came back carrying a platter with a chunk of provolone, a big handful olives and a string of dried figs.

"Eat up," she told him with a broad smile. "The boss and his bitch are asleep upstairs."

"You don't understand," he said with a parched voice. "I'm fasting. I'm waiting for a sign from God, a vision."

"Oh? How long have you been waiting?"

"Nine days. No. Yes. I think. Well—" He looked embarrassed. "I can't remember."

"What's your name then?" she asked, smiling at his confusion.

"Fidèle," he said. "At least I can remember that."

"I'm Serafina," she told him. Then she tore one of the figs from the string with her teeth. "You're not from around here."

"I was brought up in Palermo at the Orphanage of Saint Jerome and now I'm a student at the seminary next door to the orphanage."

"So you're running away?" Her sea-green eyes shone with delight. "I'd like to do that."

"Oh, no," Fidèle said, startled. "I came out here to pray and fast and wait for a sign from God, a call to the priesthood."

"What a waste," she said without thinking. "I mean, why do you need a sign from God? Doesn't the abbot take care of all that?"

"Because I don't feel fit to be a priest!" he cried. "Because I'm tormented by terrible visions. Because despite all my prayers—even in the middle of my prayers—something breaks into my head and distracts me. I thought if I left the city and came out to this simple, this bare, this, this—" He fumbled for the right word.

"To this God-forsaken wilderness of dry dirt and stones. Yes, go on," she prompted, sinking her strong white teeth into another fig.

"I thought if I came out here and prayed and fasted and mortified my flesh, purifying myself, then God would give me a vision, a blessed light to let me know for certain that I was clean enough and strong enough to serve Christ at the altar. But instead the distractions have been growing worse. I try to pray and it's as if someone were singing in my head, singing not words but single notes, weightless shimmering notes that hang in the air like flakes of gold. A beautiful voice, a woman's voice." He closed his eyes and wiped the sweat from his eyelids with his palms. "She's a contralto," he added shakily.

"Are you getting enough sleep?"

"When I sleep I have nightmares." He swung his fists down on the table so hard—*crash!*—that the bucket jumped, quite startled. "Last night I dreamed of angels plunging from heaven like meteors, their wings in flames, the air sizzling. And today it feels as if my head is on fire," his voice cracked and his hands shook.

Serafina closed her hands over his and looked into his glittering eyes. "You should rest here in the shade and eat more," she told him.

Fidèle snatched back his hands. "Some days I don't even know who I am!" he sobbed. Then he lifted the bucket as high as he could and emptied it on his head.

Serafina cried Hey! and turned round to fetch a towel, but when she turned back he had already pulled off his shirt and was using it to mop his head and neck.

"I've never told these things to anyone," he murmured, clearly puzzled.

Serafina saw how his bones were beautiful and strong, the flesh of his stomach as tight as a drum, and suddenly she wanted to pull his head against her breasts, to feel his fiery cheeks and parched mouth. "You look like a bird cage," she said tenderly.

"But I feel much better. It's amazing." He smiled and looked around. "My head is clear for the first time in days. I'm ready now. I'm *ready*. All I need is a quiet place to pray." He smiled again, as if seeing her for the first time. "How old are you?"

"Eighteen. Almost eighteen. Practically eighteen. What's wrong?"

"I'm so happy—" He broke off, not knowing what he wanted to say.

"Listen. Let's get out of here. I've got some money hidden upstairs. I'll go get it."

"Money? All I need is a place to pray. They have rooms upstairs?"

In fact, the stairs had groaned and shuddered because somebody heavy was coming down. Now in strolled the boss, Mazza, a large barrel-shaped man tucking his shirt into his pants, buttoning his fly, scowling. "What's the fuss about? What's going on here?" he demanded, looking from one to the other.

"This gentleman wants a room," Serafina said.

"This gentleman without his shirt? And is that his little prayer book on the floor? He looks like a runaway priest to me. I can smell a priest even in my sleep."

"He wants a room," Serafina repeated.

"By the day or by the hour?" Mazza asked, unfolding a soiled apron.

"Until tomorrow morning," Fidèle said, picking up his prayer book and looking at it as if he had forgotten how to read.

"Up the stairs and down the hall, the room at the end. If you want the girl, you pay extra," Mazza told him.

"What?"

"He was making a bad joke," Serafina said, her cheeks reddening. "Let me show you the room."

"I'll take the money now," Mazza said evenly.

So Fidèle paid and followed Serafina up the narrow stairs and down the hall to the little whitewashed room. It had a bed over here, a table with an oil lamp over there, and in between was an open window with a brilliant blue square of sky. At that moment Fidèle was so happy that he wanted to break out singing, but when he turned to tell Serafina about it she was gone. He shut the door behind him, took off his shoes and sat on the covers with a pillow between his head and the wall. His body felt wonderfully light and at the same time it seemed to have a compressed power deep inside, as if he were about to spring up from the bed and fly off, soaring to extravagant heights in great circular sweeps and turns and rolls and volutes. In fact, he felt too giddy to pray, so he simply waited for the vision to appear. His eyelids grew heavy and then heavier and soon he was asleep.

Only God knows how long Fidèle slept. When he opened his eyes the room was dark and the open window was crowded with stars. Sweet air embraced him like an arm (smooth and soft and warm) and there came a tender ripping sound, as if his soul were being torn open. He groped for the oil lamp, struck a match and touched it to the wick, then something soared over him or through him, knocking him to the floor at the foot of the bed. Now the room was drenched with golden light and she stood just inside the window, her airy white garments floating down into silence while a luminous golden cloud hung about her head and flakes of gold lingered in the air like shimmering music. She had a scissors in one hand and a sheaf of paper money in the other. Fidèle shut his eyes, shook his head, opened his eyes again.

"I am an angel of God," she whispered.

"An *angel?*"

"Shhh." She put her finger across her lips to show he should lower his voice. "Yes. Angels are pure spirits, without bodies, having understanding and free will," she explained.

"Oh." Now Fidèle had spent a year at the seminary, but he wasn't a fool and he knew this was Serafina herself in her nightdress. "I see."

"Angels were created to adore and enjoy God in heaven," she added, just as in the Catechism.

"I know. But what are you doing in my room?"

"Angels were also created to assist before the throne of God and—and they have often been sent as messengers from God to man, and are also appointed our guardians," she recited. "I'm here to give you a message," she said.

"And what might that be?"

"There is a certain young woman who works here like a slave in the kitchen, and waits on table and cleans the rooms. Not to mention being forced to do other filthy things."

Little by little the flakes of gold floating in the air had settled to the floor, as if they were chicken feathers cut loose from a pillow and gilded by lamplight.

"Serafina?"

"Yes, that's her name. And when you wake in the morning she'll be gone, but don't believe any lies about her, because anything she took belonged to her and she earned it and didn't steal it."

"Is that why you cut open the pillow? To get at the money?"

"And if you ever see her again, take her away with you to Palermo."

Fidèle knew he would never be a priest, for the sight of her breasts through the gauze of her dress was beautiful to him, and when he looked into her eyes his heart felt as if it were being squeezed in his chest, and he thought how wonderful it must be to have a mother and father in the flesh, how fortunate to have a wife and child.

"Any other messages?" he asked her.

"You should stop fasting and eat more." The she blew into the chimney of the oil lamp and vanished, leaving him alone in the darkened room.

Fidèle's eyes gradually grew accustomed to the dark. The stars crowded back into the window, then one by one they faded and the sky began to lighten. He heard boots going down the stairs and up the stairs, doors being wrenched open and slammed shut, heard Mazza cry, "Where's the damned girl! Where's the goddamned girl!"

That afternoon (August 16, 1893) Fidèle was walking back along the dusty road from Vuccarina to Palermo. His shirt was stuffed with oranges, his pockets with provolone, prosciutto, raisins and figs. This is amazing, he thought. Here I've been eating all morning and I'm still famished. The roasted brown grass, the baked cactuses, the rocks cooking in the sun, everything—even the yellow sky heavy with sand blown over from Africa—everything looked beautiful to him. If the world were an egg I'd swallow it in a gulp, he thought. Little by little he was able to make out somebody standing on a huge boulder way ahead of him where the road forked, one road to Palermo and the other to Mondello. He prayed it was Serafina and in a while he could see that it was. When he reached the foot of the boulder he stopped and looked up at her, but Serafina was gazing steadily out the road to Mondello. "Ciao, Serafina!" he called up to her. She turned and looked down at him and smiled. "Ciao, Fidèle," she said, her voice as refreshing as a drink of cool water. She was dressed in a white dress, rather like a First Communion dress but without a head shawl, and she had a bundle of clothes under her arm and a framed photograph with a glass cover.

"Where are you going?" he asked.

"They say there's a beautiful beach at Mondello. I've always wanted to see the sea."

"Come with me to Palermo," he said.

"Whatever for?"

"I want to say good-bye to the gardener at the Seminary.

He is like a father to me. And they have a beautiful harbor at Palermo with ships that sail all over the globe. Come with me."

Serafina climbed down from the boulder and joined Fidèle.

"Who is in the photograph?" he asked.

"This is my mother," she said.

If you had been there Serafina would have shown you the photograph, because it was the only thing she had of her mother and she was very proud of it. And you could have heard them talk as they walked down the road to Palermo, their voices getting smaller in the distance, Serafina saying, "Yes. She was from Venice. And I have her eyes and hair. And I like water. That's because she was from Venice where the streets are made of water."

44

A LETTER FROM THE STRAND GALLERY ARRIVED, saying, *Dear Renato: The large painting which you have on loan to our gallery has failed to find a buyer, I'm sorry to say, despite its obvious merit. As you know, I had hoped to place your work in our exhibit schedule, but current and future commitments make that impossible and, regrettably, we will not be able to show your work at the Strand Gallery. Sincerely, Sonia Strand.* I looked at the letter a few more times to see if I had missed a merciful phrase or word, but it had only two sentences and I hadn't missed a thing. Sonia had a large signature, a sweeping S followed by a vigorous zigzag flourish.

I made a cup of coffee but then, feeling so tired, I sat down at the table and stayed there a long time looking across the room at my canvases and I saw down a long perspective how all of my life converged toward this solitary room filled with these stretched canvases, saw that my years added up to this broken wall of worthless painting. After a while I got up from the table but something happened—the chair tumbled over backwards and I fell forward, grabbed the edge of the sliding table but crashed to the floor anyway. I climbed to my feet and pulled myself up straight, focusing on my father and how he worked at his craft and took pride in his good work and how he faced the world calmly though he never got the recognition he deserved. Keeping him in mind, I walked over to the kitchen counter, started the heat under the kettle, took down a bag of Italian Roast and carefully made a cup of coffee using a paper filter and the ceramic coffee funnel which had been given to me by Brizio, who might still need my help in life; when the coffee was finished, I added a splash of whole milk and took the mug of coffee with me while I walked up and down to look at the paintings. It was hard to think and, being exhausted, I sat down at the table and was resting there when Kim came in happy to show me his school papers, a big stack of papers, and then Avalon kept saying something. "Well, do you?" she insisted. I asked her What. "Do you want me to warm up your coffee? You've got two mugs of coffee on the table and they're both cold," she said. I told her no, and she went away but came back later with Sonia's letter and said, "What's this about?"

"Don't read my mail, Avalon. How many times have I told—"

"I already read it. What does the bitch mean she won't be able to show your work?"

"The bitch means she won't show my work."

Avalon read the letter again, frowning and chewing her lip. "Well," she said, tossing the letter onto the table. "There's lots of other galleries."

"No. I've been to the other galleries. At one time or another I've been to every gallery in New England. No one wants to show me. My work is over. I'm finished."

Avalon studied me a moment, then started to open her mouth to say something but changed her mind, took the coffee mugs from the table and emptied them gently into the sink. We worked side-by-side at the counter making dinner, talking about nothing much or, to be exact, Avalon chattered while I kept thinking about the Strand Gallery and at last I said, "I'm going to go get my painting back," and I left.

I drove in and when I got close to the Strand I began to look for an empty stretch of curb but didn't find one and so went down Newbury past the gallery, maneuvering around a couple of stalled cars and onto a side street, turning up one block and down the next until I found a place to park. The evening air was dead still, as if waiting for something, and suffocatingly warm so that by the time I had hiked back to Newbury I was sweating. At the Strand Gallery half a dozen people were outside on the stone steps, chatting and laughing, drink in hand, happy in the light streaming through the Strand's open door. I crossed the street away from the gallery, tugging the damp shirt from my chest and pumping it like a bellows to cool me down. I looked at the reception crowd inside the big window, the women with bare shoulders, the men in jackets. A woman's laugh floated up from the cluster of people on the steps. I crossed over to the gallery and went in, the place alive with light and the noise of people talking. I pushed toward the back, passed the artist on display (elegant jacket, torn blue-jeans with paint smears) and was wedging my way around the wine-and-fruit table to Sonia's office when Peter Bell caught up with me. "I'm here for my painting," I told him. "Yes, of course," he said, popping in ahead of me, extending an arm to clear the way. He closed the office door behind us, caught his breath and said, "Our men aren't here tonight. Maybe it would be easier to pick it up tomorrow. What do you think? It's a big painting and it really takes two to manage it properly, two or three. I think you should come back tomorrow. It's best for the painting. What do you think?" The canvas leaned along a side wall, a gilded rococo chair at the end of it.

"I'll take it right now." I mopped my face with my sleeve.

He went reluctantly to the far corner of the room and unlocked a metal clad door, saying, "It's going to be difficult. You have to negotiate down the stairs to the ground level out back.

As you can—" But I had pulled the painting away from the wall, got in back of it, reached as wide as I could on the long crosspiece of the stretcher, then grabbed a hold and started toward the door to the showroom. "I'll go out the front. Just open the goddamn door," I told him.

"No, no, no, you don't want to do that! Mr Stillamare, please, oh—"

I leaned the painting back against the wall, pulled open the showroom door, grabbed the stretcher crosspiece, and lifted.

"Please—" he cried.

I swung around little by little to line up the forward vertical edge of the stretcher frame with the open doorway and now slowly started forward as Bell scuttled sideways ahead of me, grabbed the upright edge with both hands and helped to steer it through the doorway. "Slow, slow, slow," he said, muting his voice. "The table is out here, the credenza with food—."

Sonia Strand took me in with a glance, turning aside and spreading her arms to gently brush back the guests who were beginning to look this way, still chatting. My arms stretched along the crosspiece, my cheek pressed to the back side of the canvas and I, not being able to see much, followed Sonia, her garment of shimmering beads blue and green and violet, as she began to make a corridor through the crowd toward the open front door, rain falling through the doorlight. My stretched arms weakened and then trembled and the bottom of the frame banged on the floor. "Bell! Get on this side!" I croaked. I tried to lift the stretcher, but my arms shook and lowered it to the floor again. I waited a moment, then grabbed the crosspiece and lifted. I took a step, somebody crying *Watch out for the food!* as I fell into the canvas, tripping over the bottom of the frame and toppling all onto the edge of the table, smashing and dragging so I sprawled on the canvas under a cascading tower of plates, tumbling fruits and cheeses, a big green bottle still spinning slowly on its side, dribbling a stream of pale wine—I scrambled to my feet in the silence, grabbed the edge of the painting and hauled it face down across the floor, tilted it up on edge and dragged it out the door and down the steps, the rainy gusts snapping it this way and that like a sail until I came to a cross street where I turned the corner and leaned it, face out, against a brick wall.

I stood there, my head throbbing, while people hurried past hunched against the blowing rain, and a kid bare to the waist sailed by on a skateboard, his black hair a mass of thick ringlets, his coffee skin glistening. I jogged one block over and two blocks down, sat in the car with my head against the wheel, panting, then drove back to the canvas and parked half on the sidewalk, got out and swung the back of the canvas against the car, then shoved it up onto the roof and roped it there. I drove home and slid the canvas down from the car roof—discovered the stretcher was busted at one end—and dragged it through the apartment house door. I climbed up to the studio and Avalon came down with me to hold the trailing edge of the frame while I pulled it up the stairs. She didn't say anything while we were hauling it up, but as soon as we got inside the studio she said, "Take off your clothes and take a shower or you'll get a chill and die." I gave her my shirt, then I got a dish towel and blotted the face of the canvas, got two more and worked on the back around the stretcher while Avalon, hands on hips, watched me and when I was through she said, "Take a hot shower, *please*." I pulled off my clothes and got into a hot shower. I don't know how long I was there but Avalon reached in and turned off the water, then she grabbed my wrists, pulled me to my feet and gave me a towel. I put on a pair of pants and a sweater, and we sat side by side on the floor by my bunk and drank cheap white wine in silence for a while, then Avalon put her arm through mine and, for no reason at all, confessed about her shabby and unfortunate life in San Francisco until I went to bed.

45

MIMI'S CAFÉ HAS EXHIBIT SPACE ON THE TOP FLOOR. The roof is all skylight and there's a big square hole in the middle of the exhibit space so that light can shine down to the swank dining tables on the second floor and to the bar below that. I'd been to the Café gallery before, but only because some of my students had shows there. This day I brought one of my big Genesis pages and photographs of the others in the same series. The gallery manager, Ms Finch, looked at my handiwork and was shuffling through the photos when she said, "I don't see how I could show these." She looked up and handed the photos back to me. "The people who come to Mimi's are younger and they wouldn't go for work like this. I think they'd be put off." She smiled firmly. "I'm sorry to have taken up your time. I know you must be as busy as I am." Then she shook my hand, said goodbye and walked away.

That night I lay dead in my bunk but awake, as if I were a ghost haunting my own studio, and I wondered what would become of these paintings when I was gone, whether they would live in light or die too, because it's impossible to sell the left-behind canvases of a dead man who never was famous, never sold much, and whose reputation fell apart in his middle age, and my Alba—who never helped me get a gallery, never helped me find a dealer, never helped me sell a canvas—this Alba won't begin to nurture my work and reputation when I'm pushing up daisies. I've turned the pages of *ArtNews* and *Art in America* and caught myself witlessly looking for my name in the announcement of an exhibit or in a gallery review, because it's hard to believe my name can't be there one time or another, can't be there ever, and that in this living world I'm invisible: Alba no longer believes in my work, no longer believes in me, and this is what it feels like to be dead.

Next morning I woke up late with a headache, but I had a

good long piss, washed my face and trimmed the beard—titanium white, it looked like. I checked the big painting (*Berkshire Fields*, painted when the artist was only 61) and, although the stretcher was fractured at one end, it had survived the rain and had dried well, the canvas tightening somewhat. After breakfast I went for a slow, useless walk along the Charles, then came back to the studio and was making a mug of coffee when Kim came in the door and said somebody had phoned me at the Daily Grind. I asked him what he was doing home from school at this hour, and he said, "School's out. Yesterday was the last day. Don't you remember?" and I told him I had forgotten but, yes, now I remembered. When we got to the café Avalon told me, "Your doctor called and he wants you to call him back. Here's the number." So I phoned the doctor and his secretary said, "Oh, yes, Mr Stillamare, the blood test numbers came back from the lab and they're in the range where we look for cancer, so Dr. Cadoc would like to see you for a biopsy."

46

ALBA DROVE ME TO THE UROLOGIST'S OFFICE WHERE I introduced her to Dr. Cadoc who, I realize, I've not described before, a gentle stoop-shouldered man with bright eyes and a whimsical smile. Maybe you know that to get biopsy samples from the prostate gland they insert a firm cylindrical probe up into the rectum, like a .38 caliber handgun up your butt. I hadn't any need to think about it before. "This device does two things—it makes an ultrasound scan and takes tissue samples," Dr. Cadoc said, showing me the probe. I told him it looked too damn big. "I'll tell you each time before we take a sample. You'll hear a click and feel a tap inside, like a little hammer, but don't be alarmed." That's when the hollow needle stabs through the rectal wall to take a bite from my prostate,

I said. "Yes, but you won't feel it. And don't be alarmed if you discover blood in your urine later today. Of course, there's some discomfort from the probe. It's uncomfortable. But the procedure sounds worse than it actually is," he said. "—And this is Jane. She'll be manipulating the probe and I'll be here watching the scan and choosing the sites to sample." Jane was a beefy plain-faced woman with grayish hair which had been cut so it resembled an iron helmet. "Take off your shoes and trousers and underpants," she told me, yanking a long sheet of waxy paper onto the examination table. "Then get up here and lie on your side facing the wall. I hope you're not some nervous Nellie," she muttered.

Afterward, in the car, Alba asked me how I felt and I said I don't know, I feel OK, I think I'd like a cup of coffee. We sat side by side at a little round table in the sun, drinking our coffee and viewing the people and the cars, as if I were still part of the ordinary afternoon. A couple of bronze guys in shorts dropped their bicycle helmets on a nearby table and stood there talking, one of them unfastening his sport gloves and the other one mopping a handkerchief on his neck and throat; and beyond the bicyclists three girls were chattering, the blonde constantly sweeping up a hank of hair, holding it, letting it go, then sweeping it up again, while here in front of us a college kid had pulled his bare foot into his lap to examine the underside of his heel. "Everybody's so young and so healthy," I said.

Alba looked around. "That man over there is about twenty years older than you are," she said.

"He looks out of place."

"Well, you don't look out of place," she told me. "And I like your white beard."

I sat there and thought about going back to the studio, but I didn't want to paint or to think about painting and I didn't even want to go to the studio. Alba broke in on me, saying, "You can stay at home, you know. Why don't you stay at home?" and I said All right. Late that night we had a glass of wine and as I had been thinking of the kids most of the day I said, "They're far enough along. They'll make out all right," and Alba said, Yes, they'll be fine, and I said, "I wish Brizio would settle down, get started on something serious. He's better than what he's doing. He could use some help," and Alba said, Brizio will do fine. I said, "They're good. They're as good as anybody. That's one thing we did right."

"We did a lot of things right," she said.

That night my piss came out looking cloudy and the next morning I found I had dribbled blood onto the bed sheets. Later I phoned Tom Hay who seven years ago had told me over a café table that he had just learned he had a cancerous prostate. Now we went out to a bistro for lunch and I told him what was going on, saying, "This is only a biopsy and I'm coming apart."

"Man," he said. "I think you're doing fine."

The next day Cormac phoned me, which meant Hay had told him, so we all met for coffee at the Paradiso, sat outside under an umbrella, shaggy Cormac saying, "So, Ren, how are you doing?" I told him I was getting bored with my morbid thoughts about death, impotence and incontinence. He searched me a moment, then shifted his bulk in his chair as if to change the subject. "You look good with that beard," he said. So we began to talk politics or art or sports or something, and though I wasn't paying attention it was better than being in solitary confinement in my skull.

The next morning when I got up to piss, nothing came. Not a drop. I washed and shaved and tried to piss again, because the need was getting painful, but all that happened was a hard dry cramp deep inside. Alba drove me to the hospital emergency room and by the time we got there the pain had grown so it seemed there was only this heavy ballooning agony down low and nothing else in the world. After twenty minutes the triage nurse admitted me from the waiting room to one of the examination rooms, and by then I was sweaty and shaking somewhat but just able to unbuckle my belt and tear down my pants while

Alba rushed some paper towels onto the floor because the pain, like an enormous slowly clenching hand, now squeezed out all my crap - "Oh, God! Oh, shit!" I cried.

Somebody cleaned up the mess and somebody else came with a clipboard and asked us questions and told me to get onto the bed; ten minutes later a lanky guy appeared with a file folder, shook my hand and introduced himself as doctor somebody and asked me if I was Renato Stillamare. I said, "Yes, but I don't know for how long." He said not to worry, he would insert a catheter and I'd feel fine. I said Tycho Brahe died this way. "Tycho Brahe? I knew he had a silver nose, but I didn't know about the urinary blockage." A young woman appeared and handed the doctor a kit containing the catheter and bag. "This is Maria. Now I'm going to put some ointment on the tip of your penis, make it numb," he told me. I said Yes, do it. "It will feel chilly, cool," he added. I agreed it felt chilly. "I'm ready to insert the catheter," he said to Maria.

"*I'm not!* Let me grab a hold of something," I said and grabbed the steel bed frame. Alba had come over.

"Just a steady—" he said and shoved it in like a knife to a scabbard while my body arched up from the bed and I shouted, "*Ow! Damn!*" A moment later he asked, "How are you feeling?"

"Better than a couple of minutes ago," I said.

"I should think so," he said, ducking down to adjust the catheter and bag. He reappeared, file folder in hand. "Think about surgery," he said.

"I'm no good at surgery."

He smiled. "Dr. Cadoc can take care of that for you. He's a good surgeon. I'll send him a report. —Sorry to meet under these circumstances, Mr Stillamare."

About an hour later we left the emergency room; Alba drove and I slumped cautiously in the passenger seat with a catheter up my old prick, a water-filled balloon banging around inside my bladder and a plastic bag strapped to my leg. A day or so later Dr. Cadoc phoned and said that the biopsy had found no cancer.

Dr. Cadoc, my age, had retired from surgery, so it was performed by one of his young associates, a brisk fifty-year old. He had explained how many pieces of equipment they were going to insert up through the urethra, *my* urethra. Now it was the morning to do it. "What are you so worried about?" he asked me.

"Death and other side effects," I said.

"You won't die unless you get hit by a truck after this is over," he said.

"Incontinence."

"We've been over that. Very unlikely."

"Impotence."

"We've been over that, too. Also very unlikely."

"Retrograde ejaculation doesn't sound like fun."

"Is he always this way?" the anesthesiologist asked him.

"He's an artist, a painter."

"When does that stuff they gave me take effect? I'm not feeling happyfied," I told them.

"I'd say it took effect some while ago," the surgeon said.

The anesthesiologist asked me to roll onto my side so he could give me the spinal. I rolled onto my side.

"Maybe you've done this a thousand times," I said to the surgeon. "But it's new to me."

"No, I haven't done this before," he said. "But I've always wanted to try."

47

THREE DAYS LATER I WAS BACK AT ALBA'S, BUT before I left the hospital I was instructed not to lift anything heavier than ten pounds and not to try sex or anything similarly pleasurable, but to drink lots of water. When I pissed it felt like I had a flamethrower down there. I was tired, mostly. I lazed around the apartment and wrote letters to the children and napped. Lou Zocco came around one day and asked how it was ("I'm peeing bloody urine, looks like Chianti," I told him.) and Tom Hay came by a couple of days later ("It's the color of Calabrian Rosé. I'm waiting for the Bianco.") and they each took me out for a coffee, but mostly I stayed with Alba and read whatever she had lying about the apartment, not even reading but just looking, and Zoe came over for dinner, bringing a sweet desert each evening.

Threadbare Sebastian Gabriel, the paper-maker, came by and since I was getting my appetite back we went to lunch at a bistro in the Square. "I brought the load of paper to your studio," he said. "Your Avalon let me in."

"She's not mine," I told him.

"Anyway, she let me in and I left it stacked on the floor, but you should put in on a table or pallet. —Your new work looks great," he added. "All those new canvases, fantastic. Getting ready for a show?"

I wondered how much Avalon had told him about the Strand Gallery mess; from his skittering gaze I figured she'd told him enough to make him unsure as how to talk to me. "I'm always ready for a show. —Now tell me about that bright daughter of yours, tell me about Cait," I said, to change the subject.

"Caitlin's trying to teach me accounting." His face lit up, as it did whenever he talked about her. "She's organizing my business into folders with different colored labels on them. She loves doing that kind of stuff." He talked about his daughter, and then about his ex-wife who was already a mid-level executive at a Manhattan brokerage firm, and about his paper-making business which he felt was taking in more money this year, even if he didn't know how much or how to keep track of it, talked about what he called the yin and yang of the paper-making business, and about his favorite deep thinker, Carl Jung (alas), and about how he was going to rearrange his workshop according to the rules of Feng Shui, which I took to be some kind of screwball Chinese geometry, and how his daughter had found some great things for him to wear at a second-hand shop called Déjà Vu All Over Again, and about an eighteen-speed bicycle he had bought to save wear and tear on his car. As we parted he was quite cheerful, saying, "I'll bring a pallet to your studio and get the paper off the floor. And you get well. My father had one of those operations a year ago and he's fine now, pissing like a horse." I didn't see a lot of Sebastian and had forgotten what an amiable good guy he was, despite his head being stuffed with straw.

48

I WAS GETTING RESTLESS AT ALBA'S PLACE. SHE WAS working at her desk, a nineteenth-century escritoire with a computer, and I asked her, "Know what this apartment is like?"

"Ummmm," she says, undeflected from the computer screen.

"Alba, know what this apartment is like?"

"In a sec," she says.

"Alba."

She turned to me. "Yes, Ren, it's like a concrete box with windows, it's like a concrete rabbit warren, it's like a concrete dovecote or a row of concrete pigeon holes or a concrete mausoleum, or it's like a concrete columbarium and we're the funeral urns inside it—I especially liked that one. Did I forget something?"

"I'm bored."

"We could drive out to look at that country property I was telling you about. It's a nice day for a car trip. Want to do that?"

Alba snatched a couple of roadmaps from one of the desk's little drawers and drove us deep into the country to the real estate office where we met the property agent, a dignified old man, who led us to the farm. The sky had changed from blue to the color of old zinc. The house was a narrow two-story box, chalky white clapboard, vacant since last fall, and we walked up the stairway and through the empty rooms and down the back stairs as if exploring a gigantic dried-out seashell. It was pleasant to come out to the soft pattering rain and we set off on a footpath, picking our way between two rows of decrepit apple trees that the agent called an orchard, and came to the barn.

The broad sliding door at the front had long since dropped from the rail and jammed in the ground, unmovable, but there was enough space between the door and the frame for us go in edgewise. It had a surprisingly good interior volume, the soft gray light falling from a row of small windows set high in the long side walls and from the large open square in the distant back wall. From the dark interior you could look through the open square to the outside scene. There was a hushed drumming of rain on the roof. I walked to the far end, waiting for the familiar scent of feed and manure which I hadn't smelled for a long time, but there was no odor. There was a cantilever beam overhead sticking outside with a big rusted pulley at the end and rain was blowing in the open frame. The land slanted down and away from the back of the barn, so from where I stood there was a ten-foot drop to the black soggy ground, then the dark green field spread out and rolled downhill for a while before it leveled off against a hazy green grove of trees that marked the end of the property. It felt good, standing there.

On the drive back we discussed the property, but we reached no conclusion except that it had been pleasant to stand in the barn and look at the green horizon under the misty rain. Now the rain had stopped, the sun came out and broad wisps of steam floated up from the black road. When we got back to the apartment I was tired again—I never understood why such minor surgery made me that tired—so while Alba went back to her desk I stretched out on her cushy sofa and drifted off. When I woke up the place was as hot as a pottery kiln. I found Alba in the bedroom where she had stripped the blankets from the bed and was lying on the sheet, naked and asleep against a pillow like one of those second-rate nudes by Carl Frieske (American, 1874-1939), one of his sleepy full-breasted, satin-bellied women laid out so your only thought is to get your knees in there and fuck your way to glory.

I went to the kitchen and while I was making a glass of iced tea Alba woke up and said, "If you're making something cool make one for me too." I poured a glass for Alba and took it to the bedroom just as she was reaching for her dress. "You look good without clothes," I told her. "I wish I were up to it."

"I'm sure you will be," says Alba, lifting her arms to let the dress fall over her head and unfurl downward. "Give yourself time."

"I began to slow down a couple of years ago, you know, even before this."

"I hadn't noticed," she says.

"Which is another reason I'll love you forever."

"I hope so. Zipper," she says, turning her back so I can zip it.

"But it's true, I have less urge than I used to."

"You have plenty of urge."

"I'm down to where I have about as much craving as a woman."

"Are you trying to be clever? I'm not amused."

That evening Alba concocted a dinner which was mostly asparagus, a new recipe from France.

"I have the urge to paint," I said. "That's a start."

"Then you should paint."

"All I need is a place to exhibit."

"I've told you about Leo Conti."

I thought about that a while. "You say he likes my work?"

"What he's seen of it in galleries. That was a few years ago," she added.

"I could show him some new things."

"You should."

I drank down the last of my wine. "I wish you'd look at my new work," I said.

Alba made a display of searching for the lemon slices but didn't say anything.

"Why don't you come over to the studio?" I suggested.

"Yes. That would be delightful. For you, at least."

I poured myself a bit more wine. "I don't like the way we're living. —You and me, I mean."

She smiled, fleetingly. "Who else would you mean?"

I drained my glass again.

"And which one of us moved out?" she asks.

"I haven't moved out. I'm trying to work. I'm trying to work and I'm trying to make my life into something."

"So am I," she says, showing about as much emotion as the Queen on a playing card.

Alba and I have never completely understood each other, which I believe is a good thing, and on that occasion I understood her even less than usual. But I was healing well, due partly to nature and mostly to Alba, and I was restless to get back to my paints and canvases. The next morning I packed up my stuff—there wasn't much—looked around to see if there was anything of mine in the apartment I wanted to take back with me, asked Alba if I could borrow a book I had just noticed on her desk, *Cinéma en France* or some damn thing, and while I was at it I scooped up one of her road maps and a couple of sheets of information from the real estate agent about country properties. Then I crossed the river to Boston and my studio.

49

I OPENED THE DOOR TO MY STUDIO AND THE PAINTINGS lighted up the place. The handmade paper from Sebastian lay in a neat stack on a pallet he had brought, and on my bunk there was a big white envelope from Michiko, in which envelope I found the hundred or so photos I'd shot of Avalon. In the back room Avalon's mattress was made up with Kim's sleeping bag on one side and a few books on the other – a thick volume by Carl Jung, plus a big flat paperback called *Mehndi and Bindi* and her old *Craftsman Entrepreneur*. On the bookshelf with the lipsticks and chrome-studded leather straps she had added two stolen photos of foolish old Renato, one with his big blurred hand grabbing toward the camera and another with him saying something, his arms wide open.

I went back to the studio to look at the paintings again and the more I looked the more I was amazed that I'd ever doubted them; they were better than anything I'd ever done and looking at a couple of unfinished canvases made me hungry. Avalon had put a few tomatoes in a bowl on the kitchen counter, as I had asked her a hundred times to do—though I hadn't asked for the small box of menstrual gear—and there was half a loaf of scali in a paper bag, so I sawed off a chunk of bread, sliced the tomatoes, grabbed a handful of olives and carried everything on a plate while I walked up and down in front of the unfinished paintings, because it was a pleasure to eat and to see what to do next. It felt good to be at work on a canvass, and even though I quickly got tired and had to sit down, I was able to paint again later while sitting in a kitchen chair, and I was still painting when Avalon came in.

"You're here," she says, coming across the room and smiling broadly, this strange-looking young woman—for she did look strange after not seeing her for a while—her shaggy hair dyed purplish rose and brassy yellow, silvery rings piercing her face, this Avalon, my Avalon. I stood up and she hugged me not in the old grab-ass way but with such gentleness, as if I were an invalid, while I sucked up coffee dust, her cheap cologne and her secret Avalon smell.

"Did you notice I didn't touch a thing?" she says proudly. "Everything's just the way you left it. Sebastian brought that paper for you and Michiko brought a bunch of those photos you took of me. And your mail is on the kitchen counter—see?—right here beside the Mason jar, and a list of phone calls you got at the café. I haven't touched anything of yours or moved a thing. I kept it like a goddamned museum in here.

All I did was, I swapped around some pots and glasses in the kitchen cabinet and I put that ugly Medusa dish out of the way under the counter. I put all your winter sweaters in the bottom drawer—don't look at me that way! And I happened to see those photos and took out one snapshot of you for my wallet, but that's all. Three, I mean three, three photos. And I bought some film and for our camera, I mean your camera, and took some pictures of Kim. —What's that?"

"It's an old bamboo fishing rod."

"I know it's a fishing rod, Ren."

I told her it was for Kim. "Oh," she says, thoroughly pleased. "And what's in the little box?" she asks, and I told her it was a gyroscope for Kim in case he didn't like the fishing rod. "He's out with the Rodriguez kids, skateboarding," she says. "You go back to painting. I'm going to take a shower."

That evening Avalon cooked pasta putanesca, which she enjoyed calling whore's pasta, and afterward we walked down beside the river, me carrying the rod and Kim energetically kicking a stone zigzag ahead of us. When we got back to the studio he banished the rod to the back room and spent the rest of the evening lying on the floor, the gyroscope forgotten on the kitchen table, while he read and re-read an advertising pamphlet about skateboards.

I was tired again, so I lay on my bed and looked at my accumulated mail, threw away the Charrette catalog, threw out the glossy announcements inviting me to a dozen different gallery receptions and tore to small pieces a request for the pleasure of my company at the New England Arts Awards Ceremony where I could witness the growing fame of other painters. I put aside the letter thanking me for my annual contribution to the Robert Wren Foundation (Rob had died years ago, had a crush on Alba one summer and would come Sunday mornings with his griddle and batter to make flapjacks for her.) I kept the wedding invitation from my former student, Arthur Chan, and the hand-bound notebook by Dave Koppleman, who had come to me terrified from electro-convulsive therapy, and the thank-you poem from anxious Emily Bright who used to throw up before class. I saved the letter from my Fabrizio for last, as a desert, but it turned out to be only a brief note which said he was coming to visit us, not saying when, and P.S. he was bringing Heather with him. I read it a few times to see if there was something between the lines—the couple had been living together for two years and had seemed content to go on that way forever—then I gave up.

After Avalon put Kim to bed I took the big white packet of photos, dumped them on the table and began to sort through them. These weren't carefully controlled prints, just standard stuff, but all I wanted was the image or the *logos* of the body and these were good enough, especially some photos toward the end when Avalon was just standing relaxed and looking directly at the camera. I had covered the table top with prints and was working there, so Avalon took herself, plus her book and digital music box, to sprawl on my bunk. "Earphones, and I'll play it so low you won't even hear it," she assured me. I sorted and resorted the photos till I had what I wanted and by then Avalon had padded barefoot to the back room and returned to say that Kim was fast asleep. She sat down at the table and told me, "This is a great book. It's all about mehndi and bindi. Which, I dare say, you don't know anything about. Mehndi is the art of henna tattoos, an ancient art, like in India, and bindi is the same thing only with jewels, jewels on your face and body."

"You're right, Avalon, I don't know anything about it."

"See?" Avalon slid the book around so I could look at it. "Here. Let me show you some pictures. Move over." She sprang up, came around and sat on the edge of my chair, sliding her arm under mine to lay her hand on the page. "Look," she says, very businesslike. "This is mehndi, all this design on the woman's hands and her face. All those dots. See?" The flesh on Avalon's cheek and collar bone had a humid gloss, but because she had taken a shower there wasn't any odor of coffee or cologne and I wasn't close enough to pick up her scent. "Not on me, Ren.

On the woman in the picture." She smiled. "I know what you're thinking about. You want to know if I've found an apartment. You want to know how soon I can move out. Right?"

"No."

"Liar, liar, pants on fire."

I laughed. "I wasn't thinking that at all."

"You'll be pleased to know I've been looking at apartment rentals."

"I'm pleased."

"I thought it was expensive in San Francisco, but it's worse in Boston, it's insane. People are crazy around here. Where do the assholes get the money to pay those rents?"

"They save by not buying my paintings."

"I looked at one rental so small you couldn't keep a canary in it. Then I found some cheap places in the paper, but when I looked on Kim's map they were way out in Natick or Saugus or someplace named just as weird. I've been thinking of Somerville. What do you think?"

"Somerville used to be cheap," I said. "I'll ask Sebastian. He lives out there."

"I was talking to Garland at the Daily Grind and she said Somerville was a good place. So I've been thinking of Somerville."

I was listening but not very well because, frankly, I was ready to go to sleep. I hadn't stood up painting at Alba's and hadn't taken a walk along the river after dinner at Alba's, so I guess it was natural to be more tired here at the studio with Avalon. I don't recall what else Avalon said about rentals or what we talked about. I finished my wine, rinsed out the glass and washed up for bed. Avalon was waiting by my bunk. "Good-night kiss," she says, embracing me gently, as if I might break. Then she went to her bedroom and I slid under my covers. The bunk felt narrow after sleeping in our bed at Alba's and I missed the warm touch of her body, but before I could think about anything beyond that I was asleep.

50

I WAS STRETCHED OUT ON MY BACK, LOOKING AT THE book about French cinema—the book I had scooped up from Alba's desk—when Avalon came over, lay down on the margin of the bed and began to pester me with questions about my surgery. I told her to think of it as an old clogged pipe; an expensive plumber had cleaned out the pipe. I went back to the book. She wanted to know how much of the prostate was left. I told her I had a lot of prostate to begin with and there was a lot left, then I went back to the book and Avalon kept turning this way and that to get comfortable. Then she was quiet for a while until she said, "Who does this hot love note belong to?"

I asked her what love note.

"This one. Listen to this," she said. She began to read from a sheet of blue-tinted stationery. "*One eats this delicious flower before it has climaxed, and if it has been prepared in a certain way, kept at a loving simmer for just so long, then*—."

"Where did you get that?" I asked her.

"It was here on the floor by the bed. Let me read you some more. *The delicious petals make no resistance but fall open, hot and humid*—."

I snatched the stationery sheet from her fingers. "It says artichoke right at the top. It's a recipe for artichoke—."

Avalon grabbed it back. "Oh, sure," she said. "Let me read you—Let—Ouch! Ren! Do you want to hear the rest of this? Calm down. Remember your age."

I dropped the open book over my face.

"Where was I?" Avalon said. "Ah, here! —*The delicate petals make no resistance but fall open, hot and humid beneath one's fingertips, yielding, desiring to be eaten. Now the erotic feast begins*—."

"Let me see that," I said.

She held the little blue sheet tight between both fists, but turned so I could read.

"It says *exotic*," I said. "*Exotic* feast, *not* erotic."

Avalon turned the paper back and continued to read. "*One bites down tenderly, most tenderly, and while holding the soft petal between one's teeth, slowly*—." She had a low, rippling laugh. "Oh, oh, oh. I better stop before this excites you and hurts your, your surgery," she said.

I gave up trying to read and closed the book about French cinema. "Go away," I said.

"You sound like a travel agency," she said. She rolled onto her stomach and propped herself up on her elbows and looked at me. "We're going to be friends forever. Right?"

"Right. Now I want to get ready for bed."

"We'll still see each other after I move. Right?"

"Right."

"Somerville isn't the other end of the world," she said.

"Right. And I'm really tired."

"Just because a person— Why don't you please put your arm around me and tell me—"

I put my sleepy arms around her and drank the delicious warm smell of her skin.

"I would like us to be like blood relatives who had to put up with each other, no matter what happened," she said.

"I love you, Avalon, and it's past my bed time."

Avalon went away to her bed. Although I was tired I didn't drift off to sleep but floated between sleeping and waking, my eyes growing accustomed to the dark so the stretchers, the chairs and the table, loomed out of the shadows. I didn't want to think about my paintings because I knew no gallery would show them, knew I hadn't become famous in my time and my time was up. Avalon was looking to move out and I was almost finished with the canvases and maybe Alba was right and Conti would exhibit my work and Alba and I would live in a house in the country and our friends would come to dinner. I don't know how long I lay there tired but not sleeping and yet not thinking, an old man with withered privates in a narrow bed without his wife. At last

I got up and padded over to the sink to get a glass of water, and while I was drinking I heard Avalon stir—*bam*—we bumped into each other. "I have to tell you something," she whispers. We were both naked, the imprint of her warm flesh still vibrating along my nerves where we had collided. "I have to tell you," she whispers again.

"All right, tell me."

"I'm moving to Somerville to be near Sebastian, because I love him and he loves me and probably we'll live together, but we decided I should get a place of my own for a while before moving in with him until—"

"Sebastian? My friend Sebastian?"

"He came with his daughter to bring you his hand-made paper."

"Jesus! What happened?"

"Nothing happened. We just talked," she says.

"You just *talked?* You just *talked* and decided to go live together? Christ! What kind of a conversation was it!"

"Please, Ren."

"You and Sebastian. Horrible!"

"Please, Ren."

I sat down on the edge of my bed, exhausted. "You and Sebastian. Jesus fucking Christ!"

"You promised—"

"I'm going to bed."

"You said—"

"I'm going to sleep, Avalon."

She stood there waiting, but I didn't say a word to her, so she went away and I rolled back under the bed sheet.

I got up late the next morning, the buffoon in a comic opera, the foolish old basso profundo who guards the door while his beautiful young ward, the soprano for whom he lusts, climbs out the window with the hero, an up-and-coming tenor. The deserted look of the studio told me Avalon had gone to her job at the Daily Grind, taking Kim with her. I showered and was looking around for my underwear when the door flew open and here's Avalon. "Why aren't you at work?" I asked her, stepping into my shorts.

"Because I told them I had to have a talk with you," she says. "Garland knows how difficult you can be, so she said okay, get it over with."

I pulled up my pants, buckled my belt. "Have you notified the newspapers?"

"I want to tell you what happened when Sebastian came and I—"

"I don't need to hear this. You can go back to work."

"I'm going to tell you and you're going to listen," she says.

I ignored her by looking around for my shirt.

"I opened the door and Sebastian was standing there with his daughter," she says. "Only I didn't know it was him and his daughter. He looked—well, you know how he looks—and he said, I'm Sebastian and this is my daughter Cait, and he touched his Cait's hair just so gently on top, just stroked it down like—"

"And that did it. Suddenly you knew you wanted to go live with him," I said, ducking and grabbing her wrist as she began swatting at my face.

"You're a real bastard!" she spits out, wrenching inside my fist.

I let go of her. "Sebastian's all right. He's a good guy. Go live with him. Go, go."

"*Don't try to get rid of me!*" she shouts.

"I'm not trying to get rid of you."

"Yes you are. Because you're a selfish, vain old man. You want me out of your studio but you don't want me living with anybody else. Your feelings are hurt and you want to punish me by throwing me out of your life and turning your back on me. You can't do that! We're friends for ever. You said so yourself. *For ever.*"

"I'm going for a walk by the river."

"You can't do this. I'm special to you. *You care for me!*" she cries.

"I'm going out."

Avalon dove at the door, shot the bolt and whirled around to face me. "What can I do to heal your fucking pride! I'll do whatever you want!" she sobs.

She was out of breath and her eyes glistened and my guardian angel, disgusted with me, drove a spear into my heart. I faltered. She waited, watching me.

"Come on," I said at last in a voice that sounded strange to my own ears. I put an arm around her shoulders. "I'll walk you back. I'll never abandon you. You can tell me about Sebastian while we walk. Let's go."

Along the way Avalon told me in detail about Sebastian's visits to the café and the slow walks back to my studio and how Sebastian or, more precisely, Sebastian and his daughter Cait, had captivated her. "Like, picture this girl in braids and this tall man standing beside her, behind her but watching over her," Avalon said. They had discovered certain signs in their lives that showed they were destined to meet. Like, for example, when Sebastian was a boy his family had moved here to Boston exactly the same month that Avalon was born here, and years later young Sebastian had driven across the country to San Francisco and walked the same streets as Avalon, who was only fifteen at the time, as if he was searching for her. And for six months Avalon worked in the shop of a paper-maker named Shozo Takeda—"I told you about that job and how come I knew how to make rag paper," she said. "And don't look at me that way, Renato, because I know I told you because I remember you didn't believe me."—which was destiny preparing her to understand Sebastian's craft. And destiny prepared Sebastian to understand Avalon's life by having him take care of his daughter by himself and bring her up by himself, so he understood how hard it is being a single parent, working and bringing up a kid at the same time. Cait's mother was a total delinquent, like that bitch Linda who fucked up Avalon's life when Avalon was a girl. "Did you know Sebastian's wife didn't want the baby?"

she asked me. "She wouldn't have had it except she was such a brainy bitch she got past the third month before she even knew she was pregnant and that's when Sebastian married her, because he wanted the baby." All that was destiny and mystical, but you could see how their lives fit together in practical ways, too, because Sebastian couldn't learn the business side of his craft and was always going broke, but Avalon had money sense and for weeks before she had even met him she had been reading a book about the craftsman entrepreneur— "How do you explain *that!*"—and she could keep Sebastian's accounts for him and help him with new business ideas and, well, she had thrown away her birth control pills. So my Avalon and the gangly paper-maker had fallen in love.

"I should think you'd like him," she says. "He's like you, only younger."

I laughed briefly. "Lucky for you, he's not like me at all."

"What do you mean?"

"You two were meant for each other," I said.

"You mean it?" She had stopped in the doorway of the café, turning to search my face. "Yes. You do mean it," she says, relieved.

Garland had glanced up from behind the counter, her hands on her hips, ready to swat at me if I got close enough, but I was already gutted and boned so I took a table by the window and one of the kids brought me breakfast.

51

THE NOTE ON BLUE STATIONERY THAT AVALON HAD read to me the other night was a recipe for steamed artichokes. I figured it must have fallen from between the pages of the French cinema book I had taken from Alba's desk. The recipe wasn't in Alba's handwriting and I thought maybe Alba had borrowed the book with the folded paper in it, but Alba had scribbled here and there in the book's margins, so it was her book. Then I found four more blue stationery sheets behind the blanket chest where I had first dumped the book. All the recipes were in the same bold handwriting—artichoke, puff pastry, and an elaborate dinner that extended across both sides of two blue pages, all written in a fancy, sneaky style that made them sound like they were about something other than food.

52

LITTLE BLACK THOUGHTS WERE CIRCLING INSIDE my skull like Van Gogh crows and I wondered what somebody else would make of those recipes, but Mike Bruno wasn't around anymore and Cormac or Zocco would enjoy this too much to be helpful, so I went to the Daily Grind and showed them to Gordon who frowned and then laughed and then shrugged and handed them back, saying, "Beats me." I drove over to Zoe's studio, Blue Door Graphics. She was busy with a pair of clients, so I went upstairs and poured a cup of coffee from her breakfast pot, heated it in the microwave and took it to the sitting room, a place I've always liked—a large bay window overlooking the leafy back street, comfortable chairs and, yes, one of my painting (great slabs of clean color) stored on the wall, plus a gouache I did of Astrid when she was twelve.

Zoe arranges her books chronologically, according to when she acquired them. She says this way it's easy to find whichever book she's looking for because she can always remember when she first read it and, she says, the rows of book titles make her diary. You start at the top bookshelf on the left (Dr. Benjamin Spock's *Baby and Child Care*, paperbound, the cover bandaged together by adhesive tape) and go down the bookcase, then to the top of the neighboring one and so on around the room through new age paperbacks, plus a little white album of wedding photos, a shelf of business books, past a pamphlet on divorce, then poetry and novels, plus a leatherette folder with a second marriage certificate and a solitary wedding photo, and eventually to a pamphlet from Planned Parenthood on safe and legal abortion, then a row of feminist manuals, past the journals of Anaïs Nin and a big biography of Georgia O'Keefe and up to the present at a volume with the bookmark still in it (*The History of God* by Karen Armstrong, clothbound.) I was looking at the snapshots we'd taken of Astrid's graduation from Hampshire when Zoe came up the stairs.

"I'll take you to lunch," I said.

"You know the way to a woman's heart. Tell me how you are."

"Fine. I'm fine. Is that a sunburn?"

"Forgot my sunblocker. Want to walk? If you feel up to it, there's a place within walking distance, you know."

We walked slowly to CHEAP EATS and sat outdoors and while waiting for our eats I gave Zoe one of the recipes to read. I watched some kids playing basketball, then Zoe finished reading and looked up. "It's a recipe for puff pastry. What's so remarkable about that?" she said, handing it back to me. I asked her wasn't there something else there. "Only that it's over written," she says. "Maybe over ripe."

"Don't you think there's a hidden meaning where it talks about the dough expanding and lifting, growing five or ten times bigger than it was? And then this line—*Glorious to see, light in the hand, heaven in the mouth.*"

Zoe looked blank, then she laughed. "Oh, how shy-making. What else do you have there?"

"Nothing."

"Let's see," she says, plucking the stationery sheets from my hand. "Artichokes," she says, reading. A short while later she looks up, saying, "This other is a menu for a light dinner, very light, just an appetizer, an extraordinary appetizer. Not like that nonsense about puff pastry or those, those steamy artichokes. This is romantic. Very romantic."

"What are you talking about?

"The wine is listed. And even the candles. It's beautiful, I *love* this. And I like the description—it's flowery but forgivable—of preparing the melon and wrapping each piece in a strip of prosciutto, arranging them, sprinkling the black pepper, adding the lemon wedges. This is a preface, a foreword, a—"

"What do you mean?"

"And the dessert, the peach Melba with raspberry sauce. Sure, yes, this is a romantic dinner, a wonderful romantic dinner," she says, finally looking up.

"Meaning?"

"You eat this first, dummy, because it's light and not filling. It stimulates the appetite. It enlivens all your senses. It creates a thirst and hunger, but not the kind that can be satisfied by more food or wine." She smiled and handed the pages back to me. "These are valentines, Ren. Each recipe in this menu is a love letter. The little dinner is just a beginning, it unwraps you. Or unzips or unbuttons. —Where did you get these?"

"Never mind."

"Not that athletic Californienne you're living with," she says.

"Can't you say Avalon?"

"Yes, that's the one."

Our cheap eats had arrived. While we were eating, I asked Zoe what she had been up to.

"Over the weekend I went to Newport and watched a sailboat race," she said. "Many races, actually."

Her big bland stupid friend Derek Mallow owned a sailboat and he liked races and this was Zoe's way of telling me she had finally gone off with him. I wasn't surprised or, to be precise, I shouldn't have been surprised if I had been paying attention, but I had preferred not to think about any of it.

"The weather was beautiful, sunny with a light breeze," Zoe

continued. "We stayed through Monday and didn't come back until the next morning. We were in this extraordinary bed-and-breakfast, an old inn that dates back to the eighteenth century. The sun was glorious, but we pulled down the shades and spent most of the last day testing the bed, a huge four-poster."

"Don't tell me the details."

"You wouldn't think it to look at him, but he's insatiable. He's also somewhat rough," she said smugly. "I was shocked."

"Zoe."

"You'd never guess what he—."

"For Christ's sake, Zoe, keep your secrets to yourself. I'm not your hairdresser."

"I had a good time."

"Splendid."

"I need a good fuck every now and then," she said.

We didn't talk for a while but ate our sandwiches and watched the kids scramble back and forth across the abandoned parking lot, shouting. There's nothing to say about this Derek Mallow—whom I had hoped to omit—beyond his being a big, soft, boneless guy with his own consulting business, an ex-wife, two children in college, a sportscar that sounded like it was farting and a sailboat—and that's the whole man in a sentence. "You think I'm making a mistake," Zoe said flatly, shading her eyes with her hand as she followed the basketball players.

"Hell, Zoe, you know him a lot better than I do."

"You think I'm wasting my time again?" she asked, the fine lines at the corner of her eye deepening as she squinted at the hoop and its torn net.

"How would I know?"

The kids quit playing and ebbed to the shade where they had stashed some bottles of water.

"I suppose I shouldn't even be talking to you about this," she said, turning to me.

"I suppose not."

"Did you just laugh at me?"

"At you? No."

After lunch we headed back to her studio, passing the basketball players who were fooling around now, squirting water at each other, dodging, spitting, whooping.

"Now tell me where you got that romantic menu," Zoe said.

"At Alba's. But it's not her handwriting."

"Maybe they're written by that chef she was taking lessons from."

"Michelle?"

"Yes. —He's going back to France. I think he's already gone."

"Who's going back to France?"

"Michel, the chef. Michel Reverdy. You met him," she says. "—Ren, are you coming?"

"Michelle? Michelle? *I thought Michelle was a woman!*"

"It's a French name, after all. Can be male or female," says Zoe. "Anyway you met him. —Hey, are we walking together or not?"

"I never met him. The *chef?* Oh, God. The *chef!*"

"I thought you met him when Alba began taking lessons," said Zoe. "Those are probably his recipes. That's probably his menu. Alba really liked those classes," she added.

I groaned. "I know. I know she did."

"Frankly, I think she was a little intimidated at first. I mean, she was afraid she was going to be intimidated. But Michel isn't one of those tyrannical French chefs who makes you feel stupid and clumsy in your own kitchen. Quite the contrary. He has a nice way about him."

"You met him?"

"She took me to the class once, to show him off, I think. And afterward we had coffee with him. Late fifties, maybe older, vigorous, full of energy, overflowing with it," she said brightly.

"You think he was likeable?"

"Definitely, but I don't think *you* would have liked him."

"Why not?"

"He believes cooking is an art, like composing music or writing or painting. He talks about it that way."

I told her she was right, that I wouldn't have liked him, that we would have argued and it was best I'd never met the man, though Zoe insisted I had.

53

THAT AFTERNOON I DROVE ACROSS THE RIVER TO Alba's to ask what was going on between her and the fancy French chef. She came to the door, pen in hand and reading glasses peering from her hair. "Renato. What are you doing here?"

"I found these recipes in your book, the one I borrowed, the one called *French Cinema* or something like that. So, here they are." I had begun to feel dizzy or sick to my stomach.

"Oh, you shouldn't have driven over here for that," she said, taking the folded blue sheets. "They're only—they're not that important." She walked into the apartment, letting her voice trail over her shoulder as she placed the notes on the small desk. "Want something to drink? Cinzano, diet Coke, wine, coffee? I was about to make a fresh pot. You know what we have." She continued into the kitchen. "What will it be?"

I cleared my throat, said coffee would be fine.

"How are you feeling these days?"

I told her I felt fine, not as good as new, but at least I was able to piss.

Alba turned on the water and began to fill the pot. "Did the boy like your grandfather's fishing pole?" she asked, her back to me.

"It belonged to one of my uncles. And the boy's name is Kim, you know." My voice had come out sharper than I had expected.

"He and his mother are moving out, moving to Somerville."

Alba put the pot aside and twisted opened the coffee jar. "That should give you more room in your studio," she remarked, tightening the prissy wrinkle lines at the corners of her mouth.

"She'll be getting together with Sebastian. They're in love, the real thing, Avalon and Sebastian."

Alba refused to look my way. "Sebastian's a good man," she said at last, carefully spooning coffee into the pot. "I wonder how Caitlin will take it. She still so young and—."

"Caitlin will take it just fine," I cut in. "She likes Avalon—why not?—and Avalon likes her. Who wrote the recipes?" I was out of breath.

She looked up at me. "What recipes?"

"The recipes I brought you just now. The recipes on blue stationery."

She turned away and reached for the coffee mugs, saying, "Those were written by Michel, the chef I took cooking lessons from."

"What did you and the chef do besides cook? You and this chef, when you were alone together, what—."

She whirled around to look at me, the color leaving her face. "You have some nerve, asking me a question like that! Good God! You're incredible, unbelievable."

"So, what did you and this chef do?"

"*Who are you to ask me questions! Who do you think you are?*"

"I take it you did more than plan meals together—."

"*Fuck off!* You can take it any goddamn way you goddamn please." Her cheeks, white as paper a moment ago, were flushed now. "It's *my* life, what's left of it. I do what pleases *me!*"

"What does that mean?"

"It means I'm not going to answer your prying, domineering, selfish questions. *So don't ask!*"

I felt like telling her how ugly her face was when she was angry. "Is it finished between you and him?" I asked.

She plunged her trembling hands among the coffee mugs,

knocking them left and right, snatched one and hurled it at me but wild, the pieces exploding from the fridge to ricochet off the cabinets and go skitter scatter across the floor. "You shit!" she cries, her eyes flashing. "You bastard!"

"I'm not fucking Avalon."

"You mean you've *stopped* fucking her is what you mean! You mean you've stopped because you're still bleeding down there."

"She's in love with Sebastian."

"I don't give a rat's ass who she fucks. That's your problem."

"She's moving out. She's going to be living with him."

"Don't waste my time. Go away," she said, her body stiffening.

"I suppose Michel's gone back to wherever he came from."

"Go! You, go," she cries, waving her hand, brushing me away with a shooing gesture. "Get out!"

"Has he gone or not?"

"Fuck you, Renato! Fuck, fuck, fuck."

"Is he gone?"

"Don't you raise your hand at me!"

"I have never in my life—."

"Yes, he's gone, you poor bastard, yes. —Now get out of here."

"No. This is my—."

"Just go," she cries, her eyes brimming. "You make me sick. I don't want to see you!"

"Alba."

"I don't like you," she sobs.

My stomach lurched, my insides loose and weightless, as if I had stepped off a height and was falling and falling, endlessly.

"Don't say that. For God's sake, Alba—."

She was drying her eyes with the heels of her hands. "I don't—."

"Alba, shut up!"

"I don't like you anymore."

I put my hands over my ears, turned and left and turned again, stumbling at the door. "I'll see you tomorrow."

"I don't want to see you." She pushed the door shut, closing me out.

As I drove from Alba's I had to throw up, so I pulled over, opened the door and I must have fallen out, because I was on my hands and knees, vomiting on the curbstone and cars were going by. Afterward I was on a bench by the river, still on the Cambridge side, looking at the water. The world looked as if nothing had happened. Cars and trucks moved across the bridge and sped silently on the far side of the river. I was empty as a sack turned inside out. At the boat house on the far shore a young guy had lowered a racing shell into the water and was pulling away from the ramp, heading zigzag to the middle of the river, where he aligned his craft and then sliced downstream, farther and farther away, his oars glinting rhythmically.

54

THE NEXT DAY I TRIED TO PAINT BUT FELT LOWER than whale shit and could barely stand up and thought to lie down, but instead I wandered into Avalon's room and looked at her colored jerseys, neatly folded and stacked, and the things on the bookcase shelf—her black leather dog collar, her silver rings and chains—but I just looked and didn't pry into anything. She still had those stupid photos of me propped up against the books. I drifted back into the studio and studied the snapshots on the cork board, mostly the photos of Brizio, Astrid and Skye, then I sat down on the floor and stretched out on my back with my hands folded on my belt and let everything go blank. I don't know how long I had been lying there, waiting to die, when Kim came in the door and announced he was hungry and wanted to eat. After a while I asked him what he wanted to eat and he said a grilled cheese sandwich, so I hauled myself upright and made a grilled cheese sandwich and set the plate on the table with a glass of milk, then I laid myself down on the floor again. Kim ate, idly swinging his legs so one of his shoes rhythmically banged a table leg—bump and bump and bump and bump and bump and bump and bump. I closed my eyes. "Jamal is homey," he announced, accenting his words to sound like Jamal. I kept my eyes shut and a little later Kim said, "I ax Jamal could he teach me on his skate board. Can't nobody skate the way Jamal do." And still later he added, "He be going to the car wash wit Jeff tomorrow." I got to my feet and when our little wise-guy had finished the last of his milk I told him I had to do errands. I drove us to the Daily Grind where he was happy to stay and help Gordon roast coffee beans while I crossed the river to Alba's.

Alba opened the door, but kept her hand on the doorknob, ready to shut it in my face. "What do you want?" she said. I didn't know what to say and for a moment we just stood there while I hunted for words. Then Alba turned and walked back into the apartment, leaving the door open and I followed her. In the kitchen she didn't say anything, so I said, "Want a glass of Cinzano?" She shrugged and said she didn't care. I said, "White or red?" She shrugged listlessly and sat at the kitchen table, turning away from me to look out the window. I said, Let's try white poured over ice cubes." I took out the white but there wasn't much left. "There's only enough for one glass, so we'll have to have red," I told her. I got the ice cubes and prepared the drinks and sat across from her. Alba was still gazing out the window and she looked old, really old. I searched the lines in her face, wondering how many I had put there, and I felt rotten. I looked out the window and sipped the Cinzano. The vermouth had a satisfyingly bitter taste.

55

MORNINGS I WOKE UP EXHAUSTED. I DON'T KNOW which day I went to the Daily Grind and phoned Cormac McCormac, asked him if he wanted a visitor, and he said Yes. I lugged my gloomy self into my car and headed out to his place, which is one-third of the way to rural nowhere—the land out there going to seed—turned off the pike and went over hill and down dale, passing through a forgotten town where the movie palace had a blank sign and the church was boarded up, then into a lonely village center (Jake's Auto Body Repair, Best Wash, Tina's Lunch) and out a meandering road between a half mile of cornfield and a stony hillside with cows and a rusted bus, past an abandoned railway station and on to Cormac's place. I bumped along the ruts toward his barn to park beside one of his cairns and spied his broad white shirt in the black square of the barn doorway. He came out and halted, squinting in the sun and turning his shaggy head this way and that, like a bear from a cave, then the screen door at the house slapped shut and Karen McCormac was on her way down the path to me. We stood there talking, halfway between the house and the barn. "Want to have lunch and then look around, or want to look around first?" Cormac asked me, scratching his bearded cheek.

"Let's look around," I said.

Actually it wasn't a barn but a big work-shed that he had built a dozen years ago to replace the old barn that had been his original studio; inside he had a steel I-beam frame with a block-and-tackle hanging from it and a long bench with sculpting tools—not just mauls and chisels and rasps and sanders, but power saws, acetylene tools, riveting guns and other heavy junk. He showed me what he had been working on, particularly some metal castings which I liked, and a big bronze thing, shaped like a spinnaker, which had been commissioned by a software entrepreneur to decorate corporate headquarters. After a while, I had to sit down to take a rest; like I said to Cormac, it's surprising how a little surgery can take so much out of you. Later, while we were touring the vegetable garden, Karen called to us, saying she was hungry and why didn't we come to the house for lunch now.

Karen McCormac is a good-natured woman, a retired schoolteacher who wears her hair in braids and has a torso that is, as she says, flat as a pine plank. She had set the table on the back porch, so we ate overlooking the vegetable garden and, beyond that, the field with some of Cormac's stone pieces, and after lunch Cormac and I stayed on the porch with a few cold bottles of ale. It was good to tilt our chairs back and sit with our heels on the railing and drink and not talk, just enjoying the restful quiet while the sun shone and not much happened. The sky was brushed in very lightly with a particularly limpid blue and there was a row of painterly white clouds about a quarter way up from the horizon. "I'm glad I invited myself here," I said at last. "I like the view. And I like what you've done with the clouds. You handled the perspective just right, too, not so deep and not completely flattened out either. But it's those heaps of white clouds that impress me most."

"Yeah, the clouds were difficult. But I'm not a painter. Maybe you could have done better."

"I thought I might get a show at the Strand Gallery, but it didn't work out."

"Oh." Cormac was squinting at the horizon and he didn't move or say anything more for a while. "Yeah, I know what that's like. That can make you feel dead, real dead, as in dead dead. —And yet?" he said, turning his face toward me.

"I'm still alive."

He turned back to the horizon. "Yeah, being alive is good," he said. "Being alive beats all. —How's the plumbing repair? Everything working all right?" I told him I hadn't had a chance to try everything yet, but so far, so good.

We sat there and drank and didn't talk much, exchanged some gossip about galleries is all, and when he asked had I seen any interesting shows recently I had to tell him no, said I used to rely on Alba to tell me about interesting works but, since she quit reviewing galleries and began to review French bistros, I've fallen behind. "Alba's doing restaurant reviews?" he asked me. I said No, said she had taken a course in French cooking and got infatuated with it, that's all. When he asked about Zoe I said, "She's seeing a lot of some soft boneless rich guy named Mallow whose great ambition is to win a sailboat race at Newport." Cormac smiled at the horizon and said, "I know you're just trying to be nice, but I can tell you don't like the man." And I had to agree, I didn't.

Later he asked where I was living now and I told him, "I'm back in my studio. I'll stay there until I finish up this batch of paintings. They're not going to Newbury Street but they'll go someplace. I hope." Cormac said he was sure of it, said my paintings were destined to find a gallery, said the problem was that most galleries were run by timid assholes. Then he asked what happens when you do finish these paintings, meaning, would I stay in my studio or go back to living in that concrete tomb with Alba. I told him we want to buy a place in the country. "I don't want to live without her," I said. "In fact, I can't live without her. The only reason I'm at my studio is to paint." Cormac glanced at me and then gazed out at the field and the horizon and I knew he didn't believe me. "Sometimes Alba's hard to live with," I added. He thought about that a while and then said matter-of-factly, "They all are, sooner or later, one way or the other." But I felt I had been unfair. "Of course, Alba puts up with a lot," I emended.

He laughed and said, "She puts up with you, you mean."

"Mostly she puts up with me. But she's not perfect. She has lapses. Don't be deceived. There are times when she turns into her other self and recites all my sins, which she's carefully memorized, so she can go out and do something nasty, which she's been thinking of and longing for, some act of revenge."

"Whatever that might be," says Cormac. But I said only Yes, whatever that might be, and I left it at that. Later he asked about that woman in the studio, and I said Avalon's fine. I was about to tell him she's moving out, when he said, "I can barely manage one woman. How do you juggle three? Bigamy is difficult enough, I should think. But trigamy, or whatever it's called—."

"It's called trigonometry," I said.

"How do you do it, Ren?"

"I don't do it. You have it backward. They do it. And anyway, Avalon's moving out. She's moving in with Sebastian."

"Gabriel? Sebastian Gabriel?" I was gratified to see Cormac as surprised as I had been. "It's a match made in heaven," I said.

Later we got onto wise-ass art critics, Cormac telling me a story about Greenberg and how Greenberg ruined some of David Smith's sculptures, a story I think he'd told me before. Cormac had met Greenberg years ago. "The guy was a great fucker. That was a different epoch when I was married to number two and she was crazy about that whole freaky New York crowd. She had a friend on the Bennington faculty who taught literature, so we'd drive up there and Rachel would try to meet the artists who taught there or who hung out in the hills around there. I think she married me so she could meet these sculptors and painters and if she got lucky she'd get laid by someone important. I figured that out later. I still haven't figured out why I married her—or number one or number three, for that matter." So we were back to talking about women and Cormac said he was thinking of doing some figurative pieces because then he'd be able to say he needed a model. "That would be fun, a young woman with breasts up here like apples. —Though I'm beginning to wonder if I'd be able to do it," he muttered. I told him I was sure he'd be able to do figurative pieces. "No," he said. "Do the woman, the actual woman—fuck her, I mean. I can still do it in my imagination, but I'm beginning to wonder if I could do it with an actual stranger, not Karen." I told him I was sure he'd be able to do it with a stranger, too.

"But I don't know and I'm afraid to find out. I've become a dutiful husband from fear of impotence." He gave a short laugh.

"Are you serious?"

"Maybe." He studiously poured the last of a bottle into his glass. "I don't know."

Later he said he'd been thinking about Maillol being seventy-three when he got this Dina Vierny to pose for him, she being fifteen at the time. "And she had all that firmness and roundness and balance and lightness—man, she was juicy!" He laughed with pleasure, as if he were actually remembering her himself. "Then the old man died and she spent the rest of her life building him a museum, a chateau, a whole chateau devoted to him. Now she's so old and so fat she won't let anyone take her picture. And in a while she'll be as dead as Maillol," he added.

Cormac carefully lowered his empty glass to the floor, sighed, folded his big paws on his belly. There was just the sunny air over the field, a spacious quiet and the occasional buzz of a bee and the whir of grasshoppers. Cormac asked me did I ever think about death. I said Yes, too often.

"I don't understand death at all," he said. "What's it for? What's the point? I still haven't figured it out." I told him the catechism said it had something to do with Original Sin. He said, "I thought Original Sin was when Adam and Eve had their first fuck. It was so much fun they thought it must be forbidden. That's why they got fig leaves to hide their privates and pretend to God they didn't know about fucking. That's what I thought."

I said No, said they had been fucking all along like animals and they didn't know what they were doing, but after they ate from the Tree of Knowledge of Good and Evil they woke up to what they were doing and decided it was evil, so they got the fig leaves.

"There's nothing more innocent than plain fucking," Cormac

said. "Why did they think it was evil? Who put that thought into their heads? God gave them free will but when they used it God got so sore he invented death, and I still don't understand it."

I thought about that for a while. "I haven't figured out living," I told him. "I always thought I'd examine my life when I got older and had more time. I had an uncle who told me the unexamined life wasn't worth living. I think he was right, but now I'm older and I've got less time than before. The last time I had a clear view I was beginning to paint and was about to get married. I could see the way ahead, the way to go, but that was the last time. I don't know what happened next. I tried to live right, but it was all I could do just to get by. It's the same with painting. I can't paint and think about it at the same time, so I just paint."

That's the way the afternoon went. We weren't twin brothers, Cormac and me, but we'd known each other a long while and I liked him; I liked the way he did his job, happy to do it right and happy to make a living at it—yet ready to drop whatever he was doing and just sit and talk, or not talk, if that's what you needed. He was overweight and he peed a lot, I guess from diabetes, but I never heard him complain about it.

56

I DON'T KNOW EXACTLY WHEN I BEGAN TO PAINT AGAIN. Alba and I weren't all right, not at all, but we were right enough to go to Bread Alone together for cinnamon rolls or to the Mondello for an espresso. So I was painting again and feeling good about that, good enough to go to the Daily Grind when I needed a break, and there I bumped into the skinny guy I'd met at the Pixels exhibit, Vanderzee.

We exchanged hellos and because I felt guilty about not having gone to look at his work I told him I'd get over to his studio someday soon. While we were talking, Avalon saw me and came over but before she could bawl me out I told her, "He's skateboarding with Amal because Amal has two skateboards. Mrs Gupta is at her window keeping her eye on them, so don't worry."

The next day I drove to South Boston, looking for Vanderzee's place, and ended up outside a grocery store displaying signboards written in what I guess was Vietnamese. I found a parking space and walked to his address, a dirty brick structure that had been a factory seventy-five or a hundred years ago. I hadn't phoned to tell him I was coming because, frankly, I was hoping he wouldn't be in and I'd leave a note to show my good intentions and get off without having to take a guided tour of his work. I knocked on his door, but before I could scribble my note the door opened and here was Vanderzee.

"Oh! This is great! Come on in," he said, pulling me along and turning to happily announce, "Hey! It's Stillamare. Renato Stillamare's here." The place had bare brick walls and big windows; a bunch of mismatched furniture sat in the sun to the left, a crowd of paintings stood to the right. "Gail," he said, calling to an elegant cinnamon woman with high cheekbones and large gold hoops in her ears, a child clinging to her orange dress. "This is Renato Stillamare." Gail and I shook hands, her ivory bracelets clicking, and she said she was glad I had come by. "You're the one who paints nudes like landscapes and landscapes like nudes. Right?" Vanderzee had scooped up the child and was steering me toward a young man in a white suit whose name I didn't catch, only that he was a magician. We shook hands. "I'd like to stay but I'm about to disappear," the magician said cheerfully. He strolled out the door accompanied by a pale woman, a pre-Raphaelite redhead in a translucent paisley dress, leaving us at a long plank table cluttered with crockery and the scraps of a meal. I apologized for arriving unannounced, told Vanderzee I was sorry I hadn't phoned ahead, but I'd been driving through the neighborhood and thought I'd knock on his door with the hope of finding him in. "And I'm glad you did," he said, setting the little kid down on his feet. "We had a late lunch and would never have stopped talking. Want anything?" he asked, reaching toward the beer bottles on the table. But I was distracted by the wild splashes of color on the canvases in the background. "Or let me show you some paintings," he said.

I had already walked over to the stack of very large stretchers that were leaning against a pair of posts. "Yes," I said. "Show me." Vanderzee lifted the first canvass, stepped sideways several paces and leaned it against a studio easel, then came back to my side to view it. I knew he was good from the first glance. "Great," I said and told him what I liked. He pulled out a dozen big stretchers one at a time, letting them stack against each other at the easel. Some were stronger than others, but none of them was a mess and when he occasionally failed it was because of boldness or misapplied energy; he was good and he was going to get better.

He took up the last canvas, lifted it gently sideways to lean against the others, unwittingly exposing behind it a busted sofa where a woman lay curled around the baby in her arms. She blinked and squinted in the sudden light, raising her head to look at us. "Oh! You remember Winona," Vanderzee told me. And, yes, it was the flaxen-haired woman who had been pouring wine at the Pixels exhibit. Winona sat up and buttoned her blouse, still cradling the baby. "Can I get you something to eat or drink?" she asked. "I've been napping. I think it was the beer," she added. Winona and Gail cleared a patch of table and Vanderzee stoked a leaky espresso machine while I give him the names of some New York galleries I thought would welcome his work, and I would have helped him more if I could. I stayed there the rest of the afternoon, for Vanderzee was congenial and I enjoyed the distraction of his company and his women, but on the slow drive home I returned to myself who was melancholy, lonely and old.

57

I HAVE NO THEORIES ABOUT WOMEN. IN MY TWENTIES I read a deep book about female psychology, hoping it would help get them into my bed, but that never worked, so I gave up on theories. I couldn't theorize about Alba and live with her at the same time, so she remains as much a mystery to me as I do to myself, inexplicable and contrary—Alba, that is—all of which is to say that when I asked Alba would she come to the studio on Sunday for brunch with me and Sebastian Gabriel and his daughter Caitlin and Kim and, sure, Kim's mother, she said, "Yes."

I doubt that Alba herself knows for sure what goes on in her opaque heart. She may have wanted to get a look at Avalon because Zoe had gone to the Daily Grind more than once to watch Avalon and to chat her up and then—I'm certain—had reported to Alba that the skanky bitch wore rings in her face and she, Zoe, didn't know who to feel more sorry for, Renato or Avalon. And Alba may have wanted to see Avalon right now and not later, not at some other place but here in the studio, so as to get a better sense of what was going on between me and Avalon. Or maybe she decided to come merely to display her power. That would be easy enough because Alba has such a long history in this studio that if she walked in tomorrow the walls would recognize her voice, the chairs would welcome her and every little thing—dishes, cups and even the spoons in the drawer—would proclaim loyalty to her, our Alba.

The brunch was Avalon's idea. I went along with it to show her what an open-hearted man I was and to show Sebastian that Avalon and I were merely friends, buddies, pals, and if I had ever given her a second thought or, silly old man, ever kissed her on the cheek, it was purely paternal and not something weird like, say, fucking her frontward and backward on that narrow bunk over there.

Now as soon as Alba surprised me with her "Yes," I began

to think of the four of us and what kind of quartet we would make, each of us singing from a different page. I tried to see Alba coming in on Renato as he was setting the breakfast table with young, barefoot Avalon—that stopped the action right there. I rearranged the scene and had Sebastian and his daughter enter first, then Alba enters and is greeted by the happy couple, Sebastian and Avalon. The next morning I went to the Daily Grind and phoned Sebastian, told him the brunch would begin at ten, then I phoned Alba and told her to come to the studio at ten-thirty, for brunch would not begin until sometime after that, maybe at eleven.

As it happened, they both arrived at the same time, their chat and laughter floating up the stairway ahead of them, at which sound Avalon came running from the back room, flung open the door and eagerly stepped out—"Hi!"—into Alba who had started to step in—*wham!*—clutched each other to keep from falling, then awkwardly disentangled, Avalon backing into Sebastian with a brief laugh while Alba slipped sideways into the studio with a carved smile. That took care of the introductions.

Alba was in a summer dress she knew I liked, one with a long slit up the side, though this morning the slit ran only a hand's breadth above her knee. Avalon wasn't wearing those black velvet shorts that let a crescent moon of flesh hang beneath each rear hem, no; for I'd told her that Sebastian, after his divorce and accompanied by his daughter, liked a softer, more womanly woman—which was probably true— so Avalon had visited the Next-To-New shop and the Déjà Vu All Over Again boutique and was now wearing a filmy dress with sleeves of curtain lace, plus turkey feather earrings. As for Sebastian, apparently he had stolen his clothes from a scarecrow and left the poor thing naked in a corn field. I had lugged two saw horses, a couple of wood chairs and a plank tabletop from the back room, so we had more space than we needed and that was probably a good thing.

At first the conversation was stiff, but innocent Sebastian had discovered that he liked to talk, now that his wife wasn't around to correct him, and Avalon always had something to say, so Alba and I had only to add a few words now and again to keep them going. We heard about Sebastian's eighteen-speed bicycle and about windmills that could generate enough electricity to free us from dependence on foreign oil. I learned about undyed, unbleached cotton, and a lot about *chi*, which is a natural vital energy flowing through ghostly channels or meridians on the non-physical or, as they say, subtle body, and I listened while Avalon and Sebastian unfolded secrets about the seven chakras, which are places on the subtle body where the energy gathers, or flows to, or from or through. Caitlin said she didn't believe in chakras or meridians or *chi*, especially since she had seen the diagrams and thought them ugly, but she did like Tarot cards, not for telling fortunes, which she told us was a scam, but because the cards were beautiful and she and her friend Noel had invented a game where they played the Tarot cards and made up fabulous stories about the images on them. Young Caitlin was especially pretty, I thought, as she had unbraided her hair that morning and brushed it smooth, so it hung half-way down her back, glossy as a chestnut just hatched from its shell. Avalon, on the contrary, had somehow dyed the roots of her own hair a russet brass.

After the brunch, Avalon and Sebastian went off with the kids to amble along the river while Alba and I washed the dishes. While I was cleaning the waffle iron Alba walked to the doorway of the back room and stood there a few moments, looking where Avalon and Kim slept. She came back and wiped a bowl, set it on the shelf. "Kim has a nice new basketball," she remarked, breaking her silence. I said Yes, but I learned he's not much interested in basketball. Alba dried the last of the tin ware, laid it in the drawer and drifted away. "Are these photos of Avalon?" she asked. I turned and found her at the cork board, looking at some snapshots. I told her there were no photos of Avalon there. "Who is it then?" she asked. I went over to look. There was the same old jumble of overlapping photos—Brizio, uncle Zitti,

Galaxy, father, mother, Skye, my lost aunt Vivianna, Alba, and a dozen other relatives— and slid in among them were old snapshots of Avalon that she had taken from her albums. Yes, I said, that's Avalon. I went back to the sink, squeezed out the wash rag and hung it up. I said, "I think the brunch went well." Alba didn't answer. She had gone to the window and was looking out. "There's some Asti left in the bottle," I told her. "Want a glass?"

"I'll be leaving," she said, not turning around.

I poured the last of the Asti into a glass and took a swallow. "Stay a while," I said.

'No." She turned. "Enough is enough."

I had an impulses to throw her out the door or to pull off her clothes and fuck her, I couldn't tell which. "Are you going to help me choose paintings to show to Conti?" I asked her.

"You've decided to get in touch with Conti?"

"I'm thinking about it, yes."

"I think you should," she said.

"You'll come around to look at the paintings," I said. I offered her a drink from my glass of Asti, but she shook her head no.

"Some time when she's not around would be good," Alba said.

So we left it at that.

58

LATE ON FRIDAY I DROVE OVER TO ZOE'S AND ARRIVED as she was closing her studio. "I'm going to the sailboat races at Marblehead this weekend," she announced. That was her way of saying that she was going to spend the weekend with Derek Mallow.

"Well. Good luck at the races," I said.

She turned off her computer and began to gather the scattered papers and file folders from her desktop. "Some of the excitement has worn off. No man's perfect, I suppose. We stayed in an expensive cottage on the Vineyard last weekend. Anyway, I don't think you and I should talk about it. About him, I mean."

"Right, you're right."

"Did you know he's younger than me?" she asked, jamming the folders into an open file drawer.

"That doesn't make any difference."

"It does if you're in the middle of menopause." She slammed the drawer shut with her knee.

"He doesn't expect to have more children, Zoe."

"He doesn't expect problems in bed, either."

"You're going to give him problems?"

She had turned away and was putting an armful of catalogs on a shelf. "Menopause is wonderful but I don't want to talk about it."

"All right."

She straightened out the catalog shelf and turned to me. "I'm drying out, Ren. And you know it. I'm dry everywhere. My hair is brittle. My skin is cracked. My lips are dry. My eyes are dry. I'm dry *inside*. Have you forgotten? Have you forgotten how it hurts when we do it, I'm so dry!"

"There are ways around that. There are—"

"This is nature's way of telling women they're finished."

"Come on, Zoe. You're in a mood. You're not thinking clearly."

"What has thinking got to do with it!" she said, flaring at me. "Thinking isn't going to change a thing!"

"Zoe, you're a good looking woman, one of the most interesting—"

"Is that the same thing as a good time in bed?" she cried. "I don't think so! A good time in bed is when you're fucking Avalon! Warm and wet. Right?"

"Should I leave?"

"No," she said. She sighed and glanced around the studio, one hand on the light switch. "Come upstairs for a drink."

"Come to dinner at my place."

"With that Avalon?" Zoe switched off the studio lights and we went up the stairs. "You want everyone to love everyone, but that's not the way it works, Renato."

I helped her open the large window in the sitting room. I told her Avalon was leaving, was going to be moving in with Sebastian Gabriel. Zoe listened and said nothing. "Why not come to dinner?" I asked her.

"What a strange-looking couple they'll make. —I'm going to wash up. Even if you don't want a drink you can get one for me. There's a fresh bottle of Australian Chardonnay in the refrigerator. I'm not fussy."

I went to the kitchen, uncorked the bottle and poured a glass of cold Australian Chardonnay. Zoe came in from the bathroom, saying, "—Because I agree with her not only about baths and flowers but about touch, too."

I gave her the glass and asked what she was talking about.

"I agree with Alba about what happens when our kids grow up and we can't cuddle with them or even hug them when they're naked and kiss their necks. After twelve years old they keep their clothes on and don't want to be touched by their mothers. If I had a house full of four-year-olds I wouldn't need men." She walked through the sitting room and into her bedroom.

"Well," I said. "Maybe. But I don't think—"

"You know you're old when nobody touches you and you're not allowed to touch anybody. That's how they punish you for growing old. Then you wither and die, from lack of touch."

"Why are we talking about old age? Where do you get these ideas?"

"They're mine, my ideas. —I think I'll change," she added.

"I hope so. I'd be sorry if you had to live with that view of life."

"No, Renato. I'm going to change *this*," she said, plucking at her shirt. "I put this on for a business lunch. I'm getting into something more comfortable. I'll keep my ideas."

Zoe pulled off her shirt and skirt, hung them quickly in the closet, unfastened her bra and tossed it onto her bureau. The bra had incised the flesh beneath her breasts, leaving a cruel pink line which she now rubbed tenderly with her finger tips, as if to erase. "We're born in the flesh and we die of it, or from it, because of it. I haven't worked this up to a philosophy yet," she said.

"I hope there's more to me than flesh," I told her. "My flesh is betraying me. It's letting me down. It's failing."

"Well, so is mine," she said. "But that doesn't mean we have something else or something more than our bodies."

"You have to get beyond that, beyond flesh," I told her.

"Please, Ren, you're *not* the one to tell me to renounce my body." She began flipping through the dresses in the closet.

"I'm not saying renounce your body. I'm saying there's more to you than mere flesh."

"When I think of what you've spent your life painting—"

"Everything I've painted shows there's more. There's meaning. We crave meaning as much as we crave anything."

"Oh, we crave it all right," she said. "But is it there?"

"There's meaning or there's no point to painting or to living. By the way, I've just finished a group of paintings."

She drew out a dress, saying, "I'll wear this. No bra. What do you think?" It was a kind of thin white shift with big pale splashes of blue and green.

"Fine. It looks fine."

"As for your paintings, Ren, they show a lot of different things." She plunged her hands into the coiled cloth and lifted her arms, letting the dress slide down over her.

"There's more to a living body than flesh," I insisted.

"Maybe that's true for you and not for me," she said, looking into the mirror on the closet door. "I'd love for you to be a woman for just one month."

"What's *that* got to do with it?"

She drained her glass. "I'm hungry. Are we going to your place for dinner now or not? I can look at your new works." But she went to the mirror and began to brush her hair back, first one side then the other.

"Your hair looks fine, Zoe. Let's go."

"I bet you don't know the difference between a ketch and a sloop. I keep getting them confused. It's quite boring. Why is it that the more I get to know a man, the more I feel like I'm going to jail?"

"The door's over here, let's go."

"And my sexual fantasies bore me. Does that ever happen to anyone else? Does that ever happen to Alba?" she asked as we went out.

59

One night Avalon told me I owed her half a dozen photos, and I said Since when do I owe you photos? and she said Since I give you those photos of me, and I said What photos of you? and she said The photos I put up on the wall where you keep your other relatives.

"Oh, *those* photos," I said.

"Yes, those."

"I didn't know you wanted me to—I mean, I didn't know I could keep them."

"Yes. You keep those and you give me some of yours," she informed me. Then she flipped open her small square album, the glossy lilac one that holds one photo per page, and showed me the empty pages. "I've rearranged everything so yours can go in here. See?"

I saw. I went to the blanket chest at the foot of my bed, took out the cigar box crammed with unsorted photographs and brought it to the table. "Help yourself," I told her. Then I put on those tiny earphones she bought for me and listened to her music player while she sorted through the photos. She worked with a business-like frown of concentration and after twenty minutes she had chosen maybe four snapshots. She went off, came back with two water glasses full of wine, and plucked the earphones from my ears. "How about one of these olden-time photographs where your ancestors are dressed up like, you know, historical," she said. She went over to the cork board and studied the black-and-white studio portrait of my mother as a teenage flapper—cloche hat, bobbed hair, flat body. "I think that was taken in 1925," I told her.

"How old is this one?" Avalon asked, looking at the brown photograph in the pressed cardboard frame.

"That was taken around 1917 or 1918. It had to be before the influenza epidemic. There was no money for fancy photographs after that. My father's about eighteen or nineteen. His sister is about fourteen."

"She was the wild one."

"So I've heard"

"Wild how?" Avalon asked.

"She got pregnant at seventeen, I think, and—"

"She didn't *get* pregnant. Some man *got* her pregnant," Avalon informed me.

"Right, some man *got* her pregnant. In fact, his name was Zampa. They got married about six months before the baby was born, and the baby lived only a few days. I heard a lot about that. After the baby died, Zampa went to Las Vegas and Vivianna went back to live with her brother—that's my father—in the apartment over the store. Zampa deserted her, is what I was told. Maybe he went off before the baby was born. I don't know."

"You never met her, the wild one."

"She was long gone before I was born."

"She died?"

"All I know is that my father got her a job with my mother's father, in his store. That was when my father and mother were engaged to be married. After the wedding, they sailed off to France and Italy, mostly Italy, and when they got back Vivianna was gone again. She was always taking off. Then she'd send a postcard from wherever when she got there. Maybe she hooked up with Zampa again. I don't think they ever got a divorce. Anyway, nobody ever saw her again."

Avalon had the photograph in her hand and turned it over —I knew there was nothing on the back—and now she had turned it face up and was studying the image once more. "I do like these old-time pictures," she said. It was clear she wanted that photo.

"That won't fit in your album," I said, which was the truth, after all. "I'll get you a different one."

I went back to the blanket chest and dug out the cardboard letter box that had the papers from my father's family. I emptied it onto the table. The biggest item, which was wrapped in tissue paper, was the tintype photograph of my father's mother's mother, Serafina's mother, who lived in Venice where, she liked to say, the streets were made of water. There was a lot of junk—a couple of canceled passbooks from the Shawmut Bank, a paid-off mortgage, my father's Social Security card, his old passport from their wedding trip—stuff like that, but of Vivianna there was only a baptismal certificate and a picture postcard, which I showed to Avalon. The postcard said, *Here I am but not for long. Leaving for San Francisco on Monday & will write from there. Love to all, Viv.* The picture on the other side was of the Hotel National which was shaped like a shoebox, had two storeys and maybe eighteen rooms, each window with a striped awning. "I wouldn't have stayed there a week either," Avalon said. "Why did she go to Las Vegas?"

"I don't know. Maybe her husband was still out there. Italians built Las Vegas. —I can't find any small size photos of her. I thought I remembered some, just little snapshots. Sorry about that."

Avalon said That's all right, I'll go get one I took of you and you can write on the back, and I said What do you want me to write? and she said Jesus, Ren, do I have to do everything?

60

ALBA CAME TO THE STUDIO ON A HOT WEDNESDAY afternoon to look at the paintings and to tell me whatever she knew about Leo Conti before I approached him about getting a show at his gallery. I had thought because of the heat she might arrive wearing that same dress with the slit up the side, opened higher this time—which would be a good sign—but, no; she was outfitted from an L. L. Bean sportswoman's catalog, a sleeveless top with a high neck and a wraparound skirt that looked to be sewn shut. To relax us I asked did she want something to drink, maybe a glass of wine over ice, but she said No, it's too early in the day, and she even said No to a glass of water with a sprig of mint in it. I asked did she want to take a look around the place, meaning I had nothing to hide, but she said No, she'd just look at the paintings, and she walked over to the canvases. I discovered Avalon's bottle of shampoo glitter on the kitchen counter and shoved it under the sink with the soaps and sponges.

"These look good," Alba said.

"Yeah. Well. Maybe. Some of them. I hope."

"They're really good, Ren. Mind if I move them around?"

"Move anything."

While Alba looked at the paintings, I ducked into the bathroom to see what else Avalon might have left out and, in fact, found an apple-green thong hanging from the showerhead. I put in my pocket, drifted into the back room and slipped it into the plastic box where she kept her underthings, then ambled back to the studio and, because I didn't want to stand there looking at her while she looked at the paintings, I told her I was going out for a minute. "Good idea," she said, not turning from the painting she was gazing at. I went downstairs and walked through Ashcan Alley to the John Sloan realism backyard where Kim was playing with Jamal and the Gupta kids. For a while I watched them scooting around, oblivious to the heavy heat, then I went back through the alley and climbed upstairs to the studio. Alba greeted me with, "These are really great, Ren. These are the best things you've done yet. They're marvelous."

"You think so?" I was sweating from the climb.

"Yes. And if you take photos or slides to Conti, these over here are the ones I'd show."

"What's wrong with those others?"

"Nothing. But these are the ones I'd show him, that's all."

"You don't like the others?"

"That's *not* what I said, Ren. You asked me to pick out the ones I'd show Leo, and I've picked them out."

"I thought you were going to pick out the ones you liked."

"I like them all. But these are the ones I'd show him."

"What about the ink-brush nudes or semi-nudes or whatever, what did you think of them?"

"The ones you did of Avalon?"

"All right, the ones I did of Avalon, if you want to think of them that way."

"I don't think they'd show up well in a big gallery with these other paintings on the wall."

"Oh, sure! You're saying that just because it's Avalon. They're good and, in fact, they're very good. I got a vigorous line in there and not a starved thin anemic line, but a good thick powerful line that's fluid at the same time. That's something I can do."

"You asked for my opinion. You got it. All I'm saying is that they'll get overwhelmed by the canvases." The humidity had caused some loosened tendrils of hair to curl against her temple. "Believe me."

I went to the window and looked out, not to see anything but to think about what Alba had said and to calm down. I recognized that she knew more about Leo Conti and his gallery than I did, and I knew that after she left here I'd sort through the canvases to see how I felt about the ones she had chosen, and I figured I'd mostly agree with her choices, as usual. I was still at the window with my hands in my pockets, brooding on these things, when Alba came up. "What are you thinking?" she asked. I caught the fleeting scent of her perfume, not the cologne she sometimes dabbed on herself before going out, but the perfume she reserved for the evening and, more precisely, for the two of us, a light scent with a hidden muskiness someplace down there. "Are you sure you wouldn't like a drink?" I asked her. "Cinzano over ice?"

"I could do that, yes," she said slowly, apparently thinking it over.

I hurriedly groped into the back of the cabinet and retrieved the bottle, then pulled the ice tray from the refrigerator, letting Alba take two water glasses from the cupboard shelf.

"I haven't had a Cinzano for a while," she said.

"Nor have I." Alba remembered as well as I did the dead day we had a Cinzano. There was a growing silence as I broke the ice cubes from the try, dropped them into the glass, and poured the Cinzano. "So," I said, handing her a glass.

"So," she echoed.

"What have you been up to?"

"Not much." She put her finger against one of the ice cubes and swirled it around in the glass, studying the eddies of the wine. She looked up and I glanced away, then came back.

"What are you doing Sunday morning?" I asked her.

"I don't know.—You could come over for brunch," she added after a pause. "If you want to," she emended.

The drink was complex, smooth but with a heavy tart edge that all but obliterated its own sweet solace. "I could come over the night before, then I'd be there when morning came around."

She took a drink. "That might work."

"I'm willing, if you are."

We were standing close and the day was hot and I could see the tiny drops of perspiration on her forehead at her hairline. I didn't know what I was feeling, but I knew it was best just to keep going. The obscure evanescent scent rising from her mingled with the odor of the wine and I could feel my flesh begin to stir, which itself was pleasant and made it easier not to think of anything, not to recall anything. If Alba's eyes had changed in forty years I couldn't see the difference, one eye invisibly larger than the other, the dark sea-green irises flecked with uneven rays of lighter green and blue. Kim burst into the room, the door crashing behind him while he pulled himself head first to the sink, twisted sideways under the faucet and turned on the water, his skateboard racketing across the floor to whack into my bunk. He gulped at the stream of water, then eased himself down from the counter to stand beside us. "It's burning hot outside and I'm burning up!" he announced. "Can I have an ice cream?"

"Do you remember Alba?" I asked him.

"Yes. She's your wife. —Can I please have an ice cream bar? We have some in the refrigerator, chocolate-covered."

I told him to say hello to my wife, which he did, and I opened the refrigerator to get out a chocolate-covered ice cream bar.

"Do you like skateboarding?" Alba asked him.

"Of course. But Jamal is the best. Renato gave me the skateboard. It's mine."

I unwrapped the ice cream, gave it to him, and he went off with it, saying, "I have to go to the bathroom now." Alba said she had to get back to her place, and we agreed that I'd go over there on Saturday evening.

61

Leo Conti built a successful accounting firm (Conti, Cronin, Stein & Bradford) and then sold his share to his partners in order to open a gallery in East Cambridge—that's all I knew about him—and here he was in my studio, a short, jovial man with a round face and a head of thick curly dazzling black hair. He wore a white cotton jacket with broad rose stripes, a pink necktie and—*clump*, *clump*—platform shoes with thick heels and soles to boost himself two inches more. He studied the paintings I had set out for him and when he was through he turned to me and announced, "I love your work. You have a fresh way of looking at things, of seeing them. I don't know why you're not better known." I gave a short laugh and told him it baffled me, too. He flung out an arm toward the canvases and said, "You have a genius for color. This is great work." I thanked him. He grabbed a fistful of his own hair and tugged, peeling off the wig that had fooled me. He mopped his glistening tanned scalp with a handkerchief and said, "Too hot. Come around to the gallery tomorrow morning. We'll talk."

I don't know how Leo Conti succeeded as an accountant because, frankly, I wouldn't have trusted him with an old laundry list, much less with bills or receipts, but I went around to his gallery, a smudged brick shoebox among all the tall, shining structures being built in what used to be dumpy East Cambridge. Today he was wearing sneakers and a bright yellow polo shirt, no wig. "You still want to exhibit my work?" I asked him.

"Of *course* I want to exhibit your work," he replied, apparently astonished I would doubt him. We were standing in the middle of the gleaming gray, uneven concrete floor; the windows were made of old-fashioned glass blocks, and there was enough space around us to display a dozen automobiles or play a game of tennis. "But after this current show I'm closing the gallery. Everything comes down tomorrow," he said, nodding toward the paintings on the wall. "I'm forced to move. The building has been sold."

"The building has been sold?"

"Sold," he said. "And they want me out of here."

"Why are we talking?"

"Because I'm opening a place in Boston this fall and I want to exhibit you there. —What do you think of these?" he asked, spreading his arms toward the wall of paintings.

"I haven't really looked at them."

"Tell me anyway. What do you think?"

"There's something a little wrong with every canvass, Leo. But the work isn't all bad. In fact, some of it's all right. Somebody has energy and half a style. The painter's going to be good in ten years."

Conti laughed joyfully. "Five years. I'm betting five years or less. She's not thirty and she's already selling."

"Where are you going in Boston?"

"Not Newbury Street. There's too many galleries there already. It's glutted. I'll be in what you might call off-Newbury. Off-Newbury, but not too far off."

"When would I get a show?"

"I'm booked up for a year. I can't show you till a year from now. That's my dilemma." His face grew very sad, his head drooped a bit and he looked up at me, waiting.

I recognized my cue. "Don't take it so hard, Leo. You can put up one more show right here. I like this place."

"You deserve better than this, Renato. And there's no time. This place has been sold. It gets demolished eight weeks from today. I know you deserve better than this."

I was elated because I understood him now. "I *like* this place, it has a nice echo. We'll have to work fast."

Leo shook his head vigorously, no. "There's no time to get the word out about a new show. And I'm going on vacation. I've got *plans*."

"You can get the word out. Send invitations, glossy color prints. You can have a great party. The last, the best show. Invite everybody. My work is big and I have lots of it. I can fill this whole concrete ballroom."

"I haven't got a penny!" Like a successful pickpocket, he flung out his hands with his palms up to show me how empty they were. "I put everything into my new gallery. I've got nothing left. Your invitations, your announcements, getting the word out about your wonderful paintings—that would take money. The food, the wine—the cost of it all! I'd need help."

"We'll sell lots of paintings. I'll make you rich."

"I hope so. But I'll need help," he added.

"You used to be an accountant, Leo. Tell me how much help you'll need."

He laughed. "I want to talk art, you want to talk finances!" Then he sighed and said, "Well, all right, if you insist. Come into my office."

Leo led me to his office, a glass-walled cube which jutted into the exhibition space and, with the drapes pulled aside, gave a view of everything in the long gallery, much like the mechanic's office in an automobile repair shop, but here the floor was thickly carpeted and upon the carpet there lay a wine-colored rug with an intricate Afghan or Persian design, and a small teak desk with a matching teak file cabinet waited at the side. The place was comfortable and quiet.

"Leo," I said, "I keep sixty percent of the selling price."

"You read my mind!"

"No. Leo doesn't keep sixty. Renato keeps sixty."

"Oh." And after a pulse beat, he said, "Absolutely! Now, please take a chair. We have some things to talk about if we're going to sell paintings and we have to work fast."

62

After talking with Conti I felt good and decided not to go back to the studio, but to stay in Cambridge and plow through traffic to Alba's place. "Well, this is a pleasant surprise. I hope. Come in," she said. Her hair was pulled back tight and she was in white shorts and a black swimsuit top. "Sorry I'm sweaty. Just got back from the gym," she said. "And I thought you were coming tonight," she added, not quite frowning.

"I just finished talking with Leo Conti at his gallery," I said, following her into the apartment. Loose tendrils of her hair, damp and curled, hung above the nape of her heck. I told her I was getting a one-man show. "Hey, that's wonderful," she said, going down the hall toward the bedroom. I told her I was getting sixty percent of each sale. "*Very* good," she said, lifting her voice against the splashing rattle of water pouring into the tub.

"I'll be paying for the advertising, the announcements, the invitations, the food, the wine. Which is not so very good or wonderful." The water was making too much damn noise.

"You'll sell lots of paintings, Ren," she said, turning off the water.

I had halted outside the bathroom and was trying to figure out how she was feeling toward me today. I said, "Conti tells me he has ways of getting the word out to his regular buyers, as well as a few hundred others. He's got lists." Alba stood with her hands on her hips, her face a pleasant mask, still lightly flushed and completely closed. "I think I'll let you take your bath."

"The bath can wait. Tell me more." She folded her arms and leaned a shoulder against the door jamb, not inviting but waiting, expectant.

"I'm bringing canvases to the gallery on Monday. We'll hang the show in two days. The rest is up to him," I said.

"Skye and family might be back by the time the show opens. That would be great."

"You're right," I said. "That would be great. —Take your bath. I'll take you out to lunch. —If you want, I mean."

"Yes. A quick shower." She turned away and shut the door and I started back up the hall. "What do you think of the gallery?" she called out.

"The gallery?"

"Yeah. What do you think about it?" she asked, raising her voice against the opening hiss of the shower.

"It's ten times bigger than I thought it would be," I said.

I couldn't make out Alba's reply.

"What did you say?"

"I said, he fills it. He gets a good crowd." Alba's voice was blurred under the rushing cataract.

"I'll need a crowd, a very big crowd," I said.

Alba said something, but I couldn't make it out.

I stepped into the bathroom that was now cloudy with steam and everything there nebulous, humid, close and private. A few moments later she calls out: *"What did you think of the man himself?"*

"I don't know what to think."

"Oh! You're in here!" she says, startled.

"Should I leave?"

"Whatever you want."

"When Conti was an accountant he learned who had money and who collected paintings," I say, unbuttoning my shirt. "He knows a lot of the right people. He may be better at the artbiz than he looks."

"I heard he was moving the gallery to Boston," Alba says, her body fluid and elusive, dissolving and reappearing in the tall pleats and hollows of the shower curtain. "Renato? Are you there?" I step out of my falling clothes and into the stinging hot downpour. She says, "Oh! Here you are. —Well, well, hello."

It's never that easy, actually. I mean, it's easy for us to begin in the shower and end on the bed, but it's not that easy to talk or, more precisely, go back to sort things out. It's as bad as it gets when you've been wronged, and worse if you did wrong—don't ask me how that's possible, all I know is what I know. I prefer to go forward, prefer her warm slippery flesh in the shower or moist on the sunny bed cover and hot inside, prefer the weight and crush and being able to say, *She's mine.* We can talk another time, we always do, not on the bed and not now but some other place, talk about that event, what really happened, essentially happened, which was not what it might appear to be, but less, much less—though wrong, yes, wrong and stupid and vain and foolish. We have spent more than half our lives together, for which I'm grateful. We won't talk of forgiveness, not this Alba, not *my* Alba, for which I'm also grateful, because I've never loved or got aroused amid forgiveness.

63

A LETTER ARRIVED FROM INDONESIA (BADLY DEsigned stamps) from Skye, saying they were getting ready to leave, were already beginning to pack, would be flying from Jakarta and arrive, after a stop in Los Angeles, in Boston around the time the exhibit opened at the Conti Gallery. Meanwhile, Alba had received an e-mail from Brizio, telling her no more than what he had written earlier to me, that he was coming to visit us and was bringing his friend Heather with him; I had a photo of Brizio and Heather taken at a picnic two years ago and knew about her only that she had a college degree, ran in marathons and grew herbs for a living. I didn't have time to think long about these things as I was at the gallery every day that week to work with Leo Conti and his associate Ms Monday, hanging the show. By the way, Leo was surprisingly efficient in spreading information about the exhibit—little hand-written notes, e-mails, the Conti Gallery newsletter and his gallery web site, a few last-minute ads—and he even persuaded a printer to do a rush job turning out a tri-fold brochure which showed three of my paintings. "What do you think of this?" he asked, taking off his new glasses and using them to point dramatically at the brochures on his desk. I told him they looked great and had very good color reproduction. "What? No, no, not the brochures. These, *these*," he said, waving the glasses. "Do you think they make me look authoritative and smart, or just bookish?" I told him authoritative. He looked at the glasses skeptically—gigantic lenses with thin black frames—and said, "It's just window glass, but I thought they might help with the image." I told him he absolutely didn't need any help with his image. He studied the glasses a moment longer, then tossed them aside on his desk. "Image is everything," he told me.

After leaving Conti's I wedged into the traffic and drove around to Alba's, thinking of lunch, but she wasn't in so I got back in the car and joined the traffic over the river into Boston and swung down to Zoe's. I parked and walked into her studio, but before I could open my mouth she had clutched my arm, saying, "Galaxy phoned a minute ago. She's pregnant."

"Wait a minute—"

"She and Weston want to get married in a couple of weeks."

"She's thought she was pregnant before. Twice before. What makes her think—"

"She's pregnant, Ren. Galaxy says they plan to get married in a week or two. Or three."

"What's the rush? How pregnant is she? And what does she—"

Zoe had clapped her hands over her ears and walked away, but now she dropped her hands and turned, saying, "We haven't even met this man, this Weston! I *told* you we should have gone down to New York. We should have gone down when she told us she wanted to marry him. I *told* you."

"I've been trying to paint. I've been trying to get a show. Not to mention, I've been—"

"This is your *daughter* we're talking about," she cried.

"And isn't she supposed to bring him to us? Isn't that the way it's done or have they changed the rules?"

Zoe stopped walking back and forth and looked at me. "She'll come to your exhibit, I'm sure, so we can tell her to bring Weston along. Right? And she will, I'm sure. Right?"

"Absolutely."

"And then she'll get married," she added, sounding as if the idea had struck her so hard it left her dazed.

"You could look a little happier. Listen, let me take you out to lunch."

Zoe looked at her wristwatch. "How did it get so late?" She went to her desk, shut down her computer and gathered up a dozen large square envelopes in her arm, then she stopped. "What's going to happen to me after she gets married?"

"You're going to be fine," I said. She had remained standing there motionless, so I touched her shoulder and murmured, "Come on, Zoe. We'll have lunch."

Her eye had started to glisten and, as she turned to get a tissue from the box on her desk, the envelopes slipped from under her arm and slid to the floor. She sobbed. I picked up the envelopes while she wiped her eyes, blew her nose. "I've had a bad week," she said, her voice shaky. "Things haven't been going well for me."

"We'll talk about it over lunch." I put my arm around her shoulders.

"I don't want to talk about it. —Have you seen my keys?" she asked, peering into her purse. "Where are my envelopes?"

"Your keys are there and I've got the envelopes. Let's go."

Over lunch we talked some about Galaxy and Weston, but more about Zoe herself— "Because if Galaxy is married well, and I hope she does marry well, she's going to love him more and more and me less and less." I told her that's not the way love works. "That's what you think because you've been lucky. And when Galaxy's safely married you'll have less reason to see me, too." I told her that's not the way I work, but she simply turned her face away and stared out the café window. On the way back to her studio she told me she had broken up with Derek Mallow. "You never liked him, anyway," she added.

"That's not why you split."

"I split because we didn't have anything to talk about. I'm not interested in boats and he's not interested in anything else. That's why we spent too much time, you know, fucking. And one weekend was all it took to exhaust his repertoire in that area."

When we arrived back at her studio she asked me what I

thought of Emerson Ripley, and I said I thought he was a good guy and I liked him. "He asked me out to dinner tonight and I said yes, but he's so poor I don't know where we'll eat." I told her he was a nice guy and that was enough. "But what does he do?" she asked. I said he sold books and wrote book reviews. "You can't make a living that way," she said. He lives simply, I said. "I've decided to become celibate," Zoe said.

64

LATE ONE NIGHT — IT WAS OUR LAST NIGHT — I BEGAN hunting for those little photos of Vivianna which I remembered seeing, because it was so clear in my mind, my finding them some years ago among a sheaf of old letters and documents. I went back to the chest at the foot of my bunk, got down on my creaky knees, and fished out the letter box which had all the Stillamare papers. I emptied it onto the floor and then looked at each scrap as I put it back into the box, but again there wasn't any photo of Vivianna. "You look like you're praying over there," Avalon informed me. I dug my way down into the chest, lifting layers of sketch books, photo albums, art reviews, book lists handwritten by uncle Zitti, my high-school yearbook, down through a strata of bank statements and tax returns, then sideways past a sealed bundle of Polaroids (Alba and me fooling around) to the big business envelope with the label *P. Cavallù & Co.* I got to my feet, opened the envelope and poured everything onto the table. It was junk.

"That's not junk," Avalon told me. "Those are family documents. They're valuable. You should treat them with respect, carefully."

"It's junk. I'm looking for some old photos."

"Let me—"

"Damnit, Avalon—"

All the letters were carbon copies, some about a shipment of shoe machinery to Sicily and others about a commercial building in Palermo, plus there were six pocket calendars running from 1925 to 1931, each advertising P. Cavallù & Co., stock certificates totaling forty shares of Stanley & MacGibbons, Co., sheet music for "Cosa Ne Hai Fatto Del Mio Cuore?" (What have you done to my heart?), some receipts from a typewriter repair company, a couple of invoices and— Ha!—five little snapshots of Vivianna in her mid-twenties.

"Hey, maybe we're rich," Avalon said, studying the worthless stock certificates.

Two of the snapshots were taken indoors and they're dark; in one, Vivianna, her hair fashionably bobbed, sits in a heavy swivel chair beside a broad black desk, and in the other she's by a window where the light leaves almost half her face in shadow. Frankly, they're lousy photos. The remaining three snapshots were taken out of doors on a breezy summer day. Her pale blouse opens wide at the throat and her hair blows across her cheek in a short dark crescent. The sun is bright and there's no blurring, even though she's turned her head and is laughing. In this other snapshot she represses a smile, trying to hold still for the photographer, and in this last one—caught unaware, her skirt flapping in the wind—she's stepping down from a boulder to a beach, most likely the same rocky beach that shows in the background of the other outdoor shots.

"So that's her," Avalon said. "The wild one."

Vivianna appears to be twenty-five, but there's no date or writing of any kind on the back of the photos.

"You should put them in an album," Avalon said. "Why do you keep them in the envelope with all this business stuff?"

"That's how I found them, sandwiched in between all this business stuff."

"How much do you think these stock certificates are worth?" she asked.

"I think they're worth zero."

Avalon set aside the certificates and took up one of the little photos. "She's good-looking. If you ask me, your grandfather took these snapshots and kept them hidden at his office where no one else would know, that's how come they wound up in this envelope, because your Pacifico and your Vivianna were close, real close, and nobody else knew. That's what *I* think."

"That's what *you* think. Actually, she was still working for my grandfather that summer while my parents went on their wedding trip to Europe. That's what *I* know. That's probably his office over the store."

"And this is probably the beach they played on together. They were lovers, is what I think," said Avalon

"That was 1929. My aunt Vivianna was about twenty-five. My grandfather must have been at least fifty. And you think they were *lovers*?"

"Of course it wouldn't happen nowadays," Avalon said sarcastically. "Not now. Not here. Not in this room with you and me. But maybe back then young women and older men weren't so choosey who they went to bed with."

"Well, she was out of the picture when my mother and father got back in September. That was 1929 and nobody ever heard from her again, except for that one solitary postcard from Las Vegas my father got."

I went back to the chest, found the Stillamare letter box and fished out the postcard from the Hotel National.

"That lousy hotel," Avalon said. "But look when she sent it. See?"

"She didn't say when she—."

"Up here, see?"

The faded postage cancellation mark was a circle with **LAS VEGAS NEV** printed around the inside and **APR 3 1930 P.M.** down the middle. "So Vivianna didn't go to Las Vegas until the next year," Avalon said. "Before that, she was still around here. If nobody saw her, she must have been hiding."

"She could have been anywhere. Why would she be hiding?"

"Don't tell. Let me guess."

"I have a long day tomorrow. I should go to bed."

"Don't you want to hear the rest?"

"I want to give you this. Here. It's for you." I gave her the portfolio I had put together a couple of days earlier—big ink-on-paper works done with a calligraphic brush, each one of her, and damned good ones though I say so myself.

65

ALL I NEEDED TO DO WAS SHOWER AND PULL ON some fresh clothes, but I was distracted by the lonely emptiness of the studio, my big canvases gone, all that life and color gone, and especially Avalon and Kim gone, because for three days Avalon had been cleaning our place, scrubbing the kitchen and bathroom and back room, then packing up her stuff, all her cheap things—every jersey and blue jeans, every pair of shorts, all the cut-offs, sweatshirts, fishnets, vinyl, all the wire rings, black leather bracelets, chokers, chromium chains, spikes, studs, lipsticks, eye pencils, hair sparkle, all her books, postcards, bottle caps, corks, seashells, and all Kim's toys—every goddamned rag and scrap, left nothing behind except the door key, which lay so lonely on the kitchen counter, though I had emphatically told her she could keep it.

The back room felt especially lonely with that bare floor space, the sleeping bag and backpack gone, the mattress up on edge over here and the bookcase pushed back over there, and she'd swept all her little things from the shelves and returned my books in neat rows, arranged—why not?—by height. There wasn't anything for me to straighten up or put away or save, so I took a shower and when I pulled open my drawer to get a shirt there was a letter addressed to me, two folded sheets of lined notebook paper covered on both sides with Avalon's jagged handwriting. It was a thank-you note. *Dear Renato, As you see, I am writing a letter now that I have somebody to write to. There's many things I want to thank you for and I have been making a list, it's incomplete but here it is—*" Frankly, I was pleased that she appreciated those things, but as I read I began to weep and I don't know why. She was thankful for so many little, little things. Now, let me say this about Avalon—the multicolored hair, the jewelry stuck to her face, those were distractions and I've spent too much time talking about them, because if you ever knew Avalon you'd know she was beautiful and good. She was beautiful not like those women who are so pretty they think they don't fart, but beautiful when she was smeared with coffee dust from hauling sacks of coffee beans or when she was quietly watching Kim draw one of his maps, or when she tossed her head back and laughed or simply whenever. And she was good and true.

Anyway, I got myself together, got into fresh L. L. Bean chinos and a pair of paint-spotted running shoes, which shoes I felt were enough, a kind of signature at the bottom of the image to assure the buyer that I was the painter. I tried on the white wash-and-wear jacket which I had worn to get married in and which Galaxy had returned to me a year ago; it looked good, so I kept it on. I trotted downstairs, got in the wagon drove through the rain to Cambridge and Conti's gallery. The reception was scheduled from six to nine and I was almost an hour late.

There was a good enough crowd in the gallery, but before I could take a step Leo Conti popped up, whispering, "Where have you been? All these paintings and no painter!" I told him my daughter and her family had flown in from Indonesia this morning and that I'd been running late and that—. But Conti had thrust his arm through mine and was pulling me on a long diagonal across the floor. Tonight he was wearing black trousers and a black jacket over black turtleneck jersey. I said, "Leo, why are you dressed like a mortician? You sold three paintings before we even opened." He tugged my arm, tilted me down toward him to speak into my ear, saying, "Listen, buyers come to receptions to see the *painter*, not the paintings. Some of these people have money to spend and you've got to *help* them." He told me who they were and what they were, so I could perform properly as an artist, which is to say like a trained circus lion, all wild display and no bite. I chatted in a surly yet respectful way with these potential buyers, then merciful Alba came up to hand me a glass of soda water, so they withdrew, after which she took my arm, saying, "Galaxy's over here."

And here's my daughter, her face luminous and her eyes dancing, as if the room is filled lighted candles, coming to give me a hug. "Dad, this is Weston," she tells me, conjuring out of the empty air beside her a thin young man with an amiable angular face. We shake hands and agree it's time for us to meet, since we've heard so much about each other, and I turn to Galaxy to say, "I heard some news about you, I heard—" but before I can finish, she says, "Yes, I'm having a baby, really, truly, a baby," and I said, "That's wonderful, that's great, that beats all."

At first there were only people standing together in islands, a long archipelago which began at the food table and curved gently across the glassy gray concrete floor, but when I next had the time to look around the place was full. Vanderzee had come wearing what I thought was a backpack but which turned out to be a baby carrier with a little kid peering out. "These are really great. This is a great show. I love it," Vanderzee said, looking around, apparently quite pleased at what he saw. "It's a great party, too. Which reminds me," he added, turning to me, "I play Dixieland with a jazz group and I can get them over here to play a set, if you want." And before I could ask Vanderzee was he joking or simply crazy he had swung into an energetic talk with Leo, their heads together. Then a couple of gallery patrons engaged me in conversation, but sometime later I saw Vanderzee's Winona and Gail, she with a sleepy toddler in her arms. I asked the women if Vanderzee played in a jazz group. Oh, yes, they assured me, he plays the clarinet, and he's good at it.

I'm happy to say I didn't know most of the people who came, but friends did show up and I was grateful for that, too. From Copley College came Azarig and his wife, and loyal Nils Petersen, whose Pixels show I had attended, and Nils's wife Hanna, and five of my former students or, to be precise, three former male students and a couple of their women. Karl Kadish came, as did Tom Hay and his wife, and Cormac with Karen McCormac drove in from the middle of Massachusetts, the Scanlons from Connecticut, and Zocco came, and Michkio with a tall fellow named Quincy, and Gordon Levy and Garland from the café—Gordon, bless him, bought a small painting—and to my surprise boyish Peter Bell, Sonia Strand's assistant, turned up and introduced me to his companion, David Somebody.

I was talking with a twenty-something internet entrepreneur (blue jeans, yellow cotton jersey) who fancied himself a collector of contemporary art when I saw Zoe approaching. After the kid left, Zoe asked had I talked yet with Galaxy and Weston, and I said, "Yes. And they make a good-looking couple. Galaxy knows what she's doing." We could see them over by the wine table, chatting with Cormac. We watched as Galaxy, gesturing in a great zigzag, said something to Cormac, then Cormac smiled and said something in reply which caused Galaxy to laugh. While she went on talking, her hand at her side brushed against Weston's hand and returned, fingers outspread, seeking it again. Zoe turned to me and said, "We all did all right with Galaxy. I know we made a few mistakes, but we did good." And I said, "Yes, we did." Zoe had come to the exhibit with Emerson Ripley who had been at the wine table to fill two glasses and was now maneuvering through the crowd toward us. "Emerson's actually good company," Zoe told me. "But I need more time, lots more time, before I let myself—you know—get involved. Deeply," she added.

"I thought you were going to be celibate," I said.

"I am. I've been celibate for days. I'm celibate right now."

Our Avalon and Kim came with Sebastian Gabriel and his

daughter Cait, making a family. Avalon was in a fanciful dress, a colorful paper confection which Sebastian had probably made for her, and Sebastian himself was wearing a sky-blue jacket decorated with gold braid, and bogus military insignia, including a shoulder patch from Sgt. Pepper's Lonely Hearts Club Band and a breast-pocket crest from Monty Python's Flying Circus. "I don't know which one of you looks more magnificent," I said. As a matter of fact, Avalon had a beautifully weird aura about her, perhaps because of the strange dye job she had done on her hair, the tips being pale pink which shaded into a glorious rose as it neared her scalp.

Zoe took my hand and turned me around, telling me, "Look who's here," and here was Alba and our traveling daughter, Skye, who gave me a long, long hug. "We're all jet-lagged!" says Skye, holding both my hands. "Eric's at the apartment looking after the kids or he'd be here too." You look wonderful, I tell her, and behind Skye comes our son Brizio, taller than I remembered, so tall he seemed to hunch down to give me a hug. Then he swung his backpack to the floor and brought forward the young woman at his side—clear green eyes, no lipstick and a plain silver clip in her smooth chestnut hair—his companion for the last two years. "You remember Heather," Brizio says. I say, Yes, of course. "We're getting married," Brizio says. "And having a baby," Heather adds, shaking my hand.

I don't know exactly when Vanderzee's Dixieland band began to play, but by then the evening was coming to a close so there was open space on the floor and people began to dance, turning my paintings to wallpaper. Frankly, I thought the exhibit had been too damn much of a party all along and I was sore at Vanderzee and angry with Conti or, actually, I would have been if I had been sober, but because of the wine in my veins, or because I could see Brizio and Heather and Galaxy and Weston talking together, I felt elated, expansive and warm-hearted toward everyone. I had started to tell Scanlon my plans to paint frescos in a barn, but he interrupted to tell me his theory that artists shouldn't move to the country, that painting should never be done out of doors, that it's essential to paint indoors and under artificial light, otherwise the colors will look off key, because paintings are destined to be seen in the artificial light and canned air of galleries. I told him we had already signed a lease to rent a country place for a year with an option to buy.

My conversation with Scanlon was interrupted by a writer from the *Boston Phoenix* who leaned in to confide that the exhibit was the best bash he'd been to all summer, and then his tall blond companion, who said she wrote for *Art New England*, remarked on Conti's having made a killing when he sold this piece of real estate to a builder eager to put up another office building. I went looking for Conti, the man with empty pockets who had induced me to pay for all the advertising and half the wine, but he found me first, catching my arm and turning me round to meet a man whom I'd seen chatting idly with Conti when I began delivering my paintings to the gallery, a middle-aged pear-shaped man with a soft, formless face and gentle eyes. He had looked over my work a couple of days ago and was buying one of my paintings—a huge canvas, *Charles River Basin*, delicious licks of ultramarine and green and black, velvety black, and gray and blazing white— on which Conti had slapped a handsome high price. We three stepped into Conti's and the buyer told me, "That painting is better than any Kokoshka," and I agreed, said it was a hundred times better (though it was a brainless comparison) and we exchanged other such pleasantries, after which I gave him my studio address and we shook hands.

I returned to the gallery floor feeling very good; the band was swinging into "Sensation Rag," and that's when Avalon came up, telling me, "I have an idea about your aunt Vivianna."

"Another one?" I said Hi to Kim who was beside her.

"We agree that your grandfather got her pregnant and then—" she says.

"I don't remember agreeing." We were standing in front of the band and it was hard to hear. I asked Kim how he liked his new place.

"—She went into hiding but didn't go out to Las Vegas until after the baby was born," Avalon says, lifting her voice above the music.

"That's your idea."

"No, Ren, those are more or less the facts. My idea is she left her baby on your grandfather's doorstep and bought a ticket to Las Vegas a couple of weeks later."

At first I didn't understand her. All around us people were dancing and laughing and Vanderzee's clarinet was making neon-colored scribbles that hovered in the air, entangling everything, and I began to laugh, shaking my head, partly to clear it and partly to say no, not at all, never. Alba had come up and was talking with Avalon. Kim said he guessed his new place was all right and asked when was I coming to visit him. "When would you like?" I asked him

"Tomorrow," he said.

"Not tomorrow," I said. "Tomorrow I'm going out to the country."

"I could get a ride out to the country. You could show me water bugs," Kim said. Alba looked at him a moment and then asked him, "Would you like to come to a picnic tomorrow?"

By the end we had invited not only Kim but, naturally, Avalon and, of course, Sebastian and his daughter Cait, and Cormac and Karen McCormac and, though Scanlon and his wife had to return to Connecticut, we did get Vanderzee and his kid or kids and whoever. And then—because I didn't want to see my paintings as backdrop to a near-deserted ballroom where every chair and window displayed a handful of used plastic glasses and wadded paper napkins, and the caterer's table was littered with mangled piles of fruit, cheese wedges and cracker bowls with only crumbs in the bottom—I said to Alba, "Let's get out of here." We had dinner with Brizio, Heather, Galaxy, Weston, Zoe and Emerson, after which we said goodnight to everyone and, because Alba's place was crammed full with Skye and her family, plus Brizio and Heather, and my studio quite empty, we bedded down there.

66

God made us mortal, and all we have to assuage us is this perishable art and human love. At one of my exhibits I was greeted by a woman pushing a wheelchair from painting to painting—Nancy Lorette she was, whom I had last seen sprinkling confectioner's sugar into her navel, and in the wheelchair sat her little old mother Avril, bright-eyed and completely puzzled. While I was writing these pages I got word that my enduring friend Max, who brought me food when I was sick in the city, had died of prostate cancer, and a couple of days ago I learned that bright Odine, who let me draw with crayon on her beautiful long back, had died of congestive heart failure.

Looking back, I'm baffled that I haven't done better. I don't mean painting; I've done all right painting even if nobody knows it. But I could have given more time to my friends, could have listened more and complained less, could have been more generous to everyone. And I could have taken Avalon more seriously, including her notion that I'm the child of my aunt Vivianna and my grandfather Pacifico—which might be true, but Avalon is always trying to tie loose ends into a family. I've loved greedily and not with perfect chastity and I don't even know why I love the people I do. I know only that I love them. Montaigne, speaking of his dead friend Ètienne, could never explain the depth of their friendship, could say only that such friendship came because "he was he and I was I"—which is another reason to think Montaigne was Italian. I miss Mike Bruno.

I saw my first actual painting high on the wall of our Post Office, where Paul Revere galloped through the blue moonlit morning of April 19, 1775, to warn us villagers that the British were coming, galloped on the road just outside our Post Office door, his arm flung out as he thundered past. Ever since then I've always wanted to paint a mural, and may still get around to it. I wake up in the morning—flex my fingers and toes, stretch my legs—and I'm delighted to find that my body still works, that I can paint at least one more day, and especially happy I paint better than anyone else. I paint to give viewers solace for being human. A couple of years ago I drove down to Hartford to see the paintings of Pieter de Hooch (1629–1694), because he was having his first solo show. So maybe like him I'll have a retrospective three hundred years from now, or maybe, like my friend who worked by torchlight in those caves above the waters of the Ardeche, I'll wait thirty-one thousand years.

67

NEXT MORNING THE SKY WAS CLEAR BLUE, WASHED by the drenching rain of the past few days, and the deep grass around the old white farm house shimmered in the sun like shallow sea water. We unlocked the doors, threw open the windows, carried a couple of crates of wine from the wagon, and I was lugging a pair of sawhorses when Brizio and Heather pulled in, bringing food they had bought from a local farmer who, they said with satisfaction, used only natural organic fertilizers and natural organic pesticides; then Skye and Eric and their four kids drove up in a rented van with a carton of paper plates, cups, napkins, loaded from Alba's concrete storage box in Cambridge.

Later, Skye's Eric and I unhinged the board door from the kitchen closet and carried it outside where we laid it across the sawhorses for a makeshift table. We set it up by the house and figured we could spread some tablecloths on the grass a ways beyond it, under the apple branches that faced out across the hay fields toward the woods—our own paradise, though, as I pointed out to Alba, all of the apples were flawed and some had worms. As we were standing there surveying the landscape I asked Eric where his anthropology was going to take him next, which I believed was a better way of asking a son-in-law was he ever going to get a goddamn job with a decent goddamn wage and settle down within five goddamn hundred miles of here. He took my meaning and smiled, a likeable man, I believe, though it's hard to know him well when he's always at some distant edge of the map. He told me he had a letter from a friend at the University of Massachusetts about a job opening there, which he thought would be convenient for all of us, and he guessed he should write back and ask for details; on the other hand, he said, squinting at the horizon, there was some good research being done up in Toronto and some really fascinating work being talked about at a place in Saskatchewan. He looked at me and smiled, saying, "Something will turn up, I'm sure," and, after rolling that around in my head for a while, I agreed, as there was no good my doing otherwise.

I went looking for my grandchildren, last seen disappearing around a corner of the house, and along the way I bumped into Brizio's Heather who was carrying a crate of wine into the shade of the apple trees. I took it from her and we began talking about how hot the sun was and how it was too bad no one had thought to bring ice, and all the while I was taking pleasure in her clear eyes and, I confess, in the knowledge that she was carrying Brizio's baby. We were discussing the herbs she was growing for gourmet restaurants when Skye walked over to us—this athlete in a flowing batik dress, my daughter. "I didn't have time to tell to you yesterday," Skye says to me. "So I want to tell you now—I'm pregnant." She watched me expectantly, then while I'm gathering my wits, she says, as if to help me understand, "We're having another baby, Dad," to which I think I said Oh and But and Well, and then as Alba came up I told her, "Everybody's pregnant," and Alba says decisively, "Yes, it's *wonderful!*"

"Yes, wonderful," I chimed, giving Skye a belated hug and a kiss. Skye and Heather went off to explore the fields, their voices diminishing in the distance as Skye told her about some kind of Asian or Indonesian sling, a kerchief knotted to make a sling, which women, someplace, use to carry a baby. I turned to Alba. "Everybody's pregnant at once. Is that possible?"

"Apparently so," says Alba.

"She already has *four* kids."

"I'm sure Skye realizes that. I'm sure they both do."

"How are they going to support *five?*"

"That's not our worry."

"It isn't?"

Then Emerson Ripley's beater hove into view, carrying not only Emerson and Zoe, but Galaxy and Galaxy's Weston, too. They had brought bread—Tuscan rounds and rolls and long baguettes—plus a couple of bottles of wine. Later I told Zoe that Skye was pregnant. "Yes. Isn't it wonderful?"

"You knew?" I said, stopping so abruptly that Zoe, who was holding the other end of the tablecloth, was yanked to a stop. "Why, yes. I think Galaxy told me," she says, opening her arms to stretch the cloth tight between us.

"When?"

"Last night. Or maybe before then. I don't remember," she says as we lowered the billowing cloth to the grass where we anchored it with a small stone at each corner.

Vanderzee and Winona and Gail and their kids arrived with more food, and so did Cormac and Karen McCormac, so we had at least three baskets full of grapes, a bushel of peaches, a dozen ears of early corn, several freshly baked loaves, a bag of tomatoes, three fried chickens (sliced and cold), sardines, more tomatoes, a couple of cucumbers, a couple of crates of wine, some bottles of Moxie if you didn't want wine, and water from the kitchen faucet if you couldn't stand the Moxie. And at last came Kim and Avalon plus Sebastian and his daughter Cait, bringing cheeses, black olives and figs—chosen, I'm sure, by Avalon.

"Isn't she beautiful?" Sebastian said to me. Anybody else might have said Avalon looked bizarre, for she was wearing a dress again, as she had last night, but this one was composed of filmy white material with burnt umber trim and its huge sleeves were pleated like fans, so when she lifted her arms they looked like angel wings. "Oh, did you ever see anyone so beautiful?" he said, his voice hushed with awe. We were standing in the shade and Avalon, letting Kim go off to the barn with the other kids, turned and walked toward us, the sun shooting clear through her dress. She must have re-dyed her hair this morning, because it was darker than last night, the luminous rose color being closer to her scalp, the tips now reddish gold, and as she walked past you could see the backs of her hands were hued like peacock feathers, her nails like emeralds and sapphires, radiant as her own mother when she was pregnant with Avalon. "She thinks the world of you," I told Sebastian.

I supposed Avalon was pregnant, too, seeing as how all the other young women were, which prompted me to tell Cormac I was going to include pregnant nudes in the frescos I was planning to paint in the barn. He laughed. "Great! But *frescos*? Don't you need special plaster for that?" he said.

"I can get it from Rome. It's ground up limestone mixed with volcanic sand. It's great stuff. I'll use powdered pigments, the kind you mix with oil to make oil paints, but I'll mix them with water and paint directly on the *intonaco*, the damp plaster. It'll be great fun." We got to the barn just as Kim and my two oldest grandchildren came popping out. The open side of the big sliding door, though still jammed into the earth, had pulled itself away from the barn and was standing at a crazy angle, giving bearish bulky Cormac almost enough room to step inside—a further shove on the door did the trick. We walked down the long interior to the big square of light at the far end where the floor was still spongy from rain water, took in the view of the green horizon, walked back to the place where we could stare up between the naked rafters to the sky —"Well, you could put in a skylight," said Cormac—then came out to bright sunshine.

"First I'll get the roof patched," I said. "And I'll put in big, big windows on both sides, high up, like clerestory windows. The barn is just the frame for the blank walls. I'll fill in the blanks, paint everything and everybody—it will be amazing, it'll be wonderful."

We got back to the others— "Hungry! Starved! Famished!" they cried—who had been waiting for Cormac and me, we raised a toast to the company, clinked our glasses and drank. In that moment of quiet we heard a very loud *CRACK*— sourceless as a thunderclap, but sharp—and a loud grinding groan came to us, we realized, from the barn, then a popping and crackling and we saw the old structure had swayed toward its back end where the land slanted steeply down so you could walk a horse in under the barn. Avalon came shooting past, holding Kim by the wrist, while Skye cried, "Where are the kids? Are any kids over there?" I must have started to run toward the barn, because I was almost there when up came a rippling snapping sound with an undertone of CRACKS and BOOMS as it began collapsing, slowly heaving itself down over its back cellar wall to crash and smash on the ground until there was only the silence of the hot sun and a long sloped tangle of broken beams, rafters, joists, shingles, planks and clapboards, over which hovered a cloud of dust, specks of straw and seed and wood a hundred and fifty years old.

No children had been inside, everyone was safe and there was nothing we could do about the barn, but the day wasn't going to last forever the way it used to when we were kids and, since the wine was uncorked and the food ready, we began to eat and drink and loaf in the shade, talking about what we were going to do next, like building a better barn, better for frescos.

BOOK THREE

After Alba

I WENT TO THE DAILY GRIND CAFÉ AND HAD A CUP of coffee at the little table where we often sat, but Alba didn't turn up, smiling and saying "I thought I'd find you here."

Because she is dead — I know, I know. What I don't know is where she went and why she hasn't come back and is she someplace I can get to without dying, because though I wanted to die and told myself over and over to die, it became clear it wasn't going to happen right away. I don't understand why we're born or why we love or why we bring children into the world if we and everyone we love are going to die.

❧

I was born at my grandfather's house in Lexington, Massachusetts, in the evening of the last snowfall of March, eighty-three years ago. You could say I was born a few days earlier, but on that snowy evening I was found in a laundry basket on my grandfather's doorstep, so that's my true birthday.

My grandfather's name was Pacifico Cavallù and here he is, four years later, my nonno, kneeling down to crush me against his scratchy vest and gold watch chain, kissing the top of my head, the air scented with bay rum cologne and Parodi cigars and filled with his *ho-ho-ho* when he lifted me up, up, too far up to the ceiling, then caught and lowered me and set me on my feet, and I ran to my mother. Nonno kept big barrels of wine sleeping on their stomachs in the dark cobweb cellar, which was two steps down from the big cellar, and the floor in the little cellar was dirt like outside.

Later, when I was six or seven, Floria led me and our cousin

Nick over the low stone wall into the old burying ground and Floria said, "Look, you can lift up the slates," and she lifted a gravestone straight up so you could see the bottom edge, damp and sharp like a spade covered with dirt. "See?" she said. "We can switch them around." She switched two gravestones, then switched them back. In those days nobody died except the people from long ago who were already dead, like the people in that old graveyard, like Isaac Stone from 1690. Then we heard aunt Lucia, Floria's mother, calling, *"Floria, vieni, vieni qui, Floria, andiamo! Andiamo!"* So we climbed over the little stone wall and into Nonno's backyard where my father and uncle Nicolo and uncle Zitti were playing bocce in the big afternoon sunshine seventy-seven years ago.

Now people die every day. Alba died on the first day of spring. She had caught a slight cold, we thought, but in the third night her cries woke me and I called 911 and the emergency team came. They took her blood pressure. "How often do you have atrial fibrillation?" someone asked her. She could barely sit in the chair without falling off. They put her on the gurney, maneuvered her down the stairway and into the EMS truck and we drove to the hospital emergency entrance. Then hours of agony and panic — her heart racing, blood pressure collapsing, kidneys failing, her gut in agonizing knots, blood turning to acid in her veins — they gave me a tiny sponge on a stick to wet her lips and mouth. "I can't stand pain the way you can," she gasped to me, then her tongue failed to obey her will she couldn't speak her eyes filled with terror, so that

and torture for twenty hours and her heart stopped. They pounded and heaved on her chest, trying to restart it, then backed off and used voltage, again and again and again and again and again, until the doctor said it was over and I rushed to grab her — "Oh, my beautiful Alba!" — got my arms around her to help her, to help her lift, help her get up from that bed, my cheek pressed to her warm breast, her sweet warm breast. Perspiration had suffused her face but, oh, she was so heavy as never in this life. Our children gathered drifted gathered here there, our children, our kids. I stroked her hair the way she always liked and I peeled away the bloody tapes and began to pull the tube from her mouth, when some busybody bitch rushed at me, saying, "No, no, not until the coroner comes!" The doctor was sitting on a small metal chair outside the glass room, writing on a long pad he held on his knees. He looked tired. He said Alba had succumbed to a bacterial infection. "You don't have to go," he told me. "You can stay with her as long, as long as you want." But it was no use, so I told him, "No. Her spirit is gone." Our kids took me home.

That was my cousin Floria, leading us on adventures over the little stone wall to the old burying ground or up to the attic and beneath the slanting roof where the steamer trunks were stored, decorated with stickers from the White Star Line and the Cunard. A year or two later she gave me her writing desk, because she was going to the villa in Sicily with her mother Lucia and Nonno. The desk had ink stains on it, but when I lifted the lid it was clean inside and smelled fresh and I could keep drawing paper and pencils there. Everyone was calling to aunt Lucia, saying, "Hurry, hurry up, Lucia. We'll miss the boat! Andiamo!" But Lucia had stopped to light her cigarette. "The boat will wait!" she said, coming into the car, an airy scarf of smoke trailing over her shoulder. Dante and Regina were in the car ahead of us, and Nonno was in the car ahead of them, and we all drove to Boston and walked up the gangway onto the ship to say goodbye. It was a bright sunny day. I don't recall if our cousin Veronica was with us, but Nick and I had a great time.

Now Nonno and aunt Lucia and Floria were at the villa in Palermo, but the rest of us still gathered every Sunday at the big house in Lexington, the same as ever, because Nanna was still there. After the long midday dinner, my father and uncle Nicolo and uncle Zitti would remain at the table with their wine and coffee and the adult aroma of tobacco smoke. Zitti and Nicolo were professors and whenever they disagreed about something they would turn to Fidèle, my father, and ask him to referee. The young uncles had no wives yet and were up on the third floor, trying to put together a bamboo fishing pole, or they were cleaning the guns — something like that. But then we heard them clattering down the stairs. Uncle Zitti and Uncle Nicolo were talking about politics or religion when Silvio and Mercurio came through the dining room, their riding boots booming on the floor. "We're going out to watch Sandro's hawk," Silvio said. "Anybody coming with us?"

"No," Mercurio told him. "They're going to sit there all day and discuss Roosevelt and Norman Thomas. Or Mussolini. Let's go."

"Tell Sandro to be careful," uncle Nicolo called after them. "That hawk is still wild."

"One of the neighbors is going to take a shot at that bird," my father murmured.

I had watched Sandro's hawk before and there wasn't much to watch; it had yellow eyes and it just flew up and around in circles, and then after a while it swooped down and landed on Sandro's arm, on his big leather glove, where he fed it. My cousin Nick said Come on, let's go outside, and I said Veronica wants to come, too. Nick went out and I would have gone with him, but now Uncle Nicolo asked Uncle Zitti what had God been doing before he created the universe — a funny kind of question and I wanted to hear the answer.

"Ah," Zitti said. He smiled and pressed the end of his silver cigarette case so it sprang open like a little book. "Saint Augustine has the answer to that one."

"And what does your Saint Augustine say?" Nicolo asked.

My father had rolled up his sleeve and tucked two walnuts into the crook of his arm, but now he paused, waiting for the answer.

"He says God was preparing hell for those who pry too deep."

My father gave a brief laugh and closed his arm, cracking the walnuts.

"Let me correct myself," Zitti said, tapping the end of his cigarette against the silver case. "Saint Augustine didn't say that, but he talks about somebody else who said that. Augustine himself takes the question seriously."

"Does he say who God is?" Nicolo asked. He had unfolded a dazzling white handkerchief and was polishing his glasses, a pair of small octogons, like Ben Franklin's bifocals.

Zitti turned to me. "Tell your Uncle Nicolo who God is," he said.

"God is the creator of heaven and earth and all things," I recited.

My father didn't say anything, but resettled himself comfortably in his chair, satisfied with my answer. He didn't go to church, nor did any of my uncles, but it was understood that I would learn the catechism and go to church every Sunday with my mother and my little brother Bart for a while longer.

"Did the universe create itself out of nothing?" Zitti asked Nicolo.

Nicolo had started to reply, but then caught himself and nodded in my direction — bringing me into the discussion, I thought. He put his glasses back on. "I don't know," he told Zitti.

"Exactly. Nothing can create itself out of nothing!" Zitti said, slapping the table in delight. "Thus, we have God. Q.E.D."

"Renato's a big boy," my father told uncle Nicolo. "You can talk in front of him."

"I'm not a philosopher," Nicolo said, sweeping his hand here and there on the tablecloth as if to iron out the wrinkles, or maybe brush something away. "I'm an engineer, a believer in the scientific method. Science finds out the way the world is made and how it works. The more science explains, the less mysterious the world is, and the less mysterious it is, the less we use God to explain how or why things happen. I don't see evidence of God anywhere." He glanced at me and added, "But that's just my opinion."

"I see God everywhere I look," Zitti countered, flinging his arms out. "This world, the stars, the gravity that holds everything together — it didn't create itself. God created it."

"And who created God?" Nicolo asked him.

"Michelangelo created God!" my father announced. He drained his wineglass and banged it down on the table. "Sistine Chapel. Fantastic work. Genius!"

I ran out and climbed over the little stone wall into the old graveyard, but by then Nick and Veronica were already going out the other side, down into the big meadow. In the field the air was extra warm and sweet with the scent of freshly mown hay, and when you looked up it was all sky and Sandro's hawk making circles higher and higher toward the sun.

I couldn't endure the thought of Alba shut in a narrow coffin, and that coffin in a concrete box lowered into a hole in the ground and then dirt shoveled on it. I let her body go clothed in one of her favorite dresses, one I loved, sky-blue with a narrow waist, let her body go up in and received her ashes in a heavy stone box, carried her in my arms against my chest to the car, and I held her while Skye drove us home in the silence, because neither of us could speak. When we had closed the front door, my daughter said, "I think we need a hug," and we hugged. Her ashes are like her dress; they are not her.

Time after time I cried Die. Die. Die. Die. Die. Die. Die.

Die. Die.
But it didn't work and I didn't die.

Scott came over to take me for a walk, because I hadn't been out of the house. He must have phoned first and Skye must have said Yes, come over, or maybe I told him Yes, because here he was and we went out. I turned up the collar of my barn jacket, buttoned everything and jammed my hands in the pockets, because I knew how to do that. My legs walked and I got a little way down the road and already I was tired and when I looked around I discovered that everything was actually fake — the flat housefronts standing beside the road had nothing behind them, the empty trees, the papery cutout clouds against the fake blue sky — all rigged up like a cheap stage set. I stopped and told him, "Everything's fake. Look at it! It's bogus, all of it." Scott said, "Where? What do you mean?" I said, "All this. See?" And I pointed to the houses and the black trees. "It's all made to look real, but it's all pretend and make-believe." He looked at me, then he said, "Let's keep walking. Where do you want to walk to?" I said I didn't know, so he said, "Let's go this way," and we turned down some other road. The road was level but it felt like it was uphill and I was getting more and more tired. We kept walking and walking. I told him, "It's not right. It's not right. Her dying, it's not right." Scott didn't say anything and we kept walking. It was a hard walk. I said, "If there's no God, who tortured her to death?" Finally he said we could go back to the house, so we turned around and headed to the house. I said, "It's not right, her dying. It's not right, Scott," and Scott didn't say anything until he said, "I know. It's not right."

Another day it was Fletcher who came to take me for a walk. It must have been windy because he said, "Let's go this way and when we come back to the house the wind will be behind us." You could see how the trees and houses were fake and I was about to say it was weird how people could live in them, because they were no thicker than cardboard cutouts, but I decided not to because he'd think I was crazy. We walked along and I told him it wasn't right, Alba's dying. Fletch gave up a long sigh and cleared his throat and said, "Yes, it was terrible." "It wasn't right," I said. "God tortured her for twenty hours until she died," I told him. Fletch hung his head and walked along looking mostly at his boots and after a while he said, "I could help you fix that chair in the living room, the one with the loose leg." I said that was good. Yes, I wanted to do that. "I'll bring my clamps the next time I come," he said, straightening up. We agreed on that.

Zoe came over to take me for a walk and when we were walking I showed her the houses and the trees and the sky, showing her how it was all made-up fake. "See. It's not real. It's a scam." Zoe looked older than usual and said, "Yes." I knew that if you go to the side of a house the front disappears from view, and then it's the side that's only as thick as a sheet of cardboard, so everything is still fake, but I knew better than to talk about it. We walked along and everything was crazy because Zoe is the mother of my third child, Astrid, but it was Alba who brought her up, and here I was walking with Zoe, and Alba was gone and everything was wrong, like Zoe wearing high-heel shoes while we were walking on this rural road with its crumbling tar, pebbles and sand. A gusty wind blew through with a spatter of raindrops, making Zoe hunch her shoulders; she looked to be freezing but she kept walking beside me.

Zoe and Scott and Fletcher came over every so often, each

alone, to take me for a walk. I marveled how they knew to take me for a walk.

I don't know what I did the first month. My daughters Skye and Astrid came, and my son Brizio, too, of course; sometimes they were all here together, sometimes only my son or one of my daughters, then they were gone and only my oldest daughter, Skye, was here. She was here for two weeks, of which I can recall nothing; then she left and Astrid came and I don't remember anything of those two weeks, either. I'm amazed they didn't go crazy, dwelling with their living-dead father. I do recall the memorial service. And I remember after the service, when all who had come were together around me, and grief had loosened their hearts and they shared this love, all of them, and as long as they talked and ate and drank and talked, just that long would Alba be here among us, but they had lives to get back to, and one by one they went and the spaces grew larger and finally they had all gone and there was only empty space. That evening Brizio returned to his home and I was by myself.

One day I carefully opened the drawers in the nightstand and scooped out the shimmering black satins, airy silks, straps and hooks and collars, crammed everything into a small white trash bag, leaving a breath of warm perfume in the air, and then I took down the shoebox from the closet shelf and poured a quiet jingling tumble of soft leather, silvery buckles, chains and rings into the trash bag. I closed the bag with two ties and carried it down to the garage where the trash barrels stood waiting. Next, I brought a larger trash bag upstairs and opened her closet and gathered all the shoes and put them carefully, two by two — and those precious gold sandals with the imprint of her slender foot — put them into the bag and closed it with two ties and shut the closet door. I couldn't touch the dresses. I carried the bag down to the garage and lowered it carefully into the barrel beside the other one. Then I went to her desk where she had idly set her purse, which no one had touched since. I gently emptied it onto the writing surface and tenderly separated out her lipsticks, the door keys and the car key, an eyebrow pencil, a mirror, crumpled paper tissues, her miniature address book, two pens, a nail file, magnifying glass, a small Florentine leather purse with change inside, a small pad of notepaper, three postage stamps, a few safety pins, and all her little private things. Afterward, there was plenty of time to sit on the foot of the bed to howl and sob.

I made a list of my friends and jotted down the date whenever I phoned them, so I wouldn't call anyone too often. Almost nobody phoned me. But Susan Salter called and suggested dinner at a restaurant, said she'd pick me up, drive us there and back. She was a friend of Alba's from *Art New England* (good-looking, witty, many lovers, never married and slightly crazy), she arrived wearing what she knew Alba would have worn — a white summer dress and a splash of color — but with more jingling jewelry on her arm than Alba wore in a lifetime. We weren't really friends and didn't have much to talk about, but I appreciated how she was trying to help me get through the day. Al Levine phoned and we went to lunch, though we knew each other only slightly and had never had lunch or even a coffee together. John Duffy phoned from Philadelphia. He and David had been living together almost as long as Alba and I, so he understood and we had a good talk. I went to lunch in Cambridge with George Agathos. We've enjoyed boisterous dinners with George and Io — quantum mechanics and Greek cooking — but now George was so concerned about me he looked ten years older. Zocco and his wife invited me to Sunday brunch with mutual friends, but it would have been too many people for me to deal with. I had dinner with Zoe and Emerson every so often, because after me and our children, no one missed Alba more than Zoe. When she learned about Alba, she came to the house, frightened and white-faced, and when she hugged me it was as if she were clinging for support. Now it was just me and Zoe and Emerson at their table, which was friendly and calm. Avalon and Sebastian had me over for dinner, too. Avalon seated me at the head of the table and made pasta puttanesca the way I had taught her. Their kitchen is always full of Sebastian's bright cut-paper art and I like being distracted that way. Nils Petersen was good to be with but he had received a grant and was off with his wife Hanna doing avant-garde computer art, or whatever they call it, in the Netherlands. Every so often, Fletcher or Scott would phone and say let's have lunch, so I saw them from time to time.

I drove to the Daily Grind café once or twice a week, the way we used to, and when I'd get out of the car it felt as if Alba was here, walking beside me the same as ever. At the café I trade a few words with Garland behind the counter, or whoever is around, then I go talk with Gordon. At the memorial service it had been painful to see him not in his white apron with its smudges of coffee dust, but in a stiff black suit and black necktie, because something terrible had happened to Alba. He still talks about politics or sports or hard times in the coffee business, and how he misses his old location in Boston. Sometimes I talk about Alba, and he listens and doesn't try to change the subject. Or I sit alone at the window, when that's what I feel like doing. Once I was sitting by the window watching it rain and I felt Alba come up behind me, as she sometimes did at home, to kiss my cheek, so I leaned back and turned my cheek toward her, not that I thought she was there, but because I wanted her to know that I felt her presence and loved her. Walking back to the car I always think about Alba and I want to have died.

Sometimes it was me who had died and Alba who was living and I'd see her walking solitary in the quiet before sunset, walking slowly along the empty sidewalk in the little college town where Skye and her family have their home, or I'd see her at the table in our kitchen where she had set out two or three yellow place mats, but only one dish, eating alone in the silent kitchen, and my heart would contract in pain.

While Alba's possessions — her dresses, her little bottles of perfume and cologne, small jars of lotion, her glasses — were charged with meaning, all the other things in the house made no sense. The pewter bowls we had arranged on the fireplace mantel, the Afghan carpets we'd bought from Morgan, every worn book in the bookcase and the Italian tiles we had set into the kitchen wall, those things had no more meaning or connection to me than items on display in a housewares shop.

There wasn't anything to do, so I went out to the studio. The ancient barn collapsed the day we had our first picnic out here, so we'd built a new one with big windows up high all around and a studio loft at the back that faced over the fields toward the woods. Years ago I had begun some frescos — the real thing on a mix of ground-up limestone and volcanic sand. I planned to build them into the walls and the barn would become a chapel of earthly delights — or so I had thought, if you can call it thinking. A few frescos leaned against the walls, rotting like everything else. Eventually I gave up on them and returned to canvas, lots of canvas. Now the studio floor creaked underfoot because I hadn't been up there for weeks. A big flat crate still stood by the door. I had packed three paintings for a group show in Worcester, but after Alba I didn't send it. I phoned the gallery, dropped out of the show and didn't send the crate. The sketches tacked to the walls had died, and the stretchers leaning here and there, the table, the jars and brushes — everything was dead. Photographs of Alba stayed on the shelf by the table, but they weren't true anymore. I opened a window and sat for a while, but there was nothing to do, so I closed the window and left.

❦

I had kept hoping to die but it hadn't happened and after a while I gave up trying and pretended to live, just doing the things that living people do. I got up and shaved and showered and got dressed in fresh clothes. I shopped for food every day, mostly just to leave the empty house. Nadeau's grocery was nearer, but Big Valley Farms was larger and extra-bright inside and there were lots of people to be around. When I got out of the car in the big parking lot I'd haul myself up straight to show I was Alba's husband and proud of it. It was hard to do. I kept my back straight and my face up, because in this whole world she had loved me best of all. Still, I would rather have been dead.

❦

I didn't know what to do with being alive. I remembered the young woman at the Barista Coffee stand whose husband had died and I thought she could tell me what to do. She was preparing coffee for me and Alba when I noticed the snake coiling down her bare white arm to her wrist, nicely tattooed in ashen blue color. The snake had Japanese kanji on it. I told her I admired the artwork, a polite lie, and asked what the Japanese writing said. "Cancer shits," she said, pressing the plastic lids onto our coffees. "It says cancer shits."

"Oh," Alba said. "I'm so sorry!"

The young woman had already turned aside and was briskly polishing the coffee machine. "Not me. My husband," she added. By then somebody was standing behind us, waiting to order, so we left. The Barista stand was halfway to Cambridge and I bought coffee there maybe two or three more times after that. She had a thin whip-like body and black hair that stood up in thick soft spikes. She was good-looking, but like she had been punched in the face a few times and was making a slow recovery. I'd say, "How are things?" She'd give me half a laugh and answer, "Different day, same old shit." One time I asked her how her husband had died. "Brain cancer," she said.

"Oh, God, that's awful. I'm so sorry."

"Shit happens," she said.

"How long ago?"

"Eleven months," she said.

So now I went to the Barista stand and bought a cup of coffee, and when she handed it to me I spoke up like a crow trying to talk, saying, "My wife died and I don't know what to do." She looked straight at me a moment, then she said, "You can phone me. Will you call if I give you my number?" I croaked Yes. She scribbled her number on a slip of paper, slid it across the counter, saying, "Call me," then she looked to the customer behind me, so I headed to my car.

I didn't call her and I decided not to see her again, but stayed home at the window and watched the rain falling. But when it stopped raining I got in the car and drove out to the coffee stand, and as I was walking toward it I saw her coming down the wet sidewalk. She saw me and said, "You lose my number?" I said No, said I didn't want to bother her. "I don't let people bother me. — How are you doing?" she asked. I shrugged and said, "I don't know how I'm doing." People were bumping into me and brushing past us and a pelting rain had begun to fall.

"How did she die?"

We stepped into a doorway to get out of the rain and away from the people going by. I told her how Alba died and while I talked and cried, she stared out at the cars flashing by in the rain. I told her I was going crazy.

"Don't worry about it," she says, carefully drying her eyes with her fingers. "Crazy's all right. Crazy is a way to cope." She wore eyeliner, a thin black line along her eyelashes, but now it was muddy. I asked her what her name was. "Shannon," she says.

"Shannon what?"

"O'Hare."

She didn't ask but I told her my name anyway.

"Are you coming to buy a coffee tomorrow?" she asked.

I said Yes.

She looked at me a moment. "Is that a crappy yes or a real yes? Because you didn't call and you said you would, you know." I told her it was real yes and she said, "I gotta catch a bus," and went off. She was thin, like a knife.

The next day at the coffee stand she slid a red iron pan full of something heavy onto the counter and into a rumpled brown paper bag and said, "Take it."

"What is it?" I lifted the edge of the bag and caught the scent of tomato sauce.

"It's lasagna."

"Lasagna?"

"You got an Italian name, right? And you don't know lasagna?"

"You made me lasagna! You can't do that!"

"It's homemade, my kitchen."

"Christ."

"You have to eat more. That'll last you a few days."

A woman with two kids in tow had come up behind me, so I said thanks to Shannon and went home.

The lasagna's fiery tomato sauce had more pepper than I use in a month, and it lasted a week because I could swallow only a few forkfuls a day and by the last day the pasta strips had turned to leather. When I brought the iron pan back to her at the Barista Coffee stand, I told her it was great lasagna. "Good," she said. "Because you need to gain weight. You look hollow. You look like you got nothing inside."

❦

I received an announcement of Frank Vanderzee's exhibit at a gallery in Cambridge, and three days later a handwritten note arrived from Winona saying how especially happy they would be if I could come to the opening, although, she added, they knew I was not going out much, which they did understand, but they still hoped I could come. Vanderzee was maybe half as old as I was. I liked his work and we had gone to each other's shows for the last decade, but now the prospect of entering a room crowded with chattering people frightened and depressed me. I wasn't up to going by myself so I asked Scott would he drive me there and, if I needed to quit and leave without looking at anything, would he drive me right home. He said, "Sure. When do you want me to pick you up?"

So I got to the gallery and looked around and when Vanderzee saw me he came over. I told him I remembered when he was working on these canvasses and I had liked them then, and I liked them even more now. He smiled. "It's great to see you. I'm so glad you're here." Winona came and put her arm gently through mine and said, "There's a table with wine and cheese at the other end of the room. Shall we go?" I said, Yes, let's try that. I had a glass of wine and some crackers and we chatted about the kids. I had to focus my mind to make conversation, but I could do it. Gail came up and gave me a cautious hug, as if I might shatter. "Vanderzee and his wives," Alba used to say, though he wasn't married to pale Winona or cinnamon Gail.

I liked Winona and Gail, but I felt strange standing there and every so often it felt like I was going to tip over. Michiko, who had taught me all the kanji I've since forgotten, and her husband Robert arrived and we talked for a while. Michiko said she had been looking at photographs she took of Alba at our picnic last year and would make copies for me. Later I recognized Lucy Dolan, who used to babysit for us, just as she recognized me. She searched my eyes, and in a rush of sympathy threw her arms around me hard and held on like I don't know what. We talked for a moment or two — she said she was thinking of coming back to Boston now that her daughter was grown up and had left home. A few minutes later I saw Scott and asked him if he could drive me home now and he said, "Sure. Let's go." I said goodbye to Vanderzee and his wives and after I got home I sat at the kitchen table and howled, because of what God had done to Alba and how she suffered.

❦

The only widower I knew was Peter Panosian, a lawyer and amateur painter. He and his wife Helen were about fifteen years younger than we were. Helen was a vibrant woman, a prize-winning California surfer in her youth, and her slow dreadful dying had gnawed at Peter. He remained single for years, then around the time he retired he married the youngish legal assistant who had worked in his office for a decade. They moved to Pennsylvania, but we didn't lose touch and when he learned that Alba had died he wrote me a good note. So I phoned him. I think I said, Peter, this is Renato and I'm at a loss. My voice was so shaky I stopped talking, and Peter said, "Oh, Renato, oh, oh, oh." Then we talked for a while and he said, "Listen, I have to go to New York to give a talk on image and copyright — nowadays people think that whatever's on the Web is in the public domain. When I finish that business I'll come up to Boston. We'll have lunch." I said, No, that's too much trouble. He said, "No, it isn't."

So we had lunch in Boston. I think we talked for two hours, maybe more. Talking and listening to him gave me a certain relief, a sense of almost-sanity. After lunch we got into our coats and then lingered outside, talking a while longer, and he asked if I was painting. I said I hadn't picked up a brush since Alba died. "I painted a little every day," he said. "It was the only way I kept myself together. And it kept me close to her." I said I didn't see myself painting again ever. "I'm an amateur, you're an artist," he said flatly. We shook hands and embraced. "You'll paint," he told me as he headed off. I'd seen the paintings he did after his wife died. Peter liked bold primary colors, so his canvases were eye-catching, and each one was of his wife gazing straight out at you, like a series of self-portraits by Frida Kahlo. I suppose Frida had her reasons for painting that way, and I know Peter had his. The idea of painting made me sick.

Everyone was kind to me, but if I talked about Alba and went on about her it made them uneasy. So I asked Shannon her schedule and drove to the Barista Coffee stand every day to talk with her, because she didn't mind it when I talked a lot about Alba, and she didn't care if I was fifty years older than she was, and no matter what I said it didn't bother her. One day Shannon told me about Fitzpatrick, who had moved in with her a month ago. "He began hanging around," she said. "He delivers supplies for Barista. I told him, Listen, I'm not going to rearrange my place. I keep a photo of my husband in my living room and another in my bedroom, right by the bed. He says, I'm all right with that. Then he asks me, What do you want? So I told him and he says, I understand. — He thinks he does, but he doesn't," she added.

"What do you want?" I asked her.

"I want my old life back."

"Nobody understands that," I said.

"Nobody understands a fucking thing. Like at the funeral they all say, Just give me a call if you need anything. Then they disappear and I'm supposed to call up and plead with them for help. Why the hell don't they fucking phone me? What are they afraid of?"

"They're afraid the person they love most might die." I stood at the end of the counter, looking down the street at the traffic. I asked what her husband's name was.

"Robert," she said. "Everyone called him Bob or Bobby, but I called him Robert, his real name. We did everything together. He was the best person I ever knew. — Here, I'll show you," she said, taking out her phone. She flicked through some photos, then handed me the phone — big smile on his face, reddish-gold hair, striped rugby shirt.

"He's handsome," I said. "And so young. What did you do at the beginning, after he died?"

Before Shannon could answer, a guy with a computer backpack stopped by, bought a coffee, went off.

"After three months I got this job," she said. "I was running out of money and you can't pay the rent with food stamps. At night I wrote him letters. I wrote every night. I have a stack this big. Have you tried writing her letters?" she asked me.

"Only notes. Just two or three sentences."

"Whatever works," she said.

A letter arrived from Leo Conti to remind me that some time ago I had said, yes, he could come out to look at my work with an eye to showing it in his gallery. Now he was wondering if I had finished those pieces which, he said, had sounded so wonderfully interesting to him, and when should he visit my studio. Leo is short and rather round, while his wife Elena is tall, large-boned, and rather handsome. They had come to the memorial service. That day he was in a black suit with a broad black necktie, but he wasn't wearing one of his assorted wigs and at first I didn't recognize him. He looked up at me searchingly for a long moment, sad bags under his eyes, then dropped his head and said nothing. His wife said, "We're so sorry, so very sorry, we loved her." I assured her that Alba had loved them, too.

If Leo died they'd need a giant corkscrew to dig his grave, the man is so crooked. He also has a true eye for talent and if he likes your work he finds people to buy it. Leo Conti had built a successful accounting firm (Conti, Cronin, Stein & Bradford) and then, maybe fifteen years ago, he sold his share to his partners and opened a large gallery in a former automobile repair shop in East Cambridge — cement floor, glass-brick windows and a mile of wall space. Alba told me Conti wanted to be known as a patron of the arts, not an accountant, and she said he liked my work and would probably take it. At the time, I was seventy and making an assault on the top Newbury Street galleries, trying to get back to where I had been when I had a name, so I avoided Conti and told Alba I wouldn't show in his morgue unless I was dead.

But, you know, I was dying by inches and had nothing to lose, so I invited him to my studio. He arrived in a white cotton jacket with broad rose stripes, a pink necktie, platform shoes and a head of fake curly black hair. He liked what he saw. In fact, he was crazy about my work. But the building that housed his gallery was being sold, he said, and he hadn't found a new place yet, was going broke and was doubtful about fitting me into his schedule. So I volunteered to pay for the advertising and reception and — *surprise!* — he fit me into his schedule. What I mean by crooked is that on the day my show opened I learned that Leo Conti owned the building and he was the one selling it, was making big money on the deal, and could have paid for everything a thousand times. But I must add that he found buyers and, subtracting what I had given him, I still made more from that single exhibit than I had in the previous five years combined.

After the exhibit, Leo told me he was planning to move his gallery to Boston and, in fact, to locate on Newbury Street — "Not exactly *on* Newbury, not geographically speaking, but 'off Newbury,' as they say, meaning around the corner, more or less." Six months later the Conti Gallery opened south of the South End, which is in Boston all right, but geographically farther from Newbury Street than when he was in East Cambridge. I exhibited with him there and again a few years later when he cut the distance to Newbury in half by moving his gallery to Back Bay, and I always made good sales. We had lunch maybe six months before Alba — before when, before — and I talked about some new works I had completed and that's when he told me he was angling for a place on Newbury Street. I asked him if he meant on Newbury Street *geographically*. He looked injured. "Yes, yes," he said, leaning back in his chair, his hand over his heart. "What do you take me for?" he asked. I didn't say.

Now I went out to my studio to look around again. The air

in there was dead. Photographs of Alba waited on the shelf by my table. They refer to her but are not her. I looked at the big flat crate which held the three paintings that had been going to the Worcester show. I pried it open and hauled out the first stretcher and leaned it against the wall. I tried to view it, but the paint was meaningless and looking at it made me a little sick, so I slid it back into the crate and walked back to the house. I wrote a letter to Leo Conti, thanked him for asking about my work and told him I'd write again later. I couldn't paint and didn't want to.

I could not believe in the loving God and be true to Alba, so God was swept away and I stayed with Alba. Alba loved me and loved our children. God could have taken instruction from her.

We met when she was fourteen and I was seventeen. I was stacking crates of fish and ice on a dock in Newburyport when she came walking by with her arms full of long-stemmed flowers wrapped in green tissue paper. She asked me, Where's the *Saint Raphael*? and I pointed to where it was tied up and told her, That's it, the *Saint Raphael*, and she walked on. She came back later with the flowers gone and she looked at me, put her hand up to shade her eyes and looked at me, and I said, Renato Stillamare. She smiled — she had green-hazel eyes and the bridge of her nose was sunburned — then she looked away and kept walking. That evening I saw her out strolling with two other girls on the breakwater and when they saw me they nudged each other and giggled. The next night she was walking on the breakwater alone and I said, Hi, and she said, Hi, and I said, How old are you? and she said, Almost fifteen, and I laughed and said, Is that the same as fourteen? She looked off at the horizon and drew a strand of hair from her eyes, tucked it behind her ear and walked away. I caught up with her and said,

Please, I really like you, I like you. So we walked along together and that's the way it began.

We went for walks and we talked. Her parents grew flowers and had a flower shop. I told her I was going to art school in September, because I was good at drawing and wanted to be an artist. She was good at languages and said she wanted to be a diplomat and travel abroad. We lay in the freshly mowed hayfield up back of her house, the stubble sharp and prickly. I had never made love before, but I let her think I knew what I was doing and we blundered through it. The next night she told me, I'm still bleeding. I didn't know what to do and we lay in the field with our arms around each other. After two days she stopped bleeding and we made love in the field every night, even if it was raining, and when we'd get up she'd rake her hand through her hair to comb out the bits of straw. She told me the secret Algonquin name she had named herself: Ka-gi-gi, the raven. I would think of her while I was working and the first moment I'd see her in the evening I'd feel so strange, as if I had stepped off the dock and was falling, and I thought I was going crazy and was relieved when September came, because she went back to high school and I went off to the School of the Museum of Fine Arts in Boston.

The other day I began by writing *Dear Alba* at the top, but it was impossible. As a matter of fact, I can't write you if I use stationery, which is why I've been using notepaper. All I want to say is they are re-doing Nadeau's Grocery. They've pushed out the back wall so it's bigger inside and they're putting in a new tile floor and bright lights everywhere. It looks a lot brighter. I know this is trivial and stupid, but I kept thinking Oh, I should tell Alba about this. Now I'm back from Nadeau's so I'm writing you this note. Don't worry, I know this is crazy.

Scott phoned and asked did I want to have lunch someday this week. We ate at the Kitchen Table Restaurant, and when the waitress took our orders she told me, rather crisply, "Maybe you can finish your sandwich this time. You need to eat more." She was the thin one, middle-aged, named Lilian. I ordered only a half-sandwich, anyway. After she left, Scott asked me, "You come here often?"

"Not really," I said.

"She's right, you should eat more."

"I'm never hungry."

Scott hesitated, seemed about to speak, but didn't say anything. I told him, "You can't make up your mind whether to be sympathetic or critical."

"I think I'll change the subject," he said. "What do you want to talk about — sports, politics, philosophy, war, peace, the economy? How about the economy? What happened to money?"

"I haven't been keeping up with anything."

Scott sat back in his chair and studied me a moment. "How have you been?" he asked.

"I'm OK, I'm getting by. What about yourself?"

"Me?" He looked surprised. "I'm all right. My ankles were getting swollen, but my doctor reduced my blood-pressure medication and I'm fine now."

We talked about our blood-pressure medication until our waitress arrived with Scott's bratwurst and potato pancakes, and my half-sandwich which they'd purposely overstuffed. I remembered he had attended a conference in Boston a week ago, so I asked him about that. He made a brisk, dismissive gesture, as if brushing something away. "Papers and discussion groups on artificial intelligence, computers and thinking machines," he said. "Philosophers and mathematicians, mostly."

His career began in philosophy and took a turn into symbolic logic, and from there it branched into mathematics, thence computers and artificial intelligence. Now Scott, being Scott, quickly become bored by the conference discussion groups, so he went out to visit the neighborhood where he had grown up. That was Mattapan, which I should tell you is as far down the map as you can go and still be in Boston.

"I hadn't been down Blue Hill Avenue for fifty years," he told me. "And I knew I shouldn't go, but I was curious so I went. After the exodus, you know, the blacks moved in. African Americans, I mean. And Caribbeans." He paused and thought a moment. "It was a wonderful place to grow up in, years ago. And the street was lined with interesting stores and little shops. Sort of urban, but haimish. The past is memories," he decided.

It was on the tip of my tongue to tell him otherwise, but I said, "What did you do at the conference. You gave a talk, right? So how did it go?"

"Went well, I'm told." He shrugged. "Big discussion on free will. My point was that we don't have free will and if we ever get around to building a machine that thinks, it won't have free will, either."

"Are grown-up philosophers still arguing about free will? We did that in high school. No wonder you got bored. — By the way, I have free will unless someone puts a gun to my head."

"We disagree about that. — But the important thing is that I visited the scenes of my childhood. My past is intact. I have memories."

"Well-meaning people tell me I have memories of Alba. They think that's a comfort to me. They don't know what the fuck they're talking about."

"You have —" he began.

I cut him off. "If I didn't have children, I wouldn't believe I'd ever met her."

He looked at me. "I won't argue with your feelings," he said.

"Thank you."

"But you were married to a brilliant woman for —"

"The past doesn't exist, Scott."

"Time goes by fast, much too fast. I understand that. But it was at least fifty years and you know those were good years."

"The past doesn't exist. Haven't you noticed? It's gone. That's why we call it the past. It's not real anymore."

"What you had with Alba —"

"It has no more reality than a wish," I told him. "It's a romantic fiction."

He started to speak but changed his mind, shutting his mouth so abruptly I heard his teeth snap together. Looking back, I see that Scott was remarkably patient with me, for he believed wholly in reason and I was clearly mindless. His father had been a linotype operator for a Boston newspaper, his mother a Trotskyite and later a worker for the Democratic Party, and Scott had grown up a secular humanist — "a tribe without a God," he liked to say. Scott was a good guy.

It was strange to live alone, to embrace no one and to have no one put her arms around me, and sometimes it felt like my nerves were on the outside, aching to be soothed, or inside like it was thirst. But it wasn't thirst or pain, it was loneliness. Lucy Dolan who had done babysitting for us was now in her mid-fifties but still slender and straight, and at Vanderzee's exhibit she had given me a tight warm hug that lingered, the way vibrations linger after you strike the nerve strings.

I liked Shannon. I'd buy a cup of coffee, then stand under the leaky awning to watch the cars going by in the rain and talk with her between customers. She showed me she had moved her wedding ring to her right hand. "Because if I keep it where it was, people will think I'm married to Fitz and I don't want anybody to think that. I wanted to keep wearing it on my left hand at least, but it only fits my ring finger, so I had to move it to my other hand."

I told her I never had a wedding ring, but hers was beautiful, I said.

"Yeah, I know," Shannon said. "I told him not to waste the money but he insisted. The emeralds make it different."

"My wife's ring is in a little velvet bag on her bureau. I never knew her fingers were so slender. It's a small plain gold ring. That's all. With our initials inside."

"I have a friend whose husband died last year and she wears his ring on a necklace chain," Shannon said.

"That's something."

"It hangs down, you know, so it's over her heart."

When I got home I looked through Alba's jewelry and found a silver chain and put her ring on the chain and wore it. It hangs down to my breastbone. It's comforting and whenever I want I can touch it.

Before sunset I always go for a walk the way we used to at that gentle hour. It's a roundabout walk and halfway along it crosses through a field with a creek and a margin of tall grass where red-winged blackbirds nest and wild flowers grow, and eventually the path goes beside Franklin's Four Seasons, the flower nursery. Alba always took an interest in what was blossoming in the greenhouses. Then the path rises up a little slope to where we would have to lift the branches of a birch and duck under to go out the street and so to the road where we lived. Now I would remember how sometimes her hair would catch on those branches and I tried to recall just how her dress would swing as she stepped ahead. If she was here with me on these walks, all those times — and she was, she was — then I don't understand how she cannot be. You cannot be at one moment and then not be at the next.

Q. What is man?

A. Man is a creature composed of body and soul, and made to the image and likeness of God.

Q. Is this likeness in the body or in the soul?

A. This likeness is chiefly in the soul.

Q. How is the soul like to God?

A. The soul is like to God because it is a spirit that will never die, and has understanding and free will.

I understood all that. I knew what my body was and what my mind was and my personality and my character, but I didn't know what my soul was and I began to wonder about that. One day I was watching my father work on a grave marker, a rare artistic job that only he and none of the two or three workers he hired could do, because it had a butterfly carved at the top and a border of pomegranates to the left and right of the inscription, old symbols of resurrection. After a while, I asked him what the soul was. He removed his safety glasses and rubbed the two pink indents that the glasses had pinched on the bridge of his nose. He smiled a bit. "I think that's a question for your mother." I told him I had already asked her. He hesitated, then said, "Well, there's your uncle Zitti. He talks about his soul as easily as other men talk about their digestion." He put on his safety glasses and took up the chisel again, then turned to me. "Or you could ask your uncle Nicolo," he added. "He has opinions about the soul, too."

Uncle Nicolo had a big book with illustrations by Gustave Doré which Nick and I used to take from the bookcase and open on the floor to look at — dark and frightening scenes, like those naked men trapped in the ice of a frozen lake, one man gnawing on the bald head of another, or that naked woman who was twisted around, pulling out her own hair. Those were the damned being tortured forever in Hell, which was the first part of Dante's long poem. The second part was Purgatory where people got horribly punished, but after doing penance for their sins they were admitted into Paradise, which was the third part of the poem. The pictures of Hell were the ones we looked at most, because they were so gruesome and because everyone was naked there, unlike in Paradise where the souls wore clothes. The souls were really souls and not bodies, but Gustave Doré drew the bodies to show how the souls in Hell felt horrible pain forever, which Nick and I thought was terribly unfair of God, because forever was way too long a time even if they had sinned when they had been alive, but it did give you an idea of how cruel God could be when he wanted.

A few years later, Nick said he didn't believe in souls. We were walking with Veronica, coming back from the field where Sandro used to fly his hawk and where Dante and Mercurio used to shoot, but now uncle Nicolo had a Victory Garden there because of the war. We were crossing the old burying ground when Nick announced, "Frankly, I don't believe in souls." Maybe that was because his father was an aeronautical engineer at MIT and didn't believe much in religion. But Veronica said she was sure we had souls. "We have understanding and free will, which is what the soul has, and the part of us that has understanding and free will, that's the soul part." She smiled, waiting for us to see how clear and obvious it was, but I still wasn't sure if I believed in souls or not.

Nick said, "Oh, no. Because if you believe in a soul you have to believe in heaven and hell, and maybe heaven is all right, but what about hell? Do you really truly believe in hell?"

Veronica didn't answer and we walked along and climbed over the low stone wall into the backyard. "So what if there's a hell," she said lightly. "Nobody actually goes there anymore."

Some days when Shannon wasn't at the Barista stand I'd swing around to the Daily Grind to see Gordon and we'd talk about the strangeness of life or what was wrong with politicians or the Red Sox, but today he talked mostly about whether he should look for a shop with more floor space. He missed the old place in Boston, which was larger, but he liked Lexington "because this town is full of intellectuals who drink coffee all day." Here he was on the main street, but if he moved to a bigger place it would be farther from the center of town. On the other hand, if he had more floor space he could serve more people and sell more Rancilio espresso machines — but there was a lot to be said for staying in the same place, because the Daily Grind, having been here ten years, "now these fussy people know where to come to buy Hawaiian Kona or Monsoon Malabar." So Gordon went from this side to that side, debating with himself while we worked on the ancient coffee roaster, until eventually it was fixed and I held the fancy front end while he bolted it back into place. We must have talked an hour, and all that time I was able to forget who I was.

It betrays Alba to say she has died or she is dead and I say it only because that's what people can understand. I believe Alba will never die, that she has understanding and free will, and that she knows me. I would like to die and be united with her forever, the way we were. I don't know what I believe.

I drove to La Pâtisserie and bought two plain croissants, just so I could have twelve minutes of bright chat at the pastry case with Fern (twenty-five, welcoming smile, warm white arms, and a flower in her hair), but she could not rescue me so I drove away, ashamed of myself, to Café Mondello to buy a latte so I could chat up Felicia (twenty-one, blue jeans and a tight white top with a blue dab of shadow under each nipple), after which I drove home, horribly alone and feeling like shit. I do things like that every day.

One time I was having lunch with Scott and he asked what I was doing these days, and I said, "Not much, really."

"Have you been painting?"

"No. No painting."

He nodded, as if in agreement with me. "It's too early. You need more time. A little more time."

"What's the point?"

"What do you mean?" he asked.

"I mean, what's the purpose of all this — all this living, this going on? I really don't understand. I'm serious. What's the point?"

"That's a rather large question. Whole philosophies have been built —"

I cut him off. "It's not a philosophical question for me. It's in my guts. I don't understand what the fuck I'm doing here. Why am I doing whatever I do? I ask myself that every shitty day. *What's the goddamn point?*"

Scott shifted uneasily in his chair, then he looks at me a moment and says, "Did you enjoy your sandwich? Your half-sandwich, I mean."

"I guess so, yes."

"Were you enjoying our conversation?"

"Yes, sure."

"That's the point."

"*That's* the point?"

"Yes."

❦

I drifted from room to room (nothing out of place, the books in a row, the pillows smooth, the empty chairs at a conversational angle) and I realized I'm the ghost haunting this house — I'm dead and Alba is alive and this world is an illusion I have because I'm dead.

❦

Danae and Chiara will be away at college soon, so before they go they came here to be with their grandfather for the day

— you're right, Alba, we're fortunate to have such grandchildren. We were driving on Great Meadow Road after a shower when we saw a big rainbow and of course they wanted to take pictures of it, so I pulled into the parking lot at the playing fields and they took phone photos. The rainbow was large and seemed to hang in the air above the faraway soccer fields and I kept wishing I had my camera so I could send you a photo of it. That's what I mean by crazy.

It's a privilege to love someone and I loved Alba. "I'm so happy you found me," she used to say. I was handsome, her man from the sea, and the one she loved best in the whole world. She's gone, so I'm not handsome anymore. I'm an old man driving home with a pizza and I'm sobbing because some cheerful asshole is singing on the radio about his love who is gone beyond the sea and the moon and stars, but she's waiting and watching for him, and someday he'll find her there on the shore and they'll be together and he'll embrace her, just as he did before. When the song was over I stopped sniveling, blew my nose, drove back onto the road and got home in one piece.

Can you follow this goddamn story? I know it's a jumbled mess but it's what I can recall, and also some notes I wrote to Alba, plus unconnected pieces. Parts are missing and some of them may be important, but they're missing because I don't remember, or because I do remember and don't want to. I want to write about that first year, though I don't know why I want to do even that much. I'm blundering ahead, like our moronic blundering Creator.

I had figured Shannon to be forty years old — it turned out she was only thirty-three, younger than my kids and not way older than my grandkids, but her getting kicked around had added another seven years to her face. Her father owned The Copper Kettle in Charlestown and Shannon liked to brag she had grown up in a bar. Her father died when she was thirteen. When she was sixteen and pregnant she came home from school one day to find her clothes and the other ten things she owned had been dumped in a cardboard box outside the back door, which is what her mother had always threatened to do. Her mother, who used to call Shannon *The Disgrace*, died about five years ago, refusing to allow Shannon into her hospice room. Shannon dropped out of high school to have the baby and never went back, so she has that seventeen-year-old daughter, plus a teenage son from a later marriage — he's living with his father — and a daughter Robert brought with him when they married. Fitzpatrick, the guy living with her now, has a son and daughter he visits every other weekend. Fitz's ex is a bitch, Shannon tells me. "He's got hardly no money left to live on. I can't pay my rent. That's why we're living together," she says. "Pooling resources."

"It's only a matter of money?" I asked her.

"You mean do I love him? No. — Oh, the sex is good, very good, but I don't love him. How could I?"

When I go for a walk, nobody knows where I am. Together or not, Alba knew where I was and I knew where she was. Now I walk down this street and then around the corner and then along a ways and then across the field of brown grass and dried stalks where the wild flowers grew, then beside the old Franklin place and their deserted greenhouses, some of the glass busted, and up to the street. Nobody knows where I am. I've vanished. I can press my hand hard against my parka, press against my chest until I feel Alba's wedding ring in my flesh. That's our secret. My eyes are watery and I don't know if it's the icy wind or my thoughts, but no one's around and anyway it doesn't matter.

If I could slip quietly away, that would be good. My hands are cold and the sunset colorless and I'm here walking by myself or maybe I'm gone.

A letter from Leo Conti arrived, actually not a letter but a sheet from a real-estate agent's book of available properties. It displayed a big lousy color photo of a brownstone building on Newbury Street and a list of the building's basic specifications. On the back of the sheet Leo had written, *What do you think?* Only Leo and his crooked guardian angel know why he sent it to me. Newbury was one of the most expensive streets in the country. What did I think about what? Had he bought the whole damn building? Had he signed a lease for one rotten floor? Was he trying to make up his mind about where to move his gallery? I crumpled the paper and lobbed it into the kitchen wastebasket. I sent Leo a one-word postcard — *Excellent!* — which I figured would make him happy.

Nils Petersen and Hanna had returned from the Netherlands and now the DeCordova was showing some of Nils' work in an exhibit of artists' books — which is when an artist, such as Nils, makes a book out of folded paper or sheet metal or, for that matter, crispy toast, or takes a regular book and does things to it. I was happy he was making artists' books and no longer producing computer art, which I've always believed is shit without the smell. Of course, writers say that artists' books are just another way to destroy the printed word, but writers are born complaining, and at least these things are made by hand to live and die in this world, not cyberspace. Avalon and Sebastian were going, so I went with them. It was good to be with Hanna and Nils again and to have a relaxed conversation about one thing and another. Scott was there with his wife Rachel, which was good, because she has wandering pains and tends to get desperately anxious when she leaves the house. Vanderzee came with Gail and Winona, and eleven-year-old Saskia. Scott and I talked for a while and set up a lunch date at a new place called Fête Champêtre, which he said had good food despite the rococo name. And other friends and acquaintances turned up, like Barbabianco and his wife, then Tom Hay and his wife, and George Agathos and his wife, but I was getting more and more aware of Renato without his wife, so I was grateful when Avalon and Sebastian said they were ready to leave.

I carved a jack-o'-lantern for Halloween, filled a bowl with small candies, and let the neighborhood kids take however much they wanted while their parents stood at the edge of the road with flashlights, calling a cheerful, "Thank you!" as they all trooped away. Clearly, I'm learning to do things without thinking, which is good. A while later, I hauled the trash barrel out, big stupid Orion overhead, meaning it's going to get colder and darker for longer and longer.

"But what is the purpose of life?" uncle Zitti asked. That was at Thanksgiving at his house in 1949. He was back from a trip to Italy where he had taken care of his mother's property, for she had died that summer and maybe the visit to the graves of his mother and father had brought those thoughts to mind. "We're so busy living, we don't think about that," he said.

I caught the scent of Veronica's lily-of-the-valley perfume and felt her warm breath on my ear as she whispered, Here comes some philosophy.

We were a dozen people and dinner was finished, but no one had left the table — the glossy white linen was a disordered landscape of forgotten forks, nutcrackers, rumpled napkins, dessert bowls, chestnuts, ropes of dried figs, broken walnut shells, and those little paper boxes that Torrone came in, boxes with old-fashioned portraits of famous Italians. Three or four conversations were crisscrossing at once while everyone had another cup of coffee or another glass of wine. Zitti, who had been born in the Abruzzi and brought to this country by his parents when he was thirteen, was saying, "The top of the church tower was shot away and the *municipio* — you know, the mayor's building, across the square from the church — it looked like it had been used for target practice. Other than that, no change. Even the smells were the same." He smiled, remembering the smells. Then he must have thought again of his mother, his face somber once more. He sighed and said, "I should have gone back a year earlier."

Aunt Candida, his wife, said, "Zitti, please! How could you have known? They could have told you. *Ma ne anche una parola.* She could have written."

"Life —" Zitti began, then hesitated.

"It doesn't do any good to blame yourself," Candida told him, leaving to answer the phone that had begun to ring.

My father had put two walnuts in his palm and now he gently and carefully closed his fist, cracking them but not crushing them. He wasn't engaged in the conversation, because his mother and father had died when he was nineteen and death didn't interest him.

Candida returned, telling us that Mercurio said he'd be here in time for dessert. Uncle Zitti glanced at her without saying that we'd already finished dessert, and she replied, "There's still some pumpkin pie and spumoni."

"I wonder if Coral will be coming with him," my mother said.

We all knew that Mercurio and Coral weren't getting along.

"I didn't dare ask," Candida said.

My father opened his hand and began to pick out the pieces of shattered shell.

"This French philosopher, Albert Camus, he thinks life is absurd," Zitti said. "Absurd and with no purpose."

"We make up purposes as we go along," Nicolo said. "We keep changing the purpose, but the important thing is to have a purpose, a goal. Making progress toward our goal give us pleasure, and as soon as we get there, we discover another goal, further ahead."

Aunt Marissa, his wife, said, "Always going and never arriving. I don't know if that's so good."

"The purpose of life is to work," my father declared. "Work saves more souls than Jesus."

Zitti continued, "Camus says that death makes life absurd and pointless."

"You think your mother's life was pointless?" Candida asked him.

"I didn't say that. We're talking about Camus' beliefs, not mine."

"Camus is absurd," Candida murmured.

"Maybe the poor man has no family life," my mother suggested.

Zitti shrugged and opened his hands, palms up, to show he didn't know what to make of any of this. "Or maybe he says those things simply because he's French."

"You detest the French," Veronica said. "So why do you make me take French if you feel that way?"

Zitti looked at her a moment, clearly surprised. "The purpose of life is to have children," he announced to us. "That's the goal." He smiled and glanced around the table. "And we're all doing very well. *In vino veritas!*" he said, raising his empty glass. "Is there any left in that bottle or should I get another?"

Nick, across the table from me, gave me a look and tilted his head toward the door, suggesting we could escape. Veronica's brother Jason and my brother Bart had already been excused, but we were older and had to stay longer. I drained the wine from my glass and then pushed my chair back from the table.

"Where are you going?" Veronica whispered, pinching my arm.

"We're going upstairs to tear the dresses off your dolls and play doctor," I whispered. "Like we used to."

Veronica spoke up. "Can we be excused?" she asked, speaking to no one in particular.

"Take some dishes into the kitchen when you go," Candida told her.

Veronica chose the platter of turkey bones from the sideboard. Nick and I picked up our coffee cups, wineglasses, loose silverware. We three went to the jumbled kitchen, dropped everything into the crowded sink and went out the door to the backyard. The sky was a clean light blue and the air was chilly. Bart and Jason were tossing a basketball at the hoop over the garage door. Nick took out a pack of cigarettes, offered me one. "What about me?" Veronica said.

Nick laughed. "You're too young. It will stunt your growth," he said.

"I smoke all the time," she retorted.

"Oh, sure," I said.

"Let me take a puff," she said.

So I give her my cigarette and let her have a few puffs. We three walked around to the front and sat on the steps in the sun.

"I miss Nanna and Nonno's big house," Veronica said. "I liked how everybody used to go there when we were kids. I miss that."

"Nonno had to sell it," Nick said. "He had no money left after the war."

"I might go visit Nanna in the villa in Palermo," Veronica said.

"I bet Mercurio drives up without Coral," Nick said.

"I bet he drives up in his red MG," I said.

"Let me have another puff on your cigarette," Veronica said.

I had never wondered what the purpose of life was and for a while after that Thanksgiving dinner, whenever I did think about it, I figured that you lived life and that was all there was to it. Uncle Zitti's questions were puzzlers and often confusing, but uncle Nicolo's answers were understandable, like common sense. Zitti told me more than once that the unexamined life isn't worth living but I was nineteen and, the way I looked at it, you couldn't examine life and live it at the same time. I was taking courses at the School of the Museum of Fine Arts and living in Boston, in Back Bay, in my own room and on my own, and I was meeting women, not fourteen-year-old kids like Alba, and I was painting like crazy, so there was no time to examine life — that was something you might do later, maybe when you were forty years old and getting philosophical. I was living it and that's the way I liked it.

Zitti and Nicolo and my father Fidèle married three Cavallù sisters — Zitti to Candida, Nicolo to Marisa, and my father to Bianca. My father, Nicolo, and Zitti had happy marriages and enjoyed each other's company. Nicolo, a calm and gentle man, had a head as bald as the dome at MIT where he was a professor of aeronautical engineering. He was also an amateur balloonist and the author of a book on electronic orbits (highly regarded when it was published), which was rendered obsolete by quantum mechanics a year later. As a kid working in his father's grocery store, he kept Volume 1 of the 1889 edition of the *Encyclopædia Britannica* under the counter to read between customers. Zitti, a lively man with sparkling eyes, always about to break into a smile, was a professor of philosophy, inventor of an onomatopoetic language, and author of the epic poem *Luna*, about a voyage on the moon through those dark seas discovered by Galileo. As an immigrant kid, one of his jobs was to climb down into railroad tank cars with a hose and a scrub brush to wash the inside. My father, who for no particular reason would sing Puccini, or kiss my mother's cheek and pat her behind, had begun in 1920 the college education he longed for, but that same year his father and mother perished in the Influenza Epidemic. He took on his father's uncompleted masonry jobs, then kept at the work to support himself and his younger sister, became a skilled worker in stone, tile and mosaic, and an avid reader.

Those two uncles had opposing ideas about everything, including education, so when I enrolled in the Museum School they began to send me books and reading lists. From Nicolo, I still have Watts and Rule's lovely little book *Descriptive Geometry*, and Sears' *Principles of Physics*, and from Zitti, Ovid's *Metamorphoses* in Latin, plus a translation made by Arthur Golding in 1567, and a paperback edition of Castiglione's *The Book of the Courtier*. The Courtier's ideal man was athletic and bold, but even-tempered and equally good at conversation, horsemanship and poetry, so the book was a useful and practical guide, my uncle insisted, though I doubted anything written in the sixteenth century could help me much. Above all, I should strive for the Courtier's "*sprezzatura*," a wonderful word, uncle Zitti told me, that means exactly what it sounds like — nonchalance, spirit and grace, making hard things look easy. I've failed at that, too.

I walked out for a cup of coffee with the sky gray as ice on one side and already black on the other. In the cold I keep up a good pace, better than most people my age. My mother's great-grandfather was born with the hindquarters of a horse and though I'm adopted it's possible one of his rash animalistic progeny fathered me, which would be why I was left on that doorstep and why I have these legs. Alba always liked those family stories but now she's gone, so the stories don't make sense anymore. The trees are empty, exposing the bare houses. One of the shutters on the empty Franklin house is hanging upside down from the bottom hinge. I'm walking to a cup of coffee even though it will taste like yesterday's piss, so I should admit to myself that I'm going there simply to be around people but, to show I'm not a lonely old man, I'll leave after twenty minutes. Then comes the bleak walk home in the dark and I'll wonder again what the hell I'm doing here, walking alone and to where and what for.

❦

I bumped into Lucy Dolan in Cambridge in front of a delicatessen, so we went in and had lunch. She looked very good, maybe because of her bright quilted jacket and scarf, or maybe because the cold made her cheeks glow. She had come from a store auction, hoping to buy second-hand equipment for the bakery she planned to open

"Everything costs more than I can afford," she said, almost laughing. "And I mean the second-hand stuff — the new equipment is beyond-belief expensive."

I asked where she planned to have her shop.

"That's the other thing that's expensive, floor space. I want to be near Boston, but rents are so high I have to look farther and farther away. I've been asking Meg for advice. She's had that shop for years. Right now I'm living at my friend Alison's and I dread the thought of having to move from the city. — I prefer people to cows and trees," she added.

We talked about city life and country life and Lucy told me about her daughter, Jenny, who had found a job as a technical writer. "She majored in Environmental Science but she's a technical writer for a bioengineering company. I suppose she's lucky to have any kind of job in this economy." We agreed the economy was lousy and that the rich got richer and the poor got poorer, then we ordered lunch, talked about the small-size shop she was looking for, and when our sandwiches arrived she asked was I painting.

"I don't feel like painting."

"You should. You're really good at it."

I said thank you.

"I don't mean you should paint if you don't want to," she emended. "I mean, you're good at it and it would be great if you did feel like painting." She hesitated. "It must be terrible.

I mean, she was —" She broke off. "How are you?" she asked.

"I'm all right. I wish I didn't cry so much."

"I cry at least five times a week."

"Oh? What's going on in your life?" I asked.

"No, no," she said, touching my wrist reassuringly. "I'm really all right. After working fifteen years in somebody else's bakery I'm about to open my own shop and everything's too damned expensive. But I had a double major, English and Classics, so I'm prepared." She laughed. "Now tell me about Skye and Astrid and Brizio and what they're doing."

So I told her about my children and we talked and talked and she told me about San Francisco and Monterey ("Nobody thinks very hard out there. Everything's on the back burner. I may be baking bread, but I still like to read and think about things.") and about her marriage ("It wasn't toxic like some I've seen. We just got worn down until nothing was left. Maybe it was my baby being born and dying the next day, maybe it was Jenny with colic when we lived in a one-room cabin, or maybe it was Alaska or his job, or maybe it was me.") and about Jacob Bergstrom, the only father she knew ("It was easy enough for me to choose him, but amazing that he could he be so caring to somebody else's twelve-year-old kid.")

I confess that all the while she talked, I saw how good she looked, neither young nor old despite the finely etched lies around her eyes, and when she laughed it was dazzling.

Jacob — she always called him by his first name — was her mother's second husband, the wedding taking place when Lucy was five years old. Then one day in June when Lucy was twelve, her mother took her on a long automobile ride to Saratoga, in Upstate New York, where she had already secured a job on a newspaper, and she explained to Lucy that they were going to live in Saratoga from now on because Jacob was a loser, just like Lucy's father had been — and besides, her mother's old college friend from years ago lived in nearby Albany and he would be nice to them. Lucy lived with her mother in Saratoga that summer, but in September, when school was about to begin, Lucy bought a bus ticket to Albany, and from Albany she bought another to Springfield, halfway across Massachusetts, which used up almost all the money she had. She phoned Jacob from Springfield and told him she was coming home but had run out of money and could he please come and get her at the Greyhound bus station, so he drove to the bus station in Springfield and brought her back to his house, her bedroom, and her school friends. We never knew what the legal arrangements were, but Lucy, who began to spell her name Luci, grew up as Jacob Bergstrom's daughter and when she was a junior in high school we asked Luci, or Lucia Bergstrom as she then called herself, to do babysitting for us. As for Jacob, he was knocked down by a brain hemorrhage while at his desk in the cataloging department of the North Shore Library, shortly after Lucy had started her senior year in college, so she returned home to take care of him until he died nine months later.

Now as we got ready to leave the delicatessen, we were talking again about her bakery shop and pies or cookies or other delicacies, and I was raving about Italian pastries, throwing my hands around, when she caught me by my wrist and laughed and said, "If I tied your hands you wouldn't be able to say a word, you're so Italian."

"Sicilian, actually," I said, knowing only how warm her hand was.

I woke up having a wet dream about Susan Salter, or what passes for a wet dream at eighty-something. I hardly know the woman. She was Alba's colleague, not mine — bright, vivacious, and lots of jingling bracelets — so here she is rolling me onto my back and getting into the saddle. Wide awake now, just me and not much to mop up, almost nothing at all. I shaved and showered and was thinking of Alba and how she could explain me in a way that made sense, which is what I desperately need when I'm this confused.

❦

I should go back and write more about Fletcher and Katherine. Kate teaches literature at a community college and Fletch is a surrealist poet, if that means anything, a part-time novelist and the owner-editor of Prospero's Books, a small press that turns out maybe three books a year. I've never asked how they survive. They live in a three-story house with a wraparound porch and a jumble of rooms, some bedrooms, of course, but others with sports equipment and old-fashioned bookbinding gear or musical instruments, and a carriage house out back with cartons of books, and a tree house which must have been fun for their kids who are now grown up and have kids of their own. During one of those numb days after Alba was gone, Fletch brought me his wooden clamps and we repaired a chair. It took all my effort to focus on what we were doing as my vision shrank to a small circle no bigger than my two hands and there was a continuous rushing sound in my head. They invited me to dinner one evening, the three of us dining on soup and thick bread in their warm kitchen. It was a comfort and at the same time painful, because Fletch and Kate were our age and deeply enjoyed each other's company — I mean, I returned to this empty house and drifted from room to room, pulling down the shades until I was back in the kitchen, feeling lower than whale shit and stupidly puzzled that Alba wasn't here anymore.

❦

I told Shannon I'd have an espresso. She began banging coffee grounds out of the portafilter (angrily, I thought) and told me — BANG! BANG! — she was pissed because she had to sell her pickup truck, because her grandfather needed round-the-clock — BANG! BANG! — care.

"Round-the-clock is expensive," I said.

"It's fuckin' impossible," Shannon said. "He doesn't want to leave his home. He's seventy-eight. What can you do?"

I shrugged and told her I could understand her grandfather feeling that way.

"We were keeping the truck like money in the bank," Shannon said. "It was like savings. When I sell the truck we'll have nothing left. It's a good vehicle. It was one of our best things. You want spice cake with this?"

"Not this time."

"A red Nissan Titan with 110,000 miles on it," she continued. "Robert bought it new, for work, and we went everywhere in it, down the Cape and up to Montreal. I still keep his tools and things in it." Then she went silent and attended to my coffee, her face closed. "I like the way it smells," she added. "You get inside and slam the door and you feel like going places." She gave me the little espresso cup which I held in both hands to warm my fingers. "If I don't take care of my grandfather, who will? No one, that's who," she said.

My kids were coming with their families for the Christmas holidays, so I did what they asked me to do. I got a tree, and the giant who owns the farm down the road helped me set it upright in the stand. The next morning I climbed into the attic and brought down the boxes and big cartons of Christmas gear that Alba and I had wrapped and put away a year ago. That evening I strung the lights and hung all the sparkling ornaments, even those little gold balls that we got for our first little tree, though the paint was flaking away from inside the glass and we hadn't used them for years. When I had finished hanging the last of the icicles, I turned off the living room lamps, and in the dark I turned on the tree lights. And here's Renato, gathering up the empty boxes and sobbing, stumbling over a carton and landing on the sofa to bawl, because it had been so hard to do all this all alone, and now the tree is so beautiful, soft and quiet, but still Alba hasn't come back.

They came for Christmas week, one family at a time. Our Skye and her husband Eric, the perpetually displaced Canadian anthropologist, and their five kids, ranging from nine to twenty-one, came two days before Christmas, and stayed most of the day after Christmas in order to be here when our Brizio — Fabrizio on the birth certificate — and his wife Heather, a true Abenaki without an Abenaki name, arrived with their two boys. Brizio and his family stayed until our Astrid — who persists in calling herself Galaxy in the credits of her documentaries — and her husband Weston and their two kids arrived the day before New Year's Eve, so some family was here through January first. One of our secret pleasures was to be in the next room, fixing this or adjusting that, but all the while listening to our children in the kitchen catching up with each other, talking a mile a minute, laughing and gossiping. Alba and I, we'd exchange a glance, that's all.

Denise, an old friend from when I was single, had married and moved to France, sending us a yearly Christmas card with notes about herself, her husband and their two children. Her husband had died half a year before Alba. When she received the news about Alba, she phoned and we had a good talk. This Christmas her card arrived in January — *Dear Renato, I'm sorry to say the second year isn't any easier than the first, no matter what people tell you. But the children & grandchildren are well. Love, Denise.*

Around sunset the wind stopped, leaving the snow packed hard, the top flat and smooth as a sheet of fine-tooth paper.

I got into my parka and went out to shovel, but first checked my watch because no one was going to call from the door — *Renato, you've worked long enough. I've made hot chocolate!* I had a phone in my coat pocket, in case my heart jammed but left me enough time to gasp for help. The air was like ice, like that first scent of ether before you go under. I shoveled a path from the front door to my car, which I had parked farther down the driveway so I'd have a shorter distance to shovel between the car and the road. When I checked my watch again I was huffing and puffing, so I didn't get to the road. I went in, pulled off my gear, made a mug of hot cocoa for myself and sat at the kitchen table. The window reflected like a black mirror, as if I was outside seeing myself sitting alone, all alone in the lighted kitchen, so I turned off the light and my reflection mercifully disappeared. Now I could see the shed and the smooth snow all the way down to the black woods. I sat in the dark, drinking the cocoa and looking out at the snow and the woods. I wasn't thinking of Alba, or maybe I was, but anyway it felt like tears were coming, so I pulled down the window shade and turned on the light. I didn't know what to do. I went looking through the bookcase for something to read and saw one of my sketchbooks, so I took it back to the kitchen and did a line drawing of the cocoa mug and the place mat with the short fringe. It was a pretty good drawing.

I thought the album cover for *Sgt. Pepper's Lonely Hearts Club Band* was crappy art. My cousin Nick said it was a joke, all those black-and-white pop-photo faces dolled up like waxworks (I still thought it was crappy) and Veronica said the music was the important thing, not the album cover, said her kids liked the music even if they were too young to understand it, and Nick's wife Maeve said that for the first time in her life she was listening to rock and enjoying it, and not only the Beatles — which was what Alba had said five minutes ago. We were sitting on the grass by the old workshop where the faded sign still said *Stillamare's Cut Stone & Tile Company*, because my father continued to cut stone for special jobs. My father and uncle Nicolo and uncle Zitti were playing bocce. Nonno had a bocce court of fine blue gravel, but my father's was good, too, this long flat stretch of grass framed by weathered gray boards laid on their long edges. The balls were the old kind, made of wood, not plastic, so they made the satisfying, familiar *clack* sound when knocked together. It was a warm and drowsy afternoon, the air absolutely still. We had fallen silent, watching them play. Then Nick said, "We've been watching them play this same game for over twenty-five years." Then he lay back with his hands folded under his head and looked up into the tree.

"Don't be rude," Veronica told him. "We hardly ever get together and I like seeing everyone together. And it's never the same game." She shaded her eyes with her hand and watched them play.

"I'm not being rude," Nick said, closing his eyes. "I'm just saying we've watched our fathers play *bocce* for twenty-five years. And in a while my father and your father will talk politics or the meaning of meaning, and they'll ask Renato's father to decide some fine point they can't agree on." He kept his eyes closed.

"If they agreed, they wouldn't have anything to talk about," Maeve said.

At that moment, Zitti and Nicolo were watching while my father was crouched over the pallino, deciding whose ball was closest by sliding two twigs together, side-by-side, until they fit exactly between the pallino and one of the closest balls. Then, holding the twigs fixed, he tested to see if they'd fit or not between the pallino and the other close ball.

"They agree about Vietnam, anyway," Nick said.

Bennett, Veronica's husband, murmured, "Vietnam." He was lying with his eyes shut and his hands folded on his chest and I thought he had fallen asleep, but he was so political he could probably say Vietnam in his sleep.

"It's a beautiful day — why are the kids indoors?" Maeve said.

"Don't ask me," Alba said. "I'm enjoying the heat and not thinking."

Veronica stood up, brushing some stray grass from her dress. "I'm going in to help with the coffee and things." Alba and Maeve got to their feet, saying, "Wait, wait."

Nick sat up and opened his eyes. "The shade from this tree keeps moving away," he informed me. "Can't you do something about that?"

When the bocce game ended we were offered a choice of spumoni or lemon sherbet — that was cried out by Veronica from the kitchen window — along with our coffee and pasticceria. Uncle Zitti and aunt Candida and uncle Nicolo and aunt Marissa gathered the little kids and sat with them at the old plank table under the big maple where my dad and his two or three workmen used to eat their lunch in the summer. The rest of us were sitting on the grass but, naturally, the kids kept wandering from the table to wherever they wanted to go. Alba came carrying a tray with the ice cream and sherbet — a beautiful young woman in a white dress, the top part close-fitting and the bottom part long and flowing. I had lemon sherbet, tart and finely textured with vanishing ice crystals, while Alba chose the spumoni. Later, somebody passed me a plate of Italian cookies which my mother must have bought at a specialty store. "How can you tell if these are stale or not?" I asked.

"Renato," Alba said, a rebuke in her voice that only I could hear.

"All I mean is that they're born hard and taste dry from birth," I told her.

"Oh, is *that* all you mean," she said lightly.

"The French are good at pastry, the Italians are good at the main meal," Nick said.

"Cannoli are as good as anything the French make," Veronica said. "And sfogliatelle, too."

"This would be a nice day to pass a joint around," Nick said.

Bennett suddenly looked alert, even cheerful. "I have some weed in the car."

"He wants to get us arrested," Veronica said. "He thinks pot smoking is a political act. Like long hair."

"Who wants to play bocce?" Nick asked, getting up.

Nick and Bennett drifted off to play bocce, trailed by Maeve and Veronica, and I went to the table to refill my coffee cup. Uncle Zitti was talking about the Big Bang theory. Uncle Nicolo said it wasn't a theory anymore, but a fact. "They've found all that background radiation and it's everywhere," he said. "It's exactly what they predicted would be left after the Creation."

"I like the Steady State theory better," Zitti said. "I like the idea of a universe that always was and always will be, an eternal universe. Like God in the catechism," he added.

"Well, Steady State theory's gone," Nicolo told him. "Now it's all Big Bang and cosmic expansion. In fact, they calculate how fast the universe is expanding, then run the numbers backward to find when it began."

"That would be a Monday," my father said cheerfully. "The beginning took seven days and was complete by Sunday, so if you run the numbers backward it begins on Monday. I love reasoning this way. Ask me another."

"Ah, numbers," Zitti said and heaved a sigh. "People have too much faith in numbers."

"The language of nature is written with numbers," Nicolo told him. "Galileo thought so."

"And Saint Augustine believed God created the universe with a word," said Zitti.

I said, "I thought you men settled these questions thirty years ago."

Zitti smiled. "We know more now than we did thirty years ago," he said. "We can *really* settle things now."

"We're wiser," Nicolo said. "We're wise old men."

"Older, that's for sure," my father said.

"Did Augustine have anything to say about atoms?" Nicolo asked. "Atoms are getting very strange. They smash them open and all these subatomic particles fly out, like a clock with too many parts."

"No, Augustine had nothing to say about atoms," Zitti said. "That was Lucretius. Did you ever get around to reading Lucretius?" he asked me.

Lucretius was on one of the reading lists my uncle had given me years ago when I left home for art school. "I began it," I said.

"I've never read Lucretius, that's for damn sure," my father said.

"He believed in atoms and only in atoms," Zitti said. "A materialist. But brilliant."

"I thought that was Democritus," my father said, his voice vague as he searched his memory. "You know, Blake has a little poem about that. I've always liked Blake. — The atoms of Democritus and Newton's particles of light, and so forth."

"Right, Lucretius was a follower of Democritus," Zitti continued. "Said everything was composed of atoms and everything, sooner or later, dispersed back to atoms scattered through the void. He said the gods weren't interested in humans and didn't create them or anything else. Just atoms hooking onto each other, then falling apart. That's Lucretius."

" 'The atoms of Democritus and Newton's particles of light, are sands upon the Red Sea shore, where Israel's tents do shine so bright' — that's it," my father said, pleased.

Alba had come out the door with Skye. "Ren," she called to me. "Did we bring a camera?"

"I didn't," I said, putting down my coffee. "Want to go for a walk?"

Behind me, Nicolo was saying that the Red Sox were looking amazingly good this summer.

We walked down past the old grape arbor — the frame made of iron pipe almost forty years ago — the vines as thick as your arm and dense with leaves, and past the vegetable garden, sadly limited now to a dozen tomato plants and a couple of rows of garlic and peppers, then around to the remnants of the ancient canal and back up past the barn to where the others were lying or sitting on the grass in the shade of the old maple. "It's a beautiful day," Alba remarked. "Una bella giornata, like your mother says."

Yes, we made love for the first time when Alba was fourteen and I was seventeen, and at the end of summer she went back to high school and I went off to the School of the Museum of Fine Arts and we thought that was the end of it. But one winter day we bumped into each other on a sidewalk in Boston — by then she was a student at Boston University — and a couple of years later we discovered each other at a sweltering outdoor party in the West End where she was drinking straight gin, and before leaving I looked for her and found she was throwing up in the bushes, so I went off with somebody else. It was maybe two or three years afterward I got a phone call from her — she had just flown in from Paris and needed a place to crash and sleep, so I said, Yes, yes, come over. Her face was thinner than I had remembered and her faintly asymmetrical sea-green eyes darker. She had come back because she was two months pregnant and had begun to have cramps, and the next morning in my apartment when she woke up she was bleeding. I got her to the emergency room and stayed until the nurse's aide took her away in a wheelchair, then the next day I went back and watched her while she slept. I felt oddly hollow, as if some place inside me was empty. We talked the next day, a little, and she went home to Newburyport. A couple of months later I sent her an invitation to a Boston show I was in, but she didn't reply and I figured she had gone back to Paris. I moved to New York, began to paint like an abstract expressionist and tried to mingle with the big names at the Cedar Tavern, but I got a horrible case of influenza and when I recovered I saw that my New York paintings were crap. I set fire to every canvas in my studio and was tossing the flaming shit out the window when somebody called my name and she wasn't in Newburyport or Paris but here in my doorway.

"I thought you were off to Paris!" I said.

"That's tomorrow. What are you doing?" I told her I was dumping some lousy paintings. She gave me a quick smile. "I was on the sidewalk hunting for your address when these pieces of fire began to fall out of the sky. I thought it might be you." So we had a breakfast together and she said she'd write to me and, as I didn't write good letters, I said I'd send her sketches.

We corresponded and although she was still completing her work at the Sorbonne, she found a group of painters and writers and moved in with a forty-year-old man from England — a "savage intellectual who holds all social conventions in contempt," to precisely quote her letter.

I was astonished by how injured I felt, and angry at myself for feeling that way, and confused because I couldn't square anything in my mind — after all, I had gone to bed with Sophia and later with Odine and still later with Bena, and I'd never expected Alba to live like a nun. I couldn't go to Paris so I went to Montreal, to the French side, and visited an old papermaker I had known at the Museum School, and through him I met a young crowd of artists and Québécois Separatists, including Denise, a lively young woman who that first evening started to undress in my room. I said, "Wait!" and told her I was visiting Montreal only for a couple of weeks, at which she hesitated and then smiled, saying, "C'est bon cela," and pulled her jersey off over her head.

I spent the winter on Cape Ann, working for my aunt Gina who had a café there, and the following spring my friend Costas and I hitchhiked up the coast with our painting gear, aiming for Monhegan Island and those scenes where Robert Henri and his friends had done some great paintings. We never got to Monhegan, but we painted out-of-doors and though I didn't get much done, it was a lot better than painting in a hole in New York or thinking I was an abstract expressionist.

By midsummer I was back in Massachusetts, flat broke, so got a job repainting a 1930s WPA mural in a country restaurant, Lorette's Farm, a long, rambling structure where I worked at night when the place was empty and slept during the day in a stifling room in the restaurant's attic. One dawn while heading to bed I met young Nancy Lorette, who made pastry early in the morning, "Before the busybody spies are awake," she told me, laughing. One thing led to another, as philosophers say, meaning young Nancy and I met each morning on my way to bed. Then at ten each night when my room had cooled off enough for me to sleep, her mother, Avril Lorette, would tap on my door, and if I didn't jump into my pants and say *I'm awake!* she'd come in to rouse me. I'll make no excuses; one thing led to another with Mrs Avril Lorette, too.

When my various duties to the Lorettes were coming to an end, I decided to avoid bad scenes by leaving quietly, or you could say stealthily, so instead of going directly downstairs I ducked from my bedroom into the next attic, heading for the last attic and the ladder down to the storeroom. I was creeping forward, dragging my gear along with me, when I crashed through the ceiling into the room below, staggered around in a rain of crumbling plaster and bumped into Alba. "Renato!" she cried.

"I thought you were in Paris!"

She said she had gotten back a month ago and had been working there a week. "What are you doing here?" she asked.

"Murals," I said. "But now I'm escaping." By then we could hear the Lorettes' voices from an upstairs room, shouting at each other. "From Mrs Lorette?" Alba asked and I said, "Her, too."

"From Nancy? — From both?"

"It's complicated. I'm innocent." We could hear Mrs Lorette shouting and kicking my bed to pieces.

"You mean you — Complicated!" Then Alba began to laugh

and said I could take Jack's car, he being the handsome thick-necked oaf coming through the doorway in a red-striped jersey — a guy she favored, I'm sure. "Give him the keys, Jack," she told him.

I got a place in Boston in a building that was scheduled to be demolished, so the rent was cheap, and if you looked between the other tenements you could see big slices of the Charles River and Cambridge on the other side. I was invited to exhibit in a group show in Cambridge. It was a good group and my work stood out as especially strong, so I invited Alba. She came and I remember so clearly how she looked walking toward me — the trim jacket and that blazing white throat, the tight rise of her breasts -- her hair in a glossy French twist, silver buttons, flashing bracelets and high heels. It was a satisfying crowd and I met the other painters as well as the owner of a big gallery in Boston. I introduced Alba to my parents and my brother, Bart, then afterward we five went to a Greek restaurant to celebrate and agree we should all do this more often and when dinner broke up everybody hugged everybody and they drove off, leaving me and and Alba on the sidewalk.

That night we walked from the restaurant to the Charles River and then along the Charles, and as the sun came up behind Boston — the old Boston, the gold dome of the State House on the hill and a blurred mosaic of bricks and brownstones making the low city — the light came in pale blue shafts between the buildings and onto the dark glassy river to where we were standing side by side, our elbows on the railing above the edge of the water, talking and talking. Our arms brushed and — Oh! — I turned and found her watching me, waiting. Her face was bare again, the way it had been years ago, and I could see all there was to see, one eye almost invisibly larger than the other, the dark sea-green irises flecked with uneven rays of lighter green and blue, the high contour of her cheek, the nakedness of her lips, and when I kissed her mouth I got light-headed and had to grab the rail to keep from plunging into the river.

We began to walk the long bridge across the Charles, but it got longer and longer, so when a cab came by we flagged it down and rode the rest of the way to my place. When I opened the door I saw how bad it looked, so stark, with nothing but a table, a bed, some chairs and my big canvases. "Oh, I like this," Alba said. I watched her as she walked around the room, looking at my paintings, then she turned to me and said, "I love being here. All the colors and —" but she broke off as I had my hands inside the lapels of her jacket and wrenched it open, the silver button jumping away to hit the floor, ringing like a bell.

"Do you believe in God?" she asked afterward. We were naked on our hands and knees, looking under the bed for her missing button. I told her I hadn't made up my mind about that. She said, "I mean, is life just things bumping into other things and everything happening accidentally? Because if it is, then how did we meet and keep on meeting? If it's all just atoms banging into other atoms it doesn't make sense. But I feel it must make sense." All I knew was that I wanted to have her for the rest of my life. "There must be a meaning — ah!" she cried, holding up the button. She got to her feet and shook her head vigorously to untangle her hair, then began to pull a comb through it, which was a pleasure to watch, remembering how she used to rake her fingers through that mop to catch out the straw after we had laid in the field up back of her house. "I was only fifteen," she said, as if I had spoken.

"Fourteen, Ka-gi-gi, you were still fourteen."

You know this from before, because this is the way it happened.

❦

Tomorrow is Valentine's Day and I've sent flowers to the girls and, you know, there are days when I'd just as soon be dead as alive. I can't get used to the idea that I'm going to be lonely for the rest of my life. You were everyone else.

❦

Another letter arrived from Leo Conti, this one saying that by a stroke of good fortune he had been able to acquire "excellent gallery space on Newbury Street. And, Renato, I hope you notice that I said ON Newbury Street." He didn't include the address. He did say that he was having the interior redone — "stripped down to the brick walls and completely reconceived." He had been told that the space previously housed a shop that sold expensive grand pianos or expensive neckties, he couldn't recall which. He said my work was essential and he wanted to see it. "I insist, Renato, I insist." He would give me a call when he was on his way out here — with warm regards, Leo.

I didn't care piss about gallery space or Newbury Street, and I didn't know what to do with Leo's letter. I pushed it back into its envelope and set it on Alba's desk, then I got my auger, spiles and buckets, and went to tap the two sugar maples out front. We had lived here six months when the giant up the road happened by and told me, "I could loan you a couple of spiles and buckets." I asked what spiles were for. "To tap those sugar maples," he said. So that became something Alba and I did together every year when winter retreated. As the snow softened and began to sink away, we would be outside emptying the buckets into big pails, lugging those into the kitchen to boil down the sap, the kitchen windows fogging over with maple-scented steam. I still have some syrup, the last we made together, each jar neatly labeled in Alba's handwriting.

Here and now, after that job was done, I put away my auger and clomped over to the studio, but as soon as I stepped inside I knew I didn't want to be there, so I shut the place up again and clomped back to the house, wondering why I had tapped the maples when there was only me and no Alba, and why I was trudging back and forth across this stretch of snow and mud. I phoned Scott, but got no answer and left no message. I got in my car and drove to the Barista stand for a cup of coffee. I thought I'd ask Shannon what she did after her husband died and the year rolled on day by day and came again to the day when he had died, but she looked oddly sullen, so I asked her how the day was going. "I've had better," she said, pressing the lid onto the cup and handing it to me.

"What does that mean?"

"It means Fitz is full of patriarchal shit and wants to control my life. Him and his community college education."

"He seemed nice enough, the couple times I met him."

"He interviews well, if that's what you mean. — He thinks I'm going to change what I eat and give up cigarettes, all for him."

"Maybe he just wants you healthy."

"I told him, I got needs and right now I need to be left alone. So he goes off to sulk and drink too damn much, but he's feeling romantic and makes his move, and I tell him, Fuck off! and he shoves me so hard I hit the wall, so I tell him, You fuckin' touch me again and your kids'll be seeing you in Billerica on visitors' day!" She began to scrub the counter.

All I said was, "Oh," because Billerica is where the Middlesex County Jail is, and I didn't know what else to say.

"The next morning he apologizes and tells me he'll understand if I want him to pack up and get out — like I'm some kind of cold-hearted bitch." She tossed the washrag aside. "He's working three jobs," she added.

"Bad weekend," I said.

"What about yourself?" she asked. "Anything new?"

"No one's going to move in and ask me to change my menu, if that's what you mean."

She smiled. "You never can tell," she said.

"I can tell."

I went back to my car and drove home in the fading light, stopping at Big Valley Farms to buy a loaf of bread and some olives. The tall lights blazed white over the parking lot. As I got out of the car a young woman came by in a short coat and long dress or skirt — a flowing garment such as Alba would wear — and a child, a toddler, was riding tucked inside her arm, her own small hand clutching her mother's coat collar. The woman had long chestnut hair, almost like Alba's. I paced myself to follow them into the store, but inside, the young woman stopped to seat her kid in the grocery cart and I was obliged to pass them. I picked up a loaf of multigrain, and a mix of pitted Kalamata and green olives stuffed with pimientos. I turned into the next aisle and here was the young mother who just now had stopped her shopping and was leaning forward over the grocery cart to bring her face closer to her daughter's, the two of them smiling and radiant with happiness at having each other so close. She was saying something to her daughter, while the daughter put her finger across her mother's lips, as if to hush her. I hesitated, then started to edge sideways past them and the woman glanced up at me and smiled. I returned her smile and said, "Fortunate child to have such a mother," and she said, "Oh, she's wonderful."

When I pulled into the frozen mud driveway the house looked deserted for years, the windows empty and black and bare. I went in and walked from room to room, turning on the lights, pulling down the shades and closing the curtains. I sat on the sofa in a storm of tears and howled up at the ceiling to Alba, "Help me!"

❦

The anniversary of Alba's death was coming close and closer and I decided I wanted to see her medical records. My brother said, "Why do you want to do that?" and I told him I needed to know why she had died in agony. When I mentioned it to Fletcher, he didn't say anything for a moment and then asked, "Won't that upset you terribly? Why upset yourself?" I told him I was ready now. So stubborn old Renato brought proof of who he was to the clinic and the quiet-spoken woman in the records department gave him a cardboard folder three inches thick with Alba's medical papers. At home he took out the papers and saw they were stacked chronologically, the ones from the hospital on top, and some of those were handwritten. Stupid old Renato poked down a few pages from the top and began to read, but discovered he couldn't go on reading and began to cry. Now see old runny-nose Renato as he hurriedly gathers the papers in his shaky hands and stuffs them back in the folder and walks from room to room in his deserted house, embracing the folder of papers hard against his chest, all the while sobbing and saying, "Don't worry, Alba, I'll take care of you, I'll take care of you, I can do it, Alba, don't worry."

I tapped the maples, though I don't know why — a plate of ice in the bucket some mornings and the wind with a razor edge. Let the bucket hang there too long and it's so full it spills when you lift it; take it off when it's less and you have to go out twice as often. Boiling down means forty quarts of sap gets us one quart of syrup. Take it off the stove too soon and it's watery; leave it on too long and it's scorched. I did it the way we always did, but there was zero pleasure doing it without you.

On the first day of spring, Astrid phoned and so did Brizio, and Skye drove here for lunch, because Alba died one year ago on this day. I took Skye to an Indonesian restaurant and we talked mostly about the year she and Eric and the kids had spent among the Dayaks. Skye drove home, having chosen a pair of her mother's silver earrings shaped like small scallop shells and a jar of our maple syrup. Afterward, the house was empty and I walked around, not knowing what to do. The kids had been coming and going about once a month, but I still felt desolate when anyone left. Zoe and Emerson had purposely invited me to dinner this evening so I knew I was going there, and that was good to look forward to. I pulled on my parka and walked the streets where we had walked so often. When I got home I sat at the kitchen table and cried for a while, thinking of Alba and how terribly God had treated her.

I didn't know what to do. I made a cup of coffee and was still at the kitchen table when the phone rang. It was Leo Conti, telling me he was coming out to look at my work and was already on the road. Conti must have called as soon as he crossed the town line because only ten minutes later he swung his beige Mercedes into my rutted driveway, producing a big muddy splash. He got out of the car, gazed around and beamed. "Here I am again, a city boy in the country. I love it out here. Healthy air. Healthy trees. Very healthy trees. — How do I look?" He was upholstered in a thick red-and-black plaid shirt, a pair of heavy L.L.Bean boots, and a red-and-black plaid cap with fleece earflaps.

"You look ready for a winter in the Maine woods," I said.

"Exactly. I'm prepared."

"But this is Massachusetts in spring."

"You can't be too careful," he said. "Now let's go to the garage and see those works you've been keeping sequestered out here."

"Out here we call these structures barns." We headed that way.

"I thought barns were bigger and painted red," he said.

"When we got through building this, it cost as much as the house."

We went inside, the air dim and quiet and colder than outside. We climbed the stairway and as soon as we entered the studio Conti said, "Ah, wonderful! I like it up here. And the view, the view. Fantastic!"

I reminded him that I hadn't done the view, but by then he was already looking at some old canvases. "You can move them around, do whatever you want," I told him. "And there's three in that crate I was going to send to Worcester, if you want to look at them." I turned on the heat. Then I began clearing the worktable, just to have something to do while he focused on the paintings. Leo didn't say anything. For the next several minutes, he shuffled the stretchers, set this one or that one up against the wall, then simply stood there, absorbing it, his gaze flicking this way and that over each canvas, as if he were alone in the room.

"Great!" he said, startling me. "This is all good stuff, excellent, fine. But what I'm here for are the frescos you told me about years ago."

"I junked the frescos. It would take me a lifetime to get fresco colors the way I want them. I haven't got that long."

Leo ignored what I had just told him. "I want to look at them," he insisted.

They were downstairs, so we went downstairs. I opened half the shutters to let in some light, then pulled the sheets away and we looked at them. I should have destroyed them years ago. I didn't care a piss what anybody thought, I still didn't like the way the intonaco had soaked up the colors.

"Ah," he said. "Good. Very good." I didn't think so, but Leo had a faint smile on his face, as if he'd forgotten it there, and a distant speculative look in his eyes. "Now show me the big canvases, the ones you said you were going to install in this barn. — Where they'll get ruined with mold, I might add."

I opened the rest of the shutters, letting the barn fill with light, and pulled the sheets from the paintings that stood against the walls.

"Ah, yes," Leo said. He stood there and didn't say a word for a few moments, and then he added, "This is why I have a gallery."

I was pleased and then surprised that I was pleased.

After Alba died I felt like smashing everything to bits — the frescos, the seccos, and all the canvases — everything I'd brought together for the big jigsaw mural. I had filled the scene with my entire extended family, my friends and acquaintances, had brought them together at a big dinner, some of which was in the house around the table while even more was outside on the grass or among the old apple trees, under an afternoon sun, for everyone was there, mostly clothed, some unclothed, the young, the old, the dead and those not yet born, everyone talking, gesturing, listening, eating, or, like my mother and Alba's grandmother Agnes and others, in the kitchen preparing the meal, my father uncorking the wine, and also outside playing horseshoes with Alba's father or bocce with my uncle Zitti and my friend Vanderzee, arguing about art or baseball or politics, while the little ones, the toddlers, ran here and there.

Maybe I got the idea from the corkboard we had on the kitchen wall. At first that was where we tacked the kids' school bus schedule and appointment cards for the dentist, things like that, but then we added snapshots, and over the years we kept some photos there permanently — little Astrid standing up in her crib, my beautiful mother at twenty-one, Alba's father in his greenhouse, age fifty — so, unlike the photos in an album, these lost all sense of chronology and existed companionably with each other. For the mural — for all the paintings, actually, but especially for the big mural — I painted, or tried to paint, in a way not slapdash, not hasty, but with the freedom you have when you're sketching, so that even the way the paint was applied would show pleasure, deep pleasure, and I altered perspective now and then, so it looked like the wine bottle might tip out of the frame or one of the toddlers fall into your arms. I had wanted to flood the scene with so much life it would obliterate death. That was just another of my vanities and reason enough to trash the whole damned thing now. But Alba had liked it. She said I was painting better than ever, that I was at the top of my form.

So that was the first year. Before Alba died I had thought the bereaved wept because they missed the person who had died and they felt so alone, and yes, I missed Alba so much I wanted to die, but I howled because of what had happened to her, because of her struggle in pain and terror, her agony as she knew she was dying. And she is only one, as I am only one, a drop in this ocean — one *stilla* in this *mare*, as Zitti used to say, making a play on my last name. This is happening to people every day, all over the world. Crying over myself came in the second year while standing in the shower, or alone at the dinner table, or climbing the weary steps to the bedroom at the end of the day.

I had tried to hold onto our life together. Every Sunday morning I dressed up, just as we used to do, and I set out the snowy Royal Worcester plates and those beautiful cups, white as water lilies, instead of thick mugs, and I made a good breakfast with cut-up fruit, orange juice, toast and honey, and all the things we used to have if it was just us two and no guests for brunch. Then I'd eat the breakfast and read the Sunday newspaper at the empty table in the silent kitchen. After a while, holding on felt worse than letting go. I don't know how many nights I lay in bed waiting for sleep, her ring in my fist on my chest.

I put off going to bed, fearing sleep, because I was afraid I'd dream about Alba and wake to find her gone and be devastated all over again. But I rarely dreamed and when I did we were in a crowd and she would drift ahead, farther and farther ahead, until she was lost to me, or, what was worse, she would simply leave for no reason, no dispute, no anger, nothing. She was never that way in life, never did anything between us without feeling, whether rage or desire, for which I'm grateful. During the day, memories would come of our life forty-five or fifty years ago, and those memories — images, but alive — of her bathing baby Skye or breastfeeding her. Or even further back, the drives we made all over New England, wherever I could find a teaching job or a gallery with wall space, the two of us shoulder to shoulder in that tiny VW Bug — no gas gauge, leaky sunroof — the memory so clear I could see her just as she was, this beautiful bright woman whose idea of a good time was to be in my company.

Somewhere back in this defective memoir I said I'd stop

writing after I'd written about the first year. People let you grieve for a year, but after that you and your grief become an annoyance. For twelve months I had gotten through each day because I thought, without ever thinking about it, that life would get better, the way it always had after a disaster, but during the second year I saw it wasn't ever going to do that, because there was no better to get to — this was my life now and I hated it.

I had intended to stop, but here I am — scribble and scrawl — and I don't know why. I'm no closer to finding where Alba has gone and whether I can get to her without dying first, or if she no longer exists, as people say, though I still don't understand how she can be here one moment and cease to exist the next. Above all, I cannot see the point of this universal dying. When I write a note to Alba, it makes sense and I know what I'm doing, but I don't know why I continue to fill these sheets of paper.

As Denise said in her Christmas card, the second year is no better than the first. It's the same loneliness, the same abrupt collapse into tears, the same sobbing or howling, which no one wants to listen to and I don't want to talk about, and the only new thing is a growing ability to fake a life and behave like an ordinary person when other people are around. When I began this crappy chronicle, I said — or should have said if I didn't — that I'm writing this three, or now four, years after Alba died. I know she's gone and I know she's not coming back. But the other day I came into the house and saw Alba, who had finally found her way home, curled up asleep on the sofa, and even as I realized it was only our rumpled bed quilt, I knew she'd explain what had happened and how she had struggled to come home sooner, and why we had been left behind to believe she had died.

I may have written some of these events in the wrong order, scribbling things as they came to mind, and I won't bother to straighten them out because I want to finish this neuralgic scrawl before I die. We had a snow shower in late March or early April, the big flakes tumbling gently through the air and melting as they settled on the black street. The lawns along the street were white, with blades of green grass showing through here and there. I drove home through the peaceful snowfall, turning down this street and that one to go past our familiar places, all the while thinking of Alba, pretending she was sitting beside me. That may have been three years ago or last year.

❦

By the way, I did get around to reading that Lucretius book, *On the Nature of Things*, as my uncle Zitti had recommended. There it was, this small, thick, red book (ragged lines of Latin poetry on the left page, dense blocks of English on the right), and me, making my clumsy trek across it, like stumbling over every furrow of a plowed field. It turned out to be a book of atomic physics by a well-off Roman who hobnobbed with Cicero and Catullus. After the first dull pages it began to get interesting, mostly because the author was curious about every detail of the material world — the only kind of world there is, he says — and he had a theory that explained all of it. The book dazzled me.

According to Lucretius, in the beginning there's only this great void through which atoms fall endlessly, the heavier and the lighter falling at the same speed, no one atom overriding another; but now and again a spontaneous swerve occurs, two atoms connect, and one connection leads to another and another and so on to the creation of things, little things that add up endlessly and eventually lead to world upon world —infinite worlds in infinite space. That swerve was important to Lucretius, not only because it starts the compounding of matter, but also because it has no cause. It just randomly happens. So there is no iron chain of cause and effect to create a predetermined universe in which everything that happens was set at the beginning; absolutely not, the atoms simply swerve, and from those gratuitous swerves eventually comes our free will, he says.

Lucretius is more than a physicist; he's a moral philosopher who wants us to know we're free from such things as fate or destiny. And he announces early on that he's writing this book about the nature of things to liberate us readers from fear of the gods, fear of death and the afterlife, for as people are shown that the gods have no part in the creation or management of things, and once they see that all creation, including their own living body, is composed of atoms and nothing more, they'll understand that there is no life after death, no afterlife in which to suffer and fear. You, your body and your soul, are that collection of atoms and when they disperse there's no you — it's as simple as that. Lucretius's own personal atoms, body and soul, had dispersed two thousand and more years ago, and four or five hundred years later Saint Augustine died, his body but never his soul, which leaves me hanging, because I would have enjoyed introducing those two know-it-alls to each other.

"They'd make lousy dinner guests," Zocco says. "They'd end up in a food fight."

I hadn't seen Zocco for months, so I phoned him and we got together at a restaurant in Cambridge.

"No food fight," I said. "We'd have dinner here. Just the four of us — me, you, Augustine and Lucretius. They'd respect us because of our age. We're older than Augustine was when he died, and twice as old as Lucretius. Age has its prerogatives."

"I'd rather have sex."

"No, we're going to have food," I told him.

Zocco shrugged and opened his menu. "I can do that. I'm still pretty good at food."

There was a time when Lou Zocco and Cormac McCormac and Marvin Kadish and Tom Hay and I would meet — sometimes by chance, sometimes by plan — at the Café Paradiso. But the Paradiso was long gone and so was McCormac, and Kadish, too, and Tom Hay wasn't doing so well, either. Now Zocco and I had found this restaurant on Brattle Street that looked all right, especially as the windows were scrimmed with fog so the traffic outside was just blurred reds, yellows, and blues.

I don't recall what Zocco ate, but I had Italian onion soup flavorful enough to almost distract me. I asked about his wife, who had broken a bone in her foot. She was doing well, but old bones take a long time to heal, he said, much longer than you'd expect. He asked how I was doing and we talked about doctors for a brief while and about the stent that had been implanted in one of his coronary arteries a few years back. We complained about being busy and agreed that having too much to do was better than hanging around with nothing at hand. "I don't know what people who have real jobs do when they retire," Zocco said. I told him they move to Florida and play golf. "I'd go crazy," he said. "What's keeping you busy these days?"

"I shop for food, I cook, I eat, I clean up afterward. I fix leaky faucets. And every so often I think about painting and that's exhausting."

Zocco laughed. "Have you noticed how everything is so much harder and takes longer to do? When I look at some of the crazy jobs I did. Or tried to do. Remember those big plywood prints I made? I couldn't do that today."

"Those were great," I said. Zocco had made prints from huge sheets of plywood by cutting away parts of the top layer and brushing inks or paints on what remained, then covering the block with a sheet of paper big as a tablecloth and pressing it with another sheet of plywood. "I liked them."

"I made all that paper. And I had to use a paint roller to spread the inks around." He smiled, remembering. "If I got one good print out of four tries, I was lucky."

We talked about papermaking and that led to his asking had I seen Sebastian Gabriel and Avalon recently and what were they up to, so we talked about them, and later about Winthrop who I hadn't seen since he moved to Plymouth to be near his son. I said, "I think it's all those toxic lacquers and acrylics he used that rotted his nerves. His wiring was pretty far gone the last time I saw him."

"Now it's like he blew a fuse in his brain," Zocco said.

"Sometimes he makes sense, mostly not so much. He's in hospice. He's dying."

"I'm sorry —" I had thought I was going to say something more, but nothing came to mind. I looked out the window at the passing colors and that was better.

Zocco sighed. "This is glum," he said.

"I'm going to order some caffeine, an espresso, a cappuccino, anything. That might help."

"Good idea," he said. So we drank coffee and talked about Augustine's soul and Lucretius's atoms, politics and bankers and money. It was good to see Zocco again.

Alba, you'll wonder what happened. They knocked down the old Franklin house in one day. They're going to build those condominiums, just like they planned to all along. They removed all the windows but didn't save any of the fancy curlicue wood trim, then big backhoes pushed in the sides until the house collapsed in a heap — broken studs, boards, shingles. Terribly cruel and sad to see. Then they scooped the broken heap up into trucks and hauled it away. Today big earthmovers were going back and forth over what used to be the Four Seasons Gardens, scraping it flat and smooth. I'm afraid when you see it again you'll think you're lost and not find your way home.

Last year was mostly grayscale with no flavors and no smells, which I realized only later. Now, last autumn's apples are sunk brown and rotted in the long grass and Alba's gardens, those big flowerbeds she had made everywhere, are a flattened tangle of soaked, decaying leaves with reddish briars and hollow stalks sticking out every which way. After she died, the flowers must have come up by themselves to float their colors in the midsummer heat, but I hadn't seen any of it. Now all those roots and tubers were restless again, the whole amoral smelly rotten fecund world that didn't care shit about death or dying.

❦

"I'm getting good at arranging funerals," Shannon tells me. Her grandfather has died.

"I know it's a terrible time, but it sounds like you made it go well."

"First my mother, then Robert, and now my grandfather." She pressed the lid on the coffee cup and set it on the counter.

It was a sunny day and the light striking the countertop illuminated her face, a pretty woman, despite everything. I asked her what she thought about all this dying.

"I try not to think in that direction. What good did thinking ever do? There's no understanding it."

"I think about it all the time."

"Let me know if it gets you anywhere. — Did you want spice cake?"

I said yes. Shannon always slipped two slices into the bag instead of one. This time I studied her hands and saw only one piece go into the bag, but when I picked it up I felt the bulk of two.

"You're crazy. They're keeping track of every damn crumb," I told her.

"Fitz keeps track of what he delivers and what gets spoiled in transit, and I keep track of what I get and what gets tossed because it's stale or spoiled. The numbers balance, that's all that matters. — How are you doing these days?"

❦

The ophthalmologist tells me that the intraocular pressure in my right eye is so high it's damaging my optic nerve and will eventually destroy my vision. We've had this conversation before, because the same thing happened in my left eye a few years ago. I've gotten acquainted with the anatomy of my eyes, my cloudy vitreous fluid and the clogged exit canals through which it flows. We tried eye drops and laser to lower the pressure, but nothing worked. Now he suggests surgery, the same as he did on the left eye, cutting into the network of canals to open a kind of casement widow to allow the fluid a way out. I don't plan to paint anymore, but as long as I'm alive I don't want to go blind. Andrews, the ophthalmologist, is a handsome, quick, athletic man, fifty-something years old, who listens impatiently whenever I ask a question or venture an opinion. I ask how often he does such surgery. "Every Monday," he says briskly. I tell him I'll think about it. They don't respect you if you say yes on the first go-around.

Alba, I was walking past where the Four Seasons Gardens used to be, where they're building those condos. They have batter boards lined up for foundations and a red-winged blackbird flew around and landed on one of the stakes. The same kind of bird that used to nest there by the creek.

I received a letter from Elizabeth Prescott, whom I had never heard of, saying that she was writing an article on Cormac McCormac, and that she had been given my name by his wife, Karen, who spoke of me as a longtime friend of her husband. Ms Prescott hoped I would be willing to be interviewed about McCormac, the man and his work, and she would be happy to visit me for the interview at my home, my studio, or any place I preferred. She closed by saying she looked forward to my reply.

Cormac died maybe half a dozen years ago, whittled away by diabetes. He had been a big guy, built for carving ordinary New England stones into faces or parts of faces — an eye, an ear — then piling them up into cairns in his hayfield, and later in life he worked with big pieces of metal, happy with his anvil and his acetylene torch. Karen was his fourth wife. I never met his first wife, but I recall his second as a young woman with lightly flushed cheeks, as if simmering with passion or, as it turned out, resentment, while his third made a career of meeting famous artists in their beds, and the fourth was Karen, who turned out to be just right. I knew Karen had been struggling to place his sculptures in museums and private collections, but since Cormac had died the only thing written about him was a five-inch obituary in the *Boston Globe*.

Elizabeth Prescott and I agreed to meet for the interview at a restaurant in Lexington. For no particular reason I had expected somebody in her middle years but she looked to be about eighty, you could say elegantly thin or you could say bony, and with thick, silver-white hair. So she was old and I knew that I looked as old to her as she looked to me. She was pleasant, easy to talk with, and when lunch arrived she turned on her recorder and we began to discuss Cormac, with her occasional questions — a quiet, unemphatic voice — to lead the conversation. So we talked through lunch, the waitress cleared the table, brought our coffee, and Prescott asked had Cormac ever spoken about a personal artistic vision, a philosophy or esthetic that he hoped to embody in his work. I think I laughed. I said no, and told her that what struck me most about Cormac and his work was how he loved the physicality of it. He loved muscular work, loved lifting boulders or hammering metal, and he loved that his creations took up residence in three dimensions, so you could walk around them and touch them. I answered a few more questions about Cormac, then Prescott turned off her recorder.

"Thank you so much," she said, relaxing and letting her shoulders, which had been stiff as a coat hanger, droop ever so slightly. "Karen speaks very highly of you."

"Karen's very kind. I should try to get over to their place one of these days. It's somewhat out of the way. — What are you writing, exactly?"

"Karen and I met in college and we've kept in touch through the years. And since Cormac died she's been trying so hard, desperately and without much success, to establish, or reestablish —"

"I know. I've seen other widows try that. It's heartbreaking work."

"I'm not really a writer. I majored in art history in college and I've taught art history and written a few academic articles, and in Karen's eyes that makes me a writer who —. Well, anyway, she's asked me more than once if I could write a piece about Cormac and, well, I thought I'd try to help. — And my own husband died four years ago," she added.

"Oh, I'm so sorry," I said.

She hesitated. "I learned from Karen that your wife —. " She broke off.

"Yes."

"I'm sorry," she said.

"You were happily married," I said.

"Yes, very."

"I think of Alba every day. She's always there. Or here."

She smiled. "I used to think that was just a nice way of saying you missed your husband or wife, a polite way to talk about grief. But it's so true. You think of a person every day, sometimes it feels like all day. We did everything together."

"Do you have children?"

"Yes, thank God. And three grandchildren."

I asked about her husband and their life together. He had been a lawyer ("wills and mortgages and so forth") but he also did trial work for liberal causes ("obscenity cases, religious cases and things like that"). "We never got rich, but we were never poor. It was a good life." She smiled just a bit, then looked away and let her mind drift. "We liked being together," she said. "We enjoyed each other."

All the while she talked I imagined how she would have looked decades ago, her cheeks higher, full and firm, her jawline sweeping to the smooth column of her neck, for now the sacks beneath her eyes were flat and discolored and the cords along her throat hung as slack as my own. She had been loved and made love to for years, a loving and desirable woman.

"He died of emphysema. Which was horrible and unfair," she said, her voice rising in anger. "He never smoked. A little marijuana in the early years, but that's all. When we were young he ran marathons. And in the end we had to carry bottles of oxygen with us wherever we went." She sighed, looked at me again, smiled.

I said, "Cormac once told me he didn't understand death. He asked me, What's it for? What's the point?"

We talked a while longer and I thought how decayed I must appear to Elizabeth Prescott, as she does to me, and how the both of us must look to others, a very old pair sitting at a restaurant table, chatting over their coffee long after the waitress has brought the check. I said, "This conversation has been a pleasure," and she said, "The pleasure was mine," and I said, "Maybe we can get together again," and she said, "I'll be in touch to show you what I've written."

Yesterday I bought a big copper weather vane to mount on the barn — an angel flying and blowing a long trumpet, the same angel as the little ornament we set at the top of the Christmas tree. No one will think I'm crazy because I put up a weather vane, and you'll see it from far off and you'll know you're coming to the right place. If I have to move to that desolate college town where Skye lives, I'll take the weather vane along and also paint the front door same color as here, so you'll still be able to find me.

As they grew older, my uncles Nicolo and Zitti began to change their views on politics and God and everything else they always talked about, as if after all those years of disputing with each other, each had finally convinced the other of his rightness. Premises and logical deductions had clearly proven weak and unreliable for both of them. "I don't know," uncle Nicolo would say. "In fact, the older I get, the less I know." At which uncle Zitti, agreeing, would smile ever so slightly and say, "Well, in a few years we'll be dead and it won't matter what we know or don't know."

"Zitti, please!" Candida told him. "We're beginning a new year. Don't be depressing."

That would have been New Year's Day in 1976 at my parents' home. Everyone's eyesight had faded to the point where they each had a shade of night blindness and didn't drive after dark, so instead of having a New Year's Eve party my mom had invited them to celebrate New Year's Day in the early afternoon with tea or coffee, which you could have decaffeinated if you wished, and with sweetener instead of sugar, if you wanted, plus true biscotti and tiramisu.

"We'll be pushing up daises," Marissa said, sounding cheerful.

"Who wants more tea or coffee?" my mother asked, hoping to change the topic. "Renato, ask Alba if she wants to come in to get warm."

I told her Alba was fine in her warm parka and wanted to keep an eye on the kids. I didn't add that she was happy to have escaped outside with our children and my old Flexible Flyer sled which she'd taken from the cellar. I watched my father dip the end of his biscotto into his coffee and lift it with a deft roll of his fingers to shake off the lingering drop. "Is it that time moves faster as we get older," he said, "or is it just that we move slower?"

They looked unchanged to me, even though I knew it wasn't so. After all, my mother's hair was not the tumbling blue-black river of ink it had been when I was a kid, but gray, gray as Marissa's and Candida's hair. Last summer at an outdoor wedding reception, Uncle Zitti had slumped in his garden chair, his left arm having abruptly quit working, which sent him to the hospital for three days. "A very minor stroke, completely recovered now," he said, and he refused to speak about it ever again. Uncle Nicolo had slowed down and he didn't walk quite properly but shuffled and listed to one side like a wounded ship. My father had arthritis and elevated blood pressure and he complained of forgetfulness, but he looked fine and vigorous. Two winters ago he had finally ceased cutting stone and had put his tools away for the last time, and that summer he and my mom drove up to Montreal, and this past summer they stayed at the Château Frontenac in Quebec.

The conversation had drifted to political gossip — uncle Nicolo saying it looked like the Cold War was ending, Zitti declaring a different war would certainly start up someplace, my father insisting you could never trust the Soviets, Marissa and Candida saying the whole world was tired of war — and from there the talk turned to the grandchildren and then to what they were being taught in grammar school these days. Nicolo said that when he was a kid the president of Harvard announced you could get a liberal education by reading fifteen minutes a day from his five-foot shelf of books, the Harvard Classics. "There were three things I wanted to have — the Harvard Classics, the *Encyclopædia Britannica*, and a grand piano. Now we have all three." He laughed just a bit and it was impossible to say whether he was making a modest boast or tossing off a jest.

"Your son knows that story," Marissa reminded him. "And he admires you. He's told you so."

Nicolo nodded in agreement. "Yes, he did." He lingered over the thought.

I asked him what was his favorite book from the Harvard Classics.

He brightened. "Darwin. *On the Origin of Species*. It made a deep impression on me. I was fascinated by his theory of evolution. — I was so dazzled I didn't notice the dark side of it," he added.

"You see," Zitti said, turning to me. "He's changed his mind about science."

"No. I still think it's a beautiful theory, and a right one," Nicolo said. "But I've come to see evolution as tragic and wasteful. I understand how people were upset by Darwin because he said that we evolved from earlier creatures — from monkeys, as they used to say. But what's most disheartening to me is that all life arises from accidents and not because of any plan or purpose in nature. If every living thing is the result of randomness or chance or accident — call it what you want — the staggering, wasteful deaths, well —" He broke off.

"We can call it God, if you want," Zitti said. "That's the way God works his creation. Tragic and wasteful." He had finished his tiramisu and now wiped his lips with a napkin, sat back in his chair. "People have been going to church, pleading with God to behave more humanely, but so far with no luck."

"Zitti, please," Candida said. "No more about God."

Zitti laughed and opened his arms to dramatize his surprise and innocence. "I didn't bring God into this, Nicolo did," he said. "As far as I'm concerned, God is a waste of time."

"A little more coffee?" my mother suggested to everyone. "To warm up your cup."

"The longer I think about life, the more mysterious it gets," Nicolo said. "We began in some protoplasmic slime or green algae and here we are now, sitting around this table discussing our own evolution. It's stunning. I haven't thought this through but, despite the chanciness and accidents and despite all the randomness, there appears to be such a purposeful drive that . . . I don't know what to think."

My father told my mother, Yes, he'd like a little more coffee to warm his cup.

"I prefer not knowing what to think," Zitti announced. "I've always been a rationalist and a skeptic—"

I laughed. "You?" I said, interrupting him. "When did you become a rationalist and a skeptic? You must be joking."

"No. Remember, I've always liked Montaigne, a wonderfully curious and skeptical man. The older I get, the more I appreciate his refusal of certainty." He smiled. "He's an Italian, you know, transplanted to France." Zitti regarded French intellectuals as foppish dilettantes, and for those French thinkers or artists he did admire, he claimed they had Italian backgrounds.

"Can't we talk about something real for a change?" Candida said.

What am I supposed to do now? I'm a painter who had eye surgery a few weeks ago, because otherwise I'll go blind faster, my left ear doesn't hear things clearly, all my joints ache, and if I sleep the wrong way I get a pain in my hip that feels like somebody hammered a spike in there. Alba, I still wake up in the morning hard — not *hard* hard, not like when we were younger, but hard enough. So what am I supposed to do now? You're the only woman I know who understands these things. This unruly thing especially. Your man from the sea.

Katia Robinson drove up from Hartford to have lunch with me — little Katia Tsarevski, grown-up but not grown old, still very trim, still with that interested direct gaze. The Tsarevskis lived in the flat across the hall from the rent-free storage room I was using as a studio back then. Every so often I'd hear her parents' curses and rages, and skinny little Katia would come over to show me the artwork she had done in school that day. A few years later, when her mother and father got to worse fighting (screams, whacks, heavy thumps), she'd walk in with her schoolbooks and sit on the floor against the wall — knees up, underpants showing, a Balthus in my studio — and quietly do her homework while I stretched canvas or painted. Now she's about to become a grandmother. "In two weeks or so," she said.

"Raising children is the only worthwhile activity there is," I said.

She smiled. "You exaggerate, of course."

"Of course, but only a little."

"What have you been painting?" she asked.

"I haven't been painting."

We talked about my not painting and about her leaving the nondenominational church where she had been ministering for a dozen years, and about her son and daughter-in-law, and I told her this and that about my children and grandchildren. Near the end, over coffee, we talked about Alba. "For me, she was like a heroine in a book," Katia said. "I mean, really beautiful."

"Yes, she was. And she stayed that way."

I drifted into silence, then Katia added, "Not only good-looking, but . . . one day I walked in and she was in your studio arranging flowers in a glass jar. She asked me to help her, and when we were finished she broke off a blossom and tucked it in my hair. I can't tell you how extraordinary that made me feel. I know you won't understand, but it made me feel beautiful and grown-up."

"That's the way she was," I said. "That was Alba."

"I wanted to be her. I was quite envious. Or jealous." Then Katia smiled and said, "I was a jealous girl."

"Jealous? No."

"Oh, yes. I'd hear you two going into your studio and I knew what you would be doing in there. You know, on that old mattress with the sheepskin furs."

"Oh God, no!"

"You've probably forgotten, but there was a day when I took off my blouse and was bare-chested. My idea of seduction."

I had been making silkscreen prints that day and was deep into the work, pulling and lifting, when she said, What do you think of this? So I turned around and saw her.

I laughed. "I haven't forgotten. But you were just a kid, that's all."

"You were stunned. Then you said, firmly, Put on your shirt and we'll go out and I'll buy you a maple walnut ice-cream cone. — You knew maple walnut was my favorite flavor that summer."

It was a good lunch. We parted with a hug and I drove home sick with desire for Alba who was gone, gone, gone.

❦

I have plenty of time to think about the things I did. I don't meditate on the past, but every now and then a scene comes to mind, floats to the surface all on its own, and mostly it's from the early years, the two of us cozy in our second-hand VW bug (manual choke, no gas gauge) driving all over, or Alba breast feeding Skye, playing with Astrid, or just Brizio and me in the shower. Other times, it comes back like a punch in the face — my having said something that made Alba cry, or maybe it was the ugly tone of my voice. That's Renato.

Certain sexual follies don't look so disastrous from this end of life. Yes, Zoe is the mother of Astrid and so is Alba, which you understand or you don't. At the time it felt like we had wrecked ourselves, but there was nothing to do about it so we just kept on living, no matter how painfully, and after a few years we were just going along with the same ups and downs as everyone else. All that was when we were young, but we could be vain or foolish at any age. When I was seventy and Alba not much younger, we put ourselves on opposite sides of the Charles River. Alba slept in Cambridge in our overpriced Bauhaus box, a concrete columbarium with big windows and all our earthly goods. I slept in Boston in the studio with all my paintings, enough for a dozen different shows, none of which had happened in twenty years. I had been erased from the big art biz. But I had learned how to paint and was making a final attack on the galleries. Alba took up cooking with a visiting French chef.

That's when Avalon crashed from San Francisco and

knocked at my studio door — a skanky looking woman with jewelry stuck to her face, flat broke, having nothing but a backpack and a little son with Asian eyes like inkwells. I didn't know her. Her father, Brendan Flood, had been a friend of mine, but he had died when Avalon was a kid and her mother died the day she was born. Being me, I let her in and they stayed a year.

I regret being vain, oblivious, stupid and petty, regret my rants and complaints, regret talking logic when I should have shut up and listened, regret being that me. Fortunately, Alba and I craved each other's company and, above all else, craved each other.

❦

It was beginning to snow in tiny flakes, but I had decided to drive to Meg O'Brian's Trifles, a small shop in Cambridge crammed mostly with handmade jewelry, but also with scarves, fancy blouses, fripperies and second-hand clothes, all in a space no bigger than my kitchen. We both knew Meg, and I used to come here to buy Alba a little surprise — a silver seashell or a necklace of sea-glass — and I missed doing that. I longed to do it again, so I came here to get something for my granddaughters, the older ones, Danae and Chiara. And maybe I should mention right here that Meg knew Lucy Dolan.

Now Meg smiled and said, "Renato, it's good to see you," and, after a moment's hesitation, she added, "I heard, I'm so sorry." I said, Thank you, you're kind to remember. We chatted while I looked around, deciding at last on two pair of pendent earrings, glass with sparkling flakes of reddish gold inside. I confess, another reason I'd come here was so I could bring up Lucy. While Meg was putting the earrings into tiny cushioned boxes, I told her I'd bumped into Lucy and she'd told me she was going to open a bakery.

"Yes," Meg said. "She wanted me to go with her to look at a place she found, but things got busy here and I couldn't. She's calling it Peasant Bread and Fancy Pastries. I know she'll do well."

"Where is it?"

"She told me. But all I remember is it's in one of those towns out past Concord — Billerica, Acton, Westford — out that way."

❦

So the next day I drove alphabetically through snowbound towns northwest of Concord — Acton, Billerica, Boxborough, Carlisle, Chelmsford — until I found Peasant Bread & Fancy Pastries. It was a small shop, with a freshly painted yellow door and a display window where an athletic workman was coiling electric cable. I pulled open the door and a bell jingled overhead. Lucy Dolan, sliding a tray of cookies into the display case, looked up, saw me and smiled. "Renato! What a lovely surprise." Her wild thick hair was kept in check by a baseball cap with the word *Monterey* on the front.

"I was just driving through, so I thought I'd stop to say hello. — What a lie! I came hunting for your shop."

"And I'm so glad you found it."

The workman, who had hopped down from the window, smiled, told Lucy, "You're all set and good to go," and headed out to his rusty van.

"Tell me what you think," Lucy said. "Do you like it?"

I looked around. It was a bare square room with pale yellow walls, a big glass case with shelves of cookies and pastries, another case with loaves of bread, a marble-topped counter in between. "I like it very much."

"It's good, isn't it? There isn't much room out front here, but I was wondering if, anyway, I should have a couple of chairs and a small table. Make it more friendly and accommodating. And I need something for the walls."

"I like it," I told her. "It smells good in here."

She had a big beautiful smile. "Come around this way," she said. "I'll show you the bakery part."

The back room was brightly lighted and shining, divided by

a long table with a gleaming stove on one side and, on the other side, some tall aluminum racks with wheels.

"It looks wonderful," I said.

"It's a lot of work and I'm exhausted," she told me. "But I love it."

She did look tired. She was only a few years older than my oldest daughter, but she looked older than that.

"I'm in love with my bakery shop," she continued. "Is that possible? Because it's my studio, like you have a studio to paint in and I have this to bake in."

"The nice thing about your art is that people pay you so they can take it home and eat it. It's great life-sustaining art."

"Renato, you're the only person in the world who sees my baking as great art."

I laughed. "But it is," I insisted.

"You're biased in my favor."

"That, too."

You're right, there isn't enough counter space in the kitchen. And you're right about the roots from the maples making it near impossible to plant anything in the front flowerbed. I never knew how bothersome those things were. I'm trying to keep up the gardens and you know I'm not doing a good job. They were beautiful and I always said so, but I never knew how you did it and I still don't know.

I liked talking with Shannon. This morning she was wearing more makeup than usual, maybe a bit too much. "You're looking good," I told her.

She pressed the lid on the coffee cup and handed it to me, saying, "Sure. And that's all that matters. Right?"

She looked angry and I didn't know what to make of that, so I didn't say anything. I took a sip of coffee.

"You can put lipstick on a pig and rouge on a corpse. Right?" she said, insistently.

I asked her what she was so sore about.

"Sore? I found a lump and the doctor says he wants me to wait and see. In my breast. I don't want to fucking wait and see. I want it out."

It felt like somebody had kicked my head. I asked did she like her doctor.

"Why should I like my doctor?"

"I mean, do you trust his judgment. Do you think he's a good doctor?"

"How would I know?"

I couldn't figure what to say next. I asked, "What does Fitz think about this?"

She didn't say anything for a moment, then she said, "Fitz is good. He's good. He understands my feelings about this fucking shit. I think he really does."

"You're going to be OK, Shannon."

"They cut Fitz's hours. The company is trying to look super-efficient because they want Starbucks to buy them or something. So they cut his hours and I have a lump. Everything rotten happens at once."

"They'll take out the lump if they need to. You're going to be you, no matter what."

"They scheduled me a biopsy tomorrow."

"Good. You're going to be all right."

"This is all I need."

I kept telling her she was going to be all right.

❧

Alba, I wish you could see this. Summer is here and the young women shopping at Big Valley Farms are dressed for a day at the beach. Those shorts that were shaped like boxes and went halfway to the knee — they're cut high this summer, beautifully high and tight, just like you said. The younger ones are close to naked and happy about it, just a half-jersey top and shorts, and the colors for toenails in this town are rose or tangerine. I know you'd come back if you could. At dinner tonight I pushed my dish aside and put my head on the table and cried.

❦

The year wore on and I still didn't know where Alba had gone, and some days it was as if she had not been here at all, but she had been here and we had loved each other and I wanted to find her. Lucretius, writing his poem two thousand years ago, says that because space is infinite and the number of atoms is also infinite, you have to conclude that other worlds are being created out there, worlds populated by other people who, like us, are born and perish. Nowadays, up-to-the-minute physicists sound much like ancient Lucretius, for they have theories about other worlds and, in fact, whole universes, one beyond another without end. Lucretius builds his theory with step-by-step appeals to reason. I'm not wonderfully impressed by reason, though to say so is like farting in church. I mean, we have only a few ways of figuring things out and those ways are limited and fallible and it's a marvel we've come as far as we have with reasoning. Of course, these physicists who arrive at the same conclusion as Lucretius use complex mathematics to get there, but mathematics is an artifact composed by reason and when carried far enough it leads to logical paradoxes and madness.

Whatever I have of physics and mathematics comes from my uncle Nicolo. Uncle Nicolo used to present physics and mathematics as puzzles, and rather than boring me with the summation of an infinite series, he gave me Zeno's paradox of Achilles and the tortoise, and instead of quanta or wave equations, he treated me to the perplexing behavior of light. Light, he told me, passes through a solitary slit as a stream of chaotic particles, but through twin slits as a smooth continuous wave. As it happened, light had always intrigued me and by the time

I enrolled at the Museum School it wasn't simply light but color that was my heart's desire.

Uncle Zitti told uncle Nicolo that he, Zitti, was gratified by the way light acted. It appeared incomprehensible to us mortals, Zitti said, because light was a singular manifestation of God, so close to God as to be synonymous with Him, which philosophers had recognized at least as far back as the ancient Greeks. "And that new structure they've just completed at MIT," he said, tapping a cigarette on his silver cigarette case for emphasis, "that chapel or meditation building or whatever they're going to call it — it has a square block of marble as an altar and a carefully designed hole in the roof, an oculus, so that light can descend right onto it. Even at Tech they sense that light is a divine, sacred essence." At which point Nicolo would smile, sit back, and polish his Ben Franklin spectacles.

Thanks to uncle Nicolo, I was enchanted not only by Newton's vanishing infinitesimals, but by the elegant mathematical design of his cosmos, the calculated swing of the moon around the earth, the gigantic sweep of the planets around the sun, the endless trajectory of a hyperbolic comet, all traveling the conic sections of Apollonius and all drawn through their celestial courses by gravity — "Which varies inversely with the square of the distance," uncle Nicolo would remind me. That Newtonian universe, where each part moved in time with all the others, appeared reasonable to me and, above all, beautiful.

Now as I was haunting this deserted house and not painting I had plenty of time to read and it was mostly physics I read, the mathematical physics that promised other worlds, quantum mechanics. I began with Werner Heisenberg, which led me into a quicksand of mathematics and, finally, to his matrices, those tic-tac-toe arrays of numbers which were meaningless to me, because I could feel no connection between them and the howling world I lived in. On the other hand, Erwin Schrödinger's wave equations were more approachable, sensuous and beautiful in their way. In fact, Schrödinger himself came through as more approachable and I was delighted to discover that he had called Heisenberg's mathematics repellent. Even the wave equations' Greek letter psi looked good to me — if you resonate to any of this, you're doomed — just as the sigmas had looked elegant sixty years earlier when I was taught calculus.

The infinitesimal world where light is a condensation of spectral photons isn't clear as day: it's a fog of probabilities. Schrödinger's wave equations can calculate those probabilities with exquisite precision — they give the right answers every time — but what those beautiful equations say about the nature of reality is open to interpretation. Of all the probabilities, only one comes to pass, but the equations don't say the other probabilities vanish; on the contrary, they are as real as they always were, continuing forward through time, not here, but in other worlds, real worlds beyond this one. That's what I was after. Schrödinger himself shies away from speculating on the meaning of the wave function, but I'd like to ask him directly.

"There's the problem of his being dead, of course," George said. That was George Agathos and we were moving my kitchen table out the back door and past the apple trees.

"I could write him a letter," I said. "Feynman wrote a letter to his wife a year and a half after she had died. It's a heartbreaking letter."

"And it ends with his saying he doesn't know where to send it. Richard Feynman had human longings. Some people would say he was all too human."

"Did you know him?"

"No, not really. I met him a few times at conferences. I listened to some of his talks. — You forgot to tell me why we moved this table."

We had carried it past the apple trees and had finally set it down in front of the barn.

"I'm going to strip off the lacquer, take it down to the wood and resurface it," I said. "I won't go deep. Just skim the surface."

I didn't tell him I was worried that Alba wouldn't recognize it without the stains and gouges.

"I was hoping we were going to eat off it," George said. "I'm hungry."

"We *are* going to eat off it. I won't be working on it until tomorrow."

"Ah, we're dining alfresco! A picnic! Soon, I hope."

"As soon as we carry the food from the kitchen to the table."

"I'm ready."

George Agathos is the only person I know who is equally passionate about politics, quantum mechanics, and food. We brought chairs from the house and ate at the table in the cool of the barn doorway. I had made a pretty good salad — it had everything plus artichoke hearts and water chestnuts — along with a crusty Tuscan boule, some cheese and olives and a bottle of Soave.

"It's important to have wine," I said, filling his water glass with Soave. "So you'll know it's not breakfast."

George had shaded his eyes with his hand and was squinting past me. "There's a couple of small deer — fawns, I guess — over by the flower garden," he said.

I picked up a stone and threw it at them. They looked at us, then went back to nosing the grass.

"I think they know you," George said.

"They know I can't throw worth a damn. My arm is shot."

"It's a sunny day in June. Have some more wine. — Those were great brunches you and Alba had out here. Not here, exactly, but over by the house. The weather was always beautiful, too."

I don't know if you can really avoid thinking of something by trying not to, but I had tried to avoid that one. All I said was, Those were good times. Later he told me about the trip he and Io had taken to Europe and how they had visited the Large Hadron Collider. "It's a staggering piece of engineering," he said. "When that thing gets up to speed it will be seven times more powerful than any other collider anywhere." He talked about the smashup of subatomic particles at near the speed of light, the spray of exotic bits from the collision. He asked had I been doing any painting.

"No," I said. "But I miss it. I miss the desire to paint."

"It will come back."

"I don't know. Some things don't come back."

"What got you interested in Schrödinger?"

"His wave equations — how did he invent them and what do they mean?"

George smiled. "Oh, ho! You're thinking about him and that woman up in the Swiss mountains, snow outside, fire inside, making love and wave equations — fuck and scribble, fuck and scribble. That was the best two-week vacation in the history of physics."

"What do you think of the interpretation of the equations that says there must be other worlds?"

George squinted into the distance, as if to see the problem more clearly. "Ever hear the expression *Shut up and compute*?"

"Never."

"It means the equations give us the right answers — don't try to interpret them, just use them."

"You're not a big help, George."

He hesitated, then said, "I don't know if Alba is alive in another world, Ren. No one knows. Except maybe you," he added.

"Not me," I said. "I'm even less help to me than you are," I told him.

The air was warm and full of light. We drank the last of the wine, then took a slow walk up to the house with the dishes and leftovers, and back again for the chairs, talking of life on other worlds and theories of multiverses and, more locally, George's suggestion that I should lay out a bocce court on a nice stretch of flat grass alongside the apple trees. And so, goodbye. "That was a good lunch," George said. And, yes, it was a good lunch.

Alba, I have to tell you they're carving out a big new shopping plaza on the next hill beyond Big Valley Farms. And it's amazing how rapidly they're building those condos where the Four Seasons Gardens used to be. I pass it two or three times a day, and already I can't remember exactly where the old Franklin house stood. The places you and I used to walk are getting erased — everything is getting erased and there'll be no memory of us walking through that field, because memories wither when you have them all by yourself.

I hadn't seen Shannon for a month because she was off having surgery to remove the lump from her breast. "The lump was benign," she told me. "But the surgery was a bitch and it hurt."

"Doctors lie," I said. "It's part of their routine. Surgery always hurts,"

"I liked the stuff they gave me in the hospital, but when they sent me home all I had was Tylenol."

Shannon handed me my coffee and as nobody came by we talked about surgeries and pain. I told her how one of the surgeons working over me had messed up and afterward I had to have a catheter for a couple of months. "I had this hose shoved up me and a plastic bag strapped to my leg, and at night I had a big bag hanging from the bed and it would fill up with pee. In the morning when I took a shower, Alba would sit on the toilet seat and hold the bag while I showered."

"I did that for Robert when the brain cancer meant he had no control anymore. He had a catheter like that. I'd hold the bag and get in the shower with him."

"Oh."

"I didn't mind, but I was afraid he must feel humiliated or something —" She looked down at the scrub cloth and began to move it mechanically in a circle on the counter.

"He knew you loved him. You're the best thing that ever happened to him," I said. "You're the best."

That's what I think and I'm glad I told her. I saw her now and again, but a month or two later when I stopped at the stand a new woman was there who looked twenty-five and healthy. I asked if she knew Shannon. No, she didn't. I asked if she knew Fitz who delivers the supplies. She said, "The man who delivers supplies is named Fernando." I asked if the company had been bought by Starbucks. She looked blank for a moment, then said, "Do you want a coffee or a latte or something?"

❦

Leo Conti drove us to the Fête Champêtre, the expensive restaurant pretending to be a French farmhouse. Leo didn't have a wig today. His bald head was tanned and he wore a green translucent visor, rather like the ones worn by accountants hunched over their ledgers a hundred or more years ago. At the restaurant I asked him, "What's on your mind? Why this sudden lunch?"

He removed his visor and set it gently on the table. "No special reason. I'm hungry, that's all. And I thought I'd stay in touch, see how you're doing."

"I'm all right. I'm getting by. — You look fine. How's the deal for the new gallery going?"

"On schedule," he said brightly. "Next week I'll be closing the gallery."

"*Next week?* You're closing the old place *next week?*"

"I told the people who own the building I'd be leaving. I told them a year ago. No problem."

"But where will you go? Is the new place ready?"

"You mean the place on Newbury Street?" He laughed in what I took to be a purposeful display of his most jovial self. "There's a lot to be done first, beforehand, and it all takes time, especially when so many people are involved — building inspectors, finicky lawyers, expensive architects, real estate agents looking to make a quick fortune."

"You'll have no gallery for months? You'll vanish," I told him.

"No, no, no! The Conti Gallery isn't going to vanish." He leaned forward and said, "The Conti Gallery has a permanent phone number, a fax number, and a website." Now he leaned back and smiled. "And no expenses for these slack months when nobody buys paintings."

"Have you taken the new space? Are you actually there yet?"

"We're ready to go in and disembowel the place, clean it out to the brick walls. I've already hired a crew, Guatemalan immigrants, wonderful people, willing to work hard."

"When do you open on Newbury Street?"

"It will happen on schedule and have we talked about your one-man show? Your opening and the opening of the gallery — the official formal opening, not the preliminary exhibits — will be on the same date. A gala occasion. And before that happy occasion occurs, I want to select a couple of your paintings to show privately to a few buyers, people I've interested in your work — collectors, exceptional people, genuine, very genuine."

I hadn't thought about an exhibit since Leo's last visit. The prospect of a one-man show didn't excite me the way it would have in the past, and neither did the possibility of selling to a collector, even a very genuine collector. But at the same time I didn't like his gliding mention of preliminary exhibits before the gala reception for my works, and a black thought flapped through my mind that maybe the new gallery on Newbury Street was an illusion, a flashy maneuver to keep us painters distracted while Conti the Magician gathered up his goods and dropped though a trapdoor to Switzerland where he had a numbered bank account crammed with money and titles to Boston real estate. I was able to say, "That's great, Leo," and let it go at that.

For lunch, Leo had *feuillité jambon champignons*, a delicate flaky bread sandwich with ham and mushrooms, which was impressive, while I had cold chicken and raw vegetables on a split baguette. Leo talked, or thought out loud, about his getting an additional assistant or, maybe not an assistant but an intern, a really bright Art History student from, say, Yale or Harvard, or possibly Princeton, who a few years from now would write deep articles about painters the Conti Gallery had promoted. Then he debated with himself whether it would be exploitive to employ an unpaid intern. We also talked about same-sex couples having children or, to be precise, Leo talked about it and I listened, having no thoughts on the subject, and about politics, where we agreed that Congress was a dysfunctional mess and that it would be best to bring a guillotine to the House of Representatives and start over, and so on to the financial mess. I asked had the recession hurt sales. Leo made a long face and shrugged. "People are cautious these days, even rich people. What can I do? Have a fire sale? I have to appear prosperous."

"You've always appeared prosperous to me, Leo."

"Thank you. It's a disguise."

"A very good disguise," I said.

"Did I tell you I'd take care of the brochure? The entire expense, I'll take care of it."

"No, Leo, you didn't." There had always been some damn thing I was paying for in my shows at the Conti Gallery — postcards, a brochure, insurance, advertisements. "You're paying? Tell me about it."

"I see it as an illustrated exhibit catalog. Almost. Not gaudy," he hastened to add. "Not inflated. Not overdone. But something rich and fine."

Leo Conti wasn't rich. He was a gallery owner who loved art, had an eye for talent and worked ceaselessly to promote a certain vision, and he was also a former accountant with an intricate understanding of the gray areas in real estate and tax law, so I can also say he wasn't poor. Over the years I'd heard of a handful of gallery owners who made a lot of money, but I'd seen firsthand that most don't — half of them just get by and the other half go bust inside of five years. Leo was doing well, maybe very well. While we were finishing our coffee, he told me about a young painter he had exhibited a few times in group shows. "The kid's got talent but he's a difficult pain in the ass. Always complaining and asking for an advance. I told him, Give me something I can sell and I'll give you some money. Then the kid informs me about this Manhattan gallery owner who supports his artists when they're broke, gives them cash and a pat on the back. The kid tells me, As a gallery owner, you should cultivate your painters." Leo laughed quietly, reminiscently. "I told the kid, a gallery owner who cultivates his painters that way goes broke. I cultivate buyers."

That was fine by me.

❦

On this sunny day I was walking back to my car in the parking lot of Big Valley Farms, the sky a robin's-egg shade of blue with puffy white clouds here and there, like laundry baskets overfilled with freshly dried bedsheets, and just enough breeze to make the halyard slap against the big flagpole, the same sound we used to hear from the sailboats at anchor in the Merrimack, and I was so lonely, lonely, lonely. I climbed onto the car roof and shouted to the women unloading their shopping carts, I'm dying of loneliness. Rescue me! Rescue me from this terrible loneliness! Then I dropped back into my body, put my groceries in the car and drove home.

❦

I drove to Peasant Bread & Fancy Pastries to see Lucy Dolan. The little bell jingled overhead and she came in from the back room — her hair was wrapped in what looked like the colorful banner of an exotic country and her gold hoop earrings flashed. "Renato! How good to see you!"

"I'm desperate. I need a fancy pastry."

She smiled. "You came to the right place. Right now it's mostly bread, but there are some pastries over here. See?"

There were sugar cookies, fancy cupcakes, a row of Napoleons, then a small tray of ladyfingers, and next to it — "That looks like a tiramisu," I said.

"It is indeed."

"I'll take two. How's business?"

"So far, so good," she said, lifting the tiramisu from behind the glass. Lucy went on to say that she was definitely going to add a small round café table and a chair, or maybe two tables and a couple of chairs, so we talked about that, and then about the odor of freshly baked bread which, so far as she could tell, everybody liked. "There was a study they did in France," she told me. "And they found that people became more altruistic when they smelled freshly baked bread."

"I don't believe you."

She smiled. "It's a fact. A scientific fact."

"I want to believe you, but I don't."

"Maybe you're not trying hard enough, Renato."

I laughed. "I'm trying harder than you know."

She told me that the odor of freshly baked bread had such a good effect on people that chemists had come up with a concoction that smelled just like it, and now food stores that got their bread from a bakery located miles away would spray this odor in the air to make people feel more like buying a loaf. "But you haven't told me what you've doing. How have you been?"

"I'm getting by," I said.

"Getting by? Tell me more."

The bell over the door jingled and a woman came in to ask for a dozen sugar cookies. "A baker's dozen," Lucy told her, adding an extra one. It was a pleasure to watch her doing nothing more than chatting with the woman, and the woman left clearly pleased with the exchange of pleasantries. As for me, I wanted to spend the whole afternoon here, bantering with Lucy. We talked about one thing and another until I felt I should leave or I'd make a fool of myself by hanging around.

Another woman came in, bought a baguette, went out. I said, "I have to get going."

"Wait, wait! This way, come. Let me show you the table and chair I bought for the store. You can tell me what color to paint them." The back room was warm. The bent-wire chair and circular café table were just inside the rear door. "What do you think?" she asked me.

"Those are perfect," I said. "They look like you snatched them from a Parisian café."

"Actually, they're from Montreal."

"Close enough," I said.

"What colors?"

"How about a luminescent lemon yellow? Bonnard said there's no such thing as too much yellow."

"Be serious."

"Seriously, it's your café and I like what you've done here, and I'm sure you'll paint these the right colors."

"I was thinking, black table, blue chair," she said.

"Perfect."

I figured it was the right moment to leave, so I did. It was a good day, the best in a long while.

So the summer wore on and the days repeated the days of the year before, and each day was like any other. I tried to keep up Alba's many flowerbeds, which had grown to a tangle of weeds, wild grasses, and brittle paper stalks left from the end of last summer, but I didn't know a thing about flowers. My colleague Eloise Carol had retired from the Copley College of Art and was a master gardener, so I phoned her and side-by-side we dug and raked, went out to lunch, then back to the gardens. We had been coworkers but not close because, in addition to her work as a printmaker in everything from lithography to serigraphy, she had written "The Male Gaze as Rape" and other pamphlets about male painters which had set my teeth on edge.

"I don't hate men," she once told me, "I hate masculinity." We sweated over the flowerbeds for a week and got along well together, then late on Friday we sat on the porch of her large Victorian house, drank cool wine, and talked some about Alba and then about Helen, Eloise's partner of fifteen years, who had moved out one spring day two years ago, devastating Eloise. "She left me for a younger woman," Eloise said, with a short dry laugh. We watched the sky turn from light blue to pink to violet and debated desire and loss and being old, and when the first tiny stars appeared I drove home, baffled by love and grief and the ways we lived.

Some of my polo shirts needed repair and, as I can't sew to save my life, much less a shirt, I asked Felicia at Café Mondello if she knew anyone who did sewing, but no, she didn't, and neither did Katelin at La Pâtisserie, and when I asked Garland at the Daily Grind, she said, "I'm happy to tell you I haven't sewn a stich since I grew up and left home." But Roxy, who was making a latte for me, pumped her fist in the air, saying, "Hey, I know how to sew." So Roxy (who had quit doing drugs and dumped her boyfriend, and was saving her cash for Culinary Arts school) and I talked, agreed on a price, and the shirts got done.

It's happened before but it's always a rude shock when the pee comes out scarlet with blood, my faithful prostate having been abused by a couple of surgeries. I phoned the urologist's office and spoke to the doctor's assistant, told her I had seen hematuria before, told her I was drinking lots of water and would stop taking my daily aspirin tomorrow morning. "Excellent," she says. "You know the routine — and don't forget to stop the caffeine, stop the alcohol, stop spicy foods, and no chocolate, either." By day three I was peeing urine as clear as a mountain stream and the withdrawal from caffeine had tied my brain in a knot, but by the end of the summer I was back to eating and drinking like my old self. Old in that sentence means old.

I don't know how a person without children lives. Skye and Astrid (or Galaxy, as she wishes) and Fabrizio came by, one family or another almost every month, which was a pleasure while they were here but painful after they'd gone and the house had filled with empty silence again, and no Alba to talk with about the kids, about the way they're living and do they know what they're doing.

Elizabeth Prescott and I had a pleasant lunch and she gave me her article on Cormac McCormac, which I read later that night. The carefully written profile caught as much of him as an academic article could, I suppose, and reading about Cormac put me in a melancholy mood. Elizabeth and I got together for another lunch and a couple of afternoon coffee meetings, but our conversation never found its way beyond stories about our children and grandchildren or politics and the wars, and we haven't seen each other for a while.

A couple of times I had lunch with Frank Vanderzee who is always good company. He's the same age as my Brizio, give or take a year, and in some ways he reminds me of myself — my younger self, that was — especially as he loves the solitude of painting but also relishes convivial talk with friends deep into the night. We met, Vanderzee and I, a dozen years ago, because he sought me out, which was enormously gratifying to this older painter, especially as I was at the bottom of my career at the time. As for Winona and Gail, they tell me they were pals when Vanderzee met them and all three got along, one step leading to another and another leading to bed. When I met them, they were camped out in Vanderzee's studio in an old industrial building in Boston's South End — Vanderzee, Gail and her two-year-old Azizi, plus Winona and baby Saskia. That was a dozen or fourteen years ago and now they have a house with two fireplaces, a big kitchen, two bedrooms for the kids, two for the adults, and a guest room where I'm invited to spend any weekend I want, which I've not done and probably never will, being as I am old and sad and would feel like a gravestone at the breakfast table.

Andrews, the ophthalmologist, tells me he's very pleased with his handiwork on my eyes. Earlier this year, when he did the surgery to relieve intraocular pressure, he also removed the cloudy lens and inserted a clear plastic one, the same as he'd done a couple of years before in my other eye. I'm now familiar with the basic mechanics of trabeculectomies and cataract surgery. I can also describe, from the patient's perspective, a transurethral resectioning of the prostate, endoscopic gall bladder surgery, endoscopic retrograde cholangiopancreatography to insert and remove a stent from the billiary duct, and various hernia repairs.

I got around to returning Fletcher's wood clamps. We hooked up for coffee now and again, but I always forgot to bring the clamps. Finally, I put them in my van so the next time we got together I could give them to him. As it happened, Fletch gave a reading from his novel at the Aldus Bookstore, so I went to that and tucked the wood clamps into his Mini Cooper. Mostly I avoid readings. Unlike gallery receptions, which are full of chatter and cheap wine, literary readings are serious affairs where everyone is seated facing the author, like in church or a schoolroom, and some writers, mostly poets, have a lugubrious way of reading, their voices dying at the end of each line. But I liked Fletch's because when he reads or talks about his book he's so animated, as if his novel was a surprise to him — it *amazes* him — and he always has a table with a big coffeepot and sliced cake or some other confection for us to snack on.

I went out to Nils' place three or four times to help him make a swimming hole in the little stream that runs through his property. Nils and I met years ago as teachers at Copley College of Art, but he taught only half-time, which was what he wanted so that he and his wife Hanna would be at least half-free to go to foreign art festivals, learn to make mandolins, weave cloth, produce computer art — whatever that is — and mosaics. I liked Nils and I liked Hanna, despite her belief that performance art was an art. They never made much money from whatever their art happened to be, but Nils was handy at carpentry and was sought out for restorations by people who had the cash to pay for such things, and for a while Hanna had a fabric shop, then she designed and sewed glittery outfits for rock musicians and dancers, and recently she'd become a costumer for theatrical productions, so they got by pretty well.

About thirty years ago they bought a broken-down dairy farm (no cows) and had been repairing and extending the house ever since. The biggest part was up by the road with half a dozen smaller additions, halls, garages and sheds joined together behind it, one after the other, like railroad cars. The stream that ran through the bottom of their lot was narrow and shallow, but Nils figured if he cut away the bank on both sides and put some big stones where the stream narrowed, he'd have a nice waist-deep pool. So we rolled boulders and carried stones for days and I learned I wasn't as strong as I used to be.

Lucy decided to be called Lucia again, because Lucia went better with Peasant Bread & Fancy Pastries, she said. "Peasants and fancy pastries are European, and Lucia sounds more European than Lucy. — Jacob always called me Lucia. Do you remember?"

"I remember it well," I said. "We all called you Lucia back then."

She smiled, clearly gratified.

"Astrid has two names. She's known as Galaxy in her role as documentary filmmaker."

"Astrid!" She laughed. "Oh, God, we had great fun back then. Your kids were great. *Are* great!"

It was a pleasure to see Lucy, or Lucia, when she laughed, her face brightening, eyes sparkling, though in repose or when focused on a task, you saw the bones beneath the flesh and the fine net of lines around the eyes, which allowed me to pretend I was not this old man being foolish about that much younger woman. Before opening the bakery she had been staying with her friend Alison in Arlington, but now she had found an apartment, one side of a little duplex — "Out here in the country," was the way she put it.

"Out in the country?" I said. "The only country in this town is in a nature preserve."

"Too many trees, not enough people," she told me. She asked what was new in my life and I said nothing was new, absolutely nothing, then she said she was reading a biography of Abigail Adams and asked had I ever read it. I said, "No. But Alba always liked Abigail Adams and knew more about her than she knew about some of her own friends."

"They were a great marriage, Abigail and John," she said.

So we talked about the Adamses and about Jefferson, then Lucia — it's a pleasure to write her name that way — told me how to make hot flip, which was a winter drink in the late 1700s that you heated by taking a hot poker from the fire and quenching it in your tankard of rum, after which we discussed the two small round café tables she now had, and agreed she should paint them black and paint each of the four chairs a different color, the colors being harmonious with each other. As it turned out, I painted the tables and chairs a week or two later. And for the large blank wall, I agreed not to portray God transmitting the spark of life to Adam's limp hand by means of a loaf of Italian bread. "But I still think it's a good idea," I told her.

You know how when you enter Big Valley Farms the traffic bends you to the right and they've arranged the fruit and vegetable stands in the middle of your pathway, so you walk around and between them, and the other day they had pyramids of yellow grapefruit and oranges and lemons on one side and big bunches of grapes, translucent green and frosted purple, on the other, and further along a mountain of potatoes with snow-white onions in the distance, so next day I bring my camera and, of course, they had switched things around, but it was still interesting and I took some photos. When I got home, I was looking at the speckled yellow pears and glossy red peppers I had bought and I began to wonder if I picked them up simply for their color. I wish I felt like painting. On the other hand, I have more time to prepare dinner and I enjoy the meditative spell of slicing vegetables for a salad or stir-fry or, in winter, vegetable soup. The other day I did the math and I figured you made at least eighteen thousand dinners for us.

Sometimes when I'm dead and it's Alba who's alive, she's at a candlelight dinner with friends and the man seated across from Alba is her companion, a retired naval officer, or it's a summer day and those two are walking together and she's attentive to what he's saying. I know I'm dead and gone, but still I recoil at the scene. The man is one of those restrained, priggish and punctilious heroes from the Jane Austen novels that Alba liked so much.

I was online looking up bread recipes and came across an article about the aroma of baking bread and — *lo and behold!* — it said researchers at a university in Brittany had discovered that the scent of baking bread puts people in an amiable mood and they're more likely to act altruistically. So Lucia wasn't daft — she was right and I was delighted.

One Saturday morning in September, Leo Conti phoned to remind me that he was driving out to select works for the gallery. And, by the way, he was bringing his new intern with him. "She's good. Probably not what you had in mind when I said I was hiring an intern, but very good. And I'm paying her, so she's not really an intern." I remembered Leo telling me he was thinking of getting a brainy graduate from Yale or Harvard or some such place, but I'm sure I never had anything in mind about it.

Later that day his beige Mercedes dove into the ruts of my driveway, came to a jouncing halt and here he was. "I love being close to nature," he announced. Leo was in a stylish hunting vest, the kind with leather-trimmed pockets to hold shotgun shells and a leather patch up front by the shoulder to cushion the rifle butt. "And this is Quincy, my new associate," he said, introducing a woman in her thirties — violet hair hanging below her shoulders, a khaki t-shirt that looked to be made of silk, her left arm illuminated by a sinuous tattoo dense with color, short pants and delicate sandals. The short pants revealed a further tattoo descending her left leg, the empty outline of Art Nouveau scrollwork. Her skin was remarkably white and the tattoo artist must have enjoyed working on it.

Quincy and I shook hands, her straight-on gaze assessing me as I was assessing her. She said, "My daughter won't bother you. She's got a book to read and her guitar, so she can keep herself busy." She was referring to a girl of — I don't know — maybe twelve or thirteen, sitting in the backseat of the Mercedes, watching us.

We all three walked to the barn, Quincy drifting behind us, and I said to Leo, "There's something we have to talk about."

He looked at me. "What do you mean?"

"I painted a lot of these canvases for this barn. They're composed to be seen together, in a certain arrangement, in that space."

"Why are you telling me this?"

"I don't know what you want for the gallery, but a lot of these paintings aren't for sale."

"Renato, I know that. I know it because you've been telling me for five years. That's why I'm going to pick out a group of paintings and you're going to tell me which ones we can offer to those people who are eager to buy your work. Agreed?"

I said I agreed and kept quiet. I wanted an exhibit and at

the same time I didn't want to have anything to do with it and, anyway, I felt vaguely disagreeable, maybe because of Conti's assistant, and pissed at myself for feeling that way toward Conti who, after all, liked my work and sold it.

As we came along the old orchard, Leo picked one of the apples. "Is this safe to eat?" he asked me.

"It's an apple, Leo. People have been eating them for centuries."

"This one looks kind of wormy."

"That worm would never eat the apple if it wasn't a healthy apple. Eat from the other side."

While we walked, he turned the apple this way and that and looked skeptical. "I'll eat it later," he said, pushing it into his pocket.

I shoved open the barn door and we went inside. There was plenty of light pouring in from the high windows, but I showed him where the light switches were if he wanted to use them. I went upstairs to the loft and opened the studio door, then went down and told Leo he could look at anything. He was already moving some of the stretchers around. His assistant hung back, shifting from foot to foot, starting to bite a fingernail, then abruptly jamming her hand into her pocket. I told her to take a look around, make herself at home. She responded with a fleeting smile which was more like a nervous tic. I doubted she was the Art History student from Harvard or Yale that Leo had been looking for. I asked her where she had studied.

"Vermont," she said. "And Maine," she added.

What kind of an answer was that? "Those are good states," I said, after searching for something to say. "Yup, good New England states."

I told Leo I was going back to the house and would return in a half-hour or so.

Quincy's daughter had opened the car's rear doors and was sitting inside, reading. She glanced up and watched me as I went by, so I stopped to ask did she want anything, maybe a glass of water or something to eat. She hesitated, then said she had already eaten lunch, thank you anyway. I thought to ask her what she was reading, but decided against it, went inside and made myself a cup of coffee.

I had been working for thirty years to get my paintings back on Newbury Street and I wanted to get this exhibit in the new Conti Gallery on that same street, and it didn't matter to me that there might be better venues somewhere else in Boston — I wanted my work on that street — and at the same time I didn't care piss about the paintings or the exhibit. Alba had said those were good works, great works, and she had lived the life we lived, never having an extra dollar, so I could paint, and it was up to me to make sure we got this goddamn exhibit. After the show I could lie down to die, because I wasn't going to paint another canvas because there wasn't anyone to show it to. I finished the coffee, washed out the cup and the coffeepot, and headed outside.

Quincy's daughter watched from the car as I went by and I got to the apple trees before I turned around and walked back and said, "Your mother's looking at some paintings in the barn, which is where I'm going and you can come along, too, if you want." She had the guitar in her lap, which she set carefully aside before hopping out.

We walked along. I asked her, "Would you rather read or play the guitar?"

She frowned a moment, thinking about it. "I'm not too good on the guitar. I'm just learning. I like to read, too. I like to read mysteries. But I'm not so good on the guitar."

Her sunshine-blonde hair was pulled back to a short ponytail held in place with a rubber band, and she wore a dazzling white t-shirt with slight bumps there and there to indicate her breasts.

"I bet you play fine," I told her.

She smiled and made a lovely delicate fingering gesture in the air. "I'm improving, I think."

When we reached the barn, Leo was standing outside, scanning the sky. "You got fantastic clouds out here. Look at those things. And I saw a hawk!"

Quincy's daughter walked quickly ahead to her mother who was deep inside, crouched in front of one of the paintings, writing in a notebook.

"So you've met Sylvan," Leo told me. I must have looked blank, because he added, "Quincy's daughter."

"Yes, nice kid. And you say Quincy is a good assistant, or associate or something?"

"You sound doubtful, Renato. She's learning. She doesn't know your work the way I do but she's a quick study. Very bright. — She went to Harvard."

"She told me Maine and Vermont. Harvard's in Massachusetts."

"She was at Harvard for a year. Practically a year. A semester and a half, anyway. Then she took a break. Later she went to a couple of those colleges where you go for a week and they tell you what to study and then you go off to where you came from and study and write papers. Which means she's self-motivated and has lots of initiative. She's connected to the art world, maybe not exactly what you and I would call mature painters, but the coming art world. Also, she has a certain refinement and can talk well to buyers. — Good family background."

Quincy had finished her note-taking and now mother and daughter were headed our way.

"Listen," Leo said, lowering his voice. "This has been a learning experience for her. I'll come out here again without her and we'll talk, you and me. We'll go over the paintings together. This is going to be a great exhibit."

Quincy came up, now wearing eyeglasses or, more precisely, a single eyeglass — one of the lenses was missing and the hinge to the temple piece was bandaged with adhesive tape.

"I hope you like what you saw," I said.

"Oh, yes. Leo gave me photographs of your work to study and I looked forward to seeing the actual paintings. I think gallery-goers can benefit from seeing the works of the previous generation, the earlier painters. It provides historical context for the contemporary art scene." She went on a while more, but by then my head was echoing badly, blotting out whatever else she said. When she had finished, I said, "Oh. Well. Thanks. I never thought of it that way."

Luci or Lucy or Lucia, whichever way she spelled her name I liked her — in fact, I liked her a lot — and though I have more vanity and foolishness in me than most men, I don't have enough to delude myself about her and me. Conversation was easy with her and we had dinner together now and again, but she evaded coming to my home, perhaps to save me from a grotesque blunder, and we ate only in restaurants where she insisted on splitting the bill. One Wednesday she told me she was "getting away from it all, going to Montreal with a friend" for the weekend. And one Sunday morning I drove to her place on a whim to take her out for breakfast, but when I turned into the parking place behind her apartment, the guest slot was occupied by a rusted van from Boudreau Electric that had snuggled up close to her little Toyota, so without stopping I swung around and headed home.

Leo Conti drove out here to make a final selection of paintings for the show and ended up choosing the same ones Alba had told me would go best at the gallery. Conti and I argued over one painting, a four-by-six that Alba always said should be darker. I told her, I don't do darker than that. Now Leo was saying the same damn thing, Make it darker, make it darker. You began it dark, he says, so make it darker. I told him, I like color and I'm good at it and black is the absence of color so do you want me to punch a goddamn hole in the canvas? And he says, I didn't say black, I said *darker*. Then he drove off with two frescos I should have smashed long ago, but he thinks they'll interest a buyer he has in mind.

❦

Katia and I had lunch a couple of times as she crisscrossed Eastern Massachusetts, looking for a church where she and the parish were a good match, then one morning she phoned to tell me she had found what she was looking for. She said she felt like celebrating and wanted to take me out for lunch. "That's great," I said, "But I'm supposed to meet Leo Conti at noon in Boston, so he can show me the new gallery." Katia asked, Where's the gallery? and I said, On Newbury Street, if I can believe him, and Katia said, Wonderful! Because after you've inspected the gallery we can have lunch on Newbury.

And, in fact, the gallery was on Newbury, just as Leo had promised. The sidewalks were flooded with people and the street looked narrower than I had remembered, the shops smaller, but there was an excitement about this parade of outdoor cafés, fancy boutique clothiers, expensive trinket shops and pricy art galleries. The interior of the Conti Gallery had been peeled away to the brick walls, the floors had been refinished and a loose skein of electrical lines dangled from sockets in the ceiling. "I'm impressed, Leo."

"I thought you would be."

"When will the gallery be ready?"

"For you? November."

I looked around, wondering how my paintings would look in this space. Suddenly I missed Alba so much it hurt and I almost winced. Leo was watching me and waiting. "This is good, Leo," was all I said. "Very good."

As we were leaving, Leo reached up and patted my back, saying, "You're going to be all right. This is going to be great. And remember, I'm taking care of everything."

We crossed the street and walked to the Café Boul'Mich, a pleasant stroll, the air being cool and the noonday sun just warm enough, and we stood there talking about his gallery expenses until I saw Katia approaching — a big wave from her, then greetings all around, after which Leo headed off, and Katia and I found a table at the café. I had forgotten what it was like to sit at a café table with throngs of people walking by and for a moment I simply soaked in it. "I remember meeting him at some of your exhibits," she said about Leo. "But I think he had a lot of hair or was taller or something. How did the new gallery look?"

"Unfinished but good. Surprisingly good, in fact. It makes me feel like celebrating, so let me buy you lunch."

"My new church looks good, too, so let me buy you lunch, which was our plan."

We gave the waiter our orders and I asked Katia about her new parish.

"More intellectual than most," she said. "The retiring pastor was known for his brains, not his piety or good fellowship, and despite his reputation for intelligence, people come from two or three towns away to listen to him. The congregation — I think, I hope — is the kind I've been looking for. It sounds good, and at my age this is going to be my last position."

"At your age? Are you pretending to be old? You certainly don't look the part."

Katia laughed. "It's the chaste life I lead. My youth and beauty last forever because my heart is pure. No sins, no wrinkles."

You need to know something about Katia. She married her college boyfriend a month after graduating from UMass and followed that by graduating pregnant from Union Theological Seminary, but as soon as the baby was born she and her husband split. "Because at the seminary I discovered there were two things I enjoyed and was truly interested in, theology and sex. And I had intimations that these were more than interests, they were passions, and if we stayed married I'd betray him and make his life miserable and I didn't want to do that. He was a decent guy, you know. I got pregnant because I'd already had a miscarriage and I wanted a baby and I told him so and, after all, even though we had called it quits we were still sleeping in the same bed, the only difference being that our sex life was better than when we thought we were stuck with each other. He loved working on Wall Street, theology bored him, and he certainly wasn't ready to be a father, so it was best for both of us." That's what she told Alba and me.

Katia didn't intend to become a pastor when she entered the seminary; she simply loved theology and when her son turned four, Katia began a new course of study at Union Theological. We didn't see much of her during those years, but from her occasional notes and visits we understood that she was indulging her passions. We were surprised, though maybe we shouldn't have been, when she told us she had decided to become a pastor. "Obviously it can't be Catholic or Episcopalian and I'm not interested in anything less than Lutheran, but that's too confining — they're all too confining — so it's nondenominational, and I know that sounds weird, but I think I can do that. — And I love you for being so patient," she told us.

Here and now at the Café Boul'Mich, we ate lunch and talked about her new parish, about what Katia said were "all these intellectuals in Eastern Massachusetts, some of them — many of them — believe, or have a desire to believe, that there's something beyond the material world they deal with every day."

I asked were they mostly younger or mostly older.

She smiled. "Mature is the word I prefer. Most of them are mature. But there are others, of course, people who describe themselves as not religious but spiritual. Spiritual is a word that leaves a bad taste in my mouth," she added.

"We never understood how you arrived at your faith, or what kind of faith it was and, I admit, well, we didn't have the nerve to ask."

The waiter came by, flashed the dessert menu at us and confided that the crème brûlée was irresistible. We resisted and ordered espressos.

Katia said, "You two were probably wondering how I could be bedding this one and that one and be a woman of faith. I wondered that too, once in a while. I'm lucky I survived my own foolishness. But I knew there was a God. As far back as I can remember I knew there was a God. Knowing whether or not I had a calling, a true vocation — that was a puzzle, but I was willing to take that chance."

"We knew you had this natural belief in God — it was such a rare thing — but we never knew what you'd do next."

"Neither did I. I mean, I was still sleeping around, so why would God call me to religious life? To get me to stop? I don't think so. I think I'm just slow at understanding who I am. Eric and I were together long before I realized I was in love with him." Katia was referring to the man she had been living with for the last several years. "It took me a while to know I was called. I'm slow. But I go pretty far," she added, with a slight smile.

I laughed. "I remember you were celibate for a while."

"Ah, you do remember! Yes, when Theo turned thirteen and until he went off to college. It wasn't so bad. In fact, it was good."

"I can't say I ever had faith," I said. "Sometimes I believed, but it wasn't a strongly held belief, or maybe it never got to being a belief at all. When I was first in love with Alba — not when we were kids, but when we were in our twenties and found each other again — for days, for weeks, I believed in God. Everything was so stunningly right and beautiful. Actually, it wasn't so much a belief in God as it was a surge of good feelings for the whole world, the universe, an overflow of love toward everyone, including God."

"Oh, I *like* that."

"Everything's gone now," I said. "I believe in nothing."

She looked at me with those same steady, interested eyes she had as a kid, at last saying, "That's understandable."

We fell silent and watched the jumbled stream of people passing by. After a while, Katia said, "When I realized I was in love with Eric, my next thought was how devastated I'd be if anything happened to him. The world would be empty. I don't know, I can't imagine — I mean, I don't want to imagine how I'd feel."

The waiter arrived with our coffee and the bill which he placed with a flourish squarely between us, then off he went.

"You believe in God and I understand that," I said. "I don't think that's a weird belief. It makes sense to me. But who, or what, *is* this God with a capital G?"

Katia hesitated. "If I say God is the creator of heaven and earth, the seas and all things in them, will you be mad at me?"

I had to smile. "No. I won't be mad at you."

"And if I go beyond that and start listing the attributes of God, it gets rather scholastic and, well —"

I broke in, saying, "It wasn't right, Alba's dying. It wasn't right. I was in a rage about that. And I will be forever."

And Katia, all along knowing my mind, said, "Some people would hate God for that. Or they might hate a pastor, thinking she represented God, when actually—"

"I just wanted to die, that's all. I tried to will myself to death."

"The rest of us are happy you failed. And I'm particularly grateful you're right here at this table having coffee with me. You've kept going." She hesitated, then said, "Do you mind if — Can I ask you — What do you believe in that gets you out of bed every morning?"

"I don't know. I don't know much these days. And the more I think about these things, the less I know. I know Alba loved me. I believe in Alba."

I sounded stupid even to me. We drank our coffee and watched the people flowing past, this way and that, and at times overflowing into the street.

"I hope you get back to painting," Katia said. "It may be your calling."

"You're kind to say so."

She smiled. "You're probably tired of hearing me say I love and admire you."

I laughed. "No. Not at all."

It was a good lunch and a fine autumn day and Alba would have enjoyed the three of us being at the Café Boul'Mich on Newbury Street.

After my shower I was trimming my horny toenails, going over this body in the clean morning sunlight, pressing a tender area that hides a femoral hernia, finding a cyst in my groin, a numb passage along my foot, spots of scaly keratosis on my shoulder and wild sprouting hairs anyplace. Old me has become one of those whales you see heave up through tons of sea, their bodies patchy with ancient barnacles; they break into the air for a moment, fins spreading out like useless wings, then they crash down and slide under and disappear. I crave the love-making we used to do. No woman finds me attractive. I know what you're saying, and I'm grateful for it, but you're the only one who ever thought so.

Leo Conti had wanted an artist's statement for the exhibit catalog, a brief paragraph, he said, and I had said, Yes, sure, and tossed the crumpled notion into some corner of my cluttered mind and forgot about it, because it was too much work and, besides, the paintings were the goddamn statement. A couple of weeks later, Conti's associate, the one with violet hair, Quincy, turned up at my front door with a carryall under her arm and her daughter by her side, saying that Conti had sent her to get the statement from me because, she asserted, he had asked me for it a month ago and there was a deadline.

I told her to come in and asked would she like a coffee and would Sylvan like some hot apple cider. "The paintings don't need an explanation," I said.

"It's not an explanation about the paintings," Quincy tells me. "It's about you."

"I'm not going to explain me."

She hesitated a moment and was about to say something, so I said to Sylvan, "I'll make you a mug of hot apple cider with a cinnamon stick in it. Follow me."

Sylvan followed me and Quincy followed Sylvan, so we were in the kitchen now where Quincy opened her carryall on the table, telling me, "I have statements you made for other exhibits and also interviews you gave that might help you."

"I'm sure I was never so crazy as to explain myself."

She had dumped papers and magazine clippings onto the table and looked up to say, "In an interview you gave a dozen years ago you said you painted to give people solace for being human."

"That was a dozen years ago. I was young and hopeful."

"You were seventy," she informs me.

"Oh, to be seventy again."

"I thought we could start there and add to it," she says.

I poured a mug of apple cider for Sylvan and gave her a stick of cinnamon to drop into it, then I put the mug into the microwave.

Quincy was persistent, meaning we two sat at the kitchen table and debated the merits of artists' statements while her daughter, who had taken her mug of hot cider to the front room, looked through the shelf of books left behind by my children and grandchildren as they grew up. There was nothing Quincy could pry out of me because I had nothing to say. After an hour, she gave up, dropped the clippings back into her carryall, and went to the front room to get her daughter, who was seated cross-legged on the floor with an open book in her hand, studying the map of some magical kingdom that lay unfolded in her lap. "Put the book back and say thank-you and goodbye to Mr Stillamare," Quincy told her.

❦

You probably don't remember, but one day I caught you by the wrist as you were passing by in the kitchen, caught you by surprise, and you turned and asked, "Are you going to take me to your pirate ship?" I don't know why I remembered that just now, but I did. That was so long ago.

Late one fall afternoon Fletcher and I were raking leaves at his place and talking about how when we were kids our families used to rake leaves out to the street and then burn them in the gutter, so the delicately sharp odor of burning leaves became the scent of fall. "Now they don't allow it in any of these towns, not anymore," he said. We missed that odor and we talked about the smell of torn grass and damp soil that came to your nose when you were scrimmaging on the football field, and how cold you got walking home after practice with the dark coming on. I remember that part, but I don't recall how the talk got from there to books and the last chapters of novels. I know I asked him, "Why do novels always come to a satisfying conclusion, no matter what's happened, no matter what dreadful things have happened along the way, there's a sense of rightness at the end? That's not the way life is."

"That's why novels are called fictions," Fletch said. "A novel isn't life, it's fiction."

"I thought a novel was supposed to reflect life. My uncle Zitti liked to say that a novelist was like a man carrying a big mirror down the road, so it reflects everything — the blue sky overhead and the muddy road underfoot."

"I think that's from Stendhal."

"Ah, zio Zitti." I laughed. "He loved Stendhal. He couldn't bear to think of Stendhal as French and always referred to him as a displaced Italian."

"Stendhal was crazy about Italy," said Fletch. "Maybe your uncle was right."

Then we heard Fletch's Kate calling and turned to see her silhouetted in the tall yellow rectangle of the open front door. "Dinner's ready," she said. "How can you guys see what you're doing out there? It's already dark. Come in, come in."

We dragged the loaded tarpaulin to the street and dumped the leaves in the gutter where the town could vacuum them up. As we were walking back toward the house, Fletch says, "I think that sense of rightness at the end of a story is like the resolution at the end of a piece of music. Even the blues or a tragic symphony has that resolution. It doesn't mean everything turned out all right."

"It just means it's over," I said.

"Yes, that's it."

Then we went in and had dinner.

I bought vegetables today to make soup — I start with diced tomatoes and I don't use stock — but when I got home and laid the vegetables on the counter I was struck again by the colors — the yellow of the squash is really boastful, and there's the cool celery green and the harsh hue of the carrots and so on. I get into a restful, meditative calm when I cut up vegetables, like I was preparing to paint again, but first I had to slice up a batch of primary colors. It looked so good in the pot that before I ladled it out I took a photo, thinking you should see it — the craziness never goes away. I've done some line drawings and maybe I'll do some work in color.

A week ahead of the exhibit, Leo Conti sent me twenty copies of the exhibit catalog. He had outdone himself. It was extraordinary — a big, flat paperbound catalog printed on deliciously heavy glazed paper, like the pages of the art book my father had bought for our home when I was a kid. That volume was my first course in art history and I loved the big color prints and the sound of the pages sliding heavily upon each other. Now here's the catalog of *Works by Renato Stillamare* at the Conti Gallery on Newbury Street in Boston, Massachusetts. It reproduces almost every painting in the show and has not only a running text around the paintings, but also an additional two pages about the artist's oeuvre through the decades. And look at old Renato now as he takes an armful of catalogs to the barn and climbs the stairs to his studio, dropping some in his haste, so he can bring them to the shelf where the photographs of Alba wait, where he can lay a catalog open in front of her — the old bastard is sobbing now — saying, *Look, Alba. See? We made it. We got the exhibit on Newbury Street. We did it. See? We did it.*

The show was a success. The paintings looked good, the gallery was almost spacious enough, and there I was (smiling, warm-hearted, appreciative), engaging with everyone, not moving around much because friends were coming up to offer congratulations and to see for themselves if Stillamare had more or less recovered, because he went absolutely and completely, you know, *crazy*, after his wife died. The inner man was astonished at what the outer shell was capable of. Skye and Eric had driven down to my place and then to the gallery where Skye stood beside me to maneuver people this way or that, and when I hadn't caught a name she'd repeat it along with a phrase to remind me who was who. Astrid and Weston arrived at the same time as Brizio and Heather — meaning we were all together now, except their mother wasn't here.

Among my friends there was Zoe and Emerson, of course, and Zocco and his wife (still limping a bit), Avalon (in a shimmering peacock-blue dress slashed up to her thigh, because Alba had once praised her for wearing it) and Sebastian, Nils and Hanna, Scott and fragile Rachel, George Agathos (crackers and cheese in one hand, a glass of Chablis in the other, saying, "You have exceeded yourself!") and his Io, Fletcher and Kate, Lucia and her friend Alison, and others I hadn't seen in a while, like Scanlon and his wife who drove up from Connecticut, and the Goetemanns from Gloucester, plus a number of painters who had regular shows at the galley and were required to attend out of politeness.

The scattering of early-comers thickened up and the gallery grew pleasingly crowded. Quincy (high-heel shoes, trim gray suit, her violet hair held back by a silver clasp) introduced me to a trio she said were "really awesome painters" — a young man who had a degree from Copley College where I used to teach, another in a World War II airman's leather jacket, and a young African-American woman with a faint British accent in a striking red Maasai dress and jewelry. They were a decent bunch and after their polite remarks about my work (including the fifty-year-old witticism that Stillamare paints nudes as if they were landscapes and landscapes as if they were nudes) we relaxed and talked about studio space and the high cost of everything. More and more of the people were unknown to me, which was a good sign, especially when Leo introduced them to me.

Leo had chosen an authentic appearance for himself this evening — no wig, his head bald as a cannonball but slightly tanned, a plain gray suit and, peeking above his jacket's breast pocket, a pair of reading glasses as a friendly and informal touch. He wouldn't be doing any reading tonight, but he'd use the folded glasses to point out this or that when talking.

I caught a glimpse of Winona and Gail, and later Vanderzee turned up. My first exhibit with Leo had been a sprawling affair in East Cambridge and halfway through the evening Vanderzee had left, returning with his clarinet and three friends to play Dixieland until the gallery was a wreck of empty wine bottles and crumpled paper cups. Now Vanderzee shook my hand, looked around at the long dresses and money, and said, "Good crowd. Too bad I didn't bring my band."

Leo Conti introduced me to Kenneth Parkman, telling me, "Kenneth is Quincy's father." Kenneth Parkman, a tall middle-aged man with a receding hairline, shook my hand.

"Quincy's a remarkable young woman," I told him.

Parkman nodded slightly, rather thoughtfully it seemed to me. "She has an interest in art," he told me.

"She appears to have an instinct for it, a natural talent," I said.

"One can only hope so," he said, smiling. After a slight hesitation, he said, or asked, "You have children."

"Yes, and all three are here." I was about to introduce Skye, but she was in an animated conversation with a couple of people.

Parkman had looked about to say something on the subject of children, but glancing around he now said, "This is a fine exhibit, very fine." He turned slightly to the woman who had joined him, bringing her forward, saying "This is Moira, Quincy's mother."

We shook hands and she said, "My granddaughter was delighted with the book you sent her."

"A book?" I didn't know what she was talking about, then half a second later I realized the granddaughter was Sylvan. "Oh, yes! She had been reading it at my place — it belonged to my daughter — so when I came across a new copy I thought I'd send it along."

After we had exchanged a few more pleasantries, they drifted off. The party hummed along and Leo reappeared at my elbow, murmuring, "A gentleman who made a purchase at the advanced viewing is here. That's him, talking with Quincy. He wants to meet you, so let's go to my office."

We trailed Quincy who was already steering the man toward Leo's office. As usual, Leo had given certain buyers a look at the paintings a day or two early, so when the gallery opened this evening a handful of paintings had a handsome red dot beneath them to announce they'd already been sold. Leo had told me that an up-and-coming real estate trader, Mr Somebody, had bought the big semiabstract landscape. In the office we shook hands and I played my artist's role rather well, I thought, but when it was time for me to bow myself away, Leo tells me, "We're not through yet," then we push into the crowded gallery, a photographer appears out of thin air, and as people begin to turn our way, Leo puts the red dot by the painting and the photographer takes a dozen shots of the Real Estate Patron of the Arts, plus Leo Conti and the artist. I detest these stupid stunts. The buyer would really like da Vinci to paint baby Jesus surrounded by the three wise men, plus the Patron Himself, bringing gifts.

So now I told Skye I wanted a glass of goddamned wine. She took my arm, saying, Don't mutter that way, somebody might hear you, then she walked me to the table and asked, Do you want a glass of goddamned red or goddamned white? I said white and asked her did she think the exhibit was going well. And she said, "Of course it's going well. It's terrific."

Later, Astrid came by and told me, "I saw that camera business. You should rethink not letting me make a movie of one of your gallery exhibits. As part of a documentary, you know."

"Didn't we have this conversation before?"

"You gave me the wrong answer before," she said.

Wine was in my veins, I was feeling expansive and I talked with Brizio and Heather, maybe for too long. Twenty minutes earlier the gallery had been so jammed and warm that a few couples had slipped outside, lingering on the broad stone steps to chat and breathe the cold night air, but now the crowd was thinning away. Spaces were growing larger, emptier, like after Alba's memorial service. Quincy had taken off her jacket, revealing her sleeveless blouse and the brightly colored tattoo that swirled down her left arm, and now she began to clear the table of cheese platters and wine glasses. On the drive back home, Skye and Eric assured me it had been an excellent show, a great exhibit. At home I was still too accelerated to go to sleep, so I made myself a cup of hot cocoa and sat a long time at the kitchen table, waiting, though I knew Alba couldn't tell me my paintings were great, and I couldn't tell her she had been the most beautiful woman in the room tonight.

There are stupid passages in Lucretius that had me scribbling furiously in the margin. He says we're nothing but atoms that disperse when we die, and therefore death is nothing to us, and having reasoned his way to that point, he says we're now free to live like gods. But it's precisely this erasing of the self that we dread. The gods are immortal and we are not, and no, we are not free to live like gods. We die. We don't want to be dispersed or dissolved into the void, we don't want to lose each other. Death was nothing to Lucretius because he never loved and never grieved.

Take those lines where he tells us that often when a calf is slaughtered at the altar, the calf's bereaved mother — and "mother" is the word he uses — the bereaved mother wanders around, searching for her calf's familiar footprints, filling the woods with her moans, and when she returns to their stall she's pierced with longing for her calf. The passage is famous among classical scholars. But Lucretius doesn't write so much as one tender hexameter about human loss, which grief he treats with chilly reason.

The man doesn't understand people. He wrote two or three hundred lines on sexual passion, all with detachment, irony or mockery. His women are manipulating bitches, the men deluded, and those couples who enjoy each other he compares to a pair of stuck dogs — the poor hound, having mounted his hot bitch, has thrust in but can't pull back out. Lucretius is curious about everything (magnets, the growth of civilization, wet dreams, whatever) — well, so am I, and I admire him for that, but grudgingly.

His description of frenzied lovemaking is as precise as everything else he writes about. He tells us how lovers entangle, press and rub against each other, greedy mouth upon mouth. And even when they've satisfied their cravings and lie melted by the heat of their passion, it's only for a short time and "the hunger comes back, the frenzy and madness return." It's all in vain, he says. They can't wholly embrace or dissolve "or penetrate or be absorbed, body into body" — and, he says, "that's what they appear to be trying to do." Yes, Lucretius, that's what they're trying to do. But being Lucretius and literal minded, he thinks it impossible.

My friend Mike Bruno used to say that orgasms take place not down there, but in the brain. According to Mike, the tributary nerves carry only simple signals, a little vocabulary of sensations, to the spinal cord, and that bundle of signals speeds to the brain where it's parsed for meaning in the context of everything else that's going on up there, and it's the *meaning* that causes the explosion, sending messages of gratitude back to the provinces, even to the soles of your feet. I don't know if he was right or wrong — Mike was an art critic by trade and had theories about a lot of things. As for me, I can't paint and simultaneously theorize about painting, and the same goes for me and lovemaking.

But Alba and I did sometimes talk about it, awkward and hesitant even years into marriage, just the two of us at the end of the day, the children asleep upstairs. I remember a conversation that began one hot summer evening — I know it was summer because as we got deeper into it I shut the windows so our voices wouldn't carry in the humid stillness of the night — we began to talk about what it was we were doing, this or that or the other, and what it possibly meant, when we made love. In ways that Lucretius could never understand, it's possible to completely embrace or penetrate or be absorbed or dissolve, body into body. And when your beloved has gone, absolutely gone, you feel that half your body has been ripped away, and though you appear whole to everyone, you know you are not.

What I'm trying to do is to give it the sense that you're not there. Remember how you said old Fitzhugh Lane could paint silence? I'm trying to paint absence. I'm hoping the slant and color of light as it rakes across, just touching the perfume bottles, the little jewelry box, your comb, the seashell holding your earrings, and the chamber stick with no candle — I hope it works. I'm not including the big mirror, but instead a high blank wall where the mirror should be. I'm hoping it doesn't look like a neat bureau expecting someone. If I've done it right, it shows you're not here.

One day I was checking the garden fence where the snow was drifted deep and I heard something flutter this way and that in your rhododendron bush, and then a cardinal flew out and landed on the fence post, maybe three feet from me. And you know how cautious those cardinals are. She tilted her head to get a full look at me but didn't fly off, and I thought maybe this is the same cardinal that flew around us when Astrid was looking for a sign from you. Now the cardinal flew to the next fence post and looked at me again, so I went there and waited, wondering what this meant. The sun was high and there was nothing here but us two in this dead garden filled with dazzling snow. Then she flew back to the first post and hopped around to watch me again. So I walked back and watched and waited, and when she was ready she flew up, high up over the empty trees and away.

I received a letter from the New Arts Alliance announcing that in recognition of my work in the visual arts they would be honored to present me with their Biennale Award, on such and such a day in April. I assumed they'd made a mistake. I'd become a member fifty or more years ago when the Alliance was a small gang of insurgent countercultural painters living around Boston. Over the years it grew into a New England regional organization and, though I still gave them a yearly donation, I had let my membership lapse long ago — the revolution was over and the good guys had lost.

I phoned Leo and told him about the award. "Congratulations. And why are you surprised? This is new youth recognizing old youth," he said. I wrote to the New Arts Alliance to express my thanks for the honor of being a recipient of their prestigious award. Apparently they had not made a mistake because the president, Howard Chi, sent me a letter outlining the history of the New Arts Alliance Biennale Award, given every two years for the past twenty years, which was news to me, and I learned that, starting five years ago, the award was presented to two artists at the same ceremony, a "distinguished painter, such as yourself," wrote Chi, and an "emerging artist, such as Esiankiki Fields," who would be honored along with me this year. I had never come across him or her. The prize is a modest sum of money and a small silver Revere bowl.

I hadn't been to a meeting of the New Arts Alliance in thirty years, but Skye drove us to Boston, found a parking space, and stayed by my side, more or less. I was astonished by how young everyone was. There were a few familiar faces — Leo Conti, of course, had received an invitation, and Zocco was a member of the Alliance so he was there, too, with his wife, as was Vanderzee with Gail and Winona. Quincy was a familiar face, her violet hair radiating around her head as if electrified, and I recognized the young painter who had been wearing the World War II airman's jacket at my exhibit. It was a good crowd and there were some bald heads and white beards, but it looked like I was the oldest person in the room.

Two easels stood at the front of the room, one holding a canvas by Esiankiki Fields and the other holding one of mine. Before giving the awards, Howard Chi made a speech, a historical tour through my career with quotes along the way from reviews and interviews, all of which must have come from Quincy's research. The speech was mercifully short, but even before it ended it began to sound rather like an obituary — specifically, my obituary. I had started to sweat, so it was a relief when he began his remarks about Esiankiki Fields. Fields turned out to be the young African-American woman in a red Maasai dress that Quincy had introduced to me at my show a while back. This evening she was in a red sweater and black pants and wore Maasai earrings with colored beads and dangling coins, a good-looking woman.

After the awards ceremony had broken up, drinks were available, including bourbon, for which I was grateful, and it felt good to relax, have a drink with Vanderzee and his wives, and Zocco, and a handful of others I hadn't seen in years. Esienkiki caught my eye and came over to thank me for having told the Alliance to add my award money to hers. I said I remembered our conversation in the Conti Gallery about the cost of rentals and studio space. And I told her I admired her painting, especially the colors, which was true. As we talked, I learned that her mother had been a Maasai schoolteacher and her father a BBC newsman, which accounted for her slight British accent. She asked about my background and was there a difference between Sicilians and Italians. I laughed and told her, "They say Sicilians are Africans trying to be Italians." I was having a pretty good time.

On the drive home it was easy to sit quietly beside Skye and watch the lights of the city streaming past, then the lights rippling slowly on the inky-black Charles River and, at last, the miles of dark highway. I said, "I wonder how much Quincy helped get me this prize. She knows those people."

"You got the prize because you deserve it. Quincy doesn't control the New Arts Alliance."

I thought about that for a while and wished I knew what Alba would say about tonight. My mind wandered. I told Skye I didn't drive much at night. She said night driving didn't bother her. We lapsed into silence. Then later I said, "Do you think it sounded like they were giving me a lifetime achievement award?"

"Maybe. You've achieved a lot, after all."

"It sounded like an end-of-life prize," I said.

"No it didn't.

"It sounded like an obituary."

"You're being morbid," she said.

"I'm talking about what it sounded like. My life isn't over. I'm not through," I added.

"Of course you're not through."

For a while I thought of one smart thing after another to tell her, but then I thought better of it and let myself drift along with the night.

❦

Whenever it slips my mind that I'm mortal, my body comes up with an ailment to remind me. Pneumonia can do that.

❦

I came across Shannon behind the coffee bar in a café in Harvard Square! It was good to see her again. She had gained back her weight, looked fine, and had a gold ring on the fourth finger of her left hand. "Look at that," I said, and she said, "That? That's a wedding ring."

"You married Fitz," I said.

"Who else?"

"Congratulations to you both. That's so great."

"It's not all roses. But we're good," she added.

We talked a while and I learned that Fitz was working for an older guy and they repaired washers and dryers. He's quick and can learn anything, Shannon told me. I asked did she like working at this café and was it any good. She said the pay was all right and she got benefits, and as for the customers, "People are the same arrogant douchebags and dickheads the world over."

"And this has changed," I said, holding her arm where the tattooed snake coiled down toward her hand. New words ran along both sides of the snake. "Can I read it?"

Shannon turned her arm and I read *If love could have saved you, you would have lived forever.*

"That's for Robert," she said. "I got it done a couple of weeks before Fitz and I got married."

"That's beautiful. And Fitz is a lucky man. I hope you both live forever."

I can't help it. I'm moved by things like that.

I didn't get around to clearing the vegetable garden until October. I yanked out the stakes, pulled up the withered tomato plants, turned over the soil, then planted three rows of garlic and covered them with a blanket of dead leaves. Maybe next spring I'll plant the usual vegetables, but probably not. It's no fun doing this without you — the same reason I don't tap the sugar maples anymore. There are a lot of things I thought I liked, but it turns out what I liked was doing those things with you. Anyway, this frees up some time. It took me seventy years to learn how to paint so I might as well use every damned day I have left.

I didn't reread Dante, not his claustrophobic epic and certainly not his insipid love poetry, having had enough of that allegorizing sourpuss from my uncle Zitti in my twenties, and from my friend Mike Bruno in my thirties. Mike not only wrote books on art and pornography (and another on cheeses), he was also a great reader of Dante and though I loved Mike I could never love Dante. But a lot of us liked to listen to Mike talk about Dante. One summer night Alba and I drove around to Mike's place to celebrate Nixon's impeachment; the door was ajar, so we knocked and walked in and heard Mike's basso profundo from upstairs, reciting Dante, and when we got up there, yes, there he was, sitting up in bed wearing only his eyeglasses, a huge volume of Dante open in his lap, Pam on one side with a plate of cold chicken, and Clarissa on the other with a bottle of wine — all three naked as the day they were born — my own Mike Bruno, now dead twenty years and more.

Alba always liked that poem by John Donne that begins —

When my grave is broke up again,
Some second guest to entertain,
(For graves have learn'd that woman-head,
To be to more than one a bed)
And he that digs it, spies
A bracelet of bright hair about the bone,
Will he not let'us alone,
And think that there a loving couple lies,
Who thought that this device might be some way
To make their souls, at the last busy day,
Meet at this grave, and make a little stay?

Whenever Alba quoted it she skipped the part about graves learning, like women, to be to more than one a bed, and she didn't care for the later stanzas, either. She was moved by the lovers being linked by that bracelet of bright hair, and their hope to find each other on Judgement Day and to stay together, as when they were flesh and blood, before being called up for Judgement. That was in the early years of our marriage when Alba still half-believed in God and didn't believe at all in the Last Judgement.

She had a way of believing, even when she didn't believe, or maybe I should say she was always hopeful — a hopeful skeptic. Take the letter written to little Skye, when she was six or seven months old, by the priest who baptized her. That was Father Brocard, of the Carmelite Fathers, and in his letter he explained to Skye that she had become an heiress, an adopted child of God, with a right to heaven. I had read the letter and had thought it a fond gesture, but then Alba read it aloud to me, choosing certain passages, like when Father Brocard tells Skye, *I put a pinch of salt in your mouth and asked that it preserve for you a taste for divine things, for heavenly wisdom. With exorcisms I bade Satan, in the name of the Holy Trinity, depart and not molest you. And as a sign of the struggle you will have with the power of evil during life, I anointed you with oil, as formerly wrestlers were anointed. Oil makes the body supple and yet difficult for an opponent to hold. Oil is looked upon as conferring strength and giving encouragement.*

"That's beautiful," Alba said. "I love the idea of Skye having become an heiress. There's poetry in the words and another kind of poetry in the ritual. It doesn't matter that we don't believe the ritual works in some sacramental way. The ritual and what he's saying here is our hope for Skye. I *want* her to have a taste for divine things and heavenly wisdom. I *want* her to be strong and to escape the evil things in life. It's our hope."

We had the same hopes and desires, Alba and I.

Leo Conti took me out to lunch at Fête Champêtre and gave me a check for two of my frescos, the pair he had snatched before I could smash them to bits. He had made off with them two or more years ago and I had forgotten about it, so the money was like a gift. The envelope with the check also contained an accounting statement from the Conti Gallery which would satisfy scrupulous agents of the IRS and the Commonwealth of Massachusetts.

Days later, when I thought about it, it seemed to me that Leo had sold them for about half of what I figured he would have asked from a buyer. Or maybe the accounting statement was, as his defense lawyer might say, the innocent result of sloppy bookkeeping due to distraction from overwork. Or fraud. On the other hand, he had taken care of expenses and provided my exhibit with a catalog beautiful enough to make you sweat, boosting the price of every canvas ten percent, so I decided to forget about it. Some painters market their work themselves, so as not to leave forty or fifty percent with the gallery, while others, like myself, would rather paint than spend time being nice to blind blockheads who think your work is overpriced.

Leo and I don't have a written agreement, only an understanding and a handshake. He's all right, mostly. He helped raise me from the dead and I'm painting.

Quincy does a good job at the gallery as she's brought in some younger painters and, more important, younger buyers. She was flat broke and couldn't get a job anywhere when Leo hired her. "But I saw beneath the surface," he told me. "She needed a mentor. She had a good eye, but she needed someone like myself who knows the business side of the art world," he said. He went on to tell me that Quincy's father works in "that building downtown that looks like an old-fashioned washboard."

"That's the Federal Reserve Bank of Boston," I said.

"Is it? I always wondered."

"Leo."

"But I didn't know it at the time, Renato! Or if I did, it meant nothing to me. I brought her in because she's a natural. I could tell."

I know Alba's not coming back, not the way I want her back. I know she's gone. I've always known it. But I always hoped she might come back. I can wait.

So this clumsy scrawl goes limping to its end. I confess it's been pieced together from an old memoir, from jottings on the kitchen calendar, scribbled notes and my defective memory. These past few years I've thought a lot and read a lot and I'm sick to a fare-thee-well of philosophers, cosmologists, theologians and atomists, and their books, books, books. I love the things of this world — yes, the perishing things of this perishing world — and most especially I love the flesh and bone and blood that makes us as we are. I would not be the painter I am if I did not.

I remember from when I was a kid hearing uncles Nicolo and Zitti argue over reality and what was real. Nicolo always said you needed mathematics to find your way to basic reality, and what you found were atoms — a nucleus of protons and neutrons surrounded by a cloud of electrons. But Zitti, who loved words and was skeptical of numbers, believed that atoms and their electrons composed merely the distracting surface of reality or, as I recall him saying, the sensuous fog that hovers over true reality so we can grasp it with our senses. And when they'd turn to my father to settle the dispute, he'd say they should carve stone all day, as he did, to learn about reality.

I suppose both uncles were right, each in his way, but I've always liked most of all my father's common sense of things. I was adopted into the Stillamare family and into this world to live and die here. I never felt like an orphan until now, left on this doorstep to noplace. Getting to the bottom of things with the Large Hadron Collider is certainly worthwhile and it satisfies our innate curiosity to pry and penetrate the world, to find out how it works. But that's the wrong direction to go if you want to get to the meaning of anything. You can't arrive at the meaning of a story by analyzing the words and composing a dictionary or, for those who try to go even deeper, by studying the alphabet. My works are more than paint on canvas, despite the bla-bla-bla of certain moronic theorists. You can't understand anything unless you get your arms around it and grab it whole, and sometimes the whole is large, very large.

As uncle Nicolo said, atoms are very strange — you blast them open and all these particles fly out, like a clock with too many parts. He spoke those words long ago, when MIT was doing atomic research with a Van de Graaff generator, a machine that creates lightning bolts the same way pulling a wool blanket from your bed in winter generates sparks. Nowadays, physicists have exquisitely sophisticated, powerful equipment and can hurl opposing streams of protons into head-on collisions that explode into sizzling bits of energy, thus mimicking the creation of things and the beginning of time. Still, the closer we get to the bottom and beginning, the clearer it becomes that what we take as solid in this world is mutable and evanescent. It comes and goes. Human love is the only thing that lasts, as steady as Mount Monadnock and beautiful as daylight.

The question isn't whether Alba's atoms have dispersed — for certain they have — the question is whether anything remains beyond those dresses in the closet and my memory of her.

The gods have given us love instead of immortality.

It would help if you were here and we could talk about the children. Not that anything is wrong. But sometimes I wonder if they know what they're doing. I wouldn't say this to anyone else but, frankly, if two of them are all right you can be sure the third is having some kind of trouble. Not big trouble, but the sort you get when you're naive about life. And yes, I know how old they are. And if you were here you could remind me that they are grown adults — unless you had a worry of your own about them.

Driving homeward in the middle of this large midsummer day, the sun high and the heat heavy. All along the roadside there was flowering eggs-and-butter, Queen Anne's lace, blue stars of wild chicory, and I had such a longing to walk a ways into a field and lie down under the quiet air, to sleep.

Eugene Mirabelli

was born in Arlington, Massachusetts, and began writing and publishing while at university. Six of his nine novels (including those forming Renato!) create a mosaic about an Italian-American family that stretches from nineteenth-century Sicily to modern day Boston. He has received numerous awards, including a Rockefeller grant, and his many short stories, journalistic pieces, reviews and essays appear widely in magazines and anthologies, and are translated into Czech, French, Hebrew, Polish, Russian, and Sicilian. Occasionally he writes brief pieces on the arts, sciences, politics, economics at CriticalPages.com, More about his books will be found at mirabelli.ag-sites.net/index.htm and genemirabelli.com.

Photo: Lynn Finley.

The Typeface

employed for the text is Adobe Caslon Pro, a digital version of designs that William Caslon began to create around 1734 in England. His work quickly became popular throughout Europe and the American Colonies. Benjamin Franklin admired Caslon's work and rarely used any other typeface and, indeed, the first printing of the Declaration of Independence was set in Caslon. The letterforms are properly unobtrusive and maintain a subtle balance of broad and thin strokes.